By ALIX BEKINS

Published by DREAMSPINNER PRESS
http://www.dreamspinnerpress.com

Written in the Stars

ALIX BEKINS

Dreamspinner Press

Published by
Dreamspinner Press
382 NE 191st Street #88329
Miami, FL 33179-3899, USA
http://www.dreamspinnerpress.com/

Written in the Stars

Cover Art by Anne Cain   annecain.art@gmail.com
Cover Design by Mara McKennen

ISBN: 978-1-61372-444-6

Printed in the United States of America
First Edition
April 2012

eBook edition available
eBook ISBN: 978-1-61372-445-3

Special thanks to Connie and Emmet, for the review and help, and especially to Ariel, who wouldn't let me give up.

Chapter 1

Heavens Above

"NO. NO, no, no, and *no!*"

"Yes," John said, not even looking away from his computer screen.

"You can't possibly be serious," Bailey insisted. He slammed his hands down on John's desk, finally getting the attention of the magazine's editor in chief.

"Serious as a funeral," John said.

"This will *ruin* our credibility! Everything we've been working for over the last year, ever since we started! You're going to destroy it all just to pander to the masses? They don't need any more pandering! I refuse to be a part of it," Bailey said definitively. "I won't do it. I'll quit first."

John's attention had shifted back to his computer, irritating Bailey. He'd probably done it on purpose. "You won't quit."

The sound of sputtering frustration filled the office for several minutes until Bailey managed to get ahold of himself. His boss was many things, all of them annoying, but stupid wasn't one of them. "Why won't I?"

"One, because you've seen the numbers and know that we need to make some changes to keep afloat. Two, because appealing to a broader, more mainstream audience is the best way to do that. And three, because I have a bribe for you: I'll let you write the review column you've been bugging me about."

"But an article like you're suggesting is going to dumb down the whole magazine!"

"*Baaaaaileeeeey*," John said, the name sounding about three syllables longer that it actually was, each brimming with John's world-weary suffering of his senior science editor.

Bailey closed his eyes for a moment, thinking. "So you're proposing that I get to write a scathing commentary of my former peers' latest research developments every month?"

John nodded.

"I get to be rude to people, *in print*, every month—for at least twelve issues?" he clarified.

John nodded again, a smile starting to creep onto his face, starting in the fine lines around his eyes.

"And in return, you're going to make me—over my most vehement objections—write an *astrology* column?" Bailey managed to load an impressive amount of scorn into the word.

"Yes."

Huffing in justified frustration, Bailey thought for a moment again and then jerked his chin in a quick nod. "Fine. I'll do it. But!" he hurried to add before John's grin became overly smug, "I want you to guarantee the twelve-month minimum for the review column, and I insist that That Other Thing be completely anonymous. No byline, John, and no one else at *Spark* knows about it who doesn't have to. If word got out, it would destroy my remaining credibility."

"Oh, you still have some left?" John asked, eyes twinkling with laughter.

"Bite me." It was always going to smart, how the idiots at Stellar Energy had cost Bailey his reputation by refusing to listen to his advice. Well, him and the other scientists on the research team, but still.

John reached into a tray on his desk and pulled out a sheet of paper. "Here; I knew you'd want it in writing."

Bailey took the agreement back to his desk to look over thoroughly. John Forrester might be his good friend, maybe even his best friend, but he wasn't signing anything without reading the fine print. He and John had known each other too long and given each other far too much shit for him to be quite that trusting.

The two had met nearly a decade ago, when John had still been enlisted and Bailey was contracting with the military. He'd been working on a still-classified project which would one day revolutionize energy production, and John had been one of a small team of soldiers assigned to keep the scientists somewhat grounded in reality. It had turned out that John was actually quite intelligent, even had an MA in mathematics—something Bailey found difficult to believe of someone who had voluntarily signed up to be shot at—and despite the constant arguing and insults, they became friends.

They hadn't stayed in touch once the project had been completed and they were both reassigned. Bailey had finished out his contract and then gone to work for those fools at Stellar Energy. While he was grateful that John had sought him out and offered him a job at *Spark*, his gratitude only went so far. To Bailey's eternal mortification, John instinctively knew the right buttons to push, the same way he had all those years ago, to prod Bailey into doing whatever he wanted. Just like with this ridiculous astrology column.

Bailey reviewed the proposal carefully and tried not to get too upset that John had been able to predict his demands that the editorial be for a year minimum and that the astrology column remain anonymous. He signed his usual assertive scrawl and took the agreement over to Lauren, John's assistant, detouring to make himself a photocopy first.

John popped his head out the door. "Buy you a beer after work to wash away the bitter taste of defeat?" he offered.

"Go to hell. But yes, buy me a beer first."

John grinned. "So long as I know I've got company for the trip."

Bailey shook his head, flapping his hand dismissively as he headed back toward his desk. Damn John for always knowing how to get under Bailey's skin. Bailey sat down at his desk and shuddered as he started typing in search phrases to learn how to predict horoscopes.

THREE months later, John was back at the bar down the street, buying Bailey yet another in a very long—endless, maybe—string of conciliatory beers.

"I still can't believe you are making me do this."

John shrugged, bored by the same dialogue they'd had a million times but willing to recite his lines once again if that was what Bailey wanted. "People want to read about sex and romance. It's not my fault."

Bailey sat hunched over in misery, staring hopelessly at his half-empty pint glass. "This has to be punishment for something I did."

"Buck up. If you want to write the editorial column, then you have to write this one too. You're the only one who's qualified," John said, resting a consoling hand on Bailey's shoulder.

The reaction was explosive; Bailey sat up sharply, turning on John with a vengeance. "You take that back!" he spat. "I am *not* qualified to write such blatant drivel and quackery. I am so far *over*qualified, so far beyond qualified—"

"Whatever; you're the one who is writing it. It's your assignment; I'm your boss. Write the goddamned column," John said, rolling his eyes. Bailey's melodramatic outbursts, which had lost him most of his potential friends and pretty much all of his dates in the last five years, had never had very much effect on John.

"I hate you," Bailey grumbled.

"And yet somehow I manage not to cry myself to sleep at night." John smirked as he raised his glass and then drained it. "Only you would have a meltdown because your column—in an obscure new scientific journal—got praised on a morning talk show."

"That's exactly it! My astrology column—the one with *no scientific merit whatsoever*—has gained national attention, and I can't even decide if I'm more appalled that people think this bullshit is real, or that people finally approve of my work but it's *this*, or that I'm apparently shallow enough to somewhat wish I was actually getting recognition for this drivel. What am I saying—I absolutely do *not* want my name associated with this crap! John, under no circumstances are you allowed to ever reveal that I write this column. On pain of death," he said, giving John the most threatening look he could manage, which wasn't very.

John laughed. "Do you honestly think anyone would believe me anyway? Bailey McMillan, the double-PhD genius, mastermind behind Stellar Energy, writing *Spark's* astrology column?"

Bailey signaled to the bartender for another round. "I know; you're right, of course. But seriously, John, promise me—not even in your memoirs."

John rolled his eyes but nodded.

"I just don't get it. I mean, I tried—I honestly *tried*—to find some scientific basis for this garbage. Some way to use the latest research of, oh, the last two centuries of space exploration to find patterns in radiation or magnetic shifts, or anything at all that had the tiniest hint of a possibility of correlation between astronomical phenomena and human behavior, and aside from some very minor reports of a higher incidence of homicides during lunar eclipses, there is nothing. *Nothing!*"

John dared another pat on the shoulder as Bailey buried his face in his hands on the table. "It's the fact that it kind of works that really gets your goat, isn't it?"

"Yes! It's driving me insane that so many people are reporting how accurate the random crap I make up is turning out to be!"

"Only you would be so upset. Most *normal* people would simply stop worrying about it and enjoy the ride. It must suck being a genius."

"*Hate* you."

"Love you too, buddy." John laughed.

A WEEK later found them back at the same bar. It was getting to be a regular habit for them. Any time Bailey's—or rather *Spark's*—astrology column was mentioned in the news, John added an hour or two at the bar with Bailey to his evening plans. The column was turning out to be shockingly popular, and it was a good thing Bailey had insisted on keeping his agreement a secret from the rest of the staff at *Spark*, because the media had started questioning anyone they could find when neither John nor Lauren would give up the writer's name.

It seemed as if Bailey's inability to simply make up the column without doing some sort of research—mostly to prove that astrology was totally bogus—had backfired. He was running numbers, correlating everything from the levels of radiation the sun was emitting on a particular day, to meteor showers, to the slight wobble of the earth's axis and comparing it to behavioral studies, lottery winners, crime statistics, and data from suicide prevention hotlines. He remained absolutely convinced that there wasn't a shred of evidence to support any sort of relationship between the two... and yet the magazine was being flooded with e-mails from people who claimed Bailey's predictions were spot-on, including some from well-known astrologers who wanted to know his secret.

It almost made Bailey want to weep over the sheer stupidity of their readers.

"It boggles my mind that people would rather believe their lives are influenced by the movements of big chunks of rock and enormous clouds of gas two kiloparsecs away than simply accept that chaos theory makes far more sense."

"People don't want logic, Bailey, they want a sense of order in their lives." John sighed. This was becoming a very familiar conversation.

Bailey made a face. "People don't make sense! There are no numbers that are 'luckier' for a Taurus on a particular Wednesday, and there's no specific cosmological configuration that means Virgos should be careful with money or that Geminis should watch out for tall, dark strangers. And don't even get me started on the nonsense about 'love matches'. These idiots might as well be reading sheep entrails for all the 'science' involved."

"The romance stuff pisses you off the most, doesn't it?" John asked, grinning. "It's like a personal insult to your finely tuned sense of the utter randomness of love, which of course is why *you* haven't found the right person yet: sheer chance."

"It's a better answer than looking to the stars to find my soulmate," Bailey answered, tone full of distaste. "Part of it is my fault, sure, but most of it is just *life*—not ever meeting the right person at the right time under the right conditions. It doesn't have a damn thing to do with where Venus is in my chart."

John shook his head and finished his beer. "So prove it."

Bailey looked at John like he was nuts, which clearly John was, and this was simply more evidence. "Prove what, how?"

"Prove that the romance crap is wrong. Wow me," John challenged him, grinning.

"Of all the idiotic, pointless, futile theories to waste my time on…. You might as well ask me to disprove the existence of the Flying Spaghetti Monster."

"Praise His Noodly Appendage," John said, raising his glass in a toast.

"Oh for…." Bailey sighed but raised his glass to clink against John's. "Seriously. The only way to 'prove' that something doesn't work is to try it and see what happens. But anything involving human behavior is so subjective that trying to apply the scientific method is just asking for skewed results." He glanced across the room at a particularly attractive young woman seated at the bar. "I could go over to that woman and be charming and wonderful, ask her out, and then attribute her rejection to the month she happened to be born in not meshing well with the month *I* happened to be born in. Or I could give the same attribution to something slightly more logical, like the fact that she's got a tan line on her hand where a ring used to be and she might not be ready to date again yet. Or maybe she had a crappy day, or maybe her goldfish died, or maybe she hates men with blue eyes!"

"So try just the basics, like a general compatibility test," John suggested. "See which signs you're supposed to get along with the best and then date them and see if it's true."

Bailey gave him a look. "Oh please. What, you think that if I go out on a few dates and somehow magically end up getting along best with the one I'm 'supposed to'," he said, complete with air quotes, "then that will prove anything?"

"Maybe not, but you'll have a handful of dates out of it, at the very least." John smirked.

"I weep for your college professors if that's what you consider logic."

John kicked him under the table. "What do you have to lose? You go out on twelve dates, and you get to have a tiny bit of proof—"

"Flawed, subjective proof," Bailey interrupted.

"—that astrological love matches are bogus," John continued, ignoring Bailey. "Maybe you'll even get laid," he added, wiggling his eyebrows in what was probably supposed to be a suggestive way but instead looked like he had a facial tic.

"In order for an 'experiment' like that to work, I'd need to date at least one person of each sign. And I couldn't know who was who or I'd bring my own biases into it—which is going to be difficult enough to ignore, given that there is no way in hell this can work, because, and let me say this very clearly since you seem to be missing my point, *astrology is completely bogus.*"

John ignored him, as usual. "So you go out with one person of each sign within a close enough time period that you can realistically make comparisons. It's like you'll suddenly be popular," John teased. "Twelve dates in a few months; I bet that's more action than you've had in years."

Bailey made a face at him. "Why are we friends?" he asked, trying to sound genuinely curious. "I'm pretty sure I loathe you."

It wasn't as if he needed John to rub it in that Bailey didn't date much—or at all—and that the idea of finding even two dates in one month made his palms sweat. Not everyone could have the looks John had: tallish, fit, runner's body, tanned skin, hazel eyes. His hair was a perpetual disaster of cowlicks that tended to make him look sort of goofy, but even though he was nearing his midforties, John had a grace and self-confidence that drew women to him like bees to honey. He'd always been able to charm his way into any pants he'd wanted.

Bailey never even tried to compete. Sure, he was a genius and he had money, but he simply wasn't good with people and had given up in his late teens, when he'd realized that being super-intelligent didn't seem to make people want to sleep with him. He had huge blue eyes, which were his best feature by far, a stocky body that tended to look more pudgy than strong, and hair that had sadly started thinning in his midthirties. He liked sex—*loved* sex—but rarely found dealing with other people's emotions worth the effort involved.

"What have you got to lose?" John asked, a smile beginning to tug at the corners of his mouth. "Maybe you'll even find Miss—or Mister—Right."

Bailey shook his head, knowing he'd already given in the moment he'd begun thinking about all the variables involved. "I'll bet you a steak dinner that at the end of this pseudo-scientific farce, I'm still sitting here in this bar with you."

John grinned. "You're on."

Chapter 2

Leo Rising

JOHN'S brows furrowed as he approached his office. Lauren's and Bailey's heads were close together behind her desk as they both peered at her monitor. They appeared to be arguing over something—their usual form of interaction—and as John got closer, he saw that they were working on a block of text.

"Seriously, Bailey, if you don't back the hell off, I'm going to staple your hand to this desk," Lauren threatened, reaching for her trusty Swingline.

Bailey made a scoffing noise. "Right. As if I'd just let you do this out of the goodness of your heart. Let me write the damn ad, and then all you have to do is post it."

Lauren bared her teeth, and John could have sworn she was one more insult away from actually growling at his friend. "*All*? Post the advertisement. And then filter the replies, choose your dates, and—oh right—check their fucking driver's licenses! I don't want that day spa package you promised me badly enough to put up with your BS. Either back off or find someone else to be your yenta."

"Look, I'm not being that unreasonable! These are my dates, my stupid experiment; I'm not going to let you post a personals ad for me without reading it first!"

John grabbed the stapler away from Lauren moments before her fingers reached it. "What on earth is going on out here?"

Lauren glared at Bailey, one of her Level Four glares, which had been known to make lesser men wet themselves; Level Five was death by spontaneous combustion. A former Marine, she didn't take shit from anyone and had no qualms about reminding people who pissed her off that she knew more than a hundred ways to kill, most of them without even breaking a sweat. She ran John's office with an iron fist and was worth her weight in platinum.

"Bailey needs my help getting dates for his bet with you," she said with a sneer.

John let Bailey sputter for a few moments, watching the way his face turned red, with amusement. "So you've come up with a plan, then?"

Bailey closed his eyes and took a deep breath, and some of his normal color returned. "Yes. Your ridiculous idea should be easy enough to implement. Post a personals ad, weeding out a few variables so no one outrageously incompatible is selected. Limit the dates to men only so there's no gender differential or hidden bias on my part. The trick is how to find out their signs and yet still do it anonymously, since obviously I can't know which guy is an Aquarius and which is a Libra, and no, I don't trust you to do it. Lauren seemed like the most objective choice to assist, as she's your *assistant* and it's your idiotic bet anyway."

"Because Lauren doesn't have enough to do?" John asked, one eyebrow lifting.

"Because *I* am going to be wasting enough of my time going on these ridiculous dates without coordinating the whole thing, and no one else knows about the astrology column. It will just look like she's setting me up on dates—"

"Pimping him out," Lauren said with a smirk.

"—which isn't that unusual, since she's always taken a disturbing interest in my love life," he finished, ignoring the interruption.

"Or lack thereof," John added helpfully.

Bailey gritted his teeth. "If you two are quite finished, can we just get this advertisement posted so I can get on with my life?"

John took a moment to read over what they'd written already. "'Genius, late 30s, reasonably attractive, SWM seeks Mensa members for dinner dates. Must show proof of date of birth for scientific experiment.' Seriously?"

Lauren rolled her eyes. "You see what I have to work with? Just make him go away while I do this."

"What? What's wrong with that? It's simple, direct, to the point—"

"And boring as hell. You need to say something to weed out the people who you're going to be instantly incompatible with, who like hip-hop or expect you to be romantic or whatever," John added. "Say something like 'must be a *Doctor Who* fan,'" he said, nodding at Lauren, who began to type. "'Must be a fan of *Doctor Who*, Glenn Gould's *Goldberg Variations*, and know pi to at least ten places.'"

"Ten? My seven-year-old niece knows it to twenty!" objected Bailey. "If they're actually in Mensa, that would be insulting."

"Look, you do want men to respond to this, right?" Lauren pointed out. "You're not looking for a real date, just subjects for the experiment who aren't idiots and you won't hate immediately. You're going to have to be a tiny bit more lenient."

Bailey opened his mouth to argue, but John leaped in before he could speak. "Okay, strike the bit about pi and say something about the Fibonacci sequence instead. That'll weed out anyone who's not a math geek."

The three of them fussed with the wording for a bit longer. After a short argument between John and Bailey about whether or not to specify which Doctors were acceptable, Lauren declared that they were finished and that Bailey was either going to go away while she posted the ad or she was going to castrate him with a pencil. Both men fled to the safety of their desks and finally the workday began.

Four days later Lauren evidently sent an e-mail to Bailey asking if he had any life outside of work that she needed to know about or if she could assume that all of his evenings and weekends were free for her to schedule his dates. At least, John heard ranting and raving to that effect through his open office door when Bailey came by Lauren's desk to personally inform her that he went to the gym at least two nights a week and that he used his personal time for research and development, not to mention eviscerating his peers' research in finely crafted letters to the editors of the misguided scholarly journals in which they published. When the two started to bicker about whether that actually counted as recreational or not, John decided he'd had enough.

"I realize this is a pretty mellow office, and I'd like to keep it that way, but you two need to shut the hell up and quit arguing all the time!" he said, glowering. "I know you both work hard and I don't mind that you're doing this little project during office hours, but *some people* are trying to work on getting *Spark*'s profit margin up and need a little peace and quiet to hear ourselves think."

Lauren had the grace to look abashed; Bailey just rolled his eyes.

"Just make the dates; I don't care when," Bailey huffed. "No more than two during the week and one on the weekend; that will leave me enough time to get my own things done and hopefully get through this experiment in a timely manner."

"You honestly think you're going to get three dates a week?" John scoffed.

"Actually," Lauren said, "you'd be surprised. Apparently there're a *lot* of lonely geeks out there. The ad has received about fifty replies. I'm only answering the ones who don't e-mail a picture of their dick, but even still, I think we've got at least one guy of each astrological sign already."

"If there are multiple candidates, we'll have to find a way to pick the one who looks like the best match," Bailey said.

"No way; then you'll lose objectivity," John argued. "Lauren and I will do it."

"Yes, well, fine. Also make sure none of them are fellow scientists whose work I've recently annihilated. The dinner conversation might be awkward."

John rolled his eyes. "Your colleagues are a small group of academics spread across universities and research centers all over the world. What are the odds that one of them would be responding to your personals ad?"

Bailey's eyes drifted upward, his lips moving slightly as he started to do the calculations.

"Oh for Pete's sake," John said as he shoulder-bumped Bailey before he could actually estimate a number. "You do know what 'rhetorical' means, right?"

BAILEY twitched his hands in agitation, nearly knocking over his water glass. First, the guy had been late, which was inexcusable, since Bailey was using his precious free time for this dinner, and then he was... not Bailey's type at all. He was surprisingly gorgeous, and Bailey had no idea what he was doing answering a personals ad on Craigslist.

Bailey'd been pretty sure the guy was looking for someone else when he'd walked into the bar, but apparently Lauren had oh-so-helpfully shown his date a picture of him when she'd checked his driver's license at the office. Mister Tall, Dark-Skinned, and Far Too Handsome For You had sauntered directly over to Bailey, held out his hand, and smiled.

"I'm Ramses."

It was not Bailey's fault at all that his eyebrows took on a skeptical quirk. Seriously, who was named *Ramses*? Apparently the son of two archaeologists, that was who. Good-looking ones too, or perhaps their genes had come together just right, because Ramses was hot. He also seemed to be the kind of man who expected the world to do his bidding and was charming and confident enough to get it. Their waiter rushed over to take their drink order before Ramses had even removed his jacket, and Bailey knew it was going to be *that* kind of date.

Rather than waste his time trying to decide what the man's sign was—because honestly, it wasn't 1972 anymore and he wasn't going to *ask*—Bailey focused on identifying any common ground as quickly as possible. Or lack thereof. They disagreed over the wine choice; Ramses was insistent on a particular year, and while Bailey didn't care, he wasn't paying more than thirty dollars for a bottle of wine he doubted they'd finish. It turned out they were both fairly stubborn, and while Ramses didn't come out and call him cheap per se, the implication was enough for Bailey to put another checkmark in the negative column.

"So, what do you do?" Bailey asked once food and wine had been ordered.

"Own a few businesses," Ramses answered nonchalantly. "But I've just been reelected to the city council, and I'm planning to run for the state legislature next year. My CEOs can handle things without me for a while."

Bailey nodded. Well, if the man was hoping to be a politician, that explained his slight smarminess. Bailey's passionate debate about the misallocation of funds that should have been focused on social services was met with an equally spirited rejoinder about the importance of civic celebrations to foster a sense of community, but all in all, it wasn't a bad conversation, and Bailey found himself enjoying it. So few people were able to keep up with him, although yes, he was making more effort than usual to be polite. It was a date, after all.

Which meant that when Ramses somehow managed to draw the waiter into the debate when he brought over their entrees, Bailey was more than a little miffed. The man flirted without even seeming to try, as if he naturally expected anyone nearby would be drawn to him, and frustratingly enough, they were. Bailey himself wasn't immune; there was something very attractive about his date, and well, it was a bit of an ego-boost to be the one Ramses was with. At the moment, anyway.

Everything was going well—far better than any dates Bailey could remember, in fact—until the dessert menus came.

"Let's get out of here and go back to my place," Ramses suggested with a knowing look in his eye. "I've got something sweet there, I'm sure."

Bailey wasn't sure whether to be appalled by the horrible pickup line, insistent that he get his chocolate pot de crème—which was the entire reason he had chosen this restaurant in the first place—or amazed and grateful that someone seemed to want to have sex with him. Still, he hardly knew the guy; he wasn't going to go home with him after a mere two hours and fall into bed.

Was he?

No, no; of course he wasn't.

"But… the pot de crème," he said over the rushing sound in his ears and thrum of *sex, sex, sex, sex, I could have sex* in his head.

Ramses snorted. "You'd rather have custard than go home with me?" Shaking his head, he glanced at their waiter, who was hovering nearby. "Your call, of course. I don't like to waste time."

Bailey narrowed his eyes. "Well, if dinner was a waste of time…."

"We're both men, Bailey. You placed an ad; I responded. I thought we both knew what we wanted. That's how these things always go. Stop scowling like an offended maiden; I'm not the one who's out of line here."

"I didn't realize dinner had been upgraded to foreplay since the last time I dated."

Their waiter chose that moment to come by and ask, "Have you two gentlemen decided what you want tonight?" A small smile teased at his mouth, and Bailey didn't have to be psychic to know what was coming next.

"He'll have the chocolate," Ramses said, turning a shamelessly seductive grin toward the waiter. "And I'll have your phone number. When do you get off?"

Knowing that it was coming didn't actually take the shock away. Bailey considered what it would be like to get up and punch the other man right in the face, but, well. That probably wouldn't work out very well for him. Not that the evening was working out anyway, but there was no reason to add "assaulted a city councilman in a restaurant; had to have Forrester bail me out of jail" to his research notes. He briefly entertained the girlish gesture of tossing his glass of wine in the man's face, but that wasn't his style either.

Instead he crossed his arms over his chest and ignored Ramses completely, addressing the waiter. "You do know he'll dispose of you just as easily, right? And given that apparently every meal this man eats is equivalent to first base, you're going to be about as memorable to him as the next sandwich he grabs for lunch. He's already eaten, so I doubt he's going to take much time with you, and he doesn't seem like the sort of top who really cares whether you come or not, so don't get your hopes up." Bailey stood and pulled his wallet out of his pocket, then tossed down just enough cash to cover his half of the meal, not including that ridiculous bottle of wine or a tip.

"Enjoy your dessert," he added to Ramses as he shrugged on his coat and stalked out the door.

Well. So much for Bachelor Number One.

"DID you honestly say all that?" John asked, not noticing the drip heading to the base of his ice cream cone.

"Yes." Bailey was making good headway on his own, having been unable to get rid of his need for chocolate and figuring he deserved at least a double scoop of his favorite double-dark mint chip. It was strictly coincidental that his favorite ice cream parlor was on John's side of town, and frankly, John owed him dessert. This whole thing was his fault anyway.

"Wow. What a jerk."

"No kidding. I thought things were going fine, more or less, but… damn." Bailey finished off the top scoop and began on the second. "Have I been out of the game that long?" he asked in a small voice. "I mean, it's not like I'm a prude. I like sex. I even like one-night stands."

John shrugged, tipping his head sideways to finally catch the drip that had been drawing Bailey's eyes. "You've never struck me as a prude. You don't seem particularly easy, either," he added in a rush. "It sounded like that guy was just a bad match."

Bailey sighed. "He was pretty attractive, though. Maybe I should have gone home with him."

"Nah. He was a jerk," John repeated. "And you said yourself that he probably wasn't any good in bed. No point in a fling that pisses you off before the first kiss."

"True… God, I'd like to have sex though…."

John snorted. "Don't hold back, Bailey; tell me all about it."

"Bite me," Bailey said with a huff. "You probably have no idea what it's like to go so long without getting laid."

Rolling his eyes, John rebutted, "Actually, it's been quite a while for me too. Since, uh, that wedding Lauren made me go to as her date, last August."

Bailey's eyes bulged. "You did Lauren?"

"Geez, no. Me and, uh." John glanced around, clearly a reflexive habit. "Me and one of the groomsmen. Just, you know," he said, making a furtive jerking off gesture.

"Ah ha! I *knew* you were bi," Bailey crowed.

John looked around nervously again, old habits from his former life in the military apparently not yet dead. He looked like he wanted to hush Bailey, but he didn't, although he did smack him on the shoulder. "Shut up. But, uh, yeah. I don't know about 'bi' though," he said, an uncomfortable look on his face. "I don't know if I want to date women at all anymore."

That was… not unexpected either, really. John almost never talked about his personal life, although if he was bisexual or possibly gay, that would certainly explain some of his reticence. The "Don't Ask; Don't Tell" policy had been in effect throughout John's military service, and it had only been about two years since he'd been honorably discharged after an injury he still refused to talk about.

"Women are harder." Bailey shrugged. "I mean, I have no idea what anyone is thinking when they go out with me, male or female, but women in particular seem to hope I'll transform into someone completely different once we go out on an official 'date'. Men at least don't seem to have the same expectations about meeting parents or sending flowers."

John laughed. "Yeah, men are generally more direct; at least, I'd guess that. It seems like it would be nice not to have to play games, but not have to hide either."

Bailey grinned. "Another item to add to your list of benefits of getting out of the service. No uniform regs about your hair, no sucking up to jerks who outrank you, no hiding homosexual leanings, and—oh right—no *getting shot at*."

"The toys were pretty sweet, though," John reminisced. He didn't say anything about flying, but it was there in the air between them.

John hadn't flown since the accident, and Bailey didn't know if that was by choice or because he physically couldn't or what. John certainly had enough money to buy a small Cessna or something if he wanted to, and while it wouldn't be the same as the jets he'd probably flown, it was still a little surprising to Bailey that he didn't seem interested. Still, on the list of things John didn't talk about, flying was hardly the most significant.

Bailey made a noise of agreement. "I miss all the high-powered computers, to say nothing of the—ow! Why did you just kick me?" he demanded, scooting his chair away from John and giving him a glare that suggested he'd like to set his friend on fire.

"To stop you from saying anything classified," John said, scowling back. "It's still treason to talk about government secrets in ice cream parlors, in case you'd forgotten."

"I know that! I was going to say 'minions'! I miss the minions, you overly patriotic caveman. Damn it," he said, rubbing his shin. "I bet you've given me a hematoma. I have very delicate skin, you know."

John rolled his eyes. "You are such a drama queen. Do you want me to take you to the hospital?" he asked, standing up and grabbing his coat.

Bailey got up as well, started to limp, but then decided that his shin didn't hurt that badly. He sent another glare at John, though. "My date was a jerk, I had to make do with ice cream instead of chocolate pot de crème, I didn't get laid, and now I'm bruised. Today sucks."

Snorting, John said, "Well then, tomorrow can't be anything but better."

And the sad thing was, even though he was teasing—or maybe because—that right there was why Bailey liked him.

Chapter 3

Virgo Paradox

BAILEY'S second date was not late. In fact, the man was waiting outside the restaurant when Bailey arrived his usual ten minutes early—enough time to scope out the best place to sit, the fire exits, the men's room, and warn the waiter about his food allergies without looking like a hypochondriac (or pathetic, if the warning seemed to indicate a need for monetary bribery as well) in front of someone new. Bailey would have assumed the man was waiting for someone else in a three-piece suit, maybe carrying a briefcase, who also looked like a cross between an investment banker and the Mafia, and definitely not Bailey. But the man had coughed politely as he'd walked past and said, "Excuse me, Bailey McMillan?"

"Yes?" he said, giving the man—kid, actually; with cheeks that smooth, he couldn't be over thirty—a confused look.

"I'm Oliver Dumas, your, uh, dinner companion? Ms. Newman was kind enough to share a photo so I'd recognize you," he added, looking like he was making an effort to put Bailey at ease.

"Yes, yes," Bailey said, shaking the proffered hand. "Seriously? How old are you?"

Oliver's face took on a pinched, long-suffering expression. "I'm twenty-nine. Would you like to see my identification too?"

"No, no," Bailey said, realizing that would invalidate this phase of the experiment and therefore relegate the whole dinner to being even *more* of a waste of his time. "It's not that I thought you weren't legal," he added. "Just... I did say 'late thirties' in the ad, and well, I'm a little surprised someone as young as you would respond," he finished in what he hoped was a diplomatic way.

His date shrugged. "What can I say, your mention of the Fibonacci sequence intrigued me," he said, mouth curving upward at the edges. "Would you like to go inside and eat?"

Oliver turned out to be in investments, which wasn't much of a surprise given how he was dressed. Still, he had that indefinable air of someone who could easily kill you, along with excellent posture, so Bailey felt a certain amount of smugness when it turned out that his date was former FBI. "Security" was all Oliver would say, but Bailey had spent enough time around the military to know when not to pursue certain lines of inquiry, and to be honest, it didn't matter.

What was most surprising to Bailey was that he and Oliver weren't all that incompatible. They both had advanced degrees in mathematics, which led to an invigorating discussion of the various numerical sequence patterns found in nature while they ate their meal. Oliver was attractive enough to look at, in an uptight, Windsor-knotted, every-button-buttoned sort of way, and if he'd been five to ten years older, Bailey might have found himself interested. Which was totally hypocritical, he knew, given that he'd spent the vast majority of his youth surrounded by classmates and coworkers who were a good decade or two older than he was, but still. Finding himself on the other end of the equation was unsettling.

Besides, there was no chemistry between them. As in, none at all. Oliver was attractive, he was intelligent, he was... really incredibly fussy. He kept blotting up the ring of water the condensation on his glass left on the table with his napkin. Bailey knew he had his own weird little idiosyncrasies, but... Oliver was just strange. Everything about him was perfect, immaculate, prim, and repressed. Bailey couldn't imagine him naked and sweaty from sex, or even in workout clothes at a gym. And Bailey had a quite vivid imagination, so yes— definitely no chemistry.

Still, it was a nice enough meal. They got into a minor tiff when Bailey insisted on paying, finally going so far as to take Oliver's credit card away from the baffled waitress and give her his instead, saying, "Look, it was my ad, my experiment, my date. It has nothing to do with you being younger and everything to with writing this off as a business expense, okay?"

That got him another one of Oliver's apparently rare smiles. "Well, so long as it's a financially sound decision, I won't argue."

It was still relatively early, and they hesitated outside the restaurant for an awkward moment before Oliver said, "There's an exhibition at the De Young. Do you like minimalist art, by any chance?"

"I do, actually. I've been meaning to check it out but keep forgetting," Bailey admitted.

The exhibit featured a large selection of both Cubists and de Stijl art and design, and he and Oliver stayed until closing, discussing the use of color and angles and how pleasing they both found the clean linear forms. Bailey found himself going on a bit about the lack of curves and how he found it both pleasing and yet disturbingly inhuman, making a tangent into the graphable sine waves on a typical person's body. This was, of course, complete with hand-waving as he outlined what he was talking about using the curve of Oliver's ribs and waist and hip as an example, gestures that may have been inappropriate in public—to say nothing of someone he had only known for three hours—if the scandalized look of the elderly docent was anything to go by. Oliver seemed to be trying not to laugh, though, so whatever.

They walked back to where they'd left their cars at the restaurant, pointing at certain features in the architecture around them. Oliver was bemoaning the overly decorated Victorian designs in favor of the modern glass and metal of downtown San Francisco.

"The Transamerica Pyramid is my favorite building in the world," Oliver said, twisting his head to see the flashing light on top of it. "Followed closely by the St Mary Axe tower, of course."

"The Gherkin," Bailey corrected him, smirking. "I don't know; there are a lot of beautiful designs. I find the flying buttresses on the Cologne cathedral to be some pretty amazing engineering for their time."

Oliver rolled his eyes but shrugged in an amiable way. "Too much ornamental crap getting in the way."

The topic of Engineering Through the Ages, and their corresponding design details and functionality or lack thereof, carried the two of them the rest of the way back to the underground lot, and then they were there, standing next to Oliver's very practical Japanese hybrid, his keys in his hand.

They hovered for a moment and then moved closer together. Bailey was startled to find that Oliver was ever-so-slightly taller than he was, and he had to tip his head upward in order for their lips to meet. It was over before Bailey had decided whether he even *wanted* to kiss Oliver; his body had just sort of moved on autopilot, assuming that this was a) a date, and b) one that had gone reasonably well, and therefore c) they should kiss before parting for the evening.

They both blinked at each other for a moment. "Huh," Bailey said.

Oliver nodded somberly. "All right, then. Well, it was worth a shot, I suppose." They stood together for an uncomfortable pause, and then Oliver reached into his coat pocket and pulled out a business card. "Here, e-mail me if you want to go see the Dada exhibit coming up at the SFMOMA next month."

It was practical, no-nonsense, and as straightforward an offer of platonic friendship as Bailey had ever received. He took the card. "Thanks, I'll do that. This was good."

"Yeah," Oliver agreed, and they smiled somewhat tentatively and shook hands, and then Oliver got in his car and drove away while Bailey was still walking to his.

"SO LET me get this straight: you liked each other, had a ton of things in common, but since fireworks didn't go off when you kissed, you're not interested in pursuing it?" John asked.

Bailey rolled his eyes. "There was *no* chemistry whatsoever. He was a nice kid, smart, decent-looking—if way too young—but kissing him was like kissing... I don't know, a wall. A cousin. No wait, that's disturbing; a statue, maybe? A priest? Something kind of cold and unresponsive but not incestuous or immoral...."

"A lizard?"

Bailey punched him in the arm. "A straight priest, maybe. Someone who's not going to punch you but sort of wishes you would stop already."

"Why did you even kiss him, then, if he was so horribly standoffish?"

Bailey's hands flailed like they did whenever he didn't know something, usually whenever he was talking about *people*. "I don't know! It was mutual! We both leaned in; it wasn't my fault," he protested. "Besides, it wasn't like it was a huge fiasco, it was just… awkward. And a little embarrassing," he added, and then immediately wished he hadn't.

John, as expected, laughed.

"I liked him, though. We talked about architecture and engineering, which was a nice change…." There was a brief lull while Bailey thought about his date. "The whole date was like being in an endless loop, like a Penrose staircase, you know? It seems like you're getting somewhere, but you don't and there's no way out, no matter how many steps you climb up. It's impossible, a paradox."

John sighed. "All right, so that's a 'no' for Ramses, and a 'no' for Oliver."

"It wasn't a *no*." Bailey bristled. "I mean, I liked him. We might get together for an exhibit at SFMOMA, actually. And while I would love to say I rejected Ramses in favor of a chocolate pot de crème, I think in all honesty the records have to show that he threw me over for a slutty waiter twink when it seemed like I *might* not put out."

"Not to mention that you had to settle for ice cream," John helpfully pointed out.

"I should have put out," Bailey said in a glum tone of voice. "I miss sex."

"Oh, for the love of God…." John got up to refill their coffee cups. The *Spark* staff came to the café across the street from their building often enough that the employees gave them unlimited access to refills of the regular coffee. It was a quiet, informal space, and Bailey had a serious thing for their muffins.

"So," John started again, sitting down with full two cups, one with a poppy seed muffin balanced on top. "Who did you get along with better: Ramses or Oliver?"

Bailey's nose wrinkled up while he thought about it. "Well, there was more attraction with Ramses, I suppose. He was irritating, though, and very self-centered. I'd definitely rather see Oliver again, even with no chance of scoring; I had a much better time with him."

"All right, seriously, aren't you the scientist here? You need some sort of survey tool, to record your reactions to these dates in a more objective way."

Huffing a breath of frustration, clearly irritated that he hadn't thought of it first, Bailey agreed and began to pick apart his muffin and eat it. "All right. So I need to rate attractiveness without any touching, chemistry if there was touching, shared interests… what else?"

John shrugged. "Overall personality match?"

"Right, because that whole 'opposites attract' cliché is so obviously false. Lots of successful relationships are made of couples who are more complimentary than similar."

"I meant compatible, not identical," John said with a scowl. "Like there's anyone else on the planet who was unfortunate enough to be saddled with your sparkling personality."

"Fine." Bailey crossed his arms over his chest. "No one's forcing you to be friends with me." A sudden fleeting expression of worry crossed his face. "Is there? No, never mind. I'd know about it if there was; I mean, unless I'm being misdirected…. No, I'm probably just being paranoid."

John crossed his arms over his chest too. "Jesus, you are a piece of work, you know that? *Yeah*, you're being paranoid. I have no idea why we're friends; guess I'm just a glutton for punishment."

"Oh. Well, all right then." Bailey stared at John; John stared at Bailey. They blinked at each other. "So, where were we?"

With another sigh, John got out a notebook and pen. "Constructing a survey to assess different aspects of your dates' personalities."

In the end, they came up with a rating scale that included attractiveness, chemistry, shared interests, clashing interests or hobbies, ethical perspectives, politics, and a few other topics. The final result was two pages, once Bailey typed up their notes and created a form, and they both felt good about having met the objectivity requirements for a "real" experiment. John stipulated that he and Bailey should complete the survey together after each date, so that Bailey didn't simply give a guy all negative marks if they ended up hating each other.

"I wouldn't do that!"

"You so totally would," John said with a knowing glance. "I know you, Bailey, and I know how much you hate to lose."

"Not enough to tamper with the data," Bailey said, aghast.

"Enough to gloss over any outliers."

Bailey had to concede that that was a possibility. "But only for stupid social sciences research, which is so far from *real* science that I feel dirty using the same word."

John shook his head as they got up from the table. "Back to work, McMillan. Let's see some of that 'real' science make us some money."

"YOU'RE being sued," Lauren said by way of greeting when Bailey walked past her desk to get to the coffeepot the next morning.

"Uh-uh," he replied with a dismissive hand-wave. "I was up until three this morning working on monopoles. Don't speak until that pot of coffee is inside me."

Lauren looked at the circles under his eyes, shrugged, and went back to her desk. She nodded at John through the open door of his office and went back to her desk to wait.

"Did you say I'm being *sued*?" Bailey screeched about forty-five seconds later, bringing the low hum of several conversations throughout the office to a dead halt.

John's hand on his shoulder was a surprise; he hadn't noticed his friend coming up beside him. "Let's take this in my office, okay?"

John, smart man that he was, grabbed the pot of coffee and some sugar packets before ushering Bailey inside and kicking the door shut behind them.

"Sued?" Bailey asked, eyes bulging as he sucked down most of his mug in one go. "What the fuck?"

Settling down behind his desk, John motioned to Bailey to take a seat. "Dr. Gallagher's lawyer contacted our office at eight this morning. Apparently you pissed him off when you said he was 'dumber than a brain-damaged gerbil' in last month's review column."

"I'm not writing a retraction," Bailey stated, crossing his arms over his chest. "I think if a test were done, one could easily prove that Gallagher in fact *has* an IQ lower than a gerbil. And significantly fewer instincts for self-preservation as well. Not only is he happy to theorize that his proposed device to tap into geothermal energy will *not* cause a recursive power buildup that could very well blow up our whole planet, gleefully ignoring *basic laws of physics,* but now he's suing me! As if he has any chance of coming out of a confrontation with me anything other than beaten and humiliated."

"Yeah, well." John grinned. "While I agree that Pierce Gallagher is a huge douche bag and that all publicity for *Spark* is good publicity, I've still set up a meeting for you to talk to our lawyers this morning."

"Oh God." Bailey reached for the coffeepot and gave himself a refill. "When?"

There was a buzz on John's intercom.

"Pretty much right now." John said. "Don't worry, I'll stay here to translate cranky-Bailey speech for the attorneys. It wouldn't be the best move if you insulted them enough that they wanted to sue you too."

Bailey sneered but had to agree that there was some merit in that plan. "Aspirin. Food. And why is everyone so litigious these days?" he asked as John picked up the phone to Lauren, conveying Bailey's demands. "When I tell people how to do their jobs, it's because I'm a genius and they need the benefits of my knowledge to do their job well. I mean, it's not like I tell the baristas how to make me a latte unless they do it wrong."

"Or unless you see a better way that they could be doing it," John pointed out.

"Well, yes. In other words: *wrong*."

Lauren ushered in a man and woman, both in impeccably conservative suits, and deposited a plate of muffins and bottle of Advil on John's desk. "Good luck," she murmured as she closed the door behind her.

John made the introductions while Bailey crammed a muffin and another cup of coffee into his mouth, then a final pot-emptying cup while he downed a handful of tablets.

John wisely took the opportunity to outline the problem while Bailey's mouth was full. He discussed with Ms. Zhen and Mr. Tulley the possible courses of action. When the word "retraction" came up and Bailey's face began to turn red as he struggled to swallow his bite of muffin, John merely lifted a hand to hush him.

"Just trust me, all right?" he said, passing his two-thirds full cup of coffee to Bailey, along with another muffin.

Bailey shrugged and accepted the bribe.

By the time John was standing up and Bailey had consumed every crumb on the plate, the end result of an hour-long discussion about editorial opinion restrictions and allowances, libel laws, and how very clear it was that Dr. Gallagher's attorney was going to be utterly humiliated if he actually tried to file a suit, was that they decided to do nothing.

Which in no way stopped Bailey from e-mailing his former coworker and sort-of friend, Dr. Záviška, as soon as he got back to his desk. Several screens of ranting and raving later, he hit "send" and then settled down to work.

When he next glanced up and took note of the world around him, he saw that Václav had already replied in his typical succinct bullet-pointed format:

- No, I do not think Gallagher has a chance in hell. While you were the only one to say in print, I suspect most reputable scientists agree that his theories are more on the "fantasy" side of scifi than "science."

- Yes. I suspect I have seen plants with higher self-preservation instincts, to say nothing of the entire animal kingdom.

- If the USA government can trust me with top secret projects, you should be able to, too. Why would your personal security clearance be any higher?

- What are you working on, Bailey? I will not get involved in any more projects with you and corporate Americans; my reputation barely survived our last encounter. I have enough difficulty in getting all of you to forget about your so-called Cold War, never mind that you have no idea how cold it actually was behind the Iron Curtain.

- And shut up, I know you are not American, Canada is different; I do not care. When you recognize that Czech Republic is not the same as Soviet Russia, then we will talk.

- I will be in your city for the Intelligent Energy conference in two weeks. Are you attending? Come; I will shield you from the crowd armed with rotten tomatoes. Probably.

Bailey snorted at the last one, imagining the significantly shorter scientist trying to protect him from a horde of people dressed in Renaissance Faire peasant clothes, armed with produce.

"What's so funny?" John asked behind him. Bailey jumped and almost knocked over his coffee. "Jeez, over-caffeinated much?"

"No such thing," Bailey grumbled. "And stop sneaking around like some kind of jungle cat stalking its prey. What do you want?"

"What were you laughing at?" John asked again, leaning in to look at Bailey's screen over his shoulder.

"Nothing, just Záviška—Václav—you remember him? Short wiry little Czech guy, glasses, hair that could give Einstein a run for his money? We worked on the—"

"Stellar project, right. I remember him, yeah."

"He's going to be in town. He thinks I should go to the energy conference with him."

John nodded. "You have to start getting out and about sometime. I mean, I know people were mad, but the scientists know it wasn't your fault that Stellar ripped off all those people. They know what it's like when someone else takes your work and ignores the potential consequences."

Bailey shrugged. Stellar had taken his—and yes, fine, his *team's*—brilliant ideas for modernizing nuclear power and pretty much created an immediate monopoly. The US government had had to step in and break it up, but only after hundreds of people had been screwed out of millions of dollars. Even though Bailey himself hadn't done anything wrong, everyone associated with Stellar Energy had been blacklisted by the media. Furthermore, because Stellar's board of directors had cut corners by choosing not to implement the nuclear waste disposal system the science team had recommended, the general public had associated the names of all the researchers with overflowing toxic waste dumps. As the lead scientist with all the "revolutionary genius to make it happen," Bailey's name was the one everyone had focused on.

"Listen to Záviška," John said, nudging his shoulder. "He wouldn't suggest you go if he thought you were going to be eviscerated."

"True. He's surprisingly forgiving for someone who's worked with me on multiple projects."

John laughed. "It's a small club."

"Elite?" Bailey's voice was hopeful.

"More like survivors of a plague," John said thoughtfully. "Or refugees from a natural disaster who somehow escaped unscathed."

"You suck."

John ruffled Bailey's hair and then easily dodged his friend's punches. "Someone's got to keep that enormous ego in check. It's my duty to humanity." He grinned at Bailey's scowl. "So, dinner later?"

Bailey turned back to his computer and frowned at it, then opened a new window. "Yes, fine. Go away now." He started typing.

Grinning, John tiptoed away and left him to it.

Chapter 4

Libra Trine

DINNER with John was good. Not that it usually wasn't, just that usually Bailey didn't have much other company in recent memory to compare it to. It was relaxed, enjoyable even—easy conversation, no need to explain or excuse any of his personality flaws, no need to care whether or when his deodorant had given out or if his hair was sticking up. Good.

After dinner they walked a bit, John pointing out that it was practically criminal not to go and enjoy the spring evening, which was likely warmer than the summer ones would be, no thanks to the San Francisco fog. After soliciting a promise that John knew where Bailey's EpiPen was and how to use it, he consented to a stroll in the flower-and-bee-filled park.

They talked about work and about John's ongoing struggles with the new marketing team, and Bailey tried to rein in his rant about Dr. Culper at UCLA, who appeared to be attempting to steal some of Bailey's ideas to confirm string theory. They laughed and insulted each other's intelligence, but in a comfortable, friendly way, as they walked through the deepening twilight. It was so very much like a date that Bailey almost expected John to hold his hand, and there was a strange moment as they parted when there would have been a goodnight kiss, if it had been.

Which was weird, because it was just John and not a date at all.

THE next morning as Bailey walked up to the office doors, there was a scruffy guy in his early twenties leaning against the wall. He was a little too clean to be homeless, although his white-boy almost-afro, with stained trousers and button-down shirt, suggested it. The stench of pot smoke as he shoved a clipboard at Bailey and asked "Dana Bailey McMillan?" was enough to gag a horse.

"Yes? What?"

"You are being served," the guy said with a smug grin and the flourish of a pen.

"Oh for the love of God...." Bailey took the sheaf of papers and signed where the man indicated.

He didn't even see John running across the street to nearly tackle him from the side. "Wait! You don't have to take those."

"I do, actually," Bailey said, and the court's agent nodded. "I confirmed who I was." He gave John a look. "This isn't my first time at this particular rodeo, Forrester."

Bailey was still signing and thus not looking at John, who mouthed "Rodeo?" at the agent, as if somehow the guy would be able to make him understand what sort of rodeos Bailey *had* been to. The guy shrugged and looked like he was hoping to get back to his bong before it got lonely and found someone else who would love it.

"You should check that it's from a reputable law firm first," John said out loud.

"It's from Cowen, Turja, Kavalos, and Rankin—not the most reputable, but still legitimate. Maybe Gallagher has a sibling there or something and his attorney wasn't able to talk him out of this colossal mistake without ruining Christmas dinners."

The stoner guy took back his clipboard and rambled off a flat and obviously memorized spiel about how by signing, Bailey was agreeing to the summons and would be present in court on the date specified. Bailey rolled his eyes in exasperation and nodded, practically shoving the guy out of the way so he could get inside to his morning pot of coffee.

"May I?" John asked, pulling the envelope out of Bailey's hands before he could protest. "I'll call Robert and let him know you've been served. He can deal with it; you just get to work."

"But—" Bailey tried to protest.

John raised one eyebrow. "You'd rather spend your day hassling with lawyers, ranting and raving about freedom of speech, instead of that thing you were going on and on about last night, what was it, monopoles?"

Bailey scowled. "Well, no, not as such. No. I just want it handled correctly. I have an attorney I worked with before, Russell Chapman. I don't know this Tulley."

"Trust me, that's probably for the best," John said. "He doesn't need you micromanaging him. I hired him for a reason; his firm is the best." At Bailey's crossed-arm challenging glare, he added, "I met Robert Tulley when he was lead counsel for the Army Corps of Engineers. He has an MBA and JD from Harvard, and he teaches classes on libel, slander, and defamation at Stanford. Is that enough, or would you like me to get a copy of his résumé for you?"

"Fine. I have better things to do with my time anyway," Bailey grudgingly allowed.

"Exactly. Let him do his job and you do yours," John said, patting Bailey's shoulder in a placating way. "No need to worry your pretty little head about such unpleasant business."

"I am going to punch you if you don't get away from me right now."

"Aw, Bailey. Violence never solves anything," John said, grinning as he backed away into his office.

"Ironic words for the former G.I. Joe," Bailey grumbled into his *World's Greatest Mad Scientist* coffee mug. The mug didn't answer.

"BAILEY MCMILLAN?" said a tallish, blondish man in his midforties. "I'm Rich Crown." He held out a hand for Bailey to shake. "Before you say anything, I want to apologize for being late; I got caught up in my work, but that's no excuse for keeping you waiting on a first date."

The man was only about ten minutes late (all right, twelve), and Bailey hadn't begun to get irritated about it yet, but it was decidedly nice to get an unprompted apology for once. "That happens to me a lot as well, getting absorbed in a project and losing track of time," Bailey allowed. "Nice to meet you."

"So what kind of work do you do?" they both asked at the same time.

Rich laughed, a generous and warm sound, and waited until Bailey had smiled and waved his hand at him to answer first. "I'm a writer. Mystery and suspense, mostly. And before you ask: no, nothing you'd have read. I was in journalism for a long time and just recently quit to do this instead. My first novel doesn't come out until this winter."

"All right. Well, as an interesting coincidence, I'm an astrophysicist who's just recently started writing for a new science magazine, *Spark*."

Rich's eyes twinkled with amusement. "I know. I looked you up and then realized you were the genius behind the critical diatribes that always make me laugh inappropriately loudly when I'm waiting in my doctor's office. I subscribed on the website today."

"Oh. Well, ah, thank you," Bailey said, trying not to squirm. It had been a long time since he had been praised for his work, particularly from anyone not in his field.

Which Rich noticed. "I'm sorry; have I made you uncomfortable? You've won all kinds of awards and stuff, so I'd think you'd be used to accolades and praise—oh, is it the Stellar thing?" His forehead wrinkled with concern.

"Dear God, am I never going to live that down?" Bailey said, rolling his eyes heavenward. This Rich guy was entirely too perceptive, and had he memorized Bailey's entire bio or what?

A warm hand covered his briefly, a small gesture of comfort, which Bailey was surprised to find worked. "You will. It hasn't been that long, and people will forget once you impress them with your next big idea," Rich said.

It was obviously flattery, but it did the job, and Bailey felt a little better. "Thanks. So, have you been here before?" he asked in an unsubtle attempt to change the subject, picking up the menu to hide behind it for a moment.

"Yes, many times. I know it sounds absolutely flaming," Rich said, leaning close like he was about to share top secret information, "but they make a *really* good quiche here."

As his date probably intended, that made Bailey smile. "Seriously? Quiche?"

"I know, right? Not only a huge cliché, but I'm older than you are, and even I was too young for the quiche trend of the seventies. But honestly, they somehow manage to keep the crust from turning soggy and gross, and they'll put just about anything you like in it, like an omelet. My favorite is the pesto, brie, and turkey. Oh, and their waffle sundae is also amazing, if you have a sweet tooth, which I do. I recommend the chocolate syrup instead of maple, or both if you really want to indulge. We could split it," he added with a suggestive grin when Bailey looked intrigued but hesitant. "I do like to indulge."

That was when Bailey knew the date was going to be a good one.

Over dinner they discussed everything: local restaurants of the best-kept-secrets variety; the tragedy of middle-aged metabolism; the mechanics of writing, physics, and the various forms of creativity in both fields. Bailey did order the quiche—which was fantastic—and they spilt the waffle sundae. He was pretty sure his date was flirting with him—well, obviously the man was flirting; the question was whether he meant it or if he was just outgoing and liked to flirt with whomever was nearby. Rich Crown was a bit of a queen, pun completely unintentional.

Rich was also spectacularly easy to get along with. He was smart enough to understand most of what Bailey said about his string theory research when he broke it into basic concepts. His thoughts on writing and working for magazines and newspapers were insightful and often amusing. He had a dry sense of humor that Bailey enjoyed, but it was not as acerbic as Bailey's own. He was a bit wishy-washy, though; a few times Bailey expressed an opinion contradicting his, and Rich didn't exactly backtrack so much as say that he could see Bailey's points, but…. It wasn't a bad thing, really; it was nice to hang out with someone without arguing, but in the long run it would probably irritate him. Bailey did enjoy a good argument now and then.

Wait, why was he thinking about this date in terms of a relationship? As if it was a real date, not just a stupid faux experiment to prove John wrong and make him pay for an expensive dinner?

After they'd finished the last of the sundae, Bailey paid and Rich escorted him out the door, a hand on his arm. "It's a nice evening tonight; I'm having a good time, are you?" When Bailey nodded, Rich asked, "Do you want to come back to my place? I know that sounds like a line, maybe it sort of is, but our building has one of those gardens on the roof that was mentioned in *Spark* last month, the green roof kind. I thought you might be interested in seeing it." He grinned.

Bailey didn't have much interest in plants—botany, ugh—but the allure of seeing the results of some of the current sustainability attempts in urban development, and their relevance to his work on energy consumption and reduction, sucked him in. And he was having a good time with Rich, besides. It was too early to simply go home.

On the way up to the roof, they stopped at Rich's apartment, which was an extremely large one for San Francisco. It looked like it was three bedrooms at least, which was odd for a single man, but before Bailey could comment or ask, Rich asked, "Should we bring the telescope? It looks like there's shockingly little cloud cover tonight. Or are the stars boring for a genius astrophysicist like you?"

His voice had a teasing element, so Bailey shrugged. "A telescope could be fun," he allowed, and bit his tongue against saying anything about astronomy or its illegitimate—and godforsaken—cousin, astrology.

Rich indicated for him to follow and switched on the light to a bedroom that was decorated with an unusually pastel floral wallpaper for a man in his forties, no matter how gay. Bailey blinked.

"Ah. This is my daughter's room. It's her telescope, actually. She's the one fortunate result of my brief attempt at heterosexuality."

Kids were kind of a deal breaker for Bailey, and yes, he was well aware of how shallow that made him. Damn it. "How old is she?" he asked.

"Eighteen. She's a freshman at Duke," Rich said, his pride obvious. "Sorry I didn't mention her before, but you know, some guys run at the mention of breeding, and it's honestly not as relevant as it would have been a few years ago."

Ah well. A kid that was grown up and gone was different. "Not to worry," Bailey said and, feeling generous, added, "I'm technically bisexual myself."

"Oh?"

He nodded. "Yes. Things just always work out better with men."

The huge smile he got from Rich was definitely worth the self-exposure and sort of admitting that he sucked with women. Together they lugged the telescope out to the elevator and across the roof to set it up. Rich knew what he was doing, so it didn't take very long, and it actually was a clear enough night to see an impressive stellar display. Not as impressive as it would have been somewhere outside of the city, of course, but still. They got a nice view of the Great Orion Nebula, and the moon's craters were always interesting to see close up.

"This was a good idea," Bailey admitted as they lounged back onto a bench nestled between some potted plants. Rich was pointing out the solar panels strategically hidden throughout the landscaping, and talking about how the roof saved huge amounts on energy consumption and heat loss for the building.

Bailey clarified, "Coming up here, I mean. Of course the green roof was a good idea. I'm impressed that you somehow got fourteen different owners to agree on the plans and finance it."

"I can be very persuasive," Rich said with a smile that left Bailey with no doubts.

It made him a little nervous to be flirted with so boldly, not in a bad way, but in an overly hopeful yes-please-*please* anticipatory way. Which made him babble a bit. "I do seem to be easily persuaded lately, which is so not like me at all. Just a few days ago I let myself be talked into a walk at the park, completely disregarding the dangers of solar radiation, thousands of allergens, and the ever-present threat of anaphylactic shock by apitoxin. To say nothing of this stupid bet, uh"—he cringed, catching himself too late—"*experiment* with John. He always manages to talk me into things."

"Hm... are you dating him?" Rich asked, a speculative look on his face.

"What, John? No, of course not. He's my boss, and best friend, I guess, but—"

"Good," Rich interrupted, getting up. Taking Bailey's hand, Rich pulled him up from the bench too, tugging him forward until he was close enough for their mouths to meet. Both hands securely holding Bailey's, Rich kissed him.

It started out as a somewhat cautious kiss, gentle even, but as they warmed to each other, Bailey felt desire beginning to build, sudden and unexpected and frankly delicious. This was good; God, he'd missed being touched like this....

"Is this all right?" Rich asked, coming up for air and taking those soft but strong lips too far away.

Bailey pulled him back in, his answer, "Yes, yes, very yes...," muffled as he closed the gap between them.

Without consciously meaning to, Bailey slowly walked Rich backward, the long, breath-stealing kisses disorienting for both of them. When they ran up against one of the ventilation units, Rich leaned back onto its sod-covered surface with a groan, wrapping his arms around Bailey's waist. He spread his legs apart and Bailey eagerly stepped into the space, bringing their bodies flush against each other. The next kiss was even hotter than the others had been, as if someone had suddenly turned up the heat, if that was how to measure the intensity of kisses. If so, then they'd gone from 18°C to 85°C, full of urgency and nearing the boiling point—or a simmer, at least—as Rich's hands slid down to grab Bailey's ass and grind their bodies together.

Rich's hands were fantastic, roaming all over his body but not distracting from the hot-hot-hot kisses, strong hands sliding all over him, in the delicious zone between soothing, calming touches and exploring, really fucking sexy touches, like Rich was learning the shape of every part of him, every muscle and curve. When Rich's hands got to his waist, Bailey pulled back enough to accommodate them, taking the opportunity himself to untuck Rich's shirt and start unbuttoning it, so he missed the moment before Rich's hands pressed against his thighs and then moved inward to surround his erection in a confident grip.

For a moment Bailey groaned into the sensation, but then managed to gasp, "No, wait."

Rich let go immediately, hands back on Bailey's shoulders, gently pushing him away to create some space between them, and when Bailey managed to refocus his eyes—still feeling a little drunk from the really spectacular groping—his date's forehead was furrowed with concern.

"I'm sorry; damn it. Too fast?"

"What? No, no, it's good," Bailey protested, confused for a second; he might be two kinds of genius, but lust melted his brain just like anybody else's. Maybe more so, since good sex wasn't exactly something he'd had an opportunity to build up much tolerance against. "No, it's good. Great, even. Just, horizontal would be better?"

Rich grinned, both relived and lecherous. "I like how you think."

BAILEY tried not to swagger, strut, or saunter as he walked into the office the next morning. Last night had been the end of a long dry spell, or at least, by Bailey's definitions of sex, it had been. He figured that once a person stepped away from defining sex as exclusively limited to penile-vaginal intercourse, anything that resulted in mutually enjoyable naked time with orgasms counted. Last night had been one of the best hand jobs he could remember, and if it simply *seemed* better because it was so recent, that was completely acceptable to him. It had been well over a year since any hand but his own had touched his dick, therefore: Best Hand Job Ever.

So all right; he might have strutted a little bit.

When he got to his desk, he was surprised to find an enormous bouquet of stargazer lilies and sunflowers there. Given that he was allergic to almost every kind of pollen in North America, who on earth would send him flowers? Was someone trying to kill him, albeit in the most ineffective way possible?

He saw a small card nestled among the flowers and took it, half-expecting a death threat or professional taunt. Instead, a very messy scrawl said, *Thank you for such an enlightening evening. I know the date was part of an experiment, but I hope we can explore more heavenly bodies together sometime. – Rich.* He'd included his business card as well, with e-mail address and cell phone number.

Cheesy, but sort of sweet at the same time. Not unlike Rich himself.

"I take it that your date went well?" John asked, suddenly standing beside him, leaning over to read the card in his hand.

Bailey tried not to squirm. "Yes. Very well."

"*Very* well? How well?" John's voice was almost toneless.

Bailey shrugged, trying not to smile and failing. "Well enough to end that dry spell I mentioned."

Bailey had expected some sort of male-bonding punch in the shoulder or a lewd remark or an insult blended with congratulations. Instead, John's jaw clenched and he turned an angry glare on the flowers, as if he was trying to set them on fire with the power of his brain.

John's eyebrows were sarcastic, and he didn't look at Bailey as he asked, "On the first date?"

Bailey's good mood vanished. "What crawled up your ass this morning? No, forget it," he said, holding up a hand. "I don't have time for this right now. I have Simpson's article on the creation of exotic particles to review before it goes to Elizabeth for approval, and it's already over a day late because of some personal crisis of hers, which is somehow now my mess to clean up. My sex life is absolutely not an appropriate conversation for work, and I can't deal with whatever midlife crisis you're having because I had a date and you didn't when

God knows you could pick up anyone you wanted just by smiling at them."

John rolled his eyes, although this typical reaction to one of Bailey's rants seemed more irritated than usual. "Fine. Get to work, then."

"Fine." Bailey sat down at his desk and ignored John until he went away.

It just figured that he'd finally score and John wouldn't be happy for him. This was all John's stupid idea anyway, from the blind dates to the idiotic bet and the offensive astrology column in the first place. *Of course* none of the results had anything to do with anything at all; it was simple statistical probability that at least one of twelve men Bailey was scheduled to have dinner with might end up in a semi-sexual encounter. Unless John really thought Bailey was that unattractive or his personality that abrasive....

He was working up a good head of steam—all while reviewing Simpson's article and correcting the gross misinformation she had been about to publish—when the chat window on his desktop flashed at him. It was John.

King John: Lauren says to tell you that SF Roasting just delivered a ten-pound bag of that Ethiopian coffee you like.

He snorted. The idea of demanding that John bring him a cup crossed his mind, but he decided not to push his luck with the apology-cum-peace offering. John was notoriously stubborn—almost as much so as Bailey himself—and while Bailey enjoyed arguing, he didn't like it when people were actually angry with him. Well, people whose opinions he respected, anyway. So, maybe three or four people in the universe. But John was one of them, and while he was clearly in the wrong, coffee *did* in fact make almost everything better.

Genius: Thanks.

King John: Just a reminder that you're not allowed to fill up baggies of the beans and hide them in your desk so that other people won't drink all of it.

Genius: Spoilsport.

King John: Miser.

Half an hour later, John sent,

King John: My place tonight? We'll fill out your date evaluation over pizza and beer?

Genius: Yes, fine. Can I actually get some work done today or what? Elizabeth is sending me "nudge" messages every 10 minutes.

King John: Sure. Wouldn't want to get you in trouble with the boss. I hear he's a real hardass.

Genius: You have no idea.

Bailey heard John's snorting laughter all the way from his office.

Chapter 5

Scorpio Eccentricity

"HOW did I let you talk me into working for you again?" Bailey asked, sprawling onto one of the recliners in John's living room, a bottle of beer in one hand.

"I was the only one willing to offer you a job," John said with a smirk.

Bailey snorted. "Sure, if by 'job' you mean the performance of largely irrelevant tasks that make almost no use of my genius and compensation that would be commensurate to my abilities only if I were being paid in Kuwaiti dinars... or diamonds, maybe. No, gold; diamonds are laughably easy to synthesize."

"You could be unemployed," John offered. "I'd be happy to let you move on to new opportunities, let you catch up on the soaps, go for weeks without shaving."

"Just because some of us don't grow a disgusting mountain-man beard overnight...."

"Less testosterone doesn't make you less of a man," John reassured him with a huge grin.

Bailey rolled his eyes. "Schoolyard taunts are so unbecoming on a man over forty."

John stuck out his tongue like a bratty kid, and they both laughed. "Seriously," John said a few moments later, "I never expected you to stay on at *Spark* forever. Don't get me wrong, you're honestly irreplaceable as the fact-checker, but I know you're capable of a whole lot more than writing scathing commentary of your peers and proofreading everyone else's work."

Bailey was surprised to realize that it had been well over a year since John had contacted him out of the blue and told Bailey to stop screwing around in his home, ranting and raving about the Stellar fiasco, and come work for him instead. Even more of a social pariah than usual and in need of a job—not for the money but for something occupy his time—Bailey had agreed.

He shrugged. "I'll quit when I find something else to fill my days that isn't likely to get me banned from the scientific community for gross negligence. You wouldn't believe the offers I get from thugs and lowlifes; they must still think I'm desperate enough to take on whatever outrageously destructive project they couldn't find anyone else willing to do. Did you know I was contacted by the Koreans to design nukes for them?"

John blinked. "Uh. Maybe you should tell someone in the military about that?"

"Oh please; my general e-mail's been monitored by the US government since I was sixteen. I'm sure they already know."

"Huh. Remind me not to send you any illegally downloaded porn."

Bailey gave him a look. "As if I'd want your virus-ridden, skanky, fake-boobed bimbo amateur filth on my system anyway."

John laughed. "How about the stuff with overly-waxed gym-bunny college boys?"

After pretending to think about it for a moment, Bailey shrugged. "Not if they're going to give me viruses. Porn is supposed to be safe sex, you know."

After a long pull at his beer, John said, "Speaking of porn... we should get your date evaluation done before we forget about it."

Bailey narrowed his eyes. He really didn't want to deal with a grouchy John again—or in any way address the fact that apparently John saw him as a completely sexless and unappealing geek—but it *was* getting late. So he agreed, and John grabbed his laptop, and they got to work.

After giving Rich three-out-of-fives on categories like shared interests, ethics, and other dinner conversation-type compatibility areas, they moved into the more personal topics. "Attractiveness... Rich was a three? Four? Give him a three-point-five, I guess," Bailey said. "Not at all unattractive, but didn't immediately make me weak in the knees or anything."

"What are you—a swooning maiden?"

Bailey ignored him. "Good body—damn good, considering his age—nice smile, and I do like floppy hair... I don't know; is that a four?"

There was a silence. "Maybe it would help if you decided what a five was. Brad Pitt?"

"Blech," Bailey said. "David Duchovny, maybe?"

The face John made was indescribable. "Really? I mean, he's attractive, yeah, but a five? He gets you that hot and bothered?"

"Well... no, I guess not. I just have always sort of had a thing for him. He's smart *and* hot. But I guess a five should be, what, a cross between a porn star, Greek god, and Renaissance painting?"

"Right. Some guy who's astoundingly gorgeous and also makes you pop wood."

"Thank you for bringing it down the lowest common denominator."

"No problem." John smirked. "So, who's your five?"

They sat in silence for a long moment while Bailey made faces, thinking hard. After a few minutes, he shrugged. "I give up. I can't think of anyone who isn't actually a porn star, and their employment choices make me question their intelligence too much to keep them from being a five. What can I say; I'm shallow, but no one's going to be my five based on looks alone." He paused again. "Are you sure I can't just go with David Duchovny?"

John coughed. "You know, people have said I look like him."

Bailey rolled his eyes. "Don't flatter yourself; Scully would never fall for you."

"Anyway," John said, tapping the keyboard. "So Rich was a three-point-five. And the, uh, chemistry between you two?" he asked, keeping his gaze fixed on the computer screen.

"Four out of five," Bailey said decidedly. "He's flirty, and that's always flattering. Good with his hands and—"

"Whoa, that's enough!" John interrupted. "This is a rating scale, not a tell-all confessional. I don't need the sticky details, thanks."

Sighing, Bailey nodded. "Fine, what's next?"

They finished off the questionnaire, John very businesslike and Bailey resigned to John's disinterest. He supposed it made sense; he wouldn't want all the details of John's sex life either, if his friend was ever inclined to share them. Not that he wouldn't mind *some* details about the hand job John had mentioned from the wedding last summer, but he was willing to accept that that was for more prurient interests than were socially acceptable, and he'd probably end up feeling jealous anyway.

John had really nice hands, though, long fingers, strong but dexterous. They probably felt at least as good as Rich's, not that Bailey would ever find out. Which was fine; whatever. He still had nine more of these stupid dates to get through anyway. Statistically speaking, he should be able to get laid at least once more; John might not be interested, but someone else might be. Or he could always call Rich again....

Wondering why that idea wasn't as appealing as he thought it should be, he finished off the beer, called a cab, and went home. He asked Castrovalva, but as usual his cat was more focused on getting his much-delayed dinner than on Bailey's emotional conundrums. Stupid cat.

SOME weeks Bailey did all of the math, rather than simply running the numbers through the horoscope program he'd written, just to see. He couldn't find any causation, despite the patterns. It was aggravating, like being a psychic who didn't believe in the paranormal, despite every prediction coming true. The accuracy of his astrology predictions simply defied any rational understanding of the world; therefore, there must be something he was overlooking that would explain it.

His frequent rants at the bar after work with John were now met with beer and hand-waving literary references. Last time John had said, "There are more things in heaven and earth, Bailey, than are dreamt of in your philosophy."

Bailey had snorted at him. "Nonsense. If I can't understand it, it's because it doesn't exist. I *will* figure this out. I am a *genius*, not a superstitious New Ager, remember? Nor some ignorant playwright barely out of the Dark Ages."

So today was one of those days. He was caught up on the fact-checking for all of his coworkers, had written the next two scathing reviews of his colleagues' mistakes at CERN and at the proposed Neutrino Factory, where they were about to repeat the same mistakes in a brand-new location. His office-slash-lab at home was feeling small and cramped, and his string theory project was going nowhere. Now it was Monday and Bailey was scribbling algorithms on the whiteboard next to his desk, filling it with as many variables as he could, guzzling coffee and calculating the angle of entrance of various astronomical bodies into certain areas of the sky. Also mentally composing an epic rant at whomever (the Greeks?) had looked at six stars and suddenly seen a crab. Apparently the wine in ancient Greece had been fairly strong.

"How's it going?" John asked, taking a marker out of Bailey's hand and replacing it with a muffin.

Bailey obligingly crammed about a third of it into his mouth and chewed, realizing some of his irritability and shakes might be the result of a gallon of coffee on an empty stomach. "Romance is rocky for Aquarius this week."

"Sucks to be them." John shrugged.

Bailey made a face. "I'm an Aquarius. But then, I don't believe in this crap." He scowled at his equations as if the numbers were taunting him, personally.

"Lauren wants to talk to you."

"And you're her errand boy?"

John shrugged again, and Bailey was momentarily distracted by the strange expressiveness of John's body language. His shoulders and eyebrows could communicate everything from mild disinterest to a full assessment of the cost/benefits of a proposed plan of action, in detail.

"She pointed out that you didn't seem to have eaten anything, and you growled at Simpson when she tried to get some coffee earlier. So I thought I'd let you have my muffin," John said with a suggestive brow-wiggle, as if Bailey wouldn't have gotten the innuendo.

"Hm, thanks," he said, then turned and stalked over to Lauren's desk, John trailing behind him like a puppy. "What?" he asked her.

Lauren grinned. "Your Tuesday date wants to move it up to tonight. I told him you weren't busy and that was fine."

"What? It's a Monday. You can't have a date on Monday night." He looked at John for confirmation and got a shrug and nod combination in response. "See? No, that's weird. Monday nights are for whining about a new workweek and drinking too much beer, watching stupid sports, and trying to catch up on the sleep you missed over the weekend from social events and whatnot."

"You had social events and 'whatnot' over the weekend? So much that you didn't get enough sleep? Sure, pull the other one, McMillan," Lauren said, snorting.

Bailey scowled at her. He'd been up until dawn on Sunday, but she didn't need to know he had been watching a *Doctor Who* marathon with his cat. "Fine," he huffed. "But I can already tell this one isn't going to go very well."

THAT night's date was not only strange, but half an hour late. He'd arranged to meet Bailey at a taqueria downtown, where, yes, they had good burritos, but no, not a good first impression to make, choosing a place that was essentially fast food. Also, what was up with his name?

"What sort of name is Frode?" Bailey asked, not caring if it was rude because really, there was no way this was going to go well. The man was tall and lean, almost too skinny, wearing paint-splattered blue jeans, and looked vaguely stoned, although he didn't smell of anything other than a hippy scent—patchouli, maybe?—and oil paint. He had nice eyes, though, an unusual blue-green-hazel.

"It's Danish," his date said, shrugging. "Dad was from there." At Bailey's skeptical look, he added, "Mom's family was from Spain; I look more like them. Ever been there? Any family?"

"Oh yes, the Barcelona McMillans," Bailey retorted. He took a deep breath and tried to remember to be nice. Or fair, at least. "So, you're a painter? What kind of art do you do?"

Frode took a drink of the yerba mate he'd ordered, whatever the heck that was. "Mixed media—paint, poetry, photos, found objects— that sort of thing."

"Are you any good?"

Looking more amused than offended, Frode shrugged. "Some people like it. Some don't. Got a few books published, but then I own the press, so maybe that doesn't count. Had an exhibit at the gallery on Geary last month."

Bailey nodded. "Modern?"

"Abstract." Frode took another drink, calm and unruffled by Bailey's somewhat rude interrogation. "And you're a scientist. Do you like that?"

"Like it?" No one had ever asked him if he "liked" physics and/or engineering before, and he flailed for a minute before answering. "Science isn't about 'liking', it's about understanding the world we live in and the universe beyond. It's about getting the most power from the least resources, with the fewest toxic byproducts. It's about stopping people from being such absolute idiots and messing up the ecological niche that we live in while we're still, you know, *trying to live in it*!"

His date nodded. "I like the earth too."

Closing his eyes for a moment to appeal to whatever higher powers there might be, despite his not believing in them, Bailey took a breath. He opened them in time to see the glint of amusement in his date's eyes and knew he'd been successfully baited.

The rest of the evening went about the same. Not hideously badly, but not well. Frode was difficult to get talking, his soft voice making him sound more hesitant than he actually was once he got the words out. But he jumped from topic to topic, threading together his thoughts on an Argentinean media scandal, WikiLeaks, pollution in developing nations, and the declining honeybee population crisis.

It wasn't that Bailey couldn't keep up; it was that it was simply annoying to flit around like one of the insects Frode was so concerned about rather than finish any particular topic or even delve into it very deeply. He suspected the man's life—and conversation—was like the art he'd looked up on his smartphone while Frode was in the restroom: bits and pieces all over a canvas, seemingly at random, and it was up to the observer to pull from it whatever meaning was there. If there was any meaning at all.

They finished dinner and headed out, hovering on the sidewalk.

"You like things to be more direct, huh?" Frode asked.

Bailey nodded emphatically. "Yes. Yes, I do."

"Should have guessed that from your ad, probably. The *Goldberg Variations* drew me in, though. And I also like *Doctor Who*," he added in a thoughtful tone.

"Ah... did you catch the marathon on PBS over the weekend?" Bailey couldn't imagine why he felt like he should keep the conversation going. It had been less than two hours, however, and it felt like kind of a waste to call it a night so soon.

"Nope." There was a long moment of silence, awkward on Bailey's part, although Frode seemed at ease. "Well, good luck on your dating experiment. I hope I provided some interesting data. And thanks for dinner," he said, raising the bag with the remaining half of his burrito in a strange salute.

Bailey started to hold out his hand to shake, but then he realized Frode still had his drink in the other hand and nodded instead. "Okay, yes, thanks. Um. Good night?"

Frode nodded and turned away. Bailey watched as he walked down the sidewalk, stopping near the corner to give his extra food to a homeless person sitting in a doorway.

Bailey sighed. Artists; they never made any sense to him. Could have been worse, though, he supposed, thinking of Ramses. Suddenly craving chocolate ice cream, he hurried home.

King John: Are you home already or did you just leave your computer on?

Genius: Home. Date was a flop. An artist, honestly. Can you think of any sort of person I'd be less compatible with?

King John: Teen pop star. Kindergarten teacher. Fashion designer.

Genius: Bite me. Also a singer and designer fall into the "artist" category, so they don't count.

King John: Car salesperson.

Genius: God, I hate them….

King John: So, bad date?

Genius: Not bad. Just a dud. We didn't connect at all, you know? No, you probably don't know—you can charm the pants off anyone.

King John: You wanted to charm his pants off? Damn, Bailey, turning into a Casanova on me?

Genius: I don't think so; has Hell frozen over already? Because I thought there was at least half a century before the next big climactic change, even with the greenhouse gases.

King John: It must have, if you're getting laid and I'm not.

Genius: Thanks. And anyway, I didn't get "laid" by most teenage boy standards, anyhow. But to spare you the horror of imagining me as a person who sometimes has sex, I'll skip the details.

King John: I know you have sex, Bailey. At least, I would hope so; you're a little young to be celibate. Or did you take some kind of vow with the second PhD?

Genius: You'd almost think so, given the length of the dry spells. Why do astrophysicists never get the science groupies? So unfair.

King John: No kidding. Too bad the energy conference coming up isn't in Vegas. You could maybe get a group discount at the Mustang Ranch or something.

Genius: Right, because a bunch of scientists are going to trust a whorehouse nurse that the goods are clean. To say nothing of the sordid dehumanizing nature of treating sex like an exchange of services.

King John: I like how your ethics are secondary to your personal health concerns. Gives me a warm feeling inside.

Genius: If it's a burning feeling, it's probably gonorrhea.

King John: Jerk.

Genius: Yes, lately.

King John: TMI! Anyway, I just wanted to check in that you saw the e-mail from Tulley about your court date this Friday at 10AM.

Genius: Goddammit. *This* Friday?

King John: Yes. I'll be going with you. To make sure you get there and are caffeinated enough not to get thrown in jail for contempt of court. Tulley is good, but no one is that good.

Genius: Only the Java God.

King John: And wear a suit. You have one, right? Does it need dry cleaned? And a clean shirt? You want to make Gallagher look like an unstable idiot, so you need to be calm and presentable. Maybe I should sedate you....

Genius: Did I get hit on the head? Am I having memory lapses? Because last I checked, I was fully capable of taking care of myself. Have I slid into Bobby Fisher/David Helfgott savant territory and not noticed?

King John: Says the man who won't let anyone forget he's hypoglycemic but then forgets to eat at least a few times a week.

Genius: Hmm. I've been enjoying the muffins, lately. Did you just start always getting an extra or something?

King John: Or something. Gotta keep the resident genius from fainting from manly hunger.

Genius: That only happened once, and we were in the middle of a crisis. Besides, don't make me go digging up blackmail material on you, because I still have those photos from the night at the state fair that you can't remember.

King John: Great.

Genius: Checked the suit and it does need cleaned. Where do you take yours?

King John: Bring it in and I'll deal with it.

Genius: What? Why? Why are you taking care of me so much? Do you know something I don't know? Did Tulley tell you that I was going to lose this lawsuit and you're being nice to me for when I lose everything I own?

King John: Jesus, paranoid much? I was just offering to help out. I know you're busy with work stuff, and the lawsuit, and your current unusually active social life. To say nothing of trying to disprove astrology.

Genius: Hey, we had an agreement about the A-word.

King John: Astrology. Astrology. Astrology. Astrology. Astrology!

Genius: You suck.

King John: Yup.

Genius: All right then. On that note, time for bed. Good night, John.

King John: Hasta mañana.

Chapter 6

Void of Course

IN RETALIATION, Bailey assumed, for last night's accusation of coddling, the next morning John brought in a big basket of muffins for the whole office, lemon poppy seed muffins, and had clearly marked them as such because John was so very considerate of Bailey's citrus allergy.

He scowled from the coffee area over at John's office and received a grin and jaunty wave.

"My God, would you two just get a room already?" Lauren grumbled, rummaging through a white paper bag on her desk. She pulled out a bran muffin and held it out to Bailey. When he gave her a confused look, she shrugged. "The attorneys are coming to see you today, and I don't care what kind of games you two idiots are playing, I don't want *Spark* caught in the backlash of this lawsuit because you were grouchy with our lawyers."

Preening a little, Bailey went back to his desk, muffin and coffee in hand. A while later, the rest of her words sunk in. He pulled up his daily calendar—which he pretty much ignored—to see a message flashing in red that he had a meeting with Ms. Zhen in less than an hour.

After less than five minutes trying to impress Ms. Zhen with his intellectual prowess and demonstrate that he clearly would be able to handle anything the opposing counsel threw at him, Bailey gave up. The woman was a shark, the embodiment of every stereotype about lawyers—except the positive ones. Yes, she was smart, and driven, and aggressive. She was also rude and condescending, and Bailey had a nasty feeling that she was talking to him the way he typically talked to everyone else on the planet. Although he rarely gave fashion and grooming tips to people, and why did everyone seem to think he couldn't even dress himself in clean clothes lately? Just because he'd spilled coffee on the "My Gamma makes the best Pi" T-shirt he was wearing today didn't mean he was stupid enough to wear dirty clothes to court. Or a T-shirt at all, for that matter.

"I brought a suit in this morning, and I'll take it to the cleaners at lunch," he said, trying to defend himself from further criticism.

"You have a shirt—a button-down—tie, appropriate shoes?" She looked at him critically. "A plain tie, with no math jokes or other 'witticisms'?"

He tried not to cringe. "Yes? I mean, yes. Of course I do. I have a completely boring blue tie." She didn't need to know the pattern on it was of tiny zeros and ones that said "ties suck" to anyone who could read binary code.

The rest of his Tuesday didn't get much better.

"YOU'RE leaving early today?" John asked on Wednesday, leaning against the half-wall of Bailey's cubicle.

"Yes. Václav's flight gets in at eleven, and I'm taking him to my place to sleep off the jetlag."

John's eyebrows shot up with surprise. "He's staying with you?"

"Yes. Why? We're going to work on his ridiculous idea about this new ore they've found in Antarctica, and I'm going to trounce him soundly. Then, when he's been thoroughly disproven, he'll go hide out at the hotel hosting the convention and lick his wounds in solitude." Bailey tried not to sound too gleeful, but he was quite looking forward to crushing Václav's ideas into smithereens.

"Why is this man friends with you?" John mused aloud.

"Because I'm the only one at—although quite a bit above, to be honest—his level. No one else can follow him the same way I can. It's lonely being brilliant." Bailey sighed.

"It's sad to be you," John agreed. "For so many reasons."

"Don't you have anything more useful you could be doing, like counting the pencils in the supply cabinet or making sure no one's hoarding the coffee beans?"

"We're not even out of coffee yet, geez. We get down to the last quarter-pound and you panic."

"Isn't it your job to take care of the mundane things?"

John glared at him. "No, *my* job is to make sure that this magazine stays in print so the rest of you have jobs at all. My job involves strategic planning for what will keep readers interested, analyzing market research, and assessment of threats from other magazines trying to horn in on our niche."

"Sounds like your military training has been useful."

"Just a different kind of battle," John agreed. "Less likely to get killed, though, at least in a literal sense."

"No flying, though," Bailey pointed out.

There was a moment of silence, and Bailey wasn't sure what the expression on John's face was, but it definitely wasn't happy. He wasn't entirely sure whether he'd said something wrong and ought to apologize—after all, there *wasn't* any flying in running a magazine, and he honestly had no clue why John had quit flying entirely. There was a small airfield not too far outside the city, and John certainly had enough money to buy a single-engine or other small plane. So why hadn't he?

Bailey cleared his throat, feeling awkward. "Want to go down to the bar and get burgers and beers tonight?" he offered.

John did a weird movement that was half shrug, half nod. "Sure. Six all right? I've got a conference call at four and will probably want to write up notes and fire off some e-mails once it's over."

It was surprising, how relieved he felt by John's reply. Bailey nodded. "Fine, yes. I might go down a bit earlier; I suspect Daniel's article on time-travel scenarios in various sci-fi movies is going to drive me to drink." He pondered for a moment. "Actually, maybe I should start drinking *before* I read it; I suspect being inebriated will only improve the so-called 'logic' of his analysis."

John laughed and kicked Bailey's chair, sending him rolling to the side. "It's supposed to be fun, all right? It needs to be scientifically sound, but with a little whimsy, you know? Can you be whimsical, Bailey?"

Bailey carefully raised one eyebrow. "I'm writing your accursed *astrology* column," he growled, careful to keep his voice at a whisper. "That's either whimsical or brain-damaged; I'm not convinced there's a difference. So yes, I can be 'whimsical'."

"It's so sexy when you make air quotes at me," John said, wiggling his eyebrows. "I can barely keep my hands to myself."

"Go away now." Bailey turned back to his desk, making shooing motions over his shoulder. "Working here." Luckily, John went back to his office, still chuckling, and oblivious to Bailey's burning cheeks and suddenly racing heart.

It wasn't as if John had never said anything flirtatious to him before. And in fact, Bailey was being flirted with quite a lot lately—far more so than usual, anyhow. Shouldn't he be building up some kind of tolerance? He hadn't been this flustered with any of his dates, not even Rich or Ramses, and he'd known he could have had sex with either of them. But all John had to do was smirk the right way, slouch a little with his hip cocked to the side, and tease him, and his heart leapt.

He was entirely too old for a stupid crush on his friend. His *boss*. All of this thinking about dates and romance and sex was clearly having a negative impact on his intelligence. He could sort this out with logic: his increased distraction and preoccupation with mating and courtship had increased his sensitivity to the normal level of pheromones that every human produced. It was no wonder he was feeling the urge to pair-bond with the person he spent the most time near.

It was simple animal biology, that was all. Perhaps if he actually managed to have full-out sex on one of his dates, the problem would take care of itself. Or he could always call Rich….

BAILEY had an uncharacteristic bounce in his step when he arrived at work the next day. He poured a cup of coffee for Lauren (after his own, of course) and even showed up to the staff meeting without being forcefully dragged into the conference room. His eyes were sparkling in spite of the slight sleep-deprived redness, and he had a set of finger-shaped bruises encircling one wrist.

John, on the other hand, was in the pissiest mood Bailey could remember. He yelled at the three interns, griped about their advertisers, and was visibly uninterested in every single one of the stories pitched at him.

"What the hell is wrong with you today?" Bailey asked once the rest of the conference room had cleared. "I thought I was the resident curmudgeon."

John made a face. "*You* had a good time last night, I see."

"What? I mean, yes, I did. Václav and I were up until almost sunrise pounding—"

Both hands came up as John took a hurried step back. "Whoa! TMI!"

"—out the massive flaws in his proposal," Bailey said slowly, brow furrowing. "What did you think we were—oh my God, you thought we were up all night fucking and that's why I'm in such a good mood? I'm right, aren't I?"

John scowled harder but said nothing. His glare centered on Bailey's wrist for a moment before he jerked it away and looked out the window.

Bailey snorted. "We had a bit of a tussle over the dry-erase markers. Václav's got more hand-strength than you'd think for such a scrawny little guy."

Most of the tension seemed to flow out of John but was replaced with awkwardness. He still seemed annoyed, too, as he said, "Maybe that strong grip will come in useful later, then."

Tucking his netbook under an arm, Bailey scooped up his coffee mug and the remaining croissant. "Whatever; I have work to do. He's coming for lunch around one, and he wants to meet you. I thought that

Afghani place a few blocks over? You love their *aushak*, and Václav wants something spicy."

John nodded. Bailey hoped that whatever bug had crawled up his ass would be gone by the time Václav showed up.

Luckily, it seemed to be, and the three men ended up having a pretty good time together, John and Václav ganging up on Bailey about his many food allergies when he interrogated the waitstaff about the possibility of lime zest in his curry.

There was an awkward moment when lunch had finished and they all walked back to the office. Václav declined to come up and take a look around, saying he wanted to finish the revisions on his proposal. He shook John's hand formally, saying, "Was nice to finally meet you, John," and then hovered around Bailey in an uncomfortable way before clasping both shoulders and quickly kissing him on each cheek.

"What the heck was that? Two years at the CNRS and he's French now?" Bailey mused as they headed back inside.

John shrugged, the tightness around his eyes from earlier that morning returning. "Well, you two certainly seem to get along well. Hey, when's his birthday; maybe you should date him," he said in a tone that could only be called bitter, although Bailey had no idea why.

He gave John the *are you honestly that stupid* look and answered, "Are you kidding? One, dating Václav would be like dating myself, which, although easier by a factor of about twelve thousand, would also be simultaneously boring and annoying. Second, he speaks Czech when he's upset or excited, and I have no interest in learning a new language just to hear someone call me a jerk or swear during sex. And third, he doesn't have sex with men. And I like sex."

"I can see where that last one would be the critical deal breaker."

"Shut up."

John smirked. "Seriously though, didn't you once give me a lecture on how most scientists experimented with the same sex?"

Bailey nodded. "Hmm, yes. A curious mind likes to collect data, even on something as inconsistent as human sexual response. And, you know, if someone offers you a hand job at four a.m. in an empty lab in order to relieve some tension, you say 'yes', even if the hand belongs to someone you don't find particularly sexually attractive."

"So, what, Václav didn't like the experiment?"

Bailey shrugged and looked uncomfortable. "Er, I believe he implied that there was an equipment failure once the man's hand was down his pants."

"Oops." John laughed a little. "Well, at least he gave it a shot?"

"Yes, points for that, I suppose," Bailey agreed. "Plus, I think he's kind of got a thing with the woman running the oversight committee on his project in Paris, Katie something…."

"I see. Well, try not to stay up too late tonight; don't forget about your court date in the morning. Mr. Tulley and Ms. Zhen will meet us here at nine."

"You're coming?"

John gave him a look that clearly said *duh*. "*Spark* is being sued too, not just you. Of course I'll be there."

They went back inside the office, bickering about who would drive and why, and the fact that Bailey had brought his suit in and taken it to the dry cleaners but not picked it up from there yet. John insisted he go retrieve it now, before he did anything else; that way at least it would be in the office and Bailey could change in the morning if he forgot to take it home.

"I'm not some crazy-haired befuddled scientist type! I can remember simple things!"

"Oh, like eating before you get hypoglycemic, and remembering where you've parked your car at the airport, and picking up your dry cleaning?"

"Hey, I only did that thing at the airport once or twice. And it's not my fault; SFO is a maze."

John raised an eyebrow. "It's got designated numbers and maps all over the place. You made me walk around with you for over half an hour after I'd taken a red-eye from DC."

"So that means you're never going to let it go?"

"Exactly."

When he got home that night, Bailey was still grumbling to himself. His guest had no sympathy at all, of course, and Václav outright laughed when Bailey tried to defend himself against John's accusations of being an absent-minded professor.

"You are not absent-minded, no, but you carefully choose to ignore facts you deem irrelevant or distracting. Taking care of your health, your relationships, and small details you assume someone else will handle are among them. This is why you have a housekeeper who shops for you, takes care of your cat, does your laundry, no? Rather than have a wife—or husband—who would do such mundane tasks for you."

Bailey made a face. "As if I'd want to be in a relationship with someone whose life-purpose was fulfilled by washing my socks. And I go to the gym!" he argued.

"Yes, you do—when, exactly? Ah yes, when your gigantic friend Jason insists, and meets you there each time, and doesn't let you get away with canceling. On your own? You are a potato."

"There's nothing wrong with potatoes," Bailey insisted, and then realized that was exactly the opposite argument from the one he'd meant to make. "I mean... oh fine. You're right, all right? I'm an absent-minded genius, little more than a brain in a jar that needs someone to take care of the physical world around me, or I would starve to death surrounded by squalor. Fine. Now do your part and order us a pizza while I take a shower."

He huffed off to his bedroom and tried not to slam the bathroom door, which only slightly muffled Václav's laughter.

FRIDAY morning, Bailey arrived outside the office building right on time, wearing his suit and tie, with four paper cups of coffee in a container and one in his hand.

John smiled and helped himself to a cup, handing another to Ms. Zhen and then to Mr. Tulley before opening the one with his name on it. "Who's the extra for?"

Bailey blinked at him. "Me."

"Right, wouldn't want you to have to get through the next hour without a good dose of caffeine in your blood," John agreed.

The required mediation attempt was both tedious and an obvious waste of time. Gallagher's attorney clearly knew he didn't have a chance in hell of winning, so he'd decided on an aggressive course of action that would—if successful—ruin the few lingering shreds of Bailey's professional reputation and make *Spark* look incredibly irresponsible for hiring him and giving him a voice in the national media. Not a bad strategy, fighting libel with libel, but Mr. Tulley and Ms. Zhen were prepared.

They haggled and counter-offered and generally resisted all attempts to negotiate until the court's mediator declared the session a failure. They agreed to arbitration, Gallagher's attorney clearly eager to stay out of litigation and full court with a jury if he could avoid it. Tulley agreed, and they scheduled the hearing for two weeks, mid-May, hoping to get the whole thing resolved before summer vacations made scheduling time with an arbitrator or judge impossible.

All in all, it was a hideous waste of time and everyone knew it. Except Gallagher, obviously, who was basking in all the attention, delighted with the whole pointless spectacle. Bailey seriously wanted to punch him in the face, cut off that stupid curly ponytail, and burn it right before Gallagher's eyes.

"I want him to cry next time," he grumbled. "Can you do that?"

Ms. Zhen smiled. "Absolutely. He wants attention, wants to be 'heard'. We'll let him have his two seconds of glory and then eviscerate him in front of the judge."

"We could let him invite in the press," Mr. Tulley mused. "It would be unusual, but it's not disallowed…."

"I like them," Bailey said, turning to John. "Good job hiring them."

"Gee, Bailey, I'm so glad you approve." John looked pleased, though, in spite of his sarcastic tone.

"All this diabolical planning to destroy Gallagher is making me hungry. Is it lunchtime yet?"

John looked at his watch. "Close enough. Xiao, Robert, do you want to join us before you rush back to the firm to plan Gallagher's death by public humiliation?"

The attorneys declined, so it was just John and Bailey who grabbed some lunch before heading back to work. They were nearing a deadline, and while Bailey's own articles were finished, his fact-checking for the less conscientious writers meant he had a full day ahead of him unless he wanted to work over the weekend.

He stopped at Lauren's desk on his way back in. "Um. Can you do me a favor?"

Lauren narrowed her eyes at him. "I am already doing you about a million favors, McMillan. What do you want now?"

"It's something I can't do!" he protested. "Can you call the guy I'm supposed to meet tonight, Dan something, and see if he'll reschedule for Saturday? I've got too much to do, and it's been a long day already."

She shrugged. "Yeah, I can do that, I guess. For twenty bucks."

"Oh for... honestly?" Bailey sputtered.

She nodded, and he dug out his wallet, slapping a bill in her outstretched hand. He scowled in response to her grin and finally made it to his desk, turning on the computer for the first time all day.

Chapter 7

Sagittarian Straight-Shooter

THE astrology column was mentioned in the *New York Times* on Saturday, which was great for *Spark* and made Bailey want to throw himself off of a building. Václav had been let in on the secret, or rather, Bailey had spilled it without realizing while he was ranting and moaning about the level of American stupidity.

Václav, naturally, had no sympathy for Bailey's plight or the horrible abuse he was suffering at John's hands. He nodded sagely as Bailey described their "blackmail-like" agreement, where he was "forced" to write the monthly column in exchange for his "completely accurate peer reviews; it's not as if it's my fault my so-called colleagues are a bunch of gibbering imbeciles."

"Yes," his friend agreed. "Is horrible crime that John is making you do this, and one day, the gods will punish him. Meanwhile, I am laughing."

"Isn't it time for you to move to the hotel yet?" Bailey grumped. "I'm pretty sure I've completely demolished your entire proposal about using that ore as fissionable material."

Václav shrugged. "Not entirely. It can still be done, although no, not as simply as I had thought. You agreed that it would produce less radioactive waste, so the idea is still worth pursuing. Why are you not helping me, anyhow? Usually you would be excited, trying to steal my preliminary work and claim it as your own. What is wrong with you?"

Shaking his head, Bailey got up and poured himself another enormous mug of coffee; Václav made it perfectly, thick as sludge and strong enough to wake up the neighbors. "Having a social life all of a sudden is very strange. I don't know how other scientists manage to date or get married at all when I'm so much more intelligent than they are and am having so much trouble focusing on my work."

"Yes, it is a great mystery to all why you are so bad at dating." Václav snorted.

Manfully ignoring the layer of sarcasm in that, Bailey steered the discussion to the conference, which would begin on Monday. He had no intention of attending the ice-breaker reception or any of the evening events throughout the week; Václav would have to go to those solo. Bailey *was* interested in hearing some of the speakers, but he was afraid he wouldn't be able to keep his mouth shut and would end up in a verbal—or possibly physical—brawl with the CEOs of some of the more evil corporations. The idea that Halliburton was attending an "Intelligent Energy" conference was ironic in the extreme.

As always, he had no tolerance for the kind of shortsightedness that would destroy the planet for future habitation in the next century or so in exchange for a few billion dollars in the next decade. Bailey in no way considered himself a tree-hugging hippy, but it was just common sense not to foul the stream you drink from—particularly upstream of your well.

Regardless, the very idea of attending the conference made his blood pressure skyrocket. A few years ago, this would have been the sort of event Bailey lived for, a playground for his intellect and ego, ripe for the kind of verbal abuse he loved to spew the best. He and Václav had a longstanding tradition of going to the scientific community's events together and reveling in being the smartest men in the room. Bailey had skipped the last few, though, licking his wounds and staying out of the public eye. This had unfortunately led to rumors of him becoming a recluse, his absence indicating his supposed culpability for the Stellar mess. Some of his more bitter colleagues even implied that he'd come unhinged and that working as a fact-checker for a non-academic popular media magazine was all he was capable of doing now. He suspected Gallagher in particular of starting the rumor that he'd spent some time in a mental hospital.

He hoped his lawyers utterly *destroyed* Gallagher.

To say that Bailey was nervous about the coming week was a fairly massive understatement. He knew his usual bravado and superiority would get him though whatever nastiness came up, but instead of looking forward to gleefully tearing apart everyone's proposals—egged on by Václav—he was hoping to fade into the background, stay on the sidelines. Václav's offer to protect him from a hail of rotten tomatoes might have been facetious, but the verbal volley of abuse was likely to be quite real.

And if he saw that asshole Malcolm Duggan from Stellar, Bailey was going to choke him to death with his own tie.

VÁCLAV gleefully harassed Bailey while he was trying to get ready for his early dinner date on Saturday evening, an activity that resulted in Bailey calling a cab to the building and almost forcibly pushing Václav into it. He was stupidly nervous already and didn't need the ongoing commentary about his choice of clothing, restaurant, and unscented shaving gel—Václav had a European preference for assertive colognes.

By the time Bailey got into his own cab, he was sweating and convinced that the evening was going to be terrible. What was he thinking, not canceling the date entirely? It had been a long week, full of weirdness with John, all-night-long debates with Václav, and the building sense of impending doom regarding the energy conference in a few days. He was in no mood to meet someone new, let alone be polite and chatty and... *polite*.

He was scrolling through his phone at the restaurant, debating whether to call John and see if he wanted to come and meet Bailey for dinner for some in-person ranting. Bailey had been waiting for Dan for over fifteen minutes; he'd clearly been stood up. It was insulting, honestly; the man had agreed to reschedule from Friday night, but he couldn't show the simple courtesy of making a call to cancel himself? Bailey was working himself into a froth of righteous indignation when a tall, good-looking man with short dark hair pulled out the chair across from him and sprawled into it.

The man gave him a million-dollar grin and held out his hand. "Dan Harper. Captain."

Bailey frowned for a moment, then set aside his phone and shook hands. "Dr. Bailey McMillan." He squinted at the Air Force insignia on the man's coat. "Great, another flyboy. Just what I need."

Dan grinned, toothy enough for a shark, but friendlier. "Oh? Date many pilots, do you?"

"No, just. My best friend was one before he retired," Bailey said. He'd stumbled over what to call John and then felt like a ten-year-old. His *best friend*? Still, he supposed it wasn't inaccurate. "But we're not dating," he added.

Dan's wide shoulders shook as he laughed. "Relax, Bailey. I'm sure you'd never cheat on guys; you don't like the type. Sorry if my tardiness made you think I'd stood you up; there was an accident on the Bay bridge." He rolled his eyes and shrugged.

"Ah. I was just, um, looking that up on my phone," Bailey lied. Dan was incredibly attractive, the sort of man who made Bailey tongue-tied and stupid, and that was saying something. He wasn't perfect-looking like Ramses had been, but he had this aura of cocky arrogance and charm that Bailey had always been a sucker for.

"So, tell me all about yourself, Dr. McMillan," Dan suggested, flagging down their server at the same time.

They ordered drinks—beer—and Dan proved to be an affable listener, intelligent enough to ask the right kind of questions, and if he was bored by Bailey's still-somewhat-nervous chatter, he was a skilled enough actor to hide it. Like John, Dan had enough experience with the physics and engineering involved in air flight to make their dinner discussion interesting to them both. Bailey had nearly finished his steak without noticing it, he was having such a decent time. He supposed that after the exasperating week he'd had, perhaps he'd needed a night off with nothing more pressing than trying not to make a fool of himself in front of someone he didn't know.

It was, in point of fact, one of the most relaxed first dates Bailey could remember having. Maybe it was the beer… although Dan himself was quite easy to be with.

"You seem like you're usually much more high-strung," Dan teased as the waitress departed with Bailey's credit card. "I was sure that you were going to be a pain in the ass after you rescheduled on me with such late notice."

The automatic protest died on Bailey's lips as he realized that for the first time in the history of thirty-nine years, someone had just implied that he was easygoing, and he didn't want to ruin it yet. He shrugged. "It was a long week, and the mediation session at court took more out of me than I'd anticipated when Lauren originally set up our date."

"Ah yes, Lauren. So is she, what, your secretary?"

Bailey snorted. "More like my extortionist. No, actually, she's John's assistant at the magazine. She's helping with the, uh, dating experiment."

"Right, the experiment. I admit that's what intrigued me about your personals ad," Dan said. "Can you talk about it, or will it invalidate your findings?" Somehow his tone of voice, combined with another of those huge grins, made it sound suggestive.

Bailey took a sip of water, his throat suddenly tight. "It, uh, might." There was no good reason for him to feel so flustered by his date; Dan was attractive, yes, intelligent enough, but there was nothing outstanding about him. He was confident without being aggressive, charming without being oily, and gave off the aura of a man who definitely knew how to have a good time in bed. And Dan had really nice hands....

They paid the bill and walked out into the chilly breeze from the bay. Without discussion, they headed toward the Embarcadero and the ships at Pier 45. It was far too late for a tour—not that Bailey would have been interested—but the lights strung on the boats were aesthetically pleasing to look at. Pretty.

Standing there in silence, Bailey suddenly realized he had no idea why they were there or what they were doing. As he opened his mouth to say something to that effect, Dan snaked an arm around his waist and pulled their bodies close together, chest to chest. Bailey didn't resist at first because he was so surprised, but then he took an automatic step back, his hands coming up between them to make space.

Dan's chest moved under Bailey's hands as he chuckled. "No? Not romantic enough for you?"

"What? No, it's fine. Nice, even. I mean, I wasn't thinking about the setting." He took a babble-stopping breath. "I wasn't expecting that."

"Evidently not." Dan leaned down until their foreheads were touching. "I don't mind being a stand-in for the night, but I won't be offended if you're saving it for the one you'd rather be with either."

Bailey blinked, furrowed his brow in thought trying to parse that offer, and then gave up after a moment. "What?"

Dan kissed his cheek and then moved away, making Bailey feel both relieved and bereft at the same time. "So does John know you have this massive crush on him? Or is he as oblivious as you are?"

"More," Bailey answered, trying not to squirm. "And it's just a stupid little crush thing. Because I've been dating, you know, recently, and thinking. About sex and stuff. More than usual." He took a slow breath, closing his eyes, frustrated by his own incoherency. "It's nothing; it will go away on its own, I'm sure. It did last time."

"Last time?" Dan and his quirked eyebrow asked.

"I may have been a little… taken with him, when we first met and were working together for the military. But I got over it."

"Like a cold?"

Bailey snorted. "Yes, like a cold. I thought I was immune now, but, well. Biology is far too inexact to be a real science."

"Uh-huh. So you're lovesick again," Dan teased.

"Don't be ridiculous; we're *friends*."

"Not going to make a move, then?" Dan waited for Bailey's nod, then asked, "So do you want to come back to my place?"

"Um." The thing was, Bailey *did*, sort of, but now that it was clear—to Dan, as well as to himself—that he would be using Dan, it just felt wrong. He could have been blissfully ignorant and well-fucked, but no. Damn Dan for being too observant—and too direct—for their own good.

"It'd be fun," Dan cajoled, tracing a finger along the line of Bailey's jaw, making him shiver.

"Yeah, really not the problem," he grumbled.

Dan laughed again. "Wow, you are totally hung up on this guy, aren't you? You know the best way to get over someone is to fuck someone else." He gave Bailey a probing look. "Unless you're not ready to get over him yet...." He made a humming noise, and then took Bailey's elbow and pulled him into a café. "What kind of coffee do you like? Let me guess, straight-up Americano?"

"Yes, but. What are you doing?"

"It's early. We're not having sex. So I'm ordering us some coffee, and maybe one of those gorgeous cupcakes or two in the display case, and we're going to come up with a plan so you can get your man."

"I... what?"

For once in his life, Bailey felt like he couldn't keep up. He was blaming the long week and the relaxed interactions with Dan that had thrown him off his game, but still. The man was clearly not making any sense. First he was making a move on Bailey, and then he was probing about his stupid crush on John, and then he was offering to have rebound sex (not that Bailey had "bounced" against John, or however the analogy went; sports were definitely not his thing). And now Dan wanted to brainstorm seduction tactics so he could "get" John.

"Who the hell *are* you?" Bailey asked, mystified.

Just like in the beginning, Dan gave him one of those million-dollar smiles. "I'm the man who's going to get you a boyfriend."

BAILEY stayed out extremely late with Dan. By the time he got home, it was well past two in the morning; they'd closed down the bar across the street from the café. Despite the fact that they'd spent several hours talking about John and Bailey and their history, when Dan embraced him on the curb and kissed him goodbye, Bailey had almost wanted to dive into the cab and go home with him. The man could kiss, holy cow. And after a whole night talking together, he felt like he knew Dan pretty well. The sex would definitely be fantastic. Dan had a wicked sense of humor and in his ongoing flirtation and risqué jokes had alluded to a few kinks Bailey was quite interested in trying out sometime.

Perhaps the alcohol was impairing his judgment, or maybe it was simple animal lust, but Bailey barely got the door to his apartment closed and locked behind him before he was collapsing onto his sofa, one hand down his pants, wishing it was someone else's. A relatively short time later, he was sighing and then heaving himself up and into the bathroom for a quick wash before face-planting onto his bed. Sexy pilots with naughty grins and far too much charm to be allowed filled his dreams.

AND woke him up from them, far too early.

"Mmmrh?" he mumbled into his phone.

"It's almost eleven; are you seriously not up yet?" John asked.

Bailey made a garbled sound of angry protest.

"I thought we could meet for brunch. Unless you have company."

His mouth finally coming unglued, he said, "Václav went to the hotel" in a scratchy voice.

"I didn't mean Václav."

Bailey's brow furrowed in confusion, but he gave up, defeated by a lack of caffeine. "The cat?" he asked, looking at the animal in question. Castrovalva paused his grooming when Bailey looked at him, then went back to it when clearly no kitty treats were forthcoming. He'd been Bailey's pet for over five years; he knew nothing of importance was happening before the coffee machine made noises.

John made an exasperated noise. "Just meet me at Dottie's in an hour, okay? That should give you enough time to shower, drink a pot of coffee, and get there in somewhat human form, right?"

Bailey huffed but agreed. John seemed unduly eager to do the post-mortem, as he'd come to think of it, on Bailey's date with Dan. Usually Bailey was, as well, more for the company than for the data collection process, but today was different. He'd had a great time with Dan and been undeniably attracted to him, but they'd spent almost the whole night talking about *John*.

The result was that Bailey was more tight-lipped during the evaluation process than usual. There wasn't much he could say about the date, aside from the facts that Dan was sexy, they'd had a good time together, and there was no plausible reason why Bailey hadn't gone home with Dan in the wee hours of the morning. He was a terrible liar, and John in particular had always been able to see through him. The truth was that he'd really liked Dan and would have fucked him if he wasn't so stupidly hung up on John. He had almost done so anyway.

But he couldn't say that. He couldn't say that Dan was friendly and sincere and that he'd proposed a seduction campaign based on—of all insipid romcom plot devices—jealousy. That Dan had argued that a man like John would respond out of anger and frustration when he wouldn't make a move simply because he wanted to. Bailey knew John, but not *that* side of John, and honestly hadn't a clue if such tactics would work or not.

And unlike a decent *real* science experiment, the trial and error approach to problem solving with people came with some massive pitfalls: he could screw up his friendship with John forever by trying to manipulate him into a reaction. Furthermore, Bailey had no actual proof that John was interested in him that way. Sure, he was now aware of the fact that his friend was bisexual, at the very least, and had sex with men occasionally. But that was no more grounds for thinking that John might be interested in him than the fact that a woman was heterosexual meant that she'd like to go to bed with Bailey.

Finally, Bailey hadn't the first clue how to go about making John feel jealous anyway. He wasn't going to stoop to lying and pretend that he'd had a night of fabulous wild sex with Dan. He certainly wasn't going to pretend that he was "in love" after one date. He'd genuinely had a good time, though, so he tried to focus on that as they talked over brunch together.

Weirdly, the less Bailey was willing to say, the more annoyed John seemed to become. He was practically stabbing at the netbook with his fingertips, jaw clenched as Bailey danced around the topics of his conversation with Dan. One of the few things he *could* talk about with ease was how attractive Dan was, although putting his finger on what exactly made the man so appealing was difficult.

"So, what? He had a great body?"

Bailey shrugged. "Good, from what I saw. Seemed... firm, but I doubt he's the kind of guy who works out a lot or anything. But you know, he's in the military, so he's fit."

John rolled his eyes. "Fine. So decent body but not drool-inducing. Movie-star looks? Amazing eyes? Fantastic hair?"

"No, no, no. Dan was... attractive, but not a perfect ten. It was more how he was put together, you know? With a different personality, he wouldn't be noteworthy at all," Bailey mused.

"So tell me about this 'sexy' personality of his, then. God, it's like pulling teeth with you today."

Scowling back at John with an exasperated noise and hand-wave, Bailey tried. "He was... sincere. A really positive-thinking guy, you know? Not naïve, but had a hopeful outlook on life, thinks there's a solution for almost every problem. He was a good listener, funny, smart... the kind of man who wants to take care of people. Easy to work with.... In a rational world, I should definitely have gone home with him. Or at least on a second date."

Bailey stopped musing aloud and looked up at John. His friend's face had smoothed into the perfectly blank mask he wore when he was upset, but Bailey had no idea what on earth he could have said that would be so offensive.

"John?"

"I've got to go," John said, hurriedly gathering his things. He dug a twenty-dollar bill out of his wallet and slammed it on the table, not making eye contact or responding in any way to Bailey's bewildered sputtering. "See you at work Monday. Have fun with Dan."

He was gone before Bailey could protest that this *wasn't* a rational world, he had no plans to see Dan, and furthermore that he wouldn't be at work on Monday; the Intelligent Energy conference was beginning.

Utterly flummoxed, Bailey threw up his hands and went back home, determined not to leave his building again until the world made more sense.

Chapter 8

Stubborn Old Goats

THE world did not make significantly more sense on Monday morning, but Bailey caught a cab to the convention center anyway. Václav had called both Sunday night *and* Monday morning, harassing, cajoling, threatening, and even insulting Bailey by suggesting that perhaps he'd better stay at home and let the other scientists figure out a way to solve global warming if he was too busy with his astrology project. It was the physicist version of calling him a coward and suggesting he stay home to play with his dollies.

So of course by the time Bailey got his badge from the registration desk, he was already spoiling for a fight. Three cups of absolutely wretched coffee from the hotel's cart did nothing to help, and the gleam of triumph in Václav's eyes didn't either. In fact, Václav was acting like he wanted Bailey to get in a brawl, pushing him toward idiotic so-called "peers" he'd been forced to work with before, particularly the ones from his Stellar days.

"I thought you were going to keep me out of the spotlight, keep me from getting in trouble. I'd forgotten what a diabolical little imp you can be," Bailey groused. He'd finally made an excuse to get away from Dr. Cordova, a woman he'd had a humiliating crush on and who had been one of his most vociferous opponents—on any project— because of it. She was the one who had been responsible for making sure he'd been assigned to the project in Mongolia six years ago, just to get him out of her hair.

Václav shrugged. "I am keeping you out of trouble. But first I am enjoying reintroducing you to people you loathe and who wish you dead in return. Is fun to see the colors your face can turn."

"I'll turn your face colors...."

"Such violence. Threats of physical harm are so unlike you, Bailey. Perhaps all of this frustration, tension could be better expressed sexually, no?"

Bailey took a deep breath, reciting pi to fifty digits with his eyes closed. "You're doing this on purpose. Why?"

A fond smile pulled at the corners of Václav's mouth. "To distract you from the gossip which people are not even bothering to whisper, they are so rude. Better that you be furious with a few individuals than overhear the inaccurate and spiteful remarks of the many. You are an irritating and nearly insufferably arrogant man, yes, but you are my friend, and the majority of these people are fools who cannot see intelligence unless it is kneeling on the floor, kissing their asses."

There was some logic to being angry rather than hurt, Bailey supposed; he did tend to lash out when his emotions got involved. The situation with Dr. Cordova was an excellent case in point; when she'd rebuffed his advances, he had demolished her proposal on temporal anomalies, which had set her grant funding back by several years. To say nothing of the petty name-calling he'd indulged in with Gallagher that was now resulting in the libel suit. Scientists were so touchy, a bunch of bitchy little girls.

Bailey did have a few friends, though, whom Václav steered him toward as they all filed into the giant lecture hall for the day's keynote speaker. Dr. Nakamara seemed to have gotten over her awkward crush on him now that they weren't working together anymore, and Dr. Hayes was one of the few physicists who genuinely seemed to enjoy Bailey's company, for reasons he'd never been able to fathom. Perhaps the eight months they'd spent together as the only Northern Americans at the Russian research center had forged some kind of unbreakable bond, as the numbing agents of the cold, isolation, and vodka together rendered Hayes immune to Bailey's insults.

After an interminable length of self-congratulatory blathering, the corporate schmucks sat down and let their so-called scientists talk about the projects they were spearheading. Ostensibly the purpose of the week-long conference was to allow some back-and-forth, but really it was a recruitment tool for the corporations to attempt to lure in the best minds, with fresh perspectives. Most of the projects they were dumping billions of dollars into were doomed to failure, and they knew it. They had no interest in "saving the earth," just in looking like they were trying to for their corporate shareholders. It made Bailey sick.

By the second day, he was ready to throw in the towel. Unfortunately, the *Spark* office wasn't much more welcoming when he stopped by to check his e-mail and grab some decent coffee. John was giving him the cold shoulder, and while Bailey was thoughtless and rude a lot of the time and knew it, there was nothing he could recall doing that would have pissed John off so much.

To top things off, Lauren reminded him that he had a dinner date on Wednesday. "He called and asked if you were going to be at the energy conference, and said he'd meet you there. He says you'll know him."

Bailey groaned. "Great, it's going to be one of those corporate asshats, isn't it? Did you ask his name?"

Lauren's grin showed all of her teeth, which Bailey half-expected to be pointed, like a cat's or a demon's. "I said I wouldn't tell you. He had a really sexy voice, though, and that combined with his intention of making you paranoid was enough for me to be on his side. He'll meet you after the afternoon seminars finish, outside the exhibition room, on the northeast side."

"Northeast side? What is this, a scavenger hunt? Should I bring a compass?"

"I knew you wouldn't appreciate his specificity."

"*Specificity?*" he mouthed back at her, eyes wide.

"Exactitude?" Lauren scowled. "Four p.m. tomorrow, exhibition room; go away now before I maim you."

Bailey huffed and went back to his desk, casting a glance into John's office, hoping for a consolatory shrug. But no; John was on the phone, ignoring Bailey, not even bothering to eavesdrop on his admin being insolent to his best friend.

BAILEY waited outside the exhibition room, his annoyance from the morning's session having already put him in an extremely bad mood. Václav had wandered off with a small group of scientists—mostly comprised of geologists, for heaven's sake, glorified miners—trying to get them interested in his ridiculous Antarctic ore project. Bailey had disagreed vociferously with the idea of collaboration so early in the process; all it would do was diminish the credit for the concept if it worked and muddy the waters of who was in charge regardless. He'd had too many bad experiences with "sharing" to trust others with anything except the appropriate execution of tasks as needed. Better to come up with the whole project on his own and then delegate less-brilliant peons to work out the details once the big picture was already conceived.

Fuming, he wondered who this man was that was making him wait, and if he truly was someone Bailey already knew. More to the point, if he was anyone Bailey would actually *want* to know, which seemed unlikely, if the man was also in attendance at the conference.

It turned out the answer was "sort of"—Dr. Steven Severin had been and still was a chemistry professor at the university where Bailey had done his undergraduate work in his early teens. The man had been extremely harsh but fair, from what Bailey remembered, taking a no-nonsense attitude toward the fact that a hands-on class in a chemistry laboratory could result in catastrophe if the students were reckless. A lot of his fellow students had hated Professor Severin and his zero-tolerance policy toward goofing around, but Bailey had appreciated not being blown to bits by stoned football players or girls more interested in their nail polish than the similarity of the highly flammable nitrocellulose in said polish with flash paper.

The man hadn't aged particularly well, but Bailey supposed twenty-something years—especially ones filled with aggravating undergraduate idiots—were bound to leave an impact.

"Bailey McMillan, we meet again," the man said, holding out a bony hand, fingernails stained with what was probably silver nitrate. His somber black suit was loose enough to make him look gaunt, his once-black hair now threaded with silver, hanging loose down to his shoulders. The grey in his hair gave him the appearance of being covered with a layer of chalk dust, a relic from some university's distant past who had never used a whiteboard, let alone a computer. His best attribute by far was the one Lauren had noted: his voice. It was deep and resonant, with a classic British accent, and had featured prominently in Bailey's teenaged fantasies for a time.

"Professor, er, Dr. Severin. Good to see you again." They shook hands.

"Is it? I have been following your notorious career with some mild interest over the years and confess that I was quite amused to learn from your secretary that the advert on Craigslist seeking homosexual dates was for none other than Bailey McMillan. What sort of pathetic soft-sciences 'experiment' are you working on now, you misguided boy?"

Bailey tried not to bristle and failed; that sexy voice could only go so far, and he'd forgotten how condescending his former professor could be. "I can't tell you without skewing the results, and it's not *my* experiment; I'm helping a friend." A friend he wanted to track down and yell at for a good few hours at the moment for subjecting him to this "blast from the past," but a friend nonetheless.

Dr. Severin raised an eyebrow, giving Bailey a critical look. "You've lost a lot of hair."

"Since I was fifteen? Yes." The two men glared at each other for a few moments. Bailey sighed. "So. Do you want to go eat dinner and make small talk for an hour or what?"

"We did make a date," Dr. Severin said with a smile that somehow seemed oily. "Let's dine, and you can tell me all about your rise to fame and subsequent plummet into shame and obscurity. I long to hear your version of the truth on the matter."

Bailey sent a silent prayer for patience skyward and shrugged. "Fine. But you're buying the drinks."

Dinner with Dr. Severin—Bailey couldn't bring himself to think of the man as "Steven," let alone call him that, and he hadn't been invited to do so anyway—was neither horrible nor pleasant. The man had taken it personally when Bailey had chosen to go into physics, asserting that he could have been "very good" at chemistry, a rare compliment indeed. It was almost as if the one compliment his professor had ever given a student in nearly half a century of teaching had been thrown back in his face. It hadn't; Bailey was pleased to have been singled out for his brilliance, as always, but he wasn't going to change his mind about discovering how the universe was put together just to play with the elements and make them go boom.

Given the amount of time and energy he'd ended up using designing weapons for the military, it was more than a little ironic that that had been the foremost reason for his rejecting the idea of pursuing a doctorate in chemistry. Life was like that; wherever you planned to go, you were bound to end up on a path in the opposite direction entirely, at least for a while. As a teenager getting his first master's degree, he had envisioned his life at age forty to include being the head of a department at an internationally renowned research facility, having a million dollars in the bank (adjusted for inflation, of course), a brilliant wife, some children who would carry on his genius genes, and a Nobel prize. One out of five suddenly seemed quite pathetic.

Dr. Severin seemed to be holding onto the lingering resentment that Bailey had rejected his chosen field, and was gleeful at Bailey's still very public disgrace in the scientific community. He was a bit of a bastard, rubbing salt in the wounds all evening, until finally Bailey had had enough. Undergraduates might have to put up with the man, but he did not.

"This has been… well, goodnight," he said, sticking out his hand for an obligatory shake.

"Indeed. Good luck gathering the tatters of your reputation about you, Dr. McMillan. I will continue to enjoy reading your petty reviews of your less-intelligent colleagues' more promising careers."

Bailey could only blink for a moment, but then he shrugged. "At least I'm not stuck yelling at nineteen-year-olds to wear safety goggles year in and year out."

"Touché." Dr. Severin shook his hand and departed, taking his aura of sharp resentment with him.

Bailey signaled at the bartender for more whisky. He certainly deserved it.

JOHN'S good humor seemed to be restored as they went over Bailey's abysmal "date" the next afternoon at the coffee shop.

"You're a bad person, you know. The worse a time I have on these dates, the happier you are," Bailey observed.

John shrugged. "Yeah. It's really too bad that you don't have better friends, huh?"

"I have no friends, no heirs, a job no one—not even me—respects, and no Nobel."

"Suck it up. You're not in jail, you're not wounded, you're still a genius, you have money. You can turn things around whenever you decide you're done wallowing, hiding out at *Spark*. I'm sure Dr. Záviška's project would give you the opportunity to get back in the game if you wanted to."

Bailey huffed, unwilling to admit that John was right. "We'll see. Maybe once this stupid lawsuit is over and I've ground Gallagher's reputation into dust."

"Just his reputation? And here I thought you were more interested in destroying his soul."

"Same thing, really. For scientists," he clarified.

John rolled his eyes. "Oh please. You all have egos the size of blue whales, but you cringe and cry if anyone implies that you've made a mistake. Get over it. So you may have fucked up at Stellar—more by trusting them than with your actual brilliant science. So are you never going to trust anyone again, like a kid who's had his first heartbreak? I thought you were a bigger man than that, McMillan."

"I am a bigger man!"

Unfortunately this declaration was combined with a gesture that knocked his double-chocolate-chip muffin to the floor, where it fell on John's foot. They both blinked at it for a moment. John's shoulder started to shake with laughter before the sound was audible, but by that time, Bailey was laughing too.

It felt good, laughing with John. Not only to let go of the tension and crankiness that the infuriating conference had created in Bailey over the course of the week, but to be back with John, in their café, talking and laughing. John had hit a bit too close to home with his comments about Bailey "hiding." He *was* hiding, metaphorically licking his wounded ego, lashing out at his colleagues—who totally deserved it; they were just so wrong on about a million different topics—and writing an astrology column that made him want to weep with the sheer offensiveness of it all.

He'd almost forgotten that was all John's fault, actually. He glared. "I am still holding you entirely accountable for the massive insult that is the astrology farce you print once a month, sullying an otherwise acceptable scientific periodical. To say nothing of this ridiculous bet and the ensuing depression as I am forced to acknowledge the dismal state of my love life."

"Your love life is more active than it's been in decades, although if you want to 'blame' me for that, be my guest," John scoffed. "In fact, let's get the eval out of the way...." He dug the netbook out of his satchel and turned it on.

They plowed through the review of Bailey's date with Dr. Severin, and although Bailey didn't think it warranted *that* much helpless laughter, at least John seemed to be enjoying himself. The grouchiness from the last few evaluation sessions seemed to be gone, and Bailey had only been half-joking when he'd suggested it was because the last date was so bad. John wasn't that petty, he didn't think.... Perhaps he'd been more upset about the lawsuit and other things going on with the magazine than Bailey had realized.

"So, did you hear anything from Tulley this week?" he asked.

"No, why, did you? Last I heard, everything was going fine," John answered, giving him a quizzical look.

"Oh, well, good. Anything else going on?"

John's brow furrowed. "Everything is fine. Why? What have you heard?"

"Geez, and you accuse me of being paranoid. I haven't heard anything; I've been at the conference. Do you seriously think any of the leading scientists in the country read your little magazine as anything other than a guilty pleasure?"

"Well, it's not for them," John pointed out in a slightly huffy tone.

Bailey rolled his eyes. "Obviously."

"And anyway, some of them clearly *are*, or they wouldn't keep talking about it in the news. Especially the astronomers' fascination with your predictions about what to expect for the next month." John's grin was more than a little bit evil.

Bailey's face slowly turned an interesting shade of purple as he ranted and raved about the distinction between *astronomer* and *astrologer*, the idiocy of the average person, the ineptitude of his supposed peers in the scientific community, and so on and so forth. It was the same old argument, comfortable and familiar, but with the added viciousness of insulting his peers, of whom he continued to expect better despite their constant failures. The week at the conference had really pissed him off.

He ended his tirade with the firm statement, "And they definitely ought to know better than to believe such hokum."

"Hokum?" John raised one amused eyebrow.

"Hooey. Balderdash. Nonsense. Claptrap. Et cetera, et cetera," Bailey said, waving his hands.

"Did you swallow a thesaurus?"

"Yes, yes I did, you illiterate peon."

John's scowl lacked any true irritation. "You shouldn't talk to your employer that way."

"Oh please. Did it ever occur to you that I talk to you this way because I'm hoping you'll fire me?"

John laughed. Scraping his chair back, he gathered up his trash, nudging Bailey until he did the same. They headed back to the office, where nearly a week's worth of fact-checking awaited Bailey. At least it would be free of corporate evil, he thought, mentally shrugging his shoulders and following John out the door. Stupidity, well, that was a whole different matter....

Chapter 9

Age of Aquarius

THE end of the conference—to say nothing of his midweek date with Dr. Severin—had driven Bailey to drink, as he'd suspected it would. True, he'd started off with a socially acceptable dinner with the highest quality (and most alcoholic) beer the gastro-pub had, but then leaving and going back to his empty apartment, his grouchy cat, his frustrating projects, his whole futile goddamned *life*, had seemed just too pathetic. Logically he knew it was far more pathetic to sit in a bar and drink until he needed a cab to take him home, but sometimes even a genius needed to act stupidly.

The conference had ended with more of a whimper than a bang, or a fizzling grumble, to be more accurate. Václav had headed back to France with his Antarctic ore project, kissing Bailey on both cheeks again at the departure gate. They had both looked at each other uncomfortably afterward, and Václav had shrugged.

"I do not think—"

Bailey nodded. "No, let's not do that. Kissing. Again."

"Agreed." Václav nodded as well. "We will limit ourselves to caustic farewells and our usual mutually insulting correspondence."

The drive back home from the airport was long enough for Bailey to begin to feel a little bit of relief that the whole debacle was finished for another year. He hadn't been pushed to physical violence, had successfully managed to avoid most of the people he hated, and had only had one brief (albeit loud) shouting match with Malcolm Duggan when they'd run into each other at a panel.

No physical wounds, no new lawsuits, and while he wouldn't be winning any Mr. Congeniality awards, at least his attendance at the conference had dispelled the rumors that he was in an insane asylum somewhere. All in all, things had gone about as well as could be expected. Better, even.

Setting his expectations low was not something Bailey was comfortable with, but it did seem to be the key to finding this whole week a productive use of his time. Also, being drunk was helping immensely.

As he got progressively more and more drunk, he pondered calling John to come and pick him up, but there was no good reason to follow that urge. He could afford a taxi. He didn't need John haranguing him for being pathetic and whiny. He'd see John after his Saturday night date anyhow, and he probably had a dozen e-mails from the man waiting in his inbox. About important things like the corrections to Simpson's article about electron impact excitation, wanting to know where Bailey's column critiquing AI game development research was, and, of course, a nudge about the next issue's horoscope column.

Bailey sighed and signaled the bartender for another round.

THE next day Bailey really wished he'd shown a bit more restraint. He'd fiddled with some random projects during the afternoon, taken a nap, and still felt wrecked that evening as he got ready for his date. Tonight's man du jour was *also* unfortunate enough to be named John, Walker this time, and Bailey was going to have to think of him by his last name or spend all evening feeling weird. Some parents were so uncreative it was appalling. He nicked his throat shaving, badly enough to need a Band-Aid for it, and then took over fifteen minutes deciding what shirt he wanted to wear—not because he cared too much about how he looked but because he was too hungover to snap out of his daze.

Bailey's date was sympathetic, looking harried after his own evidently long week. Walker was a doctor, but the medical kind. "Hair of the dog?" he suggested, and Bailey nodded, so they headed to the bar to wait for their table. "Not the official medically approved solution, but certainly my preference. In moderation, of course."

"Of course. And after last night, just a beer or two for me," Bailey said. "I'm no longer surrounded by idiots who consider themselves my peers, and won't have to be again for several more months. God, I loathe conferences. So, what made this such an extraordinary week for you?"

"So-called 'peers' as well. Although less directly; I work doing forensics for a special crime unit. My partner can be more than a bit overbearing. This week he decided he'd test my fire investigation knowledge by hiding combustible compounds in various places in both my lab and office. If you smell smoke or chemical residue, it's probably me," Walker apologized, a weary note in his voice.

"No problem. People suck," Bailey said.

"Hate 'em," Walker agreed, raising his own beer in salute.

The two grumpy, exhausted, vaguely misanthropic men managed to find rueful grins for each other, and Bailey knew it was going to be at least a decent evening.

Walker was *smart*—not that Bailey's other dates had been idiots, at all, but still. He was able to keep up with every twist and turn of Bailey's admittedly disjointed conversation, not only tolerating Bailey's disparaging remarks about the medical profession but agreeing, to an extent, and citing the inconsistency of human biology as the reason that he had gone into research rather than private (or public) practice. Like Bailey, he didn't get along well with anyone he considered less intelligent than himself (the vast majority of everyone) but more or less felt like humanity in general was worth making an effort for. He was very loyal to his friends and employers, no matter how infuriating, and surprisingly idealistic for someone working in law enforcement. He could also be contrary just for the sake of arguing, extremely stubborn, and more tactless than direct. He was a lot like Bailey, in other words.

Walker seemed equally surprised by how similar they were, how easily they got along. "It's as if I had an only-somewhat-evil twin who was a physicist. And with entirely different parents, of course," he said as they finished their dinner. "Frankly, I expected so little from this date that I'm a bit unnerved. Most of my dates don't go well; I had to be manipulated into replying to your ad on Craigslist, even."

"Oh yeah?" Bailey asked, thinking of the bet with John that had started this whole dating farce.

"Sidney bet that you would be entertaining. In fact, now that I've lost, I'm going to owe him a house-cleaning. I should be quite annoyed about that, but damn it, I *am* enjoying myself. Maybe I can hire a cleaning service...."

Together the two of them had managed to polish off an impressive quantity of strong beer as well as some truly decadent burgers. The live band that started up around nine was far too loud, so they walked back to Walker's place to get away from it, since his apartment was close, and that was where the evening took an unexpected turn. They'd barely entered when Walker had Bailey pushed back against a wall, his tongue in Bailey's mouth.

It was good, actually, and Bailey considered protesting but, well, didn't. He was tipsy; it had been a long week; whatever. He was an adult; it felt good; why not? He wasn't devastatingly attracted to his date, but the kissing was good, the hands exploring his body felt good, and the firm muscles and sturdy frame under his own inquisitive hands were also good. It was just sex, right? What on earth was he holding out for?

Walker's bedroom was messy and grew more so with their hastily discarded clothing. Bailey was usually a little—all right, a lot—more verbose about the dynamics of sex, but Walker was somehow both easygoing and quite focused. "I want to suck you," he said, and it had been a very, very, *very* long time since Bailey had received a blowjob. Once that warm, wet, fantastic tongue was on his cock, there was no way he was going to protest; in fact, it felt as if he barely had time to enjoy the decadent pleasure of it before he was coming like a man half his age, all sweaty and gasping and utterly wrecked.

He may or may not have said "John" when he climaxed, but it *was* the man's first name, so that was all right.

Guilt and a sense of fairness motivated him to try to get his head back together when all he truly wanted to do was bask in the afterglow.

He moved down Walker's pale chest so he could reciprocate but was pulled back up for more kissing. Walker guided one of Bailey's hands to his erection instead, murmuring that he'd been looking at Bailey's fingers all night and they turned him on. Flattered, Bailey gathered enough focus to give him the best possible hand job he could, given their lack of familiarity with each other's bodies. Walker made appreciative noises, and soon enough Bailey—and Walker—were sticky and in need of cleaning up.

Which was where the evening started to get a little awkward. Walker did not seem like the sort of man who wanted company while sleeping, and frankly, Bailey wanted to get home to his own bed anyway. Not to mention that Castrovalva would be needing his kitty crunchies; Bailey hadn't planned on an overnight trip when he'd left the house that evening.

"That was nice," Walker said, getting up and grabbing a few tissues to mop up the worst of the mess.

"Ah, yes. Thank you." Bailey hovered, uncertain whether to grab his clothes or what.

"Do you want a shower before you go?"

Well, that answered that, at least. Bailey found his boxers and pants and pulled them on. "I'm good, thanks."

"Phone number? E-mail? I wouldn't mind doing this again, if you wanted to," Walker offered.

Bailey shrugged and got out his phone, dutifully inputting the information and giving his own in return. He doubted he'd call, but it wasn't like it hurt to be polite. He had no idea why he felt so empty; it had been a great blowjob, and he wasn't looking for anything more than that. Was he?

The scrape of Walker's stubble on his jaw from their brief, almost brusque, goodbye kiss made Bailey's skin itch all the way home. He'd enjoyed the evening, enjoyed the sex, enjoyed his *date*, and neither he nor Castrovalva had any idea why he felt like shit as he showered and got ready for bed.

THE thing was, if Bailey were dating like a normal person, for the usual reasons—wanting to connect with someone, have a boyfriend, have some casual sex, whatever—then his date with John Walker would have counted as a success. They were very compatible, yet didn't seem like they'd annoy the hell out of each other; they shared the same general worldview; and while the sex hadn't been mind-blowing, it had been at least a seven out of ten—not bad for a first time.

But the whole thing was soured by the fact that it hadn't really seemed like the sex was anything other than the satisfaction of a biological need, scratching an itch, uninhibited by their usual reserve. Both he and Walker kept others at arm's-length and weren't what anyone would call touchy-feely types; they'd both had emotionally taxing weeks and too much alcohol. The sex had felt more like a need to get off and a desire for something more satisfying than masturbation than actual desire for each other. And, if forced, Bailey had to admit that the lack of emotion (and timing and alcohol) was probably *why* he'd taken Walker up on the sex, where he had held out with both Rich and Dan. It wasn't that he'd liked Walker more (or less, even; they were all three quite different men), but he'd known that Walker wouldn't want anything from him that he wasn't willing to give. As in so many other things, they had been on pretty much the same page about it. Neither of them had casual sex very often, but last night it had been exactly what they'd both needed. So they'd had it. And now they were done.

It was all very logical, clinical even. So why did Bailey feel slightly ashamed and unsettled the morning after, annoyed rather than bemused by the raw patch of skin on his jawbone from where Walker's stubble had abraded him?

Evidently his week at the conference had rattled him on some deep level. Also, more moderate alcohol consumption for a while would probably be a good idea.

Sunday was another unproductive day, and by the time the ringing of Bailey's phone disturbed his afternoon session of scribbling velocity equations on one of his whiteboards and erasing them almost as fast, he was ready to bite someone's head off. Luckily—for Bailey, anyway—it was John, calling to warn Bailey that he was on his way over for dinner, pizza, and the recap of last night's date.

"I am not in a good mood. Forget the pizza; you need to bring me phanaeng curry and my own order of spring rolls, because I will stab you to death with a chopstick if you try to take any of mine."

"Extra spring rolls, got it," John said with a laugh. "Bangkok West is the place that's been browbeaten into remembering about your citrus allergy, right? Can I just tell them it's for you and they'll know what to do?"

"Yes, exactly, go there. I took one of their menus, sat down with one of the staff, highlighted all the items that I could have, laminated it, and stapled it to their desk by the phone. I order from them at least once a week."

"All right then, freak. Do you have beer, or should I get some?"

"I have plenty, and it's all yours after the bender I've been on since about Wednesday."

"You can tell me all about it in an hour or so. See you soon," John said and hung up.

When the phone rang again just as he was getting into some travel algorithms, Bailey picked it up with a rude "What do you want now?"

There was a brief pause, and then an unexpected voice said, "I was hoping for lunch next week, maybe?"

"Oh crap, who is this?"

"Rich Crown, the man who made you eat quiche with a waffle sundae for dessert a few weeks ago," the man said in a pleasant voice.

Flustered, Bailey found himself apologizing about not getting back to Rich, explaining that he had wanted to send a thank you for the flowers, but since they had been thanking *him* for the date, he hadn't wanted to get into an unending loop of thankfulness. The upshot was that Rich wanted to see him again and Bailey said yes before he could stop himself.

How had he gone from less than one date a season to having an average of two dates per week, meeting seven new men in the last month—okay, six, since he technically knew Dr. Severin already—four of whom he wouldn't mind seeing again and two whose cocks he'd touched? This was the most popular he'd ever been in his entire life; he really ought to be enjoying it more. He had a relatively slacker job compared to his usual high-stress employment contracts, and sure, he was being sued, but it wasn't like Gallagher and his lawyers were much of a threat.

Bailey was a little chagrined to realize that he could blame John for almost everything on that list, including the libel suit, since John had agreed to print his vitriolic attacks on his peers knowing full well there would be at least a minor kerfuffle at some point.

The doorbell rang, derailing Bailey's train of thought. John barely made it inside before Bailey attacked him and took away the food. Castrovalva, hearing the voice of his favorite human teasing his owner, came out to say hello. It just figured that the damn cat liked John better than Bailey.

John was in a surprisingly mellow mood, almost downcast over dinner. There was a baseball game on the TV in the background, despite Bailey's protests that it was the most boring game ever invented, even more than bowling. They filled out the survey tool for Bailey's date with John Walker, and he tried his best not to blush as he stated that they'd gone home together and gotten off.

"Wait, I thought you said the chemistry wasn't all that spectacular?"

Bailey shrugged. "It wasn't, but we were pretty compatible overall. It's not always about the supernova of lust and ripping each other's clothes off, you know."

"I know," John said in a slightly defensive tone. "I just thought you were, you know, pickier."

"No, I'm kind of a slut," Bailey admitted. "Sexual opportunities are rare enough that I usually at least consider giving it a go. The last few weeks have been massive exceptions to the rule. If my life was like this all the time, I suppose I would be a bit of a tramp. As it is, I think seizing opportunity when it tends to only present itself once a year—or less—means that I'm still essentially a celibate."

"So you don't have any standards?" John sounded skeptical.

"Of course I have standards. Someone has to at least qualify for Mensa to ride this ride. But in all honesty, I'm not positive anyone who *didn't* qualify has ever implied that they'd want to fuck me. So it's not entirely accurate to say the standards are *mine*."

That at least got a smile out of John. "So, last question: would you see him again?"

Bailey thought about it for a while. "Maybe? We got along exceptionally well. Had a good time over dinner. I kind of regret the sex, though, and annoyingly enough, I can't figure out why."

John nodded. "Some things are ruined with sex," he said sagely and finished his beer.

All of the Harp lager was gone before Bailey had finished his first bottle, and while he'd seen John drunk before, this was the first time that it had been in his home. Castrovalva was draped across John's lap, purring happily like he slut he was, being petted like it was John's new purpose in life. Lucky cat.

"You know," John said after a little while, eyes focused on the game, "these aren't the only twelve guys you're ever going to date. You don't have to pick the one you like best and move in with him or anything."

"What? I know that."

"I just mean… you don't have to settle for the best of the dozen random men who Lauren picked out from the Craigslist ad. There are a lot more people out there who might be interested in you."

Bailey gave him a skeptical look. "First off, I'm not playing *The Love Connection*; I know there's a whole world of men—and women— out there. This was a bet, remember? I don't have any interest in dating, I'm not desperately seeking someone to save me from a life of solitude, and I don't have time for relationships anyway. I mean, yes, I'm bad at them, but I genuinely do not have the energy for being nice all the time. This 'experiment' is already pushing me way past my usual reserves, and I've got to say that I'm starting to get kind of fed up with it."

He took a breath. "Second, I haven't exactly been beating potential partners off with a stick for the last decade, so you'll excuse me if I decide to take a few of them up on their offers to have sex with another real live person. After this month, I expect it will be another several months before I have the opportunity for more, and before you repeat yourself, let me say that this is at least partially by *my own choice*. I do better on my own, living my life, with my job and my friends and my annoying cat who likes you better than he likes me. I am actually happy. Dating someone tends to make me anxious and paranoid, wondering when it's all going to come crashing down," he admitted.

John made a complicated move where he seemed to shrug and nod and sigh all at the same time. "Me too."

"And third... the fuck buddies thing never seems to work out for me. I liked Walker, and the sex was about as good as can be expected when you're totally unfamiliar with each other." Bailey held up a hand. "Don't worry, that's all I'm going to divulge about it. But it just... it was so obvious we were using each other. I didn't like how that felt, even though we both knew what was going on."

"Yeah," John said. "Sometimes what you think you want in the moment, even if it makes you happy and no one's getting hurt, still leaves you feeling dissatisfied later on. Like having a fast food burger because it's easy when what you want is a steak."

Bailey pondered this for a moment. "But when you didn't even know you wanted a steak when you grabbed the burger, it's incredibly annoying."

"Yup."

"You're right; some things are ruined with sex."

"I'm a wise man," John pointed out.

"Like some ignorant sage on a mountaintop," Bailey agreed, smirking. Castrovalva hissed a moment later, disturbed from his slumber by the ensuing brief pillow fight on the sofa.

Chapter 10

Wriggly Pisces

BAILEY'S next date was on Tuesday night and was with another young, incredibly attractive man-boy. He had longish dark, curly hair, enormous eyes, and a graceful, lean build. Was it that difficult to meet intelligent gay men in San Francisco? Bailey could not figure out how both Oliver and now Fernando had become so desperate as to respond to a Craigslist ad. And being himself, he asked.

"Is it the older man-slash-'daddy' thing, or the fact that most men in their twenties are slaves to their hormones and just want sex, or what?"

Fernando seemed a little taken aback but shrugged after a moment. "Most guys my age seem more interested in a pretty face than getting to know what's inside, for sure. And it's nice to hang out with someone who isn't full of 'what am I going to do with my life?' angst. Mostly I just like to meet a variety of people, and cruising the personals ads for the one or two that aren't losers means I'll have an interesting date, at the very least."

"Interesting" seemed to be the key word for Fernando; if Bailey had to take a guess after only fifteen minutes of talking, he'd be fairly confident that being bored was Fernando's biggest pet peeve. He was a working actor, currently gearing up for *As You Like It* and *A Midsummer Night's Dream* at the annual summer Shakespeare festival. He seemed smart enough, despite an unhealthy preference for extreme sports like throwing himself off bridges with a rubber band around his ankle, and also confessed that the part of the ad that had piqued his interest was the *Doctor Who* reference.

Unfortunately, it was pretty clear to Bailey that the date wasn't going to be excellent relatively early on. Fernando was young and fun and not unintelligent, but nowhere near able to follow Bailey's conversation about his work or life. At twenty-seven, Fernando had totally different life experiences, and while it was great that he was looking for something more than a friendly fuck, he had no concept of the sort of career Bailey had or what it was like to be sued, shunned, and professionally shamed. To say nothing of Fernando being such an obviously good-looking kid that they'd never be able connect about being geeky and insecure and almost forty.

On the plus side, Fernando *had* caught most of the *Doctor Who* marathon from a couple of weeks ago, and they enjoyed discussing their favorite companions and the different personalities of the Doctor in each incarnation. It turned out that Fernando's mom had been a big fan, and it held a sort of nostalgic connection for him. For Bailey, things that reminded him of his deceased parents were things he tended to go out of his way to avoid, so it was difficult to connect over that aspect.

In the end, Fernando seemed like a nice guy, but he was too young, too carefree, and too artsy for Bailey. Or Bailey was too old, too careful, and too boring for Fernando. They parted amiably but without exchanging contact information, and that was that; it wasn't like Fernando was suddenly going to start reading physics journals for fun or Bailey was going to show up to the Shakespeare in the Park festival. Whatever; their date was still a welcome relief after the disconcerting tryst with John Walker and ordeal of drinks with Dr. Severin.

THE rest of the week went smoothly for the most part. As always, John had seemed to take undue pleasure in the fact that Bailey's eighth date hadn't gone fantastically well, and he'd supplied condolence food to make up for his teasing the following morning. Bailey felt a little chagrined that he could be bought off with a huge cup of Ethiopian coffee and a couple of pastries, but he'd always been a bit of a sucker for John. Anyone else would have had to grovel using actual words; a chocolatine from John was practically a written apology from a normal person. Well, a normal person who was appropriately awed by Bailey's sharp intellect and even sharper tongue.

The exception was that work was a giant clusterfuck on Thursday morning. Bailey found a handful of significant errors in the article Judith Mason had submitted, and since it had already gone through editing before Bailey had had a chance to review it, everyone was pissed off at *him* when it needed to be totally rewritten. As if it was his fault that she'd made a mistake in her calculations and forgotten to include the frictional coefficient and drawn entirely the wrong conclusion from incorrect data. Judith was embarrassed and angry, Elizabeth the Evil Editor was angry, and even John was annoyed, since it looked like the delay might set back the issue's release date.

"This is why we build an extra week into the schedule, people," John said during the staff meeting, speaking over all of the accusatory yelling. "It'll be close, but I think we'll be all right. Bailey, work *with* Judi, get it to Elizabeth by the end of the day. Liz, if you can get it reviewed and ready by the morning, that would be great. We'll figure out a way to cover your overtime, don't worry. Everybody else, if those three need you for anything, drop what you're doing and help them. We'll get this issue out and no one will be wiser about the whole last-minute panic, okay? Questions?"

No one had any; it seemed John's motivational speeches worked just as well in the office as they had on his high school football field and later, presumably, for military ops. The problem was identified, a plan was made, assignments handed out, and a sense of purpose replaced most of the animosity and stress. Also, free pizzas in the staff room at lunch helped a lot. By the end of the day, they were back on track, crisis averted.

"Drinks, downstairs, now," Bailey said, leaning uncharacteristically against John's office doorjamb, just after six that evening. "You're buying me the most expensive microbrew they have and a burger, and you won't say a word about the cost or my cholesterol."

"How about your blood pressure?"

"I will seriously kill you."

"Then you'd be out of a job," John pointed out, smiling.

"And my release from this purgatory would be met with celebration and carousing. Although I'm not sure if that would void our bet...," Bailey mused.

"Pretty sure murder would, yeah."

"Alas."

They were midway through dinner when John's phone rang. He groaned, pulled it out of his pocket, and gave Bailey an apologetic shrug as he answered it. He didn't say much, groaned a few times in response to whatever the person on the other end had to say, and set up a meeting for the next morning with whomever it was. He hung up, put the phone carefully on the table, pushed his place setting aside, and very carefully rested his forehead on the Formica.

Bailey snorted. He signaled the waitress and ordered another round. "Well?" he asked once she'd delivered the fresh bottles. "Are you going to actually tell me what's wrong, or do you need more time to be melodramatic? It's kind of putting me off my dinner."

John rolled his head to the side and glared at him. "You have less than a dozen french fries left on your plate. And you're eating them," he pointed out.

Bailey glared until John sat up, a slightly flat pink spot on his face from the tabletop.

"That was Robert. Apparently Gallagher's attorneys want to fight dirty. Which Robert expected from Cowen, Turja, and Kavalos but hoped their most recent partner, Rankin, would have maybe brought some common sense to the firm. Anyway, the upshot is that they think they have some kind of leverage and want to use it to strong-arm us into settling, and their settlement proposal will definitely include us printing a retraction."

"What's this leverage they think they have?" Bailey asked, trying not to either panic or fly off the handle until he got a little more information.

"I don't know. Robert and Xiao are meeting with us tomorrow to discuss it. In all probability, Robert thinks they have nothing—or at the most, nothing significant—and are just bluffing to see what they can get away with. Which makes sense… from a strategic point. They're not risking anything with this move."

"Except that I'd really like to see Gallagher bleed—now—and wouldn't be against doing it myself after a few more of those self-defense classes your friend Jason is always pushing me into."

John smiled. "Mild-mannered physicist by day, 'you-wouldn't-like-me-when-I'm-angry' destroyer of souls by night?"

Bailey shook his head. "Could have you mixed that up any more?"

"It's a gift." John paused a moment. "So hey, I didn't know you were still seeing Jason at the gym. How's he doing?"

"First, he's *your* friend; why don't you know? I just pay him to torture me, for reasons I can never quite figure out. Second," Bailey hastened to say, ignoring John's pointed look at the remains of his not-terribly-health-conscious dinner, "he seems fine. Got that puffy-faced sleep-deprived look around the eyes that all new parents have, and the entrance of the gym is plastered with the pictures of the baby, but he's still got enough energy to beat the crap out of me twice a week and text me threatening reminders to show up or else. You have really scary friends."

John grinned. "Yup. The ones who can't kill you with just their pinky fingers are either geniuses who can build weapons of mass destruction that will make you wet yourself or attorneys who can sue every last dime out of your pockets."

"Speaking of, what are we going to do? What do you think they think they know that we don't want them to?"

"Relax, Bailey; we'll handle it. Have another beer."

They had a brief glaring contest, and Bailey wanted to win, but it had been a long day, so he finally capitulated. "Fine. I'll try not to get too worked up until the meeting. Your lawyers are good, Gallagher's an idiot, blah blah blah." He took a deep, cleansing breath. "How about we spilt that chocolate cake sundae instead?"

"You always go for the chocolate when you're worried, did you know that? You only drink too much when you're being all—" John waved a hand around, searching for the right word and deciding on, "emo."

"I'm not sure whether to be more annoyed that you just called me 'emo' or surprised at your observation of my various coping methods." Bailey gave him a contemplative look. "I'll just go with being annoyed by both equally."

John made a face. "I am very observant. And you're right, you're not 'emo', you're a huge drama queen." The *so there* and childish stuck-out tongue were implied.

Bailey just sighed and signaled the waitress to order dessert.

BAILEY made a sincere effort to get into the "TGIF" mindset on his way to work the next morning, but he couldn't get over the feeling of his stomach being filled with rocks and didn't expect to until after the meeting with the attorneys. It was a mixed blessing that it was scheduled for first thing, and the other three were waiting for him with a carafe of coffee and a basket of muffins when he arrived.

Their next court date was scheduled for Monday; this last minute attempt to settle out of court/blackmail Bailey and *Spark* was irritating but not wholly unexpected, at least not according to Mr. Tulley. Bailey had actually put the lawsuit so far out of his mind—trusting the attorneys to do what they did and trusting John to deal with it—that he'd sort of forgotten about it. Admittedly, he had been distracted by his shocking social life and the energy conference and Václav's visit, to say nothing of how irritating certain monopole particles were being in relation to his superstring theory research. He'd trusted the others to deal with it, and while that often resulted in disappointment, it looked like this might not be one of those times. Perhaps he was getting better at choosing whom to trust. Or maybe he was becoming less cynical as he aged, but that seemed seriously unlikely.

He couldn't argue with Robert and Xiao's competency, though. Literally, even, for a while, as he poured coffee down his throat and chased it with a few muffins. He didn't know if it was the quality of the lawyers themselves or the fact that it was *Spark* being sued as well as himself or John's involvement or what, but the whole team was out for blood on his behalf. It was heartwarming, if a bit disconcerting. Bailey was far more used to having to verbally defend himself—even from the people who were supposed to be on his side, who historically had an irritating tendency to say he'd deserved whatever trouble he got—than he was to anyone else doing it for him.

He was touched. In the head, maybe, if he was getting all sappy about the people who were paid quite handsomely to defend him merely doing their jobs. He looked at his muffin with suspicion, wondering if John had laced it with some kind of drug that would explain this sudden flood of maudlin gratitude. Sometimes people did put booze in baked goods, after all….

"So what is it they think they know?" he asked, brushing his hands free of crumbs.

John looked at the potted plant on his desk. "They think they know who is writing the astrology column. They think that if they threaten to say that it's you, we'll cave in to their demands for a retraction and settlement."

Bailey swallowed hard and didn't look at Robert or Xiao. "Do they have any proof?"

Robert shook his head, and Xiao said decisively, "Not a shred. And if they follow through on their threat and say that you're the author in any public forum at all, we can turn right around and sue them for libel."

"Huh." He paused for a very long moment, trying to work out how to ask what he needed to without giving anything away.

John saved him. "We were just discussing the secrecy clause of the astrology column's author's contract and how if only three individuals at *Spark* know who the author is, and all three of them were willing to swear that they have not released the information either purposefully or unintentionally, then the CTK&R firm is working purely on speculation."

"Yes, and speculation is still covered under the libel rules, whether the statement is factual or not," Robert added.

"So we can operate from a 'neither confirm nor deny' position without helping the general population start narrowing down who the possible author is. It wasn't a bad move on their part," Xiao admitted, "but I bet they were hoping *Spark's* staff wasn't as loyal or close-mouthed as John seems to think they are. If more than three people know or the staff here isn't willing to run the risk of perjuring themselves in an affidavit, then we'd have a bigger problem preserving the author's anonymity. As it is, I think we can threaten a counter-defamation suit, and they'll back down."

"So the idea is to call their bluff, make them admit they have no proof, and go to court on Monday as planned?" Bailey clarified.

"Pretty much," John said, nodding.

The attorneys gathered up their papers, and John asked Lauren to call a cab for them. Nine o'clock in the morning and already the clock was ticking; they were going to have a busy day, even if all they were really doing was refusing the offer to settle.

John showed Robert and Xiao out the door and then came back to Bailey, who was practically vibrating. He raised an eyebrow, questioning.

"No, it's not caffeine poisoning; you'd think you'd know that by now. It's nerves. How the hell did they figure out it was me writing that column? I told you, John, I *told* you it had to be completely anonymous! Oh my God, what am I going to do? I'll be run out of the scientific community on a rail! I'll only be able to get a job teaching Physics to slackers at a community college. Or I'll have to work *here* for the rest of my life."

"Or until the magazine goes out of business," John suggested with a shrug. "After we lose the suit, *Spark* will be both discredited and bankrupt. Gallagher asked for a lot of money, and don't forget about the attorneys' fees."

"Oh God, I think I'm going to be sick," Bailey moaned, burying his face in his hands.

John passed over the waste bin. "Not on the carpet," he said, sitting down next to Bailey on the sofa in the conference area.

"Shouldn't have had all those muffins...."

"You'll be fine," John said, and Bailey didn't have to look up to see John roll his eyes. "You want an Alka-Seltzer or some 7-Up? Or can you just take a deep breath and calm down like a normal person? It will be *fine*."

"How can you know that? How did they find out about the column?" he wailed.

John leaned back, his hand coming to rest between Bailey's shoulder blades and starting a soothing circular motion. "First, I know everything will be fine because ultimately, this whole thing comes down to you saying something rude as an *opinion*, which is perfectly legal. Furthermore, I trust Robert Tulley; he knows what he's doing. If he and Xiao think CTK&R is bluffing, then they are. Second, we *know* they're bluffing because we know that *we* didn't tell anyone who was writing the column. I didn't tell anyone. You didn't tell anyone. And I'd bet the magazine on Lauren not telling anyone—in fact, I am betting *Spark* on it."

"But she hates me," Bailey pointed out.

"But she likes me," John said. His grin was audible, and the shrug of his shoulders was a brief hiccup in the hand rubbing Bailey's shoulders.

"Hm. Point," he conceded. He was silent for a bit, letting John keep doing what he was doing, reveling in the feeling of John's hands on him. They were warm and strong and soothing, and he felt like he was melting inside, like chocolate left out in the sun, softening and sweet....

He tensed up suddenly, undoing all of John's work. "Uh. I told Václav. It was an accident!"

John's hand stopped. "Do you think he's a security risk?" he asked carefully.

Bailey pondered it for a moment. "Well, he laughed a lot. But no, I don't think he'd tell anyone. He's my friend. And he has experience keeping secrets. Even when he drinks, he spills nothing, and I'd like to see someone drink a Czech under the table—those guys are more impervious than the Irish."

"Do you want to call and ask him if he told anyone? Would he admit it, if he'd let something slip?"

"Probably. He's got a pretty good track record for admitting his mistakes…."

John's hand began moving again. "Unlike you?"

Bailey shrugged, but it didn't interrupt the massage. "I'm getting better at it. I just refuse to be blamed for things that aren't my fault and insist on other people taking their part of the blame."

"Fair enough."

There were several long moments of the rubbing, and Bailey's stomach, which had unclenched, started to clench again for very different reasons. Or, not his stomach exactly, but somewhere a bit further down. John's hands had stopped making reassuring circles and switched to more of a light massage, thumbs pressing gently, fingers spread wide, pressure too gentle to be therapeutic and more, well, arousing.

John's hands on his body felt really, really, *really* good. In a totally inappropriate way. In a moment or two, Bailey was going to moan or something, and it would either turn into one of *those* kinds of massages, or it was going to be totally awkward, and Bailey's money was on the latter. He couldn't even excuse his response with the usual thought that he needed to get laid, because he had, just a week ago. Less, even.

No, it was John, John's hands, the feeling of being touched by John that was doing it to him. For him. With? All kinds of prepositional possibilities flickered through Bailey's head, and finally he noticed that his eyes were screwed shut, his hands clenched, and the motion of John's hand had stopped.

A moment of horrible stillness happened.

John patted him on the shoulder. "I'm going to go get you something fizzy to drink."

Bailey waited until John was gone before he let out the groan he'd been holding inside, frustration and embarrassment overshadowing the remnants of pleasure from before. He debated between walking back to his desk with what would probably be an obvious erection, ducking into the men's room to jerk off, or saving it for later, at home, when he could properly enjoy a fantasy of what might have happened if he weren't such a damn coward. If he were more willing to risk losing John.

He looked at his clenched right hand and sighed.

Chapter 11

Sextile Sexy Aries

THE rest of Bailey's Friday was ostensibly smooth sailing except for the residual grouchiness from orgasm denial. Not that he *couldn't* have gone into the restroom and had a delightful fantasy about how John's hands had felt on his back, the warmth from John's body behind him, the slight scent of his soap and other grooming products.... Instead, Bailey threw himself into another scathing critique of some of the imbeciles daring to call themselves "scientists" and tried not to look at John's office door.

Jerking off while thinking about one's colleague—never mind one's best friend—was never a good idea. Conventional wisdom suggested this, and Bailey had also unfortunately tested the theory, to his detriment, more than once. No, he would not touch his dick and think of John. That way lay madness.

However, the other way lay grumpiness.

"Your yenta wants to see you," said Simpson as she walked past Bailey's cubicle.

"My what? Oh, Lauren. Great."

Simpson gave him a probing look. "Why is she setting you up on dates anyway?"

"Because John is insane," he answered, knowing it wouldn't make sense and refusing to explain any further.

She scowled. "Whatever. I'm just passing on the message." And she continued on to her desk.

He refused to jump up and run over to Lauren like an obedient lapdog. He waited for five minutes but then got a ping on his computer from her that simply said NOW, MCMILLAN.

"What?" he demanded, crossing his arms over his chest as he tried to loom over her while she was seated behind her desk.

Lauren snorted. "You need to work on your intimidation skills, jackass, if you think I'm going to care about your huffy attitude. Your date tomorrow wants to meet at his place. He's coming by here for the ID check this afternoon, but I didn't know if you'd be worried over your virtue, meeting a strange man at his home."

Bailey scowled, trying to figure out which part of her statement was most outrageous, and settled on sputtering, "My *virtue*? What is this? The seventeenth century?"

"Careful, McMillan, or I'll tell your date you're a trollop."

Her glare was only around Level 3, but it was working up into the scary realm, and he'd had enough frustration for a day that hadn't yet reached the lunch hour. "Fine. If he's willing to make a separate trip and give you his ID, he's probably not a serial killer. And if he is, my death will be on your head."

"How would I ever live with myself?" Lauren replied, baring her teeth in what was ostensibly a grin.

Bailey fled before she could bite him.

WILLIAM HANSEN'S house was a screaming 1960s bachelor pad. The carpets were a thick white shag, the furniture and light fixtures were glass and chrome and of the rounded "futuristic" style that had been so popular in the so-called Space Age, and there was a bar in the corner. Bailey wouldn't have been the least bit surprised if it turned out that the lighting and music had a remote control or if there was a round revolving bed hidden somewhere.

The man himself looked fairly normal: a bit older than Bailey, the same sort of wide-shouldered build with an age-softened middle, surprisingly thick hair. Bill's clothing style was a tiny bit old-fashioned, but Bailey supposed that might be the current "retro" fashion; he really had no idea. Bill wasn't astoundingly attractive, but he had a lively face and an aura of charm that could either be oily or sincere—only time would tell.

"Can I offer you a drink?" Bailey's date asked after showing him into the sunken living room area. "Dinner is on its way—delivery from an Italian place around the corner. Your assistant told me about your lemon allergy, and I passed that along to the chef."

Bailey smiled and tried to relax; just because Bill's house looked like something from the Playboy mansion didn't mean he was necessarily a sleazebag. Maybe he just had weird decorating taste, or a crazy interior designer, or even perhaps that rarity known as a sense of humor. "Just a beer," Bailey said, and then added, gesturing at the décor, "This is some place."

Bill laughed. "I have an interior designer friend who asked if he could fix the place up. I didn't expect he'd go quite this far, but it always makes me laugh at the end of a long day, so I kept it. And it's a good litmus test of my guests' personalities," he added, eyes twinkling.

"I admit I'm relieved it wasn't your idea," Bailey said, taking a drink. "I have to ask—is there a circular bed?"

"You'll just have to wait and see." Bill grinned.

Their dinner was good: a simple but delicious fettuccini Alfredo and a Sunday gravy with penne, salads, bread, and tiramisu. Bailey wasn't a huge fan of having other people order for him, but the food was fantastic. Not the sort of thing his doctor would approve of, but the slight softness of Bill's tummy indicated that he didn't pay much mind to his doctor either, and Jason would almost certainly be happy to work the extra calories off of Bailey at the gym later in the week.

Their conversation revolved around the latest developments of NASA and their international counterparts. It turned out that space exploration was a bit of a hobby for Bill, and for a long, bad moment Bailey feared his date was going to start ranting about space aliens. Luckily for them both, Bill didn't, and they had a pleasant discussion about SETI and a few of the other attempts to find intelligent life. It turned out they were pretty much on the same page; it was highly improbable that intelligent life in the galaxy was limited to just one planet, but it was equally probable that any potential aliens were far too intelligent to bother with contacting idiotic and warlike Earthlings.

"So what is it you actually do?" Bailey asked after they'd finished eating. The fact that it still hadn't come up in conversation had made him wonder if his date was hiding something.

"Oh, I thought you knew," Bill said, looking a little bit uncomfortable. "I'm an actor, of a sort. I do local advertisements for travel agencies and things. I get recognized a lot; I assumed you knew."

"Hm," Bailey mused. "I did think you looked familiar, but I'm incredibly bad with names and faces and, well, people. So you're the guy I see on my TV at night?"

"Have you been watching me in your bedroom?" Bill leered, and Bailey couldn't tell if he was just that cheesy or if he was joking in an ironic way.

"Ah. The TV is in the living room," he clarified, a little uncomfortable.

Bill moved closer and put his hand on Bailey's thigh. "I guess I'll just have to take you into mine. Feel like seeing what shape the bed is now?"

Bailey did not, but before he could protest, Bill's tongue was in his mouth. It wasn't bad; it wasn't great. It was very wet, though, and he was feeling a little squeamish and a lot turned off by the time he pushed Bill away.

Breathing heavily, Bill gave Bailey a look that was almost certainly supposed to be sexy. "Ready for more?" he asked, and before Bailey could do or say anything, Bill had leaned back and grabbed the hem of his turtleneck shirt, pulling it up and over his head.

"What the—no!" Bailey was torn between amusement and confusion and a sense of some of that seventeenth century maidenly outrage that Lauren had brought up at the office. "I'm, uh, flattered and everything, but...." He debated how to say *absolutely not interested* in a polite way before giving up. "Not interested. Thanks," he added.

Also, Bill's hair seemed... askew. How the hell had that happened?

"I should go," Bailey said, jumping to his feet. "It's, uh, an early day tomorrow."

"On Sunday?"

Oh right. Damn, he was such a horrible liar when he was trying to spare someone's feelings, but he made up some excuse about breakfast with his boss that wasn't entirely untrue. Although why was he even bothering, with a guy as clueless as this? Mentally shaking his head at himself, Bailey managed to grab his jacket and apologize, giving Bill his phone number as he rushed out of the door. It was off by one digit, on purpose.

Bailey couldn't recall a time when he'd felt both apologetic and embarrassed on someone else's behalf. He wondered if this was how other people—mostly women—had felt when he'd pursued them. There was nothing to do but laugh and think of how amused John would be when they got together for brunch tomorrow.

"HE HAD a toupee? Who has a toupee these days?" John asked, incredulous. "Where did he even *get* one?"

"I know, right? Did he mail order it from some catalog specializing in things from the seventies? Maybe it was the same place his interior decorator friend got all the knickknacks for his apartment."

"What, a thrift store?"

Bailey glared at John for a moment and then considered. "Do you think you can buy a toupee at a thrift store? How would you sterilize it?"

"I don't think germs are a huge concern for the kind of man who would wear a wig," John said in a thoughtful tone.

"All right, be honest—I know my hair is thinning, but it's not *that* bad, right? I mean, not bad enough for wigs or implants or anything extreme? Not yet?"

John rolled his eyes. "Your hair is fine, Bailey."

Bailey made a face at him. "As if you know anything about the woes of male pattern balding, Mr. Hedgehog Hair. How long does it take you to get it to stick up like that, anyway? You could probably have solved cancer or something in the time you spend doing your hair in the mornings, or at least set a new flight record."

Visibly taking a deep, calming breath, John said, "It just sticks up like this all by itself. Cowlicks. They used to drive my father crazy."

Bailey made a thoughtful noise, studying John's hair and trying to decide if it would be rude to touch it and see if he was telling the truth or if it was crunchy with hair product. He decided that he didn't care and reached out a hand to touch.

"Huh. Soft."

John's face looked like it was caught between conflicting expressions of surprise, exasperation, and amusement. He blinked. "Stop touching my hair! We're in the middle of a restaurant, for fuck's sake!"

"I just wanted to see for myself," Bailey said more than a little defensively as he snatched his hand back.

Holding up a fork in a threatening manner, John glared at him. "Back off."

"Fine, fine. No hair gel, just naturally sticky-uppy, perfect hair." He squinted at it again. "And not thinning even the slightest. That's so unfair; you're at least a couple of years older than me."

John shrugged. "You keep complimenting my hair like that and I'll think you're flirting with me."

To his horror, Bailey felt his face flush. "I was just making an observation! I never really looked all that closely before now." He paused. "It's kind of grown on me, I suppose. The overall style, I mean. You just stop noticing how your friends look after a while," he added, thoughtful.

John nodded. "Unless they do something dramatic, like that time Lauren went platinum blonde for a few months."

"Or when Jason cut off his dreads," Bailey agreed. There was a semi-awkward silence, so he said, "It's funny how sometimes you forget that someone's good-looking after a while."

"Well, it's not like you're going to keep thinking 'damn, she's hot' all the time if you're married to a supermodel," John said. "But it goes the other way too. Like, you may not notice anything spectacularly great about how someone looks, but over time, you kind of start to think they're attractive."

"I don't know. First impressions last a long time," Bailey disagreed.

"No, I mean like over years," John clarified. "You know, like how an actor or actress isn't that amazing-looking the first time you see them, but after a few seasons of a TV show, you like them enough that you like *them*, and somehow that makes them seem more appealing. Maybe I'm not saying this right…."

"No, I think I get it. It's the same dynamic as on a first date, where the person is gorgeous but a total ass, and they start to look 'ugly' by the end of the date, even though objectively how they *look* hasn't changed at all. You don't like them, so they seem to be less attractive than when you first met. And vice versa."

John nodded. "Like Ramses?"

"Exactly who I was thinking of, yes." Bailey grinned. "Or, you know, Rich Crown. He wasn't gorgeous or anything, but I really liked him, and by the time we started making out, he seemed pretty hot."

John's face fell. "Yeah, like that." He took a few bites of his probably now-cold eggs and then glanced around for the waitress as if he had to go.

"What, you have a date or something?" Bailey asked.

"Nah. Just thought I'd go in to the office and make sure everything was ready for tomorrow. You've got clean clothes, right? The court date? Judge and everything?"

"Yes, dear." Bailey huffed. "I'll try not to embarrass you too much in front of all the big important people."

"Oh, I'm not gonna hold my breath for anything that extreme," John said with a laugh. "Just try to look appropriate and let the lawyers do the talking. Don't hit Gallagher in the face. And no hair-pulling; I know how you physicists get."

THE rest of Bailey's Sunday was spent standing in front of the whiteboards in his home office, scribbling and erasing until he was covered in a fine layer of dry-erase ink dust, sneezing and wondering how much it would cost to get some SMART Boards in there. Not that he didn't have the money, but still, no point in being wasteful.

He sat down at his desk, browsed for a few minutes, and considered his options. Was he willing to spend five thousand dollars for one? No, he was not. But could he make one on his own…? Better yet, did he know anyone at SMART Tech that he could bribe or harass into giving him one? His time would be far better spent browbeating an underling into making or acquiring one for him than it would be in trying to make one himself.

He pondered the unfairness of a world that had supplied him with so much brilliance and so few minions, before hitting on two possible solutions: one, ask John to have someone at the office do it; or two, ask Václav to find someone to give him one. Václav was probably the best bet—that Czech bastard probably had a few of last year's models sitting around unused at the CNRS. And he knew all about creative paperwork; maybe Bailey could do some "consulting" for them in exchange, go over there and yell at people, or give a presentation, or something. He fantasized about Parisian food for a few minutes until his stomach grumbled.

His kitchen cupboards were disappointingly free of the tantalizing delicacies he was imagining, so he settled for peanut butter on crackers and made a note to add some foie gras and good cheese and olives to the grocery list for his housekeeper to pick up. He wasn't planning on entertaining anyone of more discerning tastes than John—whom Bailey had once seen check an expiration date on a cup of yogurt, shrug, and eat it anyway—but Bailey deserved the finer things in life occasionally. Oooh, and he'd have to tell her to get some Belgian chocolate, too….

He fired off an e-mail to Václav, one to Ms. Castillo (specifying about the gourmet snacks until his stomach rumbled *again* and he called to order a pizza), and then saw that he had a new e-mail from an unrecognizable alphanumeric username, which turned out to be Oliver Dumas's.

Dear Bailey,

How are you doing? I enjoyed the latest issue of Spark, particularly your evisceration of the current problems CERN is having. As we discussed after dinner last month, the Dada exhibit is on at the SFMOMA—would you like to plan a friend-date to go see it?

I am available this coming Sunday, the 29th. Meet there at two in the afternoon? If that doesn't work but you would still like to go, suggest a date and time. If you're not interested, don't worry about it. I just thought you might be.

-Oliver

Bailey checked his schedule, and although he had a stupid astrology-inspired blind date on Wednesday and yet another one on Friday, he figured he'd need the break from the idiocy, and he had liked Oliver. No, they weren't romantically compatible, but Bailey had few enough friends that the idea of making a new one was acceptable.

Plus, Oliver had the novel aspect of being someone Bailey had kissed, who didn't hate him. And he wasn't a scientist, had never worked with Bailey, and liked both art and math. Yes, he should definitely attempt to cultivate a friendship with Oliver. He replied affirmatively to the proposed plan and then killed some time looking up the restaurants near the museum until his pizza arrived.

This coming week would include a court date, a blind date, another blind date, and then a friend-date. Add in two nights at the gym and he wasn't going to have any time to himself until a week from tomorrow. Sighing, Bailey cracked open a bottle of the good beer and settled into his favorite spot on the sofa to watch part of a *Star Trek: The Original Series* marathon. Castrovalva joined him and ate the bits of cheese that had stuck to the box. It was a good night.

Chapter 12

Eccentricities of Orbit

MONDAY'S session at the courthouse was a mixed bag. The Honorable Judge Frye had rolled her eyes at Gallagher several times and made some pointed comments about frivolous lawsuits to his attorneys. Mr. Rankin had looked appropriately chagrined, but it was obvious that the rest of the group from CTK&R couldn't have cared less.

After four long hours, the result of the arbitration was a clear win for *Spark*. No grounds for the libel accusation were found, no retraction would be printed, and the fees for the whole charade would be paid by Gallagher. Bailey thought his nemesis might have an attack of apoplexy right there in the courthouse when the amount was mentioned, and it would have served him right. Robert Tulley was coolly professional when he shook Rankin's hand; Ms. Zhen was fighting back a triumphant grin.

Bailey wanted to be excited and relieved and victorious—and he felt those things, honestly—but he was also still a little concerned. He could tell from the tightness around John's eyes that John was too, because not once during the morning's proceedings had Gallagher or his lawyers mentioned their possible leverage, that they thought they knew who was writing *Spark's* top secret astrology column. Yes, it was more blackmail than leverage, but it wasn't out of the question that it would have been used to negotiate. Bailey had been mentally prepared for that, and it was unsettling him that the word "astrology" hadn't been mentioned once. True, Gallagher didn't have any proof, but that had never stopped him from publishing his so-called "research," now had it?

So of course Bailey wasn't exactly surprised when Gallagher had spit "This isn't over" at him as they walked down the courthouse steps. His reaction was to want to shove the other scientist and watch him tumble spectacularly down to the sidewalk, but it was just a cartoonish fantasy, not an actual impulse to violence. Winning the lawsuit had soothed Bailey's temper somewhat, and he was embarrassed at how physical his violent impulses toward Gallagher had been lately. After all, he had a whole magazine at his disposal; he could use his poison pen to strike back, to tear Gallagher's career to pieces, all completely legally. Blackened eyes would heal; a destroyed career would eat at Gallagher's very core. As Bailey well knew.

"Drinks?" John offered as their group of four approached a waiting cab.

Robert paused, glanced at his watch, and then shrugged. "Perhaps one with lunch wouldn't be out of the question. Xiao?"

She nodded. "There's a gin and tonic out there with my name on it, to be paid for by those blithering idiots. Nothing like a good clean win, right, gentlemen?"

Bailey shrugged. It didn't feel like a win, since he was still waiting for the other shoe to drop, but he was always up for lunch. They went to an upscale sushi bar, and once Bailey managed to get their server to bring out one of the chefs and made him swear on a waving-cat statue that there was no citrus in their teriyaki sauce, he relaxed enough to enjoy his salmon.

After a polite celebratory lunch, the attorneys departed for their office, leaving John and Bailey lingering over the last of their edamame and a final round of beer.

"So, that went relatively well," John said.

"It didn't go badly. But now what? Gallagher—" Bailey glanced around furtively "—still thinks he knows something about the column."

"Yeah, I'm a little worried about that too. Do you really think we have a leak?" John asked. Bailey shrugged, and he sighed. "You, me, Lauren, Václav... anyone else?"

"I don't think so." Bailey sighed too. "We don't always close the doors when we talk in your office, though."

John hummed a bit to himself, thinking hard. "Well. I know several people dislike working with you and get grouchy when you correct them in your less-than-diplomatic way…. Do you honestly think they would have ratted you out to anyone?"

Bailey tried not to go with his usual knee-jerk paranoid reaction and considered it as objectively as he could for a moment. "I think people sometimes let information slip that they didn't intend, sometimes without even realizing. And as I said, we haven't been careful either. I don't know."

"I was thinking that maybe I should send out a staff memo reinforcing that the author is anonymous for important reasons and that they should all think about what it would do to their own careers if the general public thought *they* were writing a silly nonscientific column like that one."

"The walk-a-mile-in-my-shoes argument? Honestly?" Bailey rolled his eyes. "Might as well remind them of the Golden Rule while you're at it. How about threatening to fire anyone found leaking information—speculation, really, since there's no proof or paper trail?"

John rolled his eyes too. "Or I was thinking I could say it was me. To the staff, I mean," he clarified when Bailey frowned. "Not print a by-line or anything. Just some casual misdirection."

"A lie."

"You say tomato…."

"No one in the history of ever has said 'po-*tah*-toe'. That cliché has always pissed me off," Bailey groused.

John was getting an irritated look on his face. "I'm running out of options here, Bailey. You've got any helpful suggestions to make, I'd like to hear them."

"I did! Threaten to fire people. It always works for me."

"Yeah, and I try to treat people better than you do," John said with a snort.

"Wait, when did this turn into a fight? I don't get why you're mad at me now. I didn't do anything!" Bailey protested.

John leaned back in his seat and rubbed his temples for a long moment. Finally he looked up, stress and tension creasing his forehead.

It looked like he had a headache. Bailey supposed that the lawsuit and potential bankruptcy of *Spark* had probably been a bit of a strain. Not that it was anyone's fault but Gallagher's, at all, but Bailey had to admit that John had been looking a little worn out lately. Like he wasn't getting enough sleep. Or was sad, or something.

"You should take off the rest of the day," Bailey said, out of the blue. "Come on. One of the perks of owning a business is unrestricted vacation time. You need a break."

"I shouldn't. This suit has taken up a lot of my time lately, lots to do that I've been putting off."

"It's two in the afternoon," Bailey argued. "You came in on the weekend, you said, and you look like you're going to fall over if you don't relax. Let's get out of the city. Drive down the coast or something."

John's eyebrows leaped up. "Really? You're volunteering to let me drive you down the coastal highway?"

Bailey paused. "Uh. Well, I thought I'd drive." John looked like he was going to pout, and Bailey sighed. "But fine. You can have the wheel. Just try to stay somewhere in the neighborhood of the speed limit, will you? And if I get carsick, I get to take over."

Nodding, John said, "Sounds like a plan." They both got out their phones, John calling Lauren and Bailey texting Jason to cancel their session at the gym. They took a cab back to the garage by John's house and got his car, and in less than an hour, they were on Highway 1, heading south.

It was a companionable silence, John's tension ebbing as the miles between him and city increased, and once again Bailey wondered to himself why John didn't live on a ranch or something somewhere. He couldn't think of anyone less suited for city life, all the traffic and rushing and *people*. John was easygoing, sure, and he'd never complained about the city, but he had always struck Bailey as more of a modern-day cowboy type, lots of wide open sky and plenty of room. He was pretty sure John had mentioned growing up in Colorado or somewhere; his dad had been in the Air Force too, and the family had moved a lot. Maybe it had been Montana....

"Ooh, there's that bakery I like. Pull over," Bailey insisted after a while. They'd passed two signs for U-Pick Berries already, but this was the Pie Ranch, and his stomach was grumbling.

John pulled into the dirt parking area, teasing Bailey good-naturedly about his soft tummy and comparing him to Winnie the Pooh. Bailey took off for the bathroom first and then browsed the baked goods, selecting a whole ollalieberry pie, some cinnamon bread, and five jars of raspberry jam. The woman working the cash machine patiently checked the labels for citrus ingredients with him.

He deposited his goods in the car and spotted John out by the end of the parking area near the cliffs, hands in his pockets, wind teasing the top of his hair into an even more chaotic mess than usual. Bailey grabbed a sweatshirt and joined him. The waves below were mellow, high tide and not much wind. Not too far off around the next cove were three hang gliders soaring on the rising air at the cliff edge, never too far from a nice meadow to land on or a wide stretch of beach far above the tide. With the wind in his face, eyes fixed on the daring pilot whipping off a spiral of perfect loops, the expression on John's face was the very definition of wistful.

Bailey wrinkled up his face, squinted at the sun, and took a deep breath to fortify himself. "Why don't you fly anymore?"

It was sort of out of the blue, except not really, since his friend's longing and desire were so clear. John had suffered an injury, yes, but Bailey was positive the break had healed smoothly, and he couldn't think of any physical limitations that would keep John grounded. When they'd first met years ago, it had seemed like flying was John's entire raison d'être, the one thing in life that brought him joy, that made all the rules and regulations and stress of being part of the military worthwhile. Yet he'd been out for nearly two years, and Bailey hadn't heard him mention flying even once.

John sighed, wrapping his hand around the weather-beaten split-wood railing. He seemed to be having an internal debate, but was ultimately defeated in the face of Bailey's bluntness. "Can't. I got shot down in Afghanistan, and I… just can't anymore."

Bailey mulled that over for a while, reading between the lines of what John wasn't saying, deciding panic attacks or PTSD were the most likely culprits. He had a short argument inside his head that that was ridiculous, that it had been two years, that John could and should see a shrink, that it was time to man up and get over it since flying was clearly something John missed very much. It wasn't like him to *not* say those sorts of things out loud, and he got an actual cramp in his jaw from clenching it so the words wouldn't escape. Instead he awkwardly put a hand on John's shoulder and said, "I'm sorry."

"Me too."

They stood in silence for a while, watching the hang gliders. Two of them landed, but the third, the acrobatic one, kept going.

"I would be so dizzy," Bailey noted.

The side of John's mouth twitched a little in a partial smile. "You'd probably barf all over the place."

Bailey huffed. "See if I'm nice to you again."

"Better be; I'm always nice to you. I gave you a job, didn't I?" John smiled.

Bailey shook his head and tried not to smile back. "Some job. Demeaning my intelligence, forcing me to write utter tripe, and getting me sued by an imbecile just for speaking my mind."

John shrugged and said, "What can I say; I never promised you a *good* job." Bailey snorted, and he continued, "I just wanted to get you out of your house, interacting with people again. You were starting to get all hermit-like, and I worried you were going to blow up the whole city or something. And I *like* the city; it's where I keep all my stuff."

Rolling his eyes at the *Tick* reference, Bailey shook his head. "I don't need to be taken care of. But, well, thanks."

"Anytime."

Chapter 13

Clashing Horns with Taurus

IF THE satisfaction of resolving the lawsuit and the relief of trouncing Gallagher in a legal setting were fleeting, Bailey was sure it wasn't his fault. The inside of his head was a very busy place, and thoughts followed each other far faster than other people could keep up with— and faster than he could express even speaking a mile a minute. He wanted to relax and celebrate, to hold onto the peaceful feeling from the drive down the coast with John. He honestly did. But the blast of the alarm clock, the nagging worry that Gallagher knew about the astrology column, and his confusingly busy social calendar were taking a toll.

And he was also worried about John. John had been moody on the drive back—nothing unusual there—but Bailey had noticed a growing trend of silence that didn't seem to be as comfortable as it had a few months ago. When he tried to puzzle out what had changed in John's life that might be causing him stress, all he could come up with was the lawsuit and Bailey's own love life. Was John jealous? Not in a petty way, of course, but maybe the fact that Bailey was going out on all these dates had made John feel lonely or something.

Then again, who was to say John hadn't been dating, himself? He had always been pretty tight-lipped about his romantic endeavors and sexual conquests; Bailey had honestly been surprised that in the ice cream parlor last month, John had revealed that he was bisexual. And obviously if even *Bailey* could get dates through Craigslist, then John should have no problem at all, whether he wanted casual sex or a life partner. He was gorgeous, smart, interesting, and owned a business; both men and women would be his for the taking if he only asked.

In the shower, Bailey pondered why it was that John wasn't dating, and gave his morning erection a stern talking-to about inappropriate focal objects before sighing in defeat as he wrapped his hand around it. Some hair conditioner eased the way, and he leaned against the tiles, determinedly focusing his thoughts on the two overly muscled men he'd last let entertain him on an adult website. They both had tattoos and one had a tongue stud, which gave Bailey something to think about while he stroked himself. Something that wasn't John. Of course his pleasure at his success in *not* thinking about John pretty well ruined it, since now his almighty brain was picturing John as the one with the tongue stud, and that was that. He groaned as his release coated his hand, and squeezed his eyes shut, unable to rid himself of the image of John on his knees, Bailey's cock in his mouth.

The water turning cold woke him out his reverie, and he sighed and finished his shower. He pondered over coffee why it was that his brain was so disciplined when it came to science and mathematics and nearly anything academic, and so unruly when confronted with the simple proposal of *not thinking about John* while he jacked off. It was unfair that after nearly thirty years of such struggles, his libido was still the undefeated champion over his genius brain.

Castrovalva, as usual, was unsympathetic.

BAILEY'S text messages and e-mails for the day did not improve his mood.

> Gym tonight. Or else. I know where you live, you flabby scientist. If you ignore your body, it will stop working.

That was from Jason. Had it honestly been a week since Bailey had been to the gym? He'd only missed two sessions, but yes, that was a week. He sighed, thinking of the punishment he was in for. Jason was going to add an extra two miles to his treadmill course, he just knew it. That was almost enough to make him not go back, but then it would be four miles, and increase exponentially until he showed up and worked it off. Jason must have been a drill sergeant or something in another life.

Living happily ever after with your man yet? I
want an update! You buy the beer, I'll spot you
a cupcake.

That message's sender was helpfully identified by his phone as one of his former dates, Dan Harper. Bailey shivered a little, remembering their fantastic kiss and how much he'd wanted to go home with Dan. He'd been far less attracted to John Walker, whom he *had* gone home with, but wasn't that always the case? At least with Walker, Bailey hadn't felt self-conscious, and the sex had been free of complications. Plus, he remembered how frustrated he'd felt, knowing he technically *could* go to bed with Dan, but having it be out in the open that Bailey was a little hung up on John (his John) made it seem tacky.

He pondered Dan's advice for "catching" John—make him jealous. Bailey suspected it might work, possibly, but that kind of plotting was far too manipulative for him to actually attempt. For all his faults, Bailey was direct, and he didn't like the idea of tricking John into doing something he wasn't ready for. If he was even interested in Bailey that way at all, and so far there were no signs to indicate that he was.

Stupid depressing hopeless crushes. He was nearly forty, for Pete's sake; wasn't he supposed to be past this sort of ridiculous drama by now?

And finally, when he fired up his computer, there was a chat notification from Václav.

Genius: What?

ColumbaRacer: Good day to you too,
Bailey. Yes, I am doing well, so kind of
you to ask.

Genius: Blah blah blah. Stop wasting my time.

ColumbaRacer: I got your e-mail about the SMART Boards. Having looked into the resources available, I think we could send you one in exchange for a presentation on plasma windows some time in the autumn. Also, when you are asking for a favor, many people find it helpful to be polite to the person they are requesting it of. I tell you this as information only, knowing you will ignore it as you always do.

Genius: Politeness is just a waste of time.

ColumbaRacer: I'm sure your dinner dates are finding that attitude most refreshing.

Genius: Bite me. Also, yes, some of them actually do. I've had at least four good dates so far. Out of nine, before you ask. I even got flowers the morning after once, and some follow-up e-mails and phone calls.

ColumbaRacer: How sweet. Perhaps you will not die a lonely old maid after all. Are your results conforming to the predictions of your experiment?

Genius: I don't know. John and Lauren won't let me see what signs people are until after I've gone on all twelve blind dates.

ColumbaRacer: I cannot stop laughing at this entire "experiment." I would never have predicted you would abandon scientific rigor for psychology. You are not good with people.

Genius: Neither are you.

ColumbaRacer: Ah, but I am a Taurus—we are not meant to be very social.

Genius: There is absolutely NO CONNECTION between personality traits and the position of the stars at someone's birth!

ColumbaRacer: As the Americans say: duh. I am teasing you. But seriously, have you ever thought to ask yourself why you're writing an astrology column?

Genius: Many, many, many times.

ColumbaRacer: And?

Genius: I blame John.

> ColumbaRacer: Poor John.

> Genius: Poor *me*.

> ColumbaRacer: My heart bleeds for the
> injustice you must suffer. But now I
> must get back to work. Not all of us can
> write down whatever comes into our
> heads and pass it off as science.

> Genius: Yet so many of your so-called "peers"
> seem to do exactly that.

Záviška signed off with a few choice curses and insults, most of them in Czech, and Bailey began his workday.

LAUREN buzzed his phone in the evening. "Suitor Number Ten is on line three for you."

"Who?" Bailey blinked, trying to shift his focus from the horrible mess of Brad's article on temporal relativity.

"His name is Sean Ryder. I'm not meeting him; he faxed over his driver's license. Good luck on this one, McMillan," she said, laughing.

Without further ado, she transferred the call. "Hello, this is Bailey McMillan."

"I have tickets for Tuesday's performance of Verdi's *Requiem* at the symphony. Are you interested in going, or should I give them to someone else?" asked a gravelly, businesslike voice with no preamble.

A little taken aback at the man's abrupt manner, Bailey found himself agreeing to the concert.

There was a muffled "No, don't bother, we'll use them" as this Sean person apparently spoke to someone else, and then, "Good. I'll pick you up at six thirty. What's your address?"

"What? No, I can drive myself," Bailey sputtered. What was with this guy? Was he always this rude?

"This will be easier," Sean argued. "What's your address?"

Clenching his jaw, Bailey took a short breath, trying to bring his temper under control. This guy's attitude, not even pretending to listen, was aggravating. *He* was the one who usually talked over other people; it was very frustrating to have it done to him. But Bailey had agreed to the dates, and he wouldn't mind going to the concert, so he took another steadying breath and agreed, even though he knew it was going to be a bad evening before Sean even hung up.

After all, they would mostly be sitting in the concert hall and not talking. How bad could it be? He shuddered, wondering if he'd tempted fate merely by thinking that, and then mentally smacked himself for believing in fate for even a moment.

Taking a detour on his way back from refreshing his coffee mug, Bailey sprawled into one of the chairs across from John's desk. "What do you do when you know a date is going to be horrible?" he asked. Then added, "Never mind, I'm sure none of your dates have ever been bad."

John snorted. "I've had *lots* of bad dates. In fact, you could possibly infer from the fact that I'm single that I have had more bad dates than good ones."

"Hmm. Maybe. So anyway, about me now—what do you do when the other person seems like they're going to be an arrogant jerk?"

"Sounds like a perfect match for you." Bailey glared at John until he smirked an apology and continued. "I guess if I can't get out of it, I just try to make the best of it and not let the other person get under my skin. She's a bitch; I don't need to give her opinions about me or the evening any credit at all. Let it roll off my shoulders. Try to enjoy the food or the entertainment or whatever, and ignore her as much as I can," John said, getting a faraway look in his eyes, like he was remembering someone in particular.

Bailey thought for a moment, nodding. "Yeah, I guess that would work. He's taking me to the symphony. Hopefully we won't have to talk much."

John shrugged. "Not during the concert, anyway. I gather you spoke to this guy on the phone or e-mail or something?" Bailey nodded again, and John said, "Well, maybe he's just like that on the phone or in writing or whatever. First impressions aren't always accurate. Or maybe he was busy or something. Give him a chance."

"I'm going out with him, aren't I?" Bailey said in petulant tone. "All right, all right; yes, I will try to be more open-minded. Maybe he was busy or is bad on the phone, as you said. God knows I'm not great at talking to people either. Maybe he just issues orders as a matter of course...."

One of John's eyebrows rose. "He's ordering you around?"

"No, I didn't say that. He was really abrupt, though, and wouldn't even listen to me argue with the plans he'd already arranged. Do you know how annoying it is to be talked over like that?"

John grinned. "I have some idea, yeah."

"Oh, fuck off," Bailey said, but his return smile contradicted the words.

"Get out of my office. I was doing stuff," John said with a slight laugh.

"Solitaire?"

"Minesweeper." John made a shooing gesture.

"Fine, fine. I'm going. But you'd better be ready with food tomorrow; I have a feeling this one's going to be a disaster."

THE car sent to pick Bailey up was a shiny town car, but it had the feel of a limousine. It was also clear that it was owned by Bailey's date, not rented from a chauffeur service. On the plus side, Sean had manners enough to get out of the car and collect Bailey himself, rather than having the driver do it. They shook hands amiably, and although Sean's smile looked a little forced, Bailey had to admit that his probably was as well. Sean's grip was firm, just edging against aggressive, and his hands were calloused but well-groomed.

Bailey was rather sure his were soft and weak in comparison, but he spent all day working with computers and had a bad habit of picking at his nails when he was thinking hard. Also, there were ink stains that never came off; dry-erase markers were, in fact, not totally water-soluble.

"So, you enjoy classical music?" Bailey found himself asking idiotically.

"Yeah, I get season tickets every year. Sometimes the opera too, depending on their schedule," Sean replied. "You?"

"I don't go as often as I'd like; too busy. But I played concert piano for several years as a kid." He faltered when Sean simply nodded in reply, before asking, "Do you play anything?"

Sean shook his head. "Nope. Grew up in a family of construction workers; no time for such nonsense."

"Ah." Bailey was silent for a moment. "Oh! Are you from the Ryder Construction Group in all the billboard signs?"

Sean smiled. "Yup. I own it."

This would have been a perfect opportunity for Sean to ask Bailey what it was that *he* did, but no question came. "I'm a physicist," he finally said, making an attempt to not sound angry.

"You blow things up?" Sean asked, raising an eyebrow.

"No; that's chemistry. I mean, mostly. Okay, I guess sometimes I do blow things up, but almost always on purpose or to find something out, not just by accident. Or because some idiot didn't listen to me when I told them about the possible catastrophic results," he said defensively.

"So when you blow things up, it's on purpose?"

"Yes."

Sean hummed in a thoughtful way and then looked out the window for a while. Bailey gave up trying to make conversation and hoped the concert was worth all this awkwardness.

It mostly was, thank goodness. The orchestra and double choir blended seamlessly, the music soaring into the space of the hall and filling it with a reverberation that Bailey could feel in his bones. He might not be religious in any way or even believe in God or Spirit or the Great Pumpkin or whatever people wanted to call it, but this… this was something. He closed his eyes and let the music take him away to a different plane of reality, a place removed from the present, from the physical, from the limited.

On the plus side, his date seemed equally willing to sit in silence and let the music work its magic. They chatted briefly during the intermission, where Sean insisted on buying Bailey a glass of wine even though the bar had beer. The merlot did go with the pâté and crackers very well, though, Bailey supposed.

After the symphony, Sean ushered Bailey back to the car and they were on their way to a late dinner. When Bailey asked where they were going, Sean just shrugged and said, "A little place I like."

It was late and Bailey was tired of this bullshit. "No, honestly. I have severe food allergies. Where are we going? I may need to talk to the chef, and possibly bribe the waiters into taking me seriously."

Sean rolled his eyes. "Fine, I'll introduce you around when we get there. I'm sure there won't be any problems."

Bailey fumed. "If I go into anaphylactic shock because someone brings me a glass of water they fished slice of lemon out of rather than pour a fresh glass, you'll wish I'd slipped them a twenty."

A muscle jumped in Sean's jaw, where he was clenching it. "I'll make sure it's dealt with."

"Just tell me where we're going. I eat out a lot; places know me."

"I'm sure they do."

Bailey could hear that that was definitely meant as an insult, but he didn't care. He glared at Sean, wondering if he should demand to be taken home, but then remembered John's words. It was probably going to be a pretty nice, expensive restaurant. If they could be suitably cowed into demonstrating concern for Bailey's allergy, the food might very well be enjoyable, regardless of the company. And if it didn't look like that was going to happen or if it was a place he'd had bad experiences with, he'd call a cab and go home. Fuming, he decided to wait and see.

It turned out that he had, predictably, worked himself into a froth for nothing. The restaurant was a bistro that Bailey had been to several times before it had been closed for an almost year-long remodel. The hostess was new, but when Sean requested that she fetch the chef, the chef remembered Bailey.

She smiled in a rueful way. "You're the no-lemon-anywhere-near-my-food guy, right?"

Bailey smiled. "Yes, yes I am."

"I'll look over the menu and send out one of the servers with a list of what will work for you. If you don't like any of the options, let me know and I'll see what I can adjust."

Bailey thanked her and she shook her head, walking back into the kitchen with "Give me a little warning next time, and I can tailor a citrus-free main course" as her parting words.

"I'll try," he said, giving Sean a triumphantly smug look.

Dinner was eaten almost in silence. Bailey was annoyed, Sean was annoyed, and they didn't have much to talk about. They both tried, a little bit, but their stilted conversation about the performance could only take them so far. On the up side, Bailey's dinner was fantastic.

There was another brief argument when Sean reached for the check at the end of the meal. Bailey was getting pretty annoyed at being cast into the passive "female" role, although frankly he doubted most women would appreciate Sean's style of condescending generosity. He supposed the guy was quite wealthy, based on the fact that he owned one of the larger construction companies in California, but it wasn't like Bailey was a pauper. Not that Sean would know; he clearly didn't know anything about Bailey and didn't appear interested in him at all.

In fact, enjoying the symphony seemed to be the only thing they had in common. Sean insisted on driving Bailey back to his apartment, and they parted with cursory thank yous and disinterested waves on both their parts. It had been an evening of strange opposites: amazing music, great food, annoyance, and frustration.

Ah well. One more stupid blind date was over, making it ten down. Two more to go.

Chapter 14

Unexpected Gemini Triangles

WEDNESDAY morning John was in a meeting and Bailey had planned to meet Rich Crown, his date with the rooftop telescope and hand jobs and stargazer lilies floral pun, for lunch. They had a pleasant time; Rich was a nice guy. There was a lot of flirtation and some low-grade attraction, and Bailey had no clue why he wasn't interested in pursuing more. Rich could be someone to hang out with, talk with, have sex with—date, in other words. But Bailey had John for those first two things, and dating someone else would probably mean he would see less of John. Regular sex might be worth the trade-off, but… it might not.

In fact, Bailey left their lunch feeling incredibly frustrated. He wanted to talk to *John* about last night's date, not Rich. He wanted to know what John's reactions would be, see John's laughter, his smirks, his eye-rolls when he heard what an ass Sean had been. He wanted *John*.

And he couldn't have John. John was not an option, not interested in Bailey, didn't like to think about Bailey as a sexual person, seemed to get irked whenever Bailey mentioned sexual contact of any sort with his dates. He was a good friend, but it was clear he wasn't interested and was never going to be, and Bailey needed to get the hell over this stupid infatuation before he threw away every chance for happiness that came by. He hadn't intended this ludicrous experiment to result in real "dates," to truly meet people he was interested in. But he had met a few, and it would be foolish to pass them by in favor of something that was never going to happen. He was being an idiot, and there was nothing Bailey hated more than knowing he was being stupid.

John was wiped out after a day of nonstop meetings with potential advertisers, and he proposed that the two of them grab dinner from a taqueria they both liked that was near his house and then relax at his place to fill out Bailey's date evaluation form. John found a hockey game on ESPN, and they both settled in with their food and mindless entertainment for a while. Neither of them was watching the game, so John turned it off when they were finished eating and got out his laptop.

"All right, date number ten... I'm assuming that it didn't go very well?"

Bailey snorted. "No. I took your advice and tried to enjoy the parts that had nothing to do with Sean, but it was difficult."

They ran through the questions of shared interests, compatibility, attitude, and personality. There was a bit of a stumble on the physical attractiveness question, since Bailey couldn't make a judgment that didn't include Sean's gruff personality and ended up giving him a middle-of-the-scale mark, since he wasn't actually ugly or anything.

"Chemistry?" asked John.

"Ha ha," Bailey said, rolling his eyes. "Only in the sense of gasoline and a spark."

"Did you actually fight?"

"We argued. He was a jerk about the restaurant, although in the end it was okay, because the chef knew me from when I'd been there before. Still, he was unreasonable and controlling."

John's expression was sympathetic. "That sucks. Well, did you enjoy the symphony, at least?"

"Yes, very much. Verdi was always one of my favorites on the piano," Bailey said, smiling a little at the memory of the music the night before. His date with Sean might have sucked, but the concert made the experience well worth his time and resulting frustration.

"Huh. I knew you liked music, but I didn't know you played the piano."

Bailey shrugged. "I don't talk about it very often. I was good, though. I loved it."

"So what happened?"

"I won an award for my age group." Bailey fiddled with the wrappings from his burrito and chips, balling up the foil and bags. "And then my teacher said that I was a good technical player, but that I lacked passion and would never play professionally. So I quit wasting my time and focused on science and math instead."

"What? That sucks. How old were you?"

"Eight." Bailey shrugged again. "I loved it mainly for the math anyhow—the patterns and ratios in the music."

John shook his head. "That still sucks that you stopped playing if you enjoyed it. I'm sorry."

Giving him a somewhat puzzled look, Bailey said, "It was a long time ago."

"I guess. Anyway, I'm glad you had a good time at the symphony, even if you had to go with that jerk."

"Yeah, the company sucked. But it reminded me that I like going, so maybe I'll check out their concert series and see if they're doing anything else I'd like to hear this season."

"Definitely," John said, his face relaxing into a smile. "And let me know, will you? Classical music's not really my thing, but I don't mind giving it another chance. Especially from a math perspective."

"Yeah, okay," Bailey said, trying not to grin like an idiot. "It's a date."

BAILEY'S penultimate experimental date was scheduled for the Friday of Memorial Day weekend. His date stopped by to check in with Lauren and left directions to a gastropub in Twin Peaks Bailey hadn't yet been to. The place turned out to be divided in half with a sound-blocking wall, one side set up like a traditional British pub with a bar, dart boards, and a crowd of men gathered around a flat-screen TV showing a soccer game. Or football, he supposed, since it was clearly an international game.

The other half was a restaurant, and it looked like a pretty good one, standard pub fare with slight—or not so slight—"contemporary cuisine" twists. He was perusing his menu when a man sprawled into the seat across from him. Bailey looked up, blinked, and blinked again.

The man grinned. "Bailey, yeah?"

He was gorgeous. Not handsome in a conventional sense, although he had very nice eyes and a sinfully lush mouth; he also had a scar bisecting one eyebrow, and his upper front teeth were horribly crooked. Obviously not American, although his accent had already identified him as a Brit with just two words. But his grin was huge and genuine; he looked *happy*, like a person so full of joy that it was bursting out of him. The scars and the gang-style tattoos peeking out from under the neck of his T-shirt spoke of a shady past, and the bulk of his arm muscles was frankly a bit intimidating. He was gorgeous, and intriguing, and wearing the single ugliest tweed jacket Bailey had ever seen.

"Ah, yes. Bailey McMillan," he finally remembered to say, blinking again and feeling flustered. No one had ever looked this happy to see Bailey, except maybe John one time at the airport after a long flight. Was this guy on drugs?

"Excellent. Thought perhaps I'd got the wrong table or your assistant—sorry, *Spark's* assistant, she corrected me about that—had shown me the wrong picture or forgot to tell you about tonight or something. But I thought it was you. You look like a mad physicist."

"I... what?" Bailey had no idea how to respond to the sudden burst of explanations.

The man smiled again. "Not like Einstein, although maybe if you grew your hair out, I suppose. No, just meant you look like there are a lot of big thoughts in there. Oh, oops, where are my manners? Evans," he concluded, holding out his hand.

Bailey blinked for another moment, feeling rather like an overwhelmed goldfish, and then put down his menu and shook the other man's hand. "Evans?"

"Jamie Evans. It's horribly British, I know. I just go by Evans."

"Because that's less British?"

Evans shrugged, getting a smug look in his eyes. "It's not a girl's name, at least, Dana."

"I hate Lauren," Bailey said with a scowl.

Laughing, Evans shook his head. "Not her fault; I looked you up online once she told me your name. I like to know what to expect from an evening."

"Oh? And what do you expect?" Bailey asked, wondering if the comment and his reply sounded flirty or if it was just him.

Evans winked. "Intelligence, quick wit, an acerbic tongue—despite the citrus allergy—and no sufferance of fools. You like to eat, but you also work out. You're mostly on the dates for the experiment mentioned in the advert, not for the usual reasons, and despite your work on some somewhat shady and highly classified projects, my past makes you a little nervous." Evans grinned. "You keep glancing at the ink. Unless you're typically on edge, which I suppose you might be. Geeks often are. Means I'll have to work a little harder to charm you," he said with another wink.

"I… who are you? I mean, what do you do?" Bailey asked, baffled by all this.

"Don't worry, I'm not a con artist or anything like. I used to do profiling for the CIA, though, and I like reading people. It's always fun to tell them what you've seen, in the research and from their body language, and watch their reactions to it. You weren't surprised except by the bit about your attitude about the dates. And that I'm interested in charming you."

Bailey took a sip of his water. "Well, yes. You're, you know," he said, flapping his other hand about a little manically. "*You know*. Not like you probably have to try very hard, looking like that."

"Ah, you say the sweetest things," Evans teased. "Shall we order? They do a brilliant shepherd's pie with actual gravy, not that hideous brown sauce my mum used to pour on everything. The mushy peas are sadly all wrong: they actually taste good."

Laughing, Bailey began to relax and enjoy his evening. They ordered food, trading tastes, and had far more beer than Bailey was used to, since Evans insisted they do a tasting of all the British beers on tap so Bailey could decide for himself which ones he liked best. Evans was by turns insightful and silly, a perceptive judge of character who was clearly used to presenting himself as whatever someone wanted him to be. He looked like a thug but was astoundingly intelligent for someone who said he didn't have a college degree; Bailey suspected Evans had been to university and had possibly been recruited by the CIA or some other government organization before he could finish.

The only really obvious downside was that he was too young for Bailey, probably around five to ten years in the wrong direction. Admittedly he seemed to have had more "life experience" than Bailey, but still. If he was looking for a partner, like he was trying to remind himself he ought to be, Evans was too young.

"How old are you?" Bailey asked out of the blue.

Evans smirked. "I wondered when you'd finally give in and ask. Thirty-four. I'm guessing you think that's… five or six years too young? You like older men, don't you?"

"Ah, well, historically, yes. Not much more than my age, though, now. You're older than I thought you were."

"Sunscreen." Evans winked. "Plus, think of all the advantages of youth," he added, grinning lasciviously.

Bailey felt his face flush and his cock stir in his pants, ever hopeful. "Yes. There is that."

EVANS tricked Bailey into letting him pay. When their bill came, Bailey reached for it, and suddenly Evans was leaning across the table, his full, ale-moist lips pressing against Bailey's. Flustered, Bailey had taken a moment to respond, and even longer before he remembered that they were making out in public. By the time Evans let Bailey catch his breath and regain his senses, he had both the bill and his own credit card held out for a passing server to take away.

"Come back to mine," Evans said, licking his lips in a way that made Bailey wonder if his date was a former rent boy. "I promise I won't bite."

"Good, I bruise easily," Bailey found himself saying, his internal self-censors totally fried. There was a small voice deep inside that was telling him he was making a mistake, but he firmly ignored it.

Evans's apartment was a short walk away, small, messy, and Bailey didn't see much of it until the next morning. Evans made fabulous coffee, didn't have morning breath, and gave the best blowjobs Bailey could ever remember having, ever, not even in his very active and highly detailed imagination of what a perfect blowjob would be like. The first one, before Evans had fucked Bailey, had been amazing, and the wake-up one this morning was impossibly even better.

"How are you so good at that?" Bailey asked, and then cringed, hoping he hadn't just implied his new friend was a slut.

"Natural talent, I guess," Evans said, licking his reddened mouth. "Got soft, girly lips, and men like to see them wrapped around their cocks. I don't mind, and sucking them off usually means I get to top afterward. Win-win, I say."

"Definitely feels like a win to me," Bailey agreed. He hesitated with his empty coffee mug, wondering if he should ask to shower before heading home.

"What are you doing this weekend?" Evans asked, refilling Bailey's cup.

Bailey shrugged. "Nothing exciting. No big plans, the date with you Friday was pretty much it. Probably do some research, I suppose. You?"

"Have a weekend fling with me. That would be exciting, yeah?" Evans wiggled his eyebrows.

"I… uh… hmm. Well, maybe." Bailey thought for a moment. He'd never done anything like that before, but no one had ever asked, either. Why not? "Castrovalva will need food at some point. And I need my laptop. We can't fuck all the time, my ass is already sore."

Evans laughed, deep and loud. "Promise I'll let you top next time, sorry. You loved it, though, don't try to pretend otherwise." Bailey couldn't argue with that and shrugged. "All right, one stop back at your place for the feline beastie and your laptop, although I'm not going to let you use it much. This is a wild and sexy getaway, like I bet you've never let yourself have. I want to do it right."

"I... all right." Bailey smiled, tentative but also excited. Other people did this sort of thing all the time, didn't they? Evans was hot, intelligent, great in bed, and if he turned out to be boring or whatever, Bailey would just go home. He wasn't sure what they'd do while they weren't having sex, but the sex was great—really amazingly great—and who knew when he'd get another offer like this one? He'd be a fool to turn it down, and while Bailey may have been a fool about romance lately, he wasn't going to be any longer. Something good was standing right in front of him, asking him if he wanted it. "Carpe diem," he said aloud.

"That's the spirit," Evans agreed. "Now, how about a shower? It's big enough for two—barely."

CASTROVALVA ignored both Bailey and Evans, taking one look at them and stalking off to hide in Bailey's closet. Evans seemed more amused by the cat's hostility than anything else, so Bailey didn't feel the need to apologize for his pet's aloofness. The damn cat only liked John anyway; he seemed to mostly tolerate Bailey's presence in grudging exchange for food.

Back at Evans's apartment, they ordered a pizza and watched a hockey game and played chess. Evans was extremely good, proving himself a creative but logical thinker, bold in his moves but not careless. He wasn't anywhere near as good as Bailey, of course, but it was still a challenge and a satisfaction to declare checkmate after almost an hour.

"Guess you'll be wanting to collect your prize, then?" Evans asked, doing something suggestive with his tongue.

"My prize? We didn't bet anything."

Evans smirked and stood up, pulling off his T-shirt in slow motion. Bailey's mouth went dry, and he swallowed as Evans toed off his shoes and then bent at the waist to remove his socks, his firm, round ass on display.

"I think you should fuck me," Evans said, standing up again.

"I... I could do that. Yes." Overwhelmed—again—by how much he wanted to get his hands on Evans's gorgeous body, Bailey was stuttering like a schoolboy. A horny, excited schoolboy whose own ass was a little raw from the last time Evans had fucked *him*. It had been quite a while, after all. "Bedroom?" he suggested.

"For starters," Evans agreed, and led the way, removing the last of his clothes as he went so that he was sprawled naked on the bed in all his glory by the time Bailey got there.

Sixty minutes was not very long in many respects, and some people claimed to make love for hours and hours, but by the time an hour had passed Bailey felt like he'd been ten rounds in a boxing ring and was thoroughly worn out in the very best way possible. He'd started out doing most of the work, but Evans had ended up on top, riding him, making it last and last and last until Bailey's orgasm almost *hurt*, it felt so good.

"Did you take classes in this or something?" he asked once he had enough breath to form words.

Laughing, Evans responded, "What, like 'Sex and Seduction for Spies' when I was with the CIA or something? Or private tutorials on the Kama Sutra in India? Spent some time in professional brothels? Hardly. Although I did read *The Sex Secrets of Escorts*," he admitted.

"Must just be you, then," Bailey said, one hand trailing over the contours of Evans's shoulder and bicep.

"It helps when I have a good partner to work with," Evans agreed, leaning over to give Bailey a quick kiss. "You know what you're doing, and you're quite enthusiastic."

"'Grateful' would be more accurate."

"How about a shower, and then you can show me some more of that gratitude?" Evans suggested, wiggling his eyebrows.

Bailey groaned. "Death by sex. Oh well, at least it's how I always wanted to go."

After another round in the shower, Bailey declared that his dick was chafed and he needed some downtime, not to mention to refuel with some food and coffee and to check his e-mail. Evans left him alone while he went out for sustenance, the easy swagger in his walk of the freshly fucked almost distracting Bailey from his laptop. Almost.

Good thing it hadn't, since there was a reminder on his calendar that Bailey had arranged to meet with Oliver at the SFMOMA on Sunday afternoon.

"Fuck."

"Already? I thought you wanted to eat first," Evans said, coming back inside and tossing his keys onto the table.

"I do. I mean, I want to eat. Fucking is off the agenda for a little while longer. You have an astounding refractory period for a man in his midthirties. And stop smirking; I'm not sure that's a compliment, just an observation that you're a biological freak."

"My cock is a wondrous thing," Evans agreed.

"Oh for...." Bailey took a deep breath and tried to reassemble his train of thought. "I'd totally forgotten than I'd made some plans to go to the Dada exhibit with a friend on Sunday at two."

Evans opened a beer and made himself busy unpacking the bags of takeout he'd brought home. "So do you want to go or reschedule or what?"

"I... I don't know. It's a new friend. He was actually my second date in this godforsaken experiment. We sort of hit it off, but there was no chemistry at all between us," he clarified. "But I don't have that many friends outside my field, so I thought it was worth making the effort when he asked if I wanted to go to this."

"Well, it's not exactly against the 'fling' policy to go out and do nonsexual things. I could go with you, unless you'd rather I didn't," Evans offered.

Bailey took a moment to think about that. "Sure. I mean, there's no reason why not. Do you like abstract art?"

Evans's smile was triumphant. "I do, yes. Collage and mixed-media especially. I saw the Cubist exhibit last month, did you?"

Bailey nodded. "I did. Oliver and I went to it after our dinner, in fact, which is when we planned to see this one. Well then, this will be... fun?"

Evans touched his beer bottle to Bailey's. "Indeed it shall."

SUNDAY morning brought more incredibly good sex, and Evans's response to Bailey's moaning about how he wasn't in shape for this sort of repeated strenuous activity yielded one of the best nonprofessional massages Bailey had ever received. The man had a wide range of talents, that was for sure. They had lunch out and met up with Oliver at the museum, and Bailey collapsed into his bed that night too exhausted to do much more than throw some kitty crunchies in Castrovalva's bowl, and brush his teeth.

He woke up the next morning to a steady throbbing in his head. After several bleary, painful moments, he realized the throbbing was not actually inside his head; someone was knocking on his door. Relentlessly. Whimpering, he dragged himself to see who it was, wrapping his bathrobe around him and failing to figure out how the belt worked before he got to the door.

"What?" he demanded, wrenching it open. "Why are you punishing me like this?"

John was leaning against the wall, fist still raised to knock again. "Oh good, you're not dead," he said, scowling as he shouldered his way inside. "You ignored my texts, voice mails, and sent back a one-line e-mail that you were busy, so naturally I assumed you were kidnapped or dead, and some imposter was replying on your behalf to buy more time to dispose of your body."

"I... what? You're pissed off," Bailey said, and John snorted. "Can this wait until after coffee? Please? Pretty please?"

"You shower. I will make coffee. Then you will talk, at great length, until I am satisfied that you're not an imposter, weren't kidnapped by aliens, and didn't just fall off the grid like that for two days *on purpose*."

John looked like he was going to lose it in a few moments, and deciding that it was better to run away and live to fight another day, Bailey fled to the safety of his bathroom.

A short while later, freshly scrubbed and dressed, he returned to the kitchen. The coffee maker was just finishing the last few pops and hisses that signaled the end of its cycle, and Castrovalva was purring happily on John's lap while his favorite human rubbed all his happy spots. Bailey was jealous.

John's eyes followed Bailey as he moved around the kitchen, pouring himself an enormous bowl-sized mug, fiddling with fixing a regular cup for John—black, one sugar—and finally turning around to meet his friend's glare.

"What?"

"Where. Were. You," John demanded.

"Out." John's eyes narrowed, and Bailey flushed. Feeling ridiculously guilty, like a teenager caught sneaking inside the morning after an all-night party, he went on the offensive. "I was out! I was busy. Am I supposed to check in with you every four hours or something?"

John rolled his eyes. "No, but you had a date with a strange man, and then usually we get together to discuss it the next day, but instead you *disappeared*. You sent a very much unlike you five-word reply that you were busy, ignored my texts and phone calls, and I—" He bit off the rest of his sentence and took a deep breath. "Where were you?"

"I'm fine," Bailey answered, noticing for the first time that John was angry, yes, but he was also... worried? Tense, that was for sure, and he seemed less pissed off than relieved. Which was probably Castrovalva's doing. Bailey made a mental note to give the cat some extra treats for that trick.

John raised an eyebrow.

Bailey sighed. "I kind of… had a fling."

"What?" The incredulous tone in John's voice was not even a little bit flattering.

"A fling!"

John shook his head. "You don't have flings."

Bailey crossed his arms over his chest. "I can have a fling! I did. All weekend. I flung!"

A muscle jumped in John's jaw a few times as he gave the cat a very thorough scratch along the chin, and then he reached for his mug and drained it before looking at Bailey. "So are you dating this guy?" Bailey shook his head no. "Like a one-night stand, then?"

"Sort of," Bailey said, shrugging and feeling guilty again, which didn't make sense, since he should probably still be offended. "Like a one-weekend stand. A fling."

John blinked a few times, staring at his coffee cup like it was confusing him. "I can't believe you… flung."

"What? Why not? The sex was good, Evans was incredibly hot, and we had a good time." Honestly, Bailey was starting to get annoyed. It was one thing for John not to want to think about the details of his sex life, but come on!

"So why aren't you dating him?"

"Because it was finite from the beginning. Just for the weekend. Defined parameters." John looked baffled, which frankly baffled Bailey. It wasn't as if *John* could never have had a fling. "Besides, I think he's interested in someone else now," Bailey added, deflating somewhat.

"What? Your fling dumped you?"

"No! Geez, listen to what I say, would you?" Bailey took a deep breath, then grabbed both empty mugs and refilled them, adding plenty of sugar and cream to his this time. "It was just for the weekend, from the beginning. And then Sunday afternoon I met Oliver, from that second date, remember him? Anyway, we had planned to see the Dada exhibit at SFMOMA together, just as friends, and Evans decided to come along. And the two of them hit it off pretty spectacularly."

"So they both ditched you for each other?"

"Well… not really. Sort of. All right, technically yes."

John's raised eyebrows were simultaneously skeptical and urging Bailey to continue. He shrugged, poured himself a bowl of cereal, and then headed to the sofa, waiting for John to catch up once he had removed Castrovalva's claws from his thigh.

In short order, Bailey skimmed over the date on Friday, shrugging as he explained that Evans's proposal to have a sexy weekend fling had sounded like fun and he hadn't had any reason to refuse. Plus, he'd wanted to see what it was like, having never had a fling before, and he was nearly forty; if not now, when else would he have the chance? Leaving out the sexual marathon of Saturday made his redacted description rather obvious, which he tried to cover with strategically large bites of his breakfast.

"So then we got to SFMOMA and met up with Oliver."

"Wasn't that weird and awkward? You there with your sex-toy boy meeting Mr. Uptight and Proper?"

Bailey rolled his eyes. "Evans wasn't my sex toy. And anyway, he and Oliver seemed to hate each other at first. Well, Oliver seemed to hate him. Evans took that as a personal challenge and laid on the charm so thick I had a hard time not laughing."

"You didn't feel offended than your date was flirting with someone else?" John asked.

"How many times do I have to tell you, it was just a fling? I liked Evans. He was a lot of fun, but it wasn't as if we were going to have a relationship or anything. He's too…." He waved his hands around, futilely searching for the right words for Evans. "Effervescent? He's like the bubbles in champagne: highly enjoyable, but you wouldn't waste your time trying to make them last."

"Is that from a song?" John asked. "You did *not* just come up with that by yourself."

Bailey hummed, thinking. "Yes, probably. Regardless, he was fun, it was nice to see what a fling was like, and no, I don't feel tragically abandoned that he and Oliver will probably hook up. They're a better match anyway: closer to the same age, similar job experiences, and they fought like an old married couple from the beginning."

"Viciously?"

"No, idiot. Teasing." Bailey shrugged. "Like how I fight with you."

His words hung there, pregnant with unintended meaning. After a moment, Bailey cleared his throat, grabbed his bowl and mug, and fled to the kitchen, calling over his shoulder to ask if John wanted anything to eat or if they should go out to Dottie's for pancakes. If John's reply sounded a bit strangled, it was most likely due to something Castrovalva was doing with his claws.

Chapter 15

Cancer Inconjunct

BAILEY'S last date for the experiment was on a Thursday. It was hard to believe both that it was June already and that the stupid experiment had only taken a month and a half. Twelve dates in seven weeks was an unprecedented occurrence in Bailey's life, and he still wasn't sure what to make of it all.

He met Michael Winchester for a late dinner after a vigorous session at the gym that had left him aching everywhere. Jason teased him mercilessly about his strained hip and groin muscles, an unfortunate result of Bailey's epic weekend with Evans. As his friend pointed out, he was getting old, and he felt every second of those thirty-nine years as he slid onto a barstool to order a beer while he waited for his date.

After downing about a third of his glass, he looked around and met the eyes of the man sitting a few stools down from him. The stranger wasn't staring, exactly, but watching Bailey with a slightly puzzled expression on his face.

"Yes? What?" Bailey asked, too tired to be as sharp as he usually would have been.

"Nothing, just my dates usually sit *next* to me, not a couple seats away. Makes getting to know each other a little easier," the man answered.

It took an effort for Bailey not to give in to the urge to bang his forehead against the bar. "So much for making a good impression. You're Michael?"

"Mike, yes. Long day, Bailey?" the man asked, smiling. He had dimples, which was a little unexpected in a man in his midforties with a slightly graying short beard and a tanned face that testified to frequent outdoor activity.

"Long month and a half, actually. Twelve dates, a lawsuit over a libel claim, my aggravatingly inept peers, the general incompetence of the world, and that doesn't even cover my actual job, such as it is." Bailey had another drink and then realized he was being rude. "How are you?"

Mike shrugged. "Tired too. Not that I didn't want to meet you for dinner, but it's been a goddamned long day. I'd apologize for not having much energy, but I gather you're not your usual vivacious self either. Let's just have a mellow dinner together and see how it goes."

They decided to eat at the bar, since they were already comfortable there—once Mike moved over so they were seated next to each other. Their conversation was easy and superficial—not shallow enough to annoy Bailey, but not about anything terribly interesting either. It was clear they were both drained and didn't really have the energy for a date and probably should have rescheduled. But Mike was easy enough to hang out with, companionable and mellow, although Bailey suspected he probably had an intense side. Despite his current job as an electrical engineer, Mike was indeed quite the outdoorsman, kayaking and deep-sea fishing, and he played basketball on a regular basis. Mike struck Bailey as a pretty average guy, not someone he'd have much in common with.

"So why did you respond to my personals ad?" he asked after they were almost done eating.

"I used to work at Lawrence Livermore labs," Mike said, shrugging. "Thought it might be nice to reconnect with the science community."

"Ah. Well…." Bailey trailed off, trying to find something positive to say about his colleagues at the lab and, failing that, something neutral. "They have some interesting ideas there."

The corners of Mike's eyes crinkled with amusement, as if he knew what "interesting" meant in Bailey-speak. "Maybe you should write them up in your magazine, let them know what they're doing wrong in your opinion," he said.

"Hmm… not a bad idea, since they keep ignoring my advice in private. Maybe I can embarrass them into actually using their brains if I publish it in *Spark*."

They clinked their beer glasses in honor of the idea and made polite conversation until the meal was finished. Mike looked at his watch, and Bailey knew there wouldn't be any dessert or further activity for the night. Which was all for the best, since his lower back was aching and all he wanted to do was take an incredibly hot bath and send a vitriolic text message to Jason for leaving him incapacitated like this. And possibly a thank-you note to Evans for precisely the same reason….

It wasn't that Mike was unattractive or difficult to get along with. Probably if either one of them had had more energy, it could have been a good date. Bailey had a halfhearted urge to suggest they schedule a repeat so the experimental data would be more accurate, but he honestly didn't care enough. It was all a joke anyway; why waste more of his time?

He and Mike shook hands, both a bit rueful about how the date had gone but not willing to prolong it either. By ten p.m. Bailey was at home, basking in a steaming-hot tub and letting a wave of surprising relief that the whole dating experiment was finished wash over him along with the scented bubbles.

FRIDAY was slow enough that Bailey was able to talk John into a lunch break to go over the final date evaluation form. Yes, Mike was attractive; yes, they were fairly compatible; no, there wasn't a spark at all. Bailey conceded that there might have been a spark if either of them had had enough energy to generate one, but they hadn't and it hadn't happened… c'est la vie. He was a little surprised that John didn't insist on a do-over to get better data, but Bailey wasn't going to bring it up if John didn't.

"So what are the results?" he asked, leaning into John's space so he could see the computer screen. "Did the dates go as the stars predicted, or was it all a bunch of hocus-pocus like I've been saying?"

John made a face at him. "How would I know? I only have the info about your dates. Lauren's the only one with the stuff about when each of the guys was born."

Bailey blinked at him. "Well? Get it! I want to know how this panned out so we can put this whole ridiculous waste of time behind us and you can buy me the dinner you owe me for winning the bet. We said steak, right? I'm thinking the Steak Lounge? Then I can get those truffle-oil fries...."

"You're drooling," John pointed out. "And also, you haven't won yet. I'll get the data from Lauren and we'll go over it together so there aren't any accusations of cheating from either side."

At four o'clock, when Bailey couldn't wait any longer, he marched over to Lauren's desk and demanded the birthdates of his men. She raised an eyebrow at him. "You promised me a spa package for this."

"What? Yes, all right, fine. Give me the data."

"Give me the package."

They had a short battle of wills staring contest, and as usual, she brought out her totally unfair Level 5 glare and won.

"All right, already. How do you want to do this?"

Lauren swiveled her monitor around, the web page for a local day spa already pulled up, set on the "Buy Now" link. She'd selected one of the most expensive packages, which was both completely unfair and exactly what Bailey had expected. He dug his credit card out of his wallet, mumbling about extortion and blackmail and the unfairness of women, particularly ones who used to be in the Marine Corps and seemed to live to make his life difficult.

"Blah blah blah, McMillan. Type those numbers in faster. I damn well earned every moment of that massage, facial, and mani/pedi."

He clicked on the link to complete the transaction, and she swiveled the monitor back around, checking that he'd done it right. She nodded in approval and then took two sheets of paper out of a folder on her desk. She pressed the intercom button. "John, do you have a minute?"

John came out of his office and joined them at her desk, looking intrigued.

Lauren handed a paper to each of them. "Just ensuring that you both get the data at the same time so neither of you can whine about it later. Names and dates of birth for all twelve gentlemen are on there. Oh, and I took down the Craigslist ad, Bailey. I think I've seen enough pictures of dicks to last me a few years," she said with a shudder.

Both John and Bailey looked over their papers for a moment.

"The dates were all in calendar order," Bailey said, puzzled. "Why on earth would you do that?"

Lauren gave him a toothy grin of evilness. "I'm a Virgo. I like order."

"Argh! No! Stop it! Those two facts are unrelated!" Bailey felt his face flushing with frustration. His hands waved around in agitation as he tried to restrain himself from mock-throttling her but thought better of it, which made John laugh so hard he almost had to sit down.

Once the outrage (Bailey's), maniacal laugher (John's), and evil grinning (Lauren's) had stopped, Lauren pulled out another set of papers and again handed one to each of the red-faced men in front of her. "I took the liberty of consulting six different websites and books on synastry, which is the official name for comparisons of compatibility based on natal astrological charts. This is a very abbreviated rundown on their predictions for someone of Bailey's sign—Aquarius—with each of his twelve dates."

"Wow," John said. "Thanks. You didn't have to do this."

Lauren rolled her eyes. "Please. If either one of you had done it, the other would claim there was cheating. Besides," she added, eyes twinkling with mischief, "I've got a hundred dollars riding on the outcome of this. I made a bet with Dr. Záviška."

"Why am I not surprised?" Bailey muttered, and went to get another cup of coffee, since he was standing so near its beckoning aroma.

"Dinner tonight?" John asked him.

Bailey paused a moment to think. "Yes. I'm actually free. No date tonight, or this weekend at all. No more dates. Huh."

It was too new of a realization for him to feel anything other than somewhat surprised and relieved, but there was a small inkling somewhere inside his brain that although he would relish his solitude, it would take a little getting used to again. Not that he would be lonely, just… less busy. Which was good, because frankly he'd been slacking a bit on important scientific contributions. Václav had e-mailed him saying that he'd made some progress on the fissionable ore project, and Bailey needed to tear it apart and show Václav all the ways that he was so very, very wrong.

That would take care of Saturday.

JOHN slouched his way over to Bailey's desk promptly at five o'clock. "My stomach's growling. Let's go."

Bailey slowly turned his gaze from his monitor to look at John. He blinked a few times. "You would not believe the mind-boggling idiocy of those nitwits at Lawrence Livermore. My last date suggested I write them up, and oh my God, John, I think they've set a new bar for Dangerous Levels of Stupidity when Dealing with Nuclear Reactors. It's like they read the best-practices manual and then thought they'd just *set it on fire*! With nuclear waste!"

John laughed. "So keep Robert and Xiao on retainer, is what you're saying? Noted. Now, unplug, stop working, and let's go get some food. You've got that twitchy look that always makes me worry that you're either going to go on a murder spree or into hypoglycemic shock."

Muttering about the possible cereal-box originations of the lab's so-called "physicists," Bailey shut down his workstation and got ready to go. "Your place? Mine? An actual restaurant?"

"I think your place. I miss the cat," John mused. "I'd get my own, but I think Castrovalva would be jealous. And if we go to a restaurant, it will feel like a date."

"Well, we wouldn't want that," Bailey said with a huff, and left it to John to decide whether he was referring to his cat's jealousy or the prospect of them dating. John and Bailey, that was, not John and Castrovalva. Wow, he really did need to eat something; his low blood sugar was making him giddy.

They grabbed takeout on the way back to Bailey's, John having lost the battle to order a pizza. Bailey's cat came running up the moment he heard John's voice and started to rub himself all over his chosen human, purring like a badly tuned engine. The humans ate and talked while the cat begged and slutted around John, and Bailey once again offered to just give the beast to John, since they were obviously a match made in heaven. John said he liked the arrangement as it stood; it was like he kept his cat at Bailey's house, and Bailey got to deal with all the crappy parts of pet ownership while John got all the fun.

"I can't tell if you're lazy or diabolical," Bailey mused.

Nodding, John grinned. "Yup. It'll forever be a mystery to you."

Finally, they had finished the food, exhausted the work-related and cat-related and imbecilic-physicists-related conversation, and could no longer avoid the metaphorical elephant in the room. John got out his laptop with an air of reluctance, and Bailey fetched his copy of Lauren's printouts from his backpack. John propped the paper next to the screen, and they sat side by side, staring.

"Huh."

Bailey made a disgusted huffing noise. "It doesn't mean anything. This wasn't a proper 'experiment'. It totally lacked any semblance of scientific rigor."

John raised an eyebrow. "We made it as rigorous as possible for an experiment involving your love life. *You* set up the standards and parameters."

Opening and closing his mouth a few times didn't get Bailey any closer to a decent refutation of these facts. "But... this can't be right," he finally settled on saying. "Something must have gone wrong."

"Or you just could admit that you lost."

"But… no. I mean, sure, it looks like most of my dates went according to the predictions, but… there must be something in here that will prove that it's all just random. I need more time to look at the data."

John smirked. "Take as long as you like, Bailey. You're still buying me the biggest steak I can find in the Bay Area."

"Hah! We didn't do a control group for random chance," Bailey said, snapping his fingers in triumph. "A lot of those dates probably went well simply because there was enough information provided in the personals ad that weeded out anyone with whom I had absolutely nothing in common. True, a lot of the dates didn't have much or enough in common for it to go well, but still, we need some random guy-off-the-street dates to prove it wasn't the advertisement itself that influenced the positive outcomes."

"You date random guys off the street?" John asked, looking skeptical. "Like, just 'Hey, we should go out' to any random passersby who don't look homeless?"

Bailey huffed. "No, but… like guys at a bar or something. People you don't know anything about."

"Date many of them, do you?"

"Well, no. Not really. I suppose the majority of my 'dates' in the past have come from conferences or coworkers or fellow students, when I was in school. But you know normal people do that, right?"

"You're not normal, and this experiment was never about 'normal' people—it was about you," John pointed out. Bailey made a face, and John rolled his eyes and then shrugged. "Fine then. Go out with two more 'random' guys, and we'll get their birth dates at the end and add the data to this to see how it compares." He seemed defensive for some reason. He couldn't want to win the dinner that badly, could he?

Bailey himself didn't want to win so that John would pick up the bill for dinner in particular. It wasn't the money at all but the principle of the thing—astrology was absolute nonsense. Plus, he hated letting John win anything without a fight. Not in a mean-spirited way, but they had a vigorous and potentially unhealthy sense of competitiveness with each other; this was why they no longer played chess together. Bailey was the first to admit that he was a poor loser; being a genius and smarter than anyone else he'd ever met had not equipped him to deal with defeat with any semblance of grace. Which possibly explained an awful lot about his past dealings with family, friends, coworkers, and lovers, come to think of it....

"So, two more dates then?"

John shrugged. "Whatever. TV?"

They settled onto the sofa, John with the remote in hand and cat on lap while Bailey fidgeted with the cushions until they supported his back and neck adequately. Toeing off his shoes and tucking his feet up as well, he mused aloud about getting a more ergonomic sofa one day, if such a thing existed.

"They do. They sort of look like those creepy sex-furniture things, though. You know," John clarified to Bailey's raised brows, "the ones that are all strange curves and look like they were designed for a really athletic orgy?"

"I can't say that I've run into such things, no." This was both true and had the surprising result of causing John's face to flush. "Did you have an adventurous ex, or do you belong to kinky sex clubs, or what?"

John rolled his eyes. "As if I'd tell you. Nah, just seen them advertised on websites and stuff. And before you ask, *yes*, sex toy store websites."

"Huh." Bailey pondered the sort of toys John would have been shopping for. Cuffs? Restraints? A vibrator for a girlfriend? A vibrator for himself? Butt plugs? He shifted on the sofa, trying to subtly arrange his legs so his crotch was less visible; thinking about John and sex toys had had a predictable effect.

This shifting brought his feet into contact with John's thigh. Castrovalva sniffed his socks for a moment, found them uninteresting, and went back to sleep. John made a fond face at them both and patted Bailey's feet.

"If your cat would move, you might get a foot massage."

Bailey kicked the cat—lightly—until it huffily relocated to the back of the sofa by John's shoulder. He got a furious feline glare—Castrovalva was obviously threatening to take years off his life—and he had no doubt his cat would get its revenge later. But now he was getting a foot rub, and he wiggled his toes happily in John's lap, taking care not to get too close to any personal areas. He sighed in contentment as warm, strong hands began to knead at his instep and heel, and let out an orgasmic groan when John dug his thumb into the spot at the ball of his big toe.

The rubbing stopped. Bailey opened eyes he didn't remember closing and felt his face heating with embarrassment. "It, uh, feels good?"

John snorted. "I gathered that, yes."

"Sorry?"

"Nah, don't worry about it. Just surprised me. Wouldn't have pegged you as someone really loud in bed, but I guess I should have, the way you make those little happy noises when you eat."

Bailey thought about making a face or sticking his tongue out, but John had started rubbing again. "Strong hands," he mumbled blissfully.

John laughed. "You look like you're going to fall asleep. You and your cat... both of you just want to be petted, don't you?" he asked, one hand leaving Bailey's foot and presumably finding the cat.

Bailey made a sleepy—and probably ineffective—version of a snort. "We're more discerning than that. It's not like we're easy. We just want *you* to touch us."

John's hand paused a moment, then squeezed Bailey's foot. He was quiet for several moments, and Bailey started to drift off again, making soft little happy noises.

"I should get going," John said, sounding tired, "or I'm going to pass out too, the way you both keep purring."

Bailey huffed, shifting around to get into a more comfortable position on the sofa, one that totally coincidentally trapped John under the weight of Bailey's legs. "Too bad this isn't the bed." He yawned. "More room."

There was a soft hum of agreement, followed by silence broken only by Castrovalva's constant rumbling purr. Bailey reached up, eyes still closed, and dragged down the blanket he kept on the back of the sofa, sluggishly using one foot to kick it over John as well. He wiggled deeper into the warm cocoon, John's hands still on his feet.

Chapter 16

Degrading Orbits

SOMETIME in the quiet hours of the morning, Bailey woke up with a cramp in his arm and nudged John awake. John mumbled a protest, but Bailey's grip on his shoulder was firm as he steered John to bed. They'd both already lost their shoes earlier in the evening, and with a sleepy lack of self-consciousness, they stripped down to boxers and T-shirts and slid into bed. John was a polite sleeper, staying on his side of the bed, unmoving and silent. Bailey was neither.

He woke up to the smell of coffee, a cat who seemed to have gorged on one of the expensive cans of food based on the residual evidence in his bowl, and a note from John saying that Bailey snored and to have a good weekend. Bailey was well into his third mug of coffee before he quietly realized that he'd slept with John. Really slept, in his bed, in his house. He *never* did that—one, because he usually hooked up at his partner's house, and two, because after one night they usually concluded that among Bailey's many faults, being a snoring, squirming bed hog made the top ten. To be honest, he didn't sleep well with others—just as he didn't play well with them, most of the time—and he preferred to have his own space to sprawl out into and not worry about keeping another person awake or doing something antisocial like hitting them in the face with a sleep-flung arm, twitching every three seconds, snoring, mumbling, or farting.

But with John, he had just slept. Simple. Easy. Natural.

Bailey spent the majority of his Saturday e-mailing Václav and asking how on earth Václav thought his ideas were even vaguely plausible. Despite the eight-hour time difference, Václav replied right away, saying that he was thrilled to have Bailey's attention back and eagerly awaited his constructive criticism. "Constructive" had been struck through, and Bailey was impressed with Václav's ability to convey sarcasm in a variety of languages and communication formats.

They chatted for a while, Bailey filling up his whiteboard with scribbled equations and drawings, photographing it, sending it to Václav, and complaining about how much easier this would be if Václav would get him that damned SmartBoard already.

On Sunday there was an e-mail from Evans. Bailey read it and decided not to answer right away. He cleaned his apartment, or rather tidied it up so Ms. Castillo wouldn't berate him for being such a slob when she came on Monday. He always felt extra grouchy about cleaning up for the housekeeper, but she had a very sharp tongue and also a good point about not wanting to be responsible for moving his stacks of papers and journals and then being blamed when something got lost.

Tidying up could only occupy so much of his time, but it felt important to stay busy, so Bailey got to work on his op-ed columns. He'd been neglecting them, distracted by his overwhelming social calendar and ensuing romantic entanglements. It was June now, and he only had six guaranteed columns before his contract with John was fulfilled. John would probably want him to keep writing the astrology column, and while the resulting free license to tear apart his colleagues wasn't a bad bargain, he wasn't sure he wanted to agree to do it again. It had been good for *Spark* in terms of publicity and revenue, but... Bailey was beginning to get restless. Working for *Spark* wasn't what he was going to do for the rest of his life, and perhaps it was time to stop licking his wounds and get back to it. Without his noticing, said metaphorical wounds had pretty much healed, which was a bit of a surprise. Sure, he still wanted to murder all of the upper-level management at Stellar Energy, and he fully intended to let his peers in the scientific community feel the full weight of his wrath when they deserved it—which was often— but he no longer felt... humiliated.

He made a list of all the most egregious errors his peers were making and tried to prioritize them so he could write about the top six. He decided to leave at least one space free for whatever heinous new developments might come up, particularly at the Neutrino Factory, and one spot for Gallagher. Just because he could.

The work week was enlivened by John's reminder that he'd be hosting the start of summer/"thanks for all your hard work" barbecue at his place on Saturday. Someone—Lauren, most likely—had put a potluck sign-up sheet in the conference room with specific instructions, including threats to those who showed up with pitiful offerings like a bag of chips and liter of soda or assigned themselves to bring the paper plates. One day after that, the list was crossed out with a big red X and John had written in his messy scrawl that the party would be catered and no one had to bring anything unless they wanted to. Which was a huge relief, since most of the staff was full of geeks with questionable culinary tastes and abilities, and Bailey had not been looking forward to the resulting food poisoning if he'd tried to eat whatever concoctions his coworkers had managed to throw together.

John had been a little strange all week. Bailey had felt like he should say something about them unexpectedly sleeping in his bed together, but he couldn't figure out how—let alone what—without getting all tongue-tied about how he meant sleeping-sleeping, not euphemistic-sleeping. They'd had a very brief chat by the coffee pot on Tuesday, John pushing a blueberry muffin at him and saying they'd catch up later, since he had a meeting to run off to. But they hadn't. It didn't feel like John was avoiding him; Bailey was well aware of John rushing in and out of the office, and although he didn't technically have access to John's calendar, it was so simple to hack into it that it was practically an invitation. John was meeting with investors almost back-to-back all week. Bailey wondered if the magazine was in financial trouble, but he was relatively confident that John would have whined about it to him if that was the case; he'd bent Bailey's ear about *Spark*'s problems all last autumn until the sales had picked up.

Between John running around and Bailey trying to explain how cold fusion was a myth to his mentally challenged colleagues, the two of them didn't have a chance to talk until the party. The food was good, and Bailey happily indulged in a second helping of skirt steak and a third bowl of ice cream. He was debating between caramel sauce and chocolate and had decided on both when John found him.

"You know that food's for everyone, right?" he drawled. "Jason's going to make you work out twice as hard if your weight goes up."

"Jason's going to make me work twice as hard anyway," Bailey said with a snort. "I missed last week. So if I'm going to be punished, I might as well make the most of it. Besides, all I've eaten since breakfast is two PowerBars."

"Why do you do that?" John asked, shaking his head. "It's not like you couldn't program your watch or phone or something to ding at you and remind you to eat."

"I've tried that, obviously. I get caught up in what I'm doing, turn it off with a mental note to get something to eat in a minute, and then three more hours pass."

John shrugged and took a drink of his beer. "What were you so absorbed by today?"

They settled into two of the chairs on the deck to talk. Most of the people with families or social lives had left already, and it was just the two of them outside, with a cluster of the marketing team in the living room, watching some game on John's flatscreen as they polished off the rest of the keg. There was too much light pollution to see anything interesting in the sky and too much of the summer evening fog to see much of the cityscape. It gave the patio a sense of privacy, and there was no one to overhear when Bailey decided to ask about the lawsuit.

John sighed. "I haven't heard anything. I asked Robert to be on the lookout for anything CTK&R might pull, but so far it's all been silent on that front."

"I feel like I'm waiting for the other shoe to drop," Bailey complained. "I know you think I'm being paranoid, but…."

"Being paranoid doesn't mean they're not out to get you," John quoted with a smirk. "Seriously, though, I think you're right. That threat about the astrology column didn't come out of nowhere, and Gallagher doesn't seem the type to let something drop any more than you are. You physicists are a tenacious bunch."

Bailey snorted into his beer. "No kidding. There's a fine line between determination and bullheaded stubbornness. You need one or the other to get through the doctoral degree, let alone go on and make anything of yourself afterward."

"Yeah, I bet you wouldn't have bothered if you'd known you were going to end up working for a small science magazine," John teased.

"No kidding. And if I'd know about this accursed astrology column, I'd have stayed with the concert pianist life plan."

"Yeah. Life takes you in strange directions...."

They sat in the dark and drank for a while, the silence broken occasionally by the muffled shouts and groans from the sports fans inside the house.

"I just can't believe that you think maybe that love-match astrology bullshit is actually real," Bailey burst, out of the blue.

John laughed. "I don't, honestly, but I do love making you get all puffed up and flustered and then seeing you fall flat on your oversized ego."

"I knew it. You hate me."

"Loathe." John grinned. "That's why I'm going to make you help me clean up," he said, standing. He stretched for a moment, long arms reaching toward the sky, T-shirt riding up over his flat stomach and showing a narrow strip of belly. Bailey could see his treasure trail, not that he was looking.

John went inside and came back a moment later with two big plastic garbage bags. "Toss everything in. The food's probably gone bad by now, and I don't want to deal with a huge swarm of ants, flies, and meat bees tomorrow morning."

"They're not bees, they're *Vespula vulgaris*. Wasps, specifically yellow jackets. No apitoxins."

John rolled his eyes. "Whatever. Work, slave," he said, bumping Bailey's shoulder with his own before turning to one of the tables and beginning to throw most of the contents in his own garbage bag. On one of the tables they made a collection of all the recyclables, and they had the patio pretty much tidied up before the game inside had ended. John played the good host and showed the stragglers out, calling a cab for the two who had overindulged in their helpful attempt to empty the keg for him.

Most of the party had taken place outside, so the inside wasn't too bad except for the area in the living room. They got the mess cleaned up quickly, with Bailey on trash detail and John wiping down the coffee table and a spill on the sofa and rug.

"You should hire my housekeeper," Bailey pointed out.

"I don't like people touching my stuff. Besides, after two decades in the military, I'm used to cleaning up after myself. I don't mind it."

"Clearly you need more hobbies."

"Or a social life," John agreed, smiling.

"Speaking of which, do I have to beg Lauren to set up two more dates for a control group? You know she's going to totally blackmail me and demand another spa day or something. Did you know those three treatments plus some miniscule seaweed-based lunch cost me over $400?" he whined. "I do not understand women. She could have had at least two nice meals, with a friend, and a massage for that price!"

"Good thing you're dating men these days, huh?"

Bailey made a noise of thoughtful agreement and then shrugged. "So, you too? Committing to the gay side of bisexual these days?"

"Maybe." John cleared his throat. "Anyway, I'll set things up with Lauren. You'll still be on the hook for whatever she wants in return, of course," he said with a wink.

Lauren had an evil glint in her eye when Bailey stopped at her desk on Monday morning to ask if she was going to put up the Craigslist ad again or if she needed him to make a new one or what.

"It's all taken care of, McMillan. Don't you worry your pretty little head."

"What, already? How did you line up two 'random guys off the street' so fast? Oh my God, are you pimping me out?" He was starting to hyperventilate.

"Jesus, you are a piece of work. As a representative of all women of the planet, we want to thank you for deciding you were mostly gay, you big freak. To answer your question, one guy was an alternate from the first set of dates, and the other was someone I ran into and wanted to see how you got along with. And don't even ask; I'm not telling you which is which until after they're both done."

Bailey's mouth opened and closed on about seven different insulting comebacks at once as he squeezed his eyes shut. It was probably for the best that none of them managed to get out past the verbal traffic jam, or Lauren would mostly likely have sent him to the Emergency Room, and then Bailey would have had to sue her for assault, and then John would have had to plan Bailey's funeral because she would have murdered him. And frankly, Bailey didn't trust John to read his eulogy; he'd taken the liberty of writing up what he wanted said and appending it to his will, but John didn't seem like the sort of person who would be willing to read a litany of all the injustices Bailey had suffered at the hands of fools in the span of his far-too-short lifetime. He would likely be prone to maudlin sentimentality instead.

Bailey's midweek date was twenty minutes late and showed up out of breath, sweaty, and windblown, looking like he'd run the entire way from the BART station, which, in fact, he had done. Bernard pulled out a small bottle of hand sanitizing gel from his backpack and used it both before and after shaking Bailey's hand. He rearranged the place setting, lining everything up meticulously, and flagged down the waiter to bring him a sealed bottle of water.

It did not appear that this date was going to go well. Bernard set a new record for anal retentiveness. Bailey considered himself to be bit of a germophobe, but Bernard washed his hands a total of sixteen times during the first hour of their meal, and after he touched anything. He brought his own chopsticks, which were lacquer and sealed in an autoclave bag. When Bailey jokingly asked if Bernard did that himself, he got a very serious nod in reply.

"Yes, I have an autoclave at home and one at the office. It was too expensive to keep sending things out, and besides, you can't really trust people, you know?"

Bailey found himself nodding and wondering if this was how everyone else in the world saw *him*—paranoid and a little freaky to be around. After Bernard thanked Bailey for paying, citing how filthy paper money was and that one never knew what the waiters were doing with one's credit card when they took it away, Bailey said goodbye with a wave and fled. He drove home, counting his blessings that he wasn't *that* bad, surely. John would have pointed it out and harassed him about it if he was, right? John took great pleasure in giving him shit about his little peculiarities; it wasn't like he'd been holding back. Since John had never mentioned that he was seriously thinking about how to have Bailey committed to a mental institution, he couldn't be nearly as bad as Bernard. Right?

Still it was enough to make him reconsider the antibacterial hand-wipes that he kept in his wallet, car, desk, and backpack. He didn't want to get the flu, though…. Better safe than sorry.

JOHN laughed his ass off, as Bailey had expected, as they sat in the coffee shop and filled out the questionnaire for Control Date Number One. Bailey gave Bernard low scores for everything except shared interests, since he was a scientist of sorts: lab tech at a local medical facility.

"Well, no wonder the guy is paranoid about germs," John said. "You should cut him a little slack."

"He brought his own sterilized dining utensils," Bailey said, crossing his arms over his chest. "He has an autoclave at home *and in his office*. Which makes me wonder; I mean, he's got to have access to one in the lab."

"True. Can you imagine what sex with him would be like? You'd have to be encased in latex head to toe," John said, snickering like a teenager.

Bailey shook his head. "I doubt that guy has any kind of sex life at all. I can't imagine him wanting to touch anyone, no matter what kind of extreme precautions they took."

"Ah well. One more dud, one more to go. Friday?"

"Yes, Friday," Bailey agreed. "I'm meeting him there, according to Lauren. That restaurant I met the first guy, Ramses, at. This time I'm getting my pot de crème, damn it."

"Hey, you got ice cream last time," John pointed out, pouting a little. "It's not like you had to go without chocolate or anything traumatic like that."

On Friday, John caught Bailey in the communal bathroom after work, changing his shirt and applying more deodorant. "Not going home to change?"

"Why bother? I'm so mind-bogglingly tired of all of this. I just want to go to dinner, eat something decent, not be too annoyed or traumatized by this guy, and have some chocolate dessert. Then we can finally call this whole pseudo-scientific farce complete."

"Aw, poor baby. You have to give the guy a fair try, you know, or I'll make you go on another date. Don't want you skewing the results with a temper tantrum," John said.

"You are so mean to me," Bailey whined.

John laughed and slapped him on the shoulder. "Go get him, tiger!" he said, going back to his office.

Bailey dithered with his hair in the mirror for as long as he could without making himself late, sighed the sigh of the truly oppressed, and went to hail a cab. He sat in the restaurant for a few minutes, ordered a beer, and looked at his watch. His date was five minutes late, but he supposed it wasn't a big deal yet.

He was deciding which main course would be a good prelude to his chosen dessert when he sensed someone approaching the table. He looked up to see… John?

"Did the guy call to cancel? Did Lauren send you over to break the news so I wouldn't have a hissy fit at her over the phone?" Bailey asked.

John smirked. "Nope." He was wearing a sports coat over his shirt, and his hair was a little damp. He looked good, really good. Maybe he was there for dinner with someone else? "I'm your date," he said, sitting down.

"You're…. What?" Bailey gaped.

"Your date. I'll try not to be too annoying, but I can't promise not to traumatize you. I'm a Gemini; we're known for being unpredictable."

Bailey's brain froze. Stopped completely, his constant stream of background thoughts silenced for only the third or fourth time in his entire life, and the only time not during a near-death experience like a car crash. All of the physics, all of the math, all of the hum about allergies and idiots and things he needed to remember and experiments he wanted to run and people he should shout at—silent. Only one thought remained.

"I didn't know you were a Gemini."

Chapter 17

When Planets Align

BEING on a date with John was almost exactly like having dinner with him as friends. John had been on time—more or less—was charming, handsome, entertaining, a good listener, and of course they had a lot in common. It was unlike any of the other thirteen dates Bailey had been on, even the ones that had gone well. He and John already knew each other, so that tension and awkwardness was gone, replaced by relaxed, companionable conversation.

Well, mostly relaxed. There was still an air of tension. The game had been changed; they weren't there hanging out as friends who were hungry. This was indisputably a *date*, and Bailey wasn't quite sure what to make of it. And after a while, he got tired of wondering.

"Why are you here?"

John snorted a laugh. He shook his head a little, eyes crinkled with amusement and some other emotion that looked almost fond. "It was my turn. I'm qualified: I like *Doctor Who*, and math stuff, and I passed the entrance test for Mensa. I only decided not to join because the women there acted like they'd do anything to make terrifyingly smart babies with me." He shuddered.

Bailey rolled his eyes. "No, why are you *here*. With me. I mean, we have dinner together all the time. We're friends, good friends. Why make it a date? What, uh, what changed?"

"I can't hide it anymore," John said, looking at Bailey seriously. "I'm so attracted to you my hands sweat, my heart pounds, I can't think… I get an erection every time you walk in the room."

Bailey's eyes nearly bugged out of his head—until John ruined it by bursting out laughing.

"You are a cruel, cruel man." Bailey huffed.

It took John a moment to get himself settled down. He was still chuckling a little to himself as he said, "Seriously, no. I'm sorry, maybe that was a little mean. I guess... I guess it's true, actually, a little. Sort of," he added when Bailey gave him a skeptical look. "I hadn't really thought of you that way until you started telling me about all of your dates. I mean, we've been friends for a long time. You're, you know, cute enough, and your brain is terrifying, and you're fun to hang out with. You amuse me more than you annoy me, most of the time. And I trust you, which puts you in a highly elite group, by the way. But I hadn't thought about *dating* you until the last few months."

Bailey made a humming noise, pondering this information. "So hearing about my sexual exploits made you jealous?"

John rolled his eyes. "Yes, Bailey, I was inflamed with jealousy." He sounded sarcastic, but Bailey wasn't convinced that he was lying.

"So why now?" he pressed.

John took a drink of his beer and fiddled with the label for a moment before answering. "Well, okay. I was a little thrown when you hooked up with that Evans guy."

"My fling," Bailey said, nodding with a satisfied smile.

"Whatever. Yes." John scowled. "But what I was most surprised by was that he was your best match, according to the astrology predictions. And he's a Gemini."

"And?" Bailey prompted when John didn't seem like he was going to continue.

Shrugging, John took another drink. "Well, so am I. So I decided it was my turn. I'm supposed to be your best match. I bet I'm better than that British guy, anyway." He sounded a little sulky.

"It has *nothing* to do with—"

"—when either of us were born, yeah, yeah, I know," John finished. "I'm familiar with this monologue, trust me, unless you've added some new lines? There is, however, a fair bit of evidence that seems to indicate otherwise."

John's smirk made Bailey scowl. They could have had an argument about it, but the server arrived, interrupting their staring contest to take their order. Which was good, since it gave Bailey some time to think about this new development, evaluate the facts. John was here. On a date. With *him*. John had been jealous. John had not previously thought about Bailey sexually but enjoyed their friendship. John trusted him. John thought he was *cute*.

John thought he'd be Bailey's best match.

Bailey was still trying to process these last few thoughts, only half-participating in John's conversation about some of the topics the other writers had floated at the last staff meeting, and eating his dinner. John seemed to be aware that Bailey was thinking about something else, but didn't seem to mind; he was probably used to it. Which was a little startling and a lot reassuring. They did fit well together. And God knew Bailey had enjoyed his share of Special Alone Time over the years while trying not to think about John....

"What if we fuck up? What if we're not friends anymore after I do whatever it is I'll do and mess things up spectacularly?" Bailey asked midway through the meal.

The noise John made was halfway between a snort and a choke with a touch of laugh thrown in, and he needed a few swallows of water before he could answer. "Geez, jump ahead much? We haven't even kissed yet," he complained. "And who knows, maybe I'll be the one to fuck things up; I don't have the best track record with relationships, and I've never had one with a guy at all. But all right, fine. Worst-case scenario, you'll quit or I'll fire you—which is going to happen anyway, probably not very long from now—we'll have a few epic arguments, and then we'll never see each other again. I'll probably lose whatever clothes I've left at your place because you'll throw them away. I'll FedEx whatever electronics you've left over at mine. We'll try to avoid each other and most likely succeed, since we don't exactly move in the same social or work circles. The end."

Bailey blinked at him, feeling bereft over the end of their hypothetical relationship.

"*Or*," John said, "you scrounge up a little bit of optimism, we hook up, it'll be just like being friends only with sex, and we see how it goes. You'll annoy the shit out of me, I'll tease you mercilessly, your cat will continue to love me better than he loves you. We'll argue happily ever after."

"I like option two better," Bailey said.

John smiled. "Me too."

DINNER went well. They hovered a little outside the restaurant when they were done, asking where the other was parked, not sure whether they should go somewhere else or back to one of their homes. It was getting late, though, and it had been a long week. Without too much discussion, they agreed to go back to Bailey's place since the cat needed to be fed.

They walked upstairs together closer than usual, perhaps, although it might have only seemed like it because of the tension in the air between them. Bailey stopped to grab his mail, then juggled it awkwardly as he dug out his keys until John took them and unlocked the door himself. John turned off the burglar alarm and kicked off his shoes, and Bailey stood watching until John turned around to look at him, eyebrow raised.

"I hadn't realized how... comfortable you are here. I mean, you're welcome, of course. And I gave you the alarm code, I know, I just... never noticed until now."

"Seems to be a lot of that going around," John said, a faint smile in his eyes. He took the mail out of Bailey's hands and put it on the kitchen table. He moved closer, pushing into Bailey's space, until they were toe to toe. "Hey."

"Hey." Bailey blinked, finding his attention fixed on the stubble around the edges of John's jaw. Smelled John's soapy-clean scent. Licked his lips.

"God, it's like we're thirteen," John said, smiling a little.

Huffing, Bailey leaned forward and closed his eyes, pressing his mouth to John's. It was awkward for a moment, hesitant and strange. He carefully let his lips part, tasting John's, opening to him. John made a quiet noise, more of a hum than anything, and pressed closer, one hand coming up to cup Bailey's face. They traded slow, soft kisses, equal give and take, in perfect balance as they explored this new part of each other.

"Hmm," Bailey breathed once they parted. "I think that was a lot better than when I was thirteen."

"Definitely," John agreed, smiling.

Castrovalva meowed crankily. They turned to see him glaring at them from atop the kitchen counter, flagrantly violating the house rules to make his point about being ignored by John *and* unfed. It was clearly an outrage.

John chuckled a little, turning back to place a single lingering kiss on Bailey's mouth. "Go feed your cat. I'll stay here and try to convince him of where my affections lie."

"That had better be with me," Bailey grumped, but he untangled himself from John's embrace and went to deal with his feline obligations.

The sounds of purring and the crunching of cat food overlaid the background traffic noises of the city at night. John and Bailey sat on the sofa, still a bit awkward, unsure of how to begin. John moved closer, arm stretching over the back of the sofa.

"Subtle." Bailey snorted.

"Shut up."

John had a determined look in his eyes, and Bailey let himself be pulled back into the shared, private space of their bodies coming together. They traded kisses, eyes mostly closed, taking the time to get used to each other. They had been friends for years, but if anything, that made this more terrifying, more overwhelming. For Bailey, the potential to screw things up was intimidating, and while a big part of him (well, more average-sized, if he was forced to be honest) wanted to jump John right then and there, he was… hesitant. The few hours since John had sat down at his table and declared that they were on a date wasn't enough time to adjust to the change in their relationship.

There was a thump as Castrovalva jumped to the arm of the sofa and then planted himself in John's lap, kneading. "Your cat is not helping with the mood," John observed, breaking their kiss by a few centimeters.

"That's what you get for telling him he's the most important kitty in the universe," Bailey pointed out.

John laughed, and then appeared to surprise himself by yawning in the middle of it. Castrovalva's gravelly purr sent a vibration through John's whole body that Bailey could feel through their lips. The three of them sat pressed against each other on the sofa, the humans exploring each other's faces and mouths with gentle touches.

"Can't decide if I want to wake up and jump you or relax and go to sleep, and we can fuck in the morning," John sighed after a little while.

Bailey shrugged. "Sleep is good. It's taken us a long time to get here. And the sex will be better when we're more awake."

"So after coffee, then?"

Chuckling, Bailey nodded. "Definitely." He untangled his arms from John's and stood, tugging John up and leading the way to bed for the second time in as many weeks. It was a little startling, how domestic it felt, how easy, but it felt right. They stripped down to boxers and got into bed, arms and legs entangling naturally as if they'd been doing this forever. Somehow they had already learned each other's shape, deep in their subconscious minds, while orbiting around one another. Between one touch and the next, Bailey fell asleep with John's hand on his chest, the cat purring between their feet.

BAILEY awoke far too early for a Saturday to the smell of coffee. Groggy and disoriented—hadn't the automatic setting on the coffeemaker broken a few months ago?—he got up, used the bathroom, and went to investigate. He rubbed the sleep out of his eyes and yawned, scratching his belly.

"Good morning, sunshine," John said from his seat at the kitchen table.

"Coffee?"

"Yes, there's coffee. Drink some. Coffee, food, teeth brushing, and then sex. I've already fed the cat," John added. "Did the litter box too."

Bailey's brain struggled to wake up. Something important had been said. John pushed a cup of coffee toward him, and he lifted it to drink. He drank three swallows and then had to try very hard not to choke as his brain processed John's words. "Sex?"

"Yes." The look in John's eye was an interesting combination of arousing and terrifying, and it made Bailey feel hot all over.

"Sex would be good."

"Sex *will* be good. Eat something," John said, pushing a plate with a bagel and cream cheese at him. "I don't want to have to stop because your stomach's growling at us, and you're not allowed to faint from anything other than what I'm doing to you."

"I… am fully on board with that," Bailey said, drinking his coffee down and taking huge bites of his breakfast.

Bailey finished in record time and pushed his plate away. John raised an eyebrow at him. "Fifteen minutes to digest."

"You're like a drill sergeant." Bailey scowled. "Those sweatpants hide nothing, I can see that you're hard. Come on. It's not like swimming; I promise I won't drown in my own bed," he argued.

"Fourteen minutes," John said, drumming his fingertips on the table.

Bailey sighed. He knew that tone of voice. There was no way John was even going to kiss him until at least ten minutes had passed. "So, what then? Sit here and read the newspaper and pretend like we're not dying to rip each other's clothes off?"

John glanced at the paper, which he'd evidently already gone through. "We could fill out the date evaluation form."

"From last night? With you?"

John nodded.

"Oh for… fine, whatever," Bailey said with a sigh, getting John's messenger bag so they could use his netbook.

Five minutes later found Bailey, face buried in his hands, whining. "I can't believe you're making me do this. Fives on shared interests, conversational compatibility, attractiveness... but I'm only giving you a three-point-five for ethics since I still don't understand how you agreed to the military's bullshit."

Both of John's eyebrows show up. "I'm a five for attractiveness? You never give anybody a five. It's always four and a half or something. Seriously?"

Bailey scowled. "Shut up."

John grinned and then licked his lips in what he appeared to think was a sexy way, winking. "I'm your five. I make you hot and bothered."

"'Bothered', for sure. 'Hot' remains to be seen; how many more minutes do we have left?"

"Six minutes. And then you have to brush your teeth." When Bailey started to object, John said, "I already did mine. And morning breath plus cream cheese is not good."

"Fair point. So, next question?"

"Right. Um... it's the last one: 'If this person wanted to see you again, would you go out with him? Why or why not?'" John cleared his throat. "You never say yes to this one. I don't want to ask it."

Bailey picked up his coffee mug, which was distressingly empty. He poked a finger inside and caught a drip, running his finger around the edge until the resonant frequency produced a slight squeak. He took a deep breath, avoiding John, eyes still focused on his mug.

"Because I never wanted to date any of them if I could be with you," he said.

The words hung in the air between them for a long moment. John made a quiet noise, a slow, controlled inhale and exhale as he put the netbook aside and stood. Bailey glanced up at him.

"Jesus," John said, and all but lunged at Bailey, grabbing him by the shoulders and pulling him in. His mouth met and attacked Bailey's with urgent hunger as his arms wrapped around Bailey, bringing their bodies together.

Bailey had always wondered what John would be like full of lust. Whether he would be tightly controlled, maybe even get off on his superiority a little bit. Aloof and reserved, or possibly even self-conscious for some unfathomable reason. John never seemed like a man at ease with his bodily urges, maybe the result of years of denying them in the military. But then again, sometimes men like that used sex as the one area in their lives where they could let go of control and inhibitions, be wild and free and enthusiastic.

What Bailey should have considered was John's ability to surprise him. John's kisses bowled Bailey over, barely leaving him with enough brainpower for autonomic functions like heartbeat, breathing, kissing back. John had him pressed up against the wall, the full lengths of their bodies grinding together. They were both hard.

"Morning breath?" his stupid, unstoppable, humiliating mouth let slip.

John breathed against his neck. "Coffee mostly got rid of it, and I don't fucking care."

They kissed against the wall for a while, their soft sleep clothes doing more to tease them than actually inhibit their pleasure. Finally Bailey pushed John back enough that they could fumble their way to the sofa, still kissing. They fell with John seated and Bailey straddling him, holding his face, running his thumbs along John's morning scruff and enjoying the rasp. He caught John's indulgent smile but refused to feel embarrassed for being caught enjoying the texture.

John's hands moved from Bailey's waist down to grope his ass, squeezing each cheek for a moment before sliding up under Bailey's T-shirt, pushing it up and off. It had barely hit the floor before John's mouth was on Bailey's nipple.

"These always poke out. Sensitive?" he asked, tonguing one.

"Sometimes," Bailey answered with an inhale, John's teeth scraping a little. "Only if I'm pretty turned on, which, yeah. Harder's better, but no biting, okay?"

John's "Got it" was muffled as he let his teeth press against the sensitive flesh, pressure but not pain, and utterly perfect as Bailey groaned his approval.

"You, naked, now," he insisted a short while later, pulling away from John's delicious mouth with reluctance, feeling the tender spots that were probably already visible on his collarbone, neck, and shoulders where John had sucked up some delicious marks. He seemed to intuitively know how much was the right amount, the right kind of sucking bite that made Bailey want more. It was difficult to find the willpower to stop him.

"But—" John protested, but when Bailey scowled and got up, moving back enough to start tugging at John's clothes with all of his typical impatience, John let him. His nefarious strategy became clear when, stripped of only his shirt, John pushed down Bailey's pajama bottoms and grabbed his cock, guiding it into his mouth. Bailey braced one hand on John's shoulder, one knee on the sofa, and tried not to fall over.

"Some warning next time," he managed to complain through the pleasure of John's hungry mouth devouring him, and got a humming sort of agreeable sound in response. It wasn't very long at all before Bailey had to squeeze John's shoulder urgently. "Stop, now, you have to."

"What? What's wrong?" John asked, his eyes dilated and lips flushed red from what he'd been doing.

"What's wrong is that I'm going to come in about one second, and I've thought about this for way, *way* too long to have it be over so fast. You're not even naked yet!"

"I can fix that," John said, grinning as he lifted his hips and shoved off his sweats. He sat there, gorgeous and naked on Bailey's sofa, miles of skin marred by a few minor scars from an active life, a light dusting of hair in all the usual places. Completely real and entirely John.

"Wow," Bailey breathed, all of his usual verbal eloquence deserting him.

"Come here." Warm hands guided Bailey back down to straddle John's lap, skin to skin. They moaned into each other's mouths, overwhelmed at the first contact of so much flesh. So intimate. John's hands skimmed the length and breadth of Bailey's body—his shoulders, spine, hips, thighs, and ass—over and over. Especially his ass. "Please tell me you bottom," John begged. "I'm happy to switch, but God, your ass…. How have you been hiding something so round and perfect and firm all this time?"

Bailey pressed back into the fingers caressing him. "It's a clever disguise, the geeky lab coat," he said with a chuckle. "And yeah, I'm flexible. Slight preference to top, unless I'm feeling lazy, but you can go first. In fact, I have an idea… hmmm…." He reached over to the end table, opened the drawer, and fumbled around for a minute. With a noise of triumph, he found what he wanted, and he pressed a bottle of lube and strip of condoms into John's hand a moment later.

John leaned back into the cushions, giving Bailey his raised-eyebrow what-the-hell look.

"What?"

"Why do you keep condoms and lube in your living room?"

"It's where the TV is," Bailey pointed out. "I watch porn in here, obviously."

"That's… a little disturbing and also kind of hot, given how much time I've spent sitting on this sofa," John said. "But the condoms?"

"I can be an optimist sometimes," Bailey said with a shrug, the tips of his ears going warm from embarrassment.

"Glad you are," John said, opening the bottle and generously coating his fingers.

Bailey moaned as John slid first one and then another long finger inside him. They unerringly sought and found his prostate, and Bailey let his head fall to rest on John's shoulder and panted into the smooth skin of his neck. His breath hitched when John worked a third one in, feeling full and tight and ready. "Now, now, now," he chanted.

John made a growling noise and removed his fingers. Bailey held steady, the muscles of his thighs tense as he hovered, waiting and listening to John fumble with getting the condom on and slicked up. "Ready?"

"God yes, any more ready and I'd explode," Bailey groused. "Do it."

Bailey felt John guide his cock to the waiting opening and line up. He waited until he felt the first inch or so breach him, exhaling against the stretch. "Wait a second," he said, and John's hands came up to his sides, soothing. Bailey laughed; soothing was not what he needed. Grabbing John's hands, he pinned them to the back of the sofa, using his weight to hold them in place as he tensed his thighs, letting gravity help him sink down on the length of John's cock.

"You might have stopped me from touching you so far, but this is my show now," he said with a smug look, raising himself up. Down again, and then up, his quadriceps starting to burn because he wasn't a kid anymore, but it felt far too good to reconsider. John's cock was perfect inside him, thick and heavy and wonderful, as he angled their bodies so that it brushed across his prostate with every stroke.

"You feel amazing," John moaned. He twisted his hands in Bailey's grip but didn't break out of it, even though he definitely could have. Instead, he interlaced their fingers, holding and being held equally. He flexed his hips, lifting carefully, driving that little bit deeper inside that made Bailey groan.

"I need...," Bailey managed to say, and John untangled one set of their hands and wrapped his around Bailey's erection. They were rocking together at a steadier pace than Bailey would have anticipated, but every move sent his nerve endings tingling, the leisurely tempo seeming to push him higher and higher toward the inevitable.

"Hey," John said in almost a whisper. "Look at me."

Bailey had no idea what John was seeing when he looked at him, but whatever it was, it made John's eyes darken, the flush on his face and ears and throat spreading down his to chest, and moisture springing out all over. John's hand tightened on Bailey's cock, stroking not faster but tighter. No body of fragile flesh was designed to hold so much bliss for so long.

"Yes, oh fuck, *fuck*," John breathed, his hips jerking as he slammed up into Bailey. His eyes squeezed shut as he shook with pleasure.

Seeing John come—or maybe it was the hand convulsively tightening on Bailey's dick, or the cock thrusting into his ass—sent

Bailey's orgasm ripping through him like a bolt of lightning from the heavens. It went on and on, John's hand milking every drop out of him until he whimpered and made a clumsy grab for John's arm to make John stop tormenting his oversensitive cock.

He collapsed against John—heavy, unpleasantly sweaty, and too tired to care. His forty-year-old thigh muscles were screaming in protest of such vigorous activity without a proper warmup, and he suspected his chiropractor was going to be quite cranky with him sometime soon based on the twinges in his lower back. It was absolutely worth it.

"Good?" John asked, his sticky hands wrapping around Bailey's waist.

"Mmmm."

"Yeah." He gave Bailey a moment and then seemed to realize that wasn't encouraging him to move. "Up. Now. We need a shower, and also I can't feel my legs. You're really heavy."

Bailey's shoulders shook with laughter. "You suck at pillow talk."

"I kick ass at pillow talk. This is sofa-talk—totally different," John insisted, pushing Bailey up and off of him, both moving carefully, letting circulation return back to their protesting limbs.

"Hmph. Shower first," Bailey proposed, "and then we'll see about your pillow talk skills in an actual bed."

"Deal." John kissed him once, twice, and led the way to the shower.

Chapter 18

Cosmic Order

AFTER showers and breakfast at Dottie's—Bailey was too wired to go back to bed, much as he'd wanted to—John went home for some clean clothes, and Bailey went into his office to cheerfully prove to the world how brilliant he was by resolving one of Václav's neutron-capture problems with a bit of truly inspired math using the Oklo reactor as a model.

John came back on Sunday for dinner and television and sex, and after a few days of the same pattern, Bailey realized that he was in a relationship. The oddest part—aside from the statistical improbability of such an occurrence—was that it didn't feel like one. Or at least it didn't feel the way Bailey had always assumed a relationship should and would feel: awkward, forced, and doomed. Pretty much the same way he'd felt in a tuxedo the two times he'd had to wear one: as if he was suddenly on stage in a Noel Coward play, but no one had given him his lines, and wasn't he supposed to be sitting in the audience being bored out of his mind anyway?

He tried not to think about it too much, which was difficult but seemed to be working out rather well. He hung out with John. He argued with John. He ate breakfast and dinner and sometimes lunch with John. The only difference was that there was a lot more kissing and groping, and there was a weird sensation inside Bailey's chest, like something was unclenching. He didn't feel like John "completed him" or any ridiculous romantic claptrap like that, but he felt…. Actually, he had no words for how he felt aside from "good" and "comfortable" and "really amazingly happy from all the fabulous sex."

He didn't even get worked up when he received an e-mail from Oliver, solicitous but informative, saying that Oliver and Evans had indeed hooked up and that Evans would be "annoying the fuck out of me [Oliver] indefinitely or until I shoot him in the leg." Bailey replied that he thought they were a good match and hoped they could maybe all see each other for the next SFMOMA show in the autumn. He didn't want to jinx things with John—even though he didn't believe in that sort of superstitious nonsense—but he did say that perhaps they should double-date and left it at that.

Then he sent a short e-mail to Evans—wholly ignoring the contrite e-mail Evans had sent to him a few weeks ago—saying that he wished Evans luck with Oliver, thought they'd be good for each other, and also, had Bailey left his Schrodinger's cat "Wanted Dead and Alive" T-shirt there? It was awkward, yes, but he really wanted that shirt back. He felt like he should thank Evans for the sex and/or for the weekend fling that made John jealous, but that wasn't actually what had pushed John into action, and Evans ought to thank Bailey equally for the sex, so in the end he didn't end up saying anything about either.

The big news of the week turned out to be Gallagher. Robert and Xiao had scheduled a meeting with John and Bailey, one of those top secret behind-closed-doors affairs that made Bailey's hands sweat in nervous anticipation.

"Do you need a blowjob in the bathroom to take the edge off?" John asked when Bailey came into his office, jittering with nerves and hands flailing.

"What? I mean, yes, maybe that would help. Good idea," Bailey answered, stopping his pacing to pivot around and head toward the door.

John laughed. "Yeah, not in this universe, sorry. I was kidding; they'll be here any moment."

"It's not nice to tease geniuses with offers of sex you don't intend to follow through on," Bailey advised, crossing his arms across his chest and glowering. "I was capable of building a working model of an atomic bomb when I was in grade six, and I know where you live."

"I always suspected that a lot of the really creative ways for killing people were invented by scientists who weren't getting laid and were pissed off about it."

Bailey nodded solemnly. "Celibacy gives one a lot of time to think of creative means of revenge."

"On that note...," Lauren said, sticking her head in the doorway. "The attorneys are here." She showed the two of them into the conference room, bringing the usual tray of muffins and coffee with her, pointedly glaring at Bailey until he helped her.

Robert Tulley poured himself a cup, offered one to Xiao, who declined, and got down to business as soon as everyone was settled and the door to the conference room was firmly shut. "I have been informed by reliable sources that Pierce Gallagher's attorneys, CTK&R, will no longer be representing him. It seems Mr. Gallagher was unhappy with the results of his suit and is now trying to charge them with negligence."

Bailey snorted. "Hasn't he heard the expression about poking a bear with a stick?"

"Indeed," Xiao said with a smile that once again reminded Bailey of a shark. "His lawsuit will go nowhere, which is not only predictable but also especially humorous because he's being forced to represent himself; no firm in the state of California will advocate for him. And believe me, he's contacted almost all of them."

"The suit will almost certainly be dismissed as a waste of the court's time," Robert went on, "but we thought you would want to know, even if this is essentially hearsay, that it seems Mr. Gallagher's attentions have turned from you and onto his former representatives."

"For now," John said, shaking his head. "But what's to keep him from eventually making good on his threats regarding the exposure of our anonymous columnist?"

"Nothing, strictly speaking," Xiao answered. "But without an attorney to back him up, and given that his representatives threatened us with the exposure as leverage but didn't follow through, I would guess that he doesn't have any proof. And without proof, you're protected from anything he says, at least legally."

"Yes," Robert agreed. "He could, of course, stir up enough media attention that it would become difficult for you—and everyone here at *Spark*—to keep the secret, but he couldn't force you in any way to reveal the writer." Robert very carefully kept his gaze fixed on John. "We have ascertained that it would be something of a professional embarrassment, shall we say, for one of your higher-level staff to admit to writing such unscientific material, but even if Mr. Gallagher managed to convince a reputable source such as *Newsweek* to investigate, there's no reason your writer would have to unveil him- or herself."

"No, but there could be a leak," Bailey said, unable to stop himself. "Someone who works here might say something."

"True. Which is a whole different matter, but again, without proof it's simple hearsay, and neither you nor the magazine are under any obligation to respond in an official way. But...."

"Yes?" John and Bailey both prompted, voices overlapping.

Robert cleared his throat. "If you want my advice—which you are of course welcome to ignore—I would recommend you either come out with a byline or kill the column. It's attracted quite a bit of media attention already, which I'm sure was part of the goal in making the magazine more accessible to a larger pool of readers. But secrets like this are difficult to keep indefinitely. 'The truth will out,' as Shakespeare said."

John nodded, thoughtful. "Yeah. I think I knew that was where this was headed. No matter which staff person actually wrote the column"—he also was looking anywhere but at Bailey, who was starting to feel annoyingly invisible—"it makes all of the writers with professional reputations in the scientific community vulnerable. Because it would be such a shame to besmirch any of their CVs with the tainted byline of an astrology column."

Everyone except Bailey laughed, although he managed a weak smile when John kicked him under the table.

"Well, I'll see what I can do. Thank you for your thoughts, Robert, Xiao," John said as he stood up and held out a hand to shake each of theirs. "I assume I'll see you in here again at some point; no good work goes unpunished. But thanks for your help with all of this, and thanks for the info about Gallagher."

"Yes, thank you," Bailey said, also shaking hands and hoping his weren't too clammy. There was no way the two attorneys didn't know he was the writer of the column, and while they were of course constrained by attorney-client privilege, it still made him nervous to have two more people who knew.

The door to John's office had barely shut behind them before Bailey collapsed onto the sofa, head in his hands, elbows on his knees, breathing in deep gulps of air. "I can't do this anymore, John. I don't want to stop writing the op-ed pieces, and God knows I just got the rest of the year's targets lined up and even started writing a few of their public scoldings, but… I'm going to have to break our contract."

John raised an eyebrow at him. "Do you need me to call your lawyer for this?" It took Bailey a moment to process the teasing tone under John's sarcasm. "Of course we need to pull the plug on it, duh. And I'm the one breaking the contract, for the good of the magazine and all of my staff, not just for you. So there's no reason for you to forfeit your column. I know how much you love ripping apart your peers every month."

"They deserve it. And also, bite me."

"Later." John sat down on the sofa beside Bailey and leaned his head back against the wall, eyes closing. "It's too bad, in a way. I mean, I know you hated it, but you were really good at the predictions, and the accuracy of them got everyone talking. I know you don't want to go down in history as the genius who revolutionized astrology, but… it's a good column. You really surprised and impressed me."

Bailey snorted. "Trust me, it was totally unintentional. But I couldn't just make crap up; I had to try to bring a little science and math to it, try to find some sort of pattern…. It's my fault that it actually appeared to have made the predictions a little more accurate-ish."

"Anyway. Sucks that we'll have to pull the plug."

Bailey made a humming noise.

"Hmm? When you hum like that, you're thinking. What are you thinking?" John asked, sitting up to look at him.

"I'm thinking I did all of the calculations. I'm thinking that the column is good for the magazine. I'm thinking that I don't need to keep doing it for it to continue being written. Anyone with a brain and maybe some interest in this bastard stepchild of the sciences could do it. Especially someone who likes to meddle in other people's romantic lives."

"Lauren."

Bailey nodded. "She could consult with me about the astronomical events that come up, but she seemed pretty into the stuff she researched for our experiment. I bet she'd do it. God only knows what she'll extort from you in return for the favor, of course," he added.

John grinned. "I'm not worried about it. She owes me a few favors. Although maybe we're even by now...." He trailed off in thought for a moment and then got up, giving Bailey a quick kiss in passing. "I'm going to go talk to her. Don't you have work to do? I thought I heard Elizabeth bitching about you being behind yesterday?"

"Slave driver."

John made a whip-cracking noise and wiggled his eyebrows before turning and sauntering out the door. Bailey took a moment to indulge in the view, then got up and went back to his desk, hands already on his keyboard, responding to the editor's dinging chat window before his butt hit the chair.

AS SATURDAY approached, Bailey started to exhibit all the signs of extreme nervousness. It was John's birthday, and they had planned a nice dinner out. Yes, for steak, and yes, Bailey chose the restaurant, and *yes*, he'd be picking up the tab—not because John had won their stupid bet but because it was John's birthday. John had not won the bet. Bailey was pretty sure any impartial observer would agree that John had totally cheated by including himself in the tie-breaking "control" dates. But John had asked for steak, his eyes dancing with laughter, and Bailey had sighed and booked a reservation at the place with the delicious truffle fries.

He had a little something else planned, though, and that was what was making his palms sweat.

He collected John from his house in the early afternoon, refusing to elaborate on their destination, and drove southward out of the city. It wasn't very long after he got off the freeway that John's body language changed from one of relaxed amusement to stiff tension.

"Bailey?" he asked in a skeptical tone.

"Just wait," Bailey requested, and he turned into the parking lot for the small airfield.

John did as Bailey asked, but he could see John's knuckles turning white as they approached the private hangars and parked. Bailey turned off the ignition, and they sat in the car, silent.

"All right, I know this might be a bit much. I mean, more psychologically or emotionally or whatever"—Bailey's hands flailed— "than financially, which let me assure you might appear excessive but isn't a big deal for my bank account. It's not meant to be, you know, a big romantic gesture or extravagant or whatever. It's just... I want you to have this. And I don't know what reasons you keep using with yourself not to do it, so I decided to do it for you."

John took a deep breath, but Bailey couldn't tell if he was trying not to get angry or trying not to freak out or what. He chose his words with care, finally asking, "What did you do?"

"I, um, I bought you a plane."

There was another careful inhalation and exhalation. John nodded. "I see."

"Actually, yes; let's go see it," Bailey said nervously, and got out of the car. John seemed to hesitate for a moment but joined him without too much delay, and they walked to the hangar.

A man in blue coveralls came out, wiping his hands on a greasy cloth. "Can I help you?"

"Yes, I'm Bailey McMillan," Bailey said, holding out a hand for a second and then thinking better of it and withdrawing it before it could get covered in grease. "I'm here about the Bonanza G36?"

John's eyes widened. "A Beechcraft Bonanza G36? Those are the ones with the new aluminum alloy propeller, right? I flew one of the QU-22B models a few times in the Air Force."

"Well, yes. That's why I bought you one," Bailey said, and turned to follow the man who introduced himself as Terry-the-Mechanic over to the incredibly shiny little plane in the corner.

John hesitated and then hurried to catch up with them. He'd gone totally silent, and Bailey couldn't read the expression on John's face at all. But when they reached the tiny little airplane, John's typical childlike excitement won out over whatever internal battle he'd been fighting. His hand came up to trail a fingertip along the rivets on the edge of one wing.

"It's yours, then?" Terry asked after glancing at Bailey and getting a nod.

John nodded too. "I... yes. I guess it is."

Terry immediately launched into a spiel about the G36, its engine, fuel, and maneuverability stats, and so forth. Bailey would have been more reassured by a cataloging of its safety features, but John was letting himself get pulled into the excitement, asking questions, touching the body of the airplane, learning its shape. Eventually Bailey wandered over to a seat by the wall and sat down, taking out his phone to answer some e-mails while he waited. Every now and then he looked up and watched John, the expression on his face making Bailey feel warm and melty inside.

It was several hours later before they were finally ready to leave the airfield and return to the city for dinner. John had signed up for the lessons he would need to get his civilian pilot's license, and Terry had taken him up for a short flight in an older-model Beechcraft, partly just for fun, but also partly to compare and contrast how John's model would be different. They'd decided to save the virgin flight for John, who would be licensed in no time at all, probably before the end of the summer.

John was sort of bouncing as they walked back to Bailey's car. He looked high, intoxicated, and Bailey sighed a huge internal sigh of relief that there hadn't been an argument about the airplane. He'd wanted to give John a nudge but hadn't expected it to go over so easily.

They were almost all the way back over the San Mateo bridge when John apparently came down from his endorphin rush enough to turn around and glare at Bailey. "You shouldn't have done that. I would have bought one when I was ready."

Bailey snorted; he should have known he wouldn't get off so easily. "Maybe, maybe not," he said, and the implication that "not" was his personal opinion was clear. "Either way, I thought you needed a nudge. You miss flying. I couldn't exactly drag you to a shrink for your birthday and give you a coupon for therapy to help you get over whatever's been holding you back, but... I could give you this."

"Hrmph."

"You know you always make that noise when you know I'm right and you want to argue but can't think of anything to say, right?" Bailey didn't have to look away from the traffic to feel John's glare.

"You don't know everything," John said.

"Not everything, no, but I know a lot. And I know you."

John made that noise again, and there were several minutes of silence. "I guess you do," he admitted after a while. "Better than anyone else, anyway. You knew the only thing that would get me back up there was if you shoved me into it. I suppose if I freak out during the lessons, there'll at least be someone with me to get us back on the ground without mishap. And...." He took a deep breath. "I suppose maybe I could call a shrink if I need one."

Bailey nodded, trying not to smile with relief. "Yeah. And hey, maybe you'll be just fine. Maybe you'll be back up there, in the empty blue sky, and you'll be fine. And either way, I'll be there with you."

John snorted. "I'm assuming you mean metaphorically, since you seemed about as excited to get in that gorgeous Bonanza as you would be to get in an MRI machine."

"Yes, let's stick with the metaphor," Bailey agreed. "Although... I suppose I would be perhaps willing to place my life in your hands once you get your license, if that would give you some incentive."

"Really?" John twisted around to look at him. "You always say small planes are death traps and cite the Day the Music Died, as if you're anything near the kind of genius Buddy Holly and Ritchie

Valens were. This is even the same make and model airplane," John pointed out.

"It is? Um." Bailey cleared his throat. "You definitely should not have told me that. I mean, it's rated as one of the safest single-engine aircraft, and there are all kinds of new safety features in the G36, but still. Fuck."

"I promise not to crash into any mountains," John said solemnly.

"You'd better not. I'd hate to have to become a biologist just so I can figure out how to bring you back to life and yell at you."

John's hand came to rest on Bailey's thigh for a moment. "Not sure who that would be a worse fate for. But I promise. And I might not have said this yet: thanks for the airplane."

Bailey took one hand off of the steering wheel for a moment to hold John's. "Of course."

THE rest of the birthday celebration was less rife with anxiety and a lot more mellow. They ate at the restaurant, John insisting that it was payment for the bet he'd won and Bailey protesting vehemently that it wasn't anything other than a birthday celebration. They both had a little too much wine and decided to take a walk before going home. They passed a bakery that was still open despite the late hour—one of those fashionable new cupcake boutiques—and Bailey insisted that it was a sign from the cosmos that they should go in and eat cake. Since it was John's birthday and all.

They had a brief argument over mini-cupcakes versus full-sized ones and how many were both necessary and appropriate to consume on this, the anniversary of John's birth. They finally left with a box that was both candy pink in color and tied with enough ribbons that even the most flamboyant gay man in San Francisco would have felt a little self-conscious carrying it home.

"I might need to reaffirm my masculinity after all that," John said, licking the last of the icing with sparkly sugar crystals from his fingers.

"What, you want to go bear hunting or something?"

John made a face at him. "I was thinking more along the lines of a blowjob."

Bailey shrugged. "I don't think giving me a blowjob traditionally works for that, but hey, whatever you want—it's your birthday."

John smacked him. "I was thinking about *getting* one, jerk."

Agreeing that a blowjob could probably be arranged, Bailey led the way into the bedroom, both of them shedding clothes as they went. John stretched out on the bed, all long limbs and gorgeous maleness, and Bailey's mouth salivated a little. He decided to put that to good use, and without preamble, he got to work. He was happily losing himself in the smell, taste, and feel of John all around and in him, sliding John's cock in and out of his mouth in a steady rhythm, when a hand pulled insistently at his hair.

"Yes? Busy here."

"Turn around," John said, moaning a little on each breath. "Hips up here."

"No, I hate sixty-nine," Bailey protested. "Can't concentrate."

John's chuckle was a little ragged, since Bailey had got back to what he was doing. "So much for the genius ability to multitask."

"Orgasms are not meant to be multitasked," Bailey stated, pausing again. "Now can I do this or what?"

"By all means," John said magnanimously.

Bailey let the sensory input direct him, keeping it slow and steady, making the pleasure last for as long as John could stand it. When the noises he heard started to sound frustrated and desperate, he upped the pace, wrapping one hand around the base of John's cock with the other one cupping his balls. By the time John was invoking deities neither of them believed in, Bailey was alternating long strokes with short, rubbing his tongue against all the best spots, and then backing off to tease the crown with little licks. An occasional breath of cool air had John tensing under Bailey's hands and mouth until he was making choked-off sounds, almost there.

"Come on," Bailey said, teasing with his tongue between the words. John made a strangled noise, and the first burst of salty fluid filled Bailey's mouth, followed by others. He backed off little by little, letting John hold him in place, mouth soft and warm but not active any longer, until John tugged him upward again.

John's face was flushed red, eyes closed, mouth open. He was breathing hard, his body damp with sweat. He was the most beautiful thing Bailey had ever seen, the mysteries of the universe, the paradoxical fragility and endurance of space and time, all in one person.

"I love you."

John opened sleepy, satiated eyes and smiled a lazy grin. "I know. I love you too."

Epilogue

Twinkle

TWO weeks later and they were at the airfield again, which had sort of become John's home away from home. He was set on getting his license as quickly as possible, logging as many flight hours as he could. While he'd had a minor freak-out a few days after the first time he went up in the air, John was working through his issues. And Bailey might have left out the business card for a therapist he used to talk to sometimes when he needed a captive audience to listen to him whine about how impossible other people were, and it might have been moved from its location to a different spot, but neither of them was talking about it. Which was fine.

The airfield was evidently the best place to be for observing two different shows of fireworks in celebration of Independence Day, and as a new member of the Aviation Club, John had been invited to the celebration. Bailey tended to mock the holiday and its associated political jingoism, but John liked things that both blew up and made sparkles, and Bailey liked barbecue and free food, so they had agreed to go.

Bailey's stomach was pleasantly full as the two of them reclined on a fluffy blanket, comfortable enough in the dark night to be pressed up against each other, watching the show. John's hands were describing the trajectory of the last burst of fireworks and where the next few would be most likely to show up. It was comfortable, familiar, easy. Without even trying, John had become the gravity well at the center of Bailey's universe.

They watched the starbursts in intervals of silence punctuated by occasional gasps or laughs as their hands roamed to places they shouldn't, at least not in public. It was dark, though, so it was all right. No one was watching.

"Hm. Do you think this is happily ever after?"

He felt more than saw John shrug in reply. "Maybe, yeah. Why, do you think there's someone out there that would be a better match?"

"It's a big universe…," Bailey said, contemplating the odds.

John snorted, shoving him a little bit and leaning across to kiss him. "Yeah. And I'm right here."

ALIX BEKINS lives and writes atop a treacherous hillside in the Santa Cruz mountains. Her days start with a cup of proper British tea and end with crocheting ridiculous socks while watching TV. Alix is a sex-positive, kinky, belly-dancing bisexual pagan. (The only reason "goth" isn't on that list is because she prefers purple or pink hair to black and thinks absinthe is a terrible joke.) Her muses often wear the faces of her favorite celebrities and porn stars but are nowhere nearly as cooperative.

Alix is pretty sure she's the only person in the world who wears a plastic Viking helmet as a thinking cap when she battles writer's block. She always wins.

Visit her at http://alix-bekins.livejournal.com/, http://www.facebook.com/AlixBekins, or contact her at alixbekins@gmail.com.

Also from ALIX BEKINS

Relationships 201
Alix Bekins

http://www.dreamspinnerpress.com

Romance from ALIX BEKINS

http://www.dreamspinnerpress.com

CONTENT WARNINGS

Gore, death, murder, torture, mention of child torture, war, blood, vulgar language. violence, loss of loved one, scars, grief and hallucinations. Alcohol abuse and addiction. Depiction of depression, dissociation, catatonia and PTSD. And lastly, explicit content. This series is intended to be read by mature readers (18+) as there are several explicit scenes.

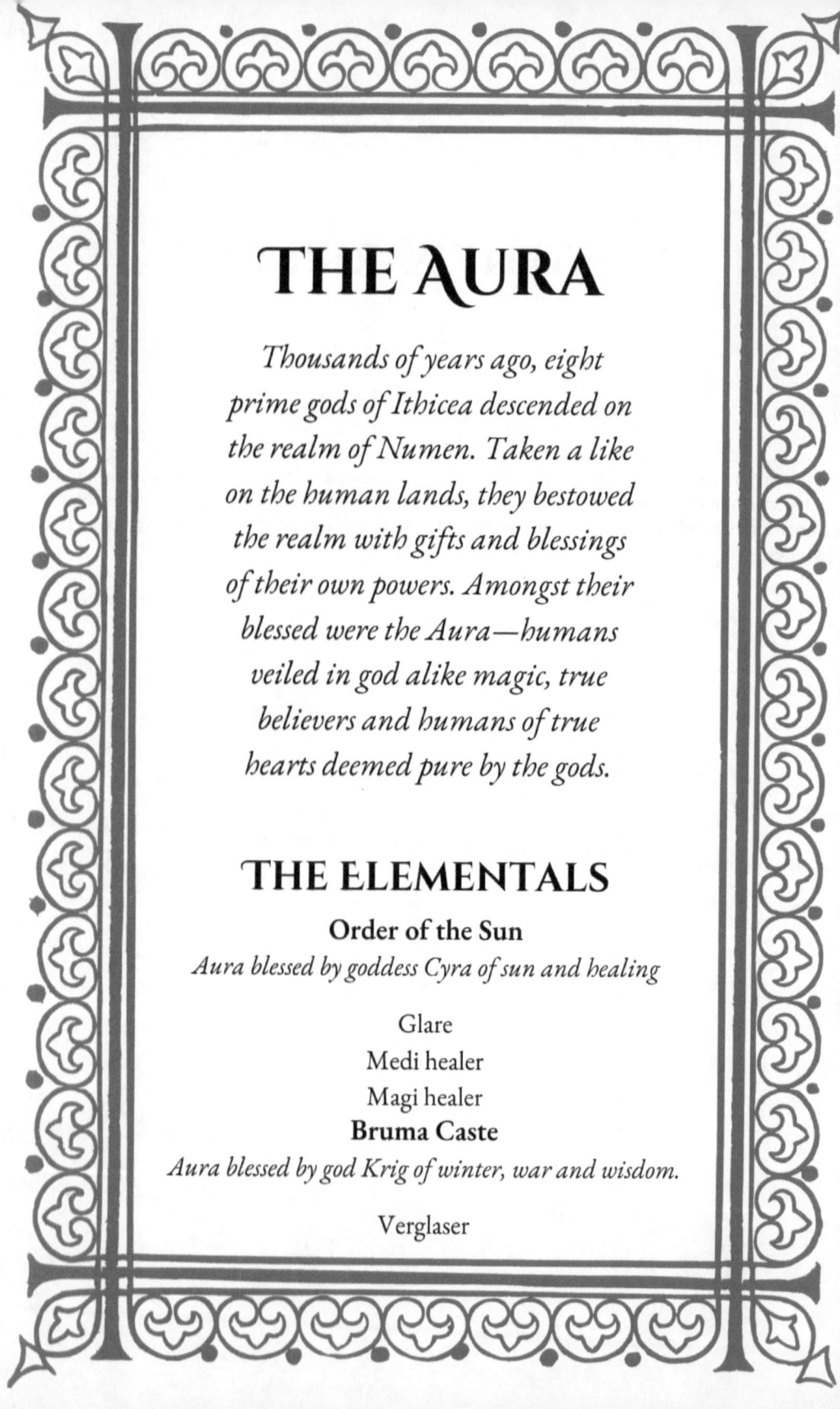

THE AURA

Thousands of years ago, eight prime gods of Ithicea descended on the realm of Numen. Taken a like on the human lands, they bestowed the realm with gifts and blessings of their own powers. Amongst their blessed were the Aura—humans veiled in god alike magic, true believers and humans of true hearts deemed pure by the gods.

THE ELEMENTALS

Order of the Sun
Aura blessed by goddess Cyra of sun and healing

Glare

Medi healer

Magi healer

Bruma Caste
Aura blessed by god Krig of winter, war and wisdom.

Verglaser

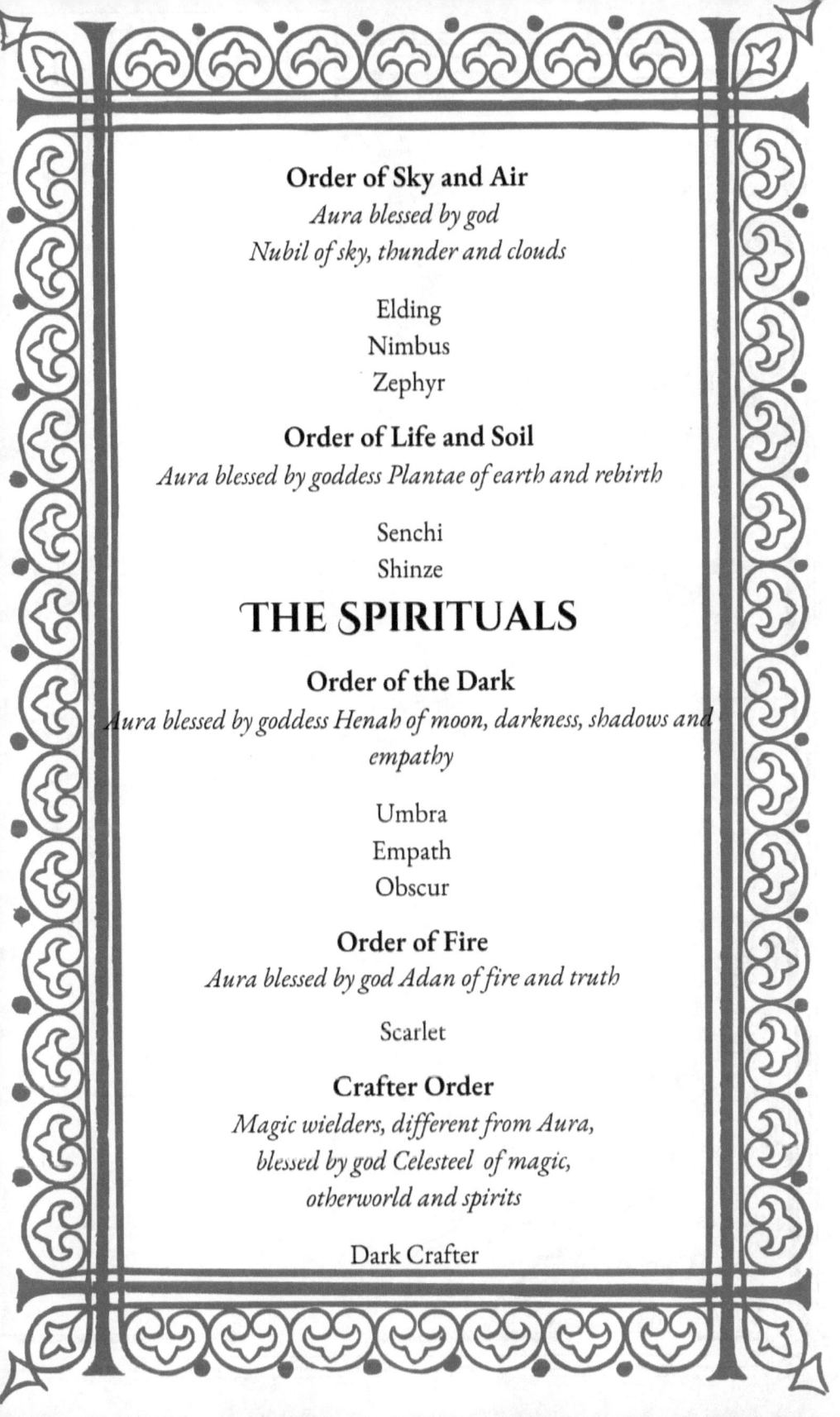

Order of Sky and Air

Aura blessed by god
Nubil of sky, thunder and clouds

Elding
Nimbus
Zephyr

Order of Life and Soil

Aura blessed by goddess Plantae of earth and rebirth

Senchi
Shinze

THE SPIRITUALS

Order of the Dark

Aura blessed by goddess Henah of moon, darkness, shadows and
empathy

Umbra
Empath
Obscur

Order of Fire

Aura blessed by god Adan of fire and truth

Scarlet

Crafter Order

Magic wielders, different from Aura,
blessed by god Celesteel of magic,
otherworld and spirits

Dark Crafter

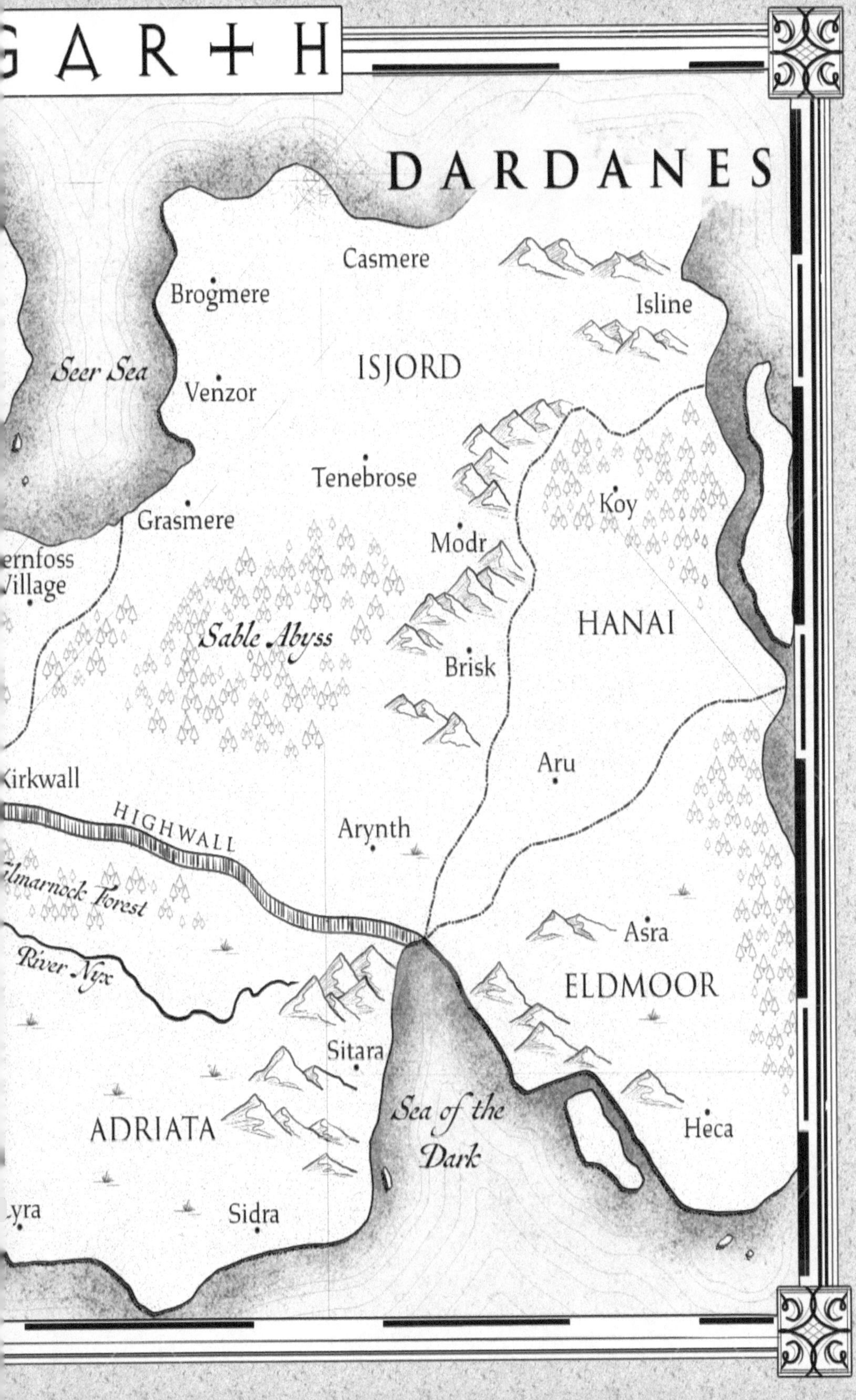

GAR+H

DARDANES

Casmere

Brogmere

Isline

Seer Sea

ISJORD

Venzor

Tenebrose

Koy

Grasmere

Modr

ernfoss
Village

HANAI

Sable Abyss

Brisk

Kirkwall

Aru

HIGHWALL

Arynth

ilmarnock Forest

River Nyx

Asra

ELDMOOR

Sitara

*Sea of the
Dark*

Heca

ADRIATA

yra

Sidra

THORA

AGE SIX

I t had been a week since uncle had brought us to a sunny land. A full week since Eren had not stopped crying. His whole body had burned in the fire, but my big brother was not crying because of that pain, the healers had healed him soon after like they had healed my own burns. Mine didn't hurt. But then mine had not been all that big—not like his. Every day, he sat at the edge of the wood house where he'd piled two separate hills of rocks. And he cried. He wouldn't tell me why. He wouldn't tell me where Snow was either. He cried harder when I said her name so I'd stopped asking.

Today he'd taken me with him to the rock piles and we'd sat beside one another for many minutes. He had not cried today. "Rora," he said hoarsely. "Remember what I told you that once when you saw Lin...when you saw your sister and I at the courts with the...man who was bleeding."

"The one who had died."

His eyes drew shut for a minute. "Yes. Remember what I told you where he had gone?"

"Up in the skies. I know, I'm not silly. Papa taught me as well."

A string of tears fell down his cheek. "That's where Lin and ma are. Up...up in the skies."

"Can't we go as well?"

"Not yet, Rora," he said, wincing as he pulled me onto his lap. "Not yet."

1

RED CARNATIONS

THORA

I had a cat once. She was white as snow and just as evil and cold as winter. My arms were almost always covered in scratches. That was until Eren and Snow found it hidden in my clothing chambers where I'd made sure no one could see her.

"Your Majesty?"

They weren't mad though. Snow and Eren took the cat, fed it and washed it for me. But uncle had found it one day, killed and skinned it, then left it on top of my bed for me to see.

"Your Majesty?"

I don't even remember crying. It was just another thing that had happened to me as a consequence of who I was and what I looked like.

My resemblance to my mother had made me uncle's target. We had the same eyes. The same hair. Snow had always hated her long hair, it got everywhere, she hated washing it, combing it, plaiting it, but she kept it nice and long, so our uncle's hate was divided in two—so I wasn't his only target. She grew loud to attract attention, I grew silent so I wasn't seen. She became defiant, I became docile. She held onto her anger, I forgot I had it altogether. She remembered every little scar, I pretended I'd never been injured in the first place. We weren't two sides of the same coin, we were two different coins altogether. She was made entirely of steel. I was made of crumbling clay. Whoever tried to use me as currency had not gotten much in exchange.

A hand touched my shoulder and I almost jerked upright. It was Nissa, my servant with warm sea blue eyes and just as kind of a smile. "It is time, Thora. Do you want to have a look in the mirror?"

Besides the white veil, dress, gloves, and diamond crown I so rarely wore, there was nothing strange in the reflection before me. I didn't feel strange either. Nor excited. Something was telling me that I should perhaps feel strange that this day felt just like another miserable sunny winter day, not the day I was about to marry the man I was betrothed to.

Ten years into my reign as an Isjordian Queen—that is how far I had made it until I was forced into choosing someone to sit beside me on the throne. A strong Isjordian Aura. Someone with good connections and an old family name just as powerful as mine. A politician who could survive my court. A businessman who could enrichen my treasury. Those had become the conditions for my affections. The very same conditions required to persuade my people against Iskyla Krigborn and her claim to my throne.

Erik was a good man. Good by most definitions that were approved by Isjordian standards. Educated. Rich. A strong lineage.

Just the thought that I needed all those meaningless titles to maintain a strong reign not threatened by men who do not desire to bow before women made me entirely too—

Another familiar hand landed on my shoulder and I breathed out a slow exhale, letting a cold mist roll for a long minute before turning to Kilian who was draped all in black as if I'd asked him to walk me to the God of Death, not my husband. "Ready?"

His smile was soft. "Are you?"

"Erik is a good man." Not the slightest clue why I had to make that statement when he hid his judgement so well from everyone. Kil did not like Erik one bit.

"You do not love him," he said matter-of-factly. "So let us not pretend this makes any sense at all beyond what it is."

"I cannot love." Not a clue why I told him that either. Not that I'd told it to anyone else before. But I suppose this was the last moment I could say it truthfully.

His brows creased, rightfully so at the idiocy I'd spewed at the most inconvenient time. "Why would you think so?"

"Because what I want is not what I deserve."

"Says who?"

"The one I wanted."

He understood. Maybe he had always understood. "You don't have to do this, Thora."

"Iskyla Krigborn has been eating through my lands inch by inch, claiming them right under my nose with my people's permission. Half of the Isline villages have already been taken, Kilian. My court has finally settled and the people are no longer talking of their fears regarding an enemy queen, but rather the incompetent one currently ruling them. This is me pushing my hand."

"Peacefully. And you know these people have never handled anything with peace in mind."

"You and Snow really need to take some time apart. She's really not rubbing on you in a good way." I grabbed my heavy skirts and led us out of my room and towards the winter gardens where the ceremony would take place. The cold...it would keep me sane. It had kept me sane for so long alone in this kingdom. The cold was my consolation price in the deal that my sister had made for me. It was now my only friend. But the cold didn't speak, and I was missing being spoken to.

Skadi stood at the garden entrance, solemn and unbothered by the marriage that she had gone to great lengths to avoid. She bowed her head at me when I passed by her but said nothing.

"I wanted you to sit amongst the guests," I said, halting.

"This marriage is not something I wish to celebrate."

"Skadi, please."

"You will be miserable."

"Yet dressed well and with an expensive taste that my father in law's diamond trade has promised to quell," I said, flashing her my emerald necklace, heavy earrings and crown. If I'd marry, I was going to marry as rich as I could. Emil, Erik's father, he was the richest there was. If he was a widower, I would have married him instead of his spoiled son.

She eyed my neck for a moment. "You've never been fond of diamonds. Your taste has always been for a much simpler rock."

That was the moment I bowed back and returned by Kilian's side to walk the remaining length to the altar.

Elias, too, had apparently refused to sit among the guests, positioned by the edge of the celebrations where my guard remained. My right-hand man only shook his head at me even though he'd been the one to introduce me to Erik.

I stopped at the entrance of the white rose gardens covered in soft snow. The small sounds at the distance where the altar had been set flew in all around—excitedly, people awed and gasped at me. All except the front row where my sister, Nia and their children were all sat.

Kilian offered me his arm. "Eren is here. He can walk you down the aisle. Or Alaric. Cai, too? Though I can't promise a ruly ceremony if he is present. He wasn't a big fan of this."

At the mention of my brother, I dropped my eyes down, forcing myself not to look his way. "I want you to do it," I said. "I don't feel comfortable with it being anyone else." Kilian was perhaps the reason why I had managed to stand this far on my own two feet.

All was so pure and white and pale while I made my way between lines of chairs framing a long altar laid with white rose petals that melted against the pristine snowy ground.

So pale the world was all of the sudden under the brisk summer sun that was but mere decoration in the skies, offering no warmth. Not even the god I served deigned us with a little ounce of his presence. Not a cloud in sight. No signs of winter anywhere but the one always present. Whatever snow surrounded us had already settled from days ago.

And the faint, strange heartbeat I'd heard in the wind all day this morning had suddenly turned so dull and faint, I could almost miss it—if only to drown out my thoughts.

Erik stood under the arbour of white roses and baby breaths. His sea-coloured eyes were pale, too. And his smile—pale. It had always been pale, empty, only a trained glamour he used as a shield when he was thrown into unflattering situations—arguments, boring conversations, and now this, our wedding. Surely, he just as everyone would have preferred to marry someone he loved, but there was very little power love could grant, and none that could help me against Iskyla.

The sound of the strange heartbeat returned, growing louder the closer I got to Erik. It wasn't my own. I could feel my own, cold heartbeat quietly in an entirely different pace from that I was hearing in the wind. So, whose heart was I hearing beat in the wind?

Kilian was reluctant to let me go once we stood close to the altar where the Isjordian priest was waiting. His hand had curled onto my forearm a little too tightly.

I shot him a pleading look and he sighed, pulling back so I could take Erik's extended hand.

"You look astonishing," my husband-to-be murmured in my ear as we turned to face the priest.

"As do you," I politely threw back at him.

Whatever words came out of the Isjordian priest's mouth bounced back into the open scenery around. Only when Erik nudged my hand did my attention return, voices returning again. The sound of the strange heartbeat disappearing.

We faced one another, waiting for the priest to say the final vows before we would be joined as one.

All so quickly, the settled snow on the ground rose in the air.

Then the wind broke.

Screams erupted.

And an arrow protruded my betrothed's chest and another between his eyes. Those sea blue eyes blew wide before going entirely dead as he sputtered and gushed blood all over me, drenching my white veil and dress in crimson.

My limbs had frozen still.

All I could see was blood.

All I could see was blood staining me.

The faint heartbeat resounded in the air. Not my own. I could already feel and hear my own beat furiously against my ribcage. Then it just disappeared. And everything else returned full force, all the noise struck me awake from the reverie.

"Thora," Eren shouted, pushing through running bodies to reach me.

Elias was quicker, his body shielding over mine while Kilian's magic roared, searching around for whoever had made the shot.

My ears rang.

But my heartbeat calmed way too soon, my pulse steady.

Yet again, I felt nothing when I saw the man who was one vow away from becoming my forever, bleed into the white snowy floor, eyes aghast and pale blond hair stained red with blood.

Shit.

A sigh left me before I could control my expression.

"Take your sister to safety," Snow said to her son, shedding her white cloak and gathering her pale blue skirts, her face marked full of rage.

Sam did as told, grabbing Rain and fading away. Then my sister followed shortly, bolting, surely to follow after whoever had been brave enough to pull this—Iskyla.

Pulling my veil off, I followed after my soldiers, only to be held back by Eren.

I hadn't seen him in so long. And so long I'd forgotten what the sight of him did to me—all that it revoked. So much betrayal. From so many of those I loved, he was the last person I'd expected to do what he did. To leave me. When he knew being left was my biggest fear.

I no longer felt that fear.

I no longer felt much.

"They are trying to lure you out," he said calmly. "Let your soldiers and everyone else chase this." He looked into the distance at where lightning was blistering skies and earth alike, probably Snow giving a show to the Isline barbarians who already feared her more than their god—just not enough to leave me alone, apparently. But they knew she would not interfere. They knew if she interfered, another war would commence. If there had been too much to lose ten years ago, there was nothing to spare today. And Iskyla was betting on that. She was betting on a war that would spare nothing and no one. Her belief was set in that war setting history back. Making Isjord what Isjord had once been. A hub of hatred, greed and conflict mongering.

Pulling my arm from his hold, I took a step away. "I'm sure no one in a while has taken such a jab at my pride."

His brows furrowed, and I knew very well the look of disappointment he flashed me. "Your betrothed just died."

"It is not yet the funeral. I'll make sure to cry then." The wind roared, obeying my command and conjoining with the falling snow to shape a dragon of frost. The earth and sky vibrated with the shrill the ice creature let as it landed to the ground, bowing so I could climb its back. No one knew Iskyla better than I did. For five years, she and I had gotten to know each other well—very well. Instead of following the direction of lightning where Snow was dealing with the men who'd carried out the attack, I headed towards where I knew the barbarian queen was intending to strike next.

Considering my dead betrothed owed half of the coastline in Casmere, and that Iskyla had gone to great lengths to try and cast her influence and grasp access to hospitable seas, she'd gone straight to where my father in law's fleet rested. My father-in-law who she'd just made a mortal enemy out of today. Emil will want a piece in the cake I was going to make out of her, so she was planning on taking him out just like she took out his son.

Smart.

I liked smart people.

Seeing smart people stress their smart little brains with useless plans brought me joy nothing else did because despite their wit, they could never realise you couldn't beat something much greater than you.

Her badly dressed soldiers all spun their heads towards the skies when I broke between clouds and then landed just merely feet away from them. The dragons roared once, causing the ships around the port city to sway and groan in their berths, and then turned into thousands of small frost serpents. They climbed and pierced through Isline bodies until a field of blood laid ahead. Not one of the soldier's attacks made it near a mile of me.

"This was upsettingly swift," I muttered to myself as the same serpents turned into wolves and began dragging and dumping the bodies into the angry half frozen sea.

The blood soon was covered by the heavy snow that was suddenly blistering furiously, and in barely a matter of minutes, the scene ahead laid as if no one had ever stepped on it. If Iskyla was going to inconvenience me, I expected her to actually put some effort in it. She was a lousy opponent. A lousy opponent my people were beginning to think was better than me—a better Krigborn. One that wouldn't smother their greed like I had for the past ten years.

An arrow whizzed past me, missing me by a foot. I'd never been so offended when I spun to the shooter. Were these the type of soldiers Iskyla sent to hunt and kill me? "This must be a joke."

Iskyla's new general who had been taunting me the same since I killed her old general three months ago, sneered and nocked back another arrow, aiming it at me.

My hand wrapped around it before the tip landed on my forehead. About a hundred ice arrows materialised and shot in the air towards him, landing in a circle around his body. When he stopped writhing like a little squirrel, I said, "Tell your queen that there are plenty of fish in the sea, Andre. She can try to kill all the men, I'll just marry a woman. She tries to kill the women, too, I'll marry a God."

"Give her what she wants."

Give—because she couldn't take. Not without making herself a queen killer, an Usurper. No, she wanted a finer title. True Queen. True Krigborn. True daughter of Winters. She wanted those. "But what she wants is mine. You can't take what belongs to others."

"It does not belong to you."

"Iskyla wants war. War she shall not have."

He scoffed. "That is the Krigborn way. Are you truly one?"

"I wasn't updated on this family tradition I supposedly have to uphold. But, nevertheless, I really don't care."

"You're a usurper. That seat is not for you."

"My carpenter would beg to differ. He made it comfortably so it fit me best."

"Hold tightly to it if you wish to keep it."

"That is very sweet of you to worry."

He jerked back when a white ghastly figure appeared right before him. Veiled entirely in a white cloak that floated as if the ground held no gravity, the creature wrapped a hand around his neck, lifting Iskyla's general up from the ground, sputtering and turning entirely too red for his own good. A frost vortex wrapped around them, cutting and tearing into the general until he was just tiny little snack pieces for seagulls.

The White Veil turned and simply bowed its head to me before vanishing into thin air. My newest mysterious ally. Perhaps my biggest at the moment. There was no one better than a godly cautionary tale. There was no one better than a vengeful spirit blessed by our Winter God to join my side. No one knew why it had returned now after centuries, or why it was on my side, but they knew to fear it.

After the guardian war, Isjordians feared nothing more than godly tales. So much so that I'd been left with no choice but to reopen and invest into building new temples everywhere.

Guards were on a strange edge when I returned back to the castle, probably meaning that whoever had just composed that attack had been amongst their ranks and they had either been taken by surprise, or known and just ignored it.

Kilian had kneeled beside Erik, studying the arrow still etched in his skull. He cast me a glance when I stood beside him and looked down at the man who'd been a sentence away from becoming my husband.

"Perhaps it was the best option for him," I said. "He would have eventually wanted out of the marriage. Erik was too proud to be my toy."

Lightning struck nearby. Snow was angry. Very angry. "Lucky bastards," my sister gritted out, dropping and sprawling on a chair. "They had gotten the kiss of death before I could give them some affection of my own kind."

"A what?" Nia asked, sending me a concerned look as she pulled her daughter, Karin, behind her.

"Kiss?" his familiar deep voice called, and my spine steeled up straight. "I wasn't that gentle, was I now, sister-in-law?"

Had my ingenuine grief made me hallucinate?

When the air fried and then thawed from the presence of his magic, I startled to my senses, my eyes slowly lifting to where he stood, leaning against the white flower archway at the start of the altar with his arms crossed over his chest.

No, he was really here.

Different, but it was him.

The scars on his right eye had grown slightly fainter, but there was a new one over his lips, and another thick one just over his brow. His hair was longer. His body had grown harder, bigger, almost taller, too. Perhaps older as well, there was a hint of grey on his temples despite his young appearance. His fingers and neck were now covered in dark tattoos. And his smile, just as dark and twisted, just as taunting, the only thing that had remained the same. I wish it had not. I had once loved that smile. Don't know if I could extend that sentiment to the rest of him.

"Little bird, if you stare at me any harder, I might just turn into stone," he said, even though he was looking at me just as intently—maybe even more.

Little bird.

Years.

Not months.

Not weeks or days.

It had been years since he had let me see him. Every spring when he returned to Dardanes from Seraphim, he came and went like summer rain. At night or on the hottest days when I couldn't bear scorching daylight, when I hid from it, when I hid from the world. Missing me intentionally as if he knew I was parched. Just as quickly as he came, he left, only touches of wet soil remained behind in the morning after, reminding me that I'd not imagined the feel or the touch of cool wet longing. Then, almost five years ago, he stopped coming altogether. He'd disappeared without trace and left only drought behind.

"I was expecting an invitation," he said, pushing from the wall. The moment he took a step forward, I unconsciously took one back, and he stopped moving when he noticed, his gaze hardening.

The thing was, I no longer missed rain. No longer desired for it. I could douse heat myself—with blistering ice. I looked between my sister and him, scolding my heart and schooling my expression. "Where are the men?"

He raised a brow, waiting a while before answering me, "Dead. Were we aiming for another outcome, Your Majesty?"

The wind felt cold. My skin felt cold. And I couldn't even feel cold. I turned to Snow, not trusting myself to say something I wouldn't regret. "All Iskyla's?" *Any mine?*

My sister nodded and I saw the rage she barely held behind a thin curtain suddenly burning and tearing and screaming to be let out. "Two words, Rora. Just two. Tell me to kill her."

Little did she know that only two words also held me back from doing the same. Fear. Panic. None of mine. My people had enough fear and panic.

Sam faded next to her, he breathed a sigh of relief as his gold and silver eyes raked over his mother, then they went wide when they landed on his uncle. "Uncle Mal?"

Malik opened his arms wide. "Missed me or what?"

Sam flew into his embrace, almost knocking him over.

He groaned, tossing him in the air like he was still three. "Hells, you've grown."

"A natural process that occurs through the years," my nephew said blankly, straightening himself. "Says quite a bit, doesn't it, uncle?"

Malik shot a look at Kilian who was wearing the strangest expression. "I was hoping you'd taken more from your mother's traits."

My nephew blinked between us all, seemingly confused. "Would you prefer it if I zapped you alive with electricity for disappearing these past five years?"

Snow nodded proudly at herself.

"Never mind," Malik said, ruffling his dark hair, and looking between the small crowd. "Where is your sister?"

"Fell asleep with Memphis. I'll go get her."

Kilian pushed forward and tipped his chin at his brother, a cold, unforgiving look falling over his eyes—he'd been the most heartbroken after Malik's disappearance. "Maybe we all will go now," he said, wrapping an arm around my shoulders. "It has been a long day for all of us, especially for Thora."

It hadn't, in fact, it had just gotten easier for me now that Erik was dead, but I nodded and glanced back at my dead betrothed sprawled on the ground, still bleeding. Kneeling before him, I shut his eyelids and ran a finger over his face. "I'm sorry," I whispered. "You deserved someone who would have wailed at this sight."

2

GREY MYRTLE

THORA

E lias and Oryn had not stopped talking and discussing for a solid second since they
came to crowd my room. Only Skadi looked pretty satisfied with the outcome,
leaning against a far wall, her eyes closed as she hummed some old tune in old Ysolt.

We were back at square one. And square one was pretty far to be in considering Elias
had taken months to scour Erik and push word of the power that would sit to reign over
Isjord once I'd marry him.

My white silk dress was stained with droplets of ruby, the last memory of what would
have been a doomed marriage. Somehow, I couldn't make myself take it off. Maybe
part of me had hoped that Erik and I would have what my sister had. Maybe I was
disappointed.

But the maybes faded away pretty quickly.

The Isline queen had finally struck inside my own walls. That did not bother me
as much as the fact that she'd managed to get her followers so close to my castle. Near
my family. Snow and her children had been sitting not even a few feet from where the
arrow had struck. A thought that had me shoot up to my feet. If her soldiers were now
disguising between mine—

"You're thinking of doing something irrational, I know that particular look," Oryn
commented, bringing me out of my daze that had somehow ignored time. It was dark
outside when it had been bright just a second ago. How long had we sat in my room for?

"To me it looks rather well calculated and rather delayed," Elias added, sending me a
look. *Fight ice with ice,* he'd told me five years ago when Sigurd Krigborn had died. *Iskyla
will not be gentle like wind. Why be wind?*

Oryn sighed, rubbing his eyes. "Thora, you have handled this situation thus far with
far too much precision to be swayed and act impulsively at this moment."

My bedroom doors swung open, and Snow stood there, a deep frown etched in her
forehead. "What is that you don't want her to do? I'll do it."

Sam walked up to me, his little face that he'd inherited from his father scrunched up
a little at my dress before his ever-composed face slipped back on. "My condolences,
aunt."

"Condolences alright," my sister scoffed, crossing her arms. "How did that bitch get
someone so close to you?"

"Ma," Sam quietly warned, taking a seat by the window, staring at the approaching
night.

Snow blinked a little. "Don't tell your father you heard me say that."

"Heard you say what?" Kilian asked, coming from behind her, his daughter's strange doll in his hand. He didn't leave her side, not a step or a full breath away unless it was for their children.

Nia pushed into the room just after him and gave me a tight hug. "I'm really sorry for your loss, Thora."

I wasn't. Not as much as I should be. The idea that I had to marry an Isjordian man to be perceived as more of an Isjordian never settled well with me. And the fact that I could only garner my people's respect by sitting a king next to my throne even less. Frankly, Erik's hand and power in Isjordian diamond trade never had boded well with me either. He was rich, filthy rich, and coin could practically buy you anything in Isjord.

Kilian's brows jerked up and he bit a smile back before Snow noticed it—he knew my truth and was trying to respect the fact that I didn't particularly want it to be known. Was I even trying to hide it?

"Let me solve this," Snow said, all threat and menace.

Nia stepped forward, "And involve not only Olympia and Adriata, but a guardian too? Do you know what that means? Are you ready to fight a holy war again?"

"Holy war?" my sister asked, her gaze sharpening. "They touched my family. There will be no holy war. Only unholy slaughter."

"There is power that lays restless in Íslines," Nia said, shaking her head. "Unleashed, it could do as much damage as Aurora did. This is why the other Krigborn are so fearlessly tempting us. Uncle Sigurd warned me, he was fearful that this would happen. This was why he held onto this life so hard after he fell sick, he knew what would happen once he'd die." She turned to me. "There are many other Krigborn who will claim the same as Iskyla, it will be never ending. This has to settle somehow. Without involving war."

"What war exactly would it be?" I asked, filling myself a glass of wine. "Would it be a fight to protect Isjordians or enslave them? They certainly don't feel the need to be protected as they see Iskyla as a possible monarch, not a threat. And do I wish to enslave?" The sip of wine tasted almost like water from the bitter words that I spoke. "I promised peace and prosperity. They do not want peace and prosperity. They want what Iskyla is willing to give them. Exalt. True Krigborn exalt led by wars and claims of power that echoes through the realm. They constantly fear now that their military is merely decor for our borders, they feel anxious that I don't call their children forward at sixteen to have them stripped of humanity so they can serve me blindly and fanatically, they are displeased that I offer their women education and not allow them to marry their daughters off at merely fifteen. They think me weak—"

"That is not true," Elias said.

I turned to him. "Then tell me, Lord Venzor, why so many men wish to see me gone?"

"Ten years is a short time to adjust to such new rules when they've abided by the old ones since the dawn of time. The new generation raised by your rule will soon come into power."

I set my empty glass down. "Maybe I should just get rid of all the old. It will make this move quicker." My eyes flashed at the idea of lining them all up and painting my white gardens red. Smiling, I added, "You all need to loosen up. Was just poking a little fun."

Snow looked disappointed, but the rest were relieved.

Filling a glass of water, I kneeled before my sister. "How is my little niece?"

"Nephew, apparently. Visha confirmed it last night." She swung the water down and then grabbed my hand to place it over her rounded stomach. "And he is feisty."

"I can see," I said, laughing when little movement grazed my palm.

"Should you be smiling like that on this very grey day?"

The room went abnormally quiet, and I froze at the sound of that voice I thought I'd forgotten until today. My smile slipped away when I lifted my attention to the door, at where he stood leaning against, a glass in hand.

Not all had changed apparently.

That still made my heart ache just a little despite everything.

His head tilted to the side, and he studied me top to bottom, slowly and attentively, swirling his drink around. Something I was wearing clearly displeased him because his face did that thing when he was angry—it turned into sculpted threat and honey coloured anger.

"Have you come to offer me your condolences?" I finally managed to gather my voice to ask. "For losing my betrothed."

His eyes dropped to my dress again. "Why for? You didn't lose anything you didn't want lost, little bird."

My pulse chilled, the cold trying to keep me calm. "Have I become your enemy?"

The glass he held stopped at his lips for a moment before he set it down on a table entirely, abandoning it to come inside the room. "Why would you say that?"

"Why are you reading me? You once said that the only privacy you violate was that of your brother and your enemies. Have I become your enemy?"

Snow chuckled and Kilian glared at his brother who had his entire attention on me as if he was seeing me for the first ever time. The older Castemont shook his head and picked up his sleepy son from the sofa. "Come, my love, let's put you both to sleep. These two can bicker all night if they wish."

"Actually," I said, standing to my feet. "You can put your brother to sleep too, Kilian. My appetite for banter has been exhausted."

"Lucky for you," Malik said, slipping further inside the room and invading what little space left that bore none of his presence—I'd made sure of it, made sure I'd burnt everything that reminded me of him. "I know how to rouse that urge."

The door slammed shut after everyone made a hasty exit, closing us together inside the room. His shadows leaned against it, towering as he was towering over me. They were just as quiet as he was being. "Were you going to really marry that poor soul?"

So many things I wanted to say, so many things I wanted him to say to me, yet he was here to mock me just like that last day before he left.

"That poor soul cared for me, liked me, and treated me kindly," I told him. "I would have not only married him, I would have made him my family, given him children and probably grown old with him."

He slowly nodded and backed away towards the door to lean against it, the move making me feel trapped all of the sudden. "Then I perhaps should offer you my condolences. Losing such an enticing business deal must indeed hurt."

"Why are you here?" After all this time? Why did he have to come back after all this time? Just when I'd gotten used to the fact that he was never coming back.

"Needed to make sure you weren't sharing my secrets with anyone."

He wasn't even trying to lie properly. "All your secrets are safe. Erik died."

"Are you saying you would have told him my secrets? Did he mean so much to you?"

"Yes," I lied.

I had lied perfectly. It had been the one lie I'd perfected in front of the mirror until I'd convinced everyone into believing—even Erik. I'd almost fooled Kilian and Snow, too.

His mouth twitched into a ghost of a smirk, not even trying to fall for my lie like everyone else was—they all wanted to believe I would and could fall in love. "I see."

"Get out, Malik. Actually, just leave again. And don't come back this time." That feeling of suffocation was wrapping like a noose around my neck, and I reached to undo the buttons at the back of my dress, needing it off my body so I could breathe.

He pushed from where he leaned and came to face me, a hand raising to my face, not touching but slowly ghosting over my skin and down my jaw. "Turn around."

Reluctantly, I did only so I didn't have to look at him any longer, gathering all my hair with a hand so he didn't touch me where I didn't want him to touch me.

His fingers were warm against my cold skin, and I'd never hated anything quite like I hated how it still hummed for him. "Did you love him?"

Sucking in a shaky breath, I said, "Yes."

"You cared for him?"

The air in the room cooled. "Yes."

"And you let him touch you?" he asked, his hand stopped pulling on the buttons and he drew a finger down my now exposed spine.

"I did," I breathed.

"And you touched him back?"

My eyes drew shut. "Yes."

He stepped closer to me, seizing what little air was left around me, his chest brushing against my back when he leaned to murmur in my ear. "I thought I'd taught you to lie better."

Was it entertaining to him? Was it funny to him that I craved to be happy to the point of madness? "I might have not loved him, nor cared for him, nor let him touch me or even touched him back, yet he would have gotten everything." Turning to him, I said, "Me and everything that came with being his." I pushed the dress off my shoulders, pulling one arm at a time until I was left in only a thin lacy white bra that Erik had gifted me. "I would have lied about loving him so perfectly, Malik, so utterly perfect. I would have put on my best show and made him the happiest man there is. Without loving, caring, touching him. He would have gone insane from happiness. I would have made it so. Because I wanted him to. I was going to give him everything. Make him my everything." Tilting my head back to look at him, I asked, "Was that a lie?"

He didn't answer me.

He was so silent all of a sudden.

Perhaps he'd always been like that.

I'd always been the one to never stop talking. Maybe I'd been the one to fill whatever void he created between us. So desperately to the point I'd made a fool out of myself.

"If you're quite done, leave."

Like a wolf looking at a strange prey for the first time, his head tilted to the side. "Are you happy, Thora?"

No matter how hard I swallowed, that lump of discomfort remained in my throat, and my voice came out too small and too broken when I replied, "Delirious." Just for him, I forced myself to smile. "Hope fate has not been as kind to you."

He chuckled, eyes raking over my blood-stained dress still hooked around my waist and the lace bra that was more lace than bra. "Heartbroken to upset you, little bird, but I've never been happier."

"How disappointing."

"I'll grow back on you."

"Like thorns and barbed wire. As always. Suffocating anything near you."

"I knew you'd turn around." He backed towards the door, eyes never leaving mine. "You looked hideous today."

"Flattered. Truly."

"Preposterous, actually, since you're fishing for compliments."

"Still very glad we repulse one another."

He pointed to my dress. "Put that back on and let's put you in front of a boiling cauldron and I'm hard as a rock."

It had been a while since anyone spoke to me as he did without consequence, so I just stood there gaping at him. At the audacity of him.

He found my reaction funny because he laughed. "Seems the Isjordian boy has been all soft on you." His smile was cruel. "But let's not speak ill of the dead."

"I've spoken ill of you every day."

"You've thought of me every day?" He grinned as he backed towards the door, the shadows sliding off the walls and sinking into the rest of the room. "Don't think about me too hard. And don't think about murdering me in my sleep. Rain and Sam are having a sleepover tonight."

"There is always tomorrow."

"There is. Dying tomorrow seems good."

"I'll prepare the decree."

"You do that, little bird."

"Don't call me that," I said, and he hissed when the door handle froze under his hold. Blowing on his hand, he made a show to bow widely. "Yes, Your Majesty."

"Clown," I whispered under my breath.

"Pretty bird," he murmured back, and then faded away.

3

VIOLET DAISIES

MALIK

Every shadow inside Tenebrose had stopped and was currently standing very still as I felt for hers. Thora had remained in one place for the past hour, by her window. Her silhouette casting the most perfect shadow onto the dark night outside. I could have forgotten everything else, but I'd never be able to forget that. How many days and nights had I spent chasing that same shadow. Sometimes without her even knowing.

She was angry with me. And she had all the right. How would I tell she could be angry at me as much as she wanted, but she also had to forgive me for whatever reason she was angry at me. I couldn't understand how she was angry at me for leaving. How can anyone be angry about losing dead weight? On the contrary, she should have been the happiest I'd forced myself to leave, that she could finally be rid of what was holding her down. I just wished the fact that she was this angry about it didn't make me grin to myself like a lunatic, wondering if she had missed me, if she had thought about me to the point of madness like I had.

I sighed, trying to roll on my bed and failing because of the two who had squeezed me between them. "Is this necessary?" I asked.

Sam shifted to look at me, and so did his sister on the other side of my bed. "It is a sleepover."

"I never agreed to it."

Rain scooted closer, yawning, her big bright grey eyes boring into me all innocence, glistening and beady. If she had not blinked when I met her earlier, I would have thought she was not real. "Can we not? I like sleepovers."

I sighed again. "Anything for you, baby doll."

It went all silent for a while, but both had not stopped staring at me.

"What now?" I asked, looking between both of them.

"Aunt Thora really doesn't like you, do you know that?" Sam whispered, and Rain nodded, yawning again and pulling close to her chest the creepiest three limbed doll with three strands of yarn for hair and only one button for an eye. The second she was asleep, it was going outside in a burning pile. Right after a Crafter exorcised it.

"Your aunt and I are friends," I said, covering Rain and her doll with a blanket so the button eye was not staring directly at me.

"*Were*," Sam said. "You used the incorrect tense."

For the uncountable time tonight, I sighed once again. "Don't read people. It's rude."

"It's not. No one knows when I do it. That's the polite thing to do."

Rain threw a small arm around my neck, suddenly overtaken with sleep. Gods, how could a small child snore this loudly.

"She didn't want to marry Erik," Sam said. "I liked Erik. He rarely lied. He didn't hide how he felt. And he liked my aunt. He liked her a lot."

"He did?" I asked, trying not to sound too detached.

"Does it matter?" he asked, laying on his back and staring at the ceiling with a look eerily similar to my brother's—unfeeling and cold. The curse of the Castemont's had not skipped him either though I'd really prayed it had. "He's dead now."

"Sam—"

"I know what death is, what it means. And ma already spoke to me about it, she told me what it should mean to me, too. You don't have to say anything."

Noise blared outside of the castle walls, and I jerked upright.

"Go," Sam said, lifting a cloud of black around the room. "Rain and I are safe. I know how to keep us safe."

He suddenly resembled another Castemont boy I knew—a boy who had told me that same sentence many times before when I'd been afraid.

Once I made sure to have shadows circling their room, I ran out, searching down the corridors filled with guards all rushing outside. Two massive shadows fell over the castle grounds poorly lit by bland moonlight and some odd torches on the far walls. The frost dragons pierced through the angry skies heading for the city and dozens of wolves prowled towards the castle gates at her command, so she couldn't be far.

"What happened?" I asked a guard.

"They set the northern halls on fire."

"What's in the northern halls?"

He swallowed. "It's where the Tenebrose Academy has classes on Fridays. Our queen lends it to the students."

"Why would they attack that area?"

"The queen...she's quite fond of the children."

A planned attack, and someone who is close enough to her to know where to attack and how to get inside the castle unnoticed.

She stood at the top of a wall tower, on the narrow edge, barely wearing anything, her long dark hair violently floating in the chilling wind, not letting me see where exactly her gaze had landed below in the city. There was nothing behind that look.

It was empty.

Too empty to belong to her.

Too empty to belong to the woman who used to possess so much colour that not even nature had.

She lifted a bare foot forward and then jumped from the tall tower, a gust of wind carrying her and making her landing soft.

"Hells, Thora," I muttered, fading just below and behind her.

Isjordians still roaming the city halted in their tracks and many others started coming out of their homes to watch her walk their streets, more giant ice wolves materialising behind her and spreading around the city. She'd gotten so much better at doing that. Her connection to the ice creatures was precise to the point she could give them life entirely, not just command them.

Isjordians looked among one another. Some unsure, some frightened, some unphased yet curious.

Thora didn't move one bit, not even lift a finger. Her eyes found me in the distance where I was watching her, leaning against the shadow of a building. She was looking at me, but she was not seeing me. Her stare was entirely lost into a void—a void I had never seen her lose herself into before.

"What have you done, Rora?" I murmured, narrowing my eyes on her.

Her wolves of ice returned. One of them holding a man between its jaws.

The creature threw the limp body to her feet. Still somehow alive.

She breathed so slow, almost as if she wasn't breathing at all. Not one word, not one movement, her eyes glued on the man with broken bones and skin, laying on the ground glaring at her.

"Get up," she ordered, and his muscles suddenly twitched and he groaned, not from pain, but utter terror. The sounds slowly turned into whimpers and pleas as he got to his feet—his broken feet held by broken knees and a broken spine.

How was he standing?

My shadows spread, searching for signs of dark craft, magic of any sort, anything to explain what I was seeing, only to return without answers. The man was moving on his own will.

"I will not bow before you," he bellowed in Old Ysolt.

"I do not need men like you to bow to me or stand beneath me. I do not need men like you to fear me. I do not need men like you at all," she said. "I do not need to kill men like you. I don't care to kill men like you. You'll do it yourself. Like the rest of you will."

The man plucked a dagger from his baldric, shakily raising the blade to his throat and sliced it through. Even after he'd choked on his own blood, stopped spurting and breathing, he remained on his feet, his lifeless eyes blown wide as they focused on her, the fear still fresh in them.

"It is late," she said to the crowd when the body collapsed to the ground. "You all might return to your homes. No more of them will make it in or out of Tenebrose after tonight. You have my promise."

Most seemed to believe her, trust her, too.

Others were still staring in disbelief at the man.

At what she'd done.

I walked behind her as she made her way back inside the castle walls, alone, barefooted and undressed, not a single guard to protect her in sight. Not once did she turn around or look around or acknowledge anyone she passed, not even when she made it to the castle wall gate. If the soldiers had not been quick to open them, she would have crashed against them. If the skies had fallen to the ground, Thora wouldn't have noticed.

Elias came running in her direction. Panic. Panic in his face and in his shadows. "Hey. Thora!" he called a bit louder, shedding his jacket and throwing it around her shoulders. Something in the way he began searching her eyes chilled my blood, as if he was looking for something that had disappeared. "Thora!"

There was a long beat of silence from everyone after his outburst. Every soldier had turned to look at their queen, and I rose a wall of deep shadows to mask her. That must have drawn her attention, because her head tipped up in their direction just slightly.

"You know that hurts my ears, right?" Thora said casually, shaking off the jacket and throwing it at him. "And your cologne hurts my lungs. Maybe that is what's warding Visha off, have you ever thought of that?"

Elias sighed. His shoulders straightened and his features returned to stone when he noticed me standing near them.

But I didn't mind the attention.

Not his.

I minded my brother's. The attention that had fallen on Thora as he walked to her. My brother rarely showed the concern he felt, but he was showing it now. "Sam notified us. You're coming to Adriata with me, and you will remain there until this is solved."

Elias nodded. "I agree. There are obviously traitors among our ranks and we've been incapable of making this a home for you."

"I don't," Thora said. "They don't want to kill me, Elias."

"No," he said. "They want to do something worse. Humiliate you in front of your whole kingdom."

"Didn't feel that in the least," she said, patting away some of the falling snow from the top of her head.

Sam cleared his throat, startling Thora when he faded by her side. "Mother says you either come with us, or she will drag you to Adriata herself."

Thora smiled at him. "Those weren't the exact words, were they?"

"Mother's vocabulary is much richer than mine."

Elias glanced over his shoulder at me, frowning. "You've aged."

That seemed to draw everyone's attention to me. Her's, too, because she stilled.

"Have you not come across a mirror these days?" I threw back.

"Nice hair."

"Nice nose. Want me to break it, pretty boy?"

He grinned. "Aw, you find me pretty?"

"The witch you're obsessed with doesn't."

He put a hand to his chest, offended. "She finds me gorgeous."

"Put words in my mouth again and I'll cut your tongue," Visha said, slipping from a portal behind me, and Elias paled. She cast me a short glance. "Was hoping the word of your return was a drunk babble."

I grinned at Elias, pushing past him and towards the woman who had continued her mindless walk inside the castle. "How do you feel that she likes me more than you?"

From the way her whole body stiffened and how her steps began almost faltering, she'd sensed me following her.

"Thora."

She flinched even though my tone had been gentle—it had always been gentle with her.

"I'll take you to Adriata," I said, keeping a small distance between us.

"No need," she said, stopping by her bedroom door and pushing it open.

Neo stood in the middle of her room, only half dressed. "You're really back." His reaction morphed from confusion to something else, something almost resembling anger. I didn't want to read him. No. If I knew he was angry about my return, I'd want to know why the man I had once considered close enough to be a brother would be angry to see me back.

Thora picked up and put on a robe. "Take me to Adriata," she said to him.

And then I had to watch her reach for his hand. I had to watch him touch her when I knew she hated to be touched. I stood there watching her in the same arms I had pushed her to.

"What?" Elias asked, appearing behind me. "Upset?"

He put a hand on my chest when I tried to go past him. "I think you should leave, Malik. Really. She'd been doing just fine."

Had the world really been so much better without me in it? "It didn't look like it."

"So what? You'll fix it? I don't think you're capable of that."

"What do you know what I am capable of?"

"Only what you're incapable of."

"How did she puppet a man to his feet?"

"I don't know what you're talking about."

I chuckled at his poor attempt at lying to an Empath. "And this White Veil I'm hearing people talk about?"

He took a step back and gave me a look that faintly resembled anger. It was hard to be angry and lie at the same time. "You've been digging around?"

"You know what I am, Elias. You've known before even knowing me. Do you think I just trained men all day and waited for some war or battle to show at my door? Who do you think did all of my brother's dirty work?"

"Why does this interest you?"

"*She* interests me."

"Why now all of this sudden interest? She's been queen for ten years. Dealt with shit like this for ten years. Where were you then?"

"I'm here now." Patting his shoulder, I said, "And I have not a single intention of ever leaving again."

4

WHITE TULIPS

Malik

I f there was one thing that made me feel right at home, it was the Adriatian council. Though Moon and Night Court had quietened in the presence of my sister-in-law, they'd not stopped glaring and huffing at one another. Currently, Moon Court stood dissatisfied with my brother's young minds that outvoted some odd regulations on shrimp fishing near Lyran shores—all the interesting and important stuff. Sometimes, I wondered if my brother instructed his side of the council to oppose Moon Court just for the fun of it. That little gleam that crossed his eyes at the banter was telling enough.

Just when Snow was about to doze off from boredom, Kilian announced, "That's enough for today." He pushed me back on my seat when I was about to stand and get the hells out of there. "Stay. The Fire Queen is here to see you."

"Why do you assume she is here to see me?"

My brother gave me an unamused look and then picked up a sleeping Snow from her chair before fading away.

Alyone waited for everyone to leave the room before she spoke, "You didn't stay for long after your return to Heyes. You ran like you'd caught fire before your feet had touched my palace for a day." When I didn't say anything, she continued, "What were the odds her betrothed would die? You must have been glad you were late and the job was finished for you."

"You came all the way to Adriata to tell me that?"

She looked around the empty meeting room. "You blame me for no reason. I didn't mean to keep the news of her marriage from you."

"Twice I asked you. Twice I *begged* you to tell me if you had heard from her. You drugged me on medicine and lied right after I was too numb to think."

"You were gone for five years. No trace. No sign. No word. Five years locked away in that portal with no way to find you, I didn't think of it as a priority especially when you turned up as injured as you did." She stepped closer to me. "Making sure you were out of danger and treated was my priority."

"I would have crawled to her if necessary, even dead," I said, propping my feet up on the meeting table. "Not good enough of an excuse."

"We all assumed you wanted to crawl away from her, not to her. Considering how you disappeared."

"You're also assuming that I disappeared on purpose. Why are you actually assuming at all, Alyone? We weren't friends. We were barely even allies." Those years I spent in Hayes, I spent drunk or drowned in work. Any work I could find. She just happened to witness one too many of my struggles at keeping my sanity intact enough to work through my issues and return to my bird.

"You had just come back from visiting Adriata the day you disappeared, and then you went into that portal without reappearing for five long years, Malik. Every time you came back from visiting your home, the man I knew you to be was gone. That last time was different, I could see it. You went inside that portal without mentioning a single word."

"The only one I owe any explanation on my whereabouts is the throne I serve."

Her face fell a little, and she frowned. "Are you saying you went in there on your brother's orders? Snowlin's, perhaps?"

"As I said."

She nodded. "When will you return to Heyes?"

"I'm not returning this time, Alyone."

Her eyes dropped to the ground as if that would hide the disappointment from her shadows. "It can't be final. You always change your mind. You see her and you will change your mind. And you know that you're always welcome in my kingdom," she said, turning to leave.

"You said I was late," I said. "I'm never late."

Alyone stopped by the doors, realisation flashing through her shadows.

Truth was, I had not made it in time to see the aftermath of her doomed marriage. I'd made it exactly in time to see the shooter take aim at her betrothed and then shoot him right between his eyes. Then I leisurely followed him towards the Sable Abyss forest, thanked him and then skinned his soul right off the bones for even thinking he could get that close to her without consequence.

The sun. I'd missed the Adriatian sun the most. Seraphim skies were still covered in thick grey fog. Though most had cleared already since after the war ten years ago, the air was still somewhat stale and the sun not warm, not bright either. And the past few days I'd spent...*spying* on my little bird had made me a little appreciative of the small luxury that Adriatian warmth was.

I laid back on the garden bench, squinting at the skies when a shade fell over me.

"What are you doing?" my brother asked, holding a sack of soil up on his shoulder. "Thought you came to help?"

"I am helping. Moral support. Keep doing whatever you do. Dig and stuff."

He raised a brow and dropped the soil sack near a ploughed patch. "Moral support? For me or you?"

"Less talking, more of that," I said, downing the lemonade Rain had made me, wincing at the bitter taste. "Crescent heaven. Have you introduced your child to the concept of sugar, or is that the evil nowadays?"

He pulled at the edges of his shirt and threw it over at the bench where I sat. "So, what moral support do I or you need?"

I let out a low whistle. "How do you still look like that at your fatherly age?"

He looked up at me, his expression all grave and much too stern. "We fuck a lot."

I coughed out my bitter drink, sputtering it all over me, while the bastard had a crooked smirk on his mouth as he continued his farming activities.

"Thought you and Snow would have finished that army of Castemonts by now," I said, shaking my wet shirt. "Eight, wasn't it?"

When his whole body turned rigid and all shadows surrounding us suddenly stiffened, I leaned on my knees to study that funny reaction. "Will you tell me what that was about, or should I ask Snow?"

He gave me a hard glare. Which, the more I looked at it, the more I realised that it wasn't directed at me. "Rain."

"As in your child or the weather?"

"Snow got really sick carrying Rain." He swallowed, his eyes darkening until the whole white and grey was a deep black. "It almost killed her at birth."

I knew. That is why I left five years ago. But Snow didn't want him to know just yet and the secret was eating at me.

He gave me that concerned look. "Are you alright?"

"Not really, but at least I'm still funny as hells despite."

"Papa," Rain screamed from somewhere in the garden and my brother faded and then returned with his little daughter in his arms.

He smacked a few big kisses on her round cheek. "Find your gloves and help me plant the tulips? Your uncle is not being useful."

She nodded and sprinted to the shed to return with a pair of small gloves in her hand. Of course he'd gotten her into this whole business. "Uncle, put my gloves on," she said, handing them to me. "Be useful."

My brother was raising demons in the making. "Where is my please?" I asked.

She giggled and squealed when I pretended to bite at her fingers. "Please, uncle."

"Well done, baby doll."

Rain ran to Kil's side and kneeled beside her father, watching him and poorly mimicking what he was doing. There was no containing Kil's happiness. Not from his shadows, nor from his face that had lit up with a grin.

I glanced up at the hot skies again and frowned. "Where is Snow?"

"With uncle Nubil," Rain said, trying to push a bunch of her dark hair away from her face and failing.

Kil pulled his gloves off and fixed her hair, securing the two tails tightly on top of her head. "Caelum. She's sat in on a meeting with them."

"Since when?" I asked, watching Rain sprint away to fetch the small pots of flowers from the green house.

My brother's jaw almost snapped from how tight it was set. "A day ago."

I raised a brow at him. "A whole day. How on Numen have you survived without wagging your tail at your wife for a whole day?"

A shadow knocked me hard behind my head. "That fucker needs to understand that our children miss her."

I chuckled. "The children miss her, huh?"

"My, my," Snow cooed, coming into the garden space. "Have I been summoned?"

Kil shot up to his feet, eyes wide. "You're back."

His wife frowned and glared at him. "Should you be so happy?"

My brother cleared his throat and tucked away his smile. "No, I shouldn't, should I?"

I held back my laughter, and my brother shot me a quick glare.

"Well," she said, looking around. "Will you not be greeting me either?"

Like that, Kil dropped everything and ran to her, gathering her body close to his and kissing her.

"Mother of skies," I murmured to myself when he began all but eating her face and pressing himself to her.

"Mama," Rain screamed once again, dropping the little flowerpot she carried and running to her parents.

Kil hoisted their little girl up and the three shared a long, long embrace. For a second,

I almost felt bitter.

When I cleared my throat, my brother looked at me with some strange realisation, and then sat his daughter on my lap. "Will you stay with uncle, my little princess? Your ma and I need to...talk for a moment."

Horny, lying piece of shit. "Don't be too loud."

He shot me a look over his shoulder and smirked. "I never raise my voice during arguments, brother. It's her you got to tell," the bastard said, pointing to his scowling wife who was about to undress him right then and there.

Before she could say anything, he pressed his mouth to hers and both faded out of sight.

"Is ma in trouble?" Rain asked, blinking those thick dark lashes at me. "Daddy gets really upset when she leaves."

Motherfu— "No, sweet baby, she's fine."

She nodded and then pushed off my lap to resume her work in the garden. She was her father's shadow. Both of them were. Sam was even worse perhaps. Speaking of demon number one, where was that child?

After she was done planting her tulips, she remained transfixed before the flowers, touching the tip of her gloved fingers on the colourful petals and then pulling her hand away, sighing and lowering her little chubby face with sadness.

"What is it?" I asked, standing and kneeling beside her.

"I can't touch them, uncle. Things die when I touch them."

I stood there silent for a moment, feeling another sort of dread fill my mind. Had she started manifesting her magic this early? Even Kil had been older. "What do you mean, baby doll?"

She finally raised her eyes to mine. "I don't have nice magic like mama or auntie Rora. Not even like papa. I have bad magic. I made Memphis sick," she silently murmured. "I touched M and made her sick. I cannot touch the flowers because I make them sick. I really love flowers, uncle. I really love Memphis, too. I didn't mean to do it."

Why had her father not told me about this? I'd been back for almost a week, and he had not mentioned a fucking thing.

"What if I tell you that your papa used to have the same bad magic?"

She went quiet and her grey eyes went wide. "He did? But he doesn't kill flowers."

"He used to."

"How did it stop?" she asked, her voice hopeful, her eyes almost teary.

In no way I will ever allow anyone to show you how. I pulled her gloves off and held her small hands in mine—they were so, so small. "How about I teach you?"

"Papa is already teaching me."

I hated how my blood chilled at those words. Not when I knew my brother couldn't be him, not when I knew Kil was nothing like our father. "He is?"

She nodded and then frowned up at me. "Why are you sad, uncle? Did I make you sad?"

"No, I was just remembering something."

Dinner was almost too silent. The kids were with Alaric, and Snow had stuffed her mouth with food, only quietly glancing between my brother and me.

"What?" Kilian finally snapped, cutting through his meal.

"You didn't tell me about Rain's training."

"I have it handled."

"Would you have locked her down there too?" I regretted the words the second I even thought of them.

He stopped eating and lowered his fork down before rolling his now black eyes up at me. "What did you say?"

"Kil," Snow called, putting a hand over his, and my brother's eyes unveiled from magic.

"How did you have it handled?" I asked.

"Why so curious, brother? All of a sudden."

"She is my niece."

"She was when she was born, on her first birthday, the day she first spoke and walked and cried and laughed. She's been your niece on those occasions too. Yet, this is what interests you the most?"

Snow closed her eyes and sighed. "Kil, please. I'll explain."

"She is like me and you. You think one can simply train our kind of magic?" I asked.

"There we are," he said, stretching back in his seat and levelling a cold look on me. "You think I'll do to her what our father did to us. Because you always have thought of me to be like him, haven't you?"

He was not wrong.

I had.

Many times.

But not just him.

Some part of me will always believe that we were brutalised beyond the point we saw the violence we inflict. That at some point, we became blind to our own violence. The abused will become the abuser without them even realising.

Snow's head turned to me and I had to look away from seeing the heartbreak written in her face. My gaze landed on steps reaching our table, on the light rose coloured silk slippers peeking from under the heavy fabric of the modest navy dress she wore—I never remembered her wearing such dull colours or such frumpy fabrics.

Thora bowed her crowned head to my brother and then went to hug her sister before quietly taking a seat on Kil's left. "I thought we'd be alone," she commented, laying a piece of cloth on her lap as her food was being served before her.

My hands itched to drag her chair closer to me. "You mind my presence that much?"

"I mind it when it disturbs those I love," she snapped, the air chilling entirely and making our breaths mist. "If you must ruin, Malik, keep ruining yourself, not others. You've done plenty of that already."

Snow's eyes widened on her sister. "Rora—"

"You two might think you owe him decency, but I owe him nothing," she replied courtly, cutting though her food.

She'd changed.

She'd changed so much.

My eyes were telling me that she was the same girl who bore all my deepest and darkest secrets like they were the most precious things she'd ever beheld, but my soul recognised the damage it had done.

"I'm afraid your peace will be disturbed a while longer," I said, reaching for my cup of water, needing to hold something to stop the shake of my hands.

Her cutlery hissed against the porcelain, and she stared ahead at nothing for a brief moment before continuing through her meal. Saying nothing.

"Won't you ask?"

"I have no interest, but it seems you're eager to tell anyway."

I turned to my brother who had stopped eating and had leaned back in his chair, a particularly confused frown directed at me. "I'll see to Rain's training."

"I can help my own child."

I scoffed. "What will you show her? How to nurture it? We can't nurture our magic, Kil, it will only eat at her. Like it still eats at you."

"And you?" Thora asked, finally looking at me. "Will you show her how to cower from it, how to drown herself in misery because of it?"

"Rora, enough," Snow calmly said, and the whole room went silent.

Cold emerald eyes were still on mine when she smirked with such disdain. "Perhaps not. Even that he's failed to do."

Unable to contain my reaction, I grinned at her. "Have you been praying for my downfall, little bird?"

"What downfall? Can someone stoop any lower than where you were last I saw you?" She raised the fork to her lips, offering me a sweet smile before biting on her food.

"That was mean."

"Aw, diddums."

I threw my head back and laughed while she glared at me. She had every weapon in her arsenal to destroy me, ruin me, humiliate me, and this was how she was choosing to do so. Using none of the ammunition I gave her, she was using her own.

"Erik's funeral is in two days," she said to Kil, angling her chair so most of her back was to me. "He will be buried in castle grounds."

"Are you certain?" my brother asked.

"He's been in my council for six years. Courted me for two. His father is one of my most trusted. He deserves to be remembered as the king who almost was."

My brother's entire mood shifted, and he smiled at her. "You want to provoke Iskyla, isn't it?"

Thora shrugged. "I killed her general, secured myself a rich ally thanks to her, and dozens of others who adored Erik and his family are in support of me. Then there is that little failed fiasco in Tenebrose which would appear quite distasteful to Isjordians who enjoy their proprietary—it only made them remember that Iskyla is a barbarian queen after all. She must be angry."

"You killed Andre?"

She nodded. "The day of the wedding right after Erik was shot, I went to Casmere. They had set an ambush for Emil's ships."

"No one mentioned anything."

"No one saw anything."

My brother tilted his head back. "She must think you have him in your dungeons. Could be the cause of the attack last night."

"Possibly," Thora calmly replied, cutting through her meal.

The playful girl was gone. The one eager for chaos. There was someone else sitting beside me. The Thora I knew had never been so orderly or calm or numb or colourless.

Something didn't exactly feel right.

Snow sat on the seat next to mine, staring out of the balcony overlooking the lily gardens. We'd not had a moment to talk after I'd returned, and now that we had it, we both found it hard to do so. She and I carried a secret no one but the two of us knew.

"I didn't think you'd disappear on me when I asked you for that favour."

"Neither did I." When I entered the portal five years ago, shortly after Snow had fallen ill during her pregnancy and almost died from Rain's magic, I'd left this realm behind with the purpose to find Astra. To find the realm we were from, to know more about our magic, to meet more like us who could help. Rain and Sam would soon grow up and manifest magic none of us had control of. When Nubil had suggested that maybe Snow hand over her children to the heavens to live among their kind, I had not hesitated. Part of me wanted to know about myself, too. To know if all my kind lived plagued by our own power as Kil and I did.

She frowned. "What do you mean?"

"I was locked in the last world that I portalled to."

"What?" She braced a hand on the railing. "Mal, I thought you found somewhere to stay, somewhere yours, somewhere you had liked."

That made me chuckle a little, especially when she knew that all what she mentioned were here in this realm. "There was no magic where I went. Nothing similar to our world. It took me months and months of searching and reading to return through a portal that they had preserved from their world's ancient civilization."

She began pacing back and forth. "Gods. What...what if you had never found a way to return?"

"Ah, my pride," I feignedly gasped, putting a hand to my chest.

"I should have destroyed that place when Kil told me to. I shouldn't have asked you. I shouldn't have sent you on this meaningless goose chase."

"It wasn't a goose chase." Especially after seeing Rain. Sam had inherited more of his mother's traits and magic, but his sister was entirely Kil. More than what Kil was, perhaps. My brother and I had found a way to tame and cope with our magic because we were brutally forced to. Even after that, we still often slipped. Thankfully, we'd never slipped long enough to cause harm. Rain, however, she was a little kid, one who I hoped my brother would never show the brutal ways of numbing what we were subject to. So, I'd gone to search for the place where more of us were—for the past five years, I'd gone to search for Astra, a realm outside Fader's reach and right inside Nihilia's watch. A place that for whatever reason, no one wanted us to find. Including Nubil.

She stopped, her head turning to me. "You...found it? You found Astra?"

"No. But I found out why we can't find it." I patted the chair next to mine. "Sit, you're tiring my nephew."

Once she was sat and calmed down, I continued, "Astra has apparently closed all doors to the outer realms after the demon gods were sentenced to Nihilia's prisons."

"I should have known," she said, sneering up at the skies. "Considering none up there will let a squeak of information out about it."

"There is another reason. Our descendants, some call them the Astral born, were the ones who captured the Demon Gods. The gates were partially shut to protect their lineage and part to prevent the Astral born from being used to rouse them from their confinement."

"It was a goose chase then," she said, heaving a sigh.

"They are out there, Snow. More like us. We don't need to find Astra at all."

She shook her head. "You're never going back. You're never entering that portal again. I'm going to have it turned into ash."

"What if I told you I might know someone across that portal who has access to that information?"

"Who?"

"Someone who teaches and trains beings like me and you. I met him during one of our travels and he owes me a favour?"

"There is a catch, isn't there?"

"The gates to his realm are also shut."

"Damn it."

"I will find a way," I said. "But it is time to tell Kil about everything. Tell him about where I went and why."

She groaned, slouching in her seat and manspreading all over my space, too. "He's so scared, Mal. I thought if I knew more about what you all are, he'd have an easier time with all this. He can barely sleep some nights. He has to check on me and the kids until sunrise as if we'd disappear into the thick of night."

I kneeled before her, taking her hands in mine. "I will be here this time. I won't go anywhere. Nothing will happen to you."

Her nose scrunched and she sniffled a little before throwing her arms around my neck. "You brought dust with you."

"Blame the little one."

"I will never blame him for anything. This is on you." She hugged me tighter. "Thank you for finding the way back to us. Can't believe I thought you settled someplace else far from here. Your timing was perfect though."

"You think it's beyond me to break a marriage if it had not been?" I whispered in her ear.

She pulled back and slapped my shoulder. "You actually did break it. Both your brother and I knew the moment you stepped inside Tenebrose, you fool. You let it happen."

"Aren't I romantic?"

Her nose scrunched. "A little."

"Knew you'd see my vision," I said, kissing her cheek and standing. "Tell Kil."

"Fine," she grumbled. "Where are you going?"

"Bird watching."

Following her from afar was harder than I had thought when I wanted nothing more than to be near to her. Her itinerary had a specific pattern and she never stayed in one place more than five minutes.

However, she'd not moved for the past half an hour.

Oblivious to anyone or anything, she remained in the middle of the winter gardens, staring ahead onto nothing, an inch of snow already forming over her.

Damn it, Thora.

"Come on, move," I murmured to myself, crouching on the height of the tower looking directly ahead at the whole space of the castle gardens. "You weren't doing that anymore. You weren't. I was sure of it. You weren't doing that before I left five years ago, Rora."

Just when I was about to fade to her, Oryn came out of the castle, hurrying towards her. A cloud of distress surrounded him as his eyes raked the space for anyone who was a witness to him shaking his queen for the next ten minutes.

I ran a hand through my hair. "You weren't supposed to do that anymore, little bird."

Something was different this time. There was almost nothing in her colours, just the odd light blue shade of calm when before...before there had been many angry dark shades of haunting emotions. Why was it still happening if none of them had triggered it? It felt like the puzzle was missing a piece—an emotion.

I faded below and stood right where she had stood a few moments ago, surveying the surroundings, until my attention landed on something sticking out of the ground a few feet away. A large arrow was nailed to the ground. One made entirely out of gold.

When I rested my palm against the ground, everything made sense. The soil below still held a taste of the power she had used that day to kill her father, it still held traces of her anger, her anguish and her pain. Right where I stood was where Thora had killed Silas.

5

THE PAST

MALIK

"You're hiding again," Thora said, settling next to me against the library shelf.

She'd found me again. Or maybe I wanted to be found and had hid in plain sight. Thora knew the Amaris library was where I chose to rot most of the days lately. Mostly because part of me knew this place was where she spent most of her time, too. I'd never been much of a fan of absolute darkness. The darker it was, the more honed my senses were. But I liked being in the dark with her.

"I'm a bit tired, little bird," I admitted, brushing my hand through her hair just once to feel if she was really beside me or just inside my head. "Though not sure why exactly."

"You're tired because everything touches you," she said, gathering her knees to her chest. "You're tired because you are never indifferent to anything around you whether you like to be or not. And it isn't because of your magic. It isn't because of your magic at all. Your magic makes it worse. You feel deeply and irrevocably. You feel so humanly. More humanly than most. And you were taught it to be wrong. It is tiring to feel you've done wrong when you doubt that you might have not. It's okay," she whispered, resting her chin on her knees and rocking herself back and forth. "It really is okay, you know."

"Were you talking about you or me?"

She glanced at me a little. "Would you hate it if I was talking about you?"

"I don't know."

After a little disappointed sigh, she said, "Then maybe I was not."

Reaching a hand forward, I pulled her hair away from her face, gathering it on the other side. She just watched me as I dared run my fingers back and forth her jaw, her eyes frozen in place, frozen on me.

"Say something. Anything," I spoke amidst the odd silence that had never fallen between us as it had now.

She raised a finger and traced the tattoo down my forearm. It always started like that. Little touches to test herself, to see if she could take it further. Because she had no reason to fear me. I had more reason to fear her. And it wasn't because she knew all my secrets. "Why do you mind the silence so much? What do you think will happen if we just don't say anything?"

"I want to know when you're with me. Sometimes, when you're quiet, I'm not sure if you are." And I was terrified that if it was quiet enough, she'd hear my heart erratically, torturously, painfully pound out her name. She couldn't know about my sickness, about my torment, the slow, slow ways it was starting to kill me. Because I didn't deserve this sickness. I didn't deserve its sweet torture. Because I was a man who'd turn this sickness into a plague, a curse, a blight to escape it, but never choose the cure. Because I did not deserve the cure either. There were better men than me who deserved that cure. Someone who deserved her back.

"I'm here."

"Good. I'm here too. All the fucking time," I said, my fingers sliding from her face to her brow. "So don't go there so often. Or at least take me with you. Wherever you go, take me with you."

She swallowed, and whispered, "You're such a bad friend, Malik Castemont."

I don't want to be your friend. "You knew I was a piece of shit when you entered this agreement. No take backs allowed."

A smile began slowly to spread over her face. "I've been defrauded."

You have. "Don't seem so upset, I might start to feel sorry for my crimes."

She buried her face in her hands and laughed.

I pulled her hands away and she startled a little. "Why hide it?"

"Hide what?"

How stunning you look when you smile, laugh, exist. "That I make you laugh."

"You want me to hide the fact that you've made me cry."

Because I'd be tempted to be good and stay away. I can't stay away. "I'm a bad friend." I wanted to be something worse to her. Anything, actually, I just wanted to be anything to her, and being a bad friend was the only way to keep her. I wanted to keep her the first moment I saw her. I wanted her to be mine to keep.

She sighed and sat up straight, dropping her head back on the bookshelf so she could stare at the library's starry ceiling made of tiny little black crystals etched in the walls that reflected the daylight outside. "Let's see the real stars next time, Malik."

"These will do."

"You said to take you wherever I go. I want to see the world."

I can see mine just fine from here.

"Settled," she said at my silence, her head lolling in my direction until it rested on my shoulder. Her dark lashes fluttered fast up at me. "Next time we will see the real ones."

"Didn't you hear me?"

"You always do as I say, so do as I say."

"You keep behaving like a spoiled little princess these days."

Her smile was coy. "I'm a spoiled princess. So, spoil me. Pet me. Pamper me. Adore me." She suddenly stood and reached out a hand to me. "Dance with me. Neo wants me to go with him to a dance hall next weekend and I can't make it past step five without injuring someone."

Before I could tell absolutely the hell not and spit about a thousand lies about Neo and his small dick, she grabbed a bunch of my shirt and pulled me up as if she exercised like a three-hundred-pound soldier. She was quick to arrange my limbs around her and hers around me.

Her eyes pinched at me with a glare. "Move."

"Say please. Say 'please, Mal, move'."

"You really think I have pride? Please, please, please!" she repeated, hoping from one foot to the other, looking up at me.

Ignoring the way she avoided saying my name how I wanted her to say it, I threw my head back and chuckled for a moment so I could gather my scattered thoughts and depleted will to hold a fort against her.

Then I moved.

My mother loved to dance, she'd made me dance with her whenever her illness had deceived her and hid away for a few tricking moments. She loved music, art and nature.

She'd loved everything beautiful and fragile and soft. She'd loved Thora, too. I was so much like my mother. But I was so much like my father, too. And he loved to break anything beautiful and soft and so colourful. He would have loved to break something like her.

Maybe I did, too, considering I'd yet to tell her to run far, far away from someone like me.

Thora's grin was huge while I twirled her around and pulled her to me closer and closer each time without her realising at all that our bodies were one broken restraint away from touching.

I touched that smile and she jolted just slightly, but not from fear. "You like it that much?"

She nodded, her eyes falling to my fingers moving over her lips. "In my head, it is so beautiful."

"Take me there."

Through the darkness, I could see her cheeks pinken, turning the same colour of ribbons she had arranged in her hair and tied around her neck. "It's the middle of April," she whispered as if she was telling me a secret, her eyes jumping from my eyes to my lips. "We're in the middle of a grand hall made of walls entirely of ice. The weather is gentle and warm, but there is snow, too. It falls like star fall. It glows as it falls to the ground. There are about a dozen violins and a grand maple piano in the middle of it all. Distant wind chimes and crystals that reflect the sun and fill the room with rainbows. There is no one, but me and you. And—"

"And?"

"I don't know. Usually there is more." She looked around, her gaze wandering lost. "But I like it here, too. This part I don't have to fantasise about. My mind could never make it this perfect." Then she whispered, "I'm happy here."

When I spun her again, I pulled her body flush against mine. She noticed it this time, she might have noticed my heartbeat, too, because she went quiet, her cheeks flushed entirely red. "Your tits are bigger than mine."

I sighed, half relieved that she so innocently ruined almost every awkward moment between us. "Thora, sweetheart, they are not tits."

"You might need a brassier or a corset if they get any bigger, Malik, I'd be careful with all those push-ups."

"You little shit."

She giggled a little and then rested her cheek on my chest, going silent again as if she could hear her name being called. "Take me to your world, too."

She'd asked me before, and as all the other times, I was going to tell her that the world she was thinking of was just a nightmare now. It wasn't a world at all. Not one I could alter. No one could alter nightmares. They were just memories. And memories were haunting. It was their job, I did not blame them. I just had a lot of haunting memories.

But this time I wanted to show her just to see if she could alter them like she'd altered my dreams. Thora Krigborn had that gift. She could make such ugly things shine. She could polish coal into diamonds. This girl had a way to make you believe anything. Perhaps she'd spent more time convincing herself of things that were not real than real, perhaps because even though she wore a tainted shell over that iron pit of a heart she had, she had never, not once, let herself believe she was anything but pristine.

"There is a condition," I said.

She lifted her head, eyes wide and hopeful. "What condition?"

"You don't say anything. Not one word. Nothing at all. No questions. I have no answers for whatever question you might have."

"None that you want to tell me, you mean?"

This girl. "Thora."

"It's okay. I agree. You will tell me eventually anyway, like you've told me every other thing."

Again, she was right.

I took her to the nightmare underneath the oldest temple there was in Amaris, at the catacomb tunnels disguised underneath. And as she had promised, she had not said a word. Occasionally, her grip on my sleeve tightened and loosened, sometimes she sighed and at others she let out a squeal of surprise when the spirits lingering the ground made themselves seen. Beneath the temple, the veil between life and death was thin, so thin you could sometimes see the gates of Keres and hear the bells of the next boat that took you through the river of Despairs to the Otherworld.

As we came to stop before a small cave with chains hanging from its walls, she tugged on my sleeve, forcing me to a stop, forcing me to look at her. Two round glassy emerald eyes looked up at me, full of knowing. Her lips pursed tightly as she struggled to hold to her promise not to say anything, not to acknowledge that she knew every sense in my body had been overwhelmed by death.

I'd told her the story, but I'd never shown her where it had taken place. This was the first time I'd come down here after my father had died.

"Five years old." The first time that he had brought me down here. "He probably knew since then what I was, what *gift* I was given. He could see the spirits, too, but he did not feel them as if they lived under his skin like I did. Every day up until the day he found out about my magic, he brought me here. He'd leave me by that corner," I said, pointing to a small alcove painted with old Darsan letters. "Chained in case I left. Sometimes he'd forget me here, but then Kilian paid off a guard and had found out about this place, so he'd sneak me out after father would bring me here. Father found out two weeks later, beat Kilian and put us in two cells next to one another. He brought me water and food while Kilian's wounds began festering, while he went through fever and thirst. My father let me feel my brother slowly die. I couldn't become his Eldritch Commander if I feared and hid from death, if I loathed and avoided it. I couldn't become his commander of Death if the dead taunted me. I couldn't become death if I couldn't bear the death of those I loved. The only way for it to obey my call, to heed to my every order, to remain undying under my magic was to numb myself out of emotions. If I feel, death will use it as my weakness and become my master instead of me becoming its master. It makes me weak." She made me weak. I made her weak, too. Pinching her chin, I forced her to look at me and I forced myself to look at those tear-filled eyes. "Is it to your taste?"

"There is nothing wrong with being weak," she spoke, her breath hitching, tears forming, and a feigned smile almost made a show. "Your father was wrong."

"You know what haunts me more than all he did? The fact that he was right. It cost me to think like you do, Thora. It costs me more each time I dare to."

She shook her head. "What is the point of being invincible if you have no one to protect?"

"You're full of smart words, little bird. Acting invincible doesn't really make you invincible either. Disappearing inside your little glitter and pony filled mind can't save you from your fears. It can't protect anyone else either."

"This isn't about me."

"I showed what you asked to see. I didn't ask for ways to be fixed."

"Does that make you feel better? Does being cruel to me make you feel better?"

"Immensely."

"Then go on. Make yourself feel better."

"Always the punch bag, little bird," I said, pulling hair behind her ear. "Do you like that?"

"*Immensely*," she said, two stray tears falling down her cheeks.

I clicked my tongue, stepping closer to her. "The tears," I murmured, watching them trail down her neck and soak into the rose-coloured dress she wore. "The damn tears."

Refusing to look anywhere else but straight into my dark soul, she said, her mouth quivering, "Had your fun?"

"Not quite. Tell me honestly," I said, picking up a long strand of black hair that had fallen over her shoulder and twirling it around my finger. "Why do you let me touch you?"

"Find out for yourself."

"What if I offer you a secret for it?"

"None is worth enough."

This girl. This maddening girl. "I will find one worth enough, and then you will tell me why you don't mind my hands on you," I said, wiping her tears away, my thumbs skating across her smooth skin to brush against her mouth. Gods, I loved her mouth.

"Good luck with that," she almost whispered, looking up at me, her breaths coming in shallow when my thumb slipped between her slightly parted lips.

If there was one thing I could thank the old fuck that had sired me for, it was the self control I sometimes realised I had.

Somehow, I had managed to pull away from her before committing to my thoughts.

6

SAGE ZINNIAS

THORA

My fingers were sore from the number of arrows I'd shot. The torches lining the temple altar that led to Krig's statue stirred when I shot another one that etched right on his left eye, cracking the old stone.

Skadi clicked her tongue at the number of arrows already piling around the castle temple where no one but me was allowed to enter.

A small whine leaked out of the man tied in front of the sculpture—in the front of the God that would abandon him at my hands. Iskyla's husband had soon run out of curses and was now on the last leg of his fate—begging. But I was no god. At least he'd said so. That meant begging wouldn't work on me, unfortunately.

"Look at that. I missed again," I said, nocking my last arrow back and aiming it right between his eyes.

He shook his head hard, moaning and groaning as he struggled against the binds containing him.

"You're going to anger her by keeping him here any longer," Skadi said, settling against a wall.

"Why for?" I asked, releasing my bow. When the arrow hit just a hair away from his brains, I gave Skadi a grin. "An eye for an eye. Why would she be upset?"

"Your wolves raided her village searching for him. You breached her territory."

I'd waited and anticipated her attack on Tenebrose that night. I had been waiting for a reason to enter her land and she'd given it to me. "She breached first, and my ladies hurt no one," I said, placing my bow back on its quiver and bending to give my wolves some scratches. "Not a single person. They didn't even hurt *him*. I'm playing by the book."

"How long do you think you can cheat the rules for?"

"I didn't cheat. Those rules were put by me. They can also be void when I decide so." She shook her head and made her exit. "You have a guest."

Moriko looked around the temple and frowned, just not at the man I'd tied and gagged. When she finally gave him some of her bored attention, she said, "I've never seen a man tied up with silk before."

"It's pretty," I said, leading her outside the temple grounds and onto my private gardens, offering her to sit down on a table already laid with drinks and snacks. "Like a little present." Silk soaked the blood better and left barely any marks on the skin if I wanted to be discreet. Silk was gentle, soft, yet one of the toughest materials to exist.

"He is still breathing."

"I have a feeling his death has not been written yet. My mark keeps missing."

"Or you're just planning to use him for something and are wearing his poor soul down first."

"Ah, but you're making it seem like I'm torturing him."

"Aren't you?"

"I don't know. He's never said anything against it."

"That might have to do with the fact that you've gagged him."

"Semantics. Tea?" I asked, picking my special porcelain tea set that Nia had gifted for my engagement to Erik. She knew my taste well. It had been too pretty to not use.

"I'm sure my advisors would strongly suggest I say no," she muttered, but pushed her teacup for me to fill. "I thought you would have released him back to her by now."

"Are you here advocating on Iskyla's behalf?" I sipped my warm tea. "That would really upset me."

She sighed the same type of sigh she usually sighed at my sister. "I'm here about the White Veil. There are rumours of its sighting circulating in Hanai now, too many people are talking. Different from Isjordians, my people seem to believe that the odds might turn, that we could possibly be facing the anger of the gods yet again."

"I hope you've put those doubts and fears to rest."

"When it comes to my people, the only one who can put that fear to rest is the White Veil itself."

"I'm afraid it doesn't take appearance requests."

She narrowed her eyes on me over her teacup as she took a sip. "I'm sure you could arrange something with *it*, since you two are so closely knit together."

Giving her a smile, I said, "I will see what I can do."

Moriko cocked her head back, observing me under her straight dark lashes. "Why don't you show this kingdom the woman who killed the *kingdom slayer*? Five years is a long time to drag this out for. Why leave it in the hands of such an...untrusted figure to deal with Iskyla. Give her the woman who fought Silas Krigborn alone and took his life one hundred times."

It was like time had stood still since that very exact day ten years ago. I could suddenly remember every noise around me, the taste of smoke in the air, the reek of rotting bodies leaving graveyards at Malik's command, the exact smell of my father's blood, the exact warmth of it. "She died in this very garden ten years ago. I do not raise the dead."

"No," she said, glancing behind me. "But someone else does."

I set my teacup down and looked over my shoulder where her attention had just fallen. Nia and Malik were deep in conversation, she scowled and he laughed. It was so easy for him to pretend nothing had changed, to pretend as if he had never even left.

"Use him well."

I swallowed, trying not to let myself spin into the abyss of memory that I thought I'd successfully banished. "I will do no such thing."

She leaned back in her seat, crossing her arms over her chest. "Too proud?"

"Too much self-respect."

"It's been five years now, Thora."

"And I'm sure there will be five more without his help. I promised to ever use only one man for help. And that will be the one I will strap on the throne next to mine and spoon feed him orders like a good boy." I reached for the teapot. "More tea?"

She glanced at my shaking hands holding the teapot and making the lid rattle. "I trust you, Thora. More than I usually deign someone of any of my trust, especially a Krigborn. But Iskyla has gone too far because you have let her. End this before it gets worse. Because it will. I do not know what your reasons for holding back are, and though I still respect them, I urge you to put them aside."

My reasons.

The reasons buried in this very garden.

My head buzzed yet it was the quietest it had ever felt.

A hand fell over my own and my body slowly began locking. Pale. Scars on top. Moriko's. It was Moriko's hand. Only Moriko's. "Thora?" Her voice felt distant, as if she were miles away from me.

It was only Moriko's hand.

Only Moriko's.

My vision tunnelled, every muscle in my body cramped all at once and my jaw locked tightly, a dull and pounding ache pulsed all over my stiff limbs. It could have been seconds, barely any of that, maybe minutes or hours when someone grabbed hold of me by the shoulders, the same hands began kneading down my body, loosening each muscle one after the other until they somehow began unlocking, melting away from the painful stiffness.

"Welcome back," Malik boredly said, his hands still massaging through my body and down my legs.

I pushed his hands away and stood, trying to put distance between him and I. "Where is Moriko?"

He wasn't looking at me when he said, "Left about an hour ago."

"A-an hour ago?"

I might have flinched when he looked up at me as if I were some injured doe needing to be put down. "Yes, an hour."

"Don't look at me like that."

"Since when have you started doing that again?"

"I don't know what you're talking about," I said, spinning on my heels and heading towards the castle. My chest fell quickly, and I was struggling to catch my breaths. Yes, since when was I doing that again?

I'd forgotten why I rarely stayed when I visited Adriata. This room…I hated it. It was filled with so many things I wanted to forget. One being the sofa by the balcony doors, the one he had usually laid every night I had spent here. I wondered if it still smelled like him.

Just when I laid down, a chill speared down my spine, making me shoot upright again. The room was dark enough to see the shadow under the door seal. Could even imagine him sitting on the ground, his back pressed to my door.

He used to let himself in before, simply barge in and sit on his designated sofa, blabbering and joking away until I gave up to sleep. The memory was a lifetime away, yet it felt so fresh, only as if to taunt me.

"Go away," I whispered to no one. Not that anyone would have heard it. Not even whatever spirit lingered inside the castle walls.

He remained behind that door for minutes and then hours. Robbing me of sleep and assaulting me with all sorts of resentful feelings I thought I'd long gotten over them.

Night was fully in when I got up and reached the door, pulling it open. It was dark and most of the corridor candles had blown off from the swift autumn wind slipping through windows left open.

He didn't stir despite the groan of the heavy doors, his head had fallen to an odd angle, his chest rising steady.

He was asleep.

Since when could he fall asleep so easily?

Since he left me?

Two of my guards found that particular moment to march back to my doors.

They froze on the spot and bowed at the both of us. "Apologies, Your Majesty, there was a shift change."

"She was well guarded," Malik's voice boomed over the hallow corridors, and I inwardly winced.

My guards shifted their attention between him and I before bowing again and stepping back to give us the privacy I did not need with him.

"You should—"

"Don't tell me to go," he said just as I was about to head back inside.

"I can't tell you to stay either."

"But you want me to stay."

I stopped again, my grip on the door becoming painful. "I don't want anything, Malik. I've learnt to want nothing."

"You were doing it again."

"Leave."

"Why are you doing it again?"

"Why do you care?"

"It had stopped. I swear you had stopped doing it."

Just when I was about to shut the door on him and return to bed, he faded before me, a hand gripping the door to keep it open.

"You didn't answer me."

Glaring at him, I backed away into my room.

He stepped inside and I stepped further away from him. His head tilted to the side, studying me. "Stop moving, Thora."

"Why?"

"Do you want to turn this into a chase? I can do that. I can tire you until you surrender to me. You wouldn't like it though."

"I'm not scared of you."

"I've never wanted you to be."

I stepped a little further back and stopped when he tilted his head to the side in warning. He was going to hold to his promise. And I really wouldn't like it. Not when I lacked the energy to fight him back.

"Don't loom over me."

I could see his eyes glitter even in the darkness. "Loom?"

In a flash, he faded right in front of me, a piece of my hair between his fingers, the scent of eucalyptus overwhelming me with all sorts of memories. "I really was hoping the fringe was a phase. Hoping you'd grown out of it."

"Don't mock me."

He leaned forward, close to my face, his eyes closing as he took a deep inhale. "Mock? Why would I mock you, Your Majesty?"

I snatched my hair out of his grip. "Don't patronise me."

His hand shot to my face, cupping my jaw and titling my face up to his. "Ask me, Thora. Ask about what you want to know. I've never hid a thing from you. Ask me. Don't be angry at me. You can't be angry at me. You out of all cannot be angry at me."

"I am not angry."

"When you lie like this," he started, stepping even close to me, my chest brushing against his. "It makes it more fun."

"Don't make me hurt you, Malik."

"Please do," he crooned, tipping his head forward until his nose brushed against mine.

My eyes drew shut when my treacherous heart started reminding me how much it still cared for him. "Malik—"

"Do it, Rora. You want to be angry at me? Do it properly." His hand lowered from my jaw to my neck, his fingers brushing my pulse. "Come on, sweetheart, no one better than you knows how to hurt me. So hurt me. Otherwise I won't know to stay away."

He knew—he knew I couldn't.

His hand slipped away from me and he backed away, starting to take off his jacket and dropping to the sofa he used to sleep on ten years ago.

"What are you doing?"

Putting an arm under his head, he closed his eyes and yawned. "I can't sleep. You can't sleep. Let's commiserate how we used to."

"I can sleep just fine, and we aren't—"

"We aren't what? Friends?" He chuckled, closing his eyes again. "I have no interest in being your friend again, Thora."

"Then what do you want? Is this fun for you?"

"Yes."

"Get out."

"Lay down. Or I'm going to do it for you."

Humour was gone from his voice. And I knew right then that he was no longer playing with me. After considering my chances, I ran out towards Rain's room, his laughter following me all the way down the corridor and even after I'd closed the door behind me.

Rain stirred. "Auntie?"

"Auntie is scared," I whispered, panting as I stepped towards her bed.

She pulled her covers to the side. "Nothing gets under the blanket. Hide under mine."

"Aren't you a little big to believe in things like that?" When I was her age, I knew who the real monsters were and where they hid.

"Since you came to me for protection, the littlest person in this castle, I thought you might be a little *neeve*."

"You mean naive?" I asked, settling next to her.

"That one."

"That I might be," I mumbled, snuggling against her and wondering how low I had fallen to seek protection from a little kid.

Everyone was there when I went for breakfast. Rain had sat in Snow's lap, Malik and Sam were deep in some sort of conversation, and Kil was too busy admiring my sister to even notice that the world spun, so I casually slipped in a chair, hoping they would not notice me as usual.

Except that when Malik's head turned to me, every other head in the room followed. All the attention was on me for some reason, and I shifted uncomfortably in my seat.

"Good morning, auntie," Rain said, tilting her head as she studied me. "You slept late."

"Morning, my little rain cloud."

"Slept well?" Kilian asked, giving me a subtle knowing glance.

"Not quite," I mumbled, buttering some bread.

"I heard you swapped rooms last night," my brother-in-law prodded, raising a brow. His tattle-tale daughter had definitely told him about last night. "Anything not to your liking?" After a quick glance at his brother, he added, "I'm sure we can figure something out."

"Nope," I said, buttering a piece of toast. "I just need to be back in Tenebrose, not hiding here like a coward."

"There is a threat inside your castle, Rora," my sister said, oblivious to my lie. "Inside your walls. Your home. You cannot trust a servant. Not even the mice."

"I can defend myself. That is all that matters. Iskyla wouldn't kill me so discreetly, she wants a show. She wants to humiliate me. To run me off so she can sit on the throne she thinks she deserves by my hand, not murdering me like I murdered our father. Then Isjordians would just see her as another usurper."

"How can you hold against her when you can't even sleep, aunt?" Sam asked, blinking slowly at me. "And to be able to fight them off, you need energy, sustenance. You barely eat," he pointed to the piece of toast I'd dropped back on the plate. "You barely talk. Even to Elias or Oryn who are your most trusted. Though one might argue that both are very uninteresting talkers. But that is beside the point."

The table had gone entirely too quiet and Kil was barely holding a smile, doing such a terrible job at trying not to be proud of his overly intelligent and observant son.

"You'll hurt her feelings," Malik said, munching on an apple like a smug idiot, and throwing me a wink that unsettled me more than I thought it would.

Sam returned to his plate, quietly sipping his tea. "Not so easy to hurt her feelings, uncle. But you would know that, wouldn't you?"

Kilian's shoulders were shaking from silent chuckles at his brother's stunned expression. Once he was done, he turned to me, "Stay for a while longer. At least until you figure out how to sift traitors from your ranks and your home."

"Appoint me back to my position," Malik said, and everyone turned to him.

Kilian wore a stunned expression. "You want to return to duty?"

"Yes. And then give me orders to remain by the Isjordian Queen's side."

"What?" I asked, sputtering my tea.

Leaning back in his chair, he gave me a once over. "Once my Eldritch get inside your castle, we'll find out who the traitors are among your people within an hour," he casually said, turning to his brother. "I'll remain there. By her side." He cocked his head to the side to look at me. "Approve it."

The hells? "No."

He raised a brow. "No?"

"I don't need your help."

"But you do."

"I can do without it. I've done fine so far."

"My offer stands."

"Neo can still do that job just fine," I added, knowing full well that I had not a single intention of asking Neo for that sort of help, or even having ever considered it. Part of me wanted to get him mad. To see him angry. I don't know why I thought the mention of Neo would do so. But my guess was right.

His jaw twitched. "Neo probably can't still tell his dick from his toes."

Rain giggled. "Papa, what is a d—"

My sister and brother-in-law glared at Malik. "Something your papa will cut off your uncle if he repeats that again," Snow said, kissing her daughter's cheek. "If mama doesn't get to it faster."

"You made him Commander of the Eldritch," I added, confused as to why he was always so hostile towards Neo, yet he'd handed him his position of power.

"I did?" he asked, lifting a brow and turning to his brother. "Did I now?"

I looked over at Kil who gave me a blank expression. "You were fond of him," he boredly said, drinking from his teacup. "Thought it would work best between you two if he were to be in a position of power, so I put him there."

What?

"And he thought it would make you change your mind and stay," Snow said to Malik. "Obviously he was wrong to assume both."

Kilian looked heartbroken. "My love. It was simply a miscalculation."

"Can't believe my husband is such a meddler," she said, shaking her head at him and smiling.

"A meddler? Me?" he asked, stretching back on his seat. "If you want to talk about meddling, how about you tell them—"

Snow put Rain on Malik's lap and launched in Kilian's direction, putting a hand over his mouth and leaning to whisper something in his ear that had him go silent.

This morning was the most confusing event I had attended in ages.

When I glanced at Malik, I noticed he was looking at me. "You ask Neo for help a lot, little bird?"

"That doesn't concern you," I said, standing and excusing myself out.

BLACK MARIGOLDS

MALIK

Everyone had gathered at the *almost* king's funeral. All except one. His *almost* wife and my once friend. Elias was getting fidgety, and Oryn was having strong doubts that she was off doing something she shouldn't be doing. But then so was I.

Sighing, I said, "I'll get her."

"She's not going to like that," his lordship said as I faded inside the Tenebrose castle.

There was a melody seeping around the corridors. The sound of violins turned sharp and fast the closer I got to the throne room where I could feel her shadows resting.

Thora stood by the massive red stained-glass windows, eyes latched on one spot outside with no absolute focus at all.

Signalling the orchestra to stop playing, I reached her side. "There you are."

She looked at me then, surprise colouring her green eyes, and soon, something else dimmed them to a deep and dark emerald. Something that very much resembled disdain. "Who gave you permission to come here?"

"This one felt personal." I stood beside her, close, but she didn't move away from me this time. "What were we looking at?"

Nothing. That was the answer. She'd been looking at nothing because the view outside the window faced some part of the castle wall. No shrub or column or animal in sight. Just a strip of snowy land and the tall grey wall ahead. "Picturesque. My fingers are itching to paint this."

She didn't say anything, still staring ahead. But I knew she was wanting to throw something at me. Word or object, I wasn't really sure, but she was not doing either. It was like the flame she'd always carried had been put out.

"Don't ignore me."

"It comes naturally."

"Why are they all sitting and playing in the dark? Wouldn't kill them to light a candle or two, maybe pull these curtains open a little."

"It's relaxing."

"For the dead perhaps." I tugged on her hair and her mouth fell open, all surprised and offended. "Talking about the dead. They are waiting to bury your *almost husband*."

"I know." She wiped her nose with a tissue and sniffled, suddenly tearing up. Moving past me, she descended the small throne platform and patted a violinist on the shoulder. "Well done. It was lovely."

Reaching down, I picked up the tissue she'd dropped at my feet. A small leaf falling out of it.

Nettle.

Chuckling to myself, I faded just a step behind her royal ice majesty still wiping her hay fever tears away while she tried her best to appear distraught. "Pearls, really?"

Her hand went to the claps, and she threw the necklace to the floor, letting the pearls bounce all over the marble floor. "You're right. Erik's family is in diamond merchandise. They loathe pearls."

"Your hair is down."

"He liked my hair down."

A muscle ticked in my temple. "But you don't."

"I'll make sure they bury me with my hair up when my time comes."

My hand was not even an inch away from wrapping around her arm when she stopped and said, "Don't touch me." Keeping her back to me, she said, "For the last time, what are you doing here, Malik?"

"Keeping a promise." I would make sure she found what she deserved even if it was the last thing I ever did.

She finally turned to me, her eyes were red and swollen with feigned tears. "You made no promise."

"I did. And you remember it well. I know you do."

"Give me another one instead. Leave. Make sure I never see you again."

"After I do this. I'll do that then. If that is what you want."

"I only want this one thing from you. Nothing else."

"I'm not doing it for you. I'm doing it for that nineteen-year-old girl who at least had the balls to go after something she wanted."

"She had the bad habit of going after things who didn't deserve her. Didn't you tell her so yourself?"

"I was a dick."

"Incorrect. You still are."

"And you still missed me though," I said, and without thinking of it, I reached a hand to her face and wiped some of those fake tears away. "Still ugly as hells when you cry."

Gently, she pushed my hand off. She didn't have it in her to even despise me. To at least despise me. "Leave."

Even her anger was so soft that I hated myself for being the one to have softened it. "What if I can't?"

Briefly, I thought I saw doubt cross her now hardened eyes, the only thing that she'd not let soften. "You'll leave," was all she said, and then left.

She stood beside the priest the whole of the ceremony, her face solemn at all times except when she caught me staring at her. For those brief moments when she gave me her attention, she didn't try to hide her irritation.

"That throne was made for my son to sit on," a man in front of me said to the Lord of Modr. "It is fate. Destiny. He will preposition her tomorrow morning."

Lord of Modr nodded. "And so will every other eligible bachelor in the whole of Numen."

"No one is as good as my son."

"No one is as good as her. Have you thought about that? Your son wouldn't survive under her shade, not even a day."

He threw an almost disgusted and dumbfounded look at the older man. "I know it is your duty to speak highly of her, but you don't have to think the same when you're between us."

Lord of Modr drew out a polite laughter. "If you know what I thought of her, you'd believe me to be a traitor of the Isjord you know."

Obviously displeased, the man shot the Lord of Mord one last disapproving look and then moved a distance away from him, starting the same chatter with another lord.

Thora lowered a white rose over the casket and then the others followed. The nettle was still working well because tears were pouring endlessly despite the bored look on her face.

The fact that no one in that whole graveyard believed her was making it harder for me to not laugh.

"She's exemplary in her role," Lord of Modr said to no one, so I assumed he was speaking to me. "The playbook monarch. The best I've seen in the four hundred years of my life." He thrust a hand forward for me to take, either because he didn't know who I was, or those four hundred years were catching up to him and he'd forgotten that no one shook the hand of an Empath. "I care very little about pain, Prince Malik. Take my hand."

Huh. "You assume pain is the worst I can do," I said, shaking his hand.

"Who'd want to hurt an old man like me?"

"Someone who knows what an old man like you is capable of. What grave did they dig up a prime Verglasser like you from and why? Most importantly, who did?"

He gruffly laughed and pointed his chin at his queen. "Her. Dug me right up and will bury me one day, too, with how things are going," he said with a pensive grunt. "I am her mentor and...an old friend of Skadi's, if she'd allow me to call myself so. They call me Karl Modr these days."

"Mentor?"

"She knew ice, but ice did not know her. I introduced them. Then she made me wear a three-piece suit, argue with brainless men all day and sat my old arse in perhaps the most uncomfortable wooden seat there is in the entirety of Modr."

"And what is it that you want from me? Besides the entertaining conversation."

"Nothing, Your Highness. The entertaining conversation was plenty. But you might want something from me. Something along the lines of advice."

"Do I look like I need any advice?"

"With how she's been looking at you this entire time, I fear you might need more than just advice. Though I doubt anything to be proficient enough to keep her from making an example out of you. My queen likes to set examples. Very convincing examples. Examples no one wishes to follow."

I frowned down at him. "You're one of the few who does not think of her as this dolent saint she makes herself to be."

"Oh, but beneath the apple tree hide grass snakes, Your Highness. I fed that grass snake myself and have not the slightest idea how I've been doing so for the past ten years without being bitten to my death. Especially since she does not keep companions, only obedient servants. And servants come with an expiry date."

"Are you telling me to feed the snake or not?"

"You, prince, are the apple tree. She hides well beneath that unknown power which no one would believe her to possess."

She'd told him of what I'd taught her? "And what does that make you?"

"The wind I taught her to stand against."

"What was your advice?" I asked just as he bowed and was about to make his leave.

"Ah, yes," he chuckled. "Hide her again. To aid your sister-in-law possesses no danger to Adriata and Olympia. You are family, after all. Involving the Adriatian King and Queen in this equation would perhaps be unwise, but that doesn't extend to you anymore since you've revoked most duties to the Night Crown."

"She's too proud to let me." Stubborn. Angry. Know it all. And so many, many more things I couldn't name.

"I'm reluctant to believe you're anything but obedient, Prince Malik. I knew your father well and fought beside him at the Ater battles. No one becomes obedient in the hands of a man who teaches cruelty of the finest kind." He patted my shoulder. "If my queen wishes to make an example out of you, odds are that you will very much survive." Before he left, I heard him murmur to himself, "With a bruise or two."

Thora was still looking at me as her court and Erik's family began clearing the graveyard. Tilting her head to the side, she raised a brow and mouthed, *Please die next.*

Since you were so polite, I mouthed back.

She threw me a sardonic smile. *Thank you.*

My pleasure.

Isjordian funerals lasted too long for my liking. It was almost sunset when the last of Winter Court made their way back to their homes and left me an opportunity to have a lone moment with her. I was growing sick and tired watching her from afar.

Thora sat on her throne and alone in the massive room, one leg thrown over the other, her crown sitting high on her head and a glass of wine dangling between her fingers while she stared a hole up at the ceiling.

"What are you doing?"

The glass she held stopped dangling. "Ruling and stuff." Glancing around in search of something, she innocently blinked at an uneasy guard who'd half hid under the shadow of a vase. "Off with his head?" She drank the rest of her liquor and threw the glass against a wall, letting the crystal shatter to tiny pieces.

The guard shot us both a nervous look and ducked further inside the shadows he was trying to hide in.

"No? Just his legs then?" she asked him, and he almost sunk inside his steel armour like a turtle.

"Kil and your sister are waiting for us, come down," I said, reaching a hand up to her.

There was a brief pause of her gaze on my hand. "You missed that one," she said, pointing to my ring finger that was clear of any tattoos. "Did they run out of ink in whatever hole you buried yourself for the past five years?"

"Yes."

Her upper lip curled into a slight disdainful smile that was more scorn than anger. I realised that Thora Krigborn didn't have it in her to be angry—that she'd never really been angry with me either. She could be resentful or disappointed in you, never really angry. And somehow, that was worse than anger.

"Enough with that disappointed look."

"To be disappointed I have to care, Malik. I'm all *spent* on that." Her eyes darted towards the open window blowing flecks of snow and brisk wind, and then narrowed there for a moment before she almost ran towards it. "Did you see that?"

Nothing but snow, murky skies and a tall wall filled the window frame. "There wasn't anything there," I said, stretching in one of the many empty seats and plopping my feet on the one in front. "The closest breathing and feeling thing is about one hundred feet from us. Thin and short shadows. Light steps being dragged. Tired. Old. A maid."

She shook her head, still hanging out of the widow. "I saw something." Bracing a hand against the wall, she felt around it. "Can't you hear that sound?"

Without even opening my senses, I could feel anxiety rise up her body and wrap like a noose around her neck.

Had she had much to drink?

"There," she said, and then jumped out of the window, landing softly below and running towards the edge of the castle walls that had enshrouded the periphery of the castle grounds in a veil of post sunset darkness.

I faded right behind her as she tore through the snow covered ground towards...nothing.

Just before reaching the shadow cast by the castle walls, she spun round, searching the vast nothingness, her shoulders rising faster when she noticed the emptiness around us.

Worry crashed through me. "Thora."

"No. No, I saw it and I heard it. This isn't back then. I'm fine!" Swallowing, she repeated, "I said, I'm fine! Don't look at me like that."

There was no chance that I wouldn't have caught a presence near us, I could feel every living and dead thing miles around the castle. Soldiers, maids, cooks, animals, birds. Even the dead buried as deep as the solid earth beneath our feet went. But I still asked, "What did you see?"

Reluctantly, she spoke, "I'm not sure. Looked like a black animal at first, but then it looked human. Long hair. Dark, like mine." She put two fingers in her mouth and let out a sharp long whistle. Not even a few seconds later, a pack of dire wolves tore through the snow and made their way to her side. They sniffed the air, the ground, and even my hand when I reached to pet them. After whispering a string of fast orders in old Yslot, the wolves howled up at the darkening skies before obeying and heading to search through the rest of the open space.

"Just ask for my help, Thora."

"I'd rather lock myself in a dungeon and claim insanity."

"That sounds like the perfect holiday for you. And what's wrong with being insane?"

"A queen cannot be insane."

"It will be our little secret."

There it was again. That scornful look.

I chuckled. "Don't know if you look like you want to choke or stab me to death."

"Don't know why you'd think I'd have to choose. I can do both. Without even being near you."

"I've created a monster."

Briefly, I thought she almost, almost smiled. Maybe I'd imagined it because I longed to see it. I wanted her to smile for me. Like she'd done before.

The wolves returned, circling her as if she was part of their pack. Her expression fell soon after and she sighed. "Nothing."

"You speak wolf?"

Kneeling on the ground, she patted their furs one after the other, making sure to give attention to all of the toothy creatures. "Hungry, my ladies? He's not all bones. You'll have a feast with this one."

"Flattered that you're putting in a good word for me."

Just then, she smiled a little, but I didn't know whether it was directed at her wolves, or me. It had to have been at me because it was brief, and she looked angry at herself afterwards. "I'm not insane. I know what I saw."

"Nobody will burn you at the stake even if you were, little bird. Not the first or the last insane ruler sat on that throne."

"I saw it," she snapped at me.

Smiling inwardly, I said, "Then you saw it."

"You won't believe me?"

I always believed her. But she was talking to me, so I would say just about anything to keep her going, to get her to be angry at me if she must. I needed her to feel something when she saw me. Anything. "Does it matter?" It mattered. It mattered so much.

Her lashes fluttered fast and her lips parted. A sheen of unguarded innocence falling on her features. "No, it doesn't."

"Settled then." So not settled. Very much not settled.

One last time, she glanced at where she thought she'd seen something, and then let out a sigh.

"What? Nothing else to say?"

Everything but me got her attention. The boring snow, the boring skies, the boring treelines, the boring wall. She wouldn't look at me. "What? Already tired of engaging me in conversation?"

"You were usually the one who filled the empty space, Thora."

"That is not true. But I do not fault you for not remembering. You were piss drunk the majority of the time." She straightened that fringe. "There was nothing worth remembering either way."

"Such a shitty liar."

Her eyes rolled back. "Spare me."

"You can't be mad at me forever."

"Watch me," she said, marching back towards the castle, her wolves trailing along.

RED CALLA LILIES

THORA

E lias chuckled from across the training court distance, shaking his head at the man who had just brought me the heaviest assembly of flowers I'd ever held. It had been just a day since I'd buried Erik and I had already gotten three unwelcomed visits from prospective men aiming for my crown. But considering the rumours spreading regarding the man who would end up marrying me, it surprised me that I was still getting visits from potential suitors. Whoever was to become my king had a target on their back. Had Elias threatened this one?

The man still held my hand, his mouth pressed to my knuckles. "My queen," he purred, making my face curl with a wince. "I eagerly expect to court you at a time of your choosing."

Pulling my poor hand back, I reluctantly said, "I'll have someone send word for you."

Satisfied, he backed away and left me alone.

Dropping the flowers to the ground, I looked up at the snowy skies and groaned for a solid long minute.

"At least he was not in his hundreds," Elias said, walking up to me and glancing back at the man. "He'd make a fine docile king. That's what we're after. A man to solely hold the seat next to yours warm, and provide you with children of Isjordian blood, of course."

"Maybe I should force you to marry me."

His eyes drifted to the distance for a split moment before they returned to me. "We promised it would be a last resort."

"It is my last resort."

"I–"

"Yes, you," I sighed. "Still desperately in love with the woman who will not spare you a glance?"

When I heard him inhale the breath he would use to spit back something I'd confessed to him in a moment of weakness ten years ago, I put a hand to his mouth. "Say it and I will get the priest right here to marry us this second, whether you are tied to a chair, screaming and kicking, or not."

"I'm sure you'd enjoy that. The tied up part."

I shot him a cold look and he lifted both hands up in surrender. "Just make sure this one doesn't mind me going to untie him from the bed at the crack of dawn after you're done with him. Or will you actually let this one touch you? Erik was a special case you know, not sure if all will be good with your conditions."

"Since when are any of the men that serve me allowed to not comply with my conditions?"

"The unlucky soul has my undying pity."

"That unlucky soul might be you. What news do we have from Casmere?" I asked, stepping on the calla lilies laying on the floor. I hated calla lilies. Shouldn't I be getting roses or peonies at the worst? Why was I getting funeral flowers?

"You mean, what news do we have from our little spirit friend?"

"Since when did the White Veil become our *little spirit friend*?"

"Since it started mercilessly slaying Iskyla's soldiers and began bowing to you." Again, he glanced behind me briefly. "People are getting scared."

"A whole year and it hasn't hurt a single Isjordian."

"They've turned God fearing. They hear you visit the temple often. They don't hear the part where you use Nubil's statue as a shooting pole, but they hear you're praying. And that your prayers are being answered." He sighed. "Don't bulge your eyes out like that, all excited, it's really a disturbing sight. Fear is difficult to control, Thora. You control greed and desire with coin, you control power hungry vultures with empty seats in your court, you control peace by playing someone weak. But fear? Once you've spread it, there will be nothing to grant Isjordians comfort. They will want someone strong on that throne and you will be forced to hatch from this shell you've been disguising under for ten years. Fear might not work in our favour. At least not in the long term."

"You could have saved yourself a lot of talking if you'd just found me a husband."

His attention lifted to a spot behind me, and I turned to look at what had grabbed his attention only to see Malik standing a few feet away from us, his brows pulled in the deepest scowl and his jaw set tight. He didn't move at all. Only glared at us. Mostly at Elias.

Clearing my throat, I looked at Elias again. "You have a couple of days to find me a decent enough man to marry me, or you will be going down on your knees, understood?"

"As you wish, my queen," Elias said, shaking his head as he retreated.

Even though my back was to him, I knew he was looking at me. "What do you want?"

"I am well, and how are you?"

"Fabulous. What do you want?"

"I see you're still on the hunt for a king."

"Why would I hunt for one?"

"Right. They flock to you." He glanced at the flowers I'd stepped all over. "What if Iskyla kills this one, too?"

"I'll marry inside this time. Any other wedding advice for me?"

"Don't wear white."

"To my wedding?"

"To any wedding. You looked ghastly."

"You've not changed a single bit."

"Why would I change? I quite like myself. You quite liked myself, too."

Idiot. Fool. Annoying fool who was right, unfortunately. "What are you doing here?"

"Stalking you," he plainly said.

Appalled, I gaped at him. "Why?"

"Trade secrets. If every stalker started going around telling their reasons, we wouldn't be stalkers anymore."

"You're not funny."

"I'm the funniest man you know."

"If it helps you sleep at night."

"Oh, it does," he said, stepping closer.

"What are you doing?" I asked, tilting my head back to look at his towering stare.

"Looking." After a moment, he said, "Thinking."

I boredly clapped. "A milestone for you. Doing both of those at once."

"Gods have truly put you on this earth to humble me, haven't they?"

"What do you want, Malik?"

He leaned in a little. "Can't say it."

"Why?"

"You might hit me."

"Gods, you're unbearable."

"All compliments today. Glad I caught you on a good day."

"Excuse me," a foreign deep voice called from behind Malik, and we both turned at the lanky man standing there holding a bouquet of tulips—for me supposedly.

Malik threw his head back and laughed. After he was done laughing at my misery, he patted the man on his shoulder and left still chuckling to himself.

Surprisingly, the meeting Elias rushed to call me to attend apparently only required the presence of my sister, brother-in-law, him and Alaric. None of my court members were present and this seemed like a perfect ambush to get me to spend time away from court business. It would not be the first time they'd try.

"I know I should join family dinners more often, but is this truly necessary?" I asked, taking a seat.

"I've found you a king," Elias said, flashing me a grin.

I raised a brow. "You gave up and have agreed to marry me?"

"With all due respect, I would still very much like to convince a certain witch that her babies should have my eyes."

"Good luck with that," Oryn murmured under his breath, and then shot me an almost apologetic look. "It is someone else. Someone we all think would resolve many of your issues while being a great hand of help without making it look as if Adriata is being involved."

My blood grew cold. "Atlas and I get along, but he is engaged to Pen. I will not do that to either of them." He was powerful, had a great seat in Adriata and the Dardanes new council formed after the war, would continue to advise kings and queens for all of his life and was possibly the most equipped to do so, but he couldn't marry me. It would be a death sentence. And one I had no promise to give that he'd be able to get out of any time soon.

Snow suddenly blew out a cough, reaching for a glass of water and drinking it all in one go, while the rest chose to suddenly sightsee all the great wonders of my meeting room.

I blinked at all of them. "What?"

Elias, like the fool he was, smirked at me. "We weren't talking about Atlas."

Not Atlas.

It wasn't Atlas who they'd thought of.

It wasn't Atlas who'd agreed to marry me.

The man who'd agreed to marry me was waiting for me on my bed, leaning against the headboard, a bottle of unopened liquor and two glasses between his knees. A look I recognised too well etched on his face. The same look he had on his face the night he left without saying goodbye. The same look he'd worn when I'd screamed and cursed at him the last day we saw one another—that terrible day I relived for many nights. Utter dejection rested there. Like he'd travelled so far back his mind he couldn't find a way back.

"What are you doing here?" I asked, my voice echoing.

"Thought I'd celebrate with my betrothed," he casually said, and stood up, still not looking at me as he placed both glasses on my vanity and uncapped the unopened bottle, pouring some on both.

"Celebrate what?"

"Whatever you wish. Though we could start with our engagement."

Stunned, I remained staring wide eyed at him. "You agreed?" That one question felt like the wildest thing that had come out of my mouth.

"I did." And that seemed like the wildest thing that had ever come out of his.

"Then you know that nothing about this arrangement would be real," I said, starting to take my jewellery off, not believing myself for even entertaining the idea. I wasn't even going to. Not until I saw him just now. Somehow, I wanted to see him hurt, angry, helpless and at my mercy. I wanted to see what would make him leave next—what would it take. "You can fuck who you want, sleep where you want, do what you want."

"And you?"

"The same." I looked up at him. "We'd be marrying for politics, Malik. It would not be the first or the last time a monarch has done so. Once I have the Isliners off my throne's back, you will be set free from it. A temporary solution, but since it will cost you time and effort, I am willing to set a reward for it. Like Elias must have told you, you can have anything you desire."

He took a sip from his drink and swallowed hard, almost as if the taste of it made him nauseous. "Anything I desire." Not a question. Not a statement. He sounded bitter. Mulling over the words as if he didn't understand them.

"Yes."

"Anything I fucking desire," he muttered to himself, backing from me to peruse around my room, touching my furniture and inspecting odd paintings. "You will have to be married to me."

"As I said—"

"No," he interrupted.

"You won't do it, that is fine."

"I will. But not to your rules." When he put the glass down to fill it up again, I noted the shake of his hands.

Rules? What rules? "And what would those rules be?"

"No one touches you while we are married."

For a second, I was almost stunned, but I remembered that he was perhaps the most knowledgeable politician I knew. Court and war were his bread and butter. "I can control my urges. Understandably, people mustn't figure out this is a sham."

"I will be sleeping where you sleep."

What?

"Does that make you uncomfortable?" he asked.

"Yes."

"What a shame."

"What else?"

"Nothing else."

That was it? Those were his...rules?

I grabbed the bottle when he was about to take it and leave, holding it away from him. "How long? How long since your last drink?" The winces and the shakes told me more than he'd ever will.

He licked his upper lip. "A few years."

Like an arrow had struck me, my hand loosened and the bottle slipped from my grip, falling to the ground and splintering to little bits.

Malik suddenly hauled me up by my waist and put me to sit on the desk, lifting my long skirts to inspect my feet. "Fuck, Thora," he hissed, sighing and rubbing a hand over his eyes when he didn't find any glass shards on my skin. The moment he looked up at me, he froze, his face falling. "What's wrong?"

"Did Snow or Kil force you to this arrangement?"

"No."

"Someone else?"

His scowl deepened. "No one else."

"Why did you drink?"

"Why were you so against it?"

I frowned. "What?"

"Why were you so against this agreement, Thora? Why would some idiot you don't know be better suited for it than me? Why did you argue a whole afternoon against it?"

"I don't need you to be my protector," I gritted out.

"Then what do you need, sweetheart?"

"Nothing. I would never force you to do anything."

"Force me? You think someone like me could be forced?"

This whole day was giving me whiplash. The whole entirety of it was suddenly making me question if I had imagined it all in my head. "Why are you doing this? Is this a game? I really don't understand anymore."

"A game? What game?" A frown grew deeper and deeper between his brows the more he looked at me and found none of the answers he was looking for. "What is it that you don't understand about me wanting to be near you when you know damn well, Thora Krigborn, why I can't fucking stay away."

My voice was smaller than I wished it had been when I said, "You might have forgotten that night ten years ago, but I remember it well. Too well."

In moments, that frown he wore morphed into something else—realisation. "What night?"

Sickness rose to my throat at the remembrance of that day. He'd told me so much that day. So many words I hated to hear from his lips.

"Thora," he shouted, panicked as his eyes paced between mine. "What night?"

Pursing my lips tightly, I looked away, hating how my tears had remained tears after ten long years. Hating how they had never turned to rage. Hating how they still made everyone think of them as my weakness when they weren't. Not really. My tears kept me human. I would never apologise for them.

"Fuck," he muttered, reaching to wipe my eyes. "Fuck," he shouted again, standing. "Fuck!"

Then he was gone.

Skadi entered just as he left, probably having heard the noise. She handed me a tissue. "How many times do I have to tell you that you're too pretty of a girl to cry."

Why did everyone take issue with my tears? Ugly. Pretty. Didn't I have the right to cry regardless of how I looked? "Did you know that *pretty* translates as easy to love in Calgnan?" I said, bending down to pick up the glass pieces on the ground. "I've been called that since I was little. How come everyone finds it so hard to love me then? How am I so hard to love?" A shard pierced the tip of my finger and I watched a droplet of blood mix with the spilled liquor. "No one even tries. Everyone takes the easy way out and leaves." Wiping my finger on a piece of cloth, I stood and called out to my guards. "Send word for Neo."

"Now you're taking the easy way out."

"Can I be blamed?"

"Don't do it," she said. "Not this time. Don't do it anymore. You don't need Neo's help anymore, Thora."

Truth was that I did.

ORANGE ACONITES

MALIK

C ai was the first face I saw properly as I pushed past the Myrdur castle corridors. "Disappointed it took you so long after coming back to come see me. That hurt my feelings."

"What feelings exactly, you emotionless bastard."

He chuckled. "We are starting strong. Where are my kisses and hugs?"

"Out of my way, honey bun. I'll give you all my love in a minute."

He put a hand to my shoulder, stopping me. "What's wrong?"

"I need to see Visha."

He frowned, looking behind me as if he was expecting someone else with me. "Doubt she'd be interested."

"Neither am I."

"Thora not with you?"

"Why, miss her?"

"Yeah."

I pointed at him. "You'll tell me all about that when I'm done with the witch."

He followed after me. "If you go into her room now, you'll be *done by* the witch."

"Better by her hand than Thora's. She won't fucking speak to me and I'm losing my mind."

Both his brows flew up and he blinked like the dickhead he was. "Oh, we are saying things out loud now?"

"Shut up."

"Are we having an epiphany or a mental breakdown?"

I grunted in response, and then sighed. Hells, I was becoming my brother.

"Have you told her where you went? Maybe you should have started with that. Hells," he said, standing in front of me, "You can start by telling me, too."

"No."

"Very glad you're the still insufferable piece of shit, princeling."

I banged on Visha's door until she came out, trying her best to hide Elias groaning in the background. "What?" she asked, clouds of desire to maim pooling around her floating red locks.

"I've done something, and I can't remember it."

Cai pulled on my shoulder. "What are you talking about? Did you do something to Thora?" He pushed me against the wall, hard. "What did you do to her?"

"Ten years ago, before Alyone asked me to head to Seraphim with her, I went to the tavern. I had to drink. Fuck, I did a lot more than just drink. I thought I'd imagined her that night. But I think she was really there. I think she was really there, and I did something—I said something." Turning to Visha, I said, "I need you to go inside my head and find out what I told her."

"Just ask her," she boredly replied, trying to shut the door on me.

Grabbing the door, I pushed it back. "She won't tell me."

She stood there for a moment, thinking about it. "You're an Empath. What if you hurt me when I try to get inside your head?"

"I'm not an Empath, I'm *the* fucking Eldritch Commander," I said, pushing inside her room. "And wear something, Elias, for heaven's sake."

Despite the noise of the tavern, the screeching laughter in my ear from all the women who'd huddled around me, and the thuds of a few soldiers still celebrating a war we'd somewhat won a month ago, it was still not enough to drown memories and the voices in my head who kept taunting me still. I was mostly numb. Head to toe, nothing on my body felt mine. All except my mind. The only thing I really wanted to numb. It usually worked—it had worked for me since I was thirteen and had found my father's liquor one night. It wasn't working anymore.

All because I was...worried.

About her.

A chill went down my spine, feeling the cool of her magic near me.

She's found me.

Again.

Even the ghost of her had found me, because she couldn't be here. She was miles away. Ruling her little frosted kingdom. Acting like she was alright. Faking smiles left and right. She'd faked them for me, too.

"Who is she?" one of the girls on my arms asked, looking at the woman who didn't belong in a place like this enter the tavern. Even as a blurred apparition of my depraved mind, I could tell the shape of Thora Krigborn. The damn drugs were tempting me with her, reading into what I desired most and feeding her to me.

She stopped at the door, her eyes darting to the women around me, to their arms over my shoulders, around my waist, draped all around my body. It was suffocating and heavy. When she had hers around me—it never felt so heavy or suffocating.

Thora stepped before me, finally looking at me. At least I hoped so, I hoped she was looking at me. I waited for her to say something, to give me one fake fucking smile so I could explode and wipe it off the face it didn't belong on.

Tempt me. Make me say something I will not return from.

But then, even the ghost of her knew what I wanted to do. She knew long ago, this was why she had never said or done anything—she knew me too well. "May I speak to you?" she asked calmly—so calmly.

My ears rang when I said, "Then speak."

"Tell them to leave."

"Why?"

Instead of answering me, she reached for her pockets and threw bags of coins at the women. "Leave."

Celia scoffed, picking up a bag and throwing it back at her. The bag hit her shoulder and then dropped to the floor, the coins splattering everywhere. "You really think he keeps me around because of that? Silly, little girl."

I would have told her to shut the hells up and never talk to her like that, but I wanted the little bird to do it. I wanted to see her angry. I wanted her anger. Her hate. She had to give them to me. I didn't know how I would bear to leave for Seraphim without her hating me first.

Thora blinked at the ground for a few moments. When she looked up, her smile was bright and warm and so pure. "This concerns my sister, Celia. Your queen. If you hear this, you will either have to unhear it or die. By her hand or mine if you'd like. You're...a friend. I'd grant you that. Snow likes torture, but I appreciate instant death. It will be better if I do it." Her face was entirely destitute of emotion, cold despite the smile. "Let me do it."

Celia growled, unravelling from me and sauntering away along with the other women who'd already scattered at the mention of Snow.

"You lied," I said, watching her—watching this strange ghost of hers that I'd never seen before. They always came when I desired to lose my mind entirely, they came softly and gently, quietly. They guilted me with silence.

Her smile was still on though she rarely ever kept it on with me. "It was the first thing I was taught to do. How does that still surprise you?"

"What did you come here to lie for, Your Majesty? Practise? Ruling Isjord is no easy feat for someone like you. You need all the practice you can get."

The hurt was too obvious to miss, but she held behind her lie better than I expected her to. "I need," she breathed, swallowing hard, "I need your help. It keeps happening again. That day repeats over and over until I can feel his blood on my hands, Malik. I can almost smell that day in my dreams, my thoughts. Over and over. I can't sleep." Tears gathered around her emerald eyes and her lip quivered. "I really need to sleep. It has been days. I don't think I can keep going like this. I need sleep. Badly. Just one night is all I need."

There was nothing more I wanted than to grab her and hold her until she realised nothing could harm her, but this was a dream, she was a dream. I wanted to shatter it. Just like I shattered every other dream of mine. I couldn't have her in my dreams, too, asking for me and wanting my help, I'd go insane. "You'll get used to it," I said, the words tasting like poison.

Her lips parted and she stared at me as if I'd shattered every part of her little heart. "I only...I only need it this once," she murmured. "Only this once. I won't ask again. I promise."

Those words hit me like a rock. I remember using those words myself a long time ago. Just once. Just this time. It will be the last time. I will stop. I can stop. "I'm all used up."

"Malik, please."

I remember begging, too. Begging for the kind of relief she was begging. "I've told you to never beg, but it's like you're made for begging, little bird. You do it so well."

She stumbled a step back. "Please."

And I remember the desperation. Then succumbing to it.

I dropped my head back, looking up at the dented ceiling. "You're tiring me. This is tiring me. I don't want to do it anymore."

She needed my comfort. It was something I could never deny this girl or myself not even in a million lifetimes. But I was holding her hostage to me, reliant on me because of it. In truth, she did not need my comfort. It just had become something for her to cope with. And it eerily reminded me of addiction.

"Don't do this to me, please."

"I already did." For her. Only for her. She would get better. She had to. Without me. Without coping through something that would destroy her. Because I would. Everything I touched never lasted long.

She shut her eyes tightly, breathing out a shuddering sigh. Two stray tears dropped down her face, and she quickly wiped them away, righting herself. "Alright. I won't come to you anymore."

"Good. Don't."

"Is this goodbye?"

"I suppose it is."

More tears fell down her face as she stepped towards me, her hands resting on my shoulders while she leaned to press a shivering kiss to my cheek. "Goodbye," she murmured between muffled sobs.

And as she left, as her ghost disappeared behind those tavern doors, I pressed my hands to my face, feeling my entire body shake from my own cries. My heart felt raw, as if it was swimming in a pool of flames.

It wouldn't get better. Never. It had only gotten better when it had been hers. But at least she would be better. At least she would get better. It was a small price to pay to see her happy.

At some point, I'd gotten up, dragging my feet through the streets of Amaris, desperate for just one last glance at her.

I followed after her as she left the tavern, staying in the shadows, watching as she walked through Amaris, lost in her head. I couldn't let go of even this cruel apparition of her. Shadow, mirage, a dream, a nightmare, I wanted to hold onto her until she faded from me, couldn't just let go.

I watched her stumble on the rocky streets and then I watched Neo's hands catching her. The cruel illusion growing crueller. Yet, I still couldn't let go. I couldn't stop myself from witnessing the cruellest thing my mind had taunted me with.

I watched her looking at him...looking at him like I wanted her to look at me. I watched her throw her arms around his neck and I watched him wrap his around her waist as she cried in his arms like she had once done only in mine.

I only watched.

That's all I had done.

Watched.

Neo had watched me, too. He'd seen me as he'd held her, and he'd still held her.

My last words echoed around my head as Visha's magic cast out, disappearing. As the memory flared away, realisation set in. It had not been a dream, not a hallucination. She'd been there that night. I had not imagined her.

"I'm going to kill him," I said, standing.

Cai blocked my path, his hand on my shoulder. "For caring about her?"

"Care?" I barked a laugh. "That idiot saw me. He knew what he was doing."

"And what was he doing, Mal? What did he know?" He let go of me and stepped back. "Have your old room back. Don't go to her tonight. Not like this. She won't talk to you like this."

"Then I'll wait until she wants to, but I won't stay away. I didn't return to stay away. I didn't fight to come back to this world to stay away. I'm done staying away."

I'd waited in her room for almost all night. At one point, I'd considered showing up at Neo's house and dragging her back here, but I didn't want to even consider the possibility that she had gone to him. Then I'd felt her around Tenebrose, I'd felt her shadows move, she'd not gone to him. So, I'd settled to laying down. Only I had not considered falling asleep.

Something had gripped my ability to breathe. Like a heavy weight holding me in place. It wasn't just anything holding me back, it was black steel chains that brandished my skin the more I struggled, and they were forcing me to watch what laid before me, a tight iron mask over my head, not letting me even turn my head and look away from the view ahead. Snow's body hung from the ceiling, feverish children lying below her feet, more bodies scattered around. Snakes and shadows and death feasted on their bodies, draining them of blood and of their soul. All faces I knew. Faces I'd let die. Faces of people whose death I'd felt and would never be able to forget. Once you saw and felt the brand of death, you couldn't unsee or unfelt it.

"Weak," someone hissed on my ear. So many years had passed yet that voice was the one I could never forget or banish away. "So weak, my son," father continued. "How can you be one with death when you fear it so? How can you be a son of mine when you fear your own heart!" He circled me. "We must do what we have to do. Rip it, break it, drain it. All until it can no longer feel a thing. It is the only way."

He'd done as he'd said.

And he'd failed.

It would have been easier to not have failed.

At some point, I pretended I had, but I'd been found out soon after, and he'd done it all over again. Failing all over again. Many more times.

Everything before me began vanishing, one after the other they turned into ghosts of black smoke and then faltered in the wind until the dark room of my mind and the echo chamber of memories emptied. The mask slipped from my face, dropping to the ground with a thud. Then the chains slithered off my body as if they had never bound me. The creeping feel of death washed off my skin next, the scent disappearing from my lungs and the thought gone with them, too.

Shhhh, a small voice cooed, humming some intelligible soft lullaby. Gentle cold fingers raking through my hair, making my entire skin rise with chills.

Warm and cold. It had always felt like that.

Her touch had always felt like that.

Thora stood crouched before where I'd laid on the sofa, one arm hugging her knees to her chest and the other reaching towards me. Her hand dropped from my hair to tenderly stroke my arm back and forth. Her head rested on her knees, tilted to the side while her eyes were lost somewhere in the distance of the room. She hummed again, rocking herself back and forth as she ran her fingers over my arm, comforting me. As she always had.

At some point during my staring, her hand stopped moving and so did her humming. For a small moment, she remained frozen before her head slowly turned in my direction. When she noticed I was awake, she quickly pulled her hand back, staggering and trying to move away from me. Her back hit the small table behind and she winced.

I chuckled. "Too late to make a run for it."

Rubbing her sore back, she stood and made to head back to her bed, stopping when I said, "I've always been awake every time you've done it."

Every night.

Every single night I'd feel her hands on me.

Some nights, I had even wished for nightmares only so she could be there to draw me out of them.

She whipped around so fast she got dizzy. "What?"

"You used to talk to me as well." The world went so quiet after I left, and I wondered if it had always been so quiet. I wondered how I had ignored the quiet so much. She left a void that couldn't be filled with anything. No drink, no noise, no other person could fill. While I'd fought one addiction, I'd fallen into another. Every night, I'd torture myself with thoughts of her. And my mind was ever so obedient to that torture. "You'd say so many things."

Stunned, she looked at me. "You never said anything."

Because you'd stop. I didn't want you to stop. "You were not here," I said, sitting up.

Her mouth parted and closed a few times before she said, "I went for a walk."

"It was a long walk."

"It was."

"Did you go alone?"

It took her a moment to answer me. "No. My wolves were with me."

When I stood, she took a step back, putting more distance between us. I decided to stay where I was. Didn't know if I could stand seeing her walk away from me. But I did deserve that. "That night—"

She took a few more steps away and lifted a palm to me. "Don't."

"I shouldn't have done what I did."

"Don't really care."

"If I meant to you just a fragment of what you mean to me, you do care," I said, and she finally looked at me, her hand lowering just a little. "I shouldn't have done what I did, Rora, but I did it, and I don't regret doing it, just the way I did it. You relying on me was no different than me relying on a drink. If it had been someone else, someone better, they would have told you sooner."

There was nothing subtle about the way Thora felt. Every little micro expression she wore carried more meaning than one had in their entire body. From the way her eyes hardened, how that very little dip between her brows tensed, or how the corners of her mouth pulled in just the very slightest, told me enough, told me more than words could, more than my magic could. "It was easier knowing you meant every word."

"We never do anything easy." When I stepped toward her again, she didn't step away. "Me and you, sweetheart, we don't like easy."

"There is no me and you."

There were merely a couple feet keeping me away from her. That and the fact she still hadn't lowered her hand down. "There will always be me and you."

"Things have changed."

"Things can change however many times they wish," I said, dropping back on the uncomfortable sofa I'd proclaimed as my bed. "Doesn't mean I will comply with that change."

"Our agreement hasn't started yet. You can't stay here."

Fluffing my pillow, I got comfortable again. "Make me go."

"Malik."

"Harder. Try a little harder or get back in bed, little bird." I tilted my head to her. "Unless you want to get in mine."

Her frown deepened and deepened, and as she turned, she muttered, "You've lost your goddamn mind."

"I will if you keep standing there in just that," I said.

She stopped to give me an indecipherable look over her shoulder before she tucked herself in bed.

THE PAST

MALIK

I'd told her to keep a damn candle lit at night. Olympian nights were sometimes almost darker than in Adriata and she always ended up with a bruise or two in the morning when she got up to get water or use the bathroom. Of course, she had not listened to me. She laid on her stomach, face buried underneath a ton of black hair, her long nightgown had bunched around her hips, barely covering any of her. She'd also not listened to me when I'd asked her to return to Adriata. After six months in her father's dungeons, returning to not see her lay in my bed was worse than Silas's tortures. Even worse seeing a friend I'd considered a brother inviting her to his.

The drink in my hand had condensated, untouched, the ice melting and filling what little space was left in the glass. There was just one thing I was craving right now, and it wasn't the drink I was holding.

The longer I stood there in a corner veiled by absolute darkness, watching her, the more I taught myself the one type of pain I'd missed when I'd learnt the entirety of the emotion. The one type of pain that seeped like poison and killed so slowly you wouldn't even know you were dying.

Even in hell, my father won.

I'd learnt the depths of agony. Perfected pain in all its ways. Without even being chained or beaten.

"Are you just going to stand over there and watch me like a creep?" she asked, her voice sleepy and soft.

And that pain got softer, just a little gentler. I had no idea how she always knew of my presence even if she couldn't see me, but I liked it. "Would you prefer it if I did it from up-close?"

She pushed herself up on an elbow. "Much."

I dropped my head back on the stone wall, savouring the forbidding taste of desire that I'd lately not found a way to numb anymore. Staying away was no help at all. It only made me crave it harder. "Careful, Thora."

"Of what, Malik? What should I be careful of?"

Me.

There was very little holding me back. And it was all her fault.

Mine, too, for having eyes.

Laying down, she pulled the sheet over all of her body, and said, "Wake me up when you figure it out."

Through the thick darkness she struggled to see, I saw everything. From the look in her eyes, her rapidly falling chest, the sheen of sweat on her brow, to her fingers clutching and unclutching the bed sheets. There was no need to read her, she was in pain like I was. But her pain was stunning. I'd never seen pain in colours like hers.

"Aren't you warm?" I asked, rather than commit to the urge to go there myself and pull it off her.

"Would rather sweat than make you sweat. We both know you'll stop speaking to me for a few days if things get funny between me and you."

"Why would they get funny?" I asked, raising the drink to my lips and taking a bitter sip even though it was mostly water now that the ice had melted.

"Because you also want to touch what you see."

Chugging the rest of it back, I let the burn in my throat also burn away the words I truly wanted to say. "Bold assumption."

A yawn made her smile disappear. "I love how it bothers you that I can tell you what I want because you can't."

"More bold assumptions."

"You will give up this secret at some point, I'm sure of it. I have all of them. You'll give me this one, too."

"What makes you think so?"

"Because I want it. And you give me what I want."

"I do?"

"In time, I'm sure you will."

"You read the future now?"

"I'm writing it, Malik."

Finally, I lowered my glass on a table and walked to her bed, shedding my jacket before laying next to her. "You want to write history, little bird?"

After lighting a candle, she rolled on her side to face me. "Why, you want to help?"

"Depends. What do you want to write? Tragedy? I'm good with that."

Her mouth parted just slightly, and she tugged on her bottom lip as her eyes roamed all over my face. "You stink of alcohol."

"Maybe you should rub some of your perfume on me." Reaching a hand to the neckline of her nightgown, I wrapped the little bow there around my finger. "Put a bow on me, too."

Closing the space between us, she put a hand to my neck and rubbed her wrist behind my ear and down my throat. "There."

"I meant from the bottle, hellion," I groaned, wrapping a hand around her wrist and trapping it there.

"I'm stingy. Really stingy. And you're a friend in need."

She really had no idea how much in need I was.

"Don't know about the bow though. You could get all tangled up in it and end up tied up to this bed. All mine to do what I want to do." Her voice was low and thick when she asked, "Aren't you going to tell me to be careful?"

"Maybe."

Those cold delicate fingers slipped over my lips, settling there. "Now you can't say anything at all."

Apparently, I wasn't drunk enough, because I was letting her near me longer than I normally did.

"Don't know if I like that," she murmured, the tip of her finger chasing the shape of my mouth. "I like hearing you spout nonsense a bit too much."

"Is that so?"

"Yes," she murmured, too entranced by the movement of her fingers over my face.

I let her touch me.

More than touch me.

I watched her battle away her inner most frightening thoughts. Touching was different from other senses. It came from both want and need. She was made to not need or want it. Worse. She was made to fear it. I feared her touch for an entirely different reason why she feared mine. There was nothing I wanted more than help her get over it. It was for selfish reasons. Because I wanted her to fear it how I was fearing it. I wanted her to burn from the want and need like I was. I wanted to teach her all that. I wanted to teach her how to touch me and then I wanted to show her how I wanted to touch her.

Leaning forward, she left a soft kiss on my brow and then another on my eye, her lips lingering over my skin until it finally became the most torture I'd ever been subjected to. "Good night, Malik."

When she made to pull away, I held onto her tighter, not ready for it to stop.

Her lashes fluttered fast. "You should probably let me go now."

"Stay close."

After some strange, wide-eyed hesitation, she nodded just once and laid her head on my pillow, her face barely a few inches from mine. "I'm close."

My thumb moved back and forth over her rapid pulse. I wanted nothing more than to read her at that moment, to see the intensity of her colours. Fear or...fear. I could see it was fear, just from the look on her eyes. The desire to see what sort of fear was torturing me. That torture was keeping me oddly sane. "You still mind my touch?"

She thought about it for a moment and swallowed. "I touched you first, didn't I?"

"It wasn't what I asked."

"Don't make me say it out loud."

Perhaps I was drunk beyond control, because I grinned. "Why?"

"I want you to keep being my friend a bit longer."

"I am so good to you, little bird?"

"You make me forget."

"That is so unfair," I said, my smile gone. "You make me want to remember."

"Would that be so bad?" she asked, her eyes focused on the button of my shirt that her fingers were now circling.

"Very."

"Maybe we shouldn't be friends."

"Maybe you should stop throwing a fucking tantrum and come back to Adriata."

Her finger sneaked from the buttons of my shirt to the space between them, softly grazing my skin and making my mind spin. "Why do you want me back there? I thought you might want your privacy back."

"You know the innards of my mind. You think I can even have that right?"

"I can give it back to you."

"Keep it. And you're coming back."

"I am?"

"You are," I said, pulling her hand off my shirt and making to stand. Only stopped by her firm grip on my sleeve.

"Can't you stay?"

"I can't. No until you stop trying to put me together. You know how long it took me to pull apart at everything." No one but her knew, and I'd relied on her knowing that she wanted me as I was—pulled apart. But then she'd started looking for all the parts I'd buried. While I'd thought she was holding onto them, she'd tried to piece them together behind my back. Since I'd returned from Isjord, she smiled at me more, she touched me more, she looked at me more, she spoke less and listened more. All because I'd now become something for her to fix. What I'd feared most. What I hated most. Not because

I wouldn't let her do it. But because I'd disappoint her when she would fail.

"You're a problem. Worse is, you're my problem now." She gave me one last polite smile and laid back, tucking herself tightly. "Deal with it, Malik."

For a second, I stayed there, watching her stubborn head scrunch her nose all satisfied with herself and wriggle back in a comfortable sleeping position that was about to make me very uncomfortable to be clothed by the waist down.

"Leave now. You're distracting me. I need to concentrate on thinking away thoughts of murder." She sighted and then playfully murmured to herself, "Be gone treacherous thoughts. Be gone. He's an idiot, but he's my best friend. No need to think so maliciously, he needs that head and those hands. His tongue, too. I can't possibly pluck his eyes out, he'd miss looking at me like a creep."

Without even noticing it, I was smiling down at her. "You need to grow up, you know that?"

She peeled those piercing green eyes and raised a brow at me. "I'm grown enough. Just not for you, apparently. You like them wrinkly."

"You little shit."

Like the little hellion she was, she tucked a few strands of hair behind her ear, gave me another sugary smile and then closed her eyes again.

I stood, forcing myself to back away from her bed. "You better be in Adriata tomorrow night."

"Will not," she sing-songed, yawning. "You want me there? Come get me and my problem-solving self with some polite begging and a gift of some sorts. Like chocolates. Or lace trimmings for my new gown."

Throwing away her bedsheet, I pulled on a naked leg, dragging her across the mattress and then throwing her over my shoulder, before fading to Adriata.

Between Olympia and when I had her tucked back in her old bed, there was no time to get a reaction from her beside the wide eyed, open mouth look she gave me. I gave her thigh a little smack and let my hand linger there a little to feel the soft skin I knew no one had ever touched. "Night, night, bird," I said, feeling her shiver under my palm.

"No good night kiss?" she playfully asked just as I made it to leave her room.

"It would be a good night bite, so go to sleep now."

"I still want it."

Sweet, sweet hells, I hoped she wouldn't notice me laughing and grinning like an absolute idiot as I forced myself to leave her room and shut the damn door.

"Hope you didn't just murder my sister or something," Snow said as she casually passed me, wearing her night clothes and missing the usual six foot and four feet accessory drooling after her.

"Did you pet and snuggle your dog to bed?"

"Takes him more than some snuggling and petting to put him to bed, Mal sweetheart."

"Where are you going?"

"Now you're acting like a dog."

"Snow, where are you going?"

She stopped and the look she threw me over the shoulder almost made me recoil. Guilt mixed with harrowing pain laid there. And the more I looked, the more thankful I was that she had no shadows at all for me to see or feel. "Memphis chewed on some stupid daffodils and now has a bad stomach. I'm heading down to the healers to get her something while your brother is rubbing her belly."

"I'll come with."

"It's just down the corridor, you don't—"

"I'll come with you, Snow. It's late and my brother should have known better than to send you alone."

She walked beside me. "Nothing will happen to me, Mal. I'm safe here. You know it, too."

"Yeah. I know it."

AMBER DAFFODILS

THORA

C ai leaned against the stable doors, blocking my way to my horse, arms crossed over his chest as he stared at the surprisingly blue skies, looking very determined to interrupt my morning ride through Tenebrose. It had been a long while since we'd spoken to one another. Even when we had met, there had not been much to say.

"You can't just never return to Olympia," he said. "One day, you'll have to come back. You can't keep avoiding me because I remind you of it either."

It. One of the worst moments of my life did not have a name. It was just simply...*it*. "I am not avoiding you, Cai."

He finally looked at me and raised a brow. "Or blaming me why your brother left?"

"I've never blamed you for that."

"Why not?" he asked, pushing off the wall and striding to me. "It is the truth."

"He is not the first to leave me, and I suspect he won't be the last. Are you here for Alaric's monthly checks? You usually don't engage me in conversation. Or make your presence aware at all."

"You've seen me?"

"Were you trying to hide?"

He smirked at that. "Shouldn't you be angry?"

"I am angry."

His smile turned into a wide grin. "And I'm still intact."

"I'm not Snow."

"No, you're not." He shot a quick look behind me. "I'm actually scared of you."

"When you are tired playing lackey for Alaric, find me. I can get you a much nicer position in my court."

He flashed me a wolfish grin. "Are you going to offer me to be your king? Which, I am still really hurt about by the way. Why wasn't I considered? I'd make us the most handsome pair of royals in the realm."

"Because you don't want to marry me and marrying you would hurt someone."

Something flashed in his eyes. "And marrying Mal won't hurt someone?"

"Yes. It will hurt him. And he will soon make a run for it, while you could never escape me."

Cai's head dropped back, and he sighed, just staring up at the skies for a long moment. "Come to Olympia, Thora," he said after a while, still looking at the turning Isjordian ceiling that might be finally gracing us with some dull weather soon now that a few patches of white clouds were gathering above. "It's no longer a graveyard. It never will be again. So come back. Make it your battlefield if you want. Just come back."

"I will. Someday, I will," I lied, fiddling with my sleeve. "You weren't at my wedding."

"Had a hunch it would not be your last one."

"So, it had nothing to do with the fact that my brother was there?"

"He was there?" Cai nonchalantly asked, and then gave me a massive grin when I glowered. As he backed away, a portal opened just behind him. "Did he at least look like he missed me?"

"Yes." Eren looked like he'd missed everyone, but that had been his choice.

"He better. I miss him, too."

"Does he know that?"

"I hope he does. It would mean he is still thinking about me."

"It's been ten years. You should forget about him."

"I should, shouldn't I?" Before he went inside the portal, he turned to me one last time and said, "In ten years, tell me that again. I need to hear it."

"You think you'd still miss him then?"

"Probably."

My court had gathered entirely. From northern to southern lords and captains, to even a few bailiffs. The surprise only briefly crossed me because then I saw him sitting amongst my lords, taking that spot in my court like he always belonged there. He was hard to miss from the way my people had created a berth around him, all except Elias. If someone had been happy about the Eldritch Commander's ten-year long disappearance, it had been Isjordians. They'd all had witnessed a fraction of his might that day in battle, some had even fought against him and lost. Some probably still saw him in their nightmares.

Elias stood first and the rest followed, all except him, bowing when I took my seat. "Congratulations," Lord Venzor said without even hesitating. He'd been eager to close in on this charade. "On your engagement to Prince Malik, Your Majesty."

Engagement. To him.

The rest of my court followed after Elias in their congratulations, some thrilled, some caught by surprise, some anxious at the outcome, and a few livid at my choice but smartly quiet.

Snow had been against choosing some of my father's followers to be part of my court, but it was important people knew there were still voices somewhat loud as mine in this kingdom. And also because I enjoyed the banter. It got boring easily in this silent, cold kingdom of mine. One had to step up and entertain me.

Malik didn't think so, it seemed. He had directed a silent deathly glare on the part of my council that seemed somewhat in disagreement to the news.

"You suppose this will deter the Isline Queen from any future attack?" one asked to my displeasure. The firm Lord of Brisk I knew him to be faltered a little when Malik shot him a look. "But I suppose you two are, uh, in love, of course."

"Blindly," Malik boredly said, just as I said, "Unimaginably."

My court went quiet, glancing between him and I.

"I would like your blessing, Emil," I said, breaking the grave quiet and turning to Erik's father. "Without it, I will not go forth with the engagement. Despite our situation, Erik was more than just my betrothed, I wish to respect his memory if I am allowed to."

"You have my blessings, my queen," Emil said. "And my undying support from now on forth. What of my riches I would have passed to my son, I will pass on to your armoury and men who will fight against Iskyla. My campaign and support to you will die when I die, and I will not die before I see my son's murderer be punished. I do not mean death." He turned to Malik. "I am glad she chose you. Though I'm sure not everyone will take well to the news of the Eldritch Commander becoming our king, many will see its many benefits. Besides making our queen happy, that is."

"As am I," he said as if me and him were the happiest couple to have grazed this frosted earth. "But I am no longer the Eldritch Commander. That title no longer exists."

"I'm afraid that name will stick to you beyond your grave, Prince Malik," Lord of Modr added, smirking at him.

I'd seen the two talk at Erik's funeral.

The more I looked at Karl, the more the aggravating realisation struck me. Had he been the one to suggest this engagement to Elias or him?

"Besides," Karl added. "You two fought shoulder to shoulder in the Guardian war. Eldritch Commander and the Ybris. It's already a banner of your connection and power."

"Or a recipe for disaster," I said. "If I had wanted to marry into power, Karl, I would have wed myself."

Lord Kirkwall raised a brow, "Then why are you marrying him?"

"He's pretty to look at."

A few of my court members stared at me outrageously, but others simply ducked their heads and began shifting through the court documents they had brought in for me to see and discuss.

Only one was amused by what I said. Malik was grinning ear to ear.

And it was settled. Our engagement had just been recognised by the Winter Court, and within tonight, it would have reached every Isjordian home. Iskyla, too.

They all stood and left soon after.

Him, too.

"Off so soon?" I asked.

His hand stopped on the door handle, and he shot me a look over his shoulder. "Why? Miss my pretty face already?"

"Severely," I said, leaning back on my chair. "Sit. There are things I wish to discuss with you."

"Such as."

"Sit."

Crossing his arms, he leaned back on the door. "Say please."

My nerves burned. "We're not having a ceremony. Elias will get a priest and we will sign the marriage certificate in a meeting for all the court to see. Tomorrow, even."

"No."

"It wasn't a question."

"It wasn't up for discussion. There will be a ceremony. You'll get your pretty little arse in a big dress and you're going to walk up to me in front of the court, and they will witness you saying you will cherish and love me in front of a real priest."

He had to be out of his gods damned mind. "Why?"

"Personal reasons."

"Do share."

"You aren't my friend anymore. You said that. Me and you are just two people who shared secrets. Nothing more. Why would I owe you an explanation?"

I didn't...I didn't deserve this. "Why are you trying to hurt me?"

"Why would it hurt you?"

This time, I didn't look away. "Take a guess. You know all my deepest and darkest secrets. Even the last one." It was the last secret of mine I'd told him. The night before he'd left for Seraphim and not looked back.

The thing left in this realm that I hate most is that I've ever wanted you.

Good, he'd said. *Hate me.*

But I'd never really hated him. Only myself for wanting him.

"Do you still hate it?"

"Now more than ever." He was there. Before I could pull open the door to my room, I knew he was there. There was very little light inside the room, but I could make out the shape of his half naked body standing before the sofa he'd claimed as his bed. He ran a towel over his long wet hair and down his neck, stopping to look at me over his shoulder when I closed the door shut.

There was a long stretch of silence as I walked to my bed.

"No arguments, no pushing me out, or asking me to leave?" he asked, throwing a shirt over his body.

With shaky fingers I undid the back of my dress, letting the heavy fabric pool to my feet. "Do as you wish. I'm too tired to entertain you." No matter how hard I tried to grasp the laces of my corset, I couldn't force my grip to tighten and pull on them. My fingers had cramped entirely from shooting all afternoon.

Just when I gave up and decided to sleep with it on, his fingers were grazing mine, pushing my hand away as he tugged on my corset lace and began pulling the links loose with ease. He stepped closer, dousing me in his freshly showered eucalyptus scent. "When have you started wearing these?"

"Some time ago."

"And your shooting?"

"It actually helps." I turned a little to look at him over my shoulder. "How did you know I still shoot?"

He ghosted a finger over my chin, barely touching my skin yet I shivered. "That little burn on your chin from the string." His finger moved up towards my lip, and for the first time in a long while I felt the pull to lean into someone's touch, not push away. He might have noticed that too because his touch got bolder, fingers fully exploring the skin down my neck and down towards my arm until he had my hand in his. "The mark from the fletching. The dents between your middle finger and index. The slight tilt to the left of your shoulders. You must have just come back from shooting."

He was such a darned idiot. "You saw me, didn't you?"

That wolfish grin returned on his face. "Question is, how did you not? I was right there the whole time."

"You were not," I said, trying to spin to him, but he was still firmly holding onto the corset laces.

He stepped closer to me, and his scent of eucalyptus and autumn rain washed over me. "Three hours. I thought your fingers were going to start bleeding. When the arrows stopped coming, you started shooting nothing."

"That isn't true."

He continued pulling the rest of the laces off. "Isn't it?"

"Someone would have told me."

"You mean the two soldiers who were about to piss their knickers when you began nocking back invisible arrows? Sure."

"Why didn't you?"

He pinched my chin, pulling my face back to him. "Three hours, Thora. How much longer would you have gone if I'd not sent Elias to shake you off?"

He'd sent Elias? Never mind that. Why had he gotten so close to me? "Why didn't you call for me?"

"Didn't know how you would react. Elias seemed to be the safest option at the time," he gritted out. "Perhaps the last time."

I sucked in a sharp breath when the corset came loose and dropped to the ground with the rest of my garments, leaving me in a cotton chemise.

"That's more like it," he murmured, touching the little rosy ribbon that cinched the waist of the thin material. "I was wondering where they'd gone."

His hand remained there for some time, playing with the little ribbon while my gaze was fixed on his left arm. I remembered his body better than I remembered my own, it didn't take me long to notice there was something different. Without thinking about it first, my hand wrapped around his wrist, and I fully turned to him.

Between the thick old tattoos, there were new ones—not fresh, just not the ones I remembered him having before. They were dainty, almost amateurish and cartoonish compared to the rest. They were not designs made by someone who knew what they were doing. Because they were done by...me. A long time ago.

THE PAST

Thora

Twice now he'd fallen asleep in the library as we searched for answers to Aurora's weakness. Though, I was thankful he wasn't falling asleep on the tavern floor or some dark alley where I couldn't find him. At least he was sleeping. At least one of us was.

His sleeves were pulled back, revealing a map of tattoos and another path of scattered scars and burns. To know how to inflict pain on every inch of someone's body, you have to know how that pain feels on every inch of your own. That is what he'd told me.

My fingers shook as I lowered them to trace a long burn. The more of it I touched, the more did my own skin burn, like I'd been the one to get that scar. And it hurt, it hurt the same. Like someone had pressed a scalding iron rod all over me. It had hurt the same, it had burned the same when he'd told me the story of how he'd gotten it.

His shoulders rose faster when I ran the tip of my finger over a few of the jagged marks, his breathing turning shallow.

The only parts of his body that were not inked were his face, part of his hands and his scars. He'd never covered them, always had marked his body around them.

Bored out of my head, I reached for a pen and filled it with ink, starting to trace lines over those scars, drawing over them. Though the colour of the ink was starkly darker than those of the tattoos, my drawings blended quite nicely. Branches. Silly little flowers. Arrows and even some squiggly lines that from an odd angle somewhat resembled birds and wolves and deer.

Very proud of my work, I smiled down at them.

A sudden strange bone chilling sensation raised the hair on my neck, and I startled when I glanced up, catching him watching me, dark amber eyes half shut and drowsy. They first fell on the pen I held and then on his skin before they rose to mine again. Staying there a while, locked on mine.

"It will wash, it's just ink," I said quickly, standing so fast the chair groaned loudly against the tiles, the emptiness making the sound echo down the rest of the quiet library. "I'll grab a cloth."

His hand wrapped around my wrist, stopping me. "Sit and go on."

I blinked fast. "What?"

"Go on," he said, his words slurring like he'd been drinking even though he didn't smell much like alcohol. "I've got loads of them for you to draw on."

Something heavy settled on my chest and his mouth twisted into a cruel smile. "Feeling bad for me, little bird?"

"Shut up."

He chuckled, pulling me to sit down. "Love it when you boss me around. Don't you like that, Thora, taking control from me? I know I do," he murmured low. "But I am a little fucking twisted in the head."

"I hate every word you say when you are like this."

That grin turned cruel, only how he knew to be cruel—drained of emotion and drenched rancour. "Then go."

Never. I wiped a sleeve over my eyes and settled on the chair next to him, dabbing the pen in ink again with shaky hands and blurry eyes, refusing to let this side of him win.

He began undoing his shirt, not taking his eyes off me. "Have fun," he said, throwing it off and sprawling on his seat, looking the most aware I'd seen him be when he was like this.

He watched me intently through that drowsy look that made my insides twist with something worse than sickness. His head rolled back, and he let out a small groan when I lowered my hand to his stomach. His chest rising and falling fast then faster and faster the more I drew on him, the more of him I touched.

But so did mine. My heart was erratic. My lungs were strained. I wouldn't weep. I wouldn't allow myself to cry at the sight of his scars. At the cruelty behind them. At his cruelty to me.

His hand reached forward, his thumb swiping under my eye to wipe tears I didn't know were pouring. His hand slipped through my hair, and he leaned forward, his lips pressing to my cheek, then closer to my eyes. He kissed each tear away and I sobbed harder, my sounds grew hoarser and louder, they bounced so eerily around the empty library walls. I felt hands ripping me apart from the inside.

"Sooner or later, I knew you'd cry because of me, too."

"It's not."

"Then who are your tears for, Thora?"

I smacked his chest and pushed back to stand. "Not you. You don't deserve my pity or my tears." They were for another Malik, the one who'd been too young and innocent to be cruel or hateful.

He got up to follow after me as I weaved through the dark library corridors lit only by some faint distant lantern and the glistening tiny stars on the ceiling.

"Stop it," I said, stumbling in the darkness.

"Can't let you be swallowed up by some dark monster."

I hit him with a book, quickly moving backwards. "You're the only dark monster in here."

"Correct. Only I can eat you up, little bird." He backed me into a corner, caging me in between arms.

"Pleas—"

His hand pressed against my mouth, his body pressed against mine. "Scream, Thora. Bite and scratch and cry, but never beg. Don't allow anyone to see you at their mercy." Bringing his face closer, he pressed his brow to mine. "No one."

Pulling at his fingers, I breathed, "You're not just anyone."

The entirety of his half naked body was against mine, the closest I'd ever allowed anyone to be, the closest I'd allowed another body next to mine. "Then who am I, little bird? What am I?"

He wouldn't remember what I said, so I said something I needed him to forget, "Malik. M-my Malik."

His voice was thick and dark, "Is that so?"

"Isn't it?"

Even through the faint lantern light that had reached the corner where we were, I could see the gleam in his eyes. "Perhaps it is."

I put a hand over his mouth when he leaned in. "I won't let it be just another drunken mistake of yours."

"It can't be anything else."

"I know," I whispered back.

He dropped his forehead on my shoulder and let loose a long exhale, his arms tentatively wrapping around my middle to pull me close—closer than I'd ever been to him. "You smell perfect."

"You're drunk."

A pain groaned drew out of him. "Hold me back."

"You're drunk," I repeated.

"Just hold me back, Rora."

"I can't," I whispered low, holding my arms limply by my side.

"Please," he begged, his breathing growing laboured. "Please."

Shutting my eyes tightly and forcing my nausea back to the bitter pit of envy in my stomach, I did just that. I held him back. I'd held him almost all night long. That night he'd been mine. He'd been my Malik.

He'd never let me hold him again after that.

At some point, I believed I'd imagined him ever feeling like mine.

IVORY CHRYSANTHEMUMS

THORA

That night at the library seemed so far away. A different lifetime entirely.

My fingers moved up his arm, trailing the vines I'd drawn over his scars. "How?"

"After you left me alone at the library in a puddle of my own misery, I went and had them done."

I pulled my fingers back like I'd been struck by lightning. No. He'd been drunk. I remembered that much. He shouldn't though. "But—"

"They needed to be covered," he said, as if to almost spare me from my own daily dose of embarrassment. "The scars."

"Thought they hurt to cover?" I asked, gladly taking his bait, and pretending that part of the night had not happened.

"It did. They did," he said, his gaze dropping from my face to my body. He quickly averted his eyes away from me, focusing them on a distant wall as if it was the most interesting thing he'd ever seen.

I looked down on me and then sighed at my very thin and transparent slip dress I wore. "They're just tits, Malik. You need to get over the fear of them. Especially since you insisted we bunk like old soldier pals."

Those eyes were back on me, a smile stretching on his face. One he looked to be containing and failing. "You could help me."

Arching a brow, I asked, "Help? Help you? Help you get over the fear of my tits?"

"Worth a try." His eyes slid back down between us again, lingering a little this time.

"What are you doing?"

"Getting over my fears."

"I would hit you right now, but my arm has cramped up."

"Unlucky me." After one last unashamed glance at my chest, he began backing away. "Just gold," he said, dropping on his sofa. "For my ring. I'm not a diamond and rubies type of girl."

I couldn't make myself move or look away at his body stretched on the small sofa, at his skin marked with my touch or at the necklace hanging over his neck. My necklace. The one he'd given me ten years ago. The one I'd sort of given back.

"If you're going to keep staring, Thora, come and do it from up close. You'll catch all the details."

"That's mine."

His eyes remained shut, but he knew what I was talking about. "You gave it up."

"I threw it at you."

"Very hard, if I might add."

"I want it back."

"No."

Walking up to him, I reached for the necklace, but he was quick, wrapping a hand around my wrist and pulling me down to him until my face was hovering barely an inch away from his. "Say that you're sorry for throwing at me. Say 'I'm sorry for throwing the necklace at your head, Mal.'"

"In your dreams."

"Sweetheart, in my dreams you're preoccupied with other things. Say that you're sorry. It hurt." His eyes dropped to my mouth for a moment. "It's a heavy stone."

"You're just a wuss."

"This wuss is owed an apology."

"You first."

"What did I throw at you?"

"The fact that I needed you."

There was a moment of silence before he said, "You've never needed me, Thora."

"You really have no idea."

He bit down on his smile. "Don't distract me. Apologise."

"You first."

"I'm trying to be a gentleman, sweetheart."

"You're a dick."

"Leave my dick out of this." His other hand wrapped around my jaw, his fingers squeezing my cheeks hard. "Say it. Say you're sorry." He pulled my face closer. "Give me a little pout, too. And some sorry eyes. I love your sorry eyes. Best sorry eyes I've ever seen."

He was such an idiot. An idiot that my heart still felt funny around. "I'm sorry for hitting you."

"How hard was that?"

I gave him a polite smile I usually gave little kids so they wouldn't be afraid of me. "I shouldn't have wasted all that energy and just killed you."

"I would have haunted you forever, good thing you didn't."

"Your turn to apologise."

His grip on my face loosened a little. "I'm sorry for whatever I did."

"No," I said, holding onto his arm. "Apologise for leaving me."

"Can't lie to you, little bird."

"Try."

"I'm sorry for leaving you."

The worst lie I'd ever heard came out of the mouth of the man who had never lied to me. But it was good enough, I suppose. The discomfort in his eyes made it all worth it as much as a real apology.

Pulling hard at the necklace until the chain broke, I turned and headed to my bed, sinking inside the covers and cradling the amber stone between my hands like it burned. It did burn. It burned with memories.

14

THE PAST

THORA

I was unsure if my sister had finally lost her last screw, or she really thought it appropriate to throw a massive celebration through the entirety of Olympia right after the man I knew she loved had died in his arms. At least that is what Malik had told me right after he'd chosen to pretend I never existed to begin with.

A hand wrapped around my wrist and dragged me to the dance floor.

His jaw was set tight as were his eyes on my empty neck. "You took it off."

"Surprised you can actually see at this point." How much had he had to drink?

"Where is it?"

"Why?"

"I need you to go put it back on."

I scoffed. Why was he treating me like his dog? "Is it a leash? Did you give me a leash, Malik?"

"Yes."

Before I could raise my hand and smack some sense into him, he pinned both my hands behind me and leaned in my ear. "Careful putting those hands on me, Thora."

Leaning forward until my body was pressed to his, I rested my cheek on his chest, listening to his erratic heart and waiting for it to calm down again. There was something wrong. I knew it. And he wouldn't tell me. Why wouldn't he tell me?

He was either too tired or way too drunk, because he didn't push me off. "What are you doing?"

"Trying to hug you."

"Why?"

"Because you need it."

"Who needs *hugs*?"

"Idiots like you."

"Thora."

"Stop saying my name like it is a full sentence and just tell me what's wrong."

"Put the necklace back on."

Pulling back my sleeve, I lifted my arm up to his face so he could see the yellow stone dangling from its chain wrapped around my wrist. "It wouldn't go with my dress. Will you stop being pissy about it now?"

"Pissy?" he asked, almost offended.

"Yes, pissy. Why won't you tell me what happened at the lake? It's like...it was like...you were there and then you weren't."

"Don't take that necklace off, ever," he said, changing the topic entirely.

That was when I angrily began taking it off.

He was quick to wrap it back on and pull me to him. "Thora."

"Not a full sentence," I sneered.

"It is to me," he calmly replied, putting it back on after I tried to take it off a second time. "Don't take it off. Me and you are not tied beyond this realm. Something happens to me or you, I won't be able to find you. I had Oryn place some of my essence inside the stone while you were sleeping one night."

"Creep," I murmured, my struggle dying off, but something else began knocking hard against my chest. "I'm going to heavens. We won't ever be in the same place beyond."

"Sure thing."

Looking away so he wouldn't see what his words had done to me, I said, "I've done nothing to grant me hells."

"Talking back to me like this sure has, you little hellion."

"Why should I even listen to you, Malik?" He wasn't listening to me. He wasn't talking to me. We were two people who had just learnt to comfortably share the same space without doing much, and I didn't like that at all. Because I wanted to talk to him, listen to him. Since we'd left White Bridge a couple months ago, my mind wasn't drifting off so much anymore. It had been long since I suspected it was because of him. Like he said, we were two sides of the same chipped coin. It felt comfortable sharing even the worst of my thoughts with him.

He lowered his eyes to mine, taking a little time to answer. Looking at me like he'd find the answer there. "Because I am your friend. Best friend. The very best, actually. Friendship bracelets, hair braiding, secret telling best friends," he said ever so simply, folding my dress sleeve back so that the necklace was exposed, and then lowering it to my side.

The idiot. "Why would you want to find me beyond?"

After giving me one of those looks he usually wore to tell me he didn't wish to answer me, he raised a hand to my fringe, pushing it to the side. "Don't take the fucking thing off."

I shook my head, letting my fringe fall back into place. "I want to put a leash on you, too."

His mouth twitched. "You got your hands wrapped around my throat, isn't that good enough?"

"Are you sure it is my hands?"

"I'm sure. Gangly and fucking cold all the damn time."

My hands weren't gangly. Sure, they were thin and bony, but I wouldn't call them *gangly*. "If I tell you a secret I've not told you before, will you tell me what happened back at the lake?"

"And those damn little, cold fingers just keep squeezing and squeezing."

"You're letting me, and you love it, you sadistic—"

He put a hand over my mouth and grinned. "What secret?"

"You first," I sputtered, pushing his hand away from my face.

"You started it. Go on, bird. Tell me your pretty little secret," he leaned to whisper in my ear, making me shiver like I'd just experienced my first ever winter chill.

It was silly and immature, but I know he thrived on secrets that were slightly embarrassing to me. "I've never kissed. Suppose I don't have to go into detail about the lack of other things that usually follow kisses that I've not done."

"You can fuck without kissing. You can do many other things without kissing."

I sighed, trying to hide my red embarrassment. "That usually comes first in my book of rules."

"Not even once?"

I was nineteen. Was it really that late for me to have not? Was I helpless? "The closest I've let a man or a woman touch me for more than a second it's this." Looking up from his chest, I said, "It's you." Because it was how I wanted it. I only wanted to touch him.

"Why?"

"Because I can ruin you."

"You can ruin many men, Thora," he said, ghosting a finger down my cheek and wrapping a strand of hair around his finger. Watching me. Waiting for me. Smiling when I didn't react at the slightest in the way I reacted with others.

"Not like I can ruin you."

He pulled my strand of hair to his face, inhaling the scent. "I slipped."

Too distracted, I stuttered, "You...you slipped? Where?"

"Between worlds. Life and Death. Just as we crossed from one realm to the other. Not only did I feel Kil die, I felt just about everything else, too."

"Felt all what?" I asked, my voice barely a whisper clogged with tears.

"Just felt. All and everything like I've told you. A sick person in the distance. Someone in love. Another one dying. Except that we were in a graveyard of sorts filled with miserable spirits. And the woman standing over my dead brother wasn't just someone, so I presume you can connect the other dots. I can numb my body, tire it, but I can't do that to my mind." He grinned down at me. "Yet—can't do it yet, but I will find a way."

"You should have told me. Why didn't you tell me?"

A wicked smirk titled up his lips. "Because you wanted to know it. Really, really wanted it. I knew you'd give me something in exchange for it. Something you wouldn't have told me otherwise." Leaning in, he murmured right over my lips, "For whatever reason."

A heavy weight pulled between my thighs, and I barely managed to mutter a breathless, "Idiot."

He grabbed my chin and rubbed his thumb hard over my mouth and smeared my lipstick in the process. "Don't pout, you're not a duckling." His eyes darted somewhere behind me, and he dropped his hand from me. "Yes, brother?"

Kilian stood there, hands in his pockets, head cocked back and gazing back and forth between us. His grey, terrifying eyes narrowed on my face and then on Malik's hand that had just been there, stained pink with my lipstick. "Meet us in the night gardens in Amaris."

"Has Snow finally decided to sacrifice you for the greater good?"

"I'm marrying her before the gods."

Malik barked a laugh. "Look, brother to brother, she's cute, but she's a little insane. Reconsider or at least think about it for a bit longer."

Silence fell between the brothers for a while and then Mailk's smile fell. "Shit, you're not joking."

Kilian simply blinked once. "I'm a king, brother. I do not *joke*."

"Does she know you're marrying her?"

"Funny," Kilian said, and then faded away.

Malik turned to me, frowning. "You think she knows?"

"I bet it was her idea."

He still looked confused and then made to grab me to fade us both, but I stepped back and out of his hold. "Not in the mood for a game of catch, bird. Now, come here."

"I wish you had said something. I wish you'd come to me on your own instead of seeking something from me in return. I wish you had thought of confiding in me."

"Are we changing the rules now? Remember how this all started."

"Yes, I don't like those rules anymore. I want you to come to me. I want you to tell me whatever, whenever."

"Why?"

"Unsaid words leave scars."

"Maybe I deserve them."

"No one deserves scars, Malik."

"Maybe I do."

"No."

"No?"

"Just no. No, you don't deserve them. No reason. You don't need reasons to justify why you should have never and should never be harmed. It makes sense, you know. In my head. It should make sense to you."

"It isn't quite."

"Well, force it." Grabbing my skirts, I said, "Let's find out if your brother has lost his mind after returning from the dead."

He grabbed my hand. "Don't tell Snow. Kil said she doesn't know yet what happened at the lake."

VIRIDIAN CARNATIONS

THORA

Iskyla had become oddly bold again considering her husband was still leisuring in my mercy and in so many luxuries it offered. I wasn't interested in torture, much less in watching it, so keeping her husband as pawn didn't really give me much satisfaction as killing him would. And now that Iskyla was breaching past the rules of my kindness, it was time to cut the loose ribbons and kill him.

She'd gone and touched over the Modr border and into Hanai. Not only to get on my very last nerve and attack one of my strongest cities, but to apparently get on Moriko's last nerve, too.

What Iskyla didn't know was that Moriko had a different approach to threats of violence and war compared to me. I kept them at bay because one way or another, it thrilled me just a little, but the Autumn Queen would set loose her cannons if she saw a single sail in sight.

"It's just part of her propaganda," I said, fiddling with my necklace, smoothing my thumb over the rock's flat surface and smiling when I realised I remembered every little bump and dent on it. "To show Isjordians what I am not willing to do—put Isjord on top again. It hasn't been long since Brisk lands were returned to Hanai, so she is rubbing Isjordian pride on a very fresh wound. You remember the uproar back then." It had been the closest Isjordian's had tried to overthrow me. Hard to overthrow me without a head though, so I'd gone and quietly taken a few off from my father's old supporters that still had a little power and influence on the rest.

"I'd hardly say Isjord is far from the top, Thora. Even considering what it lost ten years ago."

"They don't want levelled playing fields. They want one crowned. Since they were made aware that Olympia exists, Isjordians have been wanting that even more."

Nia's all too warm of a gaze turned to me. "And what do you think?"

"That they need to get over their god damn fears and deal with it."

A sly smile overtook her face. "Marrying Mal will make them think otherwise. They will become greedy knowing that one of the most powerful men in this realm will become their king."

"He might be that, but he is just another tool."

"Oh, he is a tool alright, but you're underestimating him. Which strikes me as strange because you never before underestimated him. Better than everyone, you know how smart he is despite what he leads on. Just like Snow, his greatest power has never been his magic."

"I know."

"He will want to lead."

"As long as he does it under my guide."

"What if he doesn't?"

"I know how to make him leave." I knew many other ways to get him to abide by me, but that felt easier to say. Our strings were attached in such a way that it was impossible for him to overstep.

Nia cleared her throat and awkwardly fiddled with her blouse's neckline. "Don't know about that. He looks pretty determined not to stay away."

"If you tell me he is behind me, I'm going to scream."

She pursed her lips tightly and I sighed, my eyes suddenly feeling so tired they couldn't help but draw shut.

"You should keep your eyes open, aunt," Sam said, stepping by my side. "Considering how many enemies you have."

Perfect. Even my eight-year-old nephew was mocking me.

Nia chuckled. "Hi, kid."

"Aunt," he boredly greeted back, his eyes searching around—possibly for a girl who was a little short for her age with long, deep dark brown hair and a pair of very special but cold hazel eyes. "You came alone?"

"No, Karin is somewhere around here," Nia said, looking around for traces of her daughter.

My nephew's brows jumped just a little. "She is?"

"Isn't she a little old for you?" I asked, a little amused at my nephew's little obsession he developed since he got taller than past my knee.

"One day she won't be," he replied, fading and reappearing behind Karin.

Without turning, I said, "Yes, Malik?"

"My liege," he greeted right near my ear, and I shivered, gooseflesh spreading down all over my skin. Throwing an arm around my waist, he nodded at Nia. "Helenia."

She rolled her eyes. "Help me heavens."

Gently, I pushed his arm off my waist and stepped a little further away from him, not wanting him to see the gooseflesh spreading all over my naked arms. "What are you doing here?"

It looked like he didn't like that. "Thought I'd catch sight of a pale ghost I'm told to be wearing a rather fashionable cloak."

Nia glanced at me before asking, "The White Veil?"

He nodded. "That's the one." Tilting his head to me, he raised a brow. "Were we blessed by his presence?"

"He?" Nia asked, folding her arms across her chest. "Why can't it be a she?"

"Women are meticulous murderers. Rather tidy. This one is messy. I've not met a messy woman killer beside Snow. And it can't be Snow, can it?"

"Because we would know?"

"Because she would have shown her face from day one. People are more afraid of her when she isn't covering her face." He pointed at the tunnel that Moriko's Aura were working to seal permanently. "Iskyla is playing one hell of a game."

"If you would call it so," Moriko said, approaching us. "I suppose you got my apologies for not visiting and congratulations on your engagement along with the tea set."

"Cutlery set this time," Nia tried to correct discreetly, and Moriko's mouth twitched with humour just the slightest.

"You keep looking over at the tunnels as if they are about to return," Moriko noted, and I realised I'd craned my neck back in that direction.

I shook my head. "No, I just thought I heard something." The heartbeat. It sounded stronger here than it had sounded back in Isjord. Now more than ever, I was doubting whether it was more than just a sick game my mind had started to play on me for depriving it of the remedy I'd been rubbing on it for the past ten years—a remedy I could no longer rely on because *he*'d know. I didn't want Malik to know that I was still the same as that sick, needy, useless nineteen-year-old girl he'd left behind. I didn't want him to know that nothing had changed for me like it had for him.

Modr was oddly lively at night compared to the rest of my cities. It was the first time in a few years that I had stayed overnight in this part of Isjord. Perhaps I had something to thank Iskyla for. Making me realise the beauty of my lands, my people. Maybe it was the warmth we borrowed from Hanai, the one my lands missed and could never have. I didn't know exactly, but the city had changed from how it had been years ago.

Karl's house was right in the middle of the city square, and from the window of my bedroom I could see directly into a tea shop filled with the young, celebrating and laughing away their youth.

The door behind me cracked open, and no one other than Malik Castemont stood there, leaning against it, the light from behind him casting his face in shadows so I couldn't see what was written there.

"Candle," he said, stepping in and grabbing something from a bedside table. "Match." He lit one. "Fire." Bringing the small flame to the candles, he lit them all until the room filled with shadows and light. "Light." He blew in the match. "Why do you sit in the dark?"

"You're afraid of it."

His mouth pulled into a smirk. "Bird, I'm not *afraid* of it. I just told you that I don't prefer it."

"You're scared." That is what I liked to believe. I liked to think there was a way for me to hide from him.

He crossed his massive arms over his chest. "Is this a way to keep me away?"

"Perhaps."

He groaned, dropping his head back on the wall. "I love tasty lies. Makes me want to sink my teeth in them."

"It was not a lie."

"It's alright, sweetheart. I enjoyed it nonetheless."

"What do you want?"

"Things that you can't give me. But for now, I wanted to take you out for a walk."

"A walk? What am I? A dog?"

"We've announced our engagement, yet no Isjordian has seen us together. Cloak or no cloak, little sourpuss?"

He was right. Unfortunately. "Cloak," I said, grabbing it from the armchair and throwing it over my shoulders.

He pointed his head to the door, and I tidied my skirts, heading outside. Karl's house was massive and very dark at night despite the flickering candlelight on almost every wall. His shadow from behind me had towered over mine, eating mine entirely.

Even they looked menacing. More so than him actually.

"Why did you follow me outside that first night in Drava?" I asked as he came to stand beside me. I'd always been curious.

"Because I was envious."

The streets went quiet. Every eye turned to us as we made our way towards the city square. "Of what?"

"You. I saw myself in you. I saw what I couldn't be."

"Which is what?"

"Strong."

I stopped, turning to him. "You were wrong."

"Takes a lot of strength that I didn't have to pretend everything is fine when it isn't."

"I was just a good liar," I said, continuing our walk. Maybe I still am.

"You're a terrible liar. No one falls for your lies, they just pretend to because of how strong you show yourself to be even when you don't feel strong at all." He held a hand in front of me. "Hold it."

"I don't want to."

"Your enthusiasm makes me blush, but this isn't about what you want. It's about what they want. And they want to not doubt their queen."

Wiping my sweaty palm to the side of my cloak, I gave him my hand and he laced our fingers together, my cold skin meeting his warm one. This was officially the most awkward thing we had done. I don't ever remember holding his hand like this before.

"Don't make this awkward."

I coughed, almost choking on air. "I'm not."

"Then stop walking like I am holding a ransom over your head."

He pulled me inside a tea shop, sitting me at a small table by the far corner, beside a large window overlooking the street outside while he went to pick up tea and a plate of biscuits for us. The owner and even the customers had all gone silent, watching us. Mostly him when he returned to the table to sit across from me.

"I've never been inside one in Isjord," I said, undoing the cloak tie at my neck, not noticing him intently watching me until I had it folded on my lap. "What?"

"Do you ever wonder what it would have been like if you were not the Ybris, daughter of a king?"

His unusual question took me aback. "It might sound strange, but I don't think I ever have. Have you?"

"Have I ever thought what it would be like if I wasn't a spoiled princess?" He picked up a biscuit. "Never crossed my mind."

"Just when I thought you might have the ability to have a proper conversation," I muttered, taking the biscuit from his hand and shoving all of it in my mouth.

"I have thought about it," he said, biting down on a smile as he carefully reached across the table to swipe his thumb over the corner of my mouth. "All the time. Could have been a baker."

I coughed, patting my chest as I attempted to laugh around the large mouthful of cookie I was chewing. The images of him in a tiny apron and tiny hat almost had tears streaming down my eyes.

"That funny, huh?" he asked, stirring one cube of sugar in my tea and pushing it in front of me.

"You're ridiculous."

"Crushing my hopes and dreams is a very mean thing to do."

"You'll survive."

"Barely," he muttered, eating some of the biscuits.

Uneasiness fell over my bones. "Enough people have seen us," I said, pulling my cloak over my shoulders. "We can go back now." This was reminding me much of our time together ten years ago, and it was almost making me miss it, too.

"Spending five minutes with me is unbearable for you?"

"Yes. I don't wish to relive ten years ago. Not when I've already put that behind me."

When we returned, he followed me inside the room and dropped on the armchair in the far corner. It was pointless to argue with him. He'd end up doing whatever he felt like doing and I wouldn't have much of a choice but to accept it. "Sleep," he said. "Tomorrow will be a long day."

Shedding my cloak, I turned to him. "You don't have to watch me tuck myself into bed."

"No, but I want to."

My feet were glued on the spot. "Where will you sleep?" There was only that armchair and the bed in the room. And he was most certainly not going anywhere near my bed.

"I won't."

"You said tomorrow will be a long day."

"It will be. For you, my queen."

I pulled my dress off and lifted my eyes to his. "Undo my corset."

A smile rose on his face as he got up and reached me. "I like them," he said, expertly undoing the laces. "I like taking them off you even more."

How did he still have this power over me? Even after everything? "Must have had a lot of practice since you do it so easily."

"Wouldn't say a lot."

"Mhm."

"What's with the attitude? You can be jealous just yet, my liege, we're not even married yet."

"Shut up."

"As you wish." I felt his lips on my shoulder and then heard his footsteps retreat after he murmured in my ear, "As you wish."

Frost suddenly coated the room as I stood there reeling in shock, every fibre in my body concentrating on the spot his lips had just been. It took me a bit of strength to get myself to the bed, each of my steps slow and careful.

"Mother of skies, little bird," he said, chuckling as he spread himself on the armchair. "There isn't much you can do with me if I freeze to death."

"Don't touch me next time," I bit out, getting myself under the covers.

"I didn't touch you."

"Your mouth did."

"They call it a kiss. As far as I remember, you enjoyed it the last time I gave you one."

I held my breath, teeth digging on my bottom lip.

The kiss.

The kiss.

My eyes drew shut at the memory of his lips on mine. The cursed, cursed memory that refused to be buried anywhere.

Just like that, I fell asleep reliving that moment. Over and over. Of the first and last kiss I've given to someone.

WHITE ROSES

THORA

I'd only ever thought this would have happened either in a distant strange dream or if the world was truly ending.

All of Winter Court was present in the largest throne room in Tenebrose castle now decorated with pink roses, banners, furs and chandeliers. The contrast of the bright colour was stark against the grey of the weather, the dull of the stone walls and dark floors. The balcony I stood on overlooking the massive space was also all decorated the same, and I clutched the heavy curtain fabric I had hid behind somewhat in awe.

I liked to think I'd grown out of my love for the colour even though I used to spend what little of my childhood that I remembered turning everything pink. I'd grown envious of other girls wearing pretty things and being adored. I thought being like them would make my ma and pa adore me, too. I'd cried endlessly because of it, thinking they didn't want me because I wasn't like the other little girls. The only colour I often wore was red made of blood splatters from training—sometimes mine, mostly of others.

Snow had used her little smart brain and found rotten cherries in the kitchen bins, boiled them and dipped everything I had in white in it, turning dresses, skirts and shirts all strange colours of pink. I'd never cherished anything more. Not the scraps. Not the torn bow that had turned out with unevenly splotchy patches on it. But the memory of my sister's big smile and her happiness when she'd thought she'd made me happy. That day I learnt two things. Pretending to be happy made her happy, too. And that wearing pink did not make ma and pa adore me. Snow did though. She'd called me pretty as she'd put them all over my hair, dresses and shoes. I'd spent most of my childhood recreating memories so I didn't remember much of what truly happened, but that one memory was one I would never forget. Sometimes it tortured me, sometimes it soothed me, and I accepted it both ways.

"Malik," Elias said, stepping by my side on the small balcony overlooking the throne room that was getting crowded.

When I remained silently confused, he pointed his chin to the decor. "He gave the instructions to the servants and had a florist from Adriata bring the roses."

My fingers tightened against my tool skirts, clutching the pink fabric. "And my dress?"

He gave me a look. "You really think I'd go for that colour? He had Nia bring it from Adriata."

It didn't take me long to spot him in the crowd below. Malik stood at the centre of the hall, relaxed, hands in the pockets of his dark suit that fit his hard body too perfectly, conversing with a few of my court members. At the moment my attention fell on him, he went still as if he could sense it, and slowly turned to look up at where I stood on the balcony above.

Quickly, I pulled the curtain back and retreated, only to collapse with a hard wall—a wall who pulled me onto his arms that smelled of fresh eucalyptus.

"Are we playing hide and seek?" he crooned, his lips brushing the shell of my ear. "If so, I've found you, little bird."

My knees almost gave me away and I braced a hand on the wall beside us. "Isn't this bad luck? I'm the bride and you're the groom," I said, stating the obvious, but I had to say it out loud to actually start believing what I was about to do soon.

"You haven't looked at me yet and I've not looked at you, my pretty bride. But maybe we should. Why would we need good luck anyway? This marriage is doomed, whatever will come out of it will be doomed. You don't just want me to look pretty next to your throne, do you? You wanted *me*. Wanting me comes with consequences. Ones that your enemies will pay, it seems."

"Thought my intentions were clear when I picked you."

"Were they?" He leaned in close again, his nose pressing to my hair. "I don't think they were until you realised you can use me however you want with no objection. Back then you just did it to punish me."

"You owe me."

"And now you *own* me."

Elias cleared his throat and we both turned to him. "Marry first. I beg. A scandal is not on the list of things I am capable of dealing with."

"You deal with whatever I ask you to deal with," I said, trying to back away from Malik and failing when my back hit the wall.

My right-hand man let out an exasperated sigh and turned on his heels. "Yes, Your Majesty."

"Ready to be wed, my bride?" Malik murmured, coming to stand close, his lips brushing against my brow before he left a little lingering peck right there.

"Are you?"

"Ready as I'll ever be." Slowly walking backwards, he gave me one long once over, gaze fixing on my wrist where his necklace was wrapped around. "Perfect. Just perfect."

Then he was gone, returning back to the small crowd occupying my throne room. Kilian was looking up at the balcony where I stood, that permanent worried scowl he always directed at me etched in all his features. I'd decided to walk to my new betrothed alone this time. With Erik, it had meant something, a union that I was going to respect and obliged to in every way a man and a woman would. What Malik and I were doing meant absolutely nothing at all. A simple contract. I wanted it to remain and feel that way. I had no intention of making a mistake twice—getting attached to him twice.

Strangely, Skadi had joined the others this time, sitting at the furthest chair from the altar, her attention entirely on Malik.

Not entirely sure why, but I noticed that I was seeking validation from her. I took her presence as one. Though we'd grown to be friends over the past ten years, she'd become a little more than that to me. And like every daughter, I too seeked a mother's validation.

Every eye was on me as I walked over the rosy carpet to him. But I paid no mind to every eye. Only his. His eyes that were looking at me so strangely, with so much fascination that I had to take a glance down at myself to see what had caught his awe.

He helped me step in the altar podium, grinning ear to ear as he swivelled another look over my body. "Look how they wrapped you up for me. Hard to unwrap, but that's where the fun is."

The priest cleared his throat and Malik turned his charming smile to him. "Suppose you won't be there for that part of it."

Frustration and shock mixed in the priest's face. "I beg your pardon?"

"Begging, yes, I want her to make me do a lot of that soon. Hopefully in as many positions as possible."

I choked, coughing, and he rubbed a hand down my back. More to taunt me than to relieve me of the cough. His fingers skittered over my spine, and I arched my back, standing even more straight as heat pooled in my belly and a little further below.

"That's it, little bird. That's it," he cooed, rubbing my back until I could take a breath without coughing.

The priest rather took his time reading out the vows that neither of us two intended to keep. He drew them out, constantly throwing a menacing glance at Malik who had not stopped making crude comments in my ear but loud enough for him to hear, too. By the end of them, I wasn't sure whether I or the priest were more flustered.

The whole way through, a buzzing noise had filled my head, and the moment '*husband and wife*' were announced, all of it cleared. Malik slid my ring and then his own, his hand balling to a tight fist when it returned to his side.

This was it.

This was all it took.

"My queen," he spoke, throwing me a serpentine grin that drew chills over my skin, leaning to nudge my nose with his.

My pulse was throwing an entire tantrum when his lips slightly grazed mine.

He was going to kiss me.

And then he wasn't.

Not like I'd thought, at least.

The kiss he left on my cheek would have seemed chaste to most, but not to me. Not after he left another one on my jaw, and another on my neck, pressing his face there. "You smell delicious."

Before the metal of the ring had even warmed against my skin, before I could process over his kisses or the words he'd just told me, Malik turned to his soldiers sat in the pews and motioned his head to follow after him. "Everyone, out!" he barked, and my court members flinched, standing and rushing out except Kilian and his two kids who took it as a sign to wave goodbye and disappear. "No one leaves the castle wall before being cleared," he ordered his old Eldritch soldiers who'd stood by the whole ceremony. "Disperse all wall and castle guards back to their barracks. They are no longer needed inside the castle walls or to guard their queen."

"What?" I gathered my skirts and followed after him outside. Latching onto his sleeve, I pulled him back. "What do you mean? Have you lost your mind?"

His pupils expanded until his whole eyes were black, dark veins crawling around them. A strange sting like spices and metal permeated the air. Skeletal hands and limbs poked out of snow and over the walls, few walked through the main gates, some threw their bony bodies into the air and over the castle walls. Crawling and limping, they all took the places that the guards had abandoned. "No one with a pulse will ever be trusted enough to be near you as long as I am here. Until this is over, the dead and their Commander will guard you." He pinched my chin. "And you happen to be married to him. *Condolences*, little bird."

Neo and a few others from the Eldritch squadron approached us and I removed Malik's hand from my face.

"Who would have thought this," Neo commented. "What are the odds?"

"Lower than you getting your jaw dislocated twice by the same person within a day," another muttered under their breath. "So, shut up, Neo."

But Neo did not shut up. "Does this make me a...concubinus? Our prince is a dry lover, a selfish one, so I'm sure you'll be seeking me more often."

Malik stepped forward, but I held tightly onto his sleeve as I stepped before him to say, "You have little use for your tongue, so maybe you won't miss it when I cut it off." Looking at the soldiers who were struggling to keep a serious face on, I said, "Everyone besides Neo, leave." Without turning, I added, "You too, Malik. Let me handle this."

It seemed like he wouldn't listen for a moment, but then he glanced at my finger that was now just slightly heavy with his ring and began backing away. "Keep it short. I want you for myself after."

My face heated, but luckily, he was gone before I'd embarrass myself even more.

Once they were all gone, I said to Neo, "Respect is something I didn't know you lacked."

"Same goes. Was I taken in consideration at all?"

"Why would you be? Besides companionship which you know I've sought elsewhere, too, what else can you offer me? Protection? Malik is not offering me protection, I can protect myself just fine. He's giving me advantage. Tell me, Neo, were a couple of words worth losing my respect?" I stepped closer to him so only he could hear me say, "You're well aware that every moment I've been with you, I've thought of him. Do not speak to me in public like that. Different from my sister, I see no pleasure in torture. Instant death is more pleasing." Making sure I showed the disappointment I felt, I added, "I've always thought of you as my friend. Relied on you the same as if you were. Perhaps I was wrong to assume."

"He ruins everything he touches, Thora," he hissed, sneering. "I only worry about you."

He was wrong. Malik had ruined nothing that I didn't give him permission to ruin. "Next time, keep those concerns to yourself."

"Have you told him what about us?"

Us? "What part?"

"The part where I've been taking your emotions away for the past ten years," he said, stepping closer. "Is that why you have stopped coming to me, isn't it? Because you don't want him to know I've been doing that."

"It could have been anyone, you know. Any of your friends." I scoffed. "But I've always taken a liking for the pitiful and the poor, so I suppose this is on me."

He flinched like I'd whipped him. "Thora—"

"Your Majesty," Oryn called, coming from the castle gates. "We have a guest."

The throne room was empty, so empty that the quietness of it all, even the movement of dust in the air, all echoed. I'd had this visitor many times before, but today, I knew she had not come with empty threats.

The massive doors groaned open, letting a flash of candle brightness in the corridor fill the space with more shadows. Her steps were heavy, the thumbs on her boots making an awful scratching noise against my grey marble floors. Iskyla was not subtle by any means. Her yellow hair was in several long braids, her face was marked with white and blue paint, and even her clothes weren't just the ordinary leathers her people wore. No, they were from Isjordian markets. She wanted it known that she was roaming my cities right under my nose and no one had done anything about it.

"Welcome to my home," I said.

"Your home?" she scoffed. "You're resorting to drastic measures now. But I have to admit, marrying an Adriatian prince was not the drastic measure I was expecting. He is not just any Adriatian prince, but the famed Eldritch Commander, the general of the *Battle of Two Guardians*," Iskyla's voice boomed about the room as she strutted to stand right before the empty throne. "Do you fear me this much?"

"It seems you fear me since you came all the way down here," I said, turning to face her and offering her a smile that wiped off her crooked one. "What is it that you want, Isa?"

"Do not call me that."

"Why, does it hurt to be called by the name the father you killed called you?" Uncle Sigurd had not been just any king, he'd not been just any man, either. He'd been one of the best. And she'd killed him when her voice had no longer been heard in her attempts to attack my lands which had almost gotten her banished from Islines and her village.

"From one father killer to another, you should know that the names we were given as children only serve us as leashes that tie us down to servitude."

"How very sad of you to make fatherhood a flaw of your father's considering that uncle Sigurd's biggest flaw was you being his child to begin with."

"I'm certain Silas Krigborn bones haven't been resting well with you on the throne either."

"My father created a god, your father simply raised a greedy little girl who doesn't know how to pick her fights."

It was either hard for her to hide her displeasure and anger, or no one had ever shown her spoiled self how. "I've come to give you a wedding gift."

"How kind."

"A deal."

"Ah, but of course. Only you'd think of a deal as a gift."

"Is that supposed to offend me?"

"No, but what you just said did. Lacking comprehension is rather unfortunate." I waved my hand. "You were to hand me a gift."

"My soldiers will retreat from Modr and Hanai, if you hand over to me the Isline villages."

I snorted. "Sure, I will hand them to you."

Her brows hiked up. "You...will?"

Bones cracked and she screamed as her hands shot forwards, shaking as blood rushed to the end of the limbs, turning her pale skin an angry red.

"Yes," I said. "Sure. If you have no hands, I don't think I can *hand* anything back to you though."

Her laughter was almost maniacal as she searched around the empty throne room for what I presume either a Crafter or an Umbra. "Everyone saw me enter here with both of them. They will call you cowardly to turn a friendly meeting into a bloody match."

"Match?" I asked, standing. "You're no match to me, Isa. If you thought yourself to be a match to me, you wouldn't rely on deals. You'd simply take them from me."

She wore the grin of a sick minded fool. "Aren't I already doing that?"

She let out a grunt when her knees banged against the floor, kneeling before me, her whole body locking tight as I made my way to her. Groaning and moaning, unable to speak, she looked around as if my walls would get feet and come to her aid. "I asked we meet alone," she bellowed as if her requests even had any power in *my* kingdom. "But I should have known you'd play this dirty. Tell your Umbra to show their face!"

"We are alone, Isa. Just me and you."

Confusion tinted her red splotchy face as she looked back and forth her locked limbs, groaning as she tried to move them and failed.

"You were not able to rule like a queen," I said, bending down to her. "But look at the bright side. I can let you die as one. Crown you for a day and kill you to claim my throne back."

"You kill me and more will follow," Iskyla snarled. "Angrier. More powerful. Born and bred to take you down. Queen and Kings with more worth than you will ever have."

"Then I will kill those, too. Maybe I'll kill you all. Perhaps you are right. Maybe it is time old Isea becomes one again. No Isjordians and no Isliners. Just Isjordians."

She let out a broken wicked laugh. "No army of man will be led to that."

"Funny you think I need an army of the living."

"Your husband will not be aid to your madness, that much I know."

"Husband? No, Isa, I meant me. I'm the army." I grabbed her nape harder and I put my brow to hers, her pale yellow eyes clashing with mine. "My wolves will tear through your young and old without feel, without tire, without rest. It will be quick. So quick that history will brand me a merciful queen." Leaning in, I whispered in her ear, "I will make sure that everyone knows it was because of you. That their fate was your doing."

Pulling back, I straightened my dress. "But it would be so wasteful. At the end of the day, they are people of Isea, too. People I am trying to protect. From you." A gust of wind blew inside the empty room and pieces of snow and ice materialised behind me. Two massive ice wolves growled at her. "You have five seconds to get out of my sight."

She collapsed forward, finally in control of her limbs. Breathing hard, she snarled up at me. "You think I've not learnt your little tricks?"

"I know you're studying me, Isa. I know you have spies reporting what I do." I dragged my dagger over my palm and let the blood drip and pool to the floor. "But while you were trying to become me, I became better." My blood began shifting, morphing, taking the shape of a long-feathered serpent. "Five."

Isa sneered, glancing between me and the blood snake inching closer to her. "What is this?"

"Four."

"Dark magic? Blood magic?"

"Three."

"Is this what you've become!" she shouted, scurrying back.

"Two."

She laughed. Madly. "You've sold your soul, haven't you! You dealt a hand with hells for this? All so you could defeat me? How pathetic."

I'd sold my soul over a thousand times. One more time wouldn't kill me. "One."

Isa's eyes blew wide when the serpent shot in the air like an arrow, aiming in her direction. It tore through her barrier of ice, almost melting through it.

Blood was indeed thicker than water. Scorching against ice. Denser than ice.

Dropping the bloodied dagger, I took a seat on my throne, watching it all unfold before me—the red serpent circling Isa who helplessly blew all of her mana in magic to try and keep it away.

Just before the blood serpent was about to make the final blow, its body melted into a puddle of crimson liquid. At my command, Isa would live. She was my stepping stone to have this kingdom become entirely mine. My people only had to choose right. Isa would help them choose right—she would help them choose me. If I intended to join Isjord again, she had to be part of the game—a game entirely of politics. She just had to play it my way.

"Why?" she asked, trying to lift her body up from the ground and failing.

"It's time you start playing by the rules, Isa. You want to win this, them, this kingdom?

Follow the damn rules."

"Your rules, you mean?"

"Why would there be any others? My rules are the only rules. I am queen. King. God. You name it."

"There will never be any winning."

"Then I'm fine with playing until my very last breath. But stray from the rules and gone will the game be. Do not touch my people if they choose to not follow you. Do not threaten them. Do not do anything at all. Preach your little tales and sing your pitiful songs, buy them with coin and promises of power. I do not care, but you do not touch what is mine to protect. You don't want to see me play without rules."

"You'll give me my war, then?"

"I'll give you your ruin, and your ruin alone. Be grateful I am giving you a fighting chance. Be grateful that I want Isjordians to be free of the shackles rulers like you put on them. Be grateful I am offering them a choice. Change. A new future."

"I don't know if you're stupid or plainly naive."

"It's concerning that you think trying to protect this kingdom could mark me as naive, Isa."

Her pale eyes narrowed as if she couldn't grasp a single word I had just said.

"Toss her back to her people," I said when Elias stepped inside.

He sighed, shaking his head. "Again?"

"Yes, Elias, again."

If not for the way my skin prickled, I wouldn't have noticed any other presence in the room but my own—so lost in my own head. Malik pushed inside the room. Not even acknowledging Isa's bleeding body being dragged out the corridor. He simply raised a brow at the whole scene.

"What?" I asked.

Stopping in the middle of the room, he inspected everything slowly and then me. "Frankly, you're scaring me a little."

"I don't bite, Malik."

"Have no idea why you think I'd be opposed to that."

My smile was sardonic. "I'd rather die."

He threw me a wink as he marched closer. "Whatever you're into, sweetheart."

Kneeling before me, he took my hand and wrapped a torn piece of his shirt over it. He didn't ask why or how, even though he wanted to. I knew he wanted to because he kept looking at the puddle of blood behind. At the dagger. At my only wound.

He cupped a hand around my jaw and forced me to look up at him, the cold metal of his ring pressed against my cheek. "What's with the disappearing act?"

"I didn't disappear."

"I know when Thora Krigborn graces me with her precious attention and when not."

"No, you don't."

"Did you hear what I said before?"

"Nothing important if I didn't catch it. Can you take your hands off my face?"

"What pretty little manners," he mocked, pulling my face closer to him. "You want something? Order me. You want me to do something? Command me. You want me to kill someone for you, hurt them for you? Just order me. Enough with this polite shit. You're a queen now, not some twirly little princess."

"I never asked for it."

"Isn't that tough."

I glared at him and he dared to laugh.

"Really scary, aren't you, *wife*?"

"Pretend wife."

"Kinky. I like that, too."

"You really think this is a game, don't you?"

"It is. And you've forced me to play it. What if you lose, huh? What then?"

"Then I lose."

His grip on me tightened. "You never lose, Thora. You can never lose."

"What happens after this?"

"Put me on a leash and show me off to the world."

"Are you my dog now?" Quickly, I put a hand over his mouth. "Bark and so help me heavens."

Instead of making another animal sound, he bit my hand. Bit is perhaps too strong of a word, but he did have his teeth on my skin. "I've rounded up your guard on the training grounds outside the castle. I'm going to have a nice word with them all. Then I'll come here, to you. So wait me up for dinner. I want to have a nice word with you as well."

"I'm out of nice words for today."

"I'm good with bad words, too." He stood, dusting his clothes straight as he backed towards the exit still facing me. "You looked beautiful today, little bird."

"It's only my second wedding. I'm sure I will do better next time."

His response before fading away was throwing his head back and laughing.

BLUE BELLADONNAS

MALIK

N o one was giving me any answers at all. It wasn't because they were entirely unaware as much as it was because they had no care to know anything at all. They preferred it that way.

The White Veil had turned into something more than just a strange occurrence. By the time I saw someone do the holy greeting at the mention of the phantom creature, it had become part of Isjordian folklore. They feared it, but they respected Thora.

Kneeling on the thick snowy ground, I dug a hand through the snow and felt the cool wet earth beneath my fingers. Along with the traces of death and odd life, there was something else.

The Isjordian soldiers accompanying me looked uneasy, surveying the empty and silent village as if it would grow teeth and swallow them whole.

"How do so many Isliners get into the villages without being noticed?"

They exchanged glances, but ultimately knew they couldn't lie their way out of this one. "We believe," one piped up, "some of our own are letting them through. Or at least the villagers who keep mind of the guard rotations or know some of the guards and their habits."

Another stepped forward. "Also, they attack certain villages. Mostly the ones who are majorly against our queen."

"Against?"

They all winced despite my calm tone. "I...I didn't mean it like that. Not in support of the way she rules," he quickly corrected. "She had adapted methods that we as a kingdom have always strayed away from. They're...eccentric some would say."

"Eccentric?"

"We worship the God of War, and for our armies to be reduced to not even a quarter of what they've always been is seen as abnormal. Some fear we are no longer following our ways anymore. Boys and girls do not need to be taught about strategies, tactics, and philosophies of war, they need to experience it while holding their steel and learning to fight. We are born with tactics and strategies, it is the Isjordian way."

We were all born with them, it wasn't a matter of being born with them. It was a matter of knowing how to use them. "Worship? You? Since when?"

"Our beliefs might not have been strong, but our ideologies are. All which stem from our faith and our blessing."

"Clearly, since you let war ridden thoughts rot the very soil you stand on. So much so that it was going to kill the entire realm. Do you know who brought life back?"

They all exchanged some more uncomfortable looks. "Queen Snowlin, I believe.

After she defeated the White Flame Guardian."

"Wrong. Your queen, her magic and her damn tactics. You talk about worship, yet you worship the wrong god."

Walking deeper in the village, I inspected the house painted with blood and the words our famous mythical creature in a white cloak had taken time and patience to write so neatly and with excellent penmanship. Any more perfect of an execution and I would have thought a god themselves had done it.

The old gods are gone and so are their kings.

Where had I heard that before?

She had waited for me. Standing against her room window and leaning on the sill while wind blew snow inside, coating her long hair and the ground. On the small table by the sofa I slept in were a few dishes covered with silver domes to keep them warm.

"Were you nice to my poor soldiers?" she asked, sipping her drink one last time before setting the crystal tumbler on the windowsill.

"I'm always nice, sweetheart."

She pushed away from the window and took a seat on a velvet stool across from me. "Any traitors?"

I sighed, leaning back on my seat. "Only confused subjects."

Her head tilted to the side, studying the whole of me for a moment. "What does that mean?"

"They knew who they served, but they weren't past finding loyalty elsewhere."

"And? What happened to them?"

"Dealt with."

"The way an Eldritch Commander deals with almost traitors?"

"Only this Eldritch Commander. I'm the nice one, remember?"

"What did you want to talk to me about?" she asked, pulling the domes from the food plates.

"That clown who keeps painting your villages with motivational quotes."

Her glass of water stopped midway to her lips. "The White Veil? What about it?"

"*It*? So, you don't think it's not someone playing dress up?"

"It has never interested me much."

"Lying eyes and all."

She raised those same lying eyes to me. "Eyes don't lie, Malik."

"Yours do. But why are they lying to me?" Leaning forward to pry a piece of bread from her fingers, I said, "People say it comes to you, it heeds to your call for help, bows to you, follows you. Why does this thing do all that, Thora?"

Her eyes dropped to the piece of bread that I plopped in my mouth. "What are you asking?"

"I'm asking, what did you do?" Had this been ten years ago, I would have known, I would have been the first to know. She would have whispered it in my ear like she whispered all other secrets of hers, she would have giggled, feeling coy. She would have looked up at me, so innocently, blinking those dark lashes until I'd agreed that what she'd done was fine, that it wasn't wrong. I would have told her it was dangerous without her turning to give me the dismissive looks she now gave me when I showed any ounce of concern or care. She would have glared at me, argued with me, she would have pushed me until I would have broken apart and let it go. I would have broken and accepted it before she would have told me anything at all, but I loved seeing every flash of emotion across her face when she would have argued with me. There was nothing I liked more.

"You think I have somehow summoned it?" She sat back, crossing a leg over the other, the frilly cotton nightgown parting at the side to reveal one long lean leg. "You think I've grown myself some dark powers and called for the gods to send me a little helper? Seduced, perhaps?"

"Did you?" I asked, leaning forward and pulling the material of her nightgown over her bare leg.

Her eyes chased the motion and then rolled back to mine. "What if I did?"

"I'd be very impressed. The Dark God must be very impressed if he sent such a helpful divine weapon."

"But there is no weapon, Malik. It is the Winter God's doing. The wind, the snow, the people all say he is displeased. Reasonably so," she said, the lies melting off her tongue like butter.

"That's working oddly well in your favour."

"What can I say? The odds treat me kindly." She leaned over her knees and picked through her meal to dip her spoon straight into the pudding, ignoring the untouched main course. "Now I have two divine beings acting on a displeased god's behalf. Condolences, *husband*," she said, licking the spoon clean. "I promise your suffering will be for a good cause."

"Why are you in such a good mood?"

"Why do you always assume I've done something?"

"Because you have."

She threw her dessert spoon on the table a little ungently, letting the metal thud hard against the wood. "And if I have?"

"Stop spinning us in circles."

"I'll do whatever I wish."

Ignoring the cold glare she had fixed on me, I picked up the spoon she dropped and her pudding bowl. "Owning up is more honourable than having to find out for myself that even the wind beats at your pace in this kingdom, yet every Isjordian seems to think *you* go against the wind, challenge the wind, lose against it, too. The Thora Krigborn I know doesn't lose, she only gracefully pretends to."

"Don't pretend you know me."

"There is one person who pretends well here, Thora. And it is not me."

After a few moments of what seemed less like contemplation and more like spiteful seconds, she said what she'd told me many times before, "I will not become what I hate."

"You're not him." Thora Krigborn was nothing like her father. She could pass a dandelion without blowing it just in case someone needed that wish more than her. Her rage was also just as soft as the rest of her, but when need be, she sent it to war for the sake of those she loved. But that was it. How could anyone ever think she was her father's daughter? Sometimes, it hurt to think how much violence it had taken this girl to be as soft as she was.

"You don't know what I am."

"You are not Silas Krigborn, and I need you to say that back to me."

She shook her head. "You don't know what I am capable of."

"No one knows what you're capable of. But I am *someone*—someone you trusted with a lot of knowledge."

"A mistake," she dismissively said, uncapping a bottle of wine and filling two cups. She pushed one before me. "Don't you think? You only told me something of yours because you wanted something of mine. You never intended to tell me anything. It was purely a transaction which you realised a little too late just how to your disadvantage it was."

"On the contrary," I said, pushing the glass back to her. "I told you everything of mine because I wanted everything of yours."

"You weren't supposed to do that," she said, resting her tired, lying eyes on the cup I'd put in front of her. "You weren't supposed to get better without me."

"I got better because of you." Her eyes rose back to me then, still lying and all. "If I wanted to come back, I had to. There was never something wrong with you, Thora. To hurt is human. To hurt as intensely as you do is no fault of nature, only of man. I played a part in making you feel as if there truly was something wrong with you. When I found that day you in that forest, I suddenly felt tired of feeling insane alone, so I never told you that there was nothing wrong with you to begin with. I wanted to keep you, Thora. If I kept you, I would have ruined you like I ruined everything. I was so close to committing to it. But each time you begged me for help, it reminded me of myself. Except I didn't beg for help, I begged for desolation. But when you are desperate enough to beg at all, help and ruination do not seem so far off one another. You wouldn't have even noticed me slowly kill you from the inside out. It is what I did best. I was the master of it."

She just looked at me. Utterly lost. Her heart was so loud and mad that I could hear it all the way across from her.

"It is just grape juice. I don't really drink either," she said, rubbing a hand down her arm and standing towards the bathroom.

It had really been just that.

I didn't blame her for wanting to see, to test me. I didn't blame her at all. The way I was before I left...I was not an easy person to trust. Somehow, she had trusted me then still.

My brother sat back on a sun chair facing the daisy gardens, watching the kids surround Snow who had laid on the grass, snoring away. Rain was weaving daisies in her hair and Sam had one of her hands in his, trying his best to massage it.

"How is married life treating you, little brother?" Kil asked, offering me a glass of his daughter's famous lemonade which I was about to refuse when Rain turned to show me a big, hopeful grin.

I took a sip, trying not to wince, and gave her a thumbs up. "Could be worse."

"Then you're having a great time. Fantastic, even. As someone married to a Skygard sister, might I give you some advice? If she tells you to shut up, just do it," he said, grinning in his wife's direction.

"I don't know if you're really that happy or just love being miserable."

"Are you kidding me?" he asked, chugging the rest of his bitter lemonade down, wincing and coughing hard at the taste. "She needs to get up, she wants me to help. She needs a bath, she wants me to bathe her. Her feet hurt, she wants me to massage them. She can't reach for something, she wants me to do it for her. On top of that, she's having my child. Best nine months of my life."

"Then give her what she wants." Strange how ten years ago, it had been him who'd wanted more children.

Slowly, he turned to me, took a sip from his lemonade, and said, "No."

"That's a good way to ruin what you two have."

"That's a fantastic way to lose the love of my life and the mother of my children."

Snow laughed as Rain ran circles around her, singing some song in Calgnan while she clutched the odious cloth doll she loved.

"Where the hell did she get that thing?"

My brother hesitated a little, meaning that he was debating if the next words he'd say would somehow irritate me. "Driada had made it. When I cleaned out her room, I found that, some baby clothes, and a few sets of sheets with different patterns of flowers embroidered in it."

We'd never talked about her after that night at her grave. Never stepped in her room again. Never mentioned her name again. She was dead, and that was it. There was nothing more to it. Only pain. I know my mother wouldn't wish for her name to invoke pain in others, so I tried my best to not mention it. Not even to myself. "You cleaned out her room?"

"I found Sam there one day. He asked me about her, and I found out that day that I couldn't just let dust pile up on her memory. I either had to forget her, or remember the best of her."

I took the lemonade from his hand and drank until the bitterness of it softened the burning at the pit of my stomach. "Back with the sappy shit?"

"Thora said that to me when she found me there the next day, staring at the white sheets covering her furniture, not knowing what to do." He drank straight from the lemonade pitcher, coughing and sputtering. "I thought she'd resented me that day after she begged me to save her and I didn't. She hadn't, though."

"You can't save everyone, brother."

The sappy bastard just looked at me for a few silent seconds. "Not everyone. Was hoping I could save just a few at least."

Rain ran up to us and climbed my lap. "You finished the lemonade?"

Kilian and I both stared at the empty pitcher and then winced when our stomachs groaned in unison at the pain we'd inflicted to ourselves without realising. "I guess so, baby doll."

She giggled and shot up, snatching the pitcher from her father's hands and shoving her doll on his lap. "I'll go make more!" she exclaimed, running towards the castle. "Aunt Penny! Let's pick some lemons!"

"Hells save us all."

"You will drink my daughter's lemonade and you will love it," my brother said, patting my shoulder and handing me her doll.

"What do you know about the White Veil?" I said, throwing it back at him.

His head turned to me, brows furrowing. "She isn't telling you anything?"

"Nothing."

He nodded to himself. "Then I know nothing."

The lying bastard. "I thought you wanted me to help her?"

"Help her?" He chuckled. "Thora doesn't need help dealing with Iskyla. She's been spinning that woman in circles for five years now. She just needs you to stand very handsomely next to her. So do that, my adorable little brother."

"Kilian," Snow groaned, trying to roll on her side and failing.

My brother immediately shot to his feet and gave me a lopsided smirk before running to her side and hoisting her up in his arms. "Let's get you something to eat."

"I'm not hungry," she grumbled.

"You look like you're about to tear my face off. I say you're hungry."

She leaned and whispered something in his ear that had my brother grinning.

I would have gagged, but someone dropped on Kilian's seat, and sighed. "You don't want to know, trust me," Cai said.

"Wasn't intending to ask."

Kilian went past us, throwing a wink. "Enjoy solitude, kids."

"What's the deal with this White Veil?" I asked Cai.

"She didn't tell you?"

"No?"

Leaning back on the seat, he closed his eyes. "I don't know anything."

Fisting his shirt, I pulled him to me so he could see I meant the threat beside hearing it. "If you end up knowing something and she gets her sweet backside in danger, you're the first I'm tearing to shreds, sugar plum."

He pushed my hand off him. "If you act any more obsessed, people are going to think you've built her a shrine somewhere."

He had no idea. I was the fucking shrine.

Sighing, I got to my feet and headed to find Penelope carrying Rain on her shoulders while she picked lemons from her father's lemon tree. "Baby doll. Remember about our training?"

She dropped the lemons immediately, a few hitting Penelope on the way down. "Yes. Put me down, Penny!"

"Call Atlas," I said to Pen, taking Rain down from her shoulders.

"Atlas? Why?" she asked, rubbing a bruised spot on her forehead.

"To observe." To keep me from doing something my father would do.

Everyone but me knew something in Isjord. I'd been my brother's Eldritch Commander, his eyes, his ears, I'd been his enforcer. I knew about a thousand ways to get someone to tell me all their secrets and none involved me using any magic. Perhaps I'd gotten rusty. Or perhaps I was giving a certain songbird too little credit.

Casmere had fallen silent. The one city that never fell silent. There was always a sound of nature, either it be sea or wind or a wild sailor selling his stinkiest fish. But the Seer Sea was tranquil despite the approaching harsh winter. The wind was quiet, too. And the stinking fish remained piled up in their crates, their dead eyes all on the scene laid ahead.

The scene smeared with small bits of Isline soldiers.

The third scene of the sort that I had seen this week alone.

In the midst of all the gore and death that had slapped like red oil paint in an empty canvas, stood someone donned in a white pearlescent cloak that pooled to the ground, blending with the white of snow, its face hidden under the shadow of the hood. Whatever hid under it emitted no signs of life nor death. No heartbeat, no emotions. Nothing. Empty. Only a senseless amount of magic that was somehow seeping all around it, being absorbed by the ground, air and even the stones on the village walls. I'd never seen an Aura more in sync with the nature around it. Every magical being in Numen held a specific scent, something that was modified around their magic and made it their own. There were only four other creatures who did not have that separation, whose nature blended entirely too closely with nature. My brother and the three Skygards. But one stood behind me, the other was pregnant and beside my brother who'd never lose her out of his sight, and the last one was miles away gentle parenting the future bride of

Hells.

The White Veil's head turned to Thora who stood by my side, bowing at her before evaporating into nothing, only flakes of snow remaining where it once stood. Every ounce of the magic it carried disappeared with it. Too seamlessly. As if the magic had been there to begin with.

The old gods are dead, and so are their kings, the village walls behind read in old Ysolt, written with blood.

There was a sheen of sweat on Thora's brow. But not because the scene was distressing to her or because she was afraid. I doubted it was because of something else entirely.

What had my little bird been up to all this time? Making all sorts of friends it seemed.

"Who is it?" I asked her for the dozenth time, hoping she might just answer me this once.

"I do not know," she said, spinning on her heels and heading to her dragon.

"Then how about we find out."

She stopped walking and all of her soldiers gasped at me, murmurs and prayers filling the chilled atmosphere that stank so horribly of blood that it was turning over my empty stomach.

One of her captains stepped towards me. "The last time we tested the gods, a war nearly wiped us all out. Leave alone what wants to be left alone."

"Clearly, this thing does not want to leave us all alone."

The old captain glanced between his quiet queen and me. "What does it matter? Those were Iskyla's soldiers."

"And once it is done with them, are you next?"

Her soldiers gave me the most idiotic confused look I'd ever witnessed. "It always bows to our queen. Clearly, there is no reason to believe that."

"Clearly," I said, turning to the queen herself. "Right?"

Her gaze was distant, but she was not entirely gone. "Right."

Looking around the scene of the perfect crime, I asked, "Why were her people so close to the city this time? It doesn't make sense. All of their previous attacks have been on an odd small village on the outskirts."

She nodded at her soldiers in dismissal and waited until they'd gone out of ear shot. "Because I have her husband tied up."

I knew that. "Thought you were having a more peaceful approach."

"I am. No one knows. She will tell no one because it will make her seem weak. And by attacking so close by, she is doing only one thing. Scaring Isjordians. Not me."

"Are you sure about that?"

"Put those big boy powers to some use. Do I look scared?"

No. Not even a little. And I didn't even have to use my powers to know that was the truth. I knew every little sign when this girl felt anything. Knew every little quirk that came with what she felt. The exact sound her heart made, the way she breathed, the way she shook, how she tried to calm herself down, how she talked herself out of any emotion that would have her paralysed. I knew even where she went to hide from the big ones. How she avoided feeling the small emotions no one knew she was able to feel. There was more colour in her small expressions than many carried in their entire soul. There were colours, and then there were the colours of her.

"A little?" I lied.

She rolled her eyes and adjusted her hood, shielding her face from the thickening snow. "I don't remember ever hitting your head."

A gust of wind blew and knocked her hood back. One minute I had all of her attention, the next she whipped her head to the forest surrounding the old city wall ruins, staring into the tall tree shadows. "Do you hear that?"

"Hear what?"

Just then, something made its way out of the forest. Not a creature I'd ever seen before. The body had the shape of a horse, and the head was the shape of a bull, its horns deformed and way too big for its body. With every step it took towards us, its body twisted, bones with no flesh flopping everywhere.

The hells. "What is an Isline creature doing down here?"

"I don't know. I didn't think they could come down here," she said, slowly kneeling to the ground, a hand resting flush on the snow and the other held forward to the animal.

Frowning, I asked, "Since when have you become an animal lover?"

She didn't answer me, nor blink at all. Her gaze was fixed on the animal ahead that was reaching closer to her.

"Thora," I called, "Sweetheart, that isn't some lost puppy."

There was a string of magic floating from her hand in the animal's direction, almost tying them together. Nothing sinister. Only a tangent of power connecting the two. Similar power. Almost identical. Strange.

"Rora," I warned as the creature neared her even more, calling a few creeping shadows to surround her.

The animal stopped when my shadows formed a circle around her, sniffing at the black dark tentacles that were ready to latch on any unwanted move. The creature then looked at me and began rearing away from her.

Dropping before Thora, I searched her focus first before touching her face, looking for the usual signs on her features when she went into a catatonic state and finding none. "Hey."

Her gaze snapped back. "It's gone."

"I might have scared it."

"It wouldn't do anything to us. They don't get close to humans. Not these ones."

"Why was it even down here?"

Her brows pulled to a scowl. "Iskyla is not supposed to have any sort of control over them, so it can't be because of her."

"Why were you calling it to you?"

"What?"

"Your magic was calling for it. You had tethered yourself to the animal."

She blinked between the forest and me. "I–I didn't think...I didn't realise I was doing that." She held onto my arm as she stood. "I just need some rest."

I faded us to her room. "Lay down. I will call for a Medi-healer. Just in case."

BLACK HELLEBORE

MALIK

It had been one hell of a shit day scouring around near the northern Isjordian villages to find any sign of more Isline creatures. On top of it, Rain was now curled into herself in the middle of the Adriatian training grounds, sobbing because she'd *killed* yet another flower during our training. If you could call what we did training. Rain's magic resembled her father's and mine, but only in its surface. Darkness fed from our surroundings, it drew power from spiritual mana. Rain's however, it fostered from deep within, her body only acted like its confine. She didn't only need to learn how to control it, she needed to learn to contain it. In that sense, she was entirely her mother.

"Up, baby doll," I said, picking her up. "Me and you are going to see an old uncle."

She shook her head, her pigtails flying everywhere. "No."

"He can help, Rain."

Her crying ceased just like that, and my heart shrinked at her desperation to find a solution to what she was. "Alright."

Atlas shot up from his seat on the garden bench. "Where are you taking her?"

"I'll bring her back within an hour. If I don't, tell my brother we are in Hellas."

His eyes went wide. "Hellas? Wait—"

Fading into Golgotha's domain was no different than fading in the middle of a hurricane. Easy to do, but not the smartest idea. Especially when my little companion was an impressionable five-year-old with a love for the ugly and the gory.

Rain's eyes were wide and round and her mouth was stuck in the shape of awe as she surveyed the eudemons that had stopped in their tracks and were looking at us, most hungry rather than curious.

The guard in front of the Demon God's palace didn't say a word of greeting before pulling the heavy gates open and then guiding us through the wet tunnels that stank of dead fish and mould.

Golgotha sat mighty and tall on his throne of bones, surveying our surroundings as if he was expecting someone else with us. "Long time no see."

"Wish it had been longer."

Rain stepped beside me, curiously blinking at the God of Demons. She tugged on my jacket a couple times until I lowered my ear for her to whisper, "Who is the ugly one?"

Golgotha puffed up his shoulders and sneered down at her. "You look familiar."

Rain put a finger in the middle of her cheek and tipped her chin down to glare at him under her lashes. "Everyone says I look like ma."

That made the Demon God look extremely unsettled. He stood and descended the throne steps to us. "Blessed mother of all. You're the Lightning Guardian's child."

Rain crossed her arms. "I know."

"I come to speak to you," I said before my little niece would jump on his shoulders and braid his hair until they were the bestest of friends.

"Must be important since you're being oddly courteous." At the click of his fingers, the empty cave filled with furniture of all sorts, and he took a seat on an overly decorated armchair, signalling us to sit, too.

He pointed at Rain and quickly retracted the finger when my niece glowered at it. "Did you bring her here to scare me or something?"

Scare him? "Was it the pigtails or the glittery shoes?"

Rain scooted a bit closer to my side, holding her ghastly doll tightly on her lap. "He speaks funny," she whispered.

Filling up a goblet with some thick reddish liquid that I hoped to the Moon Goddess wasn't blood of some creature, he said, "We both know what she is. Drop the act." Wiping his mouth, he turned his surveying eyes on me, his nose twitching like he was a hound of sorts. "You've got the scent of a hundred worlds on you. Is that why you are here, Godling? To help you cut your search short? No luck in finding home sweet home?"

"That—"

"That and?"

"To warn you."

"Warn me of what?"

Too much. What I'd seen and heard beyond the confines of our world wouldn't grant us the comfort of warnings and preparation. "That actions have consequences. What you did to my sister-in-law ten years ago changed the course of many worlds. I know her power lingered in your realm. I know it fed it enough for the earth to breathe again. And if the earth breathes again, so does the air. You know how this goes, I guess." Dissiri would come back to life. Would have been mildly unconcerning if the whole three demon realms weren't connected to one another. Part of the reason why Fader, the God of All, didn't even bother considering bringing Dissiri back to its glory, and had instead offered Golgotha residence here. If Dissiri came back to life, so would the other two. Heavens demanded their Gods. Wherever they were held prisoner, they would be no more.

"What has happened, has happened. No need to bother with the past."

"You will not reinstate Dissiri. Ever. Your realm was fated for doom, and we both know what is fated cannot be un-fated."

"What is it that you're asking?"

"Drain Snow's magic out of your realm. Let what is dead rest."

"My realm is not dead."

"Black mould does cause some form of delusion," I said, studying his wet and leaking cave. "But I can kill delusions, too. As I can kill you."

He leaned back in his seat. "You know what death of a God would cause. You're too much of a...samaritan to consider that, so spare me your threats."

Fading right beside him, I put a hand on his shoulder and leaned in to whisper, "Despair."

The old God choked on a pained moan, blood gurgling out of his mouth as the emotion seeped deep within his skin.

"Agony," I continued, watching his eyes roll back and then the ground shake from the loss of magic feeding it. "Pain."

Then I decided to give him a little taste of his future. "Death."

Blood erupted from all over him, and he put a shaking hand to mine.

Pulling back and letting him catch his ragged breath, I said, "I don't have to kill you at all to *kill* you. I just need to put you in a constant state of dying. Which would have been the case if I wasn't so kind as I am to pull away all of it. Or was I?"

"What do you want from me?" he gritted out, shaking and letting a touch of his magic encircle me with its retching scent. But even rot could die off. The cloud of his magic dying around me.

"Drain Snow's magic and help me open a portal in Nihilia's realms."

A choked laughter left him, and he spat blood at my feet. "You don't know what you're asking."

"Your brothers are imprisoned, not dead. If your realm breathes even a whiff of life, it will feed your brothers' realms. The more Snow's magic lingers in there, the better are the chances some of it might harbour just enough energy to help your brothers escape."

From the way he lowered his eyes to some odd dent in his floor, told me that he'd thought about it. He'd known about it and hadn't even given it a single thought of fixing it. "How did you know that Nubil's guardian had left magic behind?"

"There are perks to being what I am, to being one with death and life. It gives me access to worlds across that portal no one else has. You should have seen the surprise on my face when I crossed a lowly hell guarded by one of your former guardians and he looked like he'd had a fresh facial. So energised and full of life. So unlike the rest of your folk trapped under here."

He grunted dismissively. "Why don't you ask the Lightning Guardian to open your portal?"

"Nubil won't allow her out of his domains and she has no jurisdiction in Nihilia's realms either. But you do, little mama's boy. We'd go in and out unnoticed entirely."

His eyes narrowed on me and then drifted on Rain who as predicted had fallen asleep, already bored with us. "She will be much more dangerous than you and your brother, or even the Guardian herself. Whatever answer you are looking for will only make you more aware and terrified of her. Hand her over to Nubil. She belongs ruling a heaven. Away from causing carnage." He shrugged. "At least carnage on human panes. Gods love their carnage, they will love her."

"Never. She's not a tool. She's not carnage. She's a child. Who will grow up to be a woman living a normal life. Away from all of it."

"You might not like the answers you find."

"Like them or not, those are for us to decide on."

"My brothers still have supporters all over Nihilia's realms. Do you have any idea what will happen if they know the Astral born Godlings are returning from their hiding?"

"Good thing no one will know."

"Good thing."

"At the next red moon. Bring a vessel, something that can hold inside the guardian's power without breaking. Something hollow and without soul itself."

I nodded. "At the next red moon then." Only eight months from that day.

"The Mother Goddess would never allow them to escape," Golgotha called as I hoisted a sleeping Rain in my arms.

God or not, all creatures had the same signature colour of distress and worry. Human or God, we all lied the same, and we all forced ourselves to believe our own lies. "No, she would not."

"Which realm?" he asked again.

"Valinhel."

Golgotha looked taken aback. "How do you know about Valinhel?"

"During a visit to one of Henah's realms, I had the unfortunate luck of meeting a

Shadow Guardian who'd gone to recruit a student for some academy of his."

Kilian was waiting right at the castle entrance, a look of pure rage etched on his face and blacked out eyes. "You had no right to go down there!"

At the first sign of the darkening skies, I stopped right where I was even though his daughter was still in my arms. "And you know that I'd never let any harm come near her. Even if it meant giving my life for it."

"That is it," he shouted, taking steady steps towards me despite knowing he wanted nothing but to unleash on me. "That is it, Malik! Don't you understand? Do you ever understand? I do not want you to be put in the position to ever make that choice." He stopped only a foot away from me. "I equally wish to never lose a child or my only brother. Enough, I beg. Enough making yourself to be something I get to spare!" Unlike always, he made sure I saw the disappointment he felt this time. "I'd hoped...had hoped you'd found something to want to live for. Hope, anger, pity, anything, I hoped you'd clung to something. If not for the sake of my sanity, at least for one of those reasons," he said, taking his daughter from my arms and pressing his lips to her brow, breathing a sigh of relief when she stirred in his arms.

"Forgive me," I said, and his attention rose to me again, pulled in a strange confusion. "For all the times I've given you grief."

"You've never given me grief," he quickly replied.

"I wish you were a dick to me just once. At least once, please."

He smiled, shaking his head. "Go back to your *wife*. She was looking for you."

"She was?"

He stopped again and looked at me over his shoulder, raising a brow. "Should she not be looking for you?"

"I'm not her favourite person at the moment."

"She can tell me all about it," the bastard murmured to himself.

"Kil," I called before he entered the castle.

"Yeah?"

"I'm doing better, you know."

He nodded. "I know."

Maybe I had lied to my brother.

Maybe I even lied to myself.

Because I was doing better. Just...not the whole time.

Like now.

She wasn't there. The more I searched, the more I started feeling the weight of what I did to Golgotha. The cost an Empath had to pay. Violent regret. I'd felt everything I'd inflicted on him. It was like poison. You built a resistance to it the more you drank. But just because I was numbed to the effects of it, didn't mean I didn't feel them entirely. They didn't hurt me anymore, but the memories always did.

She wasn't in her room.

Not in her damn dressing room either.

But it was dark there and it smelled a lot like her, so I decided to remain there when my sight began fogging over.

Lightheaded, I braced both hands on a wall and tried to breathe in and out. It had been a while since I'd had to ride these waves of crushing panic out without numbing help.

Her footsteps were light when she entered the dark room. Tripping once or twice on her way to where I was. Carefully and slowly, she put a hand on my back, letting it rest there for a minute before she reached closer, sliding between my arms.

It was so damn quiet I could hear her heart and she could probably hear mine. "What happened?"

"Can't," I panted. "You might use this one secret against me."

"I might." Her hand dropped down my chest until her fingers rested on my stomach, reluctant to leave my body. "But you'd let me. Isn't that why you told them all to me in the first place? Because one day you wanted me to use them against you?"

"Yes," I admitted, some air returning to my lungs, my focus falling on her standing so closely to me. "Partly. Yes."

Her hand slowly slipped a little lower and every limb in my body weakened. "Tell me."

"I went to see Golgotha. To seek his help with finding something I couldn't find for the past five years. Some damn answers."

"Answers? Is that where you have been when you left? Looking for answers?"

"Yes."

"Of what sort?"

"Kil and I...we're not from here, from this realm. Our kind left another realm, Astra, and came to Numen back when gods remained here. They settled in Adriata with the permission of Henah, hiding under the guise of being her Aura. We aren't Aura. We aren't blessed by her either, but by her mother, Goddess Nihilia." I rubbed a hand over my pounding head. "We aren't blessed at all. We're born with magic and by magic. Wherever her blood has been spilled, my kind would rise."

"Godling," she murmured to herself.

"You knew?"

"The God of Waters kept calling you and Kilian godlings." She swallowed and whispered even lower, "I might have been curious and had a look through the locked Esmeray Diaries. But none mentioned godlings settling in Numen, so I didn't think much of it."

"They had left Astra after the Demon Gods were imprisoned. My ancestors were obedient servants of Nihilia, they'd been the ones to capture them prisoner and only they could be the ones to free them. Nihilia had granted my ancestors permission to flee Astra and seek refuge somewhere followers of the Demon Gods wouldn't be inclined to find them to use as a way to free them again."

"Did you find Astra?"

"No. The gates to that realm were closed after the Demon Gods were imprisoned as a way to keep outsiders from finding the entry to where they were kept inside Astra. It would be suicide to return there."

Her frown deepened a little. Turning from curious to confused. "Why did you wish to find it?"

"No other child beside me and Kilian will ever get to know what and who they are the way we did. If there was some other way to be taught to control what we are, I was going to find it."

A small smile graced her lips and she drew her eyes shut. "You went for Rain and

Sam," she murmured, realising, carefully reaching her hand to me again, resting just the tips of her fingers on my chest, right where my heart was. "It's better now."

"Is it?"

"I hope it is," she whispered.

She sucked a breath when I stepped closer, her eyes jumping around the darkness, and when she found no answer there, she reached for me, her hands resting on my waist. To hold me back or pull me closer, I didn't know. It looked like she didn't know either.

So I decided for us, wrapping my body around hers. I held her—I finally got to hold her again. "Just for a minute let me hold you. Hate me after all you want. Forever, if you must."

Even though she said nothing, it really wasn't silent at all. It was loud, the loudest it had ever been when she put her hands on me, her fingers tightly clutching to the thin material of my shirt. "I don't think I hate you, Malik."

"No?"

"No. But I hate that you left me. Forever, if I must. I'll hate you forever for it."

"So will I."

"You shouldn't have done it to begin with. Not just after you left for Rain and Sam."

"You know how messed my mind was after the war, Thora. I did no one any favour staying. Especially you. I'd drag you down with me. I was already doing so." She pushed from me, but I only held her tighter. "Three minutes left."

"Did I ask you to leave?"

"I had to, little bird. I saw you lose your wings that day, and I wanted you to find them again. You'd never find them with me holding you back. Leaving you," I confessed, "was the hardest thing I've ever done."

Quiet fell again. But then her body loosened in my hold, and she pressed her brow to my chest. "You smell like rain."

One minute. Just a minute more, and she'd go back to telling me nothing.

"I want to bargain for five more minutes."

"It will cost you," she said.

"Name your price."

She thought about it for a moment. "Could you cut my hair?"

I ran my fingers through her long locks, and she pressed herself even closer to me. "You have yourself a bargain."

"I'm bad at business, should have asked for more."

"Yes, but you're a good politician. Ruthless."

"How was I ruthless?"

"I never had to pay a price to do things for you, to care, to want to hold you, touch you. You don't know it, but you're using it against me. Or maybe you do know."

She came out of the bathroom, wearing a long cotton gown that had soaked in spots from her wet hair. After a short glance at me, she sat in front of the mirror, nervously fiddling with a piece of ribbon. "Not too short."

I'd done it for her at least a good dozen times, but it had been ten years since she'd let me get this close to her. Not physically. To her, letting me do this meant more than any physical contact. It was the most intimate thing she'd let me do to her. So, I took my time running my fingers through her hair that had grown the longest I'd ever seen it, way past her back.

Once I'd had my fair share of admiring her, I knelt behind her, lining the scissors at her waist and cutting through her locks.

She breathed faster with each snip, her fingers digging in the velvet of the stool she sat on. When I put the comb on the vanity, she spun to look at the hair I'd cut off, but I'd been quicker. Both the scissors and the cut hair had disappeared from sight. They were gone before she'd look at them and panic like she usually did. "Done."

With a shaky hand, she touched the ends of her hair, eyes glazing over with relief when she realised not all of it was gone. "F-feels much lighter."

"Like it?" I asked, pushing her fringe to the side.

She straightened it back. "Yeah. Did you cut it straight?"

"You're nitpicking so you can ask for another price."

A small smile graced her lips, her emerald eyes shining like they had shined ten years ago. It was like time had stopped before that day. Maybe time had stopped the very first day when I pulled that hood down, when she first looked at me. She already knew a secret of mine that very first moment we met, she could see right through me.

"Why do you look guilty?" she asked me while Snow was telling Eren all that had happened.

"Guilty?"

She nodded. "When you look at Snow, I see guilt."

"Are you going after my job now?"

"Have you ever seen yourself in the mirror? You wear that guilt like a ball gown. A big, pink and sparkly ball gown." She pried her chestnuts from my hand and pushed the basket full of the nuts away from my reach. "So, what is it?"

Never before had I wanted to tell someone something I hid as much as I had wanted to tell her that moment. There was so much understanding in her innocent young eyes. She'd been ready to bear the weight of anything I would have told her.

"You won't share a single chestnut with me and now you want me to share my secrets with you?"

She'd grabbed a chestnut and threw it at me. "Go on."

Too stunned to laugh, I'd just stared at her. "I wrote off your death. Signed it. Twelve years ago, I was the one who approved the order of the attack. Not my brother."

Thora glanced at her sister, not a single reaction crossing her features. I'd been so tempted to just read her, but I wanted to see if I could read her just as well as she could read me without magic. "Snow seems to think it was your brother."

"Yes."

"Then you better stop looking at her like that if you don't want her to know."

"You won't tell her?"

"Why would I do that?"

Thora stood, looking down at me. If I wasn't already on my knees, the look in her eyes would have made me go lower. "It was nice doing business with you."

"What are friends for?"

"You aren't my friend."

Standing and towering over her, I said, "You must be tired."

Her eyes dropped down my body when I pulled my shirt off and backed towards the bathroom. "I must be."

She was right. I wasn't her fucking friend. What friend would think of doing to her what I was thinking of doing to her. "Thora."

"Yes?"

"Go to bed."

Her dark lashes fluttered fast, and she lowered her head before quickly walking to her bed and jumping inside the thick duvet cover, ducking her head under it, too.

19

GOLDEN SUNFLOWERS

THORA

He was too good at this. At acting like someone he didn't want to be. We'd toured almost every city in Isjord as tradition required after the queen or king was wed, and he'd entertained every fisherman, villager, child and animal that had come to greet us. He was the man from ten years ago, but something was oddly different. He looked...alive. Like he was just seeing the world for the first time. Everything caught his eye. Everything impressed him. Everything entertained him.

Without realising, he was beside me, my hand was in his, our fingers intertwined. "Were you thinking about me?"

"What? N-no," I stuttered, looking down at our hands.

"You better be making those faces only when you're thinking of me." He threw me a wink. "Your dear husband." He tapped a finger on his cheek. "A kiss and I'll forgive you."

He sighed after I stood there stunned for a good chunk of a minute. "Fine. We'll consider this our first marital fight."

"You can let me go now."

"I don't particularly want to," he said, stretching back, still holding my hand in his. "If I let go, will you slip away again?"

"Malik—"

My words were cut off when he shot me a withering glare. "Why are you holding secrets from me?"

"I don't owe you any answers."

"You do. Secret for a secret. We promised. If there is one thing I know about Thora Krigborn, it's that she will not go back on the word she gave me."

"Things have changed."

"Not this. I didn't say it could."

"Will you really let me go if I tell you?" Truth was, I wanted to tell him everything. It was a terrible urge I was struggling to suppress.

He raised our clasped hands up. "This is my favourite hand, little bird, I've got to have it back at some point. Unless you volunteer to take on its duties."

My face scrunched. "Ugh, you're a pig."

He reached to my ear and snorted like a proper and true pig. "Tell. I'm getting numb and your hand is sweatier than a bull's arse in hell."

"I can't control it anymore," I confessed. My mind. I'd lost control of it at some point again.

"That much I guessed. Where do you go?"

I bit my lip until I felt a gush of blood explode in my mouth. "Places." Sometimes memories. Sometimes nowhere at all. It was as if I'd lost my way inside my head, too.

He tilted his head back to look at me, his eyes dropping to my mouth. Reaching his other hand forward, he swiped a thumb over my lower lip. "What places, Thora?"

"Your turn."

He sent me a cold, disapproving look. "What do you want to know?"

"Since you know the truth about what you are, has it gotten better?"

"No. But things make sense now, and I think of less *whys*. Your turn."

"I go back in time."

"How far?"

"Your turn. Why didn't you tell me what my sister had asked you to do?"

"Because I gave her my word. It is not the first secret of hers I've not told you. Mine you can have. But hers, she'll have to give them to you. How far back in time?"

"Three years ago."

"What happened?"

I took our hands in my lap, watching our linked fingers. "It is not a story I'm ready to tell," I said, trailing a finger down his hand, over the thorny vines tattooed on his skin, "but it's something that reminded me how helpless I am."

I froze when a familiar colour flashed from under his sleeve. Before he could pull away, I tugged the sleeve down to reveal a ribbon wrapped around his wrist like a bracelet. It wasn't just any ribbon. It had my initials on it and a little rose embroidered. An awful embroidery that Driada had tried hard to teach me how to do for weeks. I'd stopped embroidering them after she'd died, and I no longer wore ribbons in my hair, so this was an old one. A very old one.

"You can't have it back," he said absently, letting go of my hand and pulling down the sleeve. "Your turn."

"Why do you have that?"

"Because it reminded me of a pretty pink princess."

I'm sure my cheeks were burning just like my ears were. "Why did you want to be reminded of me?"

"Your turn, little bird. Did you run in Neo's arms after that night to spite me?"

"Yes," I sort of lied.

"You didn't mind him touching you?"

"There are ways around it, Malik." Ways he can never know about. I lifted my palm to him. "Give me the ribbon."

His head snapped to me, hurt written all over the man who was supposed to show none of it. I'd never understood how no one could read what he felt when his eyes told everything. "Rora."

I bit into my lip so hard I winced just so I wouldn't smile. "I'll give you a new one that hasn't gone almost white."

That silly grin returned to his face. "Did you miss me?" he asked all of a sudden. "Say you missed me." Groaning, he buried his face on my lap. "Forgive me already, this is stressing me out too much."

That drew out a giggle out of me, and he looked up, his head resting on my thigh.

"I didn't miss you at all," I said, trailing a finger down the scar on his eye.

"Neither did I."

My fingers slipped down his cheek and over the scar on his lip. "Not even for a second."

"No, not even for a second."

"In fact—"

"Yes?"

"In fact," my voice was low as I struggled to breathe. "I didn't think of you at all."

After we dined with the Lord of Modr, I followed Skadi to the hot springs. She'd left me alone after being called by a soldier, but the emptiness was rather comforting, and strangely, my mind wasn't wandering, only thinking and thinking. Remembering. Recalling. It had been a while since I'd had the time to think. Maybe it was the pungent sulphur smell of the hot spring that could raise the dead right back that was keeping me pretty grounded.

"Now you were thinking about me," his voice whispered in my ear, and I blinked to myself a couple of times, wondering if I had imagined. But the overpowering scent of eucalyptus he carried made me jump upright, holding a hand over my chest.

"Malik, hells."

He threw off his shirt and started unbuttoning his trousers before sliding in the water. "You need to stop wandering off, little bird."

"I wasn't wandering off, you were just so quiet I thought I was imagining it," I said, trying to not ogle his naked body.

"Yeah? You always have my voice whispering in your head?"

"More like an evil and conniving voice that tells me to do very bad things and happens to resemble yours," I said, swimming back a little.

He leaned back against the edge of the spring rocks, elbows resting on it, drawing my attention to his bulging arm muscles. "He must be handsome, too."

"Horrendous," I said, letting my eyes shamelessly roaming down the rest of his body that wasn't submerged in water. "All crooked everywhere. Very similar to you, actually."

He crossed a hand over his chest. "Stop eyeing me up like that. I'm feeling very objectified right now."

A laugh sputtered out of me, and I covered my face with both hands, full on chuckling.

"Now she laughs at me."

Swimming forward, I splashed water right on his face. And before I could make my escape, he grabbed me around the waist. I held in a breath and waited for him to dunk me, throw me or splash me back. And I waited. After a while, I slowly faced him.

He poked a finger on my cheek until they deflated. "Thora." His tone was serious, and my heartbeat picked up. What had I done now? "What are you wearing?"

"Nothing?" I quietly responded.

"In a public hot spring?"

"Should I have a dunk while wearing my ball gown?"

"What if a man had come here?"

"One did. And I am not scared of men, Malik."

"Aren't you scared of what I would have done to them if they had seen you?"

"No man deserves my pity."

He bit into his smile. "Thora."

"Yes?"

"Wear something next time. I'm trying to be a good person and move past murdering men for just having eyes."

"Stop acting like a big brother, I have plenty of those."

His large hand flattened on my stomach. Once, then twice, he ran the tip of his thumb over the curve of my breast. The touch was so brief, so light, so gentle, that for a moment, I stood there contemplating if I'd imagined it. "Believe me, there isn't anything brotherly about that advice."

"Because you're my friend?"

"If that's what you want me to be."

"Why would I want you to be anything else?"

"I don't know, little bird. I've always wondered that myself. Why did you ever want me to be anything else to you?"

My pulse had turned erratic. "I was young and stupid."

He made a noncommittal sound, dropping his eyes at the surface of the bright blue water that was slightly transparent.

"Eyes are on my face, Malik."

"Wasn't intending to look into your eyes, Thora."

My breath was chilled despite the warm air and water. "Malik, what are you doing?"

"Taking a moment."

"For what?"

"To convince myself to let go."

"I can just hit you."

"Would be greatly appreciated."

I snorted and my head dropped on his shoulder while I laughed my sudden amusement off.

"Thora," he groaned, his palm stretching over the expanse of my lower back. It looked like he was fighting off an urge between pulling me closer or pushing me off. Like always. It had always been like that. Two magnets who had no idea what side they were until we suddenly pulled to one another.

"What? Still scared of women, Malik?"

"Just this one."

"Good. Be scared," I said, pushing from him and swimming towards the spring stairs. The mist was thick enough to cover most of my body, but he was close enough to get a glimpse as I got out, fully naked.

Skadi was waiting for me inside the Lord's quarters, and from the way she'd crossed her arms and hiked a brow up, she'd seen us.

"Don't say anything," I mumbled, drying my hair with a towel.

"I'm out of words anyway."

"No words of advice or caution?"

"None that you would accept." With a sigh, she followed after me into the bathroom, not caring that I was standing under the shower spray as naked as one came. "I do however want to remind you that the Modr Academy is due for a visit in less than an hour."

So many had joined the new academies since I'd opened them ten years ago. Most still preferred to attend the public schools, some were forced by their parents to since they upheld old Isjordian traditions that the academies refused to follow, some were unsure about joining, but at least they felt curious enough to spy the students through the barred gates. Every fine detail in the teaching program was overlooked by many scholars all over Dardanes, to ensure the kids were being taught life outside of our wintery borders as well as that inside. No generation growing under my rule would be fed the hate they were being fed before, the greed and the utter lack of empathy.

Classes were no longer small like they had been ten years ago, no longer made of only those who were old enough to choose to attend it against their parents' wishes. Many were as young as Sam.

Even though everything seemed in order, I remained in the academy's yard, hidden by a tall pear tree and watching the children leave their classes and run to their concerned parents waiting for them while others ran off into the city.

I usually always stayed and watched this part.

Half envious.

Half curious.

It was my chance to see how a family felt like, the dynamics, the banter, the simplest of interactions. Always by observing others, that's how I'd learnt what a family is supposed to look like.

The noise grew the more students came out to crowd the yard, the more the bell signalling the end of classes chimed, the more I watched their parents wave and call to their children. It grew intense. Buzzing. Blurring. Drowning.

One moment I was sinking beneath the noise, and the next, it was all gone.

Entirely quiet.

At least until the same pulse I'd heard before began overtaking all my senses. Humming against my skin. Reverberating and bouncing around my own mind. Coursing down to the tip of my fingers until I could almost touch it, feel it against my skin.

Lifting a hand forward, I swiped it across the thick snowy breeze, letting it graze my skin. Every snowflake that clung to my fingers pulsed against them with the same heartbeat I could hear and feel beneath my soles, and against my back braced on the pear tree trunk.

It was everywhere.

It felt...it felt like I stood right in the middle of a heart. All four walls were beating against me.

A hand rested on my shoulder, and then, just like that, it all went quiet. Malik's brows were pulled together as he watched me. "Where did you go just there?"

"I'm fine."

"Wasn't what I asked."

Looking around, I shook my head. "Thought I heard something."

"Just like you thought you saw something the other day?"

The sort of accusing and doubting look was annoying me. "The way you're saying it is making me look a little mad."

"Nothing wrong with that. I've accepted you as you are. Flaws and all."

"Malik—"

"I would murder in cold blood for you to just stop calling me by my ministerial name."

"You've already murdered in cold blood."

"Not right at this moment." His eyes slowly rolled up to some point over my shoulder. "Plausible to change."

Casting a quick look to where he was glowering, I said, "Leave Elias alone."

"Why is he stuck to your hip and tits, too?"

"Be kind to my right-hand man, he stuck with me no matter what I've put him through. He's my friend."

He didn't like that. Malik didn't like that at all. It was why I had said it. It was true, nonetheless, but it was not like I went around making that announcement. Especially when Elias Venzor was supposed to have a neutral stance to me in court. A lord couldn't be my friend.

"Been making a lot of friends, little bird?"

"What can I say? The position was empty and many were willing to fill it." In his defence, I did omit the fact that Elias had been forced into practically being everything to me and did not really have a choice otherwise.

He chuckled, shaking his head. "You little shit."

"That isn't very nice."

"No shit."

I sighed. "Remind me to go over ten new words a day with you every morning."

He raked a look over me and hooked a finger on the ribbon tied around my waist. "Remind me to go over what else you're hiding from me every evening." A slow smirk rose on his face. "It's blue."

"What an excellent observation, Your Majesty."

"Not your colour," he said, chasing the length of it around my stomach with his finger.

When the feel of it turned intense, I pushed his hand away and he rolled his eyes up to mine. Before he turned to leave, he taped a finger to my chin. "Next time you get naked before me, man up and turn around, too. I lack the imagination to make it up."

No matter how cold it was or how much frost I dressed my skin in, my body grew so hot I could erupt.

"I'm going to pretend I didn't hear that," Elias said, rubbing his eyes and sighing, bursting my little jittery bubble. "Can't say it will be easy."

The man had grown three layers of black circles under his eyes so I bit back a nasty reply. No one could deal with my dirty work if he dropped dead. "Yes? You came here to tell me something I suppose."

"You were right," he said, "Soldiers have spotted the Isline animals all over our forests."

"Could it mean something?"

"Oryn says so." He waved a dismissive hand in the air like the sceptic he was. "He kept rattling about the healing land."

"The land has been healing since ten years ago. Why now?"

"Want me to make a guess?"

"No?"

"Good. My guesses were shit." He raked a quick look over me. "Have you not seen Neo anymore?"

I blinked. "No, actually. It has been a while now." Almost since Malik had shown up.

"Huh."

"What?"

He shook his head. "Nothing. It's good. It's good," he repeated. "Would never trust a damn Empath to be a foot near me let alone—"

"Shhh," I hissed, going on my toes to press a hand to his mouth. Had no idea how this man had not spilled all my secrets these past ten years with how careless he was.

"Afraid Malik won't take well to your man toy messing with you?"

"One day, Elias Venzor, I'm going to cross stitch your stupid lips shut."

Glancing up at the skies with a pair of tired and lifeless eyes, he boredly said, "Heavens, let that day be today."

20

THE PAST

THORA

I was so alone I was about to lose my mind. The large room was about to eat me whole and leave nothing of mine behind. Even if I had spent six months alone in it when Malik had been taken by my father, now that I knew he was here made it feel different. Emptier.

Something crashed against my door, and I jerked upright, a hand over my heart. "How embarrassing, Thora Isa Krigborn. Grow a backbone," I murmured to myself, quickly pattering on the doors and pulling them open.

Malik's body crashed against mine, almost making me drop backwards. Bless those training sessions Cai had dragged me to.

The scent of alcohol assaulted me and made me gag. "I am going to be so cross with you if you vomit on me," I shouted, trying to get him to stand upright.

He managed to reach out one stuporous arm to the wall, bracing himself against it while the other was over my shoulders. He pressed his face to the crown of my head and hummed. "You smell so good."

"Not if you keep rubbing up on me," I said, pulling back and trying to usher him to the bathroom. Failing, by the way, because he was one massive pile of man and muscles.

My hair went loose, and I spun to him just as he pulled the ribbon out of my hair. The look of amusement on his drunken face disappeared all of a sudden, his gaze dropping to the end of the ribbon he held between his fingers, right over the embroidery on it.

"My mother makes these," he said, bunching all the ribbon in a tight fist.

"She taught me," I said, trying to pull each of his fingers back to get my ribbon back, but he wouldn't let me. "Malik, give it back."

"Were you there? When she died."

That tight noose wrapped around my neck, making my throat burn and turn hoarse. "I was."

"Did she ask for me?"

"Yes," I whispered. "Every day. She would sit and wait for you on her balcony."

His knees gave up and he dropped to the ground, two fists pressed to his eyes. For a second, he didn't look like the terrifying man he was. He looked like a grieving boy who had just realised he'd lost his mother.

I went to my knees before him, reaching a hand to his shoulder and attempting to comfort him the best way I knew how. "It's alright," I said, patting his back.

His body began shaking and then a broken sob filled the massive room.

Pulling his hands off his face, I climbed on his lap and hugged him. Burying his face on my shoulder, he only cried harder. And harder. And harder.

"You're scaring me," I said, hugging him tightly.

"Not as much as you scare me," he muttered, hiccupping.

Climbing off his lap, I tried to get his massive body up to his feet. "Come on, please." I panted. "Up, come on."

Somehow, I managed to get him to stand and carried him to the bathroom. When I loosened my hold on him to reach and turn on the tap, he lost his balance and dropped inside the bath, fully clothed. "Alright," I said to myself. "A clothed bath. I'm sure people have those."

He didn't react to the water when it started pouring and quickly filling the bath. Not to tell me if it was too hot or too cold.

Crouching down, I braced both hands on the bath edge and rested my chin on them, watching him and waiting for the water to sober him up like it usually did.

His eyes peeled open, searching the room until they landed on me. The water stirred as he lifted a hand to reach for my face, fingers briefly grazing my chin.

"Come here."

"Where?" I asked, standing.

The response was very faint and broken, so I leaned in to hear him better. When I did so, he wrapped an arm around my waist and pulled me in the water, making me squeak. "Malik!"

"Mal," he said, pulling me to lay on his chest. "How many times do I have to tell you to call me Mal."

Pulling back, I smacked a hand on his chest, sending water splashing everywhere. "Look what you did," I said, shivering, but not from the cold, I never got cold. His hand that he'd braced on my hip fell away and so did his smirk when his eyes dropped from my face to my body.

"What?"

I looked down on myself. The nightgown had turned almost transparent when it had soaked from the water, curving around my breast and clinging to every little detail on my body. I might as well have been naked.

"Get out, Thora."

I flinched back, reaching to cover my chest with my arms.

He groaned and I realised a little too late I was now sitting on his...his—

"Thora, please," he begged, eyes tightly shut and his breaths fast. "Please get out."

Bracing both shaky hands on the bath, I pulled myself out and ran outside, heading to hide inside my dressing room.

No idea how I managed to get myself out of hiding, but when he came out of the bathroom, I was already changed and tucked in bed. My cheeks flamed against the cool side of the pillow until I had to release a chill in the air for everything to cool down.

I heard him drop on the sofa he normally slept in. "Drop it, little ice princess. I'm going to catch a fucking cold."

"Oh, so you worry about a little cold?" I bit at him, pushing my blanket and sitting upright. "What about drinking yourself to stupor? No?"

He covered his face with both hands and groaned in them. "Thora, where are your own night clothes?"

"These are my own night clothes," I said, frowning.

"The normal ones."

"They are my normal ones."

"Why can I see down to your sixth rib, little bird?"

I looked down. "The fourth at best."

He laughed, his whole body shaking, and I threw a pillow at him. That only made him laugh harder. "You're so damn mean sometimes."

"And you're so damn *you* all the time."

"What is that supposed to mean?"

His laughter began to die down, and he sighed. "Don't ever leave me or I'm going to lose my mind."

Curling my arms around my legs, I pulled them to my chest and rested my chin on top of my knees, trying to collect all my senses that had gone haywire upon all recent events, and shake away those silly words he so carelessly used with my delusional self. "Where were you?"

"Right where you're thinking I was."

"I know that is not true. There was mud on your shoes, and you didn't have that stinking perfume on you or any of their lipstick. Which all means you've just lied to me."

"I did," he confessed.

"Your father is not alive, Malik. Nor is he here to haunt you. You can tell me if you were to visit Driada."

"How do you know he is not here to haunt me?"

"I've burnt sage corner to corner in this room."

He threw his head back and laughed. Once he was done mocking me, he sighed and said, "This is the safest I've ever felt from him."

Could have jumped from joy, but he already thought of me as childish, so I resisted the urge. "Great. I've got some saved up," I said, standing and reaching the vanity to pull my stack of sage. "I'll let one burn all night long."

He was still grinning when I went over to him and banged two stacks of sage together over his body in an attempt to banish any clinging souls attached to him. Like I'd been told to do.

"Not because of the sage," he said, plucking them from my hands and throwing them to the ground. "Sage only works with roasted chicken. Won't even keep away the ants in the summer, little bird, let alone spirits."

"But—" I gasped, my eyes wide. "Helenia Drava, I will kill you."

He stretched an arm out and reached to touch my leg, his fingers tickling the back of my knee. They went a little weak, but he didn't let me fall.

"What am I going to do with you?" he asked, lifting me on his lap as he sat up.

I had a few ideas, but thankfully, I managed to keep my mouth shut.

His hand dropped from my face and down my neck. He continued trailing a finger lower and lower, almost too low, leaving chills and shivers behind. "Fifth rib," he said. "You were wrong. Time to dish out a punishment."

"P-punishment? Punishment for what?"

"For getting me hard as fuck."

Instead of reeling in shock like every other scandalised fair maiden would probably have, I remained frozen at his words. *He was drunk*, I tried to tell myself, but my stubborn heart was screaming and shaking at the fact that he was attracted to my body. A fact that somehow didn't bother me like I thought it would. Ever since I was little, I'd been told by men I'd grow up to be beautiful and that I'd have men drooling and lusting after me, something that had made me wary and cautious of all my life, something I'd slowly grown repulsed to. Male attention didn't do anything for me. But not his. All I wanted was his attention.

His head fell back on the backrest. "Close your mouth or you're going to give me ideas."

"Malik—"

"Don't say my name like that."

"Like what?"

"Like that's exactly what you want me to do."

"What if it is?"

He sat me on the sofa and got up, towering over me. My mouth went dry when I saw the bulge in his trousers.

"Where are you doing?" I asked.

"To solve the problem you created."

I chased after him. "Please don't go to them." The desperation in my voice made me draw my eyes shut and bury my face in my hands from embarrassment. Sucking in a breath, I straightened. "Or do. Why would it matter, right?"

"Right," he said after a torturous while. And then he left.

Had this been my punishment?

It was the cruellest one I'd ever received. I'd never felt my heart rip the way it had that sleepless night, imagining another woman touch him. Imagining him touching her.

I'd gone so far down that helpless drain that my body had not been able to bear anymore, and I'd gotten up to retch my stomach raw on the toilet until the sun had risen.

I'd promised to never do it again—to never get close to him as I had again.

21

EMERALD DAHLIAS

THORA

There were a couple days of just...silence since after that day at the Modr academy. He'd not said much, neither had I. Then, this morning after we returned to Tenebrose last night, I couldn't find him at all.

Not one word that was said to me the whole trip to Grasmere to check on the fleet for the start of winter had gotten past my ear drum. My attention was somewhere else entirely. Not imagining away as it usually did. Well, yes, but not like that. It was doing something worse. It was becoming...paranoid.

It started with this single thought: If he wasn't anywhere he should have been, it meant he was somewhere he shouldn't be. Then it progressed to digging up past similar occurrences. Then somehow past feelings creeped up top. The crippling feeling of knowing he was somewhere I really didn't like him to be.

Straight after returning from my very short trip to Grasmere, I headed to my room—our room.

Only to find it empty.

Entirely void of life or death.

I couldn't even smell his eucalyptus perfume in the air.

It meant he hadn't been there since he left early this morning, and it was now evening time.

But he should have been there. In our room. Where he had been every day at that hour. Lounging on his sofa and waiting for me. But he wasn't today.

It suddenly felt like no time had passed. Like this was just another time I'd gotten too close to him, and he'd finally realised he'd gotten too close to me. It felt like just another time he'd abandoned me to *cleanse* himself of it. Alcohol, women, drugs. I was wondering what his poison of choice had been this time.

After an hour of tossing and turning, I got up and put a dressing gown on.

Empty.

His room in Adriata was empty. Everywhere he should be was empty. It only meant...it only meant that he was in places he always was where he didn't want to be where he was supposed to be.

It would never change, would it?

The cycle would never stop.

He wanted me close, just not that close.

I dropped to the floor, grasping at my chest for the lance that had speared through it. Cursing the way I couldn't so easily sink into my mind and not think at all since he'd returned, I grabbed at my hair, trying to forcibly will my head into obeying. But it wouldn't work. All I could think was him back then. Drunk. Entirely out of his mind in drugs. Women hanging over his arms. Their red lipstick all over him. Their pungent perfumes drowning his.

"You're an idiot, Thora," I chastised, pushing to stand up and stopping when I caught something discarded under his bed, hidden from sight. The only thing out of order in his otherwise clean room that looked like no one had slept in for months.

Sketchbooks littered the floor under his bed. The ones I'd gifted him after he'd told me he used to draw. The ones he'd always refused to use because he no longer found anything beautiful enough to draw. But they weren't brand new like I expected them to be, and when I flipped the cover open, I saw that they weren't unused either. Charcoal. He'd used charcoal to draw.

He'd drawn a portrait. A woman, long hair bound in a braid, looking ahead. My fingers went to my fringe first and then to the one on the girl's portrait before sliding to the only thing with colour on the page—on the green he'd used on her eyes. My hand shook when I flipped the page to find the same girl drawn again, her profile this time. Again, and again, the same girl was drawn in the sketchbook. Sat on a bench while reading a book. Crouched between a field of flowers. Sat on a vanity while combing her hair. By the beach, holding a wrap around her shoulders.

Alone.

From afar.

All of the drawings looked like they were sketched from afar because the girl seemed alone.

I drew a sharp breath when the next page showed the girl sleeping on the bed, tears drawn down her face while she clutched in her fist what looked like a ribbon.

The sketchbook fell out of my hand, and I braced myself on the table when the whole world around me began to spin. This is why he wouldn't apologise for leaving me. He'd never really left me. He'd only ever left my sight while I'd never really left his.

I wasn't sure how my feet carried me out of his room, but I was finally walking. I was walking away from this entire mess, and I was not going to look back. I'd given up on that once, had I not?

Then there he was. Walking towards me.

It somehow was too late to feel relief.

Malik grasped my arm when I was about to go past him. For a moment, he just looked at me, searching for answers I was not going to give him. The more he looked, the more he frowned. "Don't make me ask what's wrong."

"You just did." I pushed his hand away.

He had other plans though. Grabbing me by the waist, he put me on a stair step, letting me tower over him while his hands were planted firmly on my hips. "Tell me, Rora, or I swear I will rip an answer from the damn walls if I have to."

"Those five years when you would visit, why did you never let me see you?"

There was a brief look of surprise on his face. "Heard you were happy."

"That is such a lie, Malik Castemont. Such a horrible lie for you to say. When did you figure out that I was happy? When you were watching me in my sleep or hidden behind a wall or a tree or a shadow? Did I look happy from afar?"

The loud silence that settled confirmed everything. "Who told you?"

"People knew?" Snow and Kilian had kept this from me?

He looked away for a moment, his gaze jerking back to my hands. His hand wrapped around one of my wrists as he turned my palm and fingers stained from the charcoal. "Were you snooping around my room, little bird?"

"So what?"

"Rora," he gritted out.

"Not once," I said, trying to hold my voice steady. "Not once did you let me just see you. Nothing else. I just wanted to see you, Malik. I'd forgotten so much of you."

"You say that as if it is a bad thing."

"I take it back." My voice was barely a whisper when I said, "I do hate you."

He wore the most forlorn grin he'd ever given me, so forced, so not like him. "You don't mean that."

"With all my heart." *With what little of it was left not wanting you. With what little you'd left after taking it and disappearing with it.* "I'm past caring about you, Malik, but please refrain from showing up with a whore by your side or piss drunk when you come to Isjord."

"Is that what you think I was doing?"

"Have you ever given me any other thing to think of?"

He nodded and took a few steps away from me, seeming torn because it took him a few lingering seconds before he faded out of sight. His scent tarried behind like the most haunting spirit. But at one point, I had wanted to be haunted by it.

I think I still did.

"Get down from there and let's go home," Skadi said from where she leaned against a wall. "Go wallow with a glass of wine and some snacks before you. Misery always tastes better with some salty pickings and cheap liquor."

"I'm not wallowing."

"More shooting then?"

"Can I use a breathing target?" I asked, stepping down the stairs.

"I'm not against it, but I thought we were trying to make you the next saint queen."

"You're very unfunny."

"What's *unfunny* is the fact that you're determined not to get hands that are made for blood to be near blood."

"That's not unfunny, Skadi, that's being a smart politician. Which is what I am."

"Snow would argue another definition for what a politician is."

"If Snow wanted me to speak her language, she shouldn't have made me queen."

I halted and let out a squeak when I almost crashed against a small body. Rain tightly hugged that ugly ragdoll to her chest, blinking her massive round grey eyes up at me and then at where Skadi stood. She let out the most grown-up sigh ever, and took my hand, wordlessly pulling me towards the gardens. "You need to stop talking to that woman, aunt."

"I've told you she is nice. I promise."

Rain carefully glanced at Skadi again and shot me a strange look. "If you say so."

"Where are you taking me?"

"Uncle is building me a princess house out in the gardens."

"Is the castle not big enough for you, my little highness?"

"I want something that is mine alone."

"One day it might be."

"One day, but for now uncle is building me my own." She let out another exasperated sigh and came to a halt before the miserable scenery ahead—Malik struggling to hold a wooden structure in place while he pinned nails here and there. "But he is incredibly slow. How does a grown up not know how to build a simple house? He's taken all my day with training and I even missed my baking lessons with Penny."

Malik whipped his head to us. "Hey."

My stomach sank.

He'd been with her.

And I had been wrong.

Rain shook me back to reality. "Please, aunty, make me an ice one, or I will be as old as ten when uncle finishes that one."

"Ten is a big age," I said, smiling and trying to erase the look of discomposure from my face. "You might not even fit in it by then. You're lucky your aunt is rich and powerful."

Malik dropped his hammer and cocked both hands on his hips. "You're playing favourites, baby doll."

Rain nodded once, not even denying it. "She is my favourite, and I'm her favourite, too."

He took a seat on a garden bench and sprawled wide. "Yeah? I used to be her favourite once."

I didn't look at him. "That's a lie."

"It is not," he murmured, resting his head back and closing his eyes. "I was your favourite." When I didn't reply, he cracked open his sleepy eyes and just looked at me with a tired smile weighing down the gloom on his face. "Maybe I still am."

Tearing my attention from him, I lifted a hand forward and my magic followed the wooden skeleton of the house Malik had already built, letting ice create a thin coat of walls and a roof. Rain didn't mind the cold either. Despite her gift of death, she was also blessed by ice. Sometimes, when I watch her, I could almost swear that her grey eyes had tiny little shapes of snowflakes in them. They were like crystals. Clear. Cold. Eyes the true colour of winter.

My little odd niece squealed and giggled from happiness, squeezing the life out of that freaky doll she loved and running right inside of the makeshift tiny ice castle.

"You and Kil were training with her today?" I asked, taking a seat beside him.

"We were," he replied, his attention on our niece. "Took her inside the Danic mist before the sun rose. Kil wanted to see how the old magic would react to hers since it's the most similar to hers that we've both felt. The trip wore her out a little, so I promised to build her very own castle as per her request."

The thought that my tiny little niece was this giant storm in the making terrified me just a little. "Couldn't you just buy her a present like any normal uncle?"

"Normal uncles don't meet their nieces for the first time when they are five years old."

"Spoiling her rotten won't get her to forget you've missed all five first years of her life. You can just tell her the truth. She might spare you some grace that way. Rain's a good kid, and she's got the biggest heart. She is a bit like—"

"Kil. She's like Kil."

I turned to him and he turned to me, too. "I was going to say she's a bit like you."

He pushed my fringe to the side with a finger. "Yeah?"

"Yeah," I murmured, straightening my fringe back.

For a moment, we remained silent, refusing to look anywhere else but at each other. "You've not had anything to eat all day. Have dinner with me."

"I have eaten." Lie. I don't even remember drinking a glass of water today.

"You have not."

"You wouldn't kno—"

He gave me a pointed look. "I have eyes in every shadow. Even that of your own."

"I wish you just used your own. They're pretty nice eyes."

He was trying really hard not to laugh as he narrowed his eyes at the distance where Rain was coming in and out of her ice castle. "You like my eyes, little bird?"

"I like them when they are looking at me." The shyness had been literally ripped out of my bones at this point. He knew I've wanted him since the moment we met, and I was never shy about him knowing that. Once, I'd been cautious, yes. But only because he had drawn a line between us. Even though I'd crossed it many times, I'd always reared myself back behind it, for the sake of keeping him.

"Careful," he said, leaning both elbows back on the bench. "Those aren't things you say to friends, Thora."

"You aren't my damn friend."

His knee brushed mine and my stomach did a flip when he did it a second time. "No?"

"No."

Our knees were now resting against each other's, the hand he'd rested on the bench slightly grazed my shoulder, and every nerve ending was preoccupied with deducting the strangest mathematical problem while I remained as still as one could be. "That's a shame," he said, angling his head in my direction. "I liked being your friend." That fingertip moved back and forth just the very slightest over my skin. "But I think I might like being your husband a little better."

"*Fake* husband."

"Nothing fake about me, sweetheart," he said, standing, the sudden movement leaving me feeling entirely too empty without his little touches. I watched him pick up Rain from where she'd sprawled on the grass, sleeping like she was laying on the most royal mattress her royal bones had ever laid. "Stop ogling my fantastic backside and get up. Let's put her to bed and get you something to eat."

If there is one thing of Malik's you couldn't possibly ignore to look at, it was that. Oh, and his tiny little man waist. I could swear it was so tapered despite this massive build, he'd fit a corset beautifully. Even as I followed behind him, I took the opportunity to do just that, ogle him and those very firm thick thighs that had been squeezed onto those poor black leathers.

Malik took that moment of Rain's weakness to douse her chubby cheeks in loud smacking kisses and my little niece let out a rumble of a snore, startling him a little. "Heavens, baby doll. Trying to summon the dead or what?"

"How are her lessons coming along?"

"Kil was more patient than I, so I guess I understand why he insisted he had it under control."

"I'm sure he loves having you there with them. He's pretty busy back and forth with Olympia and Adriata, so this must be a big help to him and Rain both. You don't have to ask him to be there all the time, you know that, right? I've seen you teach your command dozens of times before. Not once—" *Have you acted like your father would have acted*, I wanted to say, but he beat me to it.

"A slip of the moment is all it takes," he said, pushing her bedroom door open with a shoulder and slipping inside the just as creepy space made of dark walls and decorated with the oddest choice of stuffed animal toys. "I could lose my temper or push her more than I should without even knowing that's what I'm doing. It is instilled in me."

"You're a trained soldier, Malik. When have you ever had a *slip of the moment*?"

As he bent down to lay Rain in bed, he turned to give me a look, his eyes dropping to my mouth. "I've had a few."

"I've never heard of any stories," I said, clearing my throat and trying to work my mind out of the crippling frustration he put me through when he carelessly ogled me back. "Someone would have told me. Adriatians are very mouthy."

"That is not what I meant," he said, taking Rain's shoes off, and then unsuccessfully attempted to pull away her doll which she clung to for dear life until he gave up. "Damn it. How can she sleep with that ugly thing?"

"It's ugly, but it's her ugly thing. That's what she says."

"She got that from you," he said, wrapping a large hand around my wrist and pulling me behind him. "Let's feed you now, little bird. Before you drop on me."

"What do we make?" I asked, holding up a pan that I most certainly had no idea how to use. Eren had done all the cooking back in White Bridge, I'd done most of the hunting.

"What do you want to eat?"

"Vanilla custard." It was one of the things that always tasted better in Adriata. The milk and eggs came from far in Tenebrose and weren't always the freshest, but Adriata was plentiful in that aspect.

His lip curled a little. "Then we make vanilla custard."

"We can make something else. You used to hate sweet stuff."

"I like you well enough," he said, taking the pan from my hand and lowering it over a hob, mercifully letting me gawk at his back instead of directly at his face. "Get me eggs, sugar and flour. I'll grab the milk and your vanilla."

After giving him the ingredients, I also grabbed a little flowery apron and slung it around his tiny little man waist. "You know how to make it without a cookbook?"

After a quick amused glance over his shoulder at me, he said, "Driada used to spend a lot of her time down here before she got as ill as she was her last few years."

A sudden quiet fell between us after that. The thing with Mal was, if he wanted to tell you something, he would. Even with me. Prying would only annoy him. If he'd made you pry, that meant he didn't want you to know. When it came to Driada, even if I wanted to annoy him on purpose, I wouldn't pry. Before, he'd usually tell me even about things he didn't want me prying on. But after he'd returned from Isjord, he'd changed.

He languidly stirred the yolks into the milk so it didn't curdle while I watched him from a safe distance. "Don't leave me," he rasped, and it took me a moment to shake the haze and grasp his words.

"I'm here."

"You almost weren't."

No one but him had noticed every time I slipped away. He'd noticed even when I hadn't. "It's like we are playing house," I said, languidly walking around him. "I've never had someone to play house with when I was little. Might as well take this off the list of things in my childhood I didn't get to do."

His eyes rose to me as I circled past him, watching me like a cat waiting to pounce on prey. "We aren't playing. You're my wife and this is one of our homes."

His wife. "Fake wife, fake home, *honey*," I said, reaching for two bowls overhead and struggling.

Before I'd resort to climbing up the shelves, Malik abandoned the stirring and lifted me around the waist, strong hands holding me up like I weighed only thoughts. He lingered a little after putting me down when he usually wouldn't hesitate to put space between us.

"There you are, *Tiny*," he spoke in my ear before moving away.

"I could have gotten them myself."

"I don't take pleasure in watching you struggle."

"Can't say the same."

There was a wicked smirk on his face as he put the tip of his finger inside the boiling custard mix and held it to me. "Tell me if it is not sweet enough."

There were tablespoons, teaspoons, soup spoons, ladles and all sorts, but I leaned forward regardless, and wrapped my lips around his finger, licking the custard off. He watched me as I did so, his eyes following every little movement I made. "Sweet enough. And oddly tasty."

"I'm a man of many skills," he said, bringing the same finger to his mouth and sucking on it.

Hurriedly, I spun round and busied myself with ladling the custard into the bowls before I'd do something that would make me too embarrassed to roam this earthly surface.

Malik didn't even give me enough time to even sit down and eat a spoonful when he asked, "Where did you disappear today?"

The taste had soured before I'd even tried it, so I lowered the spoon back on the table. "Thought you had eyes in every shadow."

"I want you to tell me. I feel like your shadow is trying to deceive and lie to me. You wouldn't do it. Keep things from me? Sure. But not lie."

"I was at court. In Grasmere. For the winter fleet checks. Got to see the new icebreakers added to the ship bows crack through ice."

Dropping the spoon on the table, he leaned back and gave me a smug look. "The White Veil made its debut in Grasmere today."

"Are you asking if I went to see the White Veil off?" I asked, gobbling down a massive spoonful of custard because he was right, I couldn't lie to him.

"Of a sort. Were you?"

"No."

"Did you engage with the White Veil in some other type of way?"

Pretending to think about it for a minute, I shook my head. "Don't think so."

"Didn't even send them a thank you note?"

"Was out of royal ink."

He ran a hand over his face to hide his smile. "You know this fucker, don't you?"

"Everyone does."

"You really want me to find out for myself? You know I will. And I like being made to work for my gold." He pointed a finger at me. "But you won't like your big fat mouse falling into one of my traps, not when it gives you the majority of the popular vote in this kingdom."

Shrugging a shoulder, I finished the rest of my custard. He could try. But he'd find nothing. I wasn't interested in giving it a face as long as it did my bidding.

He sighed, but he was not intending to give up on this, not in the least. "You're awfully quiet, little bird."

"You hate small talk."

"You never talked small before."

Shrugging again, I pulled his bowl before me and started eating his barely touched custard.

He leaned forward, giving me an odd look like he was about to offer me a brilliant deal I wouldn't be able to resist. Frankly, it worked a little until he said, "Thora, sweetheart—"

I rolled my eyes. "You whore."

His laughter filled every little spot in the massive kitchens. Every pot and pan echoed the sound until I felt my cheeks and ears turn red. I'd made him laugh a dozen times before, but this one sounded a bit different. Like he'd given up holding it back. His reactions to me had always been half of what he usually gave others. More toned down. More held back. Tamed.

Not this one though.

"I should be the one blushing, not you," he said, dragging his bowl back before him and stealing my spoon to eat what was left in there. The stretch of silence grew and grew. None of us would look at the other either. "When did we run out of things to say?"

"We haven't. You chose to be alone, and I was forced to be alone. I adapted. You haven't, it seems."

"Thora—"

"You forced me to stay in this world only for you to leave me alone in it. I wasn't even ready."

"You would have never been ready if I had stayed."

That choking feeling wrapped its hand around my throat and stung my eyes until they prickled with tears. "You think I am now? Truth is I will never be. You just made it a little easier, a little better, a little less alone, a little less haunting. You told me it would be alright, that I would be alright, and when it wasn't, you gave up on me. I needed you."

"Thora—"

"You were my friend. You knew things no one knew. You knew how much I needed you." My voice was small when I added, "I think you needed me a little, too."

"You didn't need me, Rora."

Why did I love when he called me that stupid nickname so much? "I wanted you. How about that?" I asked, scraping the bowl and angrily licking the spoon to distract myself from the way my heart was attempting to see if it could beat up my throat and outside my chest. "And I think you wanted me a little, too."

Could almost swear that the brown of his eyes was no longer brown, but a deep, endless black. "Are you still hungry?" he asked, his chest falling harder and faster than before.

I shook my head, pushing away the empty bowl with a pair of very shaky hands before I'd start chewing on the porcelain. "You?"

"Depends. Are you offering yourself up?" He grabbed our bowls and stood towards the sink, stopping a little just to lean in and whisper in my ear, "I like it when you blush for me."

"It's the irritation."

"I'm sure it is."

"You don't have to do the dishes."

"And deprive you of the chance to ogle my backside?"

"I'm certain there is nothing inside your skull but two spiders webbing the empty space," I said, tilting my head to get a better look at him.

"There is another thing."

"Certainly not a brain."

He chuckled, putting the wet dishes on the rack to dry. "A little bird."

He was an idiot. An idiot whose laughter did funny things to my body. "Sounds very painful," I said, giving him one of my polished smiles which I knew very well had always annoyed him. "Perfect."

Leaning back on the sink, he began untying the apron, his gaze never leaving mine for a second. "It is."

"Painful?" I asked, trying to keep my eyes on his upper half of the body.

"Perfect. And it was painful. It isn't anymore. I like having her in my head."

The kitchen door suddenly flew open, and Snow came into sight barefooted and wearing only a tiny white nightgown that hugged her big belly, looking confused between the two of us. Her expression widened on the pot of custard still on the stove. "I knew I smelled something. You ate without me?" she accused more than asked, waddling to the stove and lifting a hand to Malik. "Hand me a damn bowl. If I have to get on something to reach up there, it will be your head serving as a step stool."

He kissed her temple and reached for a bowl. "Love you, too, sister-in-law."

"Yeah, yeah," my sister murmured, filling herself a massive bowl of custard. She was entirely too distracted by her bowl and almost tripped over everything on the way to the table, had Malik not quite literally lifted her to a seat. "I have feet," she sneered, batting his hand away.

"Didn't they come with instructions?"

Just then, Kilian marched inside the massive space that now felt too crowded, half naked and carrying a dishevelled Rain in his arms. "Any to spare for my little princess? She is a little hungry, too."

"When is this family ever not hungry?" I murmured under my breath, reaching to fill her another bowl of custard, and Malik chuckled at my words.

Kilian sat beside Snow, wrapping her long hair in one of his hands to hold it away from her face so she could eat undisturbed, while his other hand spoon fed his sleepy, but very hungry daughter that clung to his neck for dear life.

To say I wasn't just a little envious, would be the worst lie I ever told. This was why I rarely stayed with them. Watching them like this always made me just a little...sad. I never was given what Sam and Rain had. It was ridiculous to even think about being jealous of my little niece and nephew, but little me wasn't the slightest ashamed to admit it. I had not wanted the moon or the stars, but when I had asked to be loved and taken care of, it had always felt as if I'd asked for just that, the moon and the stars—I'd asked too much, I'd asked for the impossible. But besides love and care, Snow and Kil had also given Sam and Rain the moon and the stars, even more if they asked for it, and that hurt. It really did. Like someone had taken a pickaxe to my rib cage to dig out my heart.

"I'm envious, too," Malik quietly said like the bearer of my deepest darkest secrets that he was. "It's okay to be."

"It's gone," I said, bitter tones dressing my voice and angry tears making their way down my cheeks. My childhood was gone. Robbed. "And I can never have it back. I don't even remember when I stopped being a kid, when I stopped reaching for any of my parents. Snow and Eren did their best, but they were just kids, too."

He raised a careful hand to my face and wiped all my tears back before tucking me to his chest, his arms swallowing the entirety of my frame. The safest cage I'd ever been in. "Remember what you told me?"

"I've told you too many things."

"I remember them all," he murmured, pressing his lips to my head. "I remember you telling me that it is alright to mourn what was taken from us. That is the healthy thing to do."

"I say a lot of nonsense."

"You're the smartest person I know."

"You need to get around to meeting more people."

His lips pulled into a smile where they were resting against my temple. "I think I like my person. Despite us not being friends and all anymore."

"What are you two whispering about?" my sister asked, throwing us a quick look over her shoulder before spinning to me entirely, her cheeks full. She swallowed and looked between Malik and I, almost helplessly. "Is something wrong?"

Kilian dropped his spoon and turned to us, as did sleepy Rain who wore a thick moustache of custard.

Didn't know who snorted first, Malik or me. After the fit of laughter died a little between us, Malik grabbed my hand and pulled me to the exit, gesturing to Kilian's mouth and then Rain. "All three of you need to head back to sleep. You're feeding your daughter through her nostrils."

Snow did not look convinced. It broke my heart to see my sister look so defeated. Especially when I knew she never looked like that for anyone else. She was the strongest person I knew. When I gave her a smile, she gave me a sad one back.

He faded us to Isjord, just outside my room. "I want my friend privileges back," he announced just like that, turning to leave. Not even a question or request.

"Where are you going?"

"To check on your soldiers."

"Elias does that."

"I can't come inside that room with you right now, Rora," he said, disappearing down the corridor. "I will ask for other privileges if I do."

22

BURGUNDY SNAPDRAGONS

THORA

E lias's sword whizzed straight in front of my face, cutting a few strands of my hair before I could manoeuvre back enough to avoid it. Without even giving me a chance at taking a single breath of air, he whirled around, knocking me on my back with the handle.

Dropping to the slippery gravelly ground of the training court, I held a hand to my abdomen, trying to catch the breath the hit stole out of me. Every time we had these training sessions, I regretted asking him to not hold back on me. I was useless with a sword.

Unlike usually, he didn't reach out to help at all. Instead, he sat cross legged before me, stabbing his sword on the ground and giving me a berating look, which then softened to politeness when he peeked a quick glance somewhere behind me. "You're relying too much on magic and neglecting training."

"I'm sure I'd be saying the same thing to you if we had used magic instead of swords."

"What is distracting you this much?" he asked, looking behind me again.

Groaning, I looked back at where he'd been stealing glances for the past half an hour. Malik leaned on the balcony ledge, watching us.

"He's watching you," Elias carefully announced, like Malik did not have an ear on every shadow.

"He can watch," I said, throwing my jacket off.

"Put that back on," Elias gestured, moving away from me like I was a forest fire.

"Man up, Lord Venzor." If I heard the leather squeaking one more time, I was going to have a stroke.

"I'm about to be manned down."

"He won't touch anything I don't give him permission to touch." Turning round, I looked up at him, mindful of the Isjordian soldiers around us. "Right, *honey?*"

Leaning back on a wall, he crossed his hands over his chest and gave Elias a wicked smile like only Malik Castemont knew how to give. "If I find a single bruise on my brand new wife, I'm going to pluck your soul out, tie it up and make it my bitch."

My cheeks burned. "He doesn't mean that," I said, patting his shoulder.

Very reluctantly, Elias picked his sword back up and stood, waiting for me instead of going in first like he usually did. "Is he the one distracting you?"

I shook my head. Not very strongly though because it was partially true. "Remember the noise I told you I'm hearing all the time?"

He raised an almost entirely translucent blonde brow up. "Got Visha to give you drops for that."

I went in with my attack since he usually got weak in the knees when he said her name, but he easily blocked me. "Not a case for some simple drops."

"Visha doesn't do things simply."

Could almost roll my eyes, but my heady sword was dragging all my muscles down. "Didn't work, Elias. I keep hearing it more often than before. Louder. Sometimes it's like I'm inside of it."

"Have you told him?"

"Not all of it."

"Why not?"

"Because I am waiting for it to go away."

"What if it doesn't?"

I frowned. "I keep that yellow head of yours intact with that body so you would agree with what I say and pleasantly flatter me here and there."

"Thought that was the job for the men you tie up to your bed," he said, blocking another of my attacks and pushing me back until I was stumbling on my feet and lost my balance in the gravel. He flashed me a perfect grin and pointed the tip of his sword to Malik. "I guess no more of them now that you've tied *that* knot."

"I could have your tongue cut for that."

"The lesser evil at this point."

The wind shifted a little when I braced my hands on the gravel to push myself up, the snow near my hands suddenly began moving, gathering around my fingers. Then I felt something against my palm. Like a pulse. A heartbeat. It began echoing so loud around me that every other sound muted.

It turned oddly serene. The bubbling mess in my chest suddenly disappeared. It was like I was floating. Like my heart was beating outside of my own chest. Like I was free from it.

Someone spoke behind me, the words entirely slurred and overpowered by the heartbeat. Many shadows fell over me, and the voices grew many and louder, none that I could properly hear, all were muffled.

A hand touched my cheek and I jerked, the sounds returning, the pulse disappeared from under my palm, the only thing I could feel against it was the gravel uncomfortably digging at my skin. "Rora," Malik called, brows pulled together in a scowl. "This isn't fucking funny anymore. What's going on?"

"Can't you hear that?"

"Hear what?"

"The heartbeat."

As always, he didn't doubt me, putting a hand beside mine and feeling for a few moments. When his brows began slowly pulling together, I felt the pulse beneath my palm quicken.

"Tell me that you hear it."

"I can't, but if you are hearing it, it must be there." His face was clean of any expression. Either because he was trying not to frighten me or because he really couldn't hear or feel anything. It was the first. "Do something for me," he said, his eyes blackening, dark spidery veins spreading over them. "Use your magic. As much of it as you can."

"Here?"

He nodded. "Try not to kill me. Or at least do it gently."

"So not funny," I muttered to myself, standing and moving away from him.

It was easy to draw magic, not as easy as to undraw it back to me now that the gates that used to control its flow are left for me to close myself instead of the seal. It was even harder considering I didn't only need to seal it inside myself. I had to seal the gates that flowed back to the earth.

Wind howled, ice broke and buried everything under its stiff cold coat. An entire hurricane surrounded me, ice and wind, wind and ice dancing around one another. Wherever they met, frost would splint into thousands of tiny little crystals that reflected entire rainbows around me.

Across the white of my magic, I saw his black one. Shadows that resembled black fire surrounded his body, swirling around him and then diving towards the earth fast, breaking through it with furious speed.

When his shadows began dissipating, I pulled back, too. Wind and ice disappearing.

"When?" was all he asked.

"Night before my wedding. Just...lately, it has gotten louder."

"How lately?"

"The day of the funeral was when I heard it clearly," I said, walking towards him. "What's wrong?"

"After Oryn and Visha removed your seal, I think your magic has been feeding something else beside the land."

I blinked fast. "Like?"

"Something. I just know it is now clinging to you somehow."

Trying not to gag and shiver, I murmured, "Like a...leech or something?"

"Yeah. A silent leech who has decided to show itself all of a sudden," he said, giving me a strange look, as if he was trying to see right through me.

Nausea travelled up my throat and I gagged a little. "Take it off me. Kill it or something."

"Why haven't you said anything?"

"Because of the way you are looking at me right now."

"Put your jacket on and let's go."

"I'm hot," I said, following after him. "Where are we going?"

He shed his own jacket and threw it over my shoulders. "Somewhere."

Visha didn't look pleased at all when Malik faded back along with her in his tails. She took in the meeting room and then me, blinking a little confused at both of us.

Currently, she sat before us, not moving an eyelid or breathing at all from the way her shoulders and chest didn't move. The woman was a corpse. A very pretty, red haired, corpse with a voluptuous body. She took in every word that Malik told her and then just stood there, looking more annoyed than she was when she arrived.

"What he says is possible," Visha agreed. "Something might be feeding off from your magic underneath the land. Could be anything. Whatever it is has established some sort of a tie between you and them. You can sense it and *it* can sense you back."

I shuddered.

She turned to Malik who'd remained quiet all this time. "I will need a sample of the earth and some of your blood."

Malik faded and then returned with a shovel full of mud, slamming it on the table before Visha. He handed me a handkerchief. "Do you want me to do it?"

I nodded. Extending a hand to him.

Taking a dagger from my thigh harness, he brought the blade to the tip of my finger, letting it bleed over the white handkerchief until it formed a massive red splotch.

"There," he said, throwing it to Visha who sighed, stood and grabbed it all before disappearing inside a portal.

Malik brought my finger to his mouth, sucking on the little cut. "If it happens again," he said, leaving a small kiss on the tiny cut. "You come to me, alright?"

I nodded, and abruptly stood like a firework that was about to burst.

"Where are you going?" he asked, following after me as I swerved the castle corridors.

Nope. This wasn't me running away from him. It definitely wasn't me trying to escape his presence before I did or said something embarrassing. Gods, I wanted him so badly. Ten long goddamn years had changed nothing. I still felt like that nine-teen-year-old girl who was out of mind infatuated with him. "It's Friday. I visit the Tenebrose Academy on Fridays."

"Not this Friday. Not like this."

I snorted, trying to keep my composure. "I'm fine. Nothing hurts. And it isn't like this is new or anything."

He kept following after me as I made my way out to the stables. "I'm coming with you."

No. No. No. "Aren't your soldiers already doing a fantastic job at invading every moment of privacy I have, or terrifying just about every Isjordian?"

"I want to keep an eye on you myself."

I stopped walking and turned to him. "Malik."

"You said you wanted my eyes on you," he said, stepping impossibly close. "Truth is, I want that, too. Let me."

Oh gods. "Don't scare them."

"With this adorable face? Never."

Just like he'd said, the students liked the idiot's adorable face. They'd surrounded him, asking all sorts of questions that he gladly answered with some wild exaggerations. He went against my wishes of terrifying them, but he did it in such a way that they felt protected from it—he made sure they understood that they were now his to protect and that our enemies would be the ones to face those qualms.

"Is it true that you taught the queen how to control the dead?" one of the students asked, Agnes, the granddaughter of a priestess.

"I do not do that, Agnes, despite what your old grandma says."

"She's lying," Malik said, stretching on a student's chair and engulfing the tiny space entirely. "She controls me and then I control them."

They all let out a synchronised awe and chuckled and blushed on my behalf.

"Back to your classes now," I ordered, and they all grumbled as they waved at us one last time before they left.

"They like you," he said, following me out of the classroom and onto the Academy corridors—corridors that had housed Silas's previous Bruma Command which was now extinct.

"Hard to believe I am not that dislikable?"

"Hard to believe you've opened yourself up to them enough for them to feel comfortable around you."

The bright orange sunset was blinding when we stepped outside and onto the furthest rose gardens in the castle. "They're kids. I like to think their minds have yet to twist into malicious or fearful thinking."

"They're grown up enough to know good and bad. Grown enough to choose who to trust or not. You've done good by them. You're good to them. You're good to these people even though I think the majority of them don't deserve any of it."

"I'm really not," I said. "Being good to them would mean respecting their traditions, their ways of life, and listening to their complaints. I've done none of that. I've refused to listen. Sometimes I feel just like him."

He stopped and so did I. "You're not Silas."

"No, Snow says I'm better looking."

"Where did you bury him?"

I felt blood drain out of my face. "Why would you think I've done that?"

"Because I remember telling you that burning and leaving a body unburied would let their soul roam this realm and never go beyond. I'm sure you more than most want Silas to get his proper punishment beyond. Where is he?"

How did he remember our time together more than I did? I'd been the one paying attention. "Why do you want to know?"

"Might need to take a piss."

"Don't you go to your own father's grave for that?"

"This one is closer. I hope."

"It's there."

His brow hiked up. "There?"

"Where I killed him. I buried him there."

"Under the golden arrow?"

He remembered, and he'd probably known it before even asking, he'd just wanted me to tell him. "Yes." He'd kissed me there, too. More often than I'd like to think, the place reminded me of that more than the one hundred deaths of my father. It felt like a fever dream now. Mostly by how it followed. The destruction. The deaths of millions. My sister's and Kilian's. That day had felt like one of those dreams where no matter how much or how fast you ran, you could never reach the point you were heading. We'd done everything right, but we'd been late. It had been too late. That day cost even those who had lived and survived it. Some our minds, some their souls. For some it was both.

Like him.

That day had cost Malik both.

I'd seen it.

The magic he'd used, the lives he'd taken, the pain he'd inflicted, all had dented his soul. Seeing his brother and Snow only one light breath away from death, having felt all of it, that cost him his mind.

Malik had been another sort of inconsolable after the war. Except you could never comfort someone who never cried, never raged or complained—someone who had soaked in his pain, sunken under it until it overrode his entire personality.

His finger lightly tapped my chin. "You went again."

I shook my head. "Only thinking."

"Of me, your loving husband, I hope."

"Sort of," I said, reaching to fiddle with my necklace.

"Oh?" he asked, his eyes dropping there.

Turning around, I continued our walk back to the castle. "I had my first kiss there, where the golden arrow is."

His steps slowed just a little and I stopped again so he could catch up to where I was.

"But you knew that, didn't you?" I asked.

It looked like he didn't because he looked so confused with himself. "You were with Neo."

"*Were* is a very strong word. He flirted. I flirted. That was the extent of it." Turning to fully face him, I asked, "Why, do you regret doing it?" I've always wanted to know that. If he regretted it. If he regretted the one memory I loved. "Is that why you did it? Because I was with Neo, and it was just another kiss you'd given to someone?"

Say yes, I wanted to say. *Say yes and ruin it so I could stop thinking about it every waking and dreaming moment like some foolish nineteen-year-old girl who didn't know better than to overthink just a simple kiss.* Because to him, that was probably all it had been. A simple kiss.

"Only if you tell me something."

That's how it always was with us, wasn't it? A secret for a secret. "What?"

"Did you kiss me back because I was the only one you felt comfortable enough to touch? If I had been him, would you have kissed him instead?"

My lips parted, somewhat in surprise. "How do you not already know that?"

He knew everything about me.

I knew everything about him.

There was literally nothing but a transparent sheet between me and him.

And I had been everything but subtle back then.

He angled his head to the side, still looking confused. "I was the only man you could bear to be near you, touch you, the only one you could have any sort of intimacy with. You can't tell me that isn't at least part of the reason why you've ever wanted me."

His words made me recoil like he'd struck me, and I stood there for a quiet while, gaping at him.

Turning on my feet, I marched away.

As he'd say: fuck him.

The idiot.

Just insinuating that made me furious.

How dare he.

He faded right in front of me, forcing me to stop. "Answer me or I will take that as a yes."

"Yes. Yes, that is why I did it. Yes, Malik, that is why I've been wanting to do it since the day I saw you," I lied, and continued my marching steps to the castle gates, feeling the air chill beyond the usual, and the snow under my feet turning into a sheet of ice.

Just when the soldiers pulled the entrance doors open, I stopped again. Snow had this thing when you saw her, it made you want to bow to her. An urge I always resisted at her sight. Something I always envied.

"Snow, hi!" I said, forcing a smile.

She didn't look happy. Considering she was currently generally unhappy at every little thing should have made me feel less concerned, but it didn't—not with how she was looking at me. "Visha came to me."

Of course she had.

"How come I find out about all of this now?"

"It wasn't anything concerning," I offered.

Her scowl furrowed even deeper. "You've been pushing me away," Snow said. "And I've let you."

"You're tired, Snow, we will talk another time."

"Not at all. I want to know, too, Rora. I feel like I'm the only one who doesn't know anything about you. I keep treading carefully. Why am I being so careful? I tried to think about it, but I couldn't find an answer. I just knew I had to be careful." She stepped closer to me. "Tell me, why do I have to be careful?"

The thick ball of yarn and thorns collected on my throat again and cut off my voice. My lips parted to speak but sounds and words couldn't come out.

My sister reached me and pulled me to her, hugging me. "You used to do that even when you were little," she said.

"You'd tell me the mockingbirds outside would steal my voice and put hay in my throat."

"You never believed me, did you?"

I laughed. "No. I never did. But it made you happy to know that it did."

She shook her head. "No, it made me happy because you would smile."

I buried my face in her chest and broke down, sobbing.

23

PINK ORCHIDS

MALIK

S he'd lied.

Yes, I'd used my magic to see it even though I prided myself to be pretty fucking empathetic without it.

Now she was upset with me.

Very fucking upset.

All while I was in an entire state of bliss all because of that lie. Damned painful bliss, too. Because she'd chosen an odd dress to wear at a meeting.

A meeting.

The prim and proper Thora Krigborn had found the tightest, lowest cut dress I'd ever seen on her. To wear to a meeting. And she was standing by the windows, half turned to the rest of the room, so I had a good view of all of it. Head to fucking toe.

Did I mention it was pink? Or that her hair was put up in a ponytail and tied up with the same coloured ribbon.

She looked like a god damned dream.

Like someone had cracked a heavenly door open and was letting us take a little peek behind it.

Worst was, not only had she shown me yesterday that I was the biggest fucking idiot out there, but apparently I was shitty at my job, too. An Empath like me should have been able to tell it was me she'd wanted. Maybe I just did not want to believe it. Maybe it had seemed too good to believe it.

Pushing to stand, I shed my jacket and threw it around her shoulders, catching her by surprise because she jumped a little. She smelled so damn delicious. "You look cold."

Frowning, she threw the jacket back at me. "I don't get cold."

"Sweetheart, trust me, you're very fucking cold," I said, throwing it around her shoulders again, leaning in just to catch a bit more of her perfume.

"Why are you being so weird," she hissed, glancing at her court who was pretending they weren't listening in to what we were saying.

Stepping closer until my chest brushed hers, I murmured only for her to hear, "I am so close to bending you down that table and fucking you in front of them all. So close, Thora. Friendlily, of course. Very friendlily."

She blinked a couple of times, and then her eyes widened, her pale cheeks starting to gain some colour. "Oh."

"Yes. Oh."

Pushing her arms through the massive sleeves, she quickly buttoned the jacket up until the top. "Chilly," she lightly announced to the rest of the room, pulling a chair with a shaky pair of hands.

Grabbing her chair, I pulled it out for her to sit.

She jumped in her seat just a little when I sat down next to her. "I'm not going to jump on you, little bird," I murmured in Adriatian to her, and reached for her clammy frozen hand under the table so I could cool mine down—or justify myself for holding her. "Fuck, you're cold."

"Sorry," she murmured back, glancing just about everywhere but me.

"You're finally talking to me," I said, as Elias continued counting down the number of attacks Iskyla had ordered in Isjord this past week and their calculations for the next one since there wasn't a grain of brain in her head when it came to being unpredictable.

Maybe it was because she was wanting to be caught.

I couldn't have that. Not when Thora was determined to not show that side of hers to anyone.

"I don't know what you mean," she replied, ducking her chin inside the massive jacket's opening.

"You slept in Rain's room last night." If I had not found them so cozied up, holding each other tightly, I would have taken Thora back with me. I would have taken them both, but Rain's doll wasn't going to be near where I slept at any point if I didn't want to sleep with an eye open for the rest of my life.

"She missed me."

"I missed you."

She glanced at me with the corner of her eye, not even deigning me a fraction of her attention. "Well, you left for ten years so that cancels out."

"You're going to hold that over my head until the next lifetime?" I wanted her to. I loved this—loved her torturing me like this. I wanted her to make me beg for it. I wanted her to make me get to my knees. She had to—she had to make me beg and torture me and get me to my knees because I was fairly close to doing it voluntarily.

"Why only until the next? You also insinuated that I've been trying to jump your bones since day one because apparently, you're my only shot at ever touching a man, kissing a man, wanting a man. It has to be at least five lifetimes."

"Jump my bones, huh?"

"Shut up."

Everyone on the table had a quarter of their sight on us even though they all had angled their bodies toward Elias who was still going on and on about Iskyla's methods of attack as if they mattered.

"Quieter, sweetheart, if my dick hears you one more time, I'm going to have you do something about it." Just the idea of her on her knees, lips warped around my cock, had me reaching to adjust myself.

Her hand got even colder, and she shrunk a little in her chair, going red up to her little ears.

"That's it," I cooed, bringing her hand to my lips and leaving a kiss on her almost frosted knuckles. "That's better."

Her chest fell and rose faster, but her hand warmed up.

I didn't particularly enjoy making her nervous, not when I knew that if severe, it could sometimes put her in a catatonic state—a way for her mind to block itself from going into a panic attack. But this was a different kind of nervousness. The type that had her shift in her seat, flustered. The type that made her bite into her lower soft lip as a way to control her breathing. The type where her forest green eyes darkened just a little, almost making them appear black.

The type that made me just a little curious and dared me to open my senses to see if I could tell shades of lust in her shadows. One thing held me back. I'd want to wash the curiosity away if I did find that to be the truth, and then she'd be on this table with her cunt on my face.

"Malik," Elias called, and I had to look away from her.

At least my hard on died a little at seeing his face. "Yes?"

"You've been assessing this for a couple weeks now. What are your findings?"

"You will see their results shortly."

"Results?"

Even Thora turned to me at that.

"I don't just sit and watch and take notes, Lord Venzor." Pointing to the map laid on the table, showing the north of Isjord, I added, "Notice how their attacks are concentrated there now and usually almost right at sunrise? Once or twice, even after it."

They all shared a look with one another.

"They believe old wives' tales about me. That my magic is useless in daytime so they now attack closer to sunrise. And they also attack the north, because they again believe that the further I am from Adriata, the weaker I get." I pointed to the Islines next. "Iskyla wanted to deal the Isline villages in exchange for pulling back soldiers from Modr and Hanai. Any guesses as to why she changed her strategy of obtaining Isjord from within to encircling it and eating at the edges?"

I threw a round paperweight on top of the villages. "Because she thinks I cannot use magic in her lands."

"You think she fears you?"

"No, I know she does. Just how I know her soldiers have been roaming the Dardanes markets as well as those in Whitebridge according to my informants, in search of Umbra and Dark Crafters. Iskyla feels at a disadvantage. So much so that she is breaking ancient rules her people have been abiding by for centuries. Using dark and darker magic."

"What have you done?" Thora asked, scowling at me. "I know you've done something."

I kissed her hand again. "You'll see. Soon."

"Just tell me."

Leaning in, I asked, "Like you told me yesterday?"

I'd held onto her hand all the way through the meeting and still didn't let go as the room was emptying, leaving me and her alone.

"I have to be in Rose Court in five minutes to meet with the ladies," she said, avoiding looking at me, still not pulling away from my hold though her hand had gotten unusually warm in mine—which I knew she did not like. Most heat bothered her. You'd never see her get close to a fire or a lit flame, not that she needed to.

"Some woman caught your eye?"

Confused, she finally faced me. "What?"

"What woman in Rose Court were you trying to impress today?"

"Impress?"

Letting go of her hand, I braced both my hands on her chair handles and turned it to face me with her still in it. Reaching to undo my jacket's buttons that she was wearing, I looked up at her watching me. "Yes, impress, little bird." Once I had the jacket pulled away from her body, I took in all of her. "Looking like a wet dream." My wet dream, perhaps.

Her eyes widened just a fraction—so innocently. "Nissa just wanted me to look pretty so they don't look down on me."

"Thank her for me."

"Maybe I should hold on to your jacket a bit longer," she said, reaching for it, but I held it away from her.

"In a minute. How about I walk you to Rose Court," I said, standing and reaching a hand for her.

I was there this time before the bells rang to signal Iskyla's soldiers.

The furthest village in Modr was strangely quiet considering there had just been an attack. The Isjordian guard was only about five miles away at this point, but already late by the looks of it. It seemed that I was late, too. Iskyla's soldiers had not made it far into their sudden attack. It had not been as sudden as the one carried on them either.

Bodies lay on top of one another at the village entrance. A shadowed figure standing before them and circled by white wolves—how it had been alerted before anyone else. A smart move. Training wolves was no easy feat, especially to the point they could smell danger miles before it even became dangerous.

The White Veil twisted around at the sound of my footsteps, the wolves snarling and then standing back when they took in my scent.

Before the cloaked creature was about to take off, I faded close and pulled onto the hood. Black hair half bound with a neatly tied white bow slipped free, cascading below her shoulders. Her head whipped to me, eyes wide on mine just like that first day I'd seen her in White Bridge.

I wrapped her hair around my fist and pulled her to me, her back meeting my chest. "I was starting to wonder why this pale ghost smelled like my sweet wife," I whispered in her ear, burying my face in her hair to inhale that scent that was beginning to drive me absolutely insane. Did she bathe in a fucking salad bowl? Why was she so sweet? My mouth was watering for just a tiny little taste.

"Pretend wife," she breathed, panting.

My lips curled into a smile as they rested on her neck, resisting the urge to mark her. "My pretend wife, care to tell me why you are not asleep and wearing silk bedding to terrorise your enemy? Did you get lost on your way to the bathroom?"

"I have my reasons."

"I'm sure they will be very, very good reasons," I said, spinning her to face me. "So?"

"Can't we sit down and discuss this like two grown adults?"

"I'm not the one wearing the linen, sweetheart. Besides, I've seen your disappearing tricks."

"That wasn't me. It was just ice."

I grinned. "Figured that. What about the nights we spent together? How did you tie your magic so far from Tenebrose? There isn't a chance you've left that room with me in it."

"It was Elias. He's learnt to mimic me well."

The sound of his name was starting to hurt my ears. "How did this start?"

"Well—"

"The short version. I can tell pretty well when you want to distract me and then run off when your soldiers get here."

"Snow and I read about an old Isline story about a veiled spirit we found in the library where Atlas works. The White Veil had once been a soldier in king Edric's army, said to have been buried with him as one of the most powerful Aura to live at the time.

Isjordians and Isliners alike had claimed to have seen him roam their villages at night long after he'd passed. I might have obsessed over it for a while, learning every little detail about it until I was confident enough I could act as it."

"Snow knows?"

Thora winced. "She's...been the White Veil a couple times. Before she was pregnant."

"Ah, family quality time only how the Skygards know." I leaned down until our faces were only inches apart. "The men. How do you control them? How do you move them like puppets? I'm sure I never taught you how to do that."

"Science."

"Now I need you to elaborate."

"Ice is water. Blood has water. Therefore, something I can also control. I studied. Meditated. Watched other Aura bend their magic. The closest to what I wanted to achieve was fire. It moves like liquid. But a Scarlet can also turn fire into thick lava, control it, too. Took me a while, but Karl Modr helped me master aspects of ice that I didn't know. A few old Verglassers actually used to control water in every form, too. Mist. Ice. Verglassers were also healers a long time ago and were masters of the body, using blood as a mechanism to hack at human health. Krig and the God of Waters are also brothers, so it made sense that water is familiar to us. I learnt how to turn water and blood cold enough to easily control it without killing the person. Also, our training together came to great help, learning how to tether my magic onto things."

Stunned, I just looked at her for a long minute. "Why? Why do it like this?"

"I don't want them to be afraid of me. And they would be. But they can be afraid of their God, and their *God* was on my side."

"If they fear you, then you have what you want. They will bow to you."

"Not how I want them to. I want their respect, their trust, their hope, not their fear. Otherwise, I'm just my father. What happens when they are no longer afraid of me? What about my heirs? Do I have to teach them to be vile and cruel to make people respect them? I refuse to become him. I refuse to let the other generation become like him."

"Thora, you are not Silas."

"They want Silas! They want someone like him. And that is why they are accepting Iskyla." She breathed fast. "Have you wondered why they are not revolting against the terror she's caused in these lands? They are accepting their kin being slain only because they believe they deserve it to happen since they are ruled by a weak queen. It has left me no choice. I will not match their cruelty, Malik, but I will not bow before it either. Times have changed. I will force Isjord to change one way or another. Even if it makes me look weak."

Sighing, I pulled her hood back on. "Hellion."

Her emerald eyes rounded and blinked up at me all innocence. "You're not going to tell me off?"

"Why? It's a brilliant idea."

"It is?" She frowned, almost angry, pushing her hood back to glare up at me. "Then why have you been chasing this around?"

"Because I wanted your secret. Shame you didn't come forward yourself. Made me quite sad to be excluded."

"You knew from the start?"

It almost hurt my feelings. Almost, but she was so cute all upset and angry. "Even if I couldn't hear and see, I'd recognise you anywhere, little bird."

Her eyes rounded like saucers. "You think anyone else has?"

Were they all this obsessed with her, too? If they were, then yes. "I don't believe so."

"Iskyla is scared shitless of the White Veil. I'd like to keep this ploy for as long as I need to."

"You have me, too. I can be scary sometimes."

She took a few steps back. "You scare these people shitless for other reasons."

Slowly, I caught up to her even as she kept backing away from me. "Such as?"

Her back hit a wall. "You don't bring men to submission, you bring them to their deaths."

"I will bring them to wherever you want me to bring them. It's not me they need to be scared shitless of, it's you." Tugging on the hood, I pulled it back over her head. "Go back to our room. I will be there once this mess is cleaned up."

I watched as she retreated into the darkness of the nearby forest, protected by it as she summoned one of her ice dragons and lurched up in the air, still protected by the shade of night, the dark grey clouds disguising her creature, too.

Her wolves surrounded me, demanding they be petted now that their master had left without doing so. Once they sniffed the air that took the scent of the incoming soldiers, they howled at the round moon and then took off into the forest as well, leaving me alone to deal with it.

"Was this you?" one of her captains asked, pointing to the pile of Isline soldiers as she quickly got down her horse to run at the horrid scene their queen had left behind.

"I don't leave bodies behind, Captain. Nor do I make them bleed this much."

"What do you want us to do with them?"

"Nothing, we'll send them back to Iskyla." As I'd been doing after every attack. How they had not noticed that there were no bodies to bury after these attacks, I had no idea. Maybe they thought the White Veil ate them or something.

Her eyes went wide. "We don't trespass her territory."

"Looks like she doesn't extend that grace to you. But I didn't mean I'll send you up there. Your queen would have my head. I'll take them."

"Y-you?"

"Me," I said, and the dead bodies jerked. Their limbs flailed and cracked into place as they got to their feet. Some bleeding, some limbless, some with bones sticking out of skin, the corpses all stood, marched up in a line and walked outside the village gates. Once they'd taken to my order, the dead wouldn't stop until they had obeyed it to the very last syllable. Guess Iskyla had received them all considering the measures she'd taken to avoid being met with me.

The Isjordian soldiers had all frozen in place for some reason, flinching when I said, "You can all go home."

The young captain met everyone's uneasy gaze and then returned mine. "As you say, Your Majesty," she said, bowing her head, and her soldiers followed suit, sending disturbed glances in my direction.

Thora had curled up in the middle of her big bed, her chin resting on her knees as her eyes drifted off into the distance of her mind.

"Doesn't look like you're thinking of me," I called, throwing my jacket to a chair.

Not even a flash of acknowledgement crossed her focused eyes.

The closer to her I got, the more I realised she was grinding her jaw, her eyes were out of focus entirely and her breathing was growing harder.

Careful not to startle her out of the stupor too abruptly, I sat in front of her and cupped her face, massaging my fingers down her jaw and neck to relieve some of the muscle tension. "Rora, sweetheart. Come on now. You've promised to never lock the door, to never leave me out. Why have you locked the damn door?"

Seeing her like this, I was so tempted to suck all of the emotion out of her, to take it away and make it so it never has a place inside her again. But if I did, if I brought magic in the midst of us, the lines would all blur. I'd become not something she will want or need, I'd become something she can't cope without. An addiction.

Lifting her onto my lap, I cradled her in my arms and rubbed my hands over her stiff limbs, controlling the rush of her blood until she warmed up under my touch. "You're so unfair," I murmured, studying every little dent on her face, the swollen pouty lips, the thick lashes and scattered faded freckles dusted over her nose. "This is so unfair." So close to me. Mine. All of her. Yet. None of it was for me to touch.

Her lashes fluttered and then her eyes were on me a second later. "Malik?"

"Who else would it be, little bird?"

"Forgive me for doubting my eyes. The many times I've seen you these past ten years have been purely their pity. Every time I've smelled, felt, heard you, all has been pity. Even my mind pities me."

My eyes drew shut and I dropped my brow to hers. "I don't like this nonsense, Rora." I didn't deserve it just yet. One day I would.

"I'm pitiful, aren't I?"

"This is all my fault."

She laughed, burying her face in my chest, laughing even more. Then I felt her tears soak my shirt. "I clung to the thing that felt most normal in my life. That isn't your fault. It isn't your fault that I am desperate."

"You were the most extraordinary thing that came into my life, and I boxed you like you'd fallen from the damn skies. Never let anyone see or touch or near you."

"I was happy in that box. I'm very happy in boxes."

"It is a cage, sweetheart."

"It is my cage. I chose to be in it."

"No one chooses to be in a cage."

"Perhaps not." She looked up at me. "But it's the prettiest cage I've been in."

"You should never let anyone put you in a cage, Thora. Never."

"Alright."

"You are not looking at me like you mean that."

She bit her lower lip and flashed a bright smile, her eyes all big and wide and teary, making her look like a living doll. "Sorry."

"You don't look like you meant that either."

"How do I look?"

"Like you want to lock us up inside that cage and throw away the key."

"That's why you were my best friend. You know me so well."

"That's why I *am* your best friend," I said, trailing a finger down her parted mouth. "Even though you don't tell me secrets anymore. Even though I have so many of mine to exchange for them."

"Maybe I don't want to be your friend anymore."

"Tough shit."

The way her eyes gleamed like perfect emerald fallen stars made me hate all ten years I'd spent not looking at them. "What secrets?"

"You think it will be that easy after all this?" I asked, letting my touch roam around her face, watching her lashes flutter fast and her breath hitch. My perfect torment. My biggest and most dooming secret. "When you're ready to give me yours. The deal is a deal. How about we start with what just happened?"

"But you know this one. You know this secret," she whispered. "I was just combing my hair. Some nights, I really think I can, you know, without thinking about back then. So I do it more often these days. But then it comes out of nowhere even on the best of days. My limbs just lock. My mind follows. Then I'm back at his mercy. Frozen still. Except that when it happens, Snow isn't there to drag me out of his hold before he does anything worse or lets Murdoc or Renick continue doing something worse. No one is." She lifted a hand and wiped a palm across her face. "It was gone for a while. Unless I can erase it from memory, it will always be there." She sniffled and reached a hand to my arm, fingers tracing over her tattoos. "How do you do it now?"

"Never as bravely as you."

She squeezed her eyes shut and shook her head. "Don't pity me. Even if I deserve to be pitied."

"I am pitiful myself, Rora," I said, wiping away her tears. "And so ashamed to admit that I think about ways to drown my own memories any way I can every second of the day. I just don't anymore."

"How?"

"Spite," I lied to her for a second time in my life.

A laugh bubbled out of her, and she sniffled. "Yeah?"

"Let us spite the dead fucks."

Her eyes filled with what looked like liquid guilt for a second before they strayed away from my face where they had been the entire time. She swallowed, opened her mouth to say something and then closed it. An entire too long of a second passed before she gave me a small untrue smile and said, "Lets."

Maybe I didn't feel so bad about lying to her. Because she was still hiding something. Not something I would like from the way she was fighting to avoid my gaze.

"Sleep here," she said. "That sofa must be uncomfortable." Picking up a few pillows, she put them in the middle of the bed. "There."

"What if I want to hold you?"

She shrugged, the tiny strap of her night gown falling down her shoulder. "They're only pillows," she said, the corner of her lip caught between her teeth as she nervously chewed on it.

Pulling my shirt over my head, I stood. "Get in, I'm having a shower first. I'll be done in a minute." When she peered up at me, all round forest eyes, swollen lips and flushed cheeks, I added, "Make that two."

Not that it was hard to miss, but her eyes dropped down to my lower half. "Alright," she muttered, swallowing.

I got under the shower like my body was on fire, half of my clothes coming off after they'd already been soaked by the spray.

"Fuck," I hissed, fisting my hard cock.

There was no chance of containing my grin when she softly knocked on the door, my hand tightening around myself knowing she was so close.

"Yes, Rora?" I asked, looking over my shoulder.

She cracked the door open a little, leaning against the threshold, arms crossed over her chest. Even from where she stood, I could see her nipples poking through the thin, pink fabric. "I want to watch."

Fuck me. "Yeah?"

Lifting a finger up, she motioned for me to turn. Her chest rose and fell harder and faster despite her calm expression. When I turned, her lips parted just a little and she swallowed hard, making me come up with too many vulgar thoughts that would have her running off the fastest she'd ever run.

Carefully, she took small steps inside the bathroom and sat on a bathtub corner, way too close to me.

"That wasn't smart."

"I wanted in on the details." She pointed to my cock, squirming and pressing her thighs together. "Go on." Swallowing, she added in that small, sweet voice of hers, "Pretty please."

"Up at me," I said, and her round, glassy eyes lifted to mine. "That's it," I breathed, stroking my painful erection root to tip, imagining those same eyes looking up at me when I would fuck her. "Do you like watching, little bird?"

She shrugged a shoulder, still looking up at me. "I like watching *you*. Don't stop." Clearing her throat, she added, "Please."

This girl was going to be the path to my insanity. She was even giving me a damn tour of the road, like I was a tourist in my own damn mind.

My balls tightened as my hand quickened over my length. "Come here."

Her green eyes widened just slightly before she did as told, standing about two feet away from me.

"Closer."

Her lashes fluttered fast as she took another careful step towards me, and then another until she was almost under the shower spray and close enough for me to touch.

"One more step, sweetheart, come to me."

Then she was there, the shower spray soaking her nightgown entirely.

My hand worked over my cock as I bent down to kiss her cheek, her jaw and down her neck where I pressed my face against to inhale that maddening scent of hers. Fuck, I would have come right then and there, but I had too much in my hands and I was starving to be satisfied with just a bite.

"Gods damn it, Thora," I cursed, pressing my brow to hers.

"Do you want me to help?" Going on her toes, she pressed her mouth to my shoulder, her hands falling on my chest, trailing the line of muscle further down, the touch feeling like electricity. Her fingers brushed the V on my hips until they grazed the base of my cock, and my breaths came in shallow as I felt my balls tighten.

"Fuck, Thora."

"Yes, Thora next," the little hellion said, grinning as she pressed her cheek on my shoulder and looked up at me, trailing her hands back up my chest, making sure to graze every inch.

This damn girl.

"Your body is hard as a rock," she said, pressing her lips here and there on my chest. "What did they feed you?"

"This little bird," I groaned, fucking my fist harder, faster, "If she keeps torturing me like this."

She smiled up at me, her eyes on my mouth. "Well, I am feeling very sacrificial."

"Get on your knees."

Her eyes widened just slightly, but she didn't even hesitate to do as I had told her. There was certainly something wrong with both me and her. This whole day didn't feel entirely real.

"You're going to make my cock shy if you keep looking at it like that," I said.

"Doesn't look shy to me." She pressed her thighs together, her hands clutching the end of her soaked nightgown that hid her so very little from me, the pink of her underwear visible. And my mind kept flashing with an urge to find out if she was needing me just as I was needing her.

My come shot over her chest, marking her skin, and she breathed faster, her teeth digging on her bottom lip as she raised her green round eyes up to me.

What had I done?

"Fuck." Kneeling before her, I wiped a little come that had fallen on her chin, half tempted to push it between her parted lips. "This was a lesson not to do this again, little bird."

"Which part?" she asked, watching me intently as I stood to get a cloth.

"You really need to stop that."

"What?"

"Watching me like that."

"Mhm," she hummed, still raking her heated gaze all over my body when I kneeled before her again and starting cleaning her up.

I sighed. "Rora. Enough."

"Enough what?"

I couldn't help but grin. "Little shit," I muttered, kissing her cheek and reaching for a towel to wrap around my hips. "Get in the shower and wash me off."

"What if I don't want to?"

"Rora, sweetheart, I'm going insane here," I said, putting my brow to hers and cupping her face in my hands. "Help me out, please?"

"Help you out how? I can think of a few ways."

My eyes drew shut. "Do what you're told, you hellion."

With a sigh, she went under the shower spray and began pulling her soaked nightgown off.

Somehow, my feet managed to carry me out of there in time before I lost my mind entirely.

24

YELLOW HYACINTHS

THORA

I was somewhere. Certainly, standing somewhere and with someone. Maybe a few people. My mind, however, was stuck to last night. Stuck under the shower with him.

Someone was talking, I was sure of it.

But all I could hear where his grunts from last night as he stroked his co—

"Thora," Elias snapped, and the blur of the meeting room cleared.

"Yes?" I asked, snapping straight and looking around the empty room like I'd just woken up from a dream.

He frowned. "Meeting is over. Don't you have to visit the academy?"

I blinked. "Yes." Standing, I frantically turned to search for my cloak. "Where is my cloak?"

"You came without one," Elias said, frowning even deeper.

"Oh."

"What's wrong?"

"W-wrong? Nothing is wrong," I said, hurrying outside.

I still hadn't seen him after last night when he left like his soles were on fire using the excuse of his soldiers alerting him to danger around the castle. Utter lies. My wolves would have alerted me, too, if that had been the case.

Before I reached my room, I noticed Oryn standing by the doors of my waiting chambers. The old man looked perturbed.

"She insisted," was all he said before pointing inside the room where a little girl waited on the massive sofa arrangement. Blonde hair fell straight and long to her back, pinned back and away from her face by two flowery clips. Her pale-yellow eyes had fallen on an uninteresting spot on the wall. They were not quite like Snow's or Silas's. They were lively somehow, as if she didn't know of her fate. No one who'd been born with her fate would ever have so much life in her eyes. But then again, my brother had managed to make me a mirage of propriety, too, despite all.

Lilith's mouth slowly pulled into a little smile, and she turned a look around the room, her lively yellow eyes emptily searching. "Your Majesty."

"You don't have to call me that. You're not my subject," I said, taking a seat across from her.

"You must be wondering why I've come," she said, reaching a hand forward to touch the table, her fingers searching the surface until they met the teacup.

I'd heard conversations here and there about her. The Ybris who'd barely survived her own power. Melanthe had overestimated her daughter's magic—the magic that was born to consume. Ice and death. The seal she'd put on her daughter had been insufficient compared to the one Lysander had put on us three, and the magic had consumed her ability to see.

"Does your brother know you're here?" How did a ten-year-old cross my lands and even get herself inside my castle without a single hair out of place.

The cup stopped halfway to her lips. "He doesn't. This doesn't concern Eren."

"Not much does, does it?"

After giving me an uneasy smile that reminded me too much of my own, she took another sip of her tea. "You must be close to him. He speaks so highly of you—"

"I don't care how he speaks of me. I'd rather he doesn't speak of me at all. Especially to you."

She reached to feel the table and lowered her teacup with shaky hands. "You loathe the people that birthed me, I understand why you would loathe me, too."

Even though I wished to feel spite, to loathe her as she said, somehow I couldn't. "I loathe nothing. Especially a stranger. Especially a stranger whose father I killed. Whose mother I wished I had killed. Whose memory still gives my sister nightmares even after ten long years. A stranger who would prompt those nightmares to come back. A stranger who would only invoke more than nightmares to come back, demons, too. I can't allow that. I'm very protective of my sister."

She gulped, hiding her now trembling fingers under her thighs. It bothered me how similar our mannerisms were. "I see," she said lightly, forcing a quivering smile on her face. "Not literally. Cause I can't really see, you know." After letting an uneasy little giggle, she took another sip of her tea.

The doors flew open, and we both jumped. "Who do we have here?" Malik asked, strutting inside the room. "And who is this beautiful young lady?"

She bowed her head. "Lilith Delcour, a pleasure to meet you, Your Majesty."

"Mal, little sister-in-law. Just call me Mal." The idiot took a seat beside me and threw me a wink and an arm around my shoulders. "Don't be angry at her," he murmured in my ear, and kissed my cheek with a loud smack that had me go a deep red because Lilith shyly giggled.

I was not angry at her. The only thing I wanted was to keep my sister safe. Snow was pregnant, and gods knew how she would react to seeing *her* here.

He turned to her. "How did you know it was me?"

"I'd try to explain it, but it would not make much sense at all to you just how it doesn't make any sense to me. I can see, just not how you can."

"How is Eren doing? I haven't seen him in a long while and he didn't stay long after your sister's first doomed marriage."

Sister's?

Had he lost his damn mind?

Lilith smiled at that. "He is...well. I think. Not that he says much about the state of his wellbeing." She reached a hand to a pouch tied at her waist, pulling a letter out and handing in our direction. "I don't want to hold up either of you. I'm sure you're busy, so I'll get to why I'm here. There was an eclipse in Heca two days ago. Macaria says her visions are the strongest that day as our realms align with the Otherworld at that moment. Mine are, too."

Malik took the paper, unfolding it to reveal a charcoal drawing haphazardly sketched that scarily resembled his own drawings. A woman kneeling with her head down and a skeletal form holding a crown above her head.

"Macaria and Urinthia call it transcendence—my blessing. Not quite like seeing visions. Mine are clearer, sharper. Also, not my own," Lilith explained. "I'm sometimes

overtaken by memories of the future, but not of my own. Those belonging to others."
She pointed to the drawing. "That is why I could draw it. Because you can."

"You had a vision of my future?"

She quickly shook her head. "No, I saw the future as you. The dead crowning Thora.
According to what knowledge is gifted by our God, there are a few meanings when death
crowns someone."

"If you are here to tell me that I will die, save it," I snipped.

Lilith sat up a little straighter and frantically waved her hands. "It is not that. When
I say that I felt the essence of death, I didn't mean the creature crowning you. I meant
death—death of all."

"And that is something I should worry about because?"

"Would you want the death of all?" she carefully asked. "Eren says you'd—"

"Is that all?" I interrupted.

She swallowed, nervously interlinking her fingers. "It is."

"Then I mustn't delay your journey back. Your brother, if he is the least of what he
was when he was my brother, he would worry. I don't want him gallivanting into my
kingdom searching for you. That would make us all uneasy, not just me and you."

Malik's hand slipped over mine. "You'll stay here tonight," he said to her, and we
both tensed. "I'll send word to Eren that you're safe. It gets difficult to travel through
Eldmoor at night." He turned to me as he continued, "After all, you made it through all
this journey to warn us. Right, my little bird?"

"You will have to start speaking to me again," Malik said, bracing himself against the sink
and caging me from behind as I washed my face, his body entirely too close to mine. "I
talked to your sister. She knows Lilith is here."

I spun to him so fast I knocked a few bottles behind me. "Why?"

"Because your sister is a big girl, and she can handle it like one. Cause no matter how
harsh she is, never would she have let that girl go back to Eldmoor at night. And she's a
big meanie, so imagine what that says about you."

"You didn't just call Snow a *big meanie*."

"Brace yourself, little bird. I think you're becoming worse."

"How can you say that when you know what it does to me to have her here?"

"She is a kid."

"We both know she is more than that."

"So were you. Do you deserve to be blamed for what your father was? Why does she?"

"You want me to forgive her?"

He frowned. "Forgive her for what, Thora? Being an innocent kid who is born with
the worst possible luck and living what little years she has left knowing that? Or for
stealing your brother away? If Eren had not stepped up to take care of her, Snow would
have. He did it knowing that Snow wouldn't have left that little girl to live as someone's
spare. Before Snow went to send Demir to hells, I saw them talking in the gardens.
They'd already agreed on it. He would take her. He tried to spare one sister some pain
and ended up causing it to the other."

I swallowed hard, not liking the bitter taste of the truth he just fed me. The truth I'd
been avoiding to hear. "Don't make this Snow's fault."

"It is no one's fault."

"I would have rather remained lied to."

"Is guilt that tough, huh?"

Spinning towards the sink, I said, "I don't know, you tell me."

He chuckled, wrapping his arms around my body. "Little shit."

"What are you doing?"

"Hugging this idiot I used to call my best friend. Because she needs it." He buried his face in my hair. "Because *I* need it. But gods, bending all this way down is killing my back, *Tiny*. You didn't grow into that damn quarter of an inch at all."

I elbowed his stomach hard, and that had him chuckling even more. "I did."

His eyes dropped to my breasts. "I meant vertically."

Spinning back to him, I snipped, "You absolute pig."

He snorted and then hauled me up by my waist, lifting me above his head like I was a pillow.

"Put me down, Malik!"

The idiot carried me like that to my bed and then gently lowered me down. And instead of walking around to his side, he climbed over me, and so very slowly, got himself on his side while I stood there under him, frozen in shock. He rolled to the bedside table, pulling the drawers open. "Got any of those inappropriate bedtime stories your sister reads?"

He went quiet for a moment and then began pulling a long roll of black silk ribbons. Once he'd gotten all of the six feet of it out, he gave me a look full of questions. "What are you wrapping with this?"

Shit.

I took it from his hand and then climbed on top of him, catching him by surprise this time—myself, too. Taking one of his hands, I wrapped the end of one ribbon around his wrist and then his other, binding them together and then pulling both of his arms above his head and securing them on the bed post. After I had him all tied to the bed, I leaned over the bedside table and pulled a shorter and thicker strip of black ribbon. "This one is for your eyes," I said. "Got another for your mouth, but I'm not sure how you'd feel about that."

Malik had gone the stillest I'd ever seen him be. His eyes dropped from my face to where I was straddling his stomach. Then back up to my face and back and forth his tied wrists.

"A lesson," I repeated his words from last night, leaning over to untie him, "to never touch things that don't belong to you without permission."

"Is that why you tie them to the bed? Because you don't want them touching what doesn't belong to them?" His mouth pulled into a slow grin. "Lie. Say yes."

"No."

"What if that had been my very last wish?"

"I fulfilled it. You told me to lie."

He liked that because that silly little look was back in his face. The look that made me shiver in my own skin. He knew the power he had over me. At least over my body. "Who do you belong to, my liege?"

Undoing the ribbon from the headboard, I pulled his hands to me so I could undo the ties from his wrists. "Should I lie again?"

"Depends."

"On what?"

"Whether I'd prefer to be lied to or not."

"I belong to you," I said, feeling my ears heat up. "We're married. Fake or not, I belong to you until this ends."

"Until what ends?"

I scowled. "The marriage."

"Oh, that. Yes," he said, grinning again. "Comfy up there?"

"You're nice to sit on," I attempted to casually reply while struggling to undo the last knot on his wrist.

"Mhm. Need some help?"

"No, I'm good."

"Looks like it."

Finally, I hacked the knot, setting his wrists free. I couldn't really rejoice in the achievement because his eyes had dropped to my exposed thigh that my short nightgown had not managed to cover.

He lifted a hand and touched the burnt scar there that curled all the way up to my hip and grazed my stomach just a little, too.

"It isn't as bad as Eren's," I said, tugging the nightgown down. "His are everywhere." The black craft fire from that night had managed only to lick at my skin, because Eren had protected me with his whole body. He'd curled on top of me when the ceiling had burnt and fallen on us. Despite the painful burns, he had never surrendered to the pain until I'd been safe. He'd been so worried about my little wound that he'd forgotten about his own.

The words left me before I even realised. "I miss him. I miss my big brother."

Malik's eyes drew shut. "That's lovely and all, but please don't say that when you're up there so close to my cock."

I relentlessly smacked at his chest, but that only made him laugh harder.

"You're ripping the innocence out of me, woman," he chuckled, covering his chest with both arms, acting scandalised.

"You're so vexing," I said, surrendering and laying on him, my cheek resting on his shoulder.

His arms slowly came around me and he sighed, tightening his hold as if I was suddenly going to change my mind and run off.

"Sweetheart," he groaned. "You might have to get off soon."

"Alright," I murmured, breathing him in. For a minute, I hesitated before asking, "Are you going to let me watch again?"

He groaned, tightening his grip around me and pressing his mouth on my neck. "I was thinking of something else."

My heart started to race furiously, and I sat up a little. "Like what?" I breathlessly asked, and he smiled up at me.

His hand came up to caress my cheek and then it fell to the strap of my nightgown, toying with it as he slowly pulled it down until one of my breasts was bare before him. And like I was the most delicate little thing, he ghosted his finger over my nipple.

I gasped, feeling more wetness pooling on my underwear and nerves tightening between my thighs.

He held onto me and sat up, pushing my hips to rest over his own, over his thick bulge. He buried his face on my neck, leaving gentle kisses everywhere and making his way towards my chest. The anticipation had me rolling my hips against his, trying to feel just a small friction to relieve some of that ache building there.

He groaned, holding onto my hips tightly so I wouldn't move, depriving me of just a tiny bit of relief. Just when I was about to beg him for it, his mouth closed around my nipple. "Fuck," he breathed, nuzzling his face against it. "You taste as good as you smell."

"Malik—"

"Mmm," he hummed, palming my breast and pinching my nipple between his fingers.

"Just...just," I panted, not even able to think let alone speak as he played with my body, licking and biting.

"We have a lot to talk about first before I fuck you, little bird."

"About what?"

"About one secret you're holding back from me." He kissed my neck and tortured my nipple between his fingers until I started forgetting my own name. Lifting me up, he rolled us until I was on my back and he was hovering over me. "Touch yourself. I want you to slide your fingers inside your pretty little cunt and come for me while I come for you." Pushing his hands under my nightgown, he hooked his fingers on my underwear and slowly pulled them down, dragging them down my thighs and then pocketing them. "Touch what I can't touch just yet."

Giving my nipple one last suck, he got up from the bed and headed to the bathroom, leaving me there the most frustrated I'd ever been.

Pulling back my nightgown, I lowered my hand between my thighs, feeling the slickness stick to my skin and shivering when I slid my fingers there. I'd never needed to do something so badly. Partly because I knew he was doing the same behind that door, and partly because I was on the brink of losing my mind from the pulsing ache his mouth and hands had left behind.

My fingers circled my core and I moaned from how sensitive the motion felt, making my thighs shake and my stomach quiver. I wanted him there, his mouth, his fingers, his thick cock. Gods, yes.

I slipped two fingers inside me, not even slightly enough to fill the need he'd created in me. Despite how big he was, he would have taken me so easily. So, so easily from how wet I was.

My whole body felt like a charged lightning bolt as I pumped my fingers inside my body, my other hand poorly attempting to bring back the memory of his touch on my breast as I palmed one, my fingers rubbing a taunt nipple until that coiling sensation tangled deep in my belly, desperately wanting to unfurl.

Burying my face on his pillow, I cried out a moan with his name, my whole body turning to liquid as I melted into a puddle of limbs on the white sheets. I could cry from how not nearly satisfying that was.

I needed him.

As the room was fading in the darkness and my eyes were slipping shut, I felt the bed dip and then a small, chaste kiss pressed to my cheek. "You listen so well, little bird," he whispered in my ear, leaving another kiss there. "So fucking well."

25

GREY DAISIES

THORA

He'd been up before I was, leaving the entire room for me to nervously circle around as I got ready to face him after last night. I'd even worn his nightshirt as I'd gotten myself ready, wanting his perfume soaking into my skin. Shamelessly, I'd used his soaps and shampoos, too. The entirety of my chambers had been soaked in eucalyptus by the time I'd left.

I found him sitting in the dining room I never used along with Lilith as they had breakfast. Besides the morning greetings, and the very long and very slow once over he'd given me, we hadn't exchanged any other words despite how many I had thought of on the way from my room to here.

He'd entertained every little story Lilith told him of her time in Red Coven. She called her time there 'the preparing' instead of what another would name it—being marinated in her magic like venison for her master.

The more I looked at her, the more I saw myself in her. There was a mountain of ugly hidden behind her bright smile. My breakfast soured in taste when I realised how much it resembled my own.

Lilith gave us one last wave before following Oryn towards the stables. He'd volunteered to take her back. Neither Malik nor I thought it was because of his kind old heart as much as it was to meet with the Violet Witch he so fancied but didn't have the gall to confess to.

Malik turned to press a kiss on my neck, startling me a little. "You smell like me," he groaned. After leaving a few more tortuous kisses on my face, he said, "Will be back just before lunch. We'll eat together."

I nodded, and blurted like an idiot, "Be careful."

He threw me an amused look over his shoulder. "Yeah, you too, little bird." Then I heard him chuckle to himself all the way down to where his soldiers were waiting by the castle gates.

Burying my face in my hands, I sighed. "Why am I such an awkward idiot?"

Wait a minute. Why was he such a prick, too?

Why wasn't he acknowledging anything?

Was there even something to acknowledge?

I mean, it wasn't like we did anything.

That chain of thoughts took a long time to come to an end.

I'd gotten through about half of the court reports the northern cities had brought when Neo entered the meeting room without even knocking.

He stood there for a while, silently trying to convey something to me through his disappointed stare. Sometimes, I think he forgot that the people around him weren't like him and couldn't read other's emotions.

Like always, it took him a minute or so to realise that and speak. "You've not called for me anymore."

"I know."

He threw an agitated look around the room. "So does he know then?"

I put the pen down and sighed. This conversion was bound to surface one day, and he'd decided that this was the day. "Does he know that you and I have been exchanging favours for the past couple of years?"

Stepping forward, he loudly said, "Does he know that I've been inflicting and deflecting your emotions for years?"

Not my finest of moments. "Why should he? Why should you care at all whether he knows or not? Ah, you think he will be disgusted with me."

He would.

Malik would.

And that made my stomach dip with anxiety.

"I think he should know, or will find out himself considering how close he's gotten to you again." His foot tapped on the ground, agitated. "I heard him ask around the Eldritch courts. He's already been suspecting something. Tell him, or I will have to. I cannot lie to Malik. Not about this. We swore to this brotherhood. I betrayed him and the oath I've taken, so you have to tell him, Thora."

"Is that a threat?"

"I'm saying, it will not take long for him to figure out why you're empty of certain emotions. I have no idea how he hasn't already figured it out."

"He won't kill you, Neo. If that is what you worry about."

"You don't know him."

"Quite the opposite." Because he's been doing it himself before you. Wrong or not, Malik had been my first choice of poison. He still was—just not like how it was back then, I suppose.

"Tell him, Thora," he said it almost as a warning, and I didn't like that. "Tell him that I've been taking your emotions away for almost ten years."

The meeting room door creaked just lightly, pulling Neo's attention first and then mine.

Malik was so still. Entirely focused on Neo. The moment Neo's eyes turned to me, he snapped. His face contorted to such anger. "Repeat that for me again."

Shit.

"Malik," I calmly called, standing and attempting to get between him and Neo before he committed to the thoughts written all over his face. "You heard him."

"Did I?" He let out an incredulous laugh and jabbed a finger on his temple. "There is one way this would make sense. If I'd lost it. Have I lost it, Thora?"

"It's true," Neo said.

In a flash, Malik faded beside him and crashed him hard against the nearest wall. "What have you done besides take her fear and her hurt, huh? What have you done to her?" he bellowed.

"Nothing," Neo choked. "Nothing, Mal! It isn't like that."

His elbow dug hard on Neo's throat. "See, I don't believe that. Not convinced at all, in fact. How about I find it out myself? How about I peel back every layer of emotion you've felt since you've come into this world? Perhaps put some of my own in there and force yours out like little scattering rats."

"Malik—"

"Shh, Thora. I'm thinking." His fingers twitched like he'd come to some sort of high, spidery black veins spreading around his eyes. "I'm thinking."

"You're not going to do any of that," Kilian calmly said, coming inside the room and leaning against a wall.

Sam followed after him, stopping at the door to bow his head to me and then vanish. My nephew might have just saved Neo's life.

"You knew about this?"

Kilian gave him one nod. "It would be foolish to presume it could go unnoticed. Just because you refuse to read her, doesn't mean I haven't." He tilted his head to his Empath Commander. "And Neo should have known better than to believe his command would be more loyal to him than to their king."

Malik's anger turned to his brother. "You let this go on?"

"Seemed like there was more to it." Kilian looked at me then. "Wasn't there, Thora?"

"There was."

Malik's grip on Neo only tightened and he wouldn't look at me after I said it.

"I was struggling, and Neo was kind enough to provide me with just a little relief. However dangerous it was, I was willing to give in to it. It was my choice."

"It can easily not be your choice if he puts that in your head," Malik gritted out.

"Then come and find out," I said, reaching a shaky hand to him.

Kilian pushed away from the door and called, "Neo, would you join me for a walk outside? Malik, let go of him."

Once I was left alone with him, I said, "You have no right."

"I have every right!"

"You started this, Malik! Remember!"

He stalked up to me until I was backed to a wall. "And you gave me your word you would never let any other Empath mess with you. Did you or did you not, Thora?"

"I had to," I whispered. "You don't know how it was. How bad it was back then. I had no choice. I couldn't live like that anymore! Fearing every moment I breathed because the simplest words and actions would remind me of things I didn't wish to remember. Waiting for panic to sweep in and send me spiralling inside my own mind. I was drowning, Malik. Suffocating."

The black in his eyes began dissolving, revealing amber eyes—hurt amber eyes. "Tell me one thing, then. Having gotten rid of it, has it helped at all?"

No. I just felt other things more and it wasn't always less painful. "I can sleep." At least I wasn't haunted in my dreams anymore. At least the nightmares were gone.

He barked an incredulous laugh, almost maniacal. "Tea can help you fucking sleep!"

"Malik—"

"You don't know how it is to be numbed out on purpose. Knowing how a particular emotion feels, knowing you're supposed to feel it and then nothing. No matter how deep you dig for it, no matter how hard you try to recall what you're supposed to feel and not be able to. Because I do, Thora." His shaky fingers came down on my face, torn whether to touch me or not because they only hovered over my skin. "I don't want your colours to disappear. The way you feel is one of the most beautiful things I've ever seen."

And you let him take away a piece of that. You let him touch you."

My throat felt like it was tied with barbed wire. "It. Hurt."

"I know it did, Rora. But we all must fucking hurt apparently."

"How do I stop it?"

"We will figure it out. I will figure it out," he repeated, still in a frenzy. "Right after I rip Neo's soul off his bones."

"I talked him into it."

"Don't protect him, you're only making his case worse."

"No, I did. We had an agreement." The moment the words left me, I wanted the earth to swallow me whole.

If he'd been angry a second ago, he looked furious now. "What sort of an *agreement*?"

I wasn't going to tell him that Neo had agreed to my methods of bedroom manners which were quite appalling if I was frank. There wasn't an easy way for me to be with someone. Being intimate meant touching and I didn't want anyone to touch me—anyone but him. I only wanted him to touch me. Neo wanted me despite that, so that made it our little private agreement. I confided in him because he had already accepted one other thing being wrong with me. I couldn't tell Malik that I'd agreed to Neo's company only how I allowed him to be. Tied up. In the dark. Wordlessly. No hands touching. No talking. I refused to die from embarrassment. "It is private."

Suddenly he looked taller, bigger. Somehow frightening. "Oh?"

"Yes."

"Is this how that moron got you? Is that why you've let him touch you? He'll take away your pain for a fuck?"

I flinched. "That is not what I meant." Partly, at least. Surely, there was more to the ten year long waltz me and Neo had entangled in. But the more I tried to justify the reasoning in my head, the more unreasonable it seemed. Maybe that is what I'd done—given him my body to him in exchange for freeing me of the burden of my emotions.

"Then what did you mean?"

"I don't want to tell you."

"That's cute." He backed away. "Very cute."

"Where are you going?"

"To rip an answer out of Neo's throat."

"Wait."

"Too late. You had your chance to tell me."

Ten minutes later, Nia showed up to my room. She sighed, threw a tote bag stuffed with all sorts of leaves on my bed and came to sit beside me on the sofa where I'd curled up on, holding his pillow to my chest while I'd pressed my face to it.

"You didn't have to come."

"Malik threatened to end my lineage if I didn't."

My eyes drew shut and I smiled. "What did he ask you to do?"

"To check you over."

"And?"

There was a beat of hesitation. I wouldn't like this.

"And undo what Neo has done the best I can. I'm not as good as him, but he said he was too angry to do it himself."

Tears skittered down my cheek and I sniffled, nodding and sitting up. "Alright." Though these past few weeks I'd gone without Neo's help, it was barely a fraction of what I expected it to be after she'd restored my emotions entirely. Suddenly, I remembered ten years ago, and braced myself tightly for what was about to come. I wondered if twenty-nine-year-old me was as strong as nineteen year old me had been.

I was not.

Not nearly.

"I brought all sorts of herbs for tea, as requested," she said, attempting to soften the blow.

"What for?"

"Mal said to pick something that would '*help her fucking sleep*'."

I snorted, wiping my eyes.

"You should have come to me."

"Things happen to people I keep close. They don't want to be near me anymore. I've kept you far and close enough. And look at you," I said, taking her stretched hands. "You're still around me. Don't tell me my curse hasn't been warded off."

"Thora—"

"Three years ago. I'm stuck back three years ago. It feels like my mind is constantly on a loop on that day. Constantly feeling how I felt that day. For three years," I confessed. "Then before that time, it was for two years, when I couldn't smell his scent around Adriatian corridors anymore, when I knew he'd really and truly left. Then before that, when I killed my father. He kept haunting me every waking moment. When he was done torturing during the day, it started at night, too. I could go on and on and on. No one can help me, Nia. Nothing could. In a way, this made me feel like I had some control of my emotions. If I could threaten to take them away, they'd hide and leave me alone."

It was late. Not that late, but he should have come to our room at least fifteen minutes ago. Maybe I was more anxious because part of my ability to feel fear and pain had been restored, but I couldn't bear the sting of worry. What if he'd gone and done something silly? Like actually killing Neo.

I got up. Against my better judgement, I still got up and then headed down to track someone to take me down to Adriata. Couldn't believe the idiot had left me alone with his skeletons in this god damn empty castle. Especially when he knew how queasy bones without flesh in them made me.

"He isn't in his room," Pen said just as I made to head in that direction. "Rain and Sam took pity on him sulking in the gardens, so they are doing a sleepover."

I was moving before she even finished that sentence, throwing a quick thank you over my shoulder. Gently cracking the door open, I peeked inside, not wanting to wake my niblings. Only to find out the only person I could wake up was him.

Sam was sitting on the floor, going through a massive book, while Rain was next to a snoring Malik, putting about a dozen braids in his hair and a ton more clips and bows.

"You two should be asleep."

"Cannot," Sam said disinterestedly, continuing to flip through the dusty pages. "He snores too loudly."

"So does your sister."

Sam smirked a little, but my niece looked offended. "Hey," Rain said, frowning at me. "I do not."

"Alright," I said, laying next to Malik. "You do not."

I touched a finger to his cheek. "Are you still angry at me?" Poking my finger on his cheek again, I murmured, "You can't be angry at me. I should be angry at you. You left me for ten years and I'm not going to ever let that go." When he didn't stir after my continuous prodding, I pinched his cheek. "I know you're not asleep. You told me so yourself, you're always awake."

"He's asleep," Sam casually announced after my whole speech.

I gaped, a little embarrassed of myself. "You should have told me."

"Why? You wanted to say those words anyway. Father says it's good to get things out of your chest."

"Bullshit," Rain muttered under her breath.

I gaped at my niece. "Rain Helenia Castemont, who in the hells taught you that?"

She shrugged a tiny shoulder and then continued to braid more braids in Malik's hair.

I laid beside him again, putting my head on his stretched arm. "If you weren't so damn handsome, I feel I could hate you just a little."

He stirred a little, pulling me to him and burying his face in my neck, his warm breath fanned by skin and my stomach dipped at the sensation pooling there.

"Still asleep," Sam boredly added, still flipping through the book.

"I think I lied," I murmured, racing a finger down the scar on his eye. "I don't think I can hate you even if you were ugly. You'd still be my ugly thing."

"Pink or red?" Rain asked, whispering at me while she held two pots of makeup.

26

BLUE LIATRIS

MALIK

There was a rock sitting on my chest. Another one at my side. I was sinking into the mattress entirely and this whole thing felt like one suffocating dream. Until I tried to move my limbs and cracked my eyes open to find my niece sleeping on my chest and my nephew on my right arm. "Morning, you night terrors," I groaned, my head pounding and itching and aching from some odd tension, awfully reminding me of a hangover.

After masterfully placing Rain on the bed and taking Sam off my paralysed arm, I got up and headed to the bathroom, stepping on about a dozen tiny wooden cubes that had my head spinning from pain. "Fuck. Fuck. Fuck."

Just as I finally made it out of the torture chamber that was Rain's room and into her bathroom, the glittery flower shaped mirror in front of me told me that I could potentially still be asleep and unable to wake from a nightmare.

My hair—it was sticking like horns from all sides, braided and stuck with glittery clips and bows. There was some sort of pink powder on my cheeks and another glittery blue one on my eyelids. "Fuck me."

It took me an hour to get myself sorted and then scrub my eyes raw to get the glitter specs out of my skin.

"You're up and sparkling," Kil said as I got out of his kids' room, coming in my direction. "I see you had time to touch on your makeup, too."

"Shut up."

He chuckled. "Thora was here last night."

I stilled. "You should have come to get me. Was there something wrong? Wait a fucking minute. My guard would have notified me. I would have known if something was wrong. Did she know I was with the kids?" Hells. I didn't want her thinking I was elsewhere again.

"Who do you think put the glitter in your eyes?"

She'd been here? Why had I not woken up? "The little shit."

Kil stopped by the threshold and turned to me. "Did you get any answers from Neo?"

"Yes."

My brother didn't look convinced, I just couldn't pinpoint about what exactly he looked so doubtful of. "He lives, by any chance?"

"She would never talk to me again if I'd killed him."

He shrugged and leaned against the door frame. "Could live with my wife never talking to me again if it meant taking another man out of her life."

"Because you talk enough for the both of you. If mine stops talking, my mouth will get cobwebs."

The bastard smiled and threw a look over the bed carrying his sleeping children. "Gods, Rain snores so loudly."

At that exact moment Rain stirred and shot up, wild black hair everywhere, her little face scrunching up. "Papa," she called like some wounded animal, and I swear I could see my brother's heart well and fall inside his rib cage.

"Don't act so happy, it's making me sick," I said, giving him a shove inside the room.

"What monster do you want your papa to slay for you today," I heard my idiot of a brother say as he crawled in their bed and hugged them both to his chest.

Nia was who I saw first when I stepped inside Koy's largest apothecary run by her. Grumbling as always as she did everything but spare me ten seconds of her time and day.

Though they looked nothing alike, her daughter who'd sat down on a massive wooden table gave me the same look of annoyance as her.

The two were loading and unloading a bunch of herbs from some massive crates and placing them in tiny glass jars, and for what reason, fuck knew.

"So?"

Nia shoved something to my chest. A small container with more herbs. "Took care of most, but you might have to check her through, I am nowhere as good as a true Empath. Gave her tea for sleep, too."

I lifted the container she gave me. "What's this for then?"

"That's for you."

"Poison?"

Karin giggled. "It tastes like it when ma makes it for my headache."

My eyes narrowed on the massive crates with the red painted tree of life on them littering the shelved space. "Why are you restocking so much of the Medi-Healer boxes?"

"Mor caught more of Iskyla's soldiers north of our border using the old tunnels, and all our units are preparing for potential war. They are restless when it comes to Isjord, and you know how Mor is about any slight threat. But aren't we all?" She paused. Holding one of the jars in her hand. "Some of it is actually ingredients for the monthly potions we make to send Thora for the Verglassers Silas had turned into the beasts."

"Potions? Why?"

"Did Thora not mention that some of those turned to beasts using the seedlings had their symptoms come back?"

"No, she didn't. But she's not been telling much if you have guessed."

Nia's usually stern and proud expression fell just slightly. "Silas is still torturing some of us somehow. Some more than most. Few of the Aura who turned took their own lives because the condition of their body became unbearable. Most were barely past sixteen when they'd been turned, and they didn't even make it past their twenties." She put down the boxes she was fiddling with and turned to me. "You weren't there to see the mess she had to deal with after the war. She didn't allow any of her soldiers to kill the beasts we had not managed to treat with the antidote. She did it all herself. She buried them herself, too. Some were children. Children, Mal. She was nineteen back then. A child herself. All alone, she dealt with all of it alone while you were gods knew." Nia picked up another jar and threw it at me. "Next time you ask her to put reason behind something no one can put reason behind, I want you to remember that you weren't there to help her give meaning to her reasons."

I'd been a dick, that much I knew. I'd shown up at her door about a dozen times last night, and each time I'd ended up pulling away because I didn't know how to say what a hypocrite I was for even getting mad at her.

I nodded and lifted the other jar up. "Is this for my stomach?"

"No, that's actually poison. I want you to drink it if you think you're going to do something that will hurt Thora again. Now get out."

"Bye, Malik," Karin muttered.

Elias was alone in the meeting room, the place I'd felt her last presence. "Where is she?"

"Shouldn't you know?"

"Answer me, Lord Venzor, or it will be the last time you will even have that chance."

"Your brother came to get her for dinner since she's been eating alone all day."

I was an idiot. She must be thinking I've hid from her all day. "Who is playing the ghost tonight?"

He put an elbow on the chair backrest and twisted to look at me. "Iskyla's soldiers haven't been down here for a whole week. I'm guessing they are strategizing something, or they've truly given up."

"Highly doubt it, so gear up."

His entire expression turned alert. "You've seen them?"

"No, but my shadows have. They have been lurking close to our borders for days, but their presence keeps disappearing and reappearing. They have brought down a Crafter. I can feel the rotten stench of craft all over the cities. Notify Oryn."

"He hasn't returned from Eldmoor yet."

"Get another witch."

My room was empty, but she'd been there.

I didn't even need to feel her presence to know. She'd left plenty of evidence behind and she was determined to give me a fucking heart attack. "Shit," I hissed, kicking away the empty bottles of liquor littering the floor—some of the bottles that had been hidden in my cabinets since I'd been a boy. The type of strong stuff I saved for sipping after I'd worn my organs out during a night out. It usually was the last kick of flavour to help me sleep.

"She is in the night gardens," Kilian said, leaning against my bedroom door, hands in his pockets and smirking like an idiot.

I pointed at him as I went past the corridors. "You led her to them on purpose."

"She's grown up enough to enter and roam wherever she pleases. This is also her home after all. You married her. Voluntarily. Does she even know you suggested that? Or that you threatened Elias with his life if he brought another man to see her?"

Nope. "I'm going to kill you."

"I'm your favourite brother and you would miss my cuddles!" he shouted behind me and then chuckled.

Thora laid on the grass in the middle of the night gardens, curled up in a ball while cradling a bottle of liquor to her chest. She usually had a good stomach for it, but considering how many empty bottles I'd found, I doubt even I would have been able to handle it all. But my small wife was resilient if nothing else. Sheer force of will gave her wings and sometimes it was stronger than her magic—an entirely different magic in itself. Nothing short of striking.

"Little bird," I said, standing over her.

"Sssssht," she shushed, putting a finger to her lips.

"You're not the boss of me."

Unfurling from her position, she laid on her back, eyes still tightly shut. She was so gods darn beautiful. How could anyone create something this exquisite? "I used to think death was dreadful, but death is so beautiful," she said. "After he left, I'd sometimes wish he could find me again and hold me to the edge of it, tell me all his secrets and break my heart to a million little pieces just so I didn't have to live with it beating in my chest while calling for him. He may have pushed me off that ledge if he wished. I would have gladly fallen." She opened her eyes and tipped her chin up so she could look at the bleary stars hiding between a layer of rain fog. "But he left me on a boat in the middle of the ocean. Hiding plenty of secrets in its waters. No edge to jump from in sight. And with a restless heart who didn't and won't know better than to miss him. Missing him is all it knows."

My hands seeked to touch her, everything in me seeked her, so I obeyed, crouching down, touching her hair, her face, her eyes, her little pert nose, that tiny swollen mouth. "What is this nonsense, sweetheart?" It was breaking my heart and mending it at the same time. Part of me wanted her to mean them, part of me cared too much about her to even think she meant them, that I'd done such horrors to her.

She sighed and finally rolled her drunk emerald eyes up to me—a whole viridian rain forest staring back at me. "I take it back. You're so ugly right now, your face is all wrong, all upside down. Eyes for lips and lips for eyes." Her mouth curled up with a cringe. "But why does my heart still like you?"

My sick one liked her back. "Ask her for me, too."

"She's stopped answering me since the day I swore to forget you and tried to let another man in."

"I think I like her."

"She's evil. How could she do this to me? I've been so kind and gentle to her. Worried about her to the point I took away pain so she wouldn't hurt."

Drunken Thora was a sight to behold. "I'll have a word with her."

She went on her back again and opened her arms wide. "Go ahead."

Barely holding in a chuckle, I leaned forward and left a kiss on her chest. When she sucked in a sharp breath, I left another a little lower down then I laid right beside her. "It's not her fault."

"It is," she said, her voice entirely detached. "How can it not be?

"Look at me, Thora," I said, gently turning her attention to me, trying not to startle her out of wherever stupor she was falling into. "It is not."

"Whose is it? Someone has to bear fault, Malik. I can't just be this stupid for no reason."

It was mine. For thinking I could keep her.

The skies crackled, silent lightning flashing once and then twice.

Her lips parted and she looked up again, frowning at the gathering clouds. "It's about to rain."

"You love rain."

"I do," she whispered, her voice lost. "But it never rains anymore. Not since you left. You even took rain with you."

She laid in bed across from me, sleeping soundly and breathing softly. Nothing could torment the look of calm on her face. Nothing but me, it seemed, because when I touched her rosy cheek, she stirred. Her eyes opened just that moment and landed straight on mine, as if she knew I'd been watching her. Wordlessly, she shuffled herself closer to me until her face was resting on my shoulder and her arm laid limply over my stomach.

"Pretend it's because I had to drink," she said, yawning.

"What if I don't want to?"

"Then hold me, and I'll pretend to be too drunk to remember what you did."

I didn't want to do that either. I wanted her to remember me just like I'd been remembering every little detail of hers for the past ten years. "Thora—"

"Shhh," she whispered, burying her face on the crook of my neck, her fingers moving up my stomach, over my chest until they rested on my cheek, a trail of shivers remaining behind. I could feel her lips pull into a smile over my neck as her fingers blindly grazed my nose, my eyes, my lips. "Can't believe you're real, my heart is about to leave me for dead."

I brought her hand to my lips, not believing myself she was real either. Sometimes I would think our souls might have already met in some other lifetime because of how well they knew one another. "You can have mine."

"Really?"

"Yeah."

"I'll treat it well."

"I know you will." Turning on my side, I hugged her body to me. "You've only ever been gentle to it. Even though it never knew what gentle was."

She raised her head to me, her emerald eyes were glassy and red. I kissed them both and she let out a stuttering sigh that had her shake in my hold. "Malik."

My chest rose fast, each breath was harder to take the previous. I wanted something of hers, and I wanted to give her something of mine back, but she'd gone and gotten herself drunk.

"Say something," she whispered.

"Your bony wrist is digging in my spleen."

She blinked for a moment and then began shaking from laughter. She laughed so hard that the unshed tears that had clung to her eyes suddenly skittered down her cheeks.

"If you weren't so breath-taking when you cry, I wouldn't be so tempted to make you cry."

"You said I look ugly when I cry."

"Not when you cry for me. You should see how you look when you cry for me."

Her eyes were fluttering shut, struggling to keep awake. "You're a bad man, Malik."

Leaning forward, I pressed my lips to her brow. I wanted to be all kinds of bad for her.

"Sing me a song," she whispered, snuggling against me. "So I can sleep. I didn't drink your *fucking tea* today."

"Sweetheart, I would, but that would probably make you afraid to ever sleep again."

Her light chuckles tickled over my skin. "I adore your voice. Even when it makes me afraid."

"Adore, huh?"

"Yes," she whispered even more quietly. "I adore you, Malik."

I needed her to tell me something else. "I'm not a puppy."

Her gentle fingers moved back and forth the scruff on my jaw. "No, you're a big fluffy dog."

"I'm going to let this go and pretend you were really drunk."

She pressed her lips to my cheek. "But I love big fluffy dogs."

There, laying in my arms, she looked so fragile, so soft. She was the most precious thing I'd ever held or touched, and I was not used to being let to touch or hold precious things. I had not the slightest clue how to handle her. How to touch her without tarnishing her.

"Put your hands where you want to, you coward," she murmured, drifting away to sleep.

"I need you to repeat that again for me when you're sober."

Thora had just fallen asleep when bells rang through the castle. She sprung to her feet, looking around confused until her eyes found me, her breathing calming down despite the commotion outside. "Attack. It's an attack signal from the Academy. It can't be."

"Put on a gown," I said, pushing from the bed and throwing clothes on, grabbing her the second she was covered, and fading us outside.

Elias was leading a bunch of guards down and my dead followed right behind. "It's the academy dorms," he shouted, disappearing between his men.

Thora's eyes were wide. "My wolves are with the kids. They would have warned me. No, I warned her. Iskyla couldn't have—"

27

WHITE ASPHODELS

MALIK

T he snow falling was stained with grey and crimson, it was like the skies were burning and bleeding as the whole grounds ahead had. I could feel it, sense every soul walking out of the gates of the living towards the Otherworld. I could feel the presence of the Guardian of Death reeking in the air and filling our world with despair.

The heavy scent of craft lingered in the air, signalling to what had been the one to deceive us and slip past my guards.

Thora stepped ahead. Nothing was written on her face. Nothing at all. Such emptiness that I had even seen on the dead. She rose a hand forward and the stained fog of death cleared to reveal a warm graveyard. Bodies lay slain on the ground that was no longer white, that would never be white again after today. Her white wolves lay lifeless beside them, almost protecting them in death, too.

One slow step after the other, she crossed the academy dorm gates while her soldiers fell to their knees, some sparing one lone prayer and others simply distraught, given up, and pained.

The bottom of her gown dragged along the puddle of blood, soaking in it. She knelt before a young body that was beyond saving, one of the first to have crossed the invisible gates of death. She braced both hands on the crimson ground, her fingers staining red, her head hung low and her shoulders rising fast with her heavy breathing. I didn't need to see her shadows to know she was on the verge of losing it.

Turning to Elias, I asked, "Where are the rest of the students?"

"Some were injured fighting off the Crafter and the others have been taken to their homes. The kids," he continued, struggling to speak, "they'd tried to fight back. If they had only remained inside, maybe we would have gotten to them in time."

"Elias," she quietly said. "Cancel your trip to Solarya. I need you to remain in Tenebrose for the foreseeable future."

He shot me a panicked look before asking her, "Why?"

She didn't answer him. "Oryn, gather the court and wait for me to return."

It was the old Crafter's turn to shoot me a helpless look. "Let's think this through, child."

"Let's," came her bored answer.

"If you attack Iskyla now—"

"Attack?" she asked, standing, the blood that had clung to her began trickling down the rest of her body as if it seeped from her own wounds. "I'm not going to attack her, Oryn. This wasn't an attack. In an attack, people get to at least defend themselves, don't they?" She looked at all of her people that had hung their heads low. "Don't they!" she shouted, and then took one deep breath, letting out a shaky one. She gave them all a painted-on smile, all colours of doom and disaster. But even poison could disguise itself as a flower. Everyone braced themselves for what was to come. They could feel it in the chilling air. "Iskyla will understand. Just as she expected me to."

Then the wind and snow stirred, two massive figures taking shape and an odd icy colour. The frost dragons roared, their clamour making the ground shake and stir awake the peaceful death. It was like the dead had all stopped in their tracks and turned to her attention, waiting. Waiting for more to join them.

She mounted one of the dragons and turned to me. "If anything happens, let Kilian know first, not Snow."

"You really think I'd let you leave my sight like this?"

Her dragon launched up in the air with no warning.

"Little shit!" I shouted, but she was gone.

Oryn grabbed my arm just as I was about to fade to her. "You'd be giving yourself a death sentence if you fade within the Islines, let alone use your magic."

"She already gave me that death sentence by getting on that dragon."

"You could have stopped her."

"Why? I like her a little crazy."

"A little crazy?" His eyes were wide. "You've not seen what happens when she lets go of that tight control she has on herself. She's like a daughter to me before she is my queen, I cannot allow her to get hurt. Call your brother. I beg of you."

"Nothing will touch her." I said, backing away. "Can't promise the same for the rest."

She had been quick. Quicker than I was. It had taken me four times to fade to her through the thick fog of magic that covered the Islines. She stood at the edge of the cliff overlooking the largest Isline village I'd seen. There were too many shadows around her, too many shades in her eyes, too many expressions on her face.

The wind picked up, a gentle layer of snow lifted from the ground and circled around her body to create a white cloak resembling the one she wore as the White Veil. Wolves of frost materialised next, one by one, dozens of them pranced towards the edge and then jumped off the cliff to the village below.

The ground shook as they landed one after the other, and then panicked screams filled the air. Men, women and children ran and hid as her beasts prowled closer and closer, as her dragons of frost filled the skies and poured blistering ice on everything laying below. Every counterattack from their Aura was useless, the moment pieces of ice broke, they mended a second later—indestructible. Thora had tapped into her gates of magic, feeding from them. Except that there was no gate, no bound, no restriction on what she called forth. It was just pouring out of her.

The next minute passed in a flash.

Blood soaked everything in sight. Every new wolf that formed at her command was made of red ice. Not only could the Isline Aura not stop them, but they also couldn't control them either. No one could control blood. No one but her. Even the white ice—all was tightly tethered to her, only taking orders from her command. Just how I'd taught her ten years ago.

She pushed off the cliff and jumped, the wind making her land softly below. Her creatures of ice halted their movement, and whoever had survived huddled close together, hiding and murmuring prayers to their cold god who had just suddenly left them to the mercy of another much colder god.

"It didn't have to come to this. But you have all exhausted my kindness," Thora spoke loudly, pulling her hood back, and even the wind went entirely silent like the men and women below when they realised who she was. "You didn't like my peace," she said, picking up a small wooden toy buried in the snow and bending to offer it to a child. "Why?" When he made no move to retrieve it, her fingers twisted by her side.

Suddenly, he stood on controlled steps and took it, his mother screaming when he would not obey a single one of her pleas. Thora threw an arm around his shoulders and pulled him by her side as she directed her attention over the villagers. "You know how many mothers have shed tears and screamed for their children as your people keep stepping where I do not welcome them?" Thora stood, still holding onto the terrified boy. "Where are they? Where are your kings and queens? Where are the ones who sent that order? I want nothing from you as long as you hand them to me."

No one would answer, no one would even look her in the eye. They weren't looking at her to disguise and protect someone.

At a twist of her fingers, everyone's head tipped up, their eyes popping all open. Abandoning the boy, she walked between them, looking at each pair of eyes as she went past.

"Why do you hide?" she asked, putting a finger under a man's chin. "Cousin? Uncle?"

"You're no kin of mine."

"No?" she asked, and the man's face went beet red until he stopped breathing. Thora pointed to the man and turned to the rest. "Is that who was to protect you from me?"

"You're like your father," an older woman spat in old Ysolt.

Thora's head slowly turned to her, and the woman shot to her feet, eyes wide and screaming as she made her way to her side. She smiled sweetly at the old woman, her green eyes almost shifted in colour, a gleam flickering in them. "Careful what you wish for."

The woman screamed and cried as she unwillingly walked to a cliff edge and threw herself off it, plunging to her death.

The wind picked up and Thora walked back to the little boy as one by one, the villagers began walking towards the cliff edge. All beside the children.

"Help us," some cried in my direction.

I waved at them. "On her side, I'm afraid."

"Aren't you going to tell me to stop?" she asked me. Looking ahead at the villagers, her shadows flashing uncontrollably with more shades of colour than I'd ever seen as an Empath.

"Do you want to stop?"

She cocked her head to the side and thought about it for a minute, the colour of anger and hate growing a bit more prominent than the others. "Not really."

"Then why should I tell you to stop?"

"Isn't it the right thing?"

"Since when am I a moral compass, little bird?"

"Please," the little boy beside her pleaded, crying. "Please do not hurt my grandma. She is all I have."

Everyone halted in their tracks as Thora looked down at the boy, hate and anger disappearing from her colouring entirely. A shade of gloom falling over the rest of her emotions. "Sometimes, it is better to have nothing rather than something that will corrupt you to the point that you will feel empty and alone even in the midst of a crowd, surrounded by people, being hugged by a loved one, when you desperately need comfort.

Even a rose will start to wilt next weed."

The boy shook his head. "I'll grow up to be good. You have my promise."

"I do?"

He nodded and Thora's eyes glazed over as she gave him one of her smiles. Not the one I thought she'd give him. The one she usually hid because too many had wanted to take that soft smile and twist it. "Once, I said the same. Look at me now."

A shrill pierced the silence and all of our attention rose to the hills and cliffs surrounding the village. Hundreds of six legged creatures resembling spiders and a deer melded together began descending down to us. Soon, that number turned to thousands. There were so many of them surrounding the village that I didn't know which side to be aware of first.

"Protection," Thora absently said. "They've come to protect the village."

"No," the young boy by her side murmured. "They never come close to us. The *narok* are never supposed to. They're pure magic and we could taint them, and that could kill them."

The largest among the creatures slowly made its way to where she was standing. And rooted on the spot as if she'd been bewitched, Thora did not move at all.

"Little bird," I called, readying to step ahead when the boy grabbed my hand, drawing my attention to him.

He shook his head and then pointed to the creature which had reached Thora close enough to pierce an antler through her with ease. "We do not disturb them either. If the *narok* wants to get near her, she has no choice but to let it."

As if possessed, she reached a hand forward and touched it. The spot on the creature's head lit up like a glow, and a pitched bell sound ghosted over the air. It was followed by gasps. Hundreds of gasps from the Isline villagers who watched the scene unfold with wide eyes and an expression that almost bordered between awe and terror.

"Valeria," another boy murmured. "Only she could touch the *narok*."

"What?"

"She looks like the winter bride. Krig's wife," he told me. "He was ice, and she was the brisk wind, a guardian of the Sky God. He gave the land winter and she gave it soul. Ice has no soul. Ice is ice. Winter does though. Because of Valeria."

"What does that have to do with anything?"

"Because Valeria's heart was buried here," another older kid said. "She loved this land and the mountains. It reminded her of home in the heights of Caelum. When she found out Krig's magic wouldn't let anything survive in Isea, she asked for her heart to be buried here, to keep the land and its people alive. She was the winter nature itself."

The creature suddenly stepped away, startling Thora when it shrieked loudly enough to make the ground shake.

More of a warning than a threat.

She'd not been the only one distracted, I'd been, too. An arrow pierced through the frosted wind and shot just an inch away from her face, grazing my shoulder when I faded close to push her away.

The spider-like creatures shrilled again and then marched down from the above ground towards the village, almost trampling over us and the villagers who were still frozen still under Thora's control.

Her small hand cupped my arm, trying to stop the bleeding as the animals swarmed around us, stomping and shaking the ground.

"It's nothing."

She slapped her other hand over her mouth, eyes wide on my torso where a second arrow was edged in my flesh. The metal sheath had turned a stained bronze. "It's laced with poison."

"Blood poison," I said, snapping the shaft in half. "They have a Crafter. It was a trap. Iskyla knew you'd retaliate. She wanted Isjordians to know you walked to her lands willingly seeking a fight. One she wants and thinks you will lose. If she killed you here today, she would have killed you as an invader, a threat. She'd be a queen slayer, not a usurper."

"And I gave her just what she wanted."

"Not the time to go all pessimistic on me."

Something flashed in her eyes—not metaphorically. "Malik–"

I cupped her face, tilting her head to me. Then I saw it clearly.

Her eyes.

They had changed.

28

RED TIGER LILY

THORA

I couldn't breathe. Not watching him bleed against my hand. Not knowing I'd become just what I hated. Everything was blurring. The air grew piercing cold, and the pouring snow grew sharp.

He cupped my face, frowning down at me. "Thora." His thumbs smoothed under my eyes and his chest rose faster and faster. "Your eyes."

"I need to get you somewhere safe," I choked out, barely managing to conjure magic.

"Hold tightly," he breathed, pulling me to him. "I don't think I can do this more than once."

"You can't fade, the Crafter will trace us."

"Not this time." Skeletal hands broke through the snow, the dead rising fast, so fast that a shudder travelled down my spine at the taste of death invading the air. "It will throw off the Crafter's senses. Come."

The second my hand touched his, our surroundings changed, and he collapsed forward, falling into my arms. "Oh, gods, Malik."

"Even in death you won't call me Mal," he chuckled, trying to straighten himself.

The small village was dead and empty when we stepped through it—so neat and perfect and still as wind tunnelled through the streets and the houses creating eerie tunes. Almost haunted, the shadows cast by a dim sunset crawled up the stony walls to create giants of nightmares.

"There is nothing here," Malik said as we passed through house after house. "We're safe."

"It looks so well kept. How is that possible?"

"It isn't," he said, clutching his injured side. "Not in the normal world. Not in the world that moved past gods and their gifts. The magic hovering this part of the realm preserves everything, even long after death." He pointed his head to a two-floor house with windows and doors still intact. "There. We will rest in that one tonight."

"No," I said. "No, we're almost by the border and you're injured, we cannot stop, you need a healer."

He stopped and sighed, casting me a look that made me shift on my feet. "My body can handle it."

"How do you know?"

He tilted his head back and raised a brow.

Yeah, I knew how.

"Fine," I said, leading us inside the haunted house of his choice. It was dark, but even in the dark I could tell the room was neat and dustless. Not even a cobweb in sight. "This is getting creepier by the second."

Malik dropped to a sofa, groaning and breathing heavily as he rested his head back and shut his eyes.

"Let me see," I said, kneeling before him and picking the edges of his jacket and shirt up to reveal one of the most gruesome wounds I'd ever seen, his flesh had turned a deep shade of violet around the arrowhead, red veins spreading around it.

The idiot chuckled. "Don't make that face."

I pulled my lips shut. "What face?"

"I'm not dying."

"How do you know?"

He dropped his head back and chuckled again. "Fuck, I hate this cold."

"You're cold?" I got to my feet, looking around the house, tripping and knocking myself all over the furniture draped in the darkness of night. Reaching the fireplace, my hands touched the space around all over until I reached what looked like matches.

"No fire," Malik said just as I was about to throw the match on the pieces of kindling already gathered in the fireplace. "Might as well go outside and shout that we are here."

"You'll freeze."

"I'd make a pretty ice statue."

I shed my partly bloodied gown and threw it over him, making sure to tuck the sides tightly. "You're sweating." When I rested my knuckles on his forehead, I jolted upright. "Gods, you're burning."

His breathing was slow and shallow, his eyes had completely drifted shut.

"Malik?"

Nothing.

I sat beside him, cupping his cold face in my hands. "Malik?"

He didn't answer.

Tears pricked my eyes. "Mal, please."

Slowly, his eyelids peeled open, and he gave me a little smile. "Yes?"

"Please don't die," I whispered, my voice breaking.

"Only cause you say so, sweetheart."

My body shot up and I stood, backing towards the house, searching and searching.

"Come here, little bird," he meekly called. "Don't...don't leave me alone."

Those words pierced right through me, my hands shaking hard as I rummaged through the cupboards. Once I found something that smelled like liquor, a sharp knife and some scraps of cloth, I kneeled before him again, peeling his jacket back to look at the wound that had suddenly turned a deep mauve.

He shivered when I touched his skin and I pulled back, scared I'd hurt him. "Does it hurt or are you still cold?"

His eyes were resting heavily on me. "No."

"No?"

"Touch me again."

"Silly man," I muttered, almost choking on my trembling words as I poured liquor over the knife and the pieces of cloth to disinfect them. My fingers shook when I lifted the silver blade to his skin and cut around the wound to fish out the arrowhead still embedded in his flesh.

He made no sound of pain, his chest rising fast and his hands gripping the edges of the sofa hard enough to snap the wound.

Once I felt the tip of the arrow with my fingertip, I pulled it out, making sure to move fast and sow his wound shut. My fingers slipped from the blood, but I managed to get that first stitch in, and then another, and another. It was completely dark outside by the time I finished and the furthest I could see was my crimson stained palms.

I dropped back to the ground, shaking and suddenly dizzy at the feel of his blood on my hands. Before I could feel tears sting my eyes and a cry pushed from my throat, I got up and poured all the liquor I found in the cabinets on my hands until the blood was scrubbed off.

He laid with his eyes closed, but they peeled open when I returned to his side, holding a candle. "I'm sorry," I said, pushing hair away from his sweaty brow.

"Sorry?" he breathed out, forcing a smile on his lips. "Bird, this is the best day ever."

"I'm sorry," I repeated.

He lifted a hand to my face, brushing my tears away. "Come here."

Careful not to hurt his wound, I laid beside him.

"Maybe I should get injured more often," he murmured in my hair.

When I looked up at him, he breathed out a heavy sigh and left a kiss on my brow and then another on my eye. They were gentle pecks. Nothing that should have stirred so many memories. His nose touched mine and it was too little time to comprehend anything before his mouth was pressed against mine. Gently at first. Then the little pecks he gave me turned into lingering kisses, and before we both knew, he'd pressed me under him, his tongue pushing against mine while the kiss burned.

Ten years.

Ten long years since I'd felt anything.

Ten years since the day he'd decided to leave me. And he'd only done so because he'd always known he'd do so—that he'd leave me one way or another.

He was thinking of leaving me again, wasn't he?

"Are you kissing me because you think you're going to die?" We were two people who kissed only when the world was ending. Houses on fire, earth breaking, skies falling. And my world felt like it was ending.

"I'm kissing you because I might die if I don't."

"Was that a secret?"

"No."

"So you don't want me to keep it?"

"Not this one. Do you want a secret?" he slurred, a pained moan following, and he held me tighter against him.

He had to be in excruciating pain from the craft poison and there was nothing I could do but talk to him. "Only if you want me to have it."

His hand moved from my back till it rested on the nape of my neck, fingers tracing my skin until it had lit like a match. "That night we spent in Hellas, that night was the last time I touched a woman. It was also the first time I'd touched a woman in a long while. I was so close, so close to giving it all up and making you mine. And you would have let me, wouldn't you?"

I shook my head. "But...but you went to Celia."

His brows pulled together. "Who? Oh, tossed her a bag of coins to keep her blabbering. I should have known she'd show up at the castle to know why I wasn't paying her anymore when Silas took me to Isjord."

"Why would you do that?"

"It worked, didn't it? You were disgusted by me."

I pulled back and he hissed. "I was not."

He dragged me closer to him again. "You were."

"The only thing that disgusts me is the fact that you had to go that length instead of telling me the truth. I would have stayed away from you."

"You would have?"

"It would have been hard, but I would've."

"I wouldn't have, though."

I wiped his brow with the back of my hand. "Are you in a lot of pain?"

His nose touched mine. "Mhm. Kiss me again and make me better."

"You really think you're dying, don't you?"

He chuckled. "Might be. Will you let me die then? Will you be so cruel to me even in death? Pity me," he murmured over my lips, capturing them in his again. "Please pity me."

My heart was so giddy I was about to lose my mind. "But you've been so cruel to me, too. Why should I spare you any grace?"

"You're right. But letting me die is giving me grace. I want to live and feel every punishment you have for me."

"Punish you? I'd be punishing myself, too."

"You really shouldn't be saying things like that, little bird." A strangled moan vibrated against his chest.

Cupping his face, I kissed him again, raising him from the deathly slumber pain was sending him into. "Don't hate me, but I need you to stay awake."

"I'm a man capable of many things, but hating you is not something I can ever do."

"Stay awake," I whispered, brushing his hair back.

"Command me. Even if my mind doesn't listen, my body always obeys to you."

"If you tell me again to forget this in the morning, you're going to regret it, Malik Castemont."

"I might die."

"You think it's beyond me to drag you from hell and back here?"

"A little. You'd spite me some other way. Another way that would hurt worse than hell."

"What can hurt worse than hell?"

"You in another man's arms. You wanting them. Them wanting you back and getting to have you."

"I think you really might be dying." I put a hand to my brow. "I might be, too."

He chuckled, kissing his way down my cheek and burying his face in my neck, his scruff tickling me. "Cherries. Fucking cherries."

"Cherries?"

"You smell like them."

"I don't. I use almond soap."

I gasped when his mouth suddenly latched on my neck, his tongue licking a trail to my ear. "No, you taste like sweet cherries, too."

"Malik."

"Shhh," he hummed in my ear, continuing to kiss his way around my neck. "If I am to die, I want this to be my taste of heaven. Hell is going to sting my gorgeous backside."

"I'm sure someone is going to take pity on your gorgeous backside."

"You think my backside is gorgeous?"

"What the hells was I thinking when I decided to crush on an idiot like you?"

"You had a crush on me?"

"Have. And don't pretend like you didn't know."

He shook his head. "We were complicated, Rora. You relied on me and I relied on you, one of us was bound to feel like we owed one another something. Like you owed me your affections."

"You're an absolute idiot, you know that?"

"But you kind of like me."

"Don't die and I'll show you how much."

"I must have become a saint," he groaned. "To resist the temptation and ask you to show me now."

"With how much you are bleeding, you'd end up a martyr if I showed you now."

"An honourable death. One every man wants."

"Idiot."

He chuckled, pressing his face to my hair and sighing. "Luckiest idiot."

Somehow, he'd managed to stay awake the whole night. I'd only let him sleep when his fever had gone down and when he breathed loud enough for me to hear him do so. My ear was still pressed to his chest despite, listening to his faint heartbeat. It was all I had heard beside his breathing and the wind brushing against the roofs of the empty village. All until the little scratching noise on the window.

A ghastly face flashed against it, three pairs of eyes just watching us. The creature was all bones, its insides exposed and barely hanging to its body. I could see its heart slowly pump and its lungs expand at the same rhythm. When I stood, the creature blinked all its eyes and stepped a little away from the window.

Making sure Malik was all covered up and safe, I cracked the door open and peered outside, expecting to see the creature, not the thousand others surrounding the home on all sides.

Hells.

Every fibre in my body prepared for a fight, but my senses were calm, almost in harmony with the wind, the frost, the creatures. And I knew that because their hearts beat at the same rhythm as mine and they breathed as I did. When my heart raced, so did theirs. When I held a breath, so did they.

I stepped forward and they all stepped back and away from me. Kneeling down and putting my hands towards them, I said, "I mean no harm."

"Why was your kind not spared the same sentiment?" something whispered against my ear, and my head whipped in its direction, finding no one standing close to me.

"I was owed a debt."

"A debt? Why would human lives be owed to you?"

"Because they are trying to provoke a war I cannot give them."

"But you're already at war. A one-woman army now that your general is dying."

"What?"

"He is dying, Thora," the voice crooned deep inside my mind and a chill went down my spine, making all my limbs tremble.

I ran back inside, the door flying open with a bang. He was gone. Only a massive pool of blood was left behind. "Malik!" I shouted, searching the house corner to corner. "Malik!"

My knees weakened and I dropped to the bloodied floor. The reflection shifted. Someone else was looking back at me. Young. Long blonde hair carrying in the wind. Her face had always reminded me of my own. Her eyes like Snow's. "It's just a dream," Lilith whispered, and the room carried her voice until my surroundings blurred. "Wake up. They are coming."

"Wake up," another voice called against my ear, and I gasped as the floor beneath me liquefied and pulled me under.

A hand grasped mine and air finally entered my lungs again.

"Bloodies hells, Thora," Malik sighed, putting his brow against mine. "When I was imagining you screaming my name it was nothing like this."

"You're alright?" He had to be. He'd just made a joke.

"Apart from the permanent heart condition you almost gave me, yeah, I'm alright."

And there was another joke.

I smiled, whispering to myself, "You're alright. You're alright."

Standing up, I tugged at his shirt to look at his wound. Still bruised, an angry red and desperately needing some proper attention, but it was fine. "Why did it feel so real?"

Pushing off the sofa, I unbolted the door and went outside. Just as I had thought, the same creature staring at us through the window in my dream stood by the edge of the abandoned village, blurred by the thick morning snow that was coating everything with a fresh layer of white. Stepping into the street, I took a couple steps where I remembered the other creatures standing and kneeled down, brushing my hand over the new and soft snowflakes, separating the fresh fallen snow on the ground from the permanent snowpack to reveal footsteps of all sizes and shapes embedded in it.

"What's this?" he asked, following me outside.

"It was not a dream, but it somehow was. I saw Lilith. Something is happening." I spun to him. "Why are you up?"

"I'm alive."

"Yes. Yes, you are."

"And it is tomorrow."

"It is," I agreed.

The smallest smile rose on his lips. "Good morning."

"Good morning."

Something rumbled in the distance, dragging our attention away from what was about to come next. A wall of ice quickly rose from between us, trapping him on the other side of it.

"Malik?"

"Here, sweetheart," he shouted, putting a palm against the ice wall.

"Dark Craft?"

"Don't think so. I can scent it in the air, but this one isn't a Crafter's doing. Can't you take this down? I can't risk fading or doing any magic without being scented by a Crafter. Or dying."

I tried. But it wouldn't go down no matter how many tethers of control I attached to the ice, it just wouldn't take my command. Resting my hands on it, I tried again. It had been a while since I'd gone to the basics of my magic, but this was not the rest of the realm, this was Isea, the most preserved ancient land of what our realm had once been.

"Damn it!" Pushing from the wall, my tethers reached out to merge with the snow and ice to create my creatures, but nothing. Nothing was happening. No magic. "There is something wrong," I breathed, looking down at my palms, at my skin and the blue veins below, wondering how I had ever looked so human and never noticed.

He put a palm to the wall. "Let's walk around it."

"I can't see an end."

Unsheathing a dagger, we walked along the wall, his hand against mine. Despite the thick wall of ice between us, it felt as if his skin was grazing mine.

"Talk to me," he said. "I can literally feel your unease in my stomach."

"Is that all you feel?" I asked, then saw his blurred shadow stop for a moment. Though I couldn't make out any features through the wall, somehow, I knew he had a grin on. "If we go this slow, we won't ever find an end."

"This pessimistic nonsense is really worrying me, little bird. We have to get you in the sun more."

"Not funny at all."

"Then stop smiling or I'm going to take this the wrong way."

Night had swallowed day before we'd even taken notice. There had barely been a sunset. Nothing to indicate that light would leave us stranded with miles of a wall still separating us.

Malik had leaned against the wall of ice even though I knew he was probably freezing at the contact. He was more sensitive than most to the cold, a thought that made me giggle considering the sheer size and *greatness* of him, the famed Eldritch Commander.

"Go under a tree or find a tall rock so it braces against the cold," I said. "Or you're going to freeze."

"I'm not leaving you."

"Please."

"Don't, Thora."

Sighing, I dropped my brow against the ice wall, trying to look at him through the foggy surface. I stayed like that for a long while. Long, long while. Until my eyes were drifting shut.

Trying to not nod off became harder when the forest lullaby grew louder. Birds. Wind. All sorts sang me to a devious sleep. Almost as if they were trying to lure me deep inside my dreams.

Birds.

Wind.

There were none around us.

Where were the sounds even coming from?

Jerking awake, I banged on the wall of ice. "Malik, there is something wrong." After giving him some time to stir awake and answer me, I decided to panic. "Malik?" I couldn't see him all that well now that it was so dark. "Malik?"

All then went quiet as I listened for any noise to indicate he was still there.

"This is not the time to play around, Mal, please."

The ice beneath my palms morphed and I jerked back when it took the shape of a glowy face I recognised. "Run," Lilith whispered. "Fast, Thora. Their Crafters are coming, they've followed your scent along the ice wall."

After tearing my dagger across the skirts of my nightgown, I ran until the wind almost carried me with it, her reflection following me along the ice wall.

How was she doing that?

"Towards the forest. Not along the wall or they will find you."

"No," I panted, forcing my feet to go faster. "He is on that other side."

The damn wall seemed to have no end, stretching for miles and miles. The further I went, the more it dawned on me.

"No, don't stop," the small figure in the ice said, pressing her palms to the wall surface when I slowed down.

"Lilith, why do you want me to run? I've fought Crafters with and without magic."

"They come prepared. Holding your deepest, darkest fears." She quietened for a moment and my steps faltered. "They saw right through them when they injured your husband. They will now make you face them."

"Mal. Where is Mal?"

"Far from danger."

"Put the wall down."

"I can't. It's not Craft, nor the magic of an Aura."

"Then what is it?"

"A magic of a far older kind."

"What?"

"It has a life of its own like every living thing. It was dead for a while in Isjord, but it has revived again."

"I've done that, haven't I? When Visha removed my seal."

"Yes. Macaria believes so, too. She said she felt it when your seals were removed. It seems winter wants you to find something. Something you may have maybe lost. Something you can't find without losing everything else first."

"What does that even mean?"

"I cannot give you your answers. You have to find them yourself. Otherwise nature wouldn't have gone to this extent."

Damn it. Gods dammit. I was so tired from all this bullshit. All I wanted was a nap and to be left alone. "How are you even doing this?"

"Nature doesn't view me as an anomaly either after they took off the seal my...Melanthe gave me. At least that is what I like to believe. Part of me thinks they might fear my betrothed," she said, wincing a little.

"I can't," I said, panting. I wasn't made for running or camping or any other open-air activities. My feet were made for massages. I had not grown a callus since...well, ever. "I can't go any further." I couldn't see anything ahead but the glistening stars that looked the closest to the realm I'd ever seen them. My thighs and lungs were burning. My feet ached. My poor, poor feet.

"A little further," she pushed. "Just a little, Thora."

"What is a little further?"

I halted, my chest burning from the run and the panting breaths I took as I took in what stood in the close distance.

From where I was standing, it looked like a tree made entirely of fireflies. But when I got closer, I could see that the leaves and part of the trunk glowed within itself.

"That," Lilith said just as I reached the end of the wall. "They call it the tree of life in our holy books. Blackfyre, the Red Coven's grimoire, recalls many of them to have been planted in many realms. A heart is buried under their roots so the leaves can breathe out the magic into the winter air as well as the roots spreading it in the soil."

"A heart?"

"A pure one. It was used to keep the land from dying. I figured Krig planted one in this realm, in Isjord, because his blessing would have killed the land and then starved its people. Winter and war were never meant to make humanity thrive. They were meant to extinguish it."

Realisation struck me. "The heartbeat I've been hearing. Could this be it?"

"Must be. I have to go now," she hurriedly said, looking somewhere behind her. "The scarlet stone I stole from Macaria to reach you has burned entirely. Stay under the tree and let it show you—" she warned right before disappearing.

"Show me what?"

Damn it.

Quiet.

It was so, so incredibly quiet.

The crunch of my steps in the snow echoed in the distance as I approached the tree's shade, reaching a hand forward to brace it against its trunk. It was warm. A strange sense of calm trickled over my skin when I rested both hands on it. My chest...it felt so light that I thought my body was going to float.

"Alright," I loudly said, wincing when my voice boomed around the empty air. "I'm here. What do you want to show me?"

Silence.

Nothing.

Only my pulse blasting against my ear drums.

"Talking to trees now, Thora Isa Krigborn?" I murmured to myself, walking around the tree, my fingers skimming its trunk. "That's what's wrong with you."

I paused at the sudden pulse against my palm, wondering if I had imagined it. "What?" I asked, a little embarrassed that I was now carrying full conversations with a damn tree.

Resting my ear against the trunk, I closed my eyes. "What have I lost, you stupid tree? I'm so done with all this spiritual nonsense." Banging my fist against the trunk, I groaned, "Tell me."

A squeak came out of me when the tree shifted, its trunk twisting and then splitting in half to frame what looked like a liquid mirror. The reflection however was strange. It was me, dressed the same, looking the same, just from years ago—many years ago.

Little Thora stood before me, watching me with a strange look in her eyes. They were stronger than mine were now despite the youth she still held.

Kneeling down, I tilted my head to the side to study her and she did the same, mimicking me. When I stood, she stood, too. When I spoke, she spoke, too, her small voice joining mine.

A creeping sensation travelled down my neck. "What the fuck is happening?" I murmured, and so did she. I bit my tongue. "Please don't say that word."

I sighed when she repeated my own words back to me.

Dropping to the ground, I pulled my knees to my chest and just watched her do the same. I reached a hand forward, trying to call my magic again and something strange happened, she didn't mimic me. "You can't do magic either?"

An even stranger thing happened. She said, "I am not supposed to. I promised not to ever do magic. Like Eren and Snow did."

"Oh, yeah," I said, looking around and pinching my thigh, wondering about the degree of insanity I was about to commit talking to the younger me inside the tree.

She twirled a long black strand of hair in her tiny fingers. "Isn't it lucky you can't do magic anymore? At least now we don't have to hide."

Her words struck me. "Hide?"

She nodded. "You still hide it."

"Only part of it, and it is my own choice to do so now."

"Magic is whole. That is what Eren says. We can't do just a little. We can't do a lot at once. Magic is a limb. Does it even matter whose choice it is if we are hiding such an important part of ourselves to the world?"

"I don't remember being this smart when I was little."

She smiled. "I'm smarter than you are now. More courageous, too."

"Nonsense," I muttered. "I used to be so afraid. All the time."

"Bravery has nothing to do with how afraid we are. We can fear and still be brave. You buried your fears away for many years now, that is why you can't be courageous. Eren used to say we are the bravest in front of fear."

I stood, looking around. "Now for sure I know that I was never this smart. That's not me," I said, pointing between us, and she giggled.

The smile disappeared from her face and her eyes dropped to the ground. "Why are we hiding again? I thought we were free."

"What we are can never allow us to be free."

"Snow is. Eren is. Why aren't we?"

Because I couldn't swim in the suffocating waters they had crossed through, so I had just stayed on the shore, watching them cross to safety.

"You're not me," she said, standing and reaching closer. She gave me a smile—one so genuine that I almost didn't recognise my own face. Had I ever given one of those before? "You're not me, Thora. Not anymore. You're tall and brave and powerful."

I wiped a hand over my eyes and barked a sobbing laughter. "I am not that tall."

"An ancestor surely failed us." She cleared her throat and stood tall, pushing her chin up in the air. It all made me laugh and she broke into a smile, too.

"You have to let me hurt, you know," she said, looking down at her shoes. "Don't protect me anymore. It is okay not to protect me anymore."

Sobs shook my chest. "I don't want to do that."

"I know. But I want you to. I don't want you to spend your entire life creating a safe world for me when there is such a world out there for you to live outside of your mind. I'm going to be okay," she said. "I promise. We aren't as strong as Snow or Eren, but we can be. You have to let us at least try."

I woke up with a jolt. My head was spinning. Everything around me looked surreal somehow, as if I was still dreaming.

The tree wasn't glowing anymore, my reflection gone, and the ice wall was gone, too. Even the heartbeat had disappeared.

Everything had left me behind with the winter silence surrounding me.

Rolling my shoulders and neck, I pushed up, searching the white expanse and then stepping outside the tree shadow where I'd slept, protected.

I'd only taken one step when the stench hit me.

Rotten. Sour.

The cold was doing nothing to hide it lingering in the air.

Craft—of a kind I wouldn't like from the smell of it. The kind that Oryn had told me got Crafters excommunicated from their covens.

Covered in a long cloak, the Crafter tore through the billowing snowstorm. Stopping about one hundred feet away from me, he pulled the hood back to reveal a shaved, tattooed head, and an even worse tattooed face.

I clutched my silly little dagger and stepped closer to him as he kneeled and opened his mouth widely—letting a large snake crawl out of it.

Gagging, I held my stomach, feeling bile ready to attack the snake instead of my blade.

The black snake left a trail of tar behind, slowly making its way to me, and the putrid scent it carried made me feel sicker.

Despite my best effort to seem all in control of the situation, I backed away when it got closer, hiding back under the tree's shade, my spine meeting the trunk.

"They sent you to kill me?"

He cocked his head to the side. "They sent me to get your heart."

"I need that."

"Iskyla needs it more. One bite and you can have it back. One bite is all she needs."

"Wait," I shouted, putting a hand forward, and he actually stopped, frowning at my extended limb and then up at the tree that was groaning and moaning at the sway of the wind. "Why? Why does she need my heart?"

"When you die, the land will die with you since the two are now as one." He hummed to himself. "But you didn't know that, did you?"

His snake continued circling the tree, not yet attacking me.

What was he talking about? "Know what?"

"Of your connection to winter, to the land, to the wind, and the heart buried below that has only just started beating again because of you. It is not difficult to tell. The winter creatures do not fear you. On the contrary, they see you as one of their own." He pointed to the tree. "Nature bends to you and your will. You. Are. One. Body," he said, his forked tongue slipping outside his mouth like a hissing snake.

I looked up, watching the tree's branches twisting and crawling over me like they were limbs. Hells. Was he telling the truth? How? How had I—

Oh.

Ohhhh.

My magic. The seal. Land feeding from my magic. Land finally reviving after my father's rule.

Oh.

The Crafter got closer, taking careful steps towards me as he narrowed his eyes on the space around us, watching and almost cautious of it. "You breathe, *it* breathes. Winter is no longer decaying its people and the land it has fallen upon like it was before when the kings before you reigned over it and slowly, bitterly and mercilessly began killing it." His black forked tongue swept over his dried-up lips as he chuckled. "The Krigborn Queen with emerald eyes. Who else could it be?" he asked, his voice almost mocking.

The black snake shot in my direction, and the tree bent forward just as fast, trapping the animal between its branches. Grabbing hold of its slimy tail, I slashed the dagger through its body, parting it in half.

The Crafter hissed, one side of his face turning ashen and scaly.

A gag climbed my throat, and I bent down to wash my hand in the snow until the tar disappeared from my skin.

The Crafter's hands twisted, and red, spoilt smelling magic surrounded him, lifting around in the shape of a small dome, ghastly and glowy hands rising from its surface and elongating like branches, heading towards me.

Dark shadows rose from all over and out of nowhere, thinning and towering over the Dark Crafter. Then they descended down on him, faster than anything I'd seen, collapsing against the veil of protection around him, his phantom red hands disappearing at the crash.

Both him and I spun to search our surroundings for the only one who was capable of such magic.

Malik faded right on top of the veil, holding his Adriatian steel now dressed in black burning flames. When the shadows tackled the veil again, he pierced the word right through it, surprising the Crafter who dropped on his backside.

Holding the hilt sideways, Malik pulled on the sword and then dragged it through the layer of the veil as if he was slicing a very large vegetable.

The red cocoon faltered and then disappeared altogether.

Malik's back was still to me, rising and falling fast, his breaths misting the air. In one swing, the Crafter was no more, his head rolling in the pale white snow.

He had found me.

Still breathing hard, he turned to me and pointed a finger to my necklace. "Never take that off."

Don't know how fast I ran, but when I flew onto his arms, he almost landed on his very pretty buttocks. "I thought something happened to you," I breathed, pressing my face on his warm neck.

"I'm bound to you, my liege," he said, hugging me tightly.

"What sort of punishment is that?"

"My liege needs to tell me that."

"And how is my king finding it?"

"Satisfactory," he murmured in my ear, his warm breath sending a trail of shivers down my spine.

I flinched when a fat drop of water landed on my forehead.

Then another.

And another.

We both looked up at the grey clouds gathering overhead that were now groaning with a sudden approaching storm.

Rain?

Did it even rain in the Islines?

The three drops of rain suddenly turned into a drizzle and thickened until we were caught in the middle of a rainstorm.

"It's raining," I said, reaching out my palms to catch the drops as he carried me under the tall tree of life to keep us from getting wet.

Somewhere under the downpour, I caught sight of the small figure who was still watching over me. Lifting a hand, I waved to Lilith, forgetting that she couldn't see it. But then she waved back, wearing a smile before her astral form dissolved into the rain.

I didn't even get to thank her.

"How is your wound?" I asked, trying to pull back and look at him, but he held me too tightly, face pressed to my shoulder.

"Fantastic."

I glanced at the dead remains of the Crafter. "You did magic."

"Yeah."

"How?"

"The spiritual mana was cut off, but not my physical one. At least what the infection spared."

"Kilian told me that is dangerous for you."

"I would have had a heart attack if something had happened to you so there wasn't much of a choice."

"Can I look at you? You're not letting me."

Sitting down by the tree trunk, he put me on his lap and let me have my fill of him. "Ten fingers," I counted, bringing his hands to my mouth so I could warm them up a little. "Two eyes, a silly nose, two ears and a mouth." I smiled at him. "You're all here."

He slid his hands out of my hold and cupped my face so he could bring it down to his. Then he kissed me like it was the most normal thing ever, like we'd done it ten thousand times before, while I was absolutely going out of my mind.

He pulled back and then sighed, just keeping me there, pressing his lips to mine from time to time.

"What's wrong?" I asked, running my hands over his to try and warm them up.

"I thought I wasn't going to get to you in time. You still can't do magic?"

I shook my head. "It's angry at me. My own magic is angry with me. I think I know what it is," I said to him, "the heartbeat."

"I think I do, too," he said, touching a finger to my eyes. "They've changed colour."

"They have?" I asked, a little panicked. I loved my eyes. "To what?"

"There is a ring of gold around the green. And something else."

"What else?"

"They aren't lying to me anymore."

29

GREEN BUTTERCUPS

Malik

We'd made it to the tunnel entrance by the fourth time I faded. She had her arm wrapped around my waist, still insisting I used her to stand up right. It was adorable until she really tried to do so. She'd snap in half if I did.

"Rora, sweetheart, you're going to pull a muscle."

"I've got you, lean on me."

"Stop trying to seduce me, it isn't the time nor the place." It was in fact the best place and the perfect time to wrap her legs around my waist and fuck her against the walls until she needed to lean on me herself.

Huffing all annoyed and frustrated, she moved away, letting go of me.

Not far enough for me to grab her back to my side. "Come on now, *Tiny*, I need your body heat or the upper half of me will freeze, too," I coaxed, bending to kiss her cheek and then her mouth. I'd been contemplating on doing it for the past three miles we'd walked to here, but she'd been all so worried about me, it broke my heart.

"I knew we'd make it," she said, still trying to make me lean onto her like I was wounded beyond saving. "You've got the tits. I've got the brains. It was fool proof."

I chuckled. "Sweetheart, they're not tits."

"But they are so big," she grumbled. "Why do they have to be so big? Why can't mine be that big?"

They weren't *that* big. "Because I like yours just how they are."

"Small?"

"Perfect."

She rolled her eyes up at me and glared under her thick black lashes. Despite the cool look she gave me, her pink cheeks betrayed her. "You've barely even seen them."

"I'm sure you'll show me."

"If you show me yours again."

I threw my head back and laughed, and she smiled, too. It was all I needed to see before I pulled her to me and kissed her again. We weren't going to make it back to Isjord today. Possibly not tomorrow either.

"Thora?" someone called, and I muttered a prayer to the gods that it was just the blood poison doing my head in.

Elias flashed a lantern down the tunnel and then thanked about a thousand deities as he ran towards us, even the ones no one really prayed to.

My teeth grind against one another. "Please tell me I'm hallucinating him."

When he got closer, she threw my arm over her shoulders again and gestured to Elias to do the same. "He needs a healer immediately."

"Put a finger on me Elias Venzor and it will be the last time you have fingers."

Visha was not one to fuss over people, but she was fussing over me for some reason. "Sit back down," she ordered as she searched through her cabinets for more stuff to rub on me.

"If death wanted to come for me, it would have already done so," I said, standing up from her uncomfortable rock table of torture.

"I've never seen blood poison like the one I found in your blood, so get yourself back down again. It was too—"

"Specific? Like it was made for me?" I asked, buttoning up my shirt.

She stopped fiddling with her potions and turned to me. "You knew?"

"Hard to miss when you can sense death and its ways."

"That would mean the Isline Queen is purposefully aiming for you. Perhaps the attack was not to draw in Thora after all." She picked up a massive mortar and pressed some seeds into it. "Have you told her that?"

"I will deal with it." I stood, heading to leave, but she lifted a wall of red, blocking me, "I need to study the poison."

"I need to see my wife." Thora had been attending funerals all for the kids who'd been killed at the academy, and I had not even been there for her to lean against, to console her, to held her up straight, to not let her crumble into the grief that had slammed into her the second we'd stepped back inside Isjord.

Her mouth twitched, the wall lowering. "Oh." She pointed a finger to the door while she browsed through her grimoire. "Then get out."

"Lovely as always, Visha Delcour. I see what the lordship sees in you," I said, putting my belt back on. "He must have a kink for torture."

Her mouth twitched and she almost showed me a sneer. "Likewise."

"Mhh," I hummed, making for the door. "My torture is sweet, V. So, so sweet."

The witchling rolled her eyes, her magic giving me a shove outside before pulling the doors shut with a bang.

The urge to run off to my safe space was held back only because I didn't wish to invade it with my morose thoughts, so I slowed myself on the way to her. Thinking away thoughts of anything but her. And it wasn't hard at all.

My excitement died off a little when I found her sleeping in her room. She must have been exhausted to have fallen asleep or the damn tea Nia had given her was working a little too well. "Hi, little bird," I whispered, kissing her cheek. "Didn't miss me at all, did you?"

She stirred a little, adjusting her head on the pillow and I laid close to her, my nose brushing hers. "Do you dream of me as I dream of you?" My hands tangled in her hair. "Do they haunt you as they haunt me? I hope they do. I am a cruel man like that. I've never been so glad for my cruel heart. A softer heart would have crumbled before this. How could it not? Look at you. How can anyone with a soft heart do this to you? How...how can someone with a soft heart lie to you? To you out of all."

I was so tempted to read her. To see what she was feeling. But there was a promise I had made. A bargain my cruel heart made to remain cruel. If I knew how she felt, I'd be tempted. Tempted to hope. Tempted to take her pain. Tempted to stay away. Temptation would have made my heart soft.

She stirred again, snuggling against me this time, her cheek pressed to my chest.

My eyes drew shut. "Don't make my heart soft, little bird. I don't think I can lie to you for long."

30

RED ROSES

MALIK

It had taken me an entire day to check the villages along with Oryn for any trace of dark craft, even with Memphis's help in the skies. Beside an odd trick and trap, we had not found anything that had resembled the craft we had faced in the Islines.

Oryn and Visha had called them the *Eiectus*. Crafters who had been expelled out of Eldmoor for toying with sacrifices and blood magic. Question was, how had Iskyla gotten her hands on them? If they had been capable of cutting off any supply of my magic for miles meant we had more serious things to deal with than just Iskyla's soldiers committing *anti-social* crimes in our villages—thanks to Thora and her game of dress up, that's all they had been. A noise disturbance at best.

The castle was quiet when I returned from Modr. And so was the room. Candles were dim, burning just enough light to let someone see her figure. She was laying on the bed, her face buried in her pillow, a white satin sheet haphazardly covering barely any of her. Elias had told me she'd spent all her day training her magic, just breathing and meditating—something she hated fiercely. It only meant that she was still finding it hard to call on it. It was like part of her magic had shut her out, as her head did sometimes.

Carefully not to wake her, I lowered my sword on a table and began mindlessly unbuttoning my leathers, too tired to even form a thought.

A small hand rested over mine, pulling it down and efficiently undoing the buttons for me. I'd not even heard her approach. Every sense in my body had become so accustomed to her that her presence felt like a duplicate of mine. In a sense, she was part of me. Conjoined to my soul. She did carry part of it around her neck. The good half of it. And she didn't even know it. It was how I'd found her, how I always did, how I always would. I just had to find a way to meld it to her, to convince her to never take it off even if she were to resent me again. Couldn't have her throwing it back to me again. My soul was safe only in her hands. It was hers to keep. It had been hers long ago when she began bearing all its secrets and pains as if they had been her own.

Her hands flattened against my chest and then dropped to my stomach, lightly grazing my skin—so lightly. It was tentative at first, then it became more than just exploring.

Blood immediately shot south. "Thora, don't."

Her emerald gaze rose to me, that ring of gold becoming almost luminescent in the dark. "Don't?" she asked in a trance.

"Not when I'm like this."

"Like what?"

"Not in control of what I can do." Though I was fairly sure I didn't have a single drop of blood on me, an Empath always carried the stains of death a little further inside. Until

I calmed that roaring beacon, I couldn't touch her.

The unusual ring of gold around her green eyes suddenly almost glowed. "What is it that you can do?"

I dropped my forehead to hers, inhaling and drowning in her sweet scent. "Things I shouldn't want to do to you when I'm like this."

Her hands moved up until her arms were wrapped around my neck. She rose on her toes and pressed her mouth to mine for one small moment.

It was all it took.

I pulled her to my body, and I kissed her how I wanted to kiss her. She was this fine, breakable thing, but in my hands she was iron cast in pure flames.

Pulling back, I buried my face in the crook of her neck. "Fuck."

The little hellion pressed her body to mine, letting me feel all of her and she surely felt all of me considering the way her mouth pulled to a smile where it rested against my shoulder. "I can help."

"I don't want to use you."

"Haven't we been using one another since the day we met? What's one more time?"

"Not like this."

"Then let me use you," she whispered in my ear, pulling the hand I had on her waist and bringing it between her legs. A small whimper left her when she cupped my hand against her sex.

"Thora," I warned, my voice hoarse.

Tentatively, I moved my fingers over her lace covered cunt, feeling her shake in my hold when I repeated the motion a second time. "Fuck, Thora, you've soaked them. What do you need, sweetheart, my mouth?"

I could see overwhelm cloud her. In the way her chest rose, how her tongue darted to lick her lips, how her emerald eyes quickly paced back and forth on my face, searching for clues, answers, help. Like they always did when they looked up at me. But I wanted to give none of them to her. I wanted her to find them herself. She only needed to reach for my body to know all she needed to know. To know how much I wanted her back. To know that I'd fall to my knees for her.

Grabbing her hand, I backed away until the back of my legs met the sofa, and I sat down, letting her be the one to tower over me, letting her know she had the control. I wondered how she didn't know it already. She'd always had it over me.

She bit onto that puffy lower lip that I'd almost bruised, and gathered her soft cotton gown up so she could straddle my lap. "Put your hands on me."

"Is it an order?"

"Yes."

"What is my punishment if I don't obey?"

She squirmed on my lap. "You will obey. I can ruin you."

Hadn't she already?

She watched as I trailed my hands over her legs and up her naked thighs. Her breath hitched when the material of her nightgown pulled up along with my hands and bunched until it was wrapped around her hips. Her chest rose faster and faster when I didn't stop, my hands trailing up her waist and then over her perky tits. Pulling onto the strap, I tugged it down to reveal a puckered rosy nipple.

I realised what sin looked like when I put my hands on her. It was blasphemy. The contrast of cracked and scarred skin and broken knuckles that had never healed properly. Callused and twisted fingers, hands that had been soaked in blood and ripe with murder.

It was like she could read my thoughts. Taking my hand, she brought it to her lips, kissing each finger, each scar, before bridging it to her neck, then down her chest. "You know," she said, leaning forward and taking my lips. "These are the first hands I've let touch me like this." Her hands went under my unbuttoned shirt, and she grazed her fingers over my ribs until they met over at my back. "The first lips I've kissed were yours." When she pulled back, her eyes turned glassy. "I wish you had been my every first."

"That is the worst wish I've heard," I murmured, nipping at her lips, wishing the very same thing.

"Want to hear something worse?" she asked, her hips slowly riding me as she kissed a path over my neck. "I think I've wished for you before I even saw you."

"You wished for a rotten bastard not worth anything?"

"Mhm," she hummed, sucking on my ear lobe. "You were my punishment."

"I don't want to be your punishment."

"But I love," she crooned in my ear, "to be punished."

Her teeth dug into my skin and I hissed, my cock straining painfully against my leathers. "Gods, Thora Krigborn, what are you doing to me?"

She licked a path up my throat and then kissed me, sinking her mouth to mine. "What I've wanted to do to you for a very long time," she murmured, biting my lip and then licking the sting away. "To make you mine."

I let my hands fall between her legs and her spine arched, her fingers digging in my shoulders as I prodded at her slick entrance and pushed a finger in her tight cunt. Her lips parted with a moan that had my cock almost dig itself out of my britches. "I would have hurt you, sweetheart." Her hips started riding my finger and I slipped another one, making her gasp and shake in my hold. "Fuck, Thora, how are you going to take me?"

Her eyes glazed and her swollen mouth parted open when I drove inside her faster. Delicate fingers digging in my hair as I kissed my way down to her breast, sinking my teeth on a taut nipple. "Do you know how many times I've imagined my fingers inside you, my tongue tasting you. Shit, Thora, do you know how many times I've come thinking of this."

"Later," she breathed over my mouth, licking and tasting my lips. "Show me later."

I chuckled. "You like watching me, little bird?"

She moaned when I rubbed my thumb against her core, circling them there until her limbs began shaking. "It's the single most attractive thing I've ever witnessed. Beside your tits. Those are impeccable, too."

She gave me a hard look when I pulled my fingers out of her and hooked her legs around my waist to stand. I laid her on the bed before climbing over her naked body, just looking at her. Just looking at the most beautiful thing I'd ever laid my eyes upon. Black hair spread over the white sheets, her pale skin flushed pink, her lips swollen red, and her legs spread wide open for me. It had to be a dream.

"What?" she asked, running her fingers over my lips. "Stage fright?"

"You little shit." My little shit.

"Forgot what happens now, did you?" She giggled, squirming under me and reaching for my belt. "Worry not. You're in safe hands."

I let her undress me, watching her eyes widen just slightly when she wrapped a hand around my cock, her fingers barely circling my length. "Oh."

"What? Stage fright?" Leaning in, I peppered her mouth with kisses, directing her hand to move over my very stiff cock that was practically weeping and begging just to be touched by her. "I will show you how to work the props."

"I know how to handle one, Malik."

"You don't know how to handle mine, sweetheart. I don't like being pet, so tighten your hand around me." I groaned, pushing my tongue in her mouth as she started pumping me in her little tight fist. "Fuck, that's it. Tighter, sweetheart. Shit, that's it. You're doing so well."

Her hips bucked when I reached between her legs to run my fingers over her slicken sex that was so ready to be filled, circling that spot that made her throw her back with a moan.

"So sensitive."

"Only with you," she panted, her hips rocking against my touch.

I'd been patient for ten years. I'd waited for ten fucking years. Later. We'd do this later. "Open your legs wide for me, all the petting can wait after I've thoroughly fucked you. I can't wait a second longer."

She blinked fast but did as told. Pulling her thighs wide apart and letting me see her pretty soaked cunt, weeping and begging to be filled up. I was dying to get a taste of her, but if I didn't get inside her right that moment, I was going to die a worse death. It had to wait.

"Is this alright?" I asked, lowering myself over her body and caging her in.

She nodded, a hand resting on my shoulder and the other at the back of my neck, her fingers gently stroking my scalp. "More than alright," she whispered, her chest moving fast and her eyes drawing shut.

"Let me see you, Rora."

Immediately, her chameleon gaze clashed against mine just as I pushed my thick head inside of her, her lips parting wide open as she threw her head back, breathing hard. "Hells."

I kissed her barred neck. "I've waited so long for this," I said as I filled her up entirely, my hips flush against hers. She felt like nothing I'd ever felt before. "My pretty bird, you feel so good, your cunt feels so good."

Her arms went around my shoulders when I started moving, fingers digging into my back with each thrust. "Oh, gods."

"They can't help you, I'm afraid. No one can," I said, bracing a hand on the headboard and fucking her how I've wanted to fuck her since that first day. There would be time for me to learn her body, to taste every inch of her. Today I just needed to feel her around me, fill her up with my come and claim her body as mine.

Her lips parted with a moan as I pound into her like a madman, relishing in the way she felt around my cock. Watching her perfect tits bounce with each thrust, their little perfect nipples hard and swollen.

The bed groaned with each thrust, her sweet little moans and whimpers grew even louder.

"Fuck, I'm so close, Thora."

"Yes," she breathed, tying her legs around my hips. "Come inside me."

This girl.

A drunken smile stretched on her face, but only for a moment because her lips parted with a moan, and I felt her perfect little cunt tighten around me, getting wetter with each thrust. "Oh, Malik, hells," she cried out, her thighs quivering and tightening against my hips. Her hands pushed at my chest, nails digging in my skin. "Shit. Gods."

Not long after her, I was a goner, too. My cock deep inside her as I came with a groan, filling her up.

I rolled off her before I'd suffocate her with my weight and she put a hand to her chest as if to calm her breathing down.

Her fingers slid down between her thighs, parting her swollen sex that was dripping with my come. "You fucked me," she said, awe and realisation in her breathless voice.

I grinned up at the ceiling, still panting as I said, "No take backs now. And as far as I remember, it was mutual. Friendly and mutual. *We* fucked." If anyone mentioned that word again, my cock was going to come alive and demand a redo. And I didn't want her to think I was some savage animal—not yet at least.

I'd barely taken three counts of air when she stood, wrapped a sheet around her and stiffly left towards the bathroom without even a glance at me. She left me there, spent and terribly confused.

Chasing after women or seeking their comfort after I got what I wanted was not something I did, but she was *my* woman and I wanted nothing more than to go down to my knees and beg for a sliver of her attention. I wanted her to hold me, pet my hair or whatever the fuck one did after the best fuck of their life.

Not bothering with a bath, she stood under the shower spray, head tilted up and her eyes closed.

"You wanted to get rid of me this soon after?"

She jerked, a hand flying to her chest. "I-I thought you needed a moment."

"Me? I needed a moment?" What fucking moment? The hells was she talking about?

She nodded, her eyes darting over my body, mostly my lower half, and then back up at my face, the redness of her cheeks spreading down to her neck and ears that her wet black hair couldn't cover at present since it was slicked back from the pouring shower.

"Why would I need a moment?"

"I don't know. Don't you?"

I drew closer to her and she blinked fast, squirming on the spot she stood. "You washed me off," I said, a bit lower than I intended and she shivered. "Do you know what that means?"

She shook her head.

"I'll have to do it again." Touching a hand to her cheek, I drew her closer, my nose nudging hers. "I'll have to fill you up with my come again."

"I see," she breathed in that small voice that shot blood south again.

It came out of nowhere. I laughed so hard she flinched.

"Why did you think I needed a moment?"

"I don't know. I don't usually stay after, and I try to take what I want before—"

"Before." *They come.* "You said try. Try to take what you want."

She blinked once. "I sometimes get bored before I do, so I don't, you know what." She quickly put a hand over my mouth, glaring at me. "Don't laugh. This is so embarrassing," she whispered.

I pulled her hand down. "That's sad, little bird. I wouldn't dare laugh. Did I bore you, too? Actually, don't answer that. You came all over my cock."

She went beet red. Why for I had no idea. "Malik."

"Fuck, where else do I need to fuck you to start calling me Mal."

"I like your name."

I wanted to know what else of mine she liked. "Do you mind this?" I asked, pulling onto her nipple until a squeak of a whimper left her lips.

"You don't have to be gentle with me. I know what you like. Celia talked."

My whole body froze. "Celia was a whore. Her job was to take me off the edge, not push me over to another."

Her mouth parted open, but no words came out for a while. "Isn't that what you want from me?"

"I want to stay on this edge and dangle over it until you decide to push me."

"I don't like that."

"Didn't sound like it."

"I want to be good for you."

"Sweetheart, you have no idea how good you were for me." Good? She was perfect. "Don't hold back on me."

"Do you want to be treated like a whore, Thora, is that it?"

"What if I want to?"

My silly little bird. "You can't. You're mine."

"Then treat me like I am yours."

A knock rasped at the door, and I dropped my head back. Some god was working hard against me. "Fuck off!"

"It is an emergency, Commander," one of my Eldritch soldiers called.

If it wasn't for the worry on her face, I wouldn't have given a single damn.

"Stay awake for me?" I asked. *For me, not because of nightmares, or the past, or whatever haunts your thoughts behind those vivid eyes, stay for me.* But I could not say that just yet. I couldn't say so many things, but I was hoping she'd know like she always did.

"I will wait for you," she said, lifting on her tiptoes and leaving a chaste kiss on my lips.

Despite how tempted I was to ruin every bit of innocence left in those touches, I wanted to take my time with her. I wanted to watch it all unfold before me. Slowly.

"Don't get dressed," I said, brushing a finger down her stomach, watching it rise and fall fast. "Wait for me like this."

31

PINK ROSES

THORA

I waited for him. And he did as he promised he would do. Several times. I'd barely slept for a full hour all night before he'd woken me and repeated it all over. Besides the filthy words he's whispered all over me, we'd barely spoken a word despite the eventful night. Then he'd been called away a second time, and had left me to deal with the aftermath of what we'd done all on my own.

Even though we'd not exchanged a single word after what we'd done, we'd not looked away from one another ever since we'd met this afternoon for the court meeting. Well, he'd not looked away from me and I was kind of forced to look back.

"Your hair is down today," Skadi murmured under her breath, flipping through the court paperwork handed by the lords and whatnot.

"I was in a rush." My eyes immediately returned to Mal, but his had dropped to my neck. When they returned back to mine, the corner of his lip lifted just slightly.

Skadi's hand on my forehead startled me. "Are you unwell? You've turned red."

"Just a fever."

"Didn't know you can catch that after being with a man. But what would I know? Never been with an Eldritch Commander before."

My head whipped to her like a lash, and she gave me a smirk and a little head shake.

The meeting ended shortly, and the room soon cleared, thanks to my many prayers. Even Skadi left to check on the sealines.

He didn't though.

Malik still sat across from me, tapping a finger on the table. "What's wrong?"

"Why do you think something is wrong?"

"Thora, look at me."

Was I not? "Yes?"

"Answer me."

"Why did you sit so far today? You never sit so far from me," I said, gesturing between us and his eyes fell on my agitated hand still moving back and forth between us.

"I sit beside you when Oryn is not here. He was today. I respect him."

I pointed to the chair on my left. "And this one."

"It has a bad leg and keeps creaking every time I move."

"You're my king—"

"That I am. Perhaps I should've just sat you in my lap." He grinned. "There you go again."

"What?"

He faded and leaned in to whisper in my ear, "Red like a little cherry. Don't go red unless I'm spanking your pretty little arse. I don't like others seeing you flushed. It's how you looked when you took my cock last night."

I covered my face with both hands, and he chuckled.

Kneeling beside me, he pulled my hands down. "If I knew you were going to stop looking at me, I wouldn't have touched you last night."

Opening my eyes, I looked at him. "I touched you first."

"Then what's wrong?"

"That's all I keep thinking about." What was the point in lying, and besides, what secret did I keep from him anymore?

His grin grew stupid and ridiculous. "You covered my claim," he said, touching the mark he'd left on my neck, his smile fading.

"I am a queen."

"I'm sure they all know their queen gets sucked and fucked."

"Malik!" I shrieked.

"Like a little whore even." He gripped my jaw. "Begging to be filled up."

I hid behind my hands again.

"This might just be my new favourite thing," he said, pulling them down.

"Torturing me?"

"Second favourite thing then."

"What's first?"

"Fucking you."

"I'd like to kiss you," I said more courtly than I'd intended.

"Yeah? I'd like to bend you over this table and make you scream again."

I squirmed in my seat, and he leaned forward, pressing a kiss to my mouth. Like always, they started so innocent and chaste, but always ended with his tongue on my mouth and him devouring me entirely, not even letting me breathe.

A hard knock landed on the door, but he didn't stop, and neither did I.

He pulled back to drop a few kisses on my face and then down my chest. "Maybe the fucker has come to apologize."

"Who?"

I gasped when he sucked on my skin and then gasped once more when I saw the new purple bruise he'd left right above my breast. "The one who owes you one."

Neo glanced between the two of us, and Mal's jaw ticked when his eyes raked over my dishevelled hair, swollen lip and the fresh mark that was now definitely visible.

"What?" Malik barked and Neo's expression darkened.

"Thought you finally returned from your hiding spot to actually help her."

"I am helping her. I'm a man capable of helping her in many ways."

He was.

Neo didn't think so. "How are you helping her dealing with the Isliners inching in Modr currently as we speak?"

"I'm not your daddy, Neo. If you need help, call for help. You have twelve of the men I raised and trained. Have things gone so downhill after you took over that those men are incapable of containing some elemental Aura?" A nerve twitched in his temple. "Ah, I forgot about your other activities."

"You should be out there. Aiding," Neo insisted.

"He is where I tell him to be," I said, standing. "Why are you not out there then, if it is so urgent?"

"I needed to speak with you."

"Why would you need to speak to my wife?"

"She's not your wife, Mal."

"Is she not?" He turned to me. "Are you not, sweetheart?"

"It doesn't matter to me what anyone else thinks you are to me or what I am to you, but me and you," I said to him quietly. "He is a friend, and he was yours too, if I remember correctly. He can speak to me."

"A friend, huh?"

"Yes."

"Am I your friend, too?"

I knew my cheeks and ears had heated, but I pushed my chin up and said, "A few kisses won't ruin our friendship, Malik."

His jaw twitched. "Yeah? And what will? I can try harder."

"And when you go," I choked out. "What then? Will you go back to being my friend, will you become a stranger again, or what?" Exhaling a calming breath, I stepped back. Not sure why I had just said what I did. "Never mind."

He pulled my chin up. "No. Me and you will talk about this after you have your little talk with your *friend* here," he said, brushing a hand down my cheek and leaving.

"What is it, Neo?"

"I want to apologise—"

"Accepted."

He stepped towards me and then very slowly stepped away again. "I thought me and you—" He sighed and rubbed a hand down his brow. "Perhaps not. But I want you to know that you meant and still mean a lot to me. When he leaves again, after he's had his fun with you, I will be here, I want you to know that. And I will be waiting for you. I will always wait for you."

What he said stung till my throat had swollen with frustration to the point I couldn't even spit back a single word at him.

The need to disappear inside my own thoughts grew intense. To vanish entirely. To not think of the unknown future. To wait until it got away and left me be.

But I couldn't. Not when he was still here.

He was in the middle of the training grounds, doing pull ups on a handstand, his upper half naked. Even under the thick tattoos, I could tell every muscle dent apart. He got to his feet, chest rising slowly despite the strain of the exercise.

"What are you doing?" I asked, throwing a frown all around the soldiers who had gathered around to watch him do just that. They all turned on their heels and vacated the space until my steps to him echoed from the emptiness.

He slowly raised a brow. "My body has to get used to the cold and the thicker air; it slows me."

"You didn't look slow to me," I said, swallowing as I raked a look over him.

He caught my hand and put it to his chest. "You want to touch me, touch me. You want to look at me, look at me."

"Do you want that?"

He leaned in my ear. "Why do you think I put on that little show?" His hand slid down my neck, fingers massaging my skin. "I want you to lead, I want you to command this. If you need a little prompt, I don't mind."

"Why do you want me to lead? Perhaps I want you to."

"Do you?"

"I don't know." I raised my eyes to him. "Don't."

"Don't what?"

"Don't think you made a mistake. Or that this was a bad idea."

"It is a bad idea, but it was no mistake, Thora."

Wringing an arm around his neck, I rose to my toes and sealed my lips to his. He froze for a moment and then his arms were around me, pulling me tightly to his body while he deepened our kiss. "I led," I said, panting.

"You did."

I let out a small squeal when he lifted me up in his arms., pulling my thighs around his little man waist. "Me and you need to have a conversation."

"About what?"

"About what you said before. Do I look like I'm leaving?"

"Not at the moment."

"Rora, do I look like I want to leave?" He stepped closer. "Did I look like I wanted to leave last night or this morning?"

"No."

"Ask me now. Ask me if I want to leave."

"This seems silly," I muttered to myself.

"Ask me."

Sighing, I looked up at him, "Do you want to leave?"

"No. The only one who can make me leave now is you." He touched my face. "Do you want me to?"

"Is that even a question?" Letting out a strangled breath, I said, "No. I don't want you to leave."

"Crescent heaven, you hesitated there, little bird."

I smacked his arm and his face twisted with feigned pain before he reached to hoist me up and over his head, holding me like a wooden plank.

He was a damn mountain bear. How the hell did he have this much strength?

"Who's a piglet now?" he asked, chuckling, and I stopped squealing, surrendering to him.

Lowering me a little, he kissed my lips. "You're going all quiet on me lately."

"There is a lot on my mind."

He put me down, arms banded around me as if I was going to run away from him. "I used to know everything that was in there."

"You still do. Besides, it's mostly you in there these days."

Grabbing a water bottle, he leaned back on the court fence. "Friendly thoughts, I hope."

"Thoughts of squeezing the life out of you."

He dropped his head back and smiled. "If you're going to get me hard, you're going to have to do something about it."

"Pig."

He launched in my direction, and I made a run for it.

Unsuccessfully, of course.

32

BLUE IRISES

THORA

Winter was only a week away from showing us its full blight, a week away from the solstice. Soon—Iskyla was going to make her biggest move soon, I could feel it. The weather was listless, and the skies were pale compared to other winters. There was a coat of aberrance that I couldn't exactly point out. Everything looked out of place. Down to every flake of snow that had settled on the last snow storm a few weeks ago.

Perhaps it was my connection to the land that was making me restless, that it was causing my state of alert. Or the fact that my magic had decided to play hide and seek with me all of the sudden, leaving me to the mercy of my physical training.

Elias joined me on the castle wall tower looking over the city expanse and just a little further outside as well, beyond where the old city walls had been.

A small group of Isliners awaited at the old entrance, by some of the wall ruins had been left as a reminder of the history our kingdom had gone through.

At my order, Elias had held back his soldiers from attacking, and from some point inside the city itself, Malik had held back his dead. I couldn't see him or where he was, but he must have known to retreat when the Isjordian soldiers had—maybe even before. He knew their intentions better than my guessing.

"Is this Iskyla's new strategy, send me some commoners to kill so I could be the bad guy?"

Elias shook his head. "I don't think Iskyla has sent them, and it's not just...some." He pointed his head further back where the snow mist had gathered just outside the city. "More accompanied them. Families. Elderly. Children. They've come to speak to you." He passed me a piece of paper. "From Mal."

I raised a brow at him. "He is Mal to you now?"

"He is to me whatever my queen thinks him to be," he said so officially, and then muttered between his teeth, "I'm glad he wasn't a dick to you."

"Yeah," I mumbled, a little embarrassed for some reason. Unfolding Malik's letter, I read the one word he's written and descended the tower steps, heading for the city.

Safe.

That was all he had written.

My dragon took shape before I'd stepped off the tower steps, and I jumped on its back.

A few gasps and murmurs sounded as the dragon landed only a few feet from the group of Isliners who'd shown up at my doorstep.

There were small children amongst the bunch, and I was considering how far would Iskyla go to take my throne before approaching them.

They seemed to hesitate, too. Looking back and forth the dragon and I as it began evaporating and turning back into snow.

An elderly man finally stepped forward, passing a greeting in old Yslot before saying, "We come to speak to you."

"Then speak."

"We ask that we be accepted in your lands," he said proudly and very nonchalantly, not even flinching or looking offended at my cold tone.

I blinked. "You're already in my lands."

"To remain."

Taken aback, I asked, "To remain? And your queen, your lands, your home?"

"Wherever there is winter, we are at home, and we follow no one person, only what our god guides us towards. We humans and Aura alike are merely his disciples." He threw a look over the city behind me. "However," he continued. "You do not seem to be a disciple."

"Then what am I?"

"We have no name for what you are. We have no explanation for what we saw when you came to the Islines. We have no reasoning behind why the land and the creatures would react to you the way they did. But we have faith, we listen to nature, and we recognise its affinity to you. And if winter is your kin, we have no choice but to follow you. It is what our god wants."

This seemed like the perfect trap. "Are you saying you're abandoning Iskyla because your god told you so?"

"We are only abandoning a human being. One who seems to be led astray by her own strayed beliefs. We reasoned with her, and she would not reason back with us, so we left. Thankfully, pride is an easy thing to repair."

"To remain in these lands would mean to remain under my rule. Are you ready to bow to my pride?"

"We do what the land does. And the land bowed to you as we all saw it. We will, too. And more will soon follow once the word reaches the rest of the clans."

"This seems—"

"Simple?"

"Strange."

He grunted. "You're the first of your kind, so I'd think it would be."

"First of my kind?"

"Winter has bowed to you. Winter bows before no one."

"What if you are wrong in your assumptions?"

"We are not," he confidently said. "But even if we were to be, it would not matter. It is clear even to the blindest mind that what you are is beyond what any of us can comprehend. Iskyla twisted much of our perception, but that day we say you was when her lies became undone. We didn't know you, what you are, how you rule or what you rule. We knew of you from what was told to us. Though we are firm in our ways, we've always found it in our cold hearts to at least consider change might be good for us."

A familiar face caught my eye by the old wall ruins. Karl leaned against a massive rock, listening in. Unlike very few were aware, Karl had also once been under a barbarian queen's rule. Skadi's. When he gave me a nod of approval, I managed to let out a strange sigh of relief.

"Then remain. But I wouldn't think of betraying my kindness." I said, feeling the one presence I trusted more than my own join in. "I do not believe in killing the bait, but I know someone who does."

They all shifted and bowed their heads to Malik who materialised from nothing.

I heard a prayer murmured and then another few as he made it to my side. Guess they had all either seen or heard of their dead kind walking back to their homes. And they had been right to assume it was Malik who had given the order.

The Tenebrose Academy students flocked around me, watching as the Isliners began settling in the temporary tents at the edge of Tenebrose city, by the remains of the old wall. They'd escaped their lessons with the excuse of learning more about Isean history from the barbarians themselves. Somehow, their poor elderly professor had bought it and they had dragged the sweet gentleman down here with them.

A woman who looked no older than I was came out of one of the tents, holding a young child in her arms with the same white colour of locks as his mother. She stopped when she saw me and then she gestured in holy greeting as she made in my direction.

I laughed a little when a few of the students came to stand in front of me, between the woman and me. "It is fine. The child doesn't grow tentacles and three heads to swallow me whole. Yet, I think," I whispered at them, and they all gave me some unamused glances.

Reluctantly, they backed away, but stayed close.

Reaching in her fury jacket between the child she'd tied to her front, she brought out a piece of round wood with a burnt engraving on top. The head of a wolf. "Each clan carries one," she shyly began, "We call them *makaôl*."

"A talisman," I said, taking it from her and studying the marking.

Nodding, she pulled one from her pocket, but instead of the wolf, hers had a deer engraved on it. "The three horned deer clan."

"And this?" I asked, lifting the talisman to her. "Who does it belong to?"

"You. The direwolf." She pointed her head to the students behind me. "Your clan is growing."

"My clan is my kingdom."

"Your clan is who you'd trust as family. Who you'd trust with your life. The rest are simply admirers, people who follow your rules, your guidance."

"I trust every single Isjordian with my life."

Her brows rose. "You would?"

"I do. In whoever hands it falls, it will be theirs to decide to do what they want with it. I swore to it when I wore this crown. These aren't just people who follow me. These are *my* people. Whether they like, dislike, hate or love me, loathe or admire me, every single life from the foot of the Islines to the fields of Arynth, they all are *my* people. My oath was sacred, it doesn't discriminate because of the free will we all have."

"What if they want you gone?"

"If they believe I've done something to deserve it, then I will do so."

"That simple?"

"That simple. My hands have claws. Everything I hold onto will bleed if I do. I have no desire or hunger for blood." I lifted the talisman up and nodded. "Thank you for the *makaôl*."

The students flocked around me again as the woman left, passing the talisman from hand to hand. I suppose it had turned into a history lesson after all. History might have just changed after dozens of centuries. Isliners were living in Isjordian land, accepting rule under an Isjordian queen.

"Do we trust them?" one asked.

"We do."

"Why?"

"Because they're just...people."

"They're Isliners."

I raised a brow and rubbed his head. "I wasn't sure that made them an entirely different species."

"But—"

"You were very little back then, but after the Guardians War, the rest of the realm distrusted every Isjordian the same as you are distrustful of them. We are still shunned by some. Are they right to do so?"

He rubbed his neck. "Maybe."

"Even you?"

"Not me. I didn't fight in the war."

"Not every Isjordian did, and many that did fight didn't wish to fight. However, they were all seen as the same." I pointed at the Isliners. "They didn't fight us, nor did they attack us, wish us harm or grief."

Their elderly professor waddled to us and sighed, cocking both of his shaking hands on his hips. "If only they would so intently listen to me as they listen to you. You should consider teaching a class or two, Your Majesty."

"I'm afraid mathematics makes me violently ill."

The students chuckled, agreeing with me.

"Off you go now," he ordered, and they all bowed to me before very grumpily heading back to the academy. The professor bowed, too. "You should consider what I said. They all look up to you. One day they will be your soldiers, your captains and generals, advisors or lords."

"If I am to rule for that long."

"I fear you are," he said, chuckling and waving as he followed after the kids.

My skin burned—it burned like it had burned that day twenty-three years ago. Someone had gripped my hair so tightly my scalp screamed as I was dragged through the black burning flames.

I screamed, hard until my voice was hoarse. Tears soaking my skin. But I didn't beg. Not this time. I remembered his words. And I called for him. I called for him over and over instead of begging.

Over and over.

Until everything blackened out.

My body sagged, relishing in relief.

It had been a long while since the last nightmare I'd had.

So long that panic had overthrown me more than the actual dream.

Panting, I cracked my eyes open to find him standing over me, his face twisted with worry and something else. He was breathing hard, chest almost bursting with each breath.

With a shaking hand, he pulled and hugged me to his chest.

"What is happening to me?" I panted, wiping a hand over my sweat-soaked neck.

"You called for me," he said, burrowing his face on my hair.

"I knew you'd find me."

"What are friends for?"

I chuckled, despite fear still making my limbs shake. "I'm going to kill you, Malik Castemont."

"Don't know who that is. I only know of Malik Krigborn. Crowned and wed to his loving friend."

"That was a silly thing to do."

"I'm a dedicated friend." He leaned in to kiss my ear and whisper, "I also want everything of yours. You see, I'm a little obsessed with my friend."

I was obsessed with him first.

Wrapping my arms around his neck, I rested my cheek on his shoulder. "Your friend might be going a little crazy."

"Nonsense. She already was crazy."

I laughed, pressing my face to his shirt that smelled so deliciously like him. My heart hurt—it hurt so much from holding back on telling him those cursed three words that started with the first pronoun and ended with the second.

He suddenly froze in my hold.

I froze too. Scared he somehow had found them out. Or maybe I'd spoken them out loud and not noticed.

Pulling back, I looked up at him and frowned.

Malik's gaze had trailed towards the window. He dropped a kiss on my brow and stood, pushing the window glass panes wide open. "What the fucking hells?"

"What is it?" I asked, rushing after him.

My feet came to a stop before I ever reached the window. Hundreds, no, thousands of animals were standing beneath. Not just any animal. Isline creatures. Of all sorts. All around.

"How did they get past the castle walls?"

"My dead cannot feel them, they've easily slipped through."

When I stepped forward, all of their heads rose up to where we were standing. "What do they want?"

"Not sure. I can't read something that has no soul. You think they will spare me if they know I'm friends with you?"

The intensity of the situation lessened and so did the panic in my chest as I chuckled and reached for him. Immediately, his arms banded around me again and I heaved a sigh of relief.

I'd never felt safer.

Maybe I'd scared them with my evil laugh, but the animals began backing away, either slipping past the gates in the castle walls or flying and climbing over it, disappearing away into the white landscape ahead.

"They are tied to you," he said. "Maybe they felt your distress."

"I've never seen them do that before?"

"Maybe because the part of you that could feel it was taken away. The connection between you and them was cut off. When Nia restored what was taken, it returned."

"Maybe."

"Don't freak out."

"How have you not?"

"Because it doesn't surprise me that nature adores you, too, my beautiful friend."

The silly man was never going to drop it. Tilting my head back, I looked up at him. "Maybe they have no choice."

"Do you know that spiders will cut off a weak, sick or injured limb? Starfish detach their limbs, too, for the same reasons. As do humans. I'm sure that if they had felt danger or rot from you, they would have detached themselves from you. But they haven't."

"What if they can't?"

"Nature would find a way."

"How do you know so many facts about spiders and starfish?"

"Rain told me all about them one night. Didn't let me sleep until I repeated it all back to her." He pressed his brow to mine. "Any success with magic?"

I shook my head. "I don't even know what's wrong. It just stopped obeying me. It's there, I can feel it, but it's like there is a brick wall in front of it now."

He sighed. "Maybe you should reconsider throwing the Solstice ball."

"Not this time. This is the perfect opportunity for Isliners to mingle with Isjordians."

"They will be forced to."

"Perfect plan. No?"

"You're evil," he crooned, kissing me. "So, so evil."

I tilted my head, studying Krig's statue before me. "This is your doing, isn't it?" I asked, my voice booming around the empty temple. "What the hells do you want from me?"

Balling a fistful of snow, I threw it right at it.

Skadi shook her head. "Out of everything, that somehow feels like the most disrespectful thing you've done in this holy place."

My eyes drew shut and I shook my head. "You know, Skadi, you know what is happening to me. Why won't you tell me what is happening to me?"

"Are you in the habit of speaking to what cannot answer you?" a chilling voice whispered in my ear, and I jerked forward.

The tall, blue haired man chuckled as he studied the temple space. Dressed lavishly in more blue and white, he crossed his hands behind his back and circled me. "You are one fabulous creation of nature, Thora. That nature being I, of course. Every holy entity insisted that Nubil and I interfere when one of my blessed decided to play God and mess with the rules creatures older than any god put to preserve life."

Was I hallucinating now? After a little glimpse between the statue and him, I asked, "Then why did you not?" Well, now I was talking to the hallucination. I normally never entertained my hallucinations with conversation, though.

"Because life was already dying in this and many realms. And chaos is at the centre of life and death. Your existence would be pure untameable chaos. We took a bet and wildly...hoped, as you humans would say. You would either destroy this and many other worlds, or you'd save them. We played the game of odds." He circled me, pointing at me. "Look at this. Clearly, I am favoured."

My hallucination was aggravatingly accurate. "A game, that is all of this is to you?"

The odd god tilted his head up to the skies and shut his vivid blue eyes. "On the contrary. This was a war. And I am the God of War."

"Does that make me and my siblings martyrs?"

"No war I've led has ever had such things as sacrifices. You either die a loser or live as a winner. There is no sacrifice in war, only those willing to fight." Looking back at me, he opened his eyes. "I was willing to fight."

"For your pride."

"For this realm."

"So desperate for prayers?"

"Desperate to not see loss. The God of War might I be, but I've lost, too. More than most. Beneath the snow you tread on, I've buried the heart of the one loss I will never forget."

"Touching," Malik's voice boomed around the temple. "Very touching."

Krig opened his arms like he was welcoming an old friend. "Ah, Malik, join us."

Unlike every other time, there was not an ounce of playfulness in Malik's eyes as he made his way to me. "How godly of you to just send a shadow down here."

I blinked.

He could see him?

It wasn't a hallucination.

Krig shrugged an easy shoulder. "I'm not meant to meddle, aren't I?"

"Then why are you?"

"Believe me, if this was me meddling, you would know." After our silence, he glanced at where Malik was holding me, at his hand laced with mine. "It's fascinating how chaos manages to find itself all glued back together in some shape or form. Life and death, hand in hand. Utterly terrifying, but stunning nonetheless."

"What do you want?" I asked.

"No one can give me back what I want. But I can give you what you want."

"Why would you do that?"

"Because it would mean keeping the memory of the woman I loved alive. When the land began to die under your father's rule, everything began dying with it. No prayer to me would have brought it back. No matter the faith Isjordians would cultivate. No matter how powerful I am. Winter became something one thrives in when it has a heart. Without a heart, ice is just ice. Prayer and power cannot revive something once it has died. But when you shared your power with the land, not only did the land began healing, but—"

"The heartbeat that I hear. Is that why I hear it?"

His smile was filled with tears. "Is my darling's heart strong?"

"Yes," I whispered, feeling my own heart sink at his bittersweet sadness.

The cold god nodded, looking around as if trying to feel for it. The look of pure grief on his face told me that he couldn't. "To keep alive the earth where winter falls, someone has to feed it life. Now, you're this land's beating heart. Without it, it will die again."

"It will not, my brother and sister—"

"No golden eyes," he interrupted me. "You and your brother do not have them. Your brother because he is the swift summer breeze, and you...you because you're soft autumn rain. There was already a hearth of warmth inside you, Thora. Untouched by the cruelties you endured. Untainted by the attempts made by those who wished to taint it. It's resilient—your heart—it's resilient to change. You never let anyone change it," he said, glancing at Malik and smirking before continuing, "Your sister might be more like me then she will ever be like the idiot she agreed to aid," he said, and a crack of lightning flashed over the grey skies. Krig chuckled, shaking his head. "But the hearth inside her is made of blistering frost. The coldest. The cruellest. The strongest. Unbalanced, and she would become the ruination of all. Lucky for this realm, her lover loves her eyes and the blistering frost behind. Perfect chaos, as one would call it. But you—you didn't need that reminder. Not until someone tried to take a part of your heart. For which I am sorry. I know very well how it feels."

"What is it that you want me to do?"

"What is it that you want to do, Thora? This land is now an extension of yours. A piece of you. Attached like an organ. I've got plenty more euphemisms, but I think you caught the gist."

"Detach it," Malik snipped.

Krig's brows flew up. "Detach it?"

"Sever. Separate. Disjoin. Do I need to go on?"

I wrapped my hand around his arm. "Malik—"

"I'm fucking tired of you three being tossed around like some godly game of ball. He wants to save this land, he can save it himself."

Krig shook his head. "It isn't a matter of just saving the land. The land is you, and you are the land. If one suffers, both will. If one dies, both will."

"What about my magic?"

He tapped a finger right over his heart. "Right where it has always been. It will never leave you for your heart is an infinite portal of it. As I said, you're the pure essence of chaos. Brilliant chaos. Almost if I'd melded you myself. Whatever restraint you find in your magic, you've put it there yourself."

"I don't know how."

"Then go back in time, find out how and what you put before that gate to stop it." He stepped back, his body beginning to fade. "Find what you want to do, Thora. Decide. Then let me know, too. If I should mourn my darling heart one more time."

33

WHITE SNOW FLOWERS

MALIK

She was strangely less anxious than I thought she would be. Dressed in an elegant white dress that came tight to her body and then flared at the bottom, she stood at the centre of the solstice celebrations, greeting Isjordians and the newest addition to her kingdom—Isliners. Her spine straight, her manners gentle and polite unlike how I remembered them to be ten years ago.

I hid a smile behind a glass of cold tea as I remembered the nineteen-year-old who ran her mouth saying whatever she felt like saying. Passing her judgement back then was a hard feat, now she looked like she was beyond judging others—utter bullshit. She'd perfected her role entirely.

Pushing from the far wall where I'd been hiding and watching her for the past five minutes, I cut through the thick crowd to her. I would have stood where I was, watching her, but some Isliner fool had been flirting with her for longer than my temper could hold.

A little gasp slipped past her parted lips when I slid my hand over her lower back and stood beside her. "Welcome," I said. "It was very nice of you to join my wife's and I's celebrations."

"A pleasure," he said. "Though, we aren't used to the grandness of it all."

"But you're definitely used to flirting with other people's wives," I muttered in Adriatian, and Thora's eyes went wide for a second.

"We like to exaggerate," Thora politely said, throwing me a hard side glare.

"Because we can," I added. "Isjord is a grand kingdom. It is used to grandness. Right, sweetheart?"

Her smile was uneasy. "An old tradition. I'd like it if it were more toned down, but these days people don't get much reason to celebrate, so I think we all deserve one day a year to remind ourselves of our greatness." Thora cleared her throat. "Hope it is a tradition we can share with you and the rest of your people."

"They will come around," he said to her in old Ysolt. "Once word of what we saw that day spreads, they will know who to follow. Like my clan did."

She nodded and watched him leave into the crown before she turned to give me a bewildered look. "He was being nice, and you were being so rude."

"Good thing you didn't marry me for my politeness." I leaned down and kissed her rosy painted lips. "And from what I remember, you like me when I'm rude to you. Your cunt melts around my tongue."

She shivered and took the smallest step to me, as if she couldn't help herself. Unluckily for me, she slipped off that trance state too quickly. "Your brother is watching us." Her eyes then narrowed on something behind me. "Why is the Fire Queen standing beside him?"

With a sigh, I glanced over to them. Alyone nodded and then left his side, disappearing into the white crowd. My brother had tilted his head back, raising a brow as he looked between Thora and me.

What? I mouthed.

He pointed behind me, at another Isliner fool who had gotten my bird to laugh and blush.

Thora threw me a warning look when I made to approach again, so I had no choice but to back away into my corner again, watching her.

More Isliners had joined us this past week, and from what they said, more were to come. I had no clue who I should keep an eye on more. Her. Isliners. Or Isjordians who'd become agitated at the news of their long-lost kin finally reuniting.

Against all the stark whiteness, I could spy a little ball of black. Fading to her, I picked her up and threw her in the air a couple times. "Don't you wear any other colour, baby doll?" I asked, fading us back to my hiding spot and sitting her on my knee.

"I sometimes wear grey."

"When is that?"

"When I'm really happy."

"Are you just mildly happy right now?"

She glanced around the room and scrunched her nose. "I think so. It's past my bedtime, but Sam said it would make my aunt happy if we stayed." Her small mouth opened in one impossibly large yawn. "Don't the adults like you? Why are you hiding here with me?"

"Am I annoying you, princess?"

"Yes, but that's okay. Guess some people are *amisocial*."

The little night terror. "You mean anti-social."

"Or *indoorverted*."

"Introverted, baby doll." I tapped her small button nose. "Those are some big words for you."

"Sam uses them."

"Yeah, Sam isn't like the rest of us. Bet it's tough to measure up to a big brother like that." It was for me. Kil was exactly the same. He was perfect in everything he did. I was always less than. Somehow, I had never minded. Our father had, though.

She shrugged. "He's a good big brother."

So was mine.

A pair of soft steps made their way to us. Alyone bowed her head at Rain. "Could I have a moment with your uncle, princess?"

Turning to me, Rain whispered, "Can she?"

"She can," I said, and Rain gave me a kiss on the cheek before grabbing her doll and walking away inside the celebrations, heading to hug her father's leg.

"Might we go somewhere private to discuss some matters? I can barely hear anything over the crowd."

Glancing at where my bird had been flocked by some new peacock, I nodded, leading her down the corridor. "What matters?"

"A preposition," she said. "One I've not dared make before." She shook her head. "But I don't think I could stand it anymore. Especially after seeing you with her."

"What preposition, Alyone?"

"For you to be my king."

I frowned. Was this some joke? "I am already someone's king."

She laughed a little uncomfortably. "When you're done with whatever deal you've struck with the Winter Queen, of course."

"I've struck no deal with her."

"You've rarely told me untrue words before," she said, somewhat disappointed. "Your friend, Neo, he came to me with them. Confessed that you'd come to some agreement with her. One that would soon end when she comes to defeat Iskyla."

"Alyone," I carefully said, half planning on how to murder Neo the most painful way there was. "Remember that one first night when you found me in the Heyes city ruins?" Drunk. Miserable. Calling for the woman of my heart loud enough that I'd woken the silent gods of Seraphim.

"I do."

"Do you remember me telling you that my heart was ripping apart because of this girl. That I'd have to find a way to kill my own heart if I had to continue breathing. Do you remember me telling you that I missed her like the deserts miss rain, so painfully it burns from the inside."

"Yes," she said, reaching to touch my arm. "But I also remember you being drunk."

My hand wrapped around her wrist. "If I had been any more drunk, I would have also confessed more. I would have confessed that I was going to take the hurt and the pain and the memories, I was going to stand them all just so I could be with her. I couldn't be with her how I was. I had to become worse to become better for her. And I did. I didn't leave a stone unturned in that realm, for five years, Alyone, I thought I was going to go insane if I didn't see her again."

More shadows joined around us, and I looked up at her.

Thora stood at the end of the corridor, blinking slowly between where Alyone had put her hand on me to where my hand had wrapped around her. She drew a polite smile for Alyone. "Lost?"

The Fire Queen cleared her throat, and I saw Thora clench her jaw, readying for the answer. "Actually—"

"Lost or not? It's a yes or no question."

"Not."

Thora nodded, and her smile turned sickeningly sweet as she turned to leave.

"I believe we are done here," I said, pushing Alyone's hand off me, and following after Thora. "Hey."

She heard me but didn't stop nor acknowledge me.

I faded in front of her, but she sidestepped me, and I decided then I'd let it go long enough. Hooking my arm around her waist, I lifted her up and put her on top of a table, pushing the decorative vase to the ground and letting it splinter to pieces. I pinched her chin and turned her face to me even though she refused to meet my eyes. She was too calm, meaning she was about to lock herself away from me, so I went straight to the point. "I've never touched her, never wanted to and never will. Look at me." She didn't. "When I left ten years ago, we had to work together and at some point she began to show interest in me, but I had told her everything about you. I've never hid it from anyone, Thora. You can ask her. You can ask the whole of Heyes. I swear I've spoken your name to every rock and tree." I rested my brow on hers. "I swear the wind still speaks your name for how much I've tortured it by calling your name."

Her eyes glassed over, like morning dew on croton leaves. "You just hid it from me."

"Frankly, I'm not a fan of that tone."

She pulled back. "You're unbearable."

"Drop the attitude and just hit me."

"You'd probably like that."

"Are you shaming my preferences?"

"No. I just don't want to please you at this moment as much as I want to rip your head clean off your shoulders."

"You're getting better at flirting with me, little bird."

She rolled her eyes. "Ugh."

"I know a few other sounds I could pull out of you," I said, sucking her lower lip in my mouth. "They are usually followed by some hair pulling, nail digging, skin scratching. And end with you coming all over my cock. How about some of that?" I asked, peppering her mouth with kisses until she turned into putty in my hands. "Let me sweep you away, I'm sick and tired of all the men looking at you."

"What did the Seraphim Queen want?"

"To know of my return to Heyes."

"And what did you tell her?"

"That I will leave your side only if you want me to leave." I'd tell her this over and over and over. I'd tell her this every day until she was convinced of my words.

"Is that what you really want?"

No. I never wanted to leave. Even when she would ask me to. "I'm at your mercy."

"I want you to be free to choose. I don't want you to be at anyone's mercy. Never again, Malik."

I was no longer a free man. "I want to be at your mercy. I want to be yours."

"You are mine."

I needed her to tell me that again and again. In every language she knew. "Remember it before you get jealous next time," I said, dropping my head on her shoulder. "We aren't a secret anymore, why are we being so careful with this? I wanted to pull you in my arms all night, hold you all night, keep every prying and leering eye off you, I wanted to tattoo my name across your chest, mark you as mine in every way there is."

"You'd want that?"

"I want *everything*."

Someone sighed from the end of the corridor. "This is public space as far as I was aware," Elias said, passing us on his way to the celebration hall.

"You're seeing this?" she asked him.

"Unfortunately," he boredly replied.

"See," she whispered in my ear, kissing her way down my neck. "Not a secret anymore."

"Uncle," a tired little voice called, and we both pulled away from one another. Rain yawned again and again, unable to speak for a while. "I'm sorry, auntie, but I want to go to bed. Will you put me to bed?"

Thora jumped from the table and went to pick up our niece. "Want to sleep in my bed tonight?"

My eye twitched. Would I need to fight off a five-year-old now? "Rora, sweetheart—"

"Yes," the little night terror replied. "I love your bed. Will you put the fluffies on, too?"

"I'll put on the fluffies," Thora agreed, grinning at her.

"The hells are *fluffies*?" I asked, following after her to our bedroom.

"Her dolls. She has a stack in my wardrobe for when she sleeps over. Won't ever go to sleep without them."

I paused.

A chill went down my spine.

Her dolls had been in her wardrobe all this time?

Thora glanced at me over her shoulder. "Should we tell them we've left? We're the hosts after all."

"Let Elias deal with them." Picking up Rain from her arms, I leaned it to whisper in her ear, "Why are you so cruel to me?"

"How could I say no to her little face?"

"How could you say no to my face?"

"She's cuter."

"Low blow," I said, pulling our bedroom door open for her.

Thora went inside her wardrobe room as I took Rain to wash her face and teeth. The little terror even had her own toothbrush there. Was it going to be a frequent thing?

Thora came out with some night clothes and a stack of Rain's terrifying dolls as I took off her shoes.

It looked like Thora had done it often because she expertly changed Rain into her pyjamas and had her tucked and surrounded by her creepy, button eyed dolls in a matter of minutes.

"I'm sleeping on the sofa" I said, taking a seat on the bed by her and leaning in to brush my lips on her cheek.

"There is enough space for the three of us."

"Me and those dolls aren't ever going to be sleeping on the same bed."

She touched my face, her thumb brushing my lips. "I'll keep you safe." Leaning in, she kissed me. "I'll never let the evil dolls hurt you, my precious king."

Rain giggled, ducking her face behind one of her ugly dolls to hide the embarrassment we'd just put her through.

"Your aunt is being mean to me."

She shrugged a little shoulder. "Boys deserve it."

"Rain Helenia Castemont," I said, wide eyes on her and her aunt who was in hysterics, laughing her cute arse off.

Thora squealed when I picked her up and threw her over my shoulder. "Let's put your pyjamas on, too."

"You animal."

"You didn't seem to mine this animal last night or this morning." Her dress was off her body in two seconds. Thankfully, it took me two seconds to put her nightgown on. When I spun her to face me, she had the biggest smile on. "Funny, huh?"

"I'm happy."

"I'm miserable."

"You make me happy. Do I make you miserable?"

She made me feel everything. A myriad of colours. Some which I'd been so terrified of ever feeling.

"Taking you a while to answer there, mister fox," she said, playing with my shirt's buttons.

"It has been a secret for so long that I am afraid to say it out loud."

Stepping even closer, she got to her tiptoes and lifted her ear to me, waiting for me to say it.

My lips brushed her ear as I whispered low, "You make me so happy, Thora Isa Krigborn."

34

ORANGE ALSTROEMERIAS

THORA

There was something wrong with my magic despite all my effort to restore my previous control to it. Though part of it had managed to come through, it felt all over the place. I felt all over the place.

Pulling back on the white hood, I looked around at the quiet village that had just been attacked again a second night in a row, searching for the one Isline soldier who'd managed to escape my attention while I had dealt with the rest.

"You should've been done by now," Elias hissed, running to me and looking back at the approaching Isjordian soldiers.

"I missed one."

He blinked. "You...missed one?"

Frantically, I nodded. "What do I do?"

"Did they see you?"

"I don't think so."

He sighed. "Go. I'll deal with it. They can't have gone far in this snow by foot alone."

Gathering the ends of my snow-soaked cloak, I headed for the forest by the village where my ice dragon awaited.

Something broke through the wind through the trees and I leaned back, avoiding the dagger thrown at me by a hair.

I scrunched my nose and sighed, thankful for it still being there. Once I counted all my other limbs, I felt for the warmth of blood hiding around the cold forest, listening for its flow until my senses could pick up on its vibrations. Just before I tried to squeeze every drop of my magic and reach to grasp control of them, another dagger flew my way the opposite of where they were hiding.

I felt its sting before I saw it come for me.

There were two—I'd missed two of them.

The hells was wrong with me.

The dagger had cut through the thick white robe and grazed my forearm. It didn't take long for the cloak fabric to turn red from the blood. Which would mean the both of them would know that I was human enough to bleed.

Before I could turn them both into living breathing puppets, Malik faded before me, his attention around the forest.

Like they had been called upon, both Isline soldiers walked themselves out of hiding, frozen stiff under Malik's command. Their heads twisted at an odd angle until they cracked, and their bodies thudded to the ground—dead.

"How did you know where I was?" I asked, putting a hand to my heart, thankful.

"Never take the damn necklace off."

"Oh," I said, reaching to touch the yellow stone and wincing when the wound on my arm rubbed against the cloak.

He pulled my cloak off in one move, reaching to inspect my arm. "Damn it, Rora. Told you I'd deal with them."

"No, they have to know the White Veil is still around. Do you think anyone else saw me?"

"Do you think I care about it when you're bleeding?" Malik lifted me up in his arms and faded us to Tenebrose.

"I hurt my arm, my legs work just fine," I said, wiggling them.

"I'll fix that too in a moment, don't worry."

I couldn't help but chuckle.

He looked down at me, his brown eyes dancing and glazing with amusement. "I'm funny, aren't I?"

I nodded.

"Give me your words, Thora. You know I love it when you stroke my ego. Among other things."

"You're a funny guy, Mal."

"Mal, huh?"

I'd practised. Couldn't count how many times I'd said his name to myself this morning alone. "I know so many ways to ruin you, I might as well call you Mal, right?"

He stopped in the middle of the corridor and looked down at me, his brows slowly pulling together the more he looked at me.

Had I said something wrong?

Then he lowered his lips to mine and kissed me. Tenderly at first. In the midst of it, the kiss turned burning, scorching, painful.

He was going to leave me again. And this would all be but a memory.

The realisation hit me so suddenly that I shuddered.

"One way, not many," he said. "I've grown past the rest of the stuff I've told you, they can't hurt me anymore. But there is one."

"Which?"

"Don't figure it out, I'm not ready to be ruined just yet."

"Alright," I said, running my hand through his hair. "I'll spare you."

"You're so kind to me, my liege." He chased more kisses up to my face. "Don't go around getting hurt, Thora."

"If you promise me the same."

He sighed. "You're a menace, you know that?"

"Funny word used to say incredible, amazing, blinding, beautiful, spectacular."

"Mhm," he hummed, resuming our journey to my room—ours.

Once he put me on the bed and got my heavy cloak off, he went to the bathroom and returned with a wet cloth, washing the blood off the cut on my forearm. "What?" he asked, concentrating on applying a burning salve to the shallow cut.

"Why do you think I have something to say?"

He glanced up at me briefly before resuming to treat the cut like I'd been injured beyond hope. "You don't?"

"Hurry."

His hands stopped wrapping the bandage and he glanced up at me again, raising a brow. "Hurry?"

I nodded and took his hand to put it between my legs. "I want your hands somewhere else."

"You're creating a monster, do you know that?"

"Is he mine? Do I get him on a leash?" I asked, inching closer to him. "And make him do whatever I want him to do?"

He traced kisses over my jaw before claiming my lips. "Don't know about the leash part."

I wrapped both my hands around his neck, and he groaned in my mouth. "What about one with my name on it," I said, trailing my fingers down his collarbone. "Thora's."

He climbed on top of my body within a second, pressing a knee to my core while he wrapped the rest of the bandage around my arm.

"What about my injury?" I asked, grinding myself against his leg.

"You'll live," he said, pulling his shirt over his head and throwing off.

I put a foot on his stomach, keeping him there so I could look at him a little longer. "Pull your hair down for me."

"If you put your damn bows in it, I'm going to lose this hard on."

"Lies," I crooned, grinning.

He shuddered when I slowly moved my foot further up his chiselled chest, his carved stomach falling and rising a little faster. Grabbing onto my ankle to keep me still, he chased kisses up my calf until he was lowering himself between my thighs, his scruff tickling my skin until I burst into giggles. But they soon died off when he nuzzled his face between my legs and began pulling my underwear down. "Look at needy little cunt weeping for me," he said, lifting his eyes up to mine as he put his mouth on me, licking his way up to my core and wrapping his mouth there to suck until my back was bowed off the bed. "I see I've not satisfied my friend enough this morning."

This *friend* had to run away from him this morning because he was a hungry animal, and my body could only take so much. "You're a damned idiot," I panted, my fingers dove through his hair, holding onto him as my hips rode his bloody sinful mouth and tongue.

He threw my legs over his shoulders, his large hands wrapping around my thighs to keep them parted as his tongue, mouth and teeth worked on me. "Have I told you how much I love when this cunt is on my face?"

"Mal. Mal," I chanted, gripping his hair. "Gods."

Those hungry amber eyes of his rose up to mine as he licked a finger and pushed it inside of me. "Keep quiet for me or my balls are going to burst, little bird."

I giggled. "Get them out then."

"Why? What do you want to do to them?"

So many things. "Whatever you want me to."

He rose over me, nipping at my lips as he undid his trousers. "And what do you want from me, sweetheart?"

"Thought that was obvious," I said, reaching between us to help him take his trousers off faster. "I want you to put your big cock in me and then I want you to fuck me with it until I come. Hard, preferably. Really hard."

"Filthy little bird. Your words always make my heart swell with joy," the idiot joked, pushing my thighs further apart so he could settle his humongous body between them.

"That thing is tiny so I'm glad."

I gasped when he started pushing himself inside me.

"Nothing *tiny* about me, Rora," he said between kisses as his thick cock entered me in one thrust.

I'd taken him many times already, but I don't think I'd ever get used to the feel and size of him. "Gods, you're so big," I panted, bracing my hands on his strong thighs as he shallowly started moving in and out of me.

He leaned down to kiss me. "You always take it so well." He thrust his tongue on my mouth, kissing me hard, just as hard as his hips started snapping against mine, making the sound of our bodies grow obscene.

There was nothing slow or steady with the way he fucked me. He never held back like most did, like I was this fragile soft thing that needed to be handled with gloves. It drove every nerve ending in my body insane.

"I need you deeper inside me," I told him between kisses. "Let me ride you."

"Then saddle up, sweetheart," he murmured over my mouth, and then flipped us over so I was straddling him. Holding onto my waist, he guided his cock inside of me again and pushed me down on it until my hips were flush against his and he was fully buried in me. He hissed. "Fuck."

"In a second," I whimpered against all my effort to keep my voice steady, bracing myself on his stomach to catch my breath. My whole body shook from the fullness.

Malik chuckled, pushing my hair out of my face to gather them at the back with one hand. "All good up there?"

"Yeah, the view is spectacular. But, man, it was a climb," I breathed, leaning back and rocking myself on his cock.

"Mhm, I bet," he crooned, his hands trailing down my shoulders, grazing my breast and then my stomach until they rested on my hips as I started to ride him just a little faster. "Fuck, look at that." He grinned as he watched where we joined, all so pleased with himself. "So eagerly bouncing on my cock."

I did so myself, watching his chest rise and fall faster, watching him struggle to keep himself silent. Then watching him lose that battle.

He groaned, grabbing my hips hard to keep me from moving. "Oh, fuck. Fuck, I'm going to come just watching your tight little cunt filled with my cock."

Leaning in to give him a little kiss, I said, "I can blindfold you."

"Too late, I already have the image of me balls deep inside you ingrained in my eyelids." His fingers dug through my hair, and he fisted the back, one hand holding me there and the arm banded around my waist as he thrusted from under me. "I could draw it with my eyes closed but I fear I'd do it a terrible injustice."

"You're a real pig."

"Really rich of you to say with all nine inches of me inside you."

I flushed. "Idiot."

He chuckled, sucking on my neck and palming my breasts until they moulded to his touch. "Mhm. Fuck my cock like you mean it, sweetheart," he groaned, and then reached to fist my hair again so he could pull me down for another kiss that took away what little breath there was left in my lungs. "That's it," he coaxed, meeting my pace with his own thrusts, the sounds of our fucking growing wetter. "Look how good you take it. Hells, you take it so well. Your cunt was made for me."

"I–I can't," I moaned, my body shaking and no longer feeling my own. He was going to break me one of these days.

"Time's up then," he said, rolling me under him again. He pushed up to his haunches and then braced his hands on top of my thighs so he could thrust in me hard enough to make the bed release some ugly whining noises. Then he looked down at me like some dark, tattooed god who owned every single one of my prayers. "I'm going to tattoo my name just above here," he said, spitting on his fingers and rubbing them on my sensitive core as he kept relentlessly fucking me.

My sight grew hazy, rapture pooling in my belly and making my body quiver. "Ah—Malik, I'm coming."

He didn't stop. Only pound inside me faster, more hurriedly, as a blinding wave a pleasure crashed and cascaded through my worn-out body.

Just as the spell of pleasure was about to faint, he pulled out from me and fisted his cock until his come spilled over my sex, covering my skin. "That," he breathed, pushing the thick head of his cock back inside my sore sex. "I could fucking paint that." Leaning in, he kissed me breathless again, slowly rocking his hips in shallow thrusts, prolonging my torture. "On a canvas. A massive one we could hang up on our bed."

"Pig."

"Mhm." He hugged me to his chest like it was the most normal thing for us to do. Not like we were two people who touched only at the end of the world. Or two people who had such a complicated relationship with touch. With him, it was the most mundane yet exhilarating thing I'd experienced.

He just hugged me. My heart on his. No words said. None were needed to say. We stood there for a while, him on top of me, braced on his arms so he wouldn't squish me, and I held onto his waist like I'd never held anything else before it.

I could have said it right then.

Right at that moment.

But I didn't. I'd fallen asleep.

I'd told him in my dreams instead.

That I loved him.

I threw my head back and laughed at the thousandth silly things Malik had spouted this morning alone. It was barely past dawn, barely even sunrise, yet none of us had the slightest desire to even get back to sleep so we'd asked for some food to snack on since we were both drained. Then we'd gossiped like two ladies at Rose Court. We'd badmouthed everyone from Adriata to Isjord. He knew everyone's secrets. But I was the only one who knew his.

He leaned back on his armchair, somewhat dressed if you considered the corner of a sheet he had thrown over his hips after I'd asked him to—begged almost. Did nothing to hide his huge appendage, but it certainly sort of kept my eyes off it.

Picking another grape, I threw it at his mouth, and he caught it like the professional he was, flashing me a proud grin as he chewed on it. "Come here," he said, patting his naked thigh. "This distance thing was a stupid idea."

"It was not," I said, wrapping the sheet tightly around my body and waddling to him. "I can't take it anymore."

He opened his arms wide a little too excitedly and it made me hesitate a little before curling up on his lap. "That sore?" he murmured, leaving little pecks on my lips.

"A little."

He wrapped a large arm around my neck and pulled my cheek for a kiss. "I'm sorry."

"Are you sorry about suffocating me, too?"

He chuckled, loosening his hold on me a little. "Terribly."

Resting my cheek on his shoulder, I threw an arm around his neck. "Then I forgive you."

"Rora," he said after a while.

"Yeah?"

I felt his chest under my palm raise just a little faster. "Let's start again."

"Start what again?"

"All of it. From the start. Let's do this properly. Let me make you mine properly."

Looking up at him, I said, "Are we not proper now?"

"I don't want to confess and kiss when one of us is bleeding. I want a do over."

"I liked the last one."

"You did?"

"A lot. Minus the ten years I've spent trying to loathe you, I don't want to do over any of it. I like how things were and are. I like that you were my best friend and that you still are. And most of all, I am yours. There is no other way. Will never be." I'd said too many words instead of just telling him that I loved him. I'd been ready to tell him that a long time ago, perhaps if I had been a bit more spiteful, I would have told him that night at the tavern when he pushed me away.

He put his brow to mine. "Are you still sure you're sore?"

"Are you still sure you want me?"

He searched my gaze as if he couldn't believe what I'd just asked. "There hasn't been a moment when it has been otherwise, Rora."

"If only I had known," I whispered, trying to hold back my treacherous tears. "Maybe my heart would have hurt a little less." Or more. I didn't know.

"Will you ever forgive me?"

"I'm going to try."

35

NAVY ACONITES

THORA

The attacks had gotten more frequent since more of Iskyla's old clans had made their way inside my lands, accepting me as their queen. What made me wonder was their severity. She sent less soldiers. Less trained ones, too. Which then made me think this was a tactic of hers to study me since she had no intentions of giving me a real challenge. The end was approaching, I could feel it. The end I had waited for so long. And I was finally so unready for it. Never had I been this unprepared. So weak.

Though my powers were hiding still, my people weren't. Somehow, their support had grown these past few days. Maybe it had been a blessing to lose my magic. Maybe it had been a sign.

But I missed them. Part of me had been taken. I no longer felt entirely whole.

Elias handed me a folded letter just as I stepped out of the meeting room to head for the Academy and see what mischief my students were up to. "His royal majesty wanted me to pass this to you."

"A letter?"

"Yeah, he doesn't strike me as the type to write love letters either."

A bit surprised to read what he couldn't tell in person, I unwrapped the paper fast. I shouldn't have.

Flinching upwards, I caught the letter from falling from my shocked fingers and then hugged it to my chest. "G-give me a moment?"

Elias scoffed. "Didn't think he made you that ecstatic with one sentence. Cause I'm fairly certain that is all he can write."

Malik was a military strategist. A fool, but a smart fool. A smart fool who I very much adored with all I had. I glared at Elias until he rounded the corridor and then I unfolded the most scandalous piece of paper I'd ever laid my eyes on. On top of it, it wrote:

Next time I catch you, we won't be this wasteful.
–Mal.

Then there I was. Drawn in charcoal, more naked than what the mirror showed me to be when I stood undressed before it. And like he'd told me last night—he'd drawn me just like that.

"He's lost his damn mind," I murmured to myself, securing the piece of paper inside my corset like I was some old cougar having received a message from a lover boy.

A portal cracked right before me, making me jump a few steps back. "Gods, no one knows how to knock in this gods damned castle."

Visha came out, bowed her head and said, "There is something you need to see."

No one knew to greet or exchange a polite word anymore either. "Where?"

She blinked a little more annoyed than before. "I cannot bring my work room to you."

No. No. Not Olympia. Not yet. "Is it important?" I asked, trying not to let my voice tremble like the rest of me was.

"Do you wish to know what is wrong with you and your magic?"

"Wrong? There is something wrong with me?"

Stepping sideways, she pointed to the portal. "After you."

Sweat crawled down my temple and I felt my dress suddenly sticking to my body. "V," I pleaded.

The witch's eyes somehow softened. Maybe not, maybe I imagined it because I needed that comfort. "There aren't any more bad memories there as they are here, Thora. You just want some place to blame and are doing Olympia that injustice. It's just somewhere something bad once happened. That is all. That beast will take shape only if you let it do so."

"Easy for you to say, you feed from your fears while mine feed on me." Swallowing the ball of dread down, I moved one shaky leg after the other and entered the portal to Olympia. The worst of it was, my mind had fogged over the reasons why I'd suddenly forbid myself from stepping in my sister's home, along with all Neo had done, too, it was just a mess of fear, panic and a dull ache in my chest, like a part of it was missing—like it had been ripped out of me. It just felt wrong, that was it. Terror would climb all of me. Inhibit every good memory of that place. And the fear of heights I'd long overtaken had suddenly returned as if it had never left at all.

My surroundings spun when I stepped into Visha's work room. I could hear my unpaced breaths, the thud my heart made each time it beat. I could feel my mind fog up as it always did, attempting to prevent me from remembering or reliving that moment that caused my utter terror.

"Here," Visha said, and I spun to her as if I'd just been struck.

Like a whip, the wind whipped against the open windows of her work room, as it had that day three years ago. It was just as sharp. Just as cutting.

A dull ache suddenly began deepening in my chest. One that beat at me to remember what I'd half forgotten. But that day was hazy. My mind had made it hazy. To protect me or deceive me, I didn't know.

"Thora," someone else called, putting a hand on my shoulder.

I flinched and backed away until my back met a wall.

Cai stood there, looking at me wide eyed and...guilty. "We shouldn't have done this!" he bellowed at Visha, looking at me with such repentance.

"Malik was right," Visha replied. "If he thinks Iskyla has figured out what happened to her that day in the Islines, then it won't be long until she uses it against Thora. Since she's trying her best to kill him first, it means that day is approaching. She already knows of her connection to the land since Malik caught her burning her own forests and animals with black fire—craft fire. I hope you do know what that means to the land, the air, the life around them. It is not past one Krigborn to want to kill the land to weaken the throne. One did it before her. Almost succeeded had his own daughter not stopped him."

"What?" I barely managed to murmur, my tongue feeling as heavy as the rest of my body. Iskyla—she'd done what? She knew I'd lost my magic? Tried to kill Malik?

I felt him before I saw him. Malik came inside Visha's work room, wearing the same expression as Cai was.

Guilt.

It was so raw and soft in his amber eyes that I grew even more terrified. What could he have done to me that merited that look?

Before he could step to me, Cai slid before him and gave him a shove. "You could have just told her instead of forcing her in here. Isn't that what your old man did? Throw you to the fucking waters to swim when you didn't know how to?"

"Shut up," Mal sneered, pushing him back.

"I'm taking her back," Cai said, reaching to grab me.

"Take your fucking hands off her."

Cai pulled away only to shout, "I made a damn promise to her brother!"

My feet couldn't hold me upright anymore, and my body slid against the wall until I was crouching down.

The two were at each other's throat, muttering words and threats I could no longer hear because of the noise in my ears, the old sounds and voices that had returned from that day.

A flash of the Isjordian military uniform caught my eye by the open doors. "Skadi?"

I got to my feet and followed after her, slipping past Cai and Mal.

"Hey, what are you doing here?" I called, quickly following after her. "Did Alaric call for you?"

Skadi stopped, keeping her back to me. "No, he didn't."

My mood soured. "Oh, so you must have come to see Visha. You haven't told me you've been ill again." I pointed behind me. "You passed her work room."

"I'm not ill anymore, Rora."

"You aren't?" I tried to smile, a little surprised. She'd been suffering with the effects of the turning soon after being *cured* for it. Skadi had been the first one to turn so Melanthe had not been as gentle with her as she'd been with the rest. My general had suffered and was still suffering more than anyone. But now she was suddenly telling me she didn't anymore. "That's good. That's great."

"But *you* are."

My attempt at a smile withered down. "I-I am not. I'm actually quite a healthy one," I added, forcing a grin on. "My magic will return. I'm sure. And if it doesn't, oh well, not much loss there since I was already suppressing most of it."

"Rora," Mal called, pacing fast in my direction, his steps swallowing the distance between us in a second. He pulled me to his chest, pressing his face on the crook of my neck and breathing in a sigh of relief. "Hey, sweetheart."

"Hey."

"Who were you talking to?"

I pulled back just a little to turn to Skadi. But she was gone. Frowning, I searched the wide corridors. "Skadi was here just a moment ago."

Oddly, Mal's eyes rounded in a way they had never done before. Full of beseech and torture. He raised a hand to my face, swiping a thumb back and forth my cheek until I melted onto his touch. "She was not, Rora."

I snorted. "Yes, she was. You just missed it. She's never liked you anyway, so she probably made a run for it."

"Rora—"

"Stop it," I snapped for some reason, immediately feeling guilty for doing so.

He pulled me to him again. "Thora, listen to me."

"Let's go find her. Alright? She can tell you all about it," I tried to joke as I pulled on his hand for him to follow me, but he was stuck in place.

I hated how his eyes softened at that moment, or how his touch on my cheek turned something more than intimate, or how gently he spoke to me as if he could break me when he'd always treated me as the most unbreakable thing he'd beheld, "Sweetheart, we can't speak to her."

"Why not?"

Something was wrong. Very wrong. Why was he looking at me like that?

Backing away from him, I walked towards the end of the corridor, towards where Skadi must have gone. The path led straight to the roof, and I had to stop a few times to catch my breath before powering through the next flight of stairs that took me to the tallest height I'd ever stood on. I'd forgotten how this fear felt the past ten years Neo had suppressed it.

Another one of my fears returned full force when I saw her standing right at the damn edge of the terrace, facing me.

"Skadi," I called, walking to her.

But for every step I took forward, she took one back. I stopped when she stood a foot or two from the edge of the terrace. "Skadi, please—"

I screamed when she pushed and threw herself off the ledge. My feet were heavy, but I ran to the edge with all I had. Tears and fear were spinning and blurring the surroundings. My hands were shaking when I held on to the edge, preparing myself to look at her below. "Skadi!"

But she was not there.

Had...had she escaped it?

"Where did she go?" I asked, wiping my tears away and turning to Mal. "Did you...did you catch her?"

He kneeled beside me and reached a hand out for me to take. "You trust me, right?" he asked. "At least for now?"

Frowning, I nodded and took his hand.

He faded us in the winter gardens. At the old apple tree in front of king Edric's old quarters. It felt familiar yet a creeping sensation filled my chest. Everything felt numb, tears were streaming down my face, and I didn't know why. This place was so familiar yet so unknown. It was like my mind had tried to erase it and failed, because something else remembered. Something embedded in my chest, and that had damned me with the same knowledge I'd tried to forget time and time again.

My heart.

My feet froze when we reached closer to the scaling trunk of the ancient apple tree.

Mal went and kneeled before the grey headstone sitting under its shade, pulling away at the overgrown weeds and the old flowers.

Skadi Krigborn, it read. *Queen. General. Mother.*

36

THE PAST

THORA

I t had been a tough past couple of weeks for Isjord since Iskyla started aiming her attention on someone else beside me since uncle Sigurd had passed away a couple years ago.

Her father's aunt had become her target.

Again—as I had found out.

Some time ago, Skadi had finally confessed over some heavy booze drinking that the one who'd told the Isline elders about her seeking the help of a Crafter to conceive had been none other than a teenage Iskyla, hell bound onto making her father king. Then, she'd also told me that Iskyla had been the one who'd guided my father's informants to her when she'd been overthrown and banished to live in a secluded home outside of the main villages in the Islines. Sigurd had often broken those rules and had visited her, only to find her home empty one random winter day.

I tapped Skadi's back as she retched blood and bile over a rose bush. It had started again—the sickness that she caught after what my father and Melanthe had done to her. It came and it went. Despite the fact that she no longer had the seedling or its dark magic, the dark craft had left marks behind. "Visha will find something else to take away the sickness left, I promise."

"It has been years, Rora. I'm not sure how long my body will hold." She stood and turned her half-withered gaze to me, so drowned, so defeated. "I'm old. I'm tired. I'm not sure it wants to hold anymore."

"It will hold," I said, giving her a smile. "It has to."

"Child—"

"You're not going to leave me, Skadi. It is an order from your queen." I shook my head, that selfish feeling growing heavier. "Suffer a while longer, please. Just a little longer. Visha will find something. I have the best healers and the whole of Eldmoor along with Nia looking for it. Please."

Despite the vanquish in her eyes, she nodded. "As you wish, my child."

It had been a lie.

They all had tried, but they'd found nothing.

The last attempt at it sat on Visha's worktable, dead. The girl had been young. Barely sixteen when she had joined my father's war and then forcibly turned. The dark magic had corroded firstly though her own blessing, rendering her without it and without the life sustenance it offered, and then it had gone to spread over her organs, one after the other. Because the magic was part otherworldly, there was very little one could use against it besides soothing its symptoms once it had gotten beyond the point of containment.

"Kid," Alaric sighed. "You've tried."

I could feel my heart drop and drop. "Not hard enough. My magic can heal the land, it surely can heal this, too."

"By breaking every law of nature there is," Visha agreed. "But we are not dealing with anything natural, Your Majesty. The only thing their disease will do is fight your magic, not fight itself like the land did. And the more it will absorb from it, the more the disease will feed and grow. Only to quicken the steps to death. Best we can do at this sort of stage is letting it slowly take its course. It's the least painful thing to do."

Skadi stood silent and still by a large window, looking at Taren city. She loved Taren. Taren had loved her back, too. The air in Olympia had always soothed her in nights where she'd retched her stomach almost to death or when her lungs had wished to seize breathing. The air, the nature and the people of Olympia had been more a cure than any potion she'd had. She often remained here. She would have done it more often, but she also liked being close to me. It soothed another aching part of her soul—that is what she had told me. A part of her soul that had ached long before she'd been a beast or a monster. Back when she'd just wanted to be a mother.

Skadi coughed and I pushed my chair back to hand her a handkerchief.

She turned to me at that moment. A trail of blood chasing down her eyes that looked like they'd accepted a long and tiring defeat. "This was all I could bear," she said. More blood poured down her pale face. "I hope you find it in yourself to forgive me someday. I hope you do, daughter."

One moment she was standing there, at the edge of the open window.

The next she was gone.

Right before my eyes.

My feet had stuck to the ground as everyone else rushed past me to the window, screaming and calling for her.

I couldn't move.

It had been too late even if I did move.

37

RED FOXGLOVES

Thora

Reaching to the headstone, I trailed a finger over the letters, tracing her name.

Gone.

She was gone.

All this time, she was never here.

Mal pulled me to his lap. "Rora."

The ache corroded at my chest. "Take it away. Take this one away, please."

His lips pressed to my temple. "I'm trying," he murmured, his whole body shaking. "I'm really trying. But it's not working, and I think I might have to use magic this time. I think I might have to use it this time, Rora, I don't know what else to do."

The whole world went quiet.

Even my ears stopped ringing.

There was no numbness, only heaviness weighting my mind and body, holding me earthbound as if they knew I desperately wanted to be elsewhere. "What?"

He didn't let me go even when I tried to push him back. Mal kept rocking us back and forth.

"Mal?"

"Just another minute. Please, just one more minute."

"What did you mean?" I asked, unsure if I even wanted to know.

"I've told you, little bird. You've never needed me. Not really."

"But...but...you've—" I'd felt it. That first day we met, on the castle terrace when he held me. Then outside the tavern when he'd touched my hair. And many more times I'd asked him to do it. I'd felt it. I'd felt him doing it. I'd no longer felt anguish, or terror, or hurt.

"Never. I've never touched any of it. Never taken any of it away. Only pretended to. It somehow worked."

I bitterly laughed, shaking. "It can't be. I've felt it."

"Whatever it was, it was not magic."

What?

No.

He'd lied to me?

He'd lied to me all this time?

I pushed at his chest, the air not seeming enough for my desperate lungs. "Let me go."

"One more moment. Just one more."

I pushed harder, and harder, my nails digging on his skin, scratching and making him bleed. I kicked and writhed, but he didn't let me go. "Why?" I panted, breathless. "Why did you lie to me? All this time, all this time you made me think that it made me better. That I needed it to make me better! You made me dependent on it! You made me feel like I wanted to die when you denied me it!"

"Forgive me."

He held all my secrets and I had thought I had held all of his. How...how had we told one another so, so many things, so many unsaid words and dark secrets, yet...yet we'd never confessed the simplest things? "Let me go, Malik. Let me go!" I screamed, wind blasting around us while the grounds grew thick with ice. "Why would you do this to me? Why?"

"Nothing I will tell you will justify it."

"I don't need you to justify anything, I need you to tell me the truth."

"You would leave me."

"You left me first!"

The moment his hold on me came loose, I crawled back, putting distance between us. Then I cried, like a fool, I cried. Because it didn't matter. It didn't matter at all. Truth was...truth was—what was the damn truth?

That it didn't matter, but that is actually should?

That whatever he'd done had been cure enough?

But maybe the truth was that he'd clung to me like every other poison he'd clung to. He'd clung to me because of some high it gave him. He didn't want me. He might have never wanted me. He'd gotten better and I was the last thing that stood between the old him and the new him. I was the last thing he depended on, the last thing he needed to move past so he could fully heal. Maybe he'd come back because of that. Because he couldn't clear me out of his system like he'd cleared everything else. I was his new poison.

Wiping a hand over my face, I steeled my spine to stand straight. "When were you going to tell me?"

"Every day."

"But you chose today."

"I did."

"Why?"

"Because last night I figured I can finally live without you talking to me forever. It doesn't matter if you never will, it won't change a damn thing."

Tears streamed down my face again when he said, "I love you too much for it to even matter. I'm in love with you, Thora, even if you never forgive me or love me back, I will always love you. Ten years ago I left because I had never made peace with the fact that I could love you while you could never love me back. Now I have. I've made my peace."

I should have been first.

I should have said it first.

I loved him first.

But maybe because of that, because I had loved him first, I would be the one to free him from what had been his cage all these years.

"I want you to go," I said, standing. "And I don't want you to come back this time." *Be a free man. An entirely free man.*

"Thora—"

"You owe me a promise. This—I want this. Go."

There was no emotion on his hardened face when he nodded and backed away. Lingering a bit before fading out of sight.

It was so empty.

My room was so empty.

Where he used to stand was empty.

My mind was so empty, too. Emptier than it had ever been. And ever so clear. I don't remember ever being so clear minded.

Even the mirror before me looked too...precise. Had it always been so sharp, so telling. How come I'd never noticed? Leaning forward until I was barely an inch from it, I stared at my new eyes. My pupils were now surrounded by a ring of gold that blended with the green.

The Krigborn gold.

To remind a Krigborn of the warmth of the sun despite their cold heart.

I knew exactly the moment my heart had turned cold—I had felt it. My own emotions had failed to recognise the cruelty I had wanted to inflict—the cruelty I'd already inflicted in the Islines, the same cruelty that almost became a proxy to the death of the man I loved.

It was the moment I'd felt entirely too numb. I'd almost missed my turbulent heart and my tempestuous mind.

It had been the moment I realised that all my fears had come true.

That I was my father's daughter.

That my magic was a curse.

I think I knew what door I'd shut in my heart. It was the same one I usually locked my mind behind when I wanted to shield away from the world. It was somewhere safe, somewhere no one could find, somewhere so tightly locked no one could ever get inside.

All but one.

He'd gotten behind it and saved my mind.

He'd tried to get behind it again to save my heart.

I had not allowed him.

Maybe it was for me to save myself this time.

I jumped at the soft knock on my door. Even though everything in me hoped it was him, I knew it was not him.

Snow stood at my doorstep, holding one child in each hand. "We come bearing gifts," she said, and Rain stepped forward, handing me a box of sweets and wrinkling her nose at them. Sam followed next with a bouquet of white roses.

How could I refuse that?

Rain ran past me and jumped on my bed while Sam stood there on the doorstep, staring at me, his eyes narrowed on me with confusion.

"You can just ask me, Sammy. I will tell you," I said, and my nephew's hard expression softened.

"You would?"

"You know how much I love you?"

"I do."

"I wouldn't hide anything from you by lying."

"You usually do."

"I don't have the strength to pretend or lie anymore."

"Who do you miss this much?"

"Your uncle Mal."

"Figured," he said, slipping inside the room.

Rain and Sam laid in my bed between Snow and I, huddled close to each other. "We don't mind sharing, auntie," my little niece said. "If you want our ma for a night or two, you can have her. Sam and I will be alright."

"You know she was mine before she was yours?" I asked, stroking Rain's soft hair away from her little face.

Both Sam and her turned on their sides to face me, intently concentrating on my words. They loved stories. They loved all the stories about her. Who could blame them, my sister was incredible. "She was?" they both asked.

I nodded. "She was. She got me dressed, she got me to eat, she did my hair, never let me miss a meal cause she wanted me to grow strong and big like you two, she stayed with me until I fell asleep, she rubbed my tummy when it ached, she blew on my scratches when I tripped or fell, she held me when I had nightmares. Eren said that she taught me to walk, too. You know that her name was my first word? *Snow* was my first word. Eren said that your grandmother used to insist I said it because I liked the snow outside or because I saw snow all the time, but I did like snow, I liked watching snow. Just not the snow outside, but my sister. So, she was mine first."

I looked to where she was laying, her eyes filled with tears. "Rora," she choked out, bringing a hand to my face.

Reaching over Sam and Rain, I hugged my sister tightly. "You don't have to do it anymore. You don't have to blow on my wounds anymore. I'm all grown now."

"You are, but you're still mine to look after. And I don't know, Rora, I don't know how to fix this. I'm sorry."

Cries welled on my throat, making it hard to breathe and speak. "Someone else does. He figured it out."

"Tell him to stay. He was miserable, Rora. He's always been miserable until you."

"I can't. He told me none of the secrets he confessed to me held anything over his head anymore, that he'd moved past them all. All except one. All except me. I don't know how we tangled along like this, if we meant to at all. I want him to be free, so I set him free. All I ever wanted was for him to be free, unburdened, unchained. Even if it means leaving me behind."

"I don't think he wants that, Rora."

"He's never been good at choosing what is right for him, so I'm doing it for him."

I kissed my little niece's cheek, and she stirred in her sleep. There was something I needed to know, something that would hurt younger me, but something I needed to hear. I needed to hear it to grow beyond my past, to stop wondering of what ifs, to stop doubting my denied childhood being my fault. I needed this for my younger self to stop blaming herself. "Do you...do you ever wonder if they loved us? I've always wondered." It was tiring to live with that question as an adult. As a child, it had given me hope.

Steel returned to my sister's eyes, hardening them again. "Sometimes," she said, running her fingers through her daughter's hair. "When I can't sleep at night, I go to their room and just stare at them. And then I try to think so hard that I get a headache because I can't get answers to my damn questions. How...how did anyone think of hurting us when I cannot bear to even see them cold or miss their meals. How would anyone hurt us? How did our parents hurt us the way they did? Then it makes me angry. So angry, Rora. Because even if I had to walk through fires and torture, even if there was no more blood for me to bleed, I would never, ever let anyone hurt them. I would never put anything before them. Kingdoms and realms be damned." She looked up at me. "Truth is, I don't know. I don't know if they did. Or at least not nearly enough as they should have."

"Even ma?" I forced myself to ask, feeling my younger self wither on the inside. A single tear dropped from my sister's eye. "Even her."

Lilith was there and so was my brother when I entered the meeting room the next morning. Part of me wanted to heave a sigh at the familiar presence, but my heart had spent ten years hardening and it was taking it a bit to shed its cement walls.

He spoke first, "She insisted, Rora, I'm really sorr—"

Lilith stepped before Eren, interrupting him. "I had to. For some reason my visions guide me to you over and over again and I will not choose to ignore them despite your dislike of me."

"Sit," I said to the both of them, taking a seat myself. "And go on."

Eren remained on his sport for a few moments looking somewhat surprised before he also followed suit.

"A messenger will come with the news in less than ten minutes," she said, her eyes glowing. "They've chosen something you will not be able to refuse."

"A duel," I guessed. It had always pointed to that. Now that Iskyla knew my powers had dwindled, she was confident she could take me on.

"The same as the one before you, yes," Lilith confirmed, her eyes returning back to its pale colour.

Eren glanced between me and her, looking a bit reluctant before he said, "But Iskyla has to know she will lose against you."

Maybe she would not—not while my magic had gone haywire. This was her perfect opportunity to strike. "Not just her. The claim to the throne is viable to all her sisters."

My brother's eyes widened. "Five against one?"

Her sisters were her insurance just in case she had been wrong to assume about my magic. "Are you doubting me?"

"Seems unreasonable. Isjordians will not see it well."

I shook my head. "No, they will commend it as a way to force me to prove myself, to show my strength."

"She is right," Lilith added, nodding. "The duel will happen. I've seen it happen from the eyes of many who will witness it. Your entire kingdom will stand witness to it."

Eren looked like he'd heard that for the first time. "Seen it? Lily, what have you seen?"

Ducking her head, she lowered her eyes. "I cannot speak of what I've seen, for I'd be interfering and causing much more damage by twisting the fate of tomorrow." Her hand patted against the table until her fingers touched mine. "Please, remember my warning."

Against all what some part of me wanted to say—a part that had now shrunk to a small, petty thing—I turned her hand in mine and held it. "I will. Thank you."

Lilith was almost frozen still, and then slowly, a smile made a show. One different from all the others.

I'd not realised how many decisions I had made thinking as younger me thought. Letting my past issues fill in the blanks I could have easily gotten by communicating and being understanding instead of shutting down and pushing away.

38

BLACK SPIDER LILY

MALIK

Kilian leaned against my bedroom door, watching me contemplate by a window.

"Doesn't look like you're preparing to leave."

"Don't have many shawls and corsets to pack, brother."

"And is Golgotha really agreeing to letting you remain in Hellas?"

"Yes. At least until the next red moon when the portal to Valinhel can be opened." Hellas was the only place I could think of going where I couldn't be tempted to come back to her. It had taken becoming an almost prisoner to the Demon God to keep away, to do as she had asked. Because anywhere else, I would have broken that promise.

"Yet you're here."

"Until I see her get rid of Iskyla."

"Might be sooner than later."

"I know."

His brows rose. "You know?"

"Paid a visit two nights ago to a little winter witch who might or might not have been putting a few little dreams in Iskyla's head these past few weeks."

My brother stood up straight, eyes wide and no longer amused. "You involved a ten-year-old in your plans?"

"Lilith is the only one whose craft can penetrate through the Isline magic. I had to make it believable for the queen. A sign here and there. An odd talisman. Talking shadows and trees. I had to make her believe that she was God sent. Give her ego a little power trip to beat the fear of facing Thora one to one in front of both kingdoms, and ultimately lose in front of them, too. The only way this needs to end."

"Except that she isn't facing her one to one."

"One or a thousand, she can do it."

"What if she can't?"

I stood. "She can. Don't doubt her. I don't like that."

My brother smirked. "Apologies," he said, picking some lint from my jacket. "I presume you will be there. To watch, of course."

"I will. To watch, of course."

Kilian stepped before me as I was about to step outside of my room. "You can't take control of yourself by destroying yourself before anyone else can. You can't take control of yourself by breaking your own heart before anyone else can, brother. Fix this. Try and stay to fix it."

"I've already given away that power, but I think it's too late. She doesn't even want a chance to break it anymore. She is holding my heart in her hands, not knowing what to do with it."

"It doesn't have to be goodbye."

"Goodbyes are just goodbyes until you fall in love with the person who gives you one. From her it was a death sentence, Kil. She already gave me my judgement. I am not to be spared."

My brother looked taken aback. "So, it is like that."

"It has always been like that, you blind fucker."

King Edric's grave was an entire underground tunnel maze made of encased cement coffins holding around five thousand of his finest soldiers who had given their lives to serve their first king even in death. The thick craft pouring out of the entrance was unfamiliar, ancient, and one of the most powerful barriers of magic I'd come across. Deceiving, too, because it was nothing physical. Whoever went in there surely returned with all limbs, but without their mind intact.

Cai plopped on a rock just outside the entrance and leaned back, closing his eyes. "Be done quickly. I want to see the fight. If Rora will even allow them that."

Thora wouldn't. That was the issue. By luring Iskyla into suggesting the duel, I'd forced her to face what she didn't want to face—showing the true extent of her might. She didn't want that. She'd been determined not to show that side of her ever again.

There was only one way Thora could remain powerful in the Isjordian eye without showing the full extent of her power—without losing herself in the process.

If a powerful king crowned her.

The most powerful king Isjord had before Thora.

Their first king who'd been the one to crown his first successor and banished the other. The only king who had ruled both parts of Isea, over both of its people. The only king who both sides would bow to as one, as they had only once done before. Hundreds of years ago.

"Are you sure you want to do this?" Nia asked, throwing a snowball at Cai and wincing at the bitter colour and scent of craft wafting from the gates. "Thora's control on her magic can almost surpass Snow's. Doesn't matter if there will be ten or ten thousand Krigborn coming to face her today, she will wipe their existence out of this realm without moving a single finger."

"They are Krigborn, they will play dirty, and she is determined not to. Even if she wins, this will go on forever. Today it's them, who knows who will challenge her tomorrow," I lied.

"Then we worry about that tomorrow."

"I can't worry from afar."

"You're not leaving, Mal."

Throwing her a grin, I backed towards the gates. "I've always known you love me just a little."

She rolled her eyes. "Don't let your idiot bones be chewed by some mummified corpse. I'd hate to tell that story to your brother."

Cai chuckled. "I wouldn't."

"You'd be too busy weeping for me, my muffin."

The second I stepped inside the veil, death laid a carpet before me. No matter how much I tried to ignore, look away, think it away like I'd done these past ten years, I couldn't. Forced to bear the emotions of a thousand souls still lingering around the maze, their death too, I made my way to the centre of it.

Edric had been buried with his finest Aura, his finest soldiers, in his finest weapons. Weapons of the sort that were no longer able to replicate in today's time and age because of the lack of magic lingering in nature compared to back then. Even pebble stones carried the pure magic of thousands of years ago. Metal wasn't just metal. Diamonds weren't just diamonds. Silk wasn't just silk.

Movement caught the corner of my eye instead of my senses, something that usually happened the other way around. Then shadows made their move next. Growing taller and closer to me, making the already tight corridors appear even tighter.

Pulling at my sword, I ran the tip of the Adriatian steel blade over the right wall, testing if the effect of the magic in the black metal still worked under the ancient craft. When the shadows shrieked and then dissipated, a grin stretched in my face. The black metal had been mined and used long after king Edric had been buried, so the Crafter wouldn't have accounted for it. The black blade easily cut through every shadow that hurried my way to attempt something that I would definitely not like by the way their eyes glowed red.

Possessed bodies? Yes.

Possessed shadows? First time I was seeing it. To possess something, you needed some grip into their soul, something to inhabit. Shadows had none of that, it was how Umbras could control them. They were inanimate.

Which only meant that something was controlling them.

And there it was, in the open room at the centre of the tunnelled maze. Standing right beside the first Isjordian king sat on a tall throne made entirely of gold and too many colourful jewels. The Crafter was all but bones and draped in a red cloak to hide them.

"Your gaze offends me," the Crafter's voice croaked around the room, and his skeleton raised its beady ruby eyes at me.

"Don't take it personally."

"I'm afraid I take everyone's business and intentions quite personally when they step past the doors to this grave. Ask the Isjordian king. His witch almost lost her soul attempting to thieve her way into here."

"There is a queen now."

The Crafter let out a noncommittal sound. "So she sends an...Empath to thieve her way in?" He chuckled. "Or whatever you are."

"Oh, no, this was a trip funded and planned by me." I pointed at the king's remains. "I'm only here to borrow him for a few minutes."

The Crafter threw its bony head back and laughed. "Borrow? You must have lost your mind."

"A while ago now," I said, stepping forward and into the layer of craft veiling the king, surprising the Crafter a little because he stopped laughing.

He pulled his stave forward to lean into it as he bent down to study his runes engraved on the ground. "How did you do that?"

"I forgot to introduce myself. I am married to the queen. This is why I advise men to take their wife's last name. Malik Krigborn doesn't sound so lush until you have to enter a family vault of sorts protected by a family craft."

"Smart," he said, leaning back. "But not even a Krigborn is allowed to take what belongs inside here."

"Not taking. I told you, I want to borrow."

"Borrow?"

Pulling my backpack forward, I threw it at his bony feet. "The bones of Silas Krigborn. Previous king of Isjord. His mighty crown and *anima acissor* sword, too. They can preoccupy the seat for a little while. The magic you've cast won't tell the difference. Royal bones. Rotten crown. Blade which cut through one of the mightiest wars in Numen. It's all the same."

The Crafter pulled his hood back and cocked his bony head to the side, glowing ruby eyes trailing me top to bottom. "You're a funny one."

"I will also need the soldiers buried here. About a thousand of them will do."

There was humour in his ancient voice when he asked, "Oh, will you now?"

"One thousand other dead soldiers are waiting by the entrance." Keeping Cai and Nia some warm company, I hoped.

It was then he sat up, attention going behind me, ruby eyes narrowing at the distance of the doors. "The dead raise?"

"At my order."

He was finally taking my request at *heart* because I felt the old taste of his magic coat my tongue with a taste of cyanide and thyme. "You are being serious."

"Dead. Serious."

"The hells are you?" he snarled.

"Only gods know."

39

WHITE POPPIES

THORA

There was nothing in sight beside white frost and grey skies. The elders from both the Islines and Isjord had chosen the old ground where Tenebrose had fought Isline as the place where Iskyla and I would reenact our own dispute.

Voices began filtering in the boisterous white wind filled with thick flakes of snow and howling sounds. Isjordians and Isliners alike had chosen to witness today. Remaining at a distance, I saw a few of the students from the academy push to the front lines, still in their uniforms. It took barely a full minute for those front lines to fill with more students, until the Isjordian side was just a wall of navy.

Elias and Snow followed right behind me, while Kilian, Oryn and Alaric remained somewhere in the distance where they had promised to only watch. From the corner of my eye, I could see Lilith's billowing golden hair and a taller figure beside her belonging to my brother.

The wind howled around us, the heartbeat carrying with it. Steady. Not loud. Not hindering. It was almost comforting. It was also distracting me from my erratic one.

He wasn't there.

I'd told him to go, but I had not expected he'd listen so easily. All which told me he'd probably been waiting for me to give him that permission. It was only a matter of time.

Through the blurring periphery, I could see Iskyla and her four sisters making their way to where I stood at the centre of the field.

Iskyla switched to glaring from me to Snow who had not left my side yet surely to just watch the Isline queen shake and shiver a little. "Are you here to make sure she kills me?"

Snow let out a little chuckle, patting her belly. "I don't want you to die, Iskyla, I want you to suffer. I'm here to make sure she doesn't kill you. At least not enough. But then, I only need you just a tiny little bit alive." My sister leaned in my ear to murmur. "Kill her. For her sake, kill her good. I'm not in the mood to be polite and I'm attempting to set my children a decent example."

Snow gave Iskyla one once over that had her looking away, before she bolted to stand beside Kilian.

Throwing me a confident smirk she asked, "You don't look like your usual self. Afraid?"

"And you look very much like your usual self," I said. "Very much afraid."

"No matter the power you possess, winter would only choose a true heir. One who could match to its name, to its strength, its demand. The one you can never be because of your soiled blood."

"Tell me you don't really believe that bullshit."

"Your lack of belief is what brought you to these odds with me."

"No, Iskyla. It was my kind and patient soul."

Behind her lined four other girls who looked almost identical to her. Four Krigborn princesses who without doubt had already planned the best way to tear me apart.

"This is a game of ice," Iskyla loudly called as she moved back, addressing the crowd as if she were some entertainer of sorts. "For a throne of ice. Let the best Krigborn win."

My eyes had frosted a little so they couldn't roll back, but I did sigh.

It was never about power to Iskyla.

She knew she didn't have it in her to defeat me, so she'd brought the next best thing. A crowd. Somewhere I couldn't hide behind my tricks. Somewhere where I'd be laid bare to show what I was capable of—she knew I held back on showing just what I was capable of, she'd seen what I was capable of.

"*All the old gods are gone and so are their kings,*" a girl shouted from between the crowd surrounding us, and I turned to look back at the students that had joined in, their teachers following along.

"*All the old gods are gone and so are their kings,*" another shouted even louder.

Then another.

Soon, many followed. The mountains at the distance echoing the words, louder and louder until they rumbled around like thunder.

As I looked at them, I remembered this had never been about me and my throne, or my fears. What I was and didn't want to become. This was no longer about my father or what I'd inherited from him.

As I looked at the Isliners between the crowd waving their support to me, I realised that maybe it was time all the people of Isea became one again, too. An end to the separation made by qualities of kings who I would never allow to step on the throne I held.

This was about protecting Isjordians and the new generation that would inherit this kingdom.

I couldn't fail.

Even if I had to become what I feared.

Ice began to rise from the ground, hovering midair at Iskyla's call. Her right foot moved back, and her hands rose forward almost in the shape of claws. The old ways of commanding ice. Beyond the name of a Verglasser.

There was no better way to take back control of my magic than going to the very basics of it. Just ice. Nothing else.

The way Karl had taught me, too. The ways of ice Skadi had taught me, too.

Moving just like Skadi had taught me, I waited, feeling sparks of magic start to surround my limbs, crackling and appearing out of nowhere, without even being summoned.

Iskyla and her sisters shot one another a glance, and they shifted position, ice moving along with them in tandem and howling towards me in one brutal wave.

I followed suit, the snow and the wind changing around me, intertwining together as one. After all, I was both. I was still the *Ybris*.

Then I felt it.

A small tug at first.

Then an entire grip.

Until it grew strong enough for me to grasp all the strings of magic stretching and weaving patterns in the air, attaching to the falling snow and to the billowing wind in a firm grip.

Snow halted midway from falling and the skies greyed entirely at my command without even lifting a finger or losing one breath, Iskyla's attack faltering midway to me, her ice crumbling to thin particles and disappearing in the wind.

She remained still where she was, eyes wide and stunned, commanding more and more ice with her hands while her sisters came around her and ran in my direction, swords drawn and magic following.

I slid between them, missing their attacks, and headed for Iskyla directly. All their attempts missed me entirely. Ice blowing around furiously and aimlessly, until it would melt in the air and disappear as if it had chosen to belong to no master.

Winter was not bending to her command anymore.

Eyes blown even more wide and stunned, she began backing away and looking over my shoulder to send her sister's scathing looks. "What are you doing? Get her!"

"You hide behind your young siblings? Is that why you brought them to battle today? Hoping they would tire me so you could finish me off?" I asked, walking straight through her vanishing frost attacks.

"No," she sneered, forming a small ice shield over her head as ice picks rained on her at my order. "I brought them here to see how it is done. Soon, I will grow old, and they will have to rule this kingdom for me. What a better way for them to learn and watch me do it."

The four princesses were quick on their feet, chasing fast after me to shield their sister from me, only to crash against a thin barrier of ice I'd formed around Iskyla and I.

"What is it, *true daughter of Winters*?" I asked when she turned red from blowing almost all of her mana in magic that was not obeying her and barely even grazing me. "Ice not obeying your command?"

Then it started.

She screamed, endless gales of snow and ice rose from all over, wrapping around me to trap me inside.

But ice and snow and winter was where I felt safe, the cold was home. The cold was relief. None of her attacks did anything more than trap me in my safe place. The snow and ice moulding to my control around me. And no matter how hard she fought to get back control of her own ice tethered to her, my connection to it was stronger, because even her ice suddenly obeyed me.

That was until I felt a small cut on my shoulder. Somewhere between the howl of cold magic, a thin dagger had pierced through the ice and embedded itself on my skin.

The blood matted to my navy jacket when I pulled the strange bronze blade out, starting to turn a strange shade of purple and then black.

Craft.

Blood craft.

My surroundings grew hazy, blurring and darkening for a brief moment until they grew sharp again, but different this time—the air was dressed in a dark shade of burgundy. In the distance, where Isjordians were watching, at their feet stood my students, laying on the ground, eyes wide and bleeding.

Panic climbed my throat, crawling against my mind as I spun round to see the same thing at where Snow and the rest stood. All bleeding. Sam. Rain, too. Dead. All dead. My sister screaming and crying over their bleeding bodies.

"It's just craft," I murmured to myself, over and over. But despite my heart knowing that, my mind didn't. It sunk, everything sunk under despair. It all sunk inside what I had never allowed my mind to sink against. What I'd always protected my mind from—itself. I suddenly couldn't dissociate away. It was like someone had grabbed my skull and forced me to look where I didn't want to look. Every safe place in my mind had been invaded by craft, pulling buried memories and emotions out. Forcing me to feel them all at once. All of it. All at once.

Pain struck against my temples first, travelling further down until it grasped my heart in a firm grip. "No," I cried, "No, pl—"

My lips pressed together tightly. Remembering I couldn't beg. I shouldn't beg.

Every memory returned.

All of them.

Memories I'd buried deep. Deep enough that I couldn't even remember them happening anymore. Memories, so many of them. Harrowing memories. Mostly of them. Mostly of my brother and sister. Mostly of our father. Then…then of me. Ones I thought my mind had erased.

My body shook.

My voice trapped on my throat as I relived every moment of abuse I'd buried away.

I couldn't even draw my eyes shut, the darker it was, the clearer I could see them.

Don't beg, his voice echoed in my head. *Scream and cry and bite and scratch, but never beg.*

"I won't," I whispered.

You're not me anymore, her young words echoed inside my mind. *Not anymore.*

I shook my head. "No, I'm not."

The snowstorm got thick—thick enough to help me disguise what I was about to do. The wind and air grew almost solid, too, engulfing the place in mist.

Forcing my eyes away from my dead sister's body, I looked at Iskyla. At the woman who'd suddenly grown menacing and terrifying in my craft veiled mind, the woman I was now fearing somehow—my mind working hard to project terror and forbid me from summoning magic.

"What a pretty trick," I managed to say, my jaw set tightly to stop the trembling, and breathing in until my lungs were swollen with air. And then breathing out as strings of magic spilled from my fingers again.

The Isline queen looked confused, sending looks behind me. "Strike her again", she bellowed to her sisters, her voice drowned in the snowstorm. "Strike her again. The craft hasn't taken."

"It has," I said, pushing myself to my feet. Tethers of magic grew further, slowly crawling over the ground and air. Hundreds and thousands of them, latching on every limb and drop of blood in her and her sister's bodies.

The second eldest after Iskyla dropped to her knees, clutching her chest. "Her? Are you fond of her most?"

Iskyla's eyes grew wide and mad.

Another sister dropped to the ground, screaming and writhing. "Or her?" I asked.

The third followed.

Then the fourth.

Tilting my head, I asked, "Which one do I take first? Or should I make it quick for you and take them all at once?"

Iskyla's golden stare grew violent as she foolishly ran in my direction.

I let her.

Her feet came to an immediate halt when she was but a foot from me, the tip of her dagger resting on my chest.

"Tell me, Isa. Can a human heart still freeze if it is already frozen?"

"Let go of them!" Iskyla bellowed, shaking as her hand unwillingly moved to angle her blade to her other arm and slashing across it.

Her sisters repeated the same motion at my command.

Blood gushed immediately, pooling on the snow below.

Their hands moved again to make another cut, just a little higher.

Then another, until their blades were pressed to their necks next.

One last cut.

And they would be gone.

No longer my issue.

Just when I was about to make it final, my eyes lifted to the distance around us still blurred by craft, beckoned by a strange call to my senses. I shook my head as the reality began clearing and unveiling from the dark magic.

That is when I noticed it. The wind and snow had cleared from around us. No longer shielding and disguising our fight.

The distant heartbeat returned after being gone for days, pulsing under my fingertips, below my soles, around my limbs as I spun to look at every face surrounding us.

Somewhere during that distraction, Iskyla slithered away, reaching for her sword and running towards me again full force.

Her feet halted at my command. Her whole body did. She remained still. Everything remained still. Even the wind died down. The heartbeat died down, too, when I realised everyone had just seen everything. Every Isjordian and Isliner. Even the kids.

Then I heard *his* cursed voice call to me like it did last before I nailed a dagger through his heart. Dragging me to the pits of memory I tried to forget.

"*Thora, my young rose,*" Silas's voice boomed around me, and the blood dripping down my shoulder began twisting over my skin.

The smell of craft lingered in the air again.

Murmurs travelled around me. Like a memory at first, but then they grew louder, drawing my attention to the Isjordians and Isliners watching me. Every eye was on me. Wide eyes. Fearful eyes.

I had nowhere to hide.

No way to lie.

I stood there bare. Fears in the open. Truth in the open.

But those eyes didn't remain on me for long. All of them remained wide and fearful on something else as the crowd parted for the other wonder to pass.

Against my will, against my hold on it, the wind stirred again. The skies pulled together to pour a strange shade of winter over us. A miserable shade of winter. One old as time. One tinted with raging skies.

Loud stomps shook the ground. They were coming towards me. An army of the dead all wearing silver armour, weapons and shields with the Isjordian insignia.

They parted, too. Bowing as they let only one pass. One wearing a gold armour, carrying a sword dressed all over with rubies, from pommel to hilt and along the flat centre of the blade up to the tip. The crown the skeleton wore was the same. Made entirely of gold and heavy colourful diamonds.

"*King Edric,*" a hushed whisper echoed in the wind. "*King Edric,*" it continued until everyone began murmuring it under their breath like a prayer.

Gasps were quick and hushed before all, Isjordian and Isliner alike went to their knees, bowing their heads and holding their hands in holy greeting.

King Edric's remains limped towards me, his jaw barely clinging to his skull, some bones missing here and there, the heavy armour barely hanging to them.

Everyone had gone to their knees, bowing their heads to the first ever king of Isea who was marching towards me, holding a crown and sword I'd only ever seen in history books and a few paintings and sculptures.

Iskyla kneeled next, holding a hand over her wounds and wincing at the movement that had every other injury bleed worse. Her sisters followed.

Fascinating and all, terrifying and all, but I wasn't paying mind to that.

But to the man who stood behind it all.

Malik chased King Edric's footsteps only a few feet behind him. He kneeled, too. Just not at the Isean King. He was kneeling before me. Head bowed, eyes resting on the ground.

Edric stopped a foot short from me. Even though he was merely bones and no soul, I could feel his presence everywhere, the eerie might of his still lingered in the winter air. For the first time, I also kneeled. Only because I knew I would never have to kneel ever again.

The heavy ancient crown was placed on my head. Its weight was heavier than just because of the metal.

The old king lowered the sword to my extended hands, the glistening of the gold was entirely blinding. And so were the words engraved on it.

May the winter wolf die last.

I flipped the sword the other way around.

Stormblade.

King Edric pulled onto his scabbard and handed it to me next.

When I pulled the sword back on its leather sheath, the wind calmed, the snow halted, the clouds ended their grey terror, parting in the middle to let one single stray of sunlight fall to the ground. To let it fall on me.

A crow of a large bird dragged my attention to it as it flew over my head, circling me and then launching upward the light stream and diving through the skies.

The heartbeat returned.

More noise returned.

Animals descended from the forests around, Isline creatures among them. They all descended from their hiding and headed towards Isjord.

The heartbeat grew stronger. And stronger.

Heads were raised, all looking around in wonder, whispering about the heartbeat they too could now hear.

Raising my head up to the light, I closed my eyes and let a quivering smile stretch in my face.

It was over.

When I could catch my breath like I'd never caught it before, with such ease and relief, when I couldn't feel the heavy reminder of memories curl through my hair, I opened them and stood.

The cast of light disappeared when I fully sheathed the sword back on its scabbard.

Edric's remains bowed and then began melting into dust, blown away into the wind.

A figure stood behind the crowd of Isjordians who were now bowing before me instead of their old king. Dapper in a navy suit that came high up on his neck, dark blue hair, his face young yet old, his body slender yet strong, Krig remained at the distance beside Snow who had directed the foulest side eye at him, watching me. Just before he disappeared, his eyes searched the forest around and he smiled when the heartbeat rang again in the distance.

Maybe the old gods were never gone.

Malik was the first to stand. Head still bowed, eyes still lowered. The rest all followed after their king—my king.

"You came back," I said. And he'd saved me again.

He finally looked up at me. "I will always come back. If you need me to."

"How did you know I needed you this time? I could have defeated Iskyla on my own."

"Fine. Maybe I need you."

Just when I made to say that I missed him and that I needed him, too, I heard Iskyla shout at her younger sisters who were pulling at her to stop her bleeding fists from hitting the ground in defeat.

The four all backed away when I approached. Hooking my arm under Iskyla's, I hoisted her to stand. "Enough with this tragic display, it's so unlady like."

"Finish me," she snarled.

"I see no worth in your death. But how you live the rest of your life will make me the greatest queen this kingdom will ever have."

She breathed hard, looking around her people who had now turned their backs to her to follow the rest of my people towards Isjord. "What will you do with me?"

"You will live the remainder of your days where your betrayal sent Skadi to live her last. Ulv Islet. I want you to scrub every lingering soul out of those rocks until they are so clean the ice below will shine through."

Her jaw set tightly, and she gritted out, "I'm worth more to you dead."

"You're worth nothing to me."

Elias clasped shackles on Iskyla and pulled her with no resistance at all. The fight and war in her had been doused.

"You're free to join me," I said to her sisters.

"We want exile," the eldest of the four said.

"Then have it. I'm not one to beg for you to change your mind so I'm glad you have yours set, *sweet cousins*."

After my court and the new members I'd welcomed ended their greetings and congratulations, I turned to him again, to my king still quietly waiting for me even though I'd told him to go. There were scratches all over his face, neck and hands that I had not noticed before. Blood splattered here and there on his chest.

"Where are you bleeding from?"

"Somewhere," he said, watching my search for his wound. When I made to pull away from him, he grabbed my hand and put it to his chest. "There."

This was going to be so hard. Harder than the first time. "I want to thank—"

"Nothing to thank me for, Rora," he said, interrupting me.

I shook my head. "I've got a lot to thank you for, Mal."

Not even a second later, I was pulled in his arms, in my sweet cage, the one I never wanted to leave. "I should be the one thanking you. You saved me in so many ways I didn't know I needed to be saved."

"You saved me, too."

"Forgive me."

Pulling back from his hold, I said, "No. I can't forgive you. Because if I forgive you, I can't save you one last time," I murmured, still not daring to look at him to say what I had decided to say instead of what I desperately wanted him to hear. *I love you.* "You're free, Mal."

His hands around my waist came just a little loose.

"I don't need you anymore and you do not need me," I continued. "Isn't this what we've wanted all this time? You're free. I don't forgive you. I never will." Stepping away from his hold entirely, I looked up at him, trying to hold my smile strong. "There is nothing holding onto you anymore, so go and be free. Live, Mal. How you have always wanted to." I smiled up at him despite the tears stinging my eyes. "Go and be a baker."

"Thora—"

"Don't say anything, please. I don't want to take back what I just said. I love you too much to be that selfish."

His face fell, twisting with a cry when he called my name, "Thora—"

"Please don't say anything, please," I begged, finally forcing myself to move further away from him and reaching for my necklace.

His hands wrapped around mine, pulling them from the necklace, his brow rested against mine. "No. Keep me there. Half of my soul has always been yours. Even before I wrapped it around your neck."

I felt tears rush down my face as I looked at the amber stone.

What?

40

VIOLET ALLIUMS

THORA

S now greeted my smile with a sad one of her own. "Did you banish him?"

I hugged her, holding her tightly like I'd done when I was little and afraid. "I did. But I want him back." I wanted the other half of him, too. "I just wish that was a choice he didn't make out of force or necessity. I wanted him to do it because it was what he wanted."

Kilian was looking down and frowning at me. "So, it is like that."

"It is," I agreed, and then his brows almost met his hairline.

I pulled away from Snow and hugged my nephew and my little niece hanging to my sister's skirts. "Go rest. All of you. It has been a long day."

Kilian looked behind me, at where my new court was gathering around the rose gardens, right over where I'd taken my father's life. Isjord was going to take a new life right there, where my own had started ten years ago. "It looks like it is going to be a lot longer for you."

"Nothing I cannot deal with."

He patted my head like I was still nineteen and clinging to him to teach me to be capable. "Nothing you cannot deal with."

Once everyone was there, men and women from the new and the old Isjord, I joined Elias at the centre of it. "Welcome back to those who have stood by my side for the last ten years," I said, greeting my old members, and then turning to the new. "And welcome inside my court to those that have just now joined us."

All bowed their heads and Karl Modr took a step forward. "What now, my queen?"

"Union," I said. "We join the old and the new. As by the blessing of the gods above and their gifted below, we shall be one again. One Isjord."

It had been a long, tiring day filled with much discussion and decision making. Just not long enough it seemed, because even beyond midnight, I couldn't make myself lay down or even stop thinking about him.

"I'm going to be so gentle to you," I whispered to the necklace in my hand, smoothing a finger over the amber stone. "I shouldn't have thrown you back at him ten years ago,

I'm sorry."

I smiled when the stone faintly glowed in the surrounding darkness.

A loud knock at my door almost made my soul jump out of my tired bones, and I clutched Mal's necklace to my erratic heart.

Sam came marching in. "It's mother."

He didn't even finish his sentence before I jumped out of bed and let him fade us to Adriata.

Snow's angry groans reverberated along her room. She laid on her bed, sweating and clutching her belly. Though she should be screaming in pain, she was moaning and groaning from anger. "I'm going to kill him!" she shouted, pushing the midwife and the healers off her.

Him.

As in her husband.

The man she loved.

Where was he, actually?

I paused. He'd left her side at night?

The doors slammed open, and Kilian strode in, panting and covered in a sheen of sweat and fear. He kneeled on the bed beside her, cupping her face and kissing her all over.

Her chest rose faster and faster, and she kept slapping him off her violently even though she'd asked for him up until now. "This is all your fault! You did this to me!"

"I'm sorry," Kilian said without an ounce of apology, not budging at all despite how hard she was still trying to push him away. In fact, he was grinning so brightly he was about to blind someone. "I'm so sorry. I will not do it again."

That angered my sister worse. "Get off me, you fucking bastard!"

"Alright, my love," he murmured to her, kissing her lips before standing.

"You're not staying?" I asked, shifting from one foot to another. I'd never done this before. She'd never called for me before. She had never let anyone with her in her room the two times before.

"She didn't let me stay with Rain or Sam either. I will be right by the door. If anything—"

"She will be fine," Visha assured boredly, pushing him out. "Now go so we can get your child out of her before she murders us all." Once the witch had him out, she turned to me. "You did what no Isjordian ruler has ever done, merited the praise of gods, at least act a little happier."

"You're telling me to act happier? Visha, you haven't smiled a day in your life."

"If someone had said something funny, I would have."

"Marry Elias."

She snorted and then threw her head back, laughing.

It was rather scary.

"He's going to ask you. I helped him pick the ring," I said.

She laughed harder, tears coming out of her eyes.

When I just blinked at her, her laughter died off, realisation setting in her strange but very beautiful face.

"He is?"

I nodded, grabbing the towels from her hands and heading to join my sister's side and save the healers who were hearing a pretty rough piece of her mind.

41

GOLDEN LILIES

MALIK

My brother stood facing the door long after it was shut, his shoulders rising fast, but not faster than the shadows of fear that he was suddenly not able to hide. They enshrouded the world entirely, doom dripping from his fingertips.

"She will be fine," he muttered to himself.

"They both will," I said, willing every shadow within a ten-mile radius to hold very, very still while I watched for the signs of life beyond the door before us, listening to my little nephew's strong heartbeat as well as his mother's. Kilian had not caught me far into my journey to Hellas. Thankfully, I had not made it far. Considering how distressed he was, he would have probably been caught inside the dark sea.

"Papa," Rain called from the other side of the corridor, running while clutching another of her ugly cloth dolls. My niece had an eye for horror.

Immediately, Kil's shadows pulled back and he turned to his children, giving them a bright smile. "Little princess."

I blew out a long sigh and dropped to the ground, resting my head against the wall. Sam followed suit, sitting beside me while his cold eyes remained fixed by the doors. "He will be like Rain," he said, blinking slowly.

"He will be," I agreed, making sure all my tethers attached to my nephew were strong and intact, holding his magic steady until he'd breathe with his own lungs.

Kilian sat on my other side, holding Rain on his lap and nervously rocking her.

"Dramatic bastard," I muttered.

He chuckled, his head dropping back on the wall. "One day," he said, kissing the top of his daughter's head. "Your heart will walk out of your chest, too. And you'll be left wondering if you ever were this weak and never noticed." His head turned to me and he wore a shit eating grin. "Oh, I forgot."

I only shook my head. Because he was right.

Rain stared between the both of us with beady grey eyes, wondering how our hearts could have possibly walked out of our chests considering the way she then narrowed them where our hearts had once been.

"If she gets upset seeing you being here, tell her I came to get you to keep Snow and our baby safe," my brother said.

"She won't believe it for a minute that I would have remained down there for a full day without her. I'm not going back. I'm not going anywhere. She doesn't have to speak to me. Look at me. Acknowledge me at all. She can hate me from right across her room where I will rot for the rest of this lifetime. It's a damn comfortable sofa, too."

He shook his head, chuckling. "Didn't you two have a rule about secrets? Tell each other all of them or something?"

"Yes."

"Hm."

"What is that supposed to mean?"

"For two people who share so much of their secrets, you two know nothing at all about one another."

A newborn's wailing cry rang in the air and Kil covered his face with both hands, breathing hard.

Rain hugged his neck tightly. Even Sam stood and went by his side, hiding his head in his father's chest that was now shaking from sobs.

"Congratulations, brother," I said, bringing him for a hug, too. "One more Castemont and we will be ready to take on the heavens."

He chuckled, grabbing the back of my head and hugging me like I was ten years old again. "Your turn now. I'm done, brother."

Done being afraid, he wanted to say. "Don't let Snow hear that."

He wiped a hand over his eyes. "She is already angry at me. Can't get much worse."

Patting his chest, I pulled back and hugged Sam and Rain, too. "Your little brother is lucky to have you two to protect him like your father protected me."

The two gave one another proud smiles and then hugged each other tightly.

The door to Snow's room cracked open just slightly to frame Thora's tear-streaked face. "She wants to see you," she hiccupped, beaming at Kilian, not even noticing me standing beside him.

She'd told me to go. She'd told me I was free. She'd told me she would never forgive me. But I stayed. I was never free either way. And I would beg for her forgiveness until our very next life. Or I would live like that—with her hating me. Forever, if she must.

The moment she noticed me, her lips parted, and she went stiller than the shadows around us.

Kil stood and carefully guided Thora to take his place beside me, placing Rain and Sam on her lap to trap her in place next to me.

"He's so little," she said to them, finally quenching their curiosity and trying her best to not look at me.

"It's okay, auntie," Rain said, taking her brother's hand. "We are big. Baby brother is safe."

"He sure is," she said, and then turned to me to whisper, "I think I fainted at some point. I have a bump in my head and don't recollect getting it."

That made me laugh, hard.

"I thought you'd already left," she whispered.

"Are you going to tell me to leave a second time?"

Her mouth opened and closed a few times. "No. I can only do it once. I lack the strength to do it again."

"I don't think I can ever leave even if you did. I'm not a free man, Rora. I've never been a free man since you entered my life. I'm chained to you for life, but I love you too much to tell you that there are still chains and shackles holding you back. I love you too much to be another shackle you wear."

Rain gasped as she looked up at us, and Sam took her hand. "How about we go for a walk?"

My niece giggled by her brother's side while they animatedly chatted by a far window.

"You lied to me," she said, her voice choking.

"I hope one day you might forgive me for it. For my selfishness."

Then she hit me hard and pushed to stand at least a foot away from me. "You made me wait ten years."

"I'm sorry." I slid closer to her again and she threw me a hard glare which softened when Rain laughed at her brother's magic tricks. "I missed you," I said, putting a finger on her chin and turning her face to me.

She looked out of breath. "It has been barely a day."

"I missed you so much."

"This soon?"

"I'm pitiful, aren't I?" I asked, nudging my nose to hers.

"A little," she whispered.

I bit into my smile, trying to contain it to not upset her with my happiness. "Take pity on me and let me back. I want to tell you I love you how lovers do. Everyday. As many times as I can say it. In the morning when you just wake up. At night before you fall asleep. When you ache. When you're happy. When you hate me. Or for no reason at all."

"I want that, too."

She was so soft. Like snow and spring wind. Like summer clouds and sea foam. Like a dandelion. "Let me kiss you. Forever, if you can."

Her chameleon eyes rounded and glassed over like a forest touched by the first rain and sunshine of the season. She nodded and reached for me, and I wondered how I felt in her hands. If I felt like disaster and nightmares. If I felt like gravel and thorns.

But when her lips met mine, it didn't matter. She wanted me as I was. She had always wanted me as I was.

Snow was fast asleep, her mouth slightly parted while she snored to the point the fresh Myrdur foundations were shaking.

My brother cradled his new-born son in his arms, swaying back and forth. "He looks like her," he murmured, his voice thick with tears.

"Attitude wise, I feel like he is more of a Castemont," I said, lightly pinching his fat cheek. "What's his name?"

"Jonah Malik Castemont. Snow picked it."

I chuckled, smiling down at the Castemont youngling. "What burden to carry on your tiny shoulders."

My brother glanced at Thora. "What's the verdict?"

"He can stay."

Kil nodded. "Good. I'll cut his legs if he ever tries to leave again."

"Not if I catch him first," she said.

"Will you mind holding him for a while?" he asked us.

Thora reached for him. "Thought you would never ask."

She sat beside me on the large sofa while Kil laid in bed beside his sleeping wife, his hand was on her face, his lips were on her face, too.

"Do you still hate me?" I heard my brother whisper to her.

Snow's eyes opened just slightly, and though she was exhausted, she gave him a little smile. "Are you cornering me now because I am out of it?"

"Yes. I want to know if you hate me in all of your states. If you hate me when you sleep, when you eat or think, when you don't think at all."

"I still hate you."

"Alright. I'll try harder."

"To not be afraid?"

He was silent for a moment. "I don't know about that."

"Kil, darling."

"If I lose you—"

"You will not. It will not happen."

Thora stood, also having heard their conversation. "We'll be just outside. Rain and Sam will want to see the baby."

Kil nodded and then wrapped Snow entirely into his embrace, leaning to whisper in her ear as we made our leave.

Little Jonah stirred in Thora's arms as Rain and Sam crowded around us. Thora kneeled, showing them their brand-new brother who opened his tiny eyes to look up at them.

"Krigborn gold eyes," Thora murmured, touching Jonah's face. "You're in for a ride, little boiled potato."

Rain giggled and scrunched her nose. "He does look like one."

"You looked the same," Sam said, reaching to touch his little brother.

Rain's hopeful doe eyes turned to me, horror and tears written in them. "Do I still look like a boiled potato?"

"No, baby doll, you do not look like a boiled potato," I said, sitting her on my knee.

More joined us, the corridor filling entirely with people holding and passing little Jonah from one pair of hands to the other. And like the true Castemont he was, he didn't let out a single sound, only blinking his golden eyes at the adoring people who held him.

PINK BABY BREATHS

THORA

T he fireplace crackled loudly as the flames chewed the new kindling while I was entirely swallowed by Mal's arms as he held me in his lap while we watched the Isjordian skies shift to colours of night.

"And you're back," he whispered in my ear.

"Had not gone far."

"Good," he said, leaving a kiss on my cheek. "Because I want to take you somewhere."

"Where?"

"You'll see." Standing, he threw a robe over my shoulders and took my hand, fading us in the middle of nowhere.

It was dark, the crescent moon barely giving us enough light to see where we were stepping on the snow-covered forest.

A spark glistened somewhere in the distance we were heading to. Then another. And then many others.

Not sparks.

Forest spirits.

They'd gathered around a massive weeping willow, dancing around its lean hanging branches that fell and dipped in the thick snow.

"Where did these come from?"

"Some of the kids from the academy had seen a few roam by the old wall ruins. I figured they also had returned to the land now that it bowed entirely to a new queen. Now that they are no longer afraid."

I gasped when he pulled one long, thick branch back, revealing hundreds more of the tiny glistening spirits hovering under it, dancing around the ancient giant willow trunk.

My feet halted when I noticed someone standing there, trying to buzz away the spirits that were making him sneeze.

Atlas bowed his head, almost dropping the massive book he held because of his shivering hands.

Astounded, I asked Mal, "How long has he been waiting here?"

"An hour or two."

I hit him. "He could have frozen to death."

"He wouldn't dare," he said. "Not until he has done what I brought him here to do. Then he can do whatever he wants to do."

"Which is what?"

"Give the other half of my soul to you." He touched my necklace. "To hold."

"Hold it where?" I whispered, trying to quieten my flustered heart and my stinging eyes.

"Wherever you want to. As long as it is yours to hold." He drew his fingers down my cheek. "Do you want it?"

"As long as you want mine."

He pressed his lips to my eye, catching the stray tear as it fell.

How beautiful, a tiny voice whispered and then the rest of them followed, repeating it. *And oh so sweet.*

They giggled, pushing one another and blowing more golden dust around. *The bird and the fox, the fox and the bird,* they all sang, their laughter echoing around like the purest and most magical thing I'd ever seen. *They have but one secret they carry in their hearts that no one will ever know.*

Shhhhhh, they whispered in unison. *No one can know oh how they loveeeee one another.*

There had been no red moon or wild wind, the dead or the sun, just the dark night and the crescent moon, the snow and the winter air, Atlas and the tiny glowing guests who had stopped and listened in on every vow we took before the call to the gods was made.

When Atlas had raised the burning sage between us, the smoke had curled around both mine and Mal's hand until the mark of the union had been brandished on our ring fingers, sealing our souls together.

For eternities.

Then we celebrated every night and day that followed.

Many nights and days.

All nights and days.

The end.

Or the start.

It can be whatever you wish for it to be.

THE NEXT RED MOON

MALIK

R ain had not said a single word the whole way through the dead, grey forest after we crossed the portal and into the new world. Her eyes were set straight ahead, not curious, not frightened. Only determined. She'd been so determined that she'd brought two dolls with her.

The two massive black metal gates stood tall before us, shielding a long path ahead towards a five-story old dark building made of black walls and ghastly statues engraved and carved all over its walls, and roof, and gardens.

They opened on their own, letting us pass through the empty yard filled with dead shrubs and a few empty stools. The billowing wind was our only companion, the only thing with a soul inside the ten-mile radius around us. If you didn't count the half dead one inside the building.

The entrance doors were engraved with writing in an odd language, at the top stood a coat of arms.

Rain tugged on my coat, pointing at the writing that was curling and shifting to a language I understood. Adriatian.

Arcane Academy.

Knowledge is the blood of virtue.

I pulled Rain behind me when the doors drew open, leading us into a dark corridor that began fluttering alive and bright when the torches on the walls lit one after the other until they reached the end.

We followed along even though every sense in my body hummed and warned me to run, even my magic was flaring around uncontrollably.

Another door opened and I came to a stop, narrowing my eyes on the man inside it that I had not seen in a few years.

He had white hair, cut short to his head, a few tattoos crawled up his high neckline that had failed to do its job and conceal most of them by the look of it.

"You found me," Castiel said, setting the book he held down on the table and turning to me. He pushed his dark framed glasses back and leaned onto the table, crossing his arms. "Long time no see, Malik. What do I owe this unwelcome visit?"

"Remember that favour you owe me?"

"Unfortunately."

I moved to the side so he could see Rain. "I have a student for you."

He boredly studied my niece and then rolled his unamused attention back at me. "This isn't a preschool. Bring her back when she's at least eighteen."

"You're going to help her."

His eyes narrowed and he studied me for a moment. "Are you certain this is how you wish to waste a favour? My favours are hard to come by."

"Show him, baby doll."

Rain nodded, handed me her terrifying dolls and stepped forward.

It all happened between a single second. Darkness enshrouded us entirely. We stood in the middle of a black pit only illuminated by Rain's body that had caught on black fire.

A pocket realm.

Rain had just created a pocket realm between two worlds from nothing. Purely from her mind. She could make the space as finite or infinite as she wanted. Once you were trapped in it, only she could let you out of it.

She looked back at me. "Is this alright?"

Nodding, I said, "That's enough."

The professor had a stunned expression on his face as he took his glasses off to lower them on the table. His black eyes gleamed as he bent down to kneel to her height and reach out a hand to her. "Hello, Rain. I am professor Castiel Constantine. Welcome to Arcane Academy."

Rain narrowed her eyes on the snake tattoo around his hand and then craned her neck all the way back so she could look up at me.

"Go on, baby doll. He looks stupid, but he is harmless."

When she shook his hand, the snake tattoo on his skin shifted and then moved to hide under his sleeve.

"Interesting," the Shadow Guardian said, grinning ear to ear as if he'd found a precious gem. "Very interesting." Standing, he told me, "I'd love to meet her parents."

ARCANE ACADEMY STUDENT BOARD

THE IVORY TRIBUNE

arcane academy printing services

NEW INTER-REALM STUDENT ACCEPTED INTO ARCANE ACADEMY

Rain Helenia Castemont, child of a Godling and a rare Lightning guardian, as of three days ago has been successfully accepted to attend Arcane Academy. Professor Constantine of the Dark Physics Sciences, has chosen to take the younger student under his wing. No one is fully aware as to why he has made such an acceptance and has allowed a minor to be taught magic, a rule which has never been broken by the faculty previously.

We can only speculate that the girl possesses a great deal of magic which requires her the guidance of our extraordinary teachers. Rain, at only six years old, has already shown great promise as she successfully passed the Alabaster Ministry Magical Examinations which will allow her to soon join the classes along the adult students.

STRANGE SIGHTINGS IN SILVER BAY

BY CLEOME ALKMENE

As of this week alone, three students have reported sightings of level three demons from the lower realms nearby Silver bay and two more just passing the Silent Hills. A rare occurrence through the years despite their presence north of Arcadia for more than a decade now. The ministry has yet to comment on their appearance, but they have expressed that they have a team of Halos sent to investigate and prevent any civilians from facing any potential demon on their travels.

EXTENDED EPILOGUE: A LORD'S GUIDE TO A GRUMPY WITCH'S HEART

VISHA

Though it was almost summer, the breeze in Olympia still remained somewhat chilly, and at the touch of its hands on my exposed shoulders, I shivered and so did the candlelight.

At some point over the years, I had begun waiting for him—for Elias. Just like tonight. Sat in front of my vanity while brushing a comb through my hair and impatiently glancing at the door from time to time.

Our little night meetings had started a little over ten years ago already and he still had not complained, asked for more or asked to end it. All three requests I had expected to happen at least a few months into whatever we were doing. But no, Elias Venzor was anything but unhappy with how things were going.

But he should be. Considering what Thora had told me, he must be.

He'd picked a ring. A wedding ring.

Somewhere deep into those thoughts, I had missed watching him slip inside my room.

My eyes drew shut when his body slid behind mine to wrap his arms around my waist and lower his mouth on the crook of my neck. "Your hair is going to snap if you run that brush over it one more time."

"Why? Is baldness a turn off for you?"

He chuckled in my ear right before taking a small bite. "No, you'd be cute as hells."

"Cute?"

"Pardon me, my witch, I didn't mean to offend you with such a horrible word," he cooed, slowly prying the brush from my hands as if it were to explode if he did it any less carefully. "Have mercy and let me run my fingers through your beautiful hair one last time."

I glared at him. "You're the most absurd person I know."

"That's it? I fear you've grown lenient on me."

"There is more."

"Oh, I'd love to hear more," he said, standing and starting to undress before getting comfortable on my bed.

"What are you doing?"

He yawned. "Trying to sleep. I set sail early tomorrow towards White Bridge."

And at some point, he'd started coming over to do just that. To sleep. "You can do that in your own room. In Venzor."

His eyes cracked open just a little and he patted the space next to him. "You're right. The only thing I don't have in my home is my little witch."

"How long are you staying in White Bridge?"

"Three weeks."

"Why?" Why was Thora sending him away for so long?

"Because I was asked to. Now come here and let me play with your cunt."

You'd think after ten years of this I'd be used to his absolutely filthy mouth. "Thought you wanted to sleep."

"You'll moan me a little song in my ear," he said, grinning like a fool. "Like you always do when I have my fingers inside you."

I pushed all my thoroughly combed hair back and walked myself to him. The second I managed to get both feet on the mattress, he was on me. "One day you're going to make me beg for that little favour I've been asking you since forever," he said, playing with the straps of my nightgown.

"I can't just walk around my room naked all the time, Elias."

"Why not?" he asked, chasing kisses all over my neck until every nerve on my body had tightened at his order. He pulled onto the sleeves of my nightgown until it was bunched around my waist and then palmed my breast, circling his fingers over the taunt centre until heat started pooling at the pit of my stomach. "Gods, you're the most beautiful thing I've ever seen."

Every day—he'd told me that every day since that first night he'd kissed me and then made my body feel things it had never felt before. I mainly remembered Nia's wedding day for an entirely different reason from hers. Mostly because it was the first time we'd properly fought, shouting at each other right on my bedroom doorstep. And then because ten minutes from that, he was peeling my wet dress off my body like it was nacre shell of the most stunning pearl one might have seen.

His hand came between my thighs while his mouth latched on the soft flesh of my breast, surely to leave another mark amongst the many old ones already there from the night before. Two fingers slid over my sex, and I felt his lips stretch into a smile. "Already wet," he hummed, licking a puckered nipple and circling his slick fingers over the apex of my thighs. "Did you touch yourself before I got here?"

"Yes." Another thing he'd taught me to do properly. The way he'd shown and directed me had almost made self-pleasure seem like a form of art.

"And did you come?"

"No. I wanted you."

He captured my lips and sunk two fingers inside me at the same time, making me gasp. "You wanted me what? To make you come?"

"Yes," I moaned as he slowly and torturously pumped his fingers in and out of me, spreading my legs wider when he shifted to stand between them. "Isn't that why I keep you around?"

He chuckled, sitting up and pulling his shirt and trousers off until he stood like a naked god before me. All hard muscle and an even harder cock. "I don't know, my pretty little witch, is it?" he asked, leaning in to bite my lip and wrap a hand around my throat, squeezing just enough for my breaths to come in shallower. "Put me in."

Wrapping my hand around his thick cock, I stroked his length before pressing his head to my entrance, wiggling my hips down until he slipped inside me, making him groan in my mouth.

In one shift of his hips, his cock sheathed inside me entirely and I moaned at the sting of the stretch. Bracing his other hand on the headboard, he pulled back and thrust inside me again. And again, slamming inside me relentlessly until my insides tightened like a coil.

Grabbing the hand I'd rested on his thigh, he brought my fingers to his mouth and spat. "Touch yourself while I fuck you. Let me see how you do it."

"You've seen me do it many times," I muttered breathlessly, half moaning when I started circling that sensitive spot with my fingers while his cock filled me.

"I always love a repeat performance." He groaned at the back of his throat, slowing his thrusts so he could watch where we joined. "Just like that."

My eyes almost rolled at the back of my head when his flesh started slapping against mine harder and louder. "Elias—"

My entire body shook when he pulled out of me and spun me onto my stomach. I moaned into the pillow when he thrust back inside me from behind, one of his hands coming under me to wrap around my throat again as he pressed his lips to my ear to say, "That's my good little witch, taking it so well."

"More."

His hand tightened around my throat, making it just a little harder to breathe. He knew how I liked it, and he also knew my limits. He'd been my first and he'd been the one I'd discovered and experimented all of those limits with, yet he always waited for me to demand or ask first.

The bed groaned with each thrust, his powerful hips bruising my thighs and backside as he ploughed his cock in and out of me hard, sinking me into the mattress. He left kisses on my temple, my cheek, my jaw and my ear. "You like that, huh?" He whispered in my ear and I arched my back the best I could so I could feel him deeper. "Yes, you do, don't you? So fucking wet for me."

Wetness dripped between my thighs, making the joining of our bodies grow louder and more obscene. I writhed under him, half wound up and desperate to come, and the other half silently begging for him to draw it out as long as he could, to fuck me until my vision was entirely black.

But when he braced a knee on the mattress, shifting his hips just the right amount to hit that perfect spot inside me, I cried out, digging my nails in his forearms and squirming as release crashed through my entire body a little too violently, making spots dance in front of my vision.

It was perfect. He always made it perfect for me.

He also knew that. How to fuck me. Entirely too well. Because he'd been the one to try every way there was and figure it out. He'd had the time and the practice to make him an expert.

He pulled back to sit on his haunches, taking me with him and getting me on all fours. With a knee, he pushed my legs further apart and grabbed a fistful of my hair while fucking me through a second climax. My skin, my scalp, my lungs, my insides, everything was burning and aching—burning and aching so deliciously good. A few more hard thrusts later, he came with a grunt, tugging hard at my hair until my back was flush against his chest and crashing his mouth against mine. "Is my witch happy?" he panted, pushing his tongue in my mouth to give me a sloppy kiss while his other hand came to roughly grab at my breasts that didn't quite fit even in his massive hand.

"I'm not your witch," I managed to mutter back when he let me breathe.

"Mhm," he hummed, and then his palm came down on my backside with a sharp smack when he let go of my hair, the remnants of the sting on both my scalp and skin drawing a tired moan out of me. A hand still tightly braced on my hip, he pulled out, pressing the head of his cock to my sex and collecting the come running out of me to shove it back in. He pressed a kiss to my shoulder. "Your cunt always looks so pretty when it's freshly fucked and painted with my come." Torturously, he thrust a few more times until he started dripping down my thighs and on the bedding, and my bones were so tired that my limbs were quivering, unable to hold me up.

I was covered in him and he was covered in me when I dropped on the mattress and he followed suit, breathing hard and wearing a blissful smirk. After both our breathing calmed, he turned on his side and leaned over me, tracing his thumb over my neck before bending down to kiss the skin I was sure had turned an angry red—that was the curse I carried. Not as a Crafter. As a redhead.

His touch and his mouth were so soothing, almost lulling me to sleep. Except that this beast of a man was also insatiable as I had come to discover over the past ten years. His hand and his mouth descended a little further down to my chest, tracing a finger over the nipples still sensitive from the climax he'd dragged out of me.

I grabbed a pillow and held it over his head in a very poor attempt at suffocating him. "Just go to sleep like a normal man." After sex, he only wanted more sex. Normally, so did I, but lately it was putting me on a strange high I couldn't sate without him anymore. And it was getting harder and harder to resist the urge of needing to see him at the oddest of times during the day.

He chuckled, blindly reaching to grab for me again and hoisting me over his body to straddle his hips.

Given up, I threw the pillow away from his face and accepted my fate.

The look he swept over my naked body made me straighten my spine—he had always made me feel like the most desirable woman anyone had ever laid eyes on. "Let me see you ride it. I'm gone for three weeks. I'm going to need a fresh image for all the nights and mornings I'm away from you."

"I can give you something for that."

His eyes raked over my body again, his dark irises almost expanding as he took me in. "Indeed, you can."

"A potion, Elias. Not a show."

"Yeah?" he asked, trailing a finger from my belly button and down my sore sex, making my whole body shiver. "Better than a show?"

"Yeah," I said, sliding his length between my thighs before slipping him inside me.

He sighed and put both hands under his head like he was about to sunbathe. "Nothing is better than this show."

Tradition required that we both washed up and changed the bedding in absolute silence. The only bending to the rules we'd set long ago was the fact that he'd slowly weaselled his way into sleeping entirely too closely to me, his body curved behind mine, one arm thrown over my waist and a leg over both of mine. I'd given up on demanding he won't do it because at some point in the night, either he or I would seek the other, and I much prefer it if he didn't know my body subconsciously wanted his.

And then there was his habit of counting the freckles on my shoulders when he couldn't sleep. Just as he was doing now. Four hundred and fifteen. Or so he'd told me last time he'd counted.

"Why aren't you falling asleep already?" I asked.

He pressed his nose to my hair and breathed in deeply. "I was waiting for you to do it first."

"Why?"

"Something seems odd tonight."

"Odd?"

"You're always in your head, but tonight it almost seems you're being forced to be in there. Like it isn't your choice and you're forced to hear your own thoughts."

"How do you always come up with such ridiculous conclusions?" I'd given him my body, not my mind, but somehow, he'd gotten through to that, too.

"You say I'm a ridiculous man."

I sighed, and the next words slipped out of me tonight for the first time, "I don't know what I am doing with you. Me out of all. With you out of all." If there was someone who didn't deserve to be treated and kept like a secret, it was him.

"Is that what you were not wanting to think? What you're doing with me—with someone like me?"

"Go to sleep," I said, burying my face on the pillow, but that was a short-lived effort because the bear of a man spun and hoisted me to lay on top of him.

"You want to stop this? Is that what it is?"

Pressing my cheek to his chest, I drew my eyes shut. "No, I don't want to stop it. That is the issue."

"Issue for who?"

"The both of us."

"I don't remember telling you that."

"You don't have to tell me anything," I said, glancing up at him. "I'm smart enough to come to conclusions."

"Yeah, you'd think that."

Narrowing my gaze on his, I said a little more spitefully than I intended to, "I don't think you even know what you want."

He barked a bitter laugh. "Believe me, V, I've known what I want for a very, very long time. Don't pretend you haven't known, too."

"You're a good man, Elias. You deserve better."

His brows started to slowly pull together to give me the most confused look he'd ever given me. "I deserve *you*."

"Why, what have you done to the Gods that is so bad and have you punished with me?"

"What have I done to the Sun Goddess that she won't let me have you in daylight?" he asked. "A great offence, some sort of unforgivable disservice because somehow, I crave nothing more than to pull you in my arms in the middle of the day out of all the hours. Right where everyone can see." He kissed my cheek. "But I am not an ungrateful man. The Moon Goddess keeps nights long for me these days. She must like me to give me so much pity."

My teeth dug hard on my bottom lip to bite back my smile—he got awfully smug when he made me smile, unbearably smug. "That's because it's winter, Elias."

"I wish it were winter forever."

I cupped his face, narrowing my eyes on his sleepy ones. "What the hells is wrong with you?" I asked, a tremble permeating my usually steady voice, a voice I'd trained to be steady since the day I spoke my first word. The one thing my mother had taught me perfectly was how to hide how I felt, how not to give anyone any clue to my thoughts and my feelings. How to be a blank canvas. So they wouldn't be used against me. Or to taunt me. To trick me. I'd kept that curtain on for all my life, with everyone—everyone but him. One odd day he'd pushed his head past those curtains, but for some reason, I'd never bothered to hide.

"For one, the witch that I love doesn't love me back."

An ache burned deep in my chest. I pushed away from him, settling back on my side of the bed and shaking my head. "You don't love me."

"Alright. I don't. I haven't loved you since forever. My deepest and darkest desires aren't about you." He pulled me closer to him and pressed a soft kiss on my lips. "Let's sleep now."

"I don't love you back."

Sighing, he buried his face on my chest, his arms banding tighter around my waist. "I know, my cruel little witch."

"Elias," I whispered, placing a kiss on his brow. "Elias?"

He stirred a little, but the man was gone as per usual. Deep asleep like there was no trouble in the world. I could still remember one of the first lies he'd told me. That sleeping was difficult for him and how he'd struggled since his days as a soldier. But he'd always slept so peacefully beside me even when I couldn't.

"I might have lied, too," I murmured, lacing my fingers through his long blond hair and combing through the strands just how he liked it.

"Aren't you tired of this?" I asked when I felt him carefully slip out of bed to return to Isjord like he did every morning. "Of me keeping you a secret." It was the first time I'd said that out loud. And from the look on his face, it seemed he didn't want to talk about it either. The mellowness falling over his features told me it was for a reason different than mine. That if I let the world know I had him, he might be taken from me.

"Couldn't care less, as long as you're in my arms."

"That isn't right though, is it?"

"I will have you however you let me have you."

Pushing up, I rested my back against the headboard and looked at him. "Forever?"

He grinned as he threw his clothes over his body. "If you will let me have you for that long, then yes, forever."

"Where is the ring?"

His expression slowly fell, and I watched every muscle on his body suddenly tense. "What?"

"The ring Thora helped you pick."

After a few moments of the most silence and hesitation that had ever fallen between me and him, he reached into his discarded jacket at the foot of the bed and pulled a small pouch from the breast pocket.

I blinked at him. "You keep it on you?"

"Always. Was hoping one day I'd suddenly get the courage to either lose you or have you forever."

He must have worn my heart during all these years because part of me wanted to shout that he could never lose me unless he wanted to—that I was not something to lose, only to discard. Stretching a palm in his direction, I said, "Let me see."

His fingers slightly trembled when he pulled on the pouch's strings and then deposited the ring in my hand.

It was perfect.

An oval emerald surrounded by a halo of tiny little glittering diamonds was at the centre of a shining gold band. I slid it into my ring finger and lifted my hand up to watch the twinkle dance across the diamonds. Once I was done and satisfied with my inspection, I stood, heading for the bathroom. Stopping when I noticed Elias was still frozen on the same spot. "Don't you have a ship to catch?"

"Yes," he said, snapping out of some sort of haze. "Yes, I do."

I sighed. "You're not regretting it already, are you?"

"Regretting what?"

"Wanting to marry me."

"You're marrying me?"

My eyes narrowed. "You're the one with the ring."

He slowly stepped closer as if I would fly away if he wasn't careful enough. "You're marrying me?"

"Was it just a birthday gift?"

"Say it," he whispered, resting his brow against mine and pulling me into his embrace, a place I'd found safety and peace for the first time in all my life—a life I'd mostly spent hiding, running, pretending that I didn't care, afraid fate would find reason to take more from me. "Say you're marrying me."

"You're really one hundred kilograms of a fool, aren't you?"

"I'm going to be one hundred kilograms of a dead man if you don't say it, Visha Delcour."

"I'd bring you back."

He chuckled. "What worth is a dead man in this world?"

"To me?" I asked, lifting a hand to his face and pushing a few blond strands away so I could see down the dark abyss of his eyes--down the abyss that had comforted me too many times to count. "Everything. You're like a massive thorn, Elias. Wedged deep in my chest. But if I pluck you out, I bleed."

He looked like he was trying very hard not to laugh and devour me whole at the same time. "That is the most romantic shit anyone has ever told me."

"I don't know, Elias, I don't know how to tell you that I love you properly." Not long ago, I'd been sure I'd never have this, my fate was to never have this. Now that I had it, I was afraid I might lose it, that my old fate would find me again and take me back with a tattered heart. And then, most of the time, I felt guilty for wishing it, for tasting it when he'd offered it to me, knowing that another girl had inherited my fate instead—that she had taken my place and the terrible future that came with it.

He cupped my face and kissed me. "Gods," he breathed over my mouth. "If you ever take that back, I'm going to haunt you in every dream and nightmare you ever have."

"Alright, you do that," I breathed back, and watched another ridiculous smile overtake his face.

"I love you, V." He kissed me again and again. "I can say it for the both of us."

Avoiding his eyes, I scratched my cheek, feeling my skin burn as red as my hair. "Alright, thank you." Just when I turned to enter the bathroom, I spun back to him. "Don't tell Snow just yet, I want to tell her myself." I owed her my gratitude. I had this—I had him because of her.

He pinched my chin lightly. "Alright."

"I want a small one. No crowds. No big white dress. You know I hate white."

His thumb grazed my lips. "However you like it. As long as you attend it as my bride."

I gave him a shove. "Leave."

"On second thought, fuck the trip," he mumbled, pulling his shirt off.

"Let's not," I said, trying to put his shirt back on. "And I don't like children very much."

"How they taste or—"

I glowered at him and he threw his head back, laughing his lungs out. Once he was done, he said, "Then neither do I."

He was a damn liar. Snow's kids adored him and called him the *fun* uncle despite that buffoon, Malik, being the carefree idiot that he is, competed for that same role. I wanted to see Elias as a father one day whenever that would be even though I was scared I might like him even more desperately. "Maybe just one."

"One sounds perfect."

I nodded, looking at the ring. "Maybe we should have sat to discuss all that before I put this on."

"Any request you have, write it down and let me know where to sign, but you're not taking that off."

"You might not like them all."

"I like *you*, the rest don't matter."

"That's very sad."

"I'm weeping. As you see."

When I glared up at him again, he cupped my jaw with a hand and backed me to the wall, pressing his body to mine. "Careful looking at me like that, my little witch. It makes me very fucking hard."

"When are you ever not?"

"When my little witch takes care of it. When she's a good little witch and lets me use her as I please."

"You're going to be late."

"I'm very good at apologising," he said, pulling my nightgown strap down and leaning to kiss his way all over my body.

ACKNOWLEDGEMENTS

Firstly, I'd like to thank my ARC team for being the ABSOLUTE best! I lose so much faith and confidence in my writing right before I prepare for release, but the second your messages and reviews and comments flow in, I feel on top of the world. Without you guys, I would have honestly crumbled and given up. A million thank yous.

Lizzy, bro, I don't know what I would have done without you three years ago, and I still don't know what I would do without you in the years to come. Thank you for having faith in this silly path I took. Thank you for being the first to ever listen to my rants about these stories that somehow turned out to be books.

Neta, bestie, love you.

And last but not least, to every single person who has read these books, whether you have liked them or absolutely hated them, I want to thank you for giving this story a chance.

ABOUT THE AUTHOR

Wendy Heiss is an indie author debuting with a new adult fantasy trilogy. Winter Gods & Serpents is the first book in The Auran Chronicles, releasing autumn 2021. She has graduated with honours in Forensics Science in the United Kingdom, but literature has been one of her passions since she could manage to read and write. Despite being severely tempted to ride the Agatha Christie route to crime novels, she chose to follow the Tolkien path to fantasy. She forwent fingerprint powder for ball pen ink, inevitably forgoing her parents' hope for a good life and becoming what they always feared...a figuratively starving artist.

Any whom and how, she likes cats, coffee, particularly that cr*p from instant sachets. Claims to despise mafia romance from the pits of her gall bladder but will probably end up writing one herself to try and outwrite the greatest line in history: Are you alright baby girl.

Also, fried sweet potatoes, she can definitely eat some of those without claiming to be allergic to yet another vegetable. On that last note before straying too far from a simple bio, please read her book and more to come.

If you have enjoyed the read, please consider leaving a review on Amazon and Goodreads.

ALSO BY

www.ingramcontent.com/pod-product-compliance
Lightning Source LLC
Chambersburg PA
CBHW030104260626
47156CB00008B/2516